THE
SCARLET LETTER

AN AUTHORITATIVE TEXT
BACKGROUNDS AND SOURCES
CRITICISM

❯❯❯ ❮❮❮

SECOND EDITION

NATHANIEL HAWTHORNE

THE
SCARLET LETTER

AN AUTHORITATIVE TEXT
BACKGROUNDS AND SOURCES
CRITICISM

⫸⫷

SECOND EDITION
⫸⫷

Edited by

SCULLEY BRADLEY
EMERITUS, UNIVERSITY OF PENNSYLVANIA

RICHMOND CROOM BEATTY
LATE OF VANDERBILT UNVIERSITY

E. HUDSON LONG
EMERITUS, BAYLOR UNIVERSITY

SEYMOUR GROSS
UNIVERSITY OF DETROIT

W · W · NORTON & COMPANY · INC · *New York*

For my son
Thomas L. Gross

Second Edition

Library of Congress Cataloging in Publication Data

Hawthorne, Nathaniel, 1804–1864.
  The scarlet letter.

  (A Norton critical edition)
  Bibliography: p.
  1. Hawthorne, Nathaniel, 1804–1864. The scarlet letter. I. Bradley, Edward Sculley, 1897–   II. Title.
PZ3.H318Sc 1978 [PS1868]   813'.3   ~~78-24583~~
ISBN 0-393-04495-5   77-24583
ISBN 0-393-09073-6 pbk.

1 2 3 4 5 6 7 8 9 0

Darrel Abel: "Hawthorne's Hester," from *College English*, 13 (1952), 303–9. Copyright © 1952 by the National Council of Teachers of English. Reprinted by permission of the publisher and author.

Sam S. Baskett: "*The* (Complete) *Scarlet Letter*," from *College English*, 22 (1961), 321–28. Copyright © 1961 by the National Council of Teachers of English. Reprinted by permission of the publisher and author.

Ernest W. Baughman: "Public Confession and *The Scarlet Letter*," from *The New England Quarterly*, 40 (1967), 532–50. Reprinted by permission of *The New England Quarterly* and Professor Baughman.

Nina Baym: "The Romantic *Malgré Lui:* Hawthorne in 'The Custom-House,'" from *ESQ: A Journal of the American Renaissance*, 19 (1973), 14–25. Reprinted by permission of *ESQ* and Professor Baym.

John E. Becker: "The Concluding Ritual," from *Hawthorne's Historical Allegory: An Examination of the American Conscience* (Port Washington, N.Y.: Kennikat Press, 1971), pp. 88–154. Copyright 1971 by John E. Becker. Reprinted by permission of Kennikat Press Corporation.

Charles Boewe and Murray G. Murphy: "Hester Prynne in History," from *American Literature*, XXXII (May 1960), pp. 202–204. Reprinted by permission.

W. C. Brownell: "Hawthorne: *The Scarlet Letter*," from *American Prose Masters* by W. C. Brownell, pp. 96–103. Copyright 1909 Charles Scribner's Sons; renewal copyright 1937 Gertrude Hall Brownell. Reprinted by permission of Charles Scribner's Sons.

Frederic I. Carpenter: "Scarlet A Minus," from *College English*, V (January 1944), pp. 173–80. Reprinted by permission of *College English* and the author.

Michael J. Colacurcio: "Footsteps of Ann Hutchinson: The Context of *The Scarlet Letter*" from *English Literary History*, 39 (1972) 459–94. Copyright © The Johns Hopkins Press. Reprinted by permission of The Johns Hopkins Press and the author.

Frederick C. Crews: "The Ruined Wall," from *The Sins of the Fathers: Hawthorne's Psychological Themes* (New York: Oxford University Press, 1966), pp. 136–53. Copyright © 1966 by Frederick C. Crews. Reprinted by permission of Oxford University Press, Inc.

Charles Feidelson, Jr.: From "*The Scarlet Letter*," in *Hawthorne Centenary Essays*, edited by Roy Harvey Pearce (Columbus: Ohio State University Press, 1964), pp. 31–77. Copyright © 1964 by the Ohio State University Press. All rights reserved. Reprinted by permission of the author, the editor, and the publisher.

Richard Harter Fogle: *From Hawthorne's Fiction: The Light and the Dark*. Copyright 1952 by University of Oklahoma Press. Reprinted by permission.

John C. Gerber: "Form and Content in *The Scarlet Letter*," from *The New England Quarterly*, 17 (1944), 25–55. Reprinted by permission of *The New England Quarterly* and the author.

Seymour Gross: "Solitude, and Love, and Anguish": The Tragic Design of *The Scarlet Letter*," from *College Language Association Journal*, III (March 1968), pp. 154–165. Reprinted by permission.

Daniel G. Hoffman: "Hester's Double Providence: The Scarlet Letter and the Green," from *Form and Fable in American Fiction*. © 1961 by Daniel G. Hoffman. Reprinted by permission of Oxford University Press, Inc.

Gabriel Josipovici: From *The World and the Book: A Study of Modern Fiction* (Stanford, Calif.: Stanford University Press, 1971). Reprinted by permission of Stanford University Press and Macmillan London and Basingstoke. © 1971 by Gabriel Josipovici.

Leo B. Levy: "The Landscape Modes of *The Scarlet Letter*," from *Nineteenth Century Fiction*, 23 (1969), 377–92. Copyright © 1969 by the Regents of the University of California. Reprinted by permission of the Regents and the author.

R.W.B. Lewis: "The Return Into Time," reprinted from *The American Adam: Innocence, Tragedy, and Tradition in the Nineteenth Century*, by R.W.B. Lewis, by permission of the University of Chicago Press. Copyright 1955 by the University of Chicago Press.

Roy R. Male: From *Hawthorne's Tragic Vision* (Austin, Texas: University of Texas Press, 1957) pp. 102–17. Reprinted by permission of the author and the publisher.

F. O. Matthiessen: *From American Renaissance: Art and Expression in the Age of Emerson and Whitman*, by F. O. Matthiessen. Copyright 1941 by Oxford University Press, Inc., and reprinted by permission.

Joel Porte: "The Dark Blossom of Romance," from *The Romance in America* (Middletown, Conn.: Wesleyan University Press, 1969) pp. 98–114. Copyright © 1969 by Wesleyan University. Reprinted by permission of Wesleyan University Press.

Charles Ryskamp: "The New England Sources of *The Scarlet Letter*," from *American Literature*, XXXI (November 1959), pp. 257–72. Reprinted by permission.

Ernest Sandeen: *"The Scarlet Letter* as a Love Story," from *PMLA*, 77 (1962), 425–35. Reprinted by permission of the Modern Language Association of America and the author.

David Stouck: From *The Centennial Review*, 15 (1971), 309–29. Reprinted by permission of *The Centennial Review* and the author.

John Caldwell Stubbs: From *The Pursuit of Form: A Study of Hawthorne and the Romance* (Urbana: University of Illinois Press, 1970). Copyright © 1970 by the University of Illinois Press. Reprinted by permission of the publisher and the author.

Marshall Van Deusen: From *Nineteenth Century Fiction*, 21 (1966), 61–71. Copyright © 1966 by the Regents of the University of California. Reprinted by permission of the Regents and the author.

Hyatt Howe Waggoner: Reprinted by permission of the publishers from *Hawthorne: A Critical Study*, by Hyatt Howe Waggoner (Cambridge, Mass.: The Belknap Press of Harvard University Press). Copyright 1955 by the President and the Fellows of Harvard College.

Contents

Preface to the Second Edition

For over a decade and a half the Norton Critical Edition of *The Scarlet Letter*, edited by Sculley Bradley, Richard Croom Beatty, and E. Hudson Long, has been a highly respected and successful book. A reliable text, helpful annotations, an impressive collection of background and source materials, and a representative selection from about one hundred years of criticism have made it one of the most useful works of its kind. In undertaking this revision I have kept that in mind.

The previous editors' decision to use the first edition of *The Scarlet Letter* as the text was, as recent scholarship has demonstrated, the correct one. I have reprinted that text (with a couple of emendations) because I am convinced that nothing in it impedes critical understanding and appreciation. There are, to be sure, bad texts in use; the first edition of *The Scarlet Letter* is not, in my judgment, one of them.

Except for some minor changes in the informational footnotes to the novel, I have left them pretty much what they were in the first edition. I have, however, deleted those which offered interpretation so that the reader can initially experience the novel without prompting—there is plenty of interpretation in the back of the book, where it belongs. I have, further, expanded the area of annotation to cover the back-of-the-book materials as well as the novel. It did not seem consistent to gloss what might be troublesome references in Hawthorne while allowing equally or even more obscure references by the critics to pass in silence.

In the section Backgrounds and Sources the materials in Records Based on Primary Sources could not be improved upon and so are reprinted exactly. To The Scholar and the Sources I have added essays by Ernest Baughman and Michael Colacurcio as additional examples of how critically illuminating such a traditional form of scholarship can be when practiced with tact and sophistication.

Since by my rough count almost two hundred studies of *The Scarlet Letter* have appeared in print since the first edition of this book, it is not surprising that the Criticism section has undergone the most change. Given the exigencies of space and the enormous amount of material to choose from, there was no way to feel completely satisfied with my decisions of what to drop and what to add. I did not assume, however, that later is always better. I have not only retained ten of the nineteen original selections, but I have added as well two earlier pieces: John Gerber's "Form and Content in *The Scarlet Letter*" (1944)—still one of the best analyses of the structure of the novel; and Darrel Abel's "Hawthorne's Hester" (1952)—a strongly argued disagreement with the grade given Hawthorne by Frederick Carpenter's "Scarlet A Minus."

The most obvious change in Criticism—the inclusion of a discrete section on "The Custom-House"—was the easiest to make. One of the clearest directions taken by criticism in the past twenty years has been a growing consensus that Hawthorne's introductory essay is not a detachable entity but, rather, as Sam Baskett's title has it, very much an integral part of "*The* (Complete) *Scarlet Letter*." The four essays which comprise this section display—each with its own kind of emphasis—what meanings can come into view when we, as it were, enter the novel through the door of "The Custom-House."

The previous editors began their Essays in Criticism with Henry James (1879), presumably because that's where the modern criticism of Hawthorne's novel begins. There is certainly something to be said for the position. I have, however, begun earlier—with excerpts from five contemporary reviews. I have done so not only to show, for the purposes of contrast, how mid-nineteenth-century criticism proceeded, but also to remind the present-day reader how daring was Hawthorne's treatment of The Fallen Woman to a Victorian culture which assumed that any fictional lady who stooped to folly would inevitably die an instructive death.

The twenty essays in criticism, old and new, which comprise the final section of this book are not, as the sentimental song has it, "a few of my favorite things." I have tried instead to present as wide a variety of critical approaches and opinions—many quite different from my own—as would eventuate from the suspension of my bias and the advice of other Hawthorne specialists.

It gives me great pleasure to express my gratitude to my colleagues at the University of Detroit for answering so many of my questions; to Professors Nina Baym of the University of Illinois and Sargent Bush of the University of Wisconsin for their suggestions about the contents of this book; to Miss Diane Eaton for saving this miserable two-fingered typist hours of irritation and drudgery; and to Mr. John Benedict of Norton for being as good an editor as anyone could hope for.

SEYMOUR GROSS

The Text of
The Scarlet Letter

A ROMANCE

Contents of *The Scarlet Letter*

The Scarlet Letter

Preface[1]

Much to the author's surprise, and (if he may say so without additional offence) considerably to his amusement, he finds that his sketch of official life, introductory to The Scarlet Letter, has created an unprecedented excitement in the respectable community immediately around him.[2] It could hardly have been more violent, indeed, had he burned down the Custom-House, and quenched its last smoking ember in the blood of a certain venerable personage, against whom he is supposed to cherish a peculiar malevolence.[3] As the public disapprobation would weigh very heavily on him, were he conscious of deserving it, the author begs leave to say, that he has carefully read over the introductory pages, with a purpose to alter or expunge whatever might be found amiss, and to make the best reparation in his power for the atrocities of which he has been adjudged guilty. But it appears to him, that the

---

1. Although the text of the novel given here is that of its first edition, the editors have added Hawthorne's preface to the second edition, for its historical interest.
2. That is, Salem, Massachusetts, his birthplace, where Hawthorne had recently lost his position in the Custom-house (1849) because of a Whig victory in the Presidential election of Zachary Taylor. Hawthorne's sketches of his former Whig colleagues drew fire at once from the local press. Randall Stewart, in his Hawthorne, quotes a blast from the Salem Register, a Whig paper, dated March 21, 1850: "Hawthorne seeks to vent his spite * * * by small sneers at Salem, and by vilifying some of his former associates, to

a degree of which we should have supposed any gentleman * * * incapable * * * The most venomous, malignant, and unaccountable assault is made upon a venerable gentleman, whose chief crime seems to be that he loves a good dinner."
3. The Reverend Charles Wentworth Upham of Salem, a power among the Massachusetts Whigs, whom Senator Charles Sumner called "that smooth, smiling, oily man of God," brought about Hawthorne's dismissal, and the latter, who thought him "the most satisfactory villain that ever was," probably portrayed him as the arrogant Judge Pyncheon of The House of the Seven Gables (1851).

only remarkable features of the sketch are its frank and genuine good-humor, and the general accuracy with which he has conveyed his sincere impressions of the characters therein described. As to enmity, or ill-feeling of any kind, personal or political, he utterly disclaims such motives. The sketch might, perhaps, have been wholly omitted, without loss to the public, or detriment to the book; but, having undertaken to write it, he conceives that it could not have been done in a better or a kindlier spirit, nor, so far as his abilities availed, with a livelier effect of truth.

The author is constrained, therefore, to republish his introductory sketch without the change of a word.[4]

SALEM, March 30, 1850.

The Custom-House

Introductory to "The Scarlet Letter"

It is a little remarkable, that—though disinclined to talk over-much of myself and my affairs at the fireside, and to my personal friends—an autobiographical impulse should twice in my life have taken possession of me, in addressing the public. The first time was three or four years since, when I favored the reader—inexcusably, and for no earthly reason, that either the indulgent reader or the intrusive author could imagine—with a description of my way of life in the deep quietude of an Old Manse.[5] And now—because, beyond my deserts, I was happy enough to find a listener or two on the former occasion—I again seize the public by the button, and talk of my three years' experience in a Custom-House. The example of the famous "P. P., Clerk of this Parish,"[6] was never more faithfully followed. The truth seems to be, however, that, when he casts his leaves forth upon the wind, the author addresses, not the many who will fling aside his volume, or never take it up, but the few who will understand him, better than most of his schoolmates and life-mates. Some authors, indeed, do far more than this, and indulge themselves in such confidential depths of revelation as could fittingly be addressed, only and exclusively, to the one heart and mind of per-

---

4. Probably literally true, but nevertheless certain changes, due to editorial or printers' error, appeared in the second edition.

5. Hawthorne completed *Mosses from an Old Manse* (1846) in the homestead of the Emerson family, where the Hawthornes settled after their marriage. Hawthorne's "autobiographical impulse" was displayed in the introductory essay, "The Author Makes the Reader Acquainted with his Abode," and in the sketch entitled "The Old Manse."

6. The *Memoirs of P. P., Clerk of this Parish*, an early eighteenth-century mock autobiography, was published anonymously, as were other satires emanating from the so-called "Scriblerus Club" of Pope, Swift, Thomas Parnell, Dr. John Arbuthnot, and John Gay. "P. P." satirically parodies the tedious, digressive autobiography of Bishop Gilbert Burnet, *A History of His Own Times* (1723).

fect sympathy; as if the printed book, thrown at large on the wide world, were certain to find out the divided segment of the writer's own nature, and complete his circle of existence by bringing him into communion with it. It is scarcely decorous, however, to speak all, even where we speak impersonally. But—as thoughts are frozen and utterance benumbed, unless the speaker stand in some true relation with his audience—it may be pardonable to imagine that a friend, a kind and apprehensive, though not the closest friend, is listening to our talk; and then, a native reserve being thawed by this genial consciousness, we may prate of the circumstances that lie around us, and even of ourself, but still keep the inmost Me behind its veil. To this extent and within these limits, an author, methinks, may be autobiographical, without violating either the reader's rights or his own.

It will be seen, likewise, that this Custom-House sketch has a certain propriety, of a kind always recognized in literature, as explaining how a large portion of the following pages came into my possession, and as offering proofs of the authenticity of a narrative therein contained. This, in fact,—a desire to put myself in my true position as editor, or very little more, of the most prolix among the tales that make up my volume,—this, and no other, is my true reason for assuming a personal relation with the public. In accomplishing the main purpose, it has appeared allowable, by a few extra touches, to give a faint representation of a mode of life not heretofore described, together with some of the characters that move in it, among whom the author happened to make one.

In my native town of Salem, at the head of what, half a century ago, in the days of old King Derby,[7] was a bustling wharf,—but which is now burdened with decayed wooden warehouses, and exhibits few or no symptoms of commercial life; except, perhaps, a bark or brig, half-way down its melancholy length, discharging hides; or, nearer at hand, a Nova Scotia schooner, pitching out her cargo of firewood,—at the head, I say, of this dilapidated wharf, which the tide often overflows, and along which, at the base and in the rear of the row of buildings, the track of many languid years is seen in a border of unthrifty grass,—here, with a view from its front windows adown this not very enlivening prospect, and thence across the harbour, stands a spacious edifice of brick. From the loftiest point of its roof, during precisely three and a half hours of each forenoon, floats or droops, in breeze or calm, the banner of the republic; but with the thirteen stripes turned vertically, instead of horizontally, and thus indicating that a civil, and not a military

7. Elias Hasket Derby (1739–99); as shipowner, pioneer of the oriental trade, and privateersman of the Revo- lution, he won the nickname of "Old King Derby."

post of Uncle Sam's government, is here established. Its front is ornamented with a portico of half a dozen wooden pillars, supporting a balcony, beneath which a flight of wide granite steps descends towards the street. Over the entrance hovers an enormous specimen of the American eagle, with outspread wings, a shield before her breast, and, if I recollect aright, a bunch of intermingled thunderbolts and barbed arrows in each claw. With the customary infirmity of temper that characterizes this unhappy fowl, she appears, by the fierceness of her beak and eye and the general truculency of her attitude, to threaten mischief to the inoffensive community; and especially to warn all citizens, careful of their safety, against intruding on the premises which she overshadows with her wings. Nevertheless, vixenly as she looks, many people are seeking, at this very moment, to shelter themselves under the wing of the federal eagle; imagining, I presume, that her bosom has all the softness and snugness of an eider-down pillow. But she has no great tenderness, even in her best of moods, and, sooner or later,—oftener soon than late,—is apt to fling off her nestlings with a scratch of her claw, a dab of her beak, or a rankling wound from her barbed arrows.

The pavement round about the above-described edifice—which we may as well name at once as the Custom-House of the port—has grass enough growing in its chinks to show that it has not, of late days, been worn by any multitudinous resort of business. In some months of the year, however, there often chances a forenoon when affairs move onward with a livelier tread. Such occasions might remind the elderly citizen of that period, before the last war with England,[8] when Salem was a port by itself; not scorned, as she is now, by her own merchants and ship-owners, who permit her wharves to crumble to ruin, while their ventures go to swell, needlessly and imperceptibly, the mighty flood of commerce at New York or Boston. On some such morning, when three or four vessels happen to have arrived at once,—usually from Africa or South America,—or to be on the verge of their departure thitherward, there is a sound of frequent feet, passing briskly up and down the granite steps. Here, before his own wife has greeted him, you may greet the sea-flushed ship-master, just in port, with his vessel's papers under his arm in a tarnished tin box. Here, too, comes his owner, cheerful or sombre, gracious or in the sulks, accordingly as his scheme of the now accomplished voyage has been realized in merchandise that will readily be turned to gold, or has buried him under a bulk of incommodities, such as nobody will care to rid him of. Here, likewise,—the germ of the wrinkle-browed, grizzly-bearded, careworn merchant,—we have the smart young clerk, who gets the

8. The War of 1812.

taste of traffic as a wolf-cub does of blood, and already sends adventures in his master's ships, when he had better be sailing mimic boats upon a mill-pond. Another figure in the scene is the outward-bound sailor, in quest of a protection; or the recently arrived one, pale and feeble, seeking a passport to the hospital. Nor must we forget the captains of the rusty little schooners that bring firewood from the British provinces; a rough-looking set of tarpaulins, without the alertness of the Yankee aspect, but contributing an item of no slight importance to our decaying trade.

Cluster all these individuals together, as they sometimes were, with other miscellaneous ones to diversify the group, and, for the time being, it made the Custom-House a stirring scene. More frequently, however, on ascending the steps, you would discern—in the entry, if it were summer time, or in their appropriate rooms, if wintry or inclement weather—a row of venerable figures, sitting in old-fashioned chairs, which were tipped on their hind legs back against the wall. Oftentimes they were asleep, but occasionally might be heard talking together, in voices between speech and a snore, and with that lack of energy that distinguishes the occupants of alms-houses, and all other human beings who depend for subsistence on charity, on monopolized labor, or any thing else but their own independent exertions. These old gentlemen—seated, like Matthew,[9] at the receipt of custom, but not very liable to be summoned thence, like him, for apostolic errands—were Custom-House officers.

Furthermore, on the left hand as you enter the front door, is a certain room or office, about fifteen feet square, and of a lofty height; with two of its arched windows commanding a view of the aforesaid dilapidated wharf, and the third looking across a narrow lane, and along a portion of Derby Street. All three give glimpses of the shops of grocers, block-makers, slop-sellers, and ship-chandlers; around the doors of which are generally to be seen, laughing and gossiping, clusters of old salts, and such other wharf-rats as haunt the Wapping[1] of a seaport. The room itself is cobwebbed, and dingy with old paint; its floor is strewn with gray sand, in a fashion that has elsewhere fallen into long disuse; and it is easy to conclude, from the general slovenliness of the place, that this is a sanctuary into which womankind, with her tools of magic, the broom and mop, has very infrequent access, In the way of furniture, there is a stove with a voluminous funnel; an old pine desk, with a three-legged stool beside it; two or three wooden-bottom chairs, exceedingly decrepit and infirm; and,—not to forget the library,—on

---

9. In Matthew 9 : 9, the Apostle was "sitting at the receipt of custom"—a customhouse officer—when Jesus called him to become a disciple.

1. Specifically, the ancient district of wharves in London; hence figuratively, the dockside slums of any seaport.

some shelves, a score or two of volumes of the Acts of Congress, and a bulky Digest of the Revenue Laws. A tin pipe ascends through the ceiling, and forms a medium of vocal communication with other parts of the edifice. And here, some six months ago,—pacing from corner to corner, or lounging on the long-legged stool, with his elbow on the desk, and his eyes wandering up and down the columns of the morning newspaper,—you might have recognized, honored reader, the same individual who welcomed you into his cheery little study, where the sunshine glimmering so pleasantly through the willow branches, on the western side of the Old Manse. But now, should you go thither to seek him, you would inquire in vain for the Loco-foco[2] Surveyor. The besom of reform has swept him out of office; and a worthier successor wears his dignity and pockets his emoluments.

This old town of Salem—my native place, though I have dwelt much away from it, both in boyhood and maturer years—possesses, or did possess, a hold on my affections, the force of which I have never realized during my seasons of actual residence here. Indeed, so far as its physical aspect is concerned, with its flat, unvaried surface, covered chiefly with wooden houses, few or none of which pretend to architectural beauty,—its irregularity, which is neither picturesque nor quaint, but only tame,—its long and lazy street, lounging wearisomely through the whole extent of the peninsula, with Gallows Hill and New Guinea at one end, and a view of the alms-house at the other,—such being the features of my native town, it would be quite as reasonable to form a sentimental attachment to a disarranged checkerboard. And yet, though invariably happiest elsewhere, there is within me a feeling for old Salem, which, in lack of a better phrase, I must be content to call affection. The sentiment is probably assignable to the deep and aged roots which my family has struck into the soil. It is now nearly two centuries and a quarter since the original Briton, the earliest emigrant of my name,[3] made his appearance in the wild and forest-bordered settlement, which has since become a city. And here his descendants have been born and died, and have mingled their earthly substance with the soil; until no small portion of it must necessarily be akin to the mortal frame wherewith, for a little while, I walk the streets. In part, therefore, the attachment which I speak of is the mere sensuous sympathy of dust for dust. Few of my

2. A Whig term of abuse for any Democrat, originated in 1835 by conservative Democrats of New York in derision of a radical faction which, deprived of lamplight by a prank, continued meeting by the light of candles and "locofocos," or friction matches.

3. Hawthorne's first American ancestor, William Hathorne [*sic*], came to Massachusetts from England in 1630; he became a member of the House of Delegates and major of the Salem Militia.

countrymen can know what it is; nor, as frequent transplantation is perhaps better for the stock, need they consider it desirable to know.

But the sentiment has likewise its moral quality. The figure of that first ancestor, invested by family tradition with a dim and dusky grandeur, was present to my boyish imagination, as far back as I can remember. It still haunts me, and induces a sort of home-feeling with the past, which I scarcely claim in reference to the present phase of the town. I seem to have a stronger claim to a residence here on account of this grave, bearded, sable-cloaked, and steeple-crowned progenitor,—who came so early, with his Bible and his sword, and trode the unworn street with such a stately port, and made so large a figure, as a man of war and peace,—a stronger claim than for myself, whose name is seldom heard and my face hardly known. He was a soldier, legislator, judge; he was a ruler in the Church; he had all the Puritanic traits, both good and evil. He was likewise a bitter persecutor; as witness the Quakers, who have remembered him in their histories, and relate an incident of his hard severity towards a woman of their sect,[4] which will last longer, it is to be feared, than any record of his better deeds, although these were many. His son, too, inherited the persecuting spirit, and made himself so conspicuous in the martyrdom of the witches, that their blood may fairly be said to have left a stain upon him.[5] So deep a stain, indeed, that his old dry bones, in the Charter Street burial-ground, must still retain it, if they have not crumbled utterly to dust! I know not whether these ancestors of mine bethought themselves to repent, and ask pardon of Heaven for their cruelties; or whether they are now groaning under the heavy consequences of them, in another state of being. At all events, I, the present writer, as their representative, hereby take shame upon myself for their sakes, and pray that any curse incurred by them—as I have heard, and as the dreary and unprosperous condition of the race, for many a long year back, would argue to exist—may be now and henceforth removed.

Doubtless, however, either of these stern and black-browed Puritans would have thought it quite a sufficient retribution for his sins, that, after so long a lapse of years, the old trunk of the family tree, with so much venerable moss upon it, should have borne, as its topmost bough, an idler like myself. No aim, that I have ever cherished, would they recognize as laudable; no success

4. *Cf.* "The Gentle Boy," in which Hawthorne told the story of a Quaker woman evangelist and her son, persecuted and destroyed by the severity of the Puritans.

5. Magistrate John Hathorne, a son of William, the original settler, was one of the judges during the Salem witchcraft trials in 1692; unlike the majority of his colleagues, he refused to repent his role once the hysteria had passed.

of mine—if my life, beyond its domestic scope, had ever been brightened by success—would they deem otherwise than worthless, if not positively disgraceful. "What is he?" murmurs one gray shadow of my forefathers to the other. "A writer of story-books! What kind of a business in life,—what mode of glorifying God, or being serviceable to mankind in his day and generation,—may that be? Why, the degenerate fellow might as well have been a fiddler!" Such are the compliments bandied between my great-grandsires and myself, across the gulf of time! And yet, let them scorn me as they will, strong traits of their nature have intertwined themselves with mine.

Planted deep, in the town's earliest infancy and childhood, by these two earnest and energetic men, the race has ever since subsisted here; always, too, in respectability; never, so far as I have known, disgraced by a single unworthy member; but seldom or never, on the other hand, after the first two generations, performing any memorable deed, or so much as putting forward a claim to public notice. Gradually, they have sunk almost out of sight; as old houses, here and there about the streets, get covered half-way to the eaves by the accumulation of new soil. From father to son, for above a hundred years, they followed the sea; a gray-headed ship-master, in each generation, retiring from the quarter-deck to the homestead, while a boy of fourteen took the hereditary place before the mast, confronting the salt spray and the gale, which had blustered against his sire and grandsire. The boy, also, in due time, passed from the forecastle to the cabin, spent a tempestuous manhood, and returned from his world-wanderings, to grow old, and die, and mingle his dust with the natal earth. This long connection of a family with one spot, as its place of birth and burial, creates a kindred between the human being and the locality, quite independent of any charm in the scenery or moral circumstances that surround him. It is not love, but instinct. The new inhabitant—who came himself from a foreign land, or whose father or grandfather came—has little claim to be called a Salemite; he has no conception of the oyster-like tenacity with which an old settler, over whom his third century is creeping, clings to the spot where his successive generations have been imbedded. It is no matter that the place is joyless for him; that he is weary of the old wooden houses, the mud and dust, the dead level of site and sentiment, the chill east wind, and the chillest of social atmospheres;—all these, and whatever faults besides he may see or imagine, are nothing to the purpose. The spell survives, and just as powerfully as if the natal spot were an earthly paradise. So has it been in my case. I felt it almost as a destiny to make Salem my home; so that the mould of features and cast of character which had all along been familiar here—ever, as one representative of the race lay down in his grave, another assuming, as it were, his sentry-march along the Main Street—might still in my little day be seen and recognized in the old town. Nevertheless, this very sentiment is an evidence that the connection, which has become an unhealthy one, should at last be severed. Human nature will not flourish, any more than a potato, if it be planted and replanted, for too long a series of generations, in the same worn-out soil. My children have had other birthplaces, and, so far as their fortunes may be within my control, shall strike their roots into unaccustomed earth.

On emerging from the Old Manse, it was chiefly this strange, indolent, unjoyous attachment for my native town, that brought me to fill a place in Uncle Sam's brick edifice, when I might as well, or better, have gone somewhere else. My doom was on me. It was not the first time, nor the second, that I had gone away,—as it seemed, permanently,—but yet returned, like the bad half-penny; or as if Salem were for me the inevitable centre of the universe. So, one fine morning, I ascended the flight of granite steps, with the President's commission in my pocket, and was introduced to the corps of gentlemen who were to aid me in my weighty responsibility, as chief executive officer of the Custom-House.[6]

I doubt greatly—or rather, I do not doubt at all—whether any public functionary of the United States, either in the civil or military line, has ever had such a patriarchal body of veterans under his orders as myself. The whereabouts of the Oldest Inhabitant was at once settled, when I looked at them. For upwards of twenty years before this epoch, the independent position of the Collector had kept the Salem Custom-House out of the whirlpool of political vicissitude, which makes the tenure of office generally so fragile. A soldier, —New England's most distinguished soldier,[7]—he stood firmly on the pedestal of his gallant services; and, himself secure in the wise liberality of the successive administrations through which he had held office, he had been the safety of his subordinates in many an hour of danger and heart-quake. General Miller was radically conservative; a man over whose kindly nature habit had no slight influence; attaching himself strongly to familiar faces, and with difficulty moved to change, even when change might have brought unquestionable improvement. Thus, on taking charge of my department, I found few but aged men. They were ancient sea-captains, for the most part, who, after being tost on every sea, and standing up sturdily against life's tempestuous blast, had finally drifted into

6. Hawthorne became Surveyor in the Salem Customhouse in 1846 and remained in office until 1849.
7. General James F. Miller, who had been the Collector, or chief officer, for twenty-four years. Miller had earlier distinguished himself in the War of 1812 and as first territorial governor of Arkansas.

this quiet nook; where, with little to disturb them, except the periodical terrors of a Presidential election, they one and all acquired a new lease of existence. Though by no means less liable than their fellow-men to age and infirmity, they had evidently some talisman or other that kept death at bay. Two or three of their number, as I was assured, being gouty and rheumatic, or perhaps bed-ridden, never dreamed of making their appearance at the Custom-House, during a large part of the year; but, after a torpid winter, would creep out into the warm sunshine of May or June, go lazily about what they termed duty, and, at their own leisure and convenience, betake themselves to bed again. I must plead guilty to the charge of abbreviating the official breath of more than one of these venerable servants of the republic. They were allowed, on my representation, to rest from their arduous labors, and soon afterwards—as if their sole principle of life had been zeal for their country's service; as I verily believe it was—withdrew to a better world. It is a pious consolation to me, that, through my interference, a sufficient space was allowed them for repentance of the evil and corrupt practices, into which, as a matter of course, every Custom-House officer must be supposed to fall. Neither the front nor the back entrance of the Custom-House opens on the road to Paradise.

The greater part of my officers were Whigs. It was well for their venerable brotherhood, that the new Surveyor was not a politician, and, though a faithful Democrat in principle, neither received nor held his office with any reference to political services. Had it been otherwise,—had an active politician been put into this influential post, to assume the easy task of making head against a Whig Collector, whose infirmities withheld him from the personal administration of his office,—hardly a man of the old corps would have drawn the breath of official life, within a month after the exterminating angel had come up the Custom-House steps. According to the received code in such matters, it would have been nothing short of duty, in a politician, to bring every one of those white heads under the axe of the guillotine. It was plain enough to discern, that the old fellows dreaded some such discourtesy at my hands. It pained, and at the same time amused me, to behold the terrors that attended my advent; to see a furrowed cheek, weather-beaten by half a century of storm, turn ashy pale at the glance of so harmless an individual as myself; to detect, as one or another addressed me, the tremor of a voice, which, in long-past days, had been wont to bellow through a speaking-trumpet, hoarsely enough to frighten Boreas himself to silence.[8] They knew, these excellent old persons, that, by all established rule,—and, as regarded some of them,

8. Boreas was god of the north wind.

weighed by their own lack of efficiency for business,—they ought to have given place to younger men, more orthodox in politics, and altogether fitter than themselves to serve our common Uncle. I knew it too, but could never quite find in my heart to act upon the knowledge. Much and deservedly to my own discredit, therefore, and considerably to the detriment of my official conscience, they continued, during my incumbency, to creep about the wharves, and loiter up and down the Custom-House steps. They spent a good deal of time, also, asleep in their accustomed corners, with their chairs tilted back against the wall; awaking, however, once or twice in a forenoon, to bore one another with the several thousandth repetition of old sea-stories, and mouldy jokes, that had grown to be pass-words and countersigns among them.

The discovery was soon made, I imagine, that the new Surveyor had no great harm in him. So, with lightsome hearts, and the happy consciousness of being usefully employed,—in their own behalf, at least, if not for our beloved country,—these good old gentlemen went through the various formalities of office. Sagaciously, under their spectacles, did they peep into the holds of vessels! Mighty was their fuss about little matters, and marvellous, sometimes, the obtuseness that allowed greater ones to slip between their fingers! Whenever such a mischance occurred,—when a wagon-load of valuable merchandise had been smuggled ashore, at noonday, perhaps, and directly beneath their unsuspicious noses,—nothing could exceed the vigilance and alacrity with which they proceeded to lock, and double-lock, and secure with tape and sealing-wax, all the avenues of the delinquent vessel. Instead of a reprimand for their previous negligence, the case seemed rather to require an eulogium on their praiseworthy caution, after the mischief had happened; a grateful recognition of the promptitude of their zeal, the moment that there was no longer any remedy!

Unless people are more than commonly disagreeable, it is my foolish habit to contract a kindness for them. The better part of my companion's character, if it have a better part, is that which usually comes uppermost in my regard, and forms the type whereby I recognize the man. As most of these old Custom-House officers had good traits, and as my position in reference to them, being paternal and protective, was favorable to the growth of friendly sentiments, I soon grew to like them all. It was pleasant, in the summer forenoons,—when the fervent heat, that almost liquefied the rest of the human family, merely communicated a genial warmth to their half-torpid systems,—it was pleasant to hear them chatting in the back entry, a row of them all tipped against the wall, as usual; while the frozen witticisms of past generations were thawed out, and came bubbling with laughter from their lips. Externally, the jollity of aged men has much in common with the mirth of children; the intellect, any more than a deep sense of humor, has little to do with the matter; it is, with both, a gleam that plays upon the surface, and imparts a sunny and cheery aspect alike to the green branch, and gray, mouldering trunk. In one case, however, it is real sunshine; in the other, it more resembles the phosphorescent glow of decaying wood.

It would be sad injustice, the reader must understand, to represent all my excellent old friends as in their dotage. In the first place, my coadjutors were not invariably old; there were men among them in their strength and prime, of marked ability and energy, and altogether superior to the sluggish and dependent mode of life on which their evil stars had cast them. Then, moreover, the white locks of age were sometimes found to be the thatch of an intellectual tenement in good repair. But, as respects the majority of my corps of veterans, there will be no wrong done, if I characterize them generally as a set of wearisome old souls, who had gathered nothing worth preservation from their varied experience of life. They seemed to have flung away all the golden grain of practical wisdom, which they had enjoyed so many opportunities of harvesting, and most carefully to have stored their memories with the husks. They spoke with far more interest and unction of their morning's breakfast, or yesterday's, to-day's, or to-morrow's dinner, than of the shipwreck of forty or fifty years ago, and all the world's wonders which they had witnessed with their youthful eyes.

The father of the Custom-House—the patriarch, not only of this little squad of officials, but, I am bold to say, of the respectable body of tide-waiters all over the United States—was a certain permanent Inspector. He might truly be termed a legitimate son of the revenue system, dyed in the wool, or rather, born in the purple; since his sire, a Revolutionary colonel, and formerly collector of the port, had created an office for him, and appointed him to fill it, at a period of the early ages which few living men can now remember. This Inspector, when I first knew him, was a man of fourscore years, or thereabouts, and certainly one of the most wonderful specimens of winter-green that you would be likely to discover in a lifetime's search. With his florid cheek, his compact figure, smartly arrayed in a bright-buttoned blue coat, his brisk and vigorous step, and his hale and hearty aspect, altogether, he seemed—not young, indeed—but a kind of new contrivance of Mother Nature in the shape of man, whom age and infirmity had no business to touch. His voice and laugh, which perpetually reëchoed through the Custom-House, had nothing of the tremulous quaver and cackle of an old man's utterance; they came strutting out of his lungs, like the crow of a cock, or the blast of a clarion. Looking at him merely as an animal,—and there was very little else to look at,—he was a most satisfactory object, from the thorough healthfulness and whole-someness of his system, and his capacity, at that extreme age, to enjoy all, or nearly all, the delights which he had ever aimed at, or conceived of. The careless security of his life in the Custom-House, on a regular income, and with but slight and infrequent ap-prehensions of removal, had no doubt contributed to make time pass lightly over him. The original and more potent causes, how-ever, lay in the rare perfection of his animal nature, the moderate proportion of intellect, and the very trifling admixture of moral and spiritual ingredients; these latter qualities, indeed, being in barely enough measure to keep the old gentleman from walking on all-fours. He possessed no power of thought, no depth of feeling, no troublesome sensibilities; nothing, in short, but a few common-place instincts, which, aided by the cheerful temper that grew inevitably out of his physical well-being, did duty very respectably, and to general acceptance, in lieu of a heart. He had been the husband of three wives, all long since dead; the father of twenty children, most of whom, at every age of childhood or maturity, had likewise re-turned to dust. Here, one would suppose, might have been sorrow enough to imbue the sunniest disposition, through and through, with a sable tinge. Not so with our old Inspector! One brief sigh sufficed to carry off the entire burden of these dismal reminiscences. The next moment, he was as ready for sport as any unbreeched in-fant; far readier than the Collector's junior clerk, who, at nineteen years, was much the elder and graver man of the two.

I used to watch and study this patriarchal personage with, I think, livelier curiosity than any other form of humanity there pre-sented to my notice. He was, in truth, a rare phenomenon; so per-fect in one point of view; so shallow, so delusive, so impalpable, such an absolute nonentity, in every other. My conclusion was that he had no soul, no heart, no mind; nothing, as I have already said, but instincts; and yet, withal, so cunningly had the few materials of his character been put together, that there was no painful per-ception of deficiency, but, on my part, an entire contentment with what I found in him. It might be difficult—and it was so—to con-ceive how he should exist hereafter, so earthly and sensuous did he seem; but surely his existence here, admitting that it was to terminate with his last breath, had been not unkindly given; with no higher moral responsibilities than the beasts of the field, but with a larger scope of enjoyment than theirs, and with all their blessed immunity from the dreariness and duskiness of age.

One point, in which he had vastly the advantage over his four-footed brethren, was his ability to recollect the good dinners which it had made no small portion of the happiness of his life to eat. His gourmandism was a highly agreeable trait; and to hear him talk of roast-meat was as appetizing as a pickle or an oyster. As he possessed no higher attribute, and neither sacrificed nor vitiated any spiritual endowment by devoting all his energies and ingenuities to subserve the delight and profit of his maw, it always pleased and satisfied me to hear him expatiate on fish, poultry, and butcher's meat, and the most eligible methods of preparing them for the table. His reminiscences of good cheer, however ancient the date of the actual banquet, seemed to bring the savor of pig or turkey under one's very nostrils. There were flavors on his palate, that had lingered there not less than sixty or seventy years, and were still apparently as fresh as that of the mutton-chop which he had just devoured for his breakfast. I have heard him smack his lips over dinners, every guest at which, except himself, had long been food for worms. It was marvellous to observe how the ghosts of bygone meals were continually rising up before him; not in anger or retribution, but as if grateful for his former appreciation, and seeking to reduplicate an endless series of enjoyment, at once shadowy and sensual. A tenderloin of beef, a hind-quarter of veal, a spare-rib of pork, a particular chicken, or a remarkably praiseworthy turkey, which had perhaps adorned his board in the days of the elder Adams,[9] would be remembered; while all the subsequent experience of our race, and all the events that brightened or darkened his individual career, had gone over him with as little permanent effect as the passing breeze. The chief tragic event of the old man's life, so far as I could judge, was his mishap with a certain goose, which lived and died some twenty or forty years ago; a goose of most promising figure, but which, at table, proved so inveterately tough that the carving-knife would make no impression on its carcass; and it could only be divided with an axe and handsaw.

But it is time to quit this sketch; on which, however, I should be glad to dwell at considerably more length, because, of all men whom I have ever known, this individual was fittest to be a Custom-House officer. Most persons, owing to causes which I may not have space to hint at, suffer moral detriment from this peculiar mode of life. The old Inspector was incapable of it, and, were he to continue in office to the end of time, would be just as good as he was then, and sit down to dinner with just as good an appetite.

There is one likeness, without which my gallery of Custom-House portraits would be strangely incomplete; but which my comparatively few opportunities for observation enable me to sketch only

9. John Adams (1735–1826), second president of the United States, was father of the sixth president, hence "the elder Adams."

in the merest outline. It is that of the Collector, our gallant old General,[1] who, after his brilliant military service, subsequently to which he had ruled over a wild Western territory, had come hither, twenty years before, to spend the decline of his varied and honorable life. The brave soldier had already numbered, nearly or quite, his threescore years and ten, and was pursuing the remainder of his earthly march, burdened with infirmities which even the martial music of his own spirit-stirring recollections could do little towards lightening. The step was palsied now, that had been foremost in the charge. It was only with the assistance of a servant, and by leaning his hand heavily on the iron balustrade, that he could slowly and painfully ascend the Custom-House steps, and, with a toilsome progress across the floor, attain his customary chair beside the fireplace. There he used to sit, gazing with a somewhat dim serenity of aspect at the figures that came and went; amid the rustle of papers, the administering of oaths, the discussion of business, and the casual talk of the office; all which sounds and circumstances seemed but indistinctly to impress his senses, and hardly to make their way into his inner sphere of contemplation. His countenance, in this repose, was mild and kindly. If his notice was sought, an expression of courtesy and interest gleamed out upon his features; proving that there was light within him, and that it was only the outward medium of the intellectual lamp that obstructed the rays in their passage. The closer you penetrated to the substance of his mind, the sounder it appeared. When no longer called upon to speak, or listen, either of which operations cost him an evident effort, his face would briefly subside into its former not uncheerful quietude. It was not painful to behold this look; for, though dim, it had not the imbecility of decaying age. The framework of his nature, originally strong and massive, was not yet crumbled into ruin.

To observe and define his character, however, under such disadvantages, was as difficult a task as to trace out and build up anew, in imagination, an old fortress, like Ticonderoga, from a view of its gray and broken ruins.[2] Here and there, perchance, the walls may remain almost complete; but elsewhere may be only a shapeless mound, cumbrous with its very strength, and overgrown, through long years of peace and neglect, with grass and alien weeds.

Nevertheless, looking at the old warrior with affection,—for, slight as was the communication between us, my feeling towards him, like that of all bipeds and quadrupeds who knew him, might not improperly be termed so,—I could discern the main points of his portrait. It was marked with the noble and heroic qualities which

---

1. General Miller.
2. This fortress, captured from the British (May 10, 1775) by irregulars under Ethan Allen and Benedict Arnold, had already been depicted in Hawthorne's "Old Ticonderoga, A Picture of the Past."

showed it to be not by a mere accident, but of good right, that he had won a distinguished name. His spirit could never, I conceive, have been characterized by an uneasy activity; it must, at any period of his life, have required an impulse to set him in motion; but, once stirred up, with obstacles to overcome, and an adequate object to be attained, it was not in the man to give out or fail. The heat that had formerly pervaded his nature, and which was not yet extinct, was never of the kind that flashes and flickers in a blaze, but, rather, a deep, red glow, as of iron in a furnace. Weight, solidity, firmness; this was the expression of his repose, even in such decay as had crept untimely over him, at the period of which I speak. But I could imagine, even then, that, under some excitement which should go deeply into his consciousness,—roused by a trumpet-peal, loud enough to awaken all of his energies that were not dead, but only slumbering,—he was yet capable of flinging off his infirmities like a sick man's gown, dropping the staff of age to seize a battle-sword, and starting up once more a warrior. And, in so intense a moment, his demeanour would have still been calm. Such an exhibition, however, was but to be pictured in fancy; not to be anticipated, nor desired. What I saw in him—as evidently as the indestructible ramparts of Old Ticonderoga, already cited as the most appropriate simile—were the features of stubborn and ponderous endurance, which might well have amounted to obstinacy in his earlier days; of integrity, that, like most of his other endowments, lay in a somewhat heavy mass, and was just as unmalleable and unmanageable as a ton of iron ore; and of benevolence, which, fiercely as he led the bayonets on at Chippewa or Fort Erie,[3] I take to be of quite as genuine a stamp as what actuates any or all the polemical philanthropists of the age. He had slain men with his own hand, for aught I know;—certainly, they had fallen, like blades of grass at the sweep of the scythe, before the charge to which his spirit imparted its triumphant energy;—but, be that as it might, there was never in his heart so much cruelty as would have brushed the down off a butterfly's wing. I have not known the man, to whose innate kindliness I would more confidently make an appeal.

Many characteristics—and those, too, which contribute not the least forcibly to impart resemblance in a sketch—must have vanished, or been obscured, before I met the General. All merely graceful attributes are usually the most evanescent; nor does Nature adorn the human ruin with blossoms of new beauty, that have their roots and proper nutriment only in the chinks and crevices of decay, as she sows wall-flowers over the ruined fortress of Ticonderoga. Still, even in respect of grace and beauty, there were points

3. Battles on the Niagara front that turned the tide in the summer of 1814 (during the War of 1812).

well worth noting. A ray of humor, now and then, would make its way through the veil of dim obstruction, and glimmer pleasantly upon our faces. A trait of native elegance, seldom seen in the masculine character after childhood or early youth, was shown in the General's fondness for the sight and fragrance of flowers. An old soldier might be supposed to prize only the bloody laurel on his brow; but here was one, who seemed to have a young girl's appreciation of the floral tribe.

There, beside the fireplace, the brave old General used to sit; while the Surveyor—though seldom, when it could be avoided, taking upon himself the difficult task of engaging him in conversation—was fond of standing at a distance, and watching his quiet and almost slumberous countenance. He seemed away from us, although we saw him but a few yards off; remote, though we passed close beside his chair; unattainable, though we might have stretched forth our hands and touched his own. It might be, that he lived a more real life within his thoughts, than amid the unappropriate environment of the Collector's office. The evolutions of the parade; the tumult of the battle; the flourish of old, heroic music, heard thirty years before;—such scenes and sounds, perhaps, were all alive before his intellectual sense. Meanwhile, the merchants and ship-masters, the spruce clerks, and uncouth sailors, entered and departed; the bustle of this commercial and Custom-House life kept up its little murmur round about him; and neither with the men nor their affairs did the General appear to sustain the most distant relation. He was as much out of place as an old sword —now rusty, but which had flashed once in the battle's front, and showed still a bright gleam along its blade—would have been, among the inkstands, paper-folders, and mahogany rulers, on the Deputy Collector's desk.

There was one thing that much aided me in renewing and re-creating the stalwart soldier of the Niagara frontier,—the man of true and simple energy. It was the recollection of those memorable words of his,—"I'll try, Sir!"[4]—spoken on the very verge of a desperate and heroic enterprise, and breathing the soul and spirit of New England hardihood, comprehending all perils, and encountering all. If, in our country, valor were rewarded by heraldic honor, this phrase—which it seems so easy to speak, but which only he, with such a task of danger and glory before him, has ever spoken— would be the best and fittest of all mottoes for the General's shield of arms.

It contributes greatly towards a man's moral and intellectual health, to be brought into habits of companionship with indi-

4. Tradition holds that General Miller, when commanded by General Scott to take a British battery at Lundy's Lane, replied in these words.

viduals unlike himself, who care little for his pursuits, and whose sphere and abilities he must go out of himself to appreciate. The accidents of my life have often afforded me this advantage, but never with more fulness and variety than during my continuance in office. There was one man, especially, the observation of whose character gave me a new idea of talent. His gifts were emphatically those of a man of business; prompt, acute, clear-minded; with an eye that saw through all perplexities, and a faculty of arrangement that made them vanish, as by the waving of an enchanter's wand. Bred up from boyhood in the Custom-House, it was his proper field of activity; and the many intricacies of business, so harassing to the interloper, presented themselves before him with the regularity of a perfectly comprehended system. In my contemplation, he stood as the ideal of his class. He was, indeed, the Custom-House in himself; or, at all events, the main-spring that kept its variously revolving wheels in motion; for, in an institution like this, where its officers are appointed to subserve their own profit and convenience, and seldom with a leading reference to their fitness for the duty to be performed, they must perforce seek elsewhere the dexterity which is not in them. Thus, by an inevitable necessity, as a magnet attracts steel-filings, so did our man of business draw to himself the difficulties which everybody met with. With an easy condescension, and kind forbearance towards our stupidity,—which, to his order of mind, must have seemed little short of crime,—would he forthwith, by the merest touch of his finger, make the incomprehensible as clear as daylight. The merchants valued him not less than we, his esoteric friends. His integrity was perfect; it was a law of nature with him, rather than a choice or a principle; nor can it be otherwise than the main condition of an intellect so remarkably clear and accurate as his, to be honest and regular in the administration of affairs. A stain on his conscience, as to any thing that came within the range of his vocation, would trouble such a man very much in the same way, though to a far greater degree, than an error in the balance of an account, or an ink-blot on the fair page of a book of record. Here, in a word,—and it is a rare instance in my life,—I had met with a person thoroughly adapted to the situation which he held.

Such were some of the people with whom I now found myself connected. I took it in good part at the hands of Providence, that I was thrown into a position so little akin to my past habits; and set myself seriously to gather from it whatever profit was to be had. After my fellowship of toil and impracticable schemes, with the dreamy brethren of Brook Farm;[5] after living for three years within

5. The cooperative agrarian community near Boston, founded by transcen- dentalists in 1841. Hawthorne joined, but withdrew, somewhat poorer, after

the subtile influence of an intellect like Emerson's; after those wild, free days on the Assabeth, indulging fantastic speculations beside our fire of fallen boughs, with Ellery Channing;[6] after talking with Thoreau about pine-trees and Indian relics, in his hermitage at Walden; after growing fastidious by sympathy with the classic refinement of Hillard's[7] culture; after becoming imbued with poetic sentiment at Longfellow's hearth-stone;—it was time, at length, that I should exercise other faculties of my nature, and nourish myself with food for which I had hitherto had little appetite. Even the old Inspector was desirable, as a change of diet, to a man who had known Alcott.[8] I looked upon it as an evidence, in some measure, of a system naturally well balanced, and lacking no essential part of a thorough organization, that, with such associates to remember, I could mingle at once with men of altogether different qualities, and never murmur at the change.

Literature, its exertions and objects, were now of little moment in my regard. I cared not, at this period, for books; they were apart from me. Nature,—except it were human nature,—the nature that is developed in earth and sky, was, in one sense, hidden from me; and all the imaginative delight, wherewith it had been spiritualized, passed away out of my mind. A gift, a faculty, if it had not departed, was suspended and inanimate within me. There would have been something sad, unutterably dreary, in all this, had I not been conscious that it lay at my own option to recall whatever was valuable in the past. It might be true, indeed, that this was a life which could not, with impunity, be lived too long; else, it might make me permanently other than I had been, without transforming me into any shape which it would be worth my while to take. But I never considered it as other than a transitory life. There was always a prophetic instinct, a low whisper in my ear, that, within no long period, and whenever a new change of custom should be essential to my good, a change would come.

Meanwhile, there I was, a Surveyor of the Revenue, and, so far as I have been able to understand, as good a Surveyor as need be. A man of thought, fancy, and sensibility, (had he ten times the Surveyor's proportion of those qualities,) may, at any time, be a man of affairs, if he will only choose to give himself the trouble. My fellow-officers, and the merchants and sea-captains with whom my official duties brought me into any manner of connection,

seven months. The experience is reflected in his novel, *The Blithedale Romance* (1852).

6. The Assabeth joins the Concord River near Concord. Since he was living at Emerson's home in Concord, Hawthorne came to know such members of Emerson's circle as William Ellery Channing (1818–1901).

7. George Stillman Hillard (1808–79), Boston lawyer and philanthropist, prominent in literary circles; he served Hawthorne as friend and practical advisor.

8. Bronson Alcott (1799–1888) was the most extreme and visionary of the American transcendentalists.

viewed me in no other light, and probably knew me in no other character. None of them, I presume, had ever read a page of my inditing, or would have cared a fig the more for me, if they had read them all; nor would it have mended the matter, in the least, had those same unprofitable pages been written with a pen like that of Burns or of Chaucer, each of whom was a Custom-House officer in his day,[9] as well as I. It is a good lesson—though it may often be a hard one—for a man who has dreamed of literary fame, and of making for himself a rank among the world's dignitaries by such means, to step aside out of the narrow circle in which his claims are recognized, and to find how utterly devoid of significance, beyond that circle, is all that he achieves, and all he aims at. I know not that I especially needed the lesson, either in the way of warning or rebuke; but, at any rate, I learned it thoroughly; nor, it gives me pleasure to reflect, did the truth, as it came home to my perception, ever cost me a pang, or require to be thrown off in a sigh. In the way of literary talk, it is true, the Naval Officer—an excellent fellow, who came into office with me, and went out only a little later—would often engage me in a discussion about one or the other of his favorite topics, Napoleon or Shakespeare. The Collector's junior clerk, too,—a young gentleman who, it was whispered, occasionally covered a sheet of Uncle Sam's letter-paper with what, (at the distance of a few yards,) looked very much like poetry,—used now and then to speak to me of books, as matters with which I might possibly be conversant. This was my all of lettered intercourse; and it was quite sufficient for my necessities.

No longer seeking nor caring that my name should be blazoned abroad on title-pages, I smiled to think that it had now another kind of vogue. The Custom-House marker imprinted it, with a stencil and black paint, on pepper-bags, and baskets of anatto,[1] and cigar-boxes, and bales of all kinds of dutiable merchandise, in testimony that these commodities had paid the impost, and gone regularly through the office. Borne on such queer vehicle of fame, a knowledge of my existence, so far as a name conveys it, was carried where it had never been before, and, I hope, will never go again.

But the past was not dead. Once in a great while, the thoughts, that had seemed so vital and so active, yet had been put to rest so quietly, revived again. One of the most remarkable occasions, when the habit of bygone days awoke in me, was that which brings it within the law of literary propriety to offer the public the sketch which I am now writing.

In the second story of the Custom-House, there is a large room,

---

9. Chaucer served as Controller of Customs in London from 1374 to 1386; Robert Burns was District Collector of Excise Taxes from 1789 to 1791.

1. Usually "annatto," a red dyestuff derived from the pulp of a tropical fruit.

in which the brick-work and naked rafters have never been covered with paneling and plaster. The edifice—originally projected on a scale adapted to the old commercial enterprise of the port, and with an idea of subsequent prosperity destined never to be realized—contains far more space than its occupants know what to do with. This airy hall, therefore, over the Collector's apartments, remains unfinished to this day, and, in spite of the aged cobwebs that festoon its dusky beams, appears still to await the labor of the carpenter and mason. At one end of the room, in a recess, were a number of barrels, piled one upon another, containing bundles of official documents. Large quantities of similar rubbish lay lumbering the floor. It was sorrowful to think how many days, and weeks, and months, and years of toil, had been wasted on these musty papers, which were now only an encumbrance on earth, and were hidden away in this forgotten corner, never more to be glanced at by human eyes. But, then, what reams of other manuscripts—filled, not with the dulness of official formalities, but with the thought of inventive brains and the rich effusion of deep hearts—had gone equally to oblivion; and that, moreover, without serving a purpose in their day, as these heaped up papers had, and—saddest of all—without purchasing for their writers the comfortable livelihood which the clerks of the Custom-House had gained by these worthless scratchings of the pen! Yet not altogether worthless, perhaps, as materials of local history. Here, no doubt, statistics of the former commerce of Salem might be discovered, and memorials of her princely merchants,—old King Derby,—old Billy Gray,—old Simon Forrester,—and many another magnate in his day;[2] whose powdered head, however, was scarcely in the tomb, before his mountain-pile of wealth began to dwindle. The founders of the greater part of the families which now compose the aristocracy of Salem might here be traced, from the petty and obscure beginnings of their traffic, at periods generally much posterior to the Revolution, upward to what their children look upon as long-established rank.

Prior to the Revolution, there is a dearth of records; the earlier documents and archives of the Custom-House having, probably, been carried off to Halifax, when all the King's officials accompanied the British army in its flight from Boston.[3] It has often been a matter of regret with me; for, going back, perhaps, to the days of the Protectorate,[4] those papers must have contained many refer-

---

2. William Gray (1750–1825), a wealthy shipowner, in late life became lieutenant governor of Massachusetts. Captain Simon Forrester (1776–1851), when Hawthorne wrote these words, was thought to be the wealthiest citizen of Salem.
3. Hawthorne's suggestion is whimsical —but Salem did become the colonial seat of Massachusetts when the British

closed the port and occupied Boston at the beginning of the Revolution. Washington besieged Boston in March, 1776, and Howe evacuated his British troops by ship to Halifax, Nova Scotia.
4. That phase of the English revolution during which Oliver Cromwell, as "Lord Protector," was chief of state from 1653 to 1658.

ences to forgotten or remembered men, and to antique customs, which would have affected me with the same pleasure as when I used to pick up Indian arrow-heads in the field near the Old Manse.

But, one idle and rainy day, it was my fortune to make a discovery of some little interest. Poking and burrowing into the heaped-up rubbish in the corner; unfolding one and another document, and reading the names of vessels that had long ago foundered at sea or rotted at the wharves, and those of merchants, never heard of now on 'Change,[5] nor very readily decipherable on their mossy tombstones; glancing at such matters with the saddened, weary, half-reluctant interest which we bestow on the corpse of dead activity,—and exerting my fancy, sluggish with little use, to raise up from these dry bones an image of the old town's brighter aspect, when India was a new region, and only Salem knew the way thither,—I chanced to lay my hand on a small package, carefully done up in a piece of ancient yellow parchment. This envelope had the air of an official record of some period long past, when clerks engrossed their stiff and formal chirography on more substantial materials than at present. There was something about it that quickened an instinctive curiosity, and made me undo the faded red tape, that tied up the package, with the sense that a treasure would here be brought to light. Unbending the rigid folds of the parchment cover, I found it to be a commission, under the hand and seal of Governor Shirley,[6] in favor of one Jonathan Pue, as Surveyor of his Majesty's Customs for the port of Salem, in the Province of Massachusetts Bay. I remembered to have read (probably in Felt's Annals)[7] a notice of the decease of Mr. Surveyor Pue, about fourscore years ago; and likewise, in a newspaper of recent times, an account of the digging up of his remains in the little graveyard of St. Peter's Church, during the renewal of that edifice. Nothing, if I rightly call to mind, was left of my respected predecessor, save an imperfect skeleton, and some fragments of apparel, and a wig of majestic frizzle; which, unlike the head that it once adorned, was in very satisfactory preservation. But, on examining the papers which the parchment commission served to envelop, I found more traces of Mr. Pue's mental part, and the internal operations of his head, than the frizzled wig had contained of the venerable skull itself.

5. The "Merchant's Exchange," Boston.
6. William Shirley, English-born lawyer, came to Massachusetts in 1731, later serving as governor (1741–49 and 1753–56).
7. The death of one Jonathan Pue, surveyor and searcher of Salem and Marblehead, in fact appears in the *Annals*, dated March 24, 1760 (Joseph B. Felt, *Annals of Salem from its First Settle-* *ment*, Salem, 1827). Such antiquarian records and local archives fascinated Hawthorne and gave substance to the imagination which created his writings. For Hawthorne's debt to historical sources, see Charles Ryskamp, "The New England Sources of *The Scarlet Letter*," reprinted on pp. 205–219 of this book.

They were documents, in short, not official, but of a private nature, or, at least, written in his private capacity, and apparently with his own hand. I could account for their being included in the heap of Custom-House lumber only by the fact, that Mr. Pue's death had happened suddenly; and that these papers, which he probably kept in his official desk, had never come to the knowledge of his heirs, or were supposed to relate to the business of the revenue. On the transfer of the archives to Halifax, this package, proving to be of no public concern, was left behind, and had remained ever since unopened.

The ancient Surveyor—being little molested, I suppose, at that early day, with business pertaining to his office—seems to have devoted some of his many leisure hours to researches as a local antiquarian, and other inquisitions of a similar nature. These supplied material for petty activity to a mind that would otherwise have been eaten up with rust. A portion of his facts, by the by, did me good service in the preparation of the article entitled "Main Street," included in the present volume.[8] The remainder may perhaps be applied to purposes equally valuable, hereafter; or not impossibly may be worked up, so far as they go, into a regular history of Salem, should my veneration for the natal soil ever impel me to so pious a task. Meanwhile, they shall be at the command of any gentleman, inclined, and competent, to take the unprofitable labor off my hands. As a final disposition, I contemplate depositing them with the Essex Historical Society.[9]

But the object that most drew my attention, in the mysterious package, was a certain affair of fine red cloth, much worn and faded. There were traces about it of gold embroidery, which, however, was greatly frayed and defaced; so that none, or very little, of the glitter was left. It had been wrought, as was easy to perceive, with wonderful skill of needlework; and the stitch (as I am assured by ladies conversant with such mysteries) gives evidence of a now forgotten art, not to be recovered even by the process of picking out the threads. This rag of scarlet cloth,—for time, and wear, and a sacrilegious moth, had reduced it to little other than a rag,—on careful examination, assumed the shape of a letter. It was the capital letter A. By an accurate measurement, each limb proved to be precisely three inches and a quarter in length. It had been intended, there could be no doubt, as an ornamental article of dress; but how it was to be worn, or what rank, honor, and dignity, in by-past times,

8. He later excluded this and several other tales from the volume. "Main Street," a descriptive account of old Salem, appeared in a miscellany entitled *Aesthetic Papers* (1849), edited by his sister-in-law, Elizabeth Peabody; later in *The Snow-Image and Other Twice-Told Tales* (1852).

9. Since the Pue documents and the red or scarlet letter A are fictional inventions, they were never received by the Historical Society of Essex County, Massachusetts.

were signified by it, was a riddle which (so evanescent are the fashions of the world in these particulars) I saw little hope of solving. And yet it strangely interested me. My eyes fastened themselves upon the old scarlet letter, and would not be turned aside. Certainly, there was some deep meaning in it, most worthy of interpretation, and which, as it were, streamed forth from the mystic symbol, subtly communicating itself to my sensibilities, but evading the analysis of my mind.

While thus perplexed,—and cogitating, among other hypotheses, whether the letter might not have been one of those decorations which the white men used to contrive, in order to take the eyes of Indians,—I happened to place it on my breast. It seemed to me, —the reader may smile, but must not doubt my word,—it seemed to me, then, that I experienced a sensation not altogether physical, yet almost so, as of burning heat; and as if the letter were not of red cloth, but red-hot iron.[1] I shuddered, and involuntarily let it fall upon the floor.

In the absorbing contemplation of the scarlet letter, I had hitherto neglected to examine a small roll of dingy paper, around which it had been twisted. This I now opened, and had the satisfaction to find, recorded by the old Surveyor's pen, a reasonably complete explanation of the whole affair. There were several foolscap sheets, containing many particulars respecting the life and conversation of one Hester Prynne, who appeared to have been rather a noteworthy personage in the view of our ancestors. She had flourished during a period between the early days of Massachusetts and the close of the seventeenth century. Aged persons, alive in the time of Mr. Surveyor Pue, and from whose oral testimony he had made up his narrative, remembered her, in their youth, as a very old, but not decrepit woman, of a stately and solemn aspect. It had been her habit, from an almost immemorial date, to go about the country as a kind of voluntary nurse, and doing whatever miscellaneous good she might; taking upon herself, likewise, to give advice in all matters, especially those of the heart; by which means, as a person of such propensities inevitably must, she gained from many people the reverence due to an angel,[2] but, I should imagine, was looked upon by others as an intruder and a nuisance. Prying farther into the manuscript, I found the record of other doings and sufferings of this singular woman, for most of which the reader is referred to the story entitled *The Scarlet Letter*; and it should be borne carefully in mind, that the main facts of that story are authorized

1. Anticipating a mystery unresolved in the novel, whether Hester's letter of scarlet cloth was matched by an A branded on Arthur's breast.
2. See conclusion of the last chapter of the novel.

and authenticated by the document of Mr. Surveyor Pue. The original papers, together with the scarlet letter itself,—a most curious relic,—are still in my possession, and shall be freely exhibited to whomsoever, induced by the great interest of the narrative, may desire a sight of them. I must not be understood as affirming, that, in the dressing up of the tale, and imagining the motives and modes of passion that influenced the characters who figure in it, I have invariably confined myself within the limits of the old Surveyor's half a dozen sheets of foolscap. On the contrary; I have allowed myself, as to such points, nearly or altogether as much license as if the facts had been entirely of my own invention. What I contend for is the authenticity of the outline.

This incident recalled my mind, in some degree, to its old track. There seemed to be here the groundwork of a tale. It impressed me as if the ancient Surveyor, in his garb of a hundred years gone by, and wearing his immortal wig,—which was buried with him, but did not perish in the grave,—had met me in the deserted chamber of the Custom-House. In his port was the dignity of one who had borne his Majesty's commission, and who was therefore illuminated by a ray of the splendor that shone so dazzlingly about the throne. How unlike, alas! the hang-dog look of a republican official, who, as the servant of the people, feels himself less than the least, and below the lowest, of his masters. With his own ghostly hand, the obscurely seen, but majestic, figure had imparted to me the scarlet symbol, and the little roll of explanatory manuscript. With his own ghostly voice, he had exhorted me, on the sacred consideration of my filial duty and reverence towards him,—who might reasonably regard himself as my official ancestor,—to bring his mouldy and moth-eaten lucubrations before the public. "Do this," said the ghost of Mr. Surveyor Pue, emphatically nodding the head that looked so imposing within its memorable wig, "do this, and the profit shall be all your own! You will shortly need it; for it is not in your days as it was in mine, when a man's office was a life-lease, and oftentimes an heirloom. But, I charge you, in this matter of old Mistress Prynne, give to your predecessor's memory the credit which will be rightfully its due!" And I said to the ghost of Mr. Surveyor Pue,—"I will!"

On Hester Prynne's story, therefore, I bestowed much thought. It was the subject of my meditations for many an hour, while pacing to and fro across my room, or traversing, with a hundredfold repetition, the long extent from the front-door of the Custom-House to the side-entrance, and back again. Great were the weariness and annoyance of the old Inspector and the Weighers and Gaugers, whose slumbers were disturbed by the unmercifully lengthened tramp of my passing and returning footsteps. Remembering their own former habits, they used to say that the Surveyor was walking the quarter-deck. They probably fancied that my sole object—and, indeed, the sole object for which a sane man could ever put himself into voluntary motion—was, to get an appetite for dinner. And to say the truth, an appetite, sharpened by the east-wind that generally blew along the passage, was the only valuable result of so much indefatigable exercise. So little adapted is the atmosphere of a Custom-House to the delicate harvest of fancy and sensibility, that, had I remained there through ten Presidencies yet to come, I doubt whether the tale of *The Scarlet Letter* would ever have been brought before the public eye. My imagination was a tarnished mirror. It would not reflect, or only with miserable dimness, the figures with which I did my best to people it. The characters of the narrative would not be warmed and rendered malleable, by any heat that I could kindle at my intellectual forge. They would take neither the glow of passion nor the tenderness of sentiment, but retained all the rigidity of dead corpses, and stared me in the face with a fixed and ghastly grin of contemptuous defiance. "What have you to do with us?" that expression seemed to say. "The little power you might once have possessed over the tribe of unrealities is gone! You have bartered it for a pittance of the public gold. Go, then, and earn your wages!" In short, the almost torpid creatures of my own fancy twitted me with imbecility, and not without fair occasion.

It was not merely during the three hours and a half which Uncle Sam claimed as his share of my daily life, that this wretched numbness held possession of me. It went with me on my sea-shore walks and rambles into the country, whenever—which was seldom and reluctantly—I bestirred myself to seek that invigorating charm of Nature, which used to give me such freshness and activity of thought, the moment that I stepped across the threshold of the Old Manse. The same torpor, as regarded the capacity for intellectual effort, accompanied me home, and weighed upon me in the chamber which I most absurdly termed my study. Nor did it quit me, when, late at night, I sat in the deserted parlour, lighted only by the glimmering coal-fire and the moon, striving to picture forth imaginary scenes, which, the next day, might flow out on the brightening page in many-hued description.

If the imaginative faculty refused to act at such an hour, it might well be deemed a hopeless case. Moonlight, in a familiar room, falling so white upon the carpet, and showing all its figures so distinctly,—making every object so minutely visible, yet so unlike a morning or noontide visibility,—is a medium the most suitable for a romance-writer to get acquainted with his illusive guests.

There is the little domestic scenery of the well-known apartment; the chairs, with each its separate individuality; the centre-table, sustaining a work-basket, a volume or two, and an extinguished lamp; the sofa; the book-case; the picture on the wall;—all these details, so completely seen, are so spiritualized by the unusual light, that they seem to lose their actual substance, and become things of intellect. Nothing is too small or too trifling to undergo this change, and acquire dignity thereby. A child's shoe; the doll, seated in her little wicker carriage; the hobby-horse;—whatever, in a word, has been used or played with, during the day, is now invested with a quality of strangeness and remoteness, though still almost as vividly present as by daylight. Thus, therefore, the floor of our familiar room has become a neutral territory, somewhere between the real world and fairy-land, where the Actual and the Imaginary may meet, and each imbue itself with the nature of the other. Ghosts might enter here, without affrighting us. It would be too much in keeping with the scene to excite surprise, were we to look about us and discover a form, beloved, but gone hence, now sitting quietly in a streak of this magic moonshine, with an aspect that would make us doubt whether it had returned from afar, or had never once stirred from our fireside.

The somewhat dim coal-fire has an essential influence in producing the effect which I would describe. It throws its unobtrusive tinge throughout the room, with a faint ruddiness upon the walls and ceiling, and a reflected gleam from the polish of the furniture. This warmer light mingles itself with the cold spirituality of the moonbeams, and communicates, as it were, a heart and sensibilities of human tenderness to the forms which fancy summons up. It converts them from snow-images into men and women. Glancing at the looking-glass, we behold—deep within its haunted verge— the smouldering glow of the half-extinguished anthracite, the white moonbeams on the floor, and a repetition of all the gleam and shadow of the picture, with one remove farther from the actual, and nearer to the imaginative. Then, at such an hour, and with this scene before him, if a man, sitting all alone, cannot dream strange things, and make them look like truth, he need never try to write romances.

But, for myself, during the whole of my Custom-House experience, moonlight and sunshine, and the glow of fire-light, were just alike in my regard; and neither of them was of one whit more avail than the twinkle of a tallow-candle. An entire class of susceptibilities, and a gift connected with them,—of no great richness or value, but the best I had,—was gone from me.

It is my belief, however, that, had I attempted a different order of composition, my faculties would not have been found so pointless and inefficacious. I might, for instance, have contented myself with writing out the narratives of a veteran shipmaster, one of the Inspectors, whom I should be most ungrateful not to mention; since scarcely a day passed that he did not stir me to laughter and admiration by his marvellous gifts as a story-teller. Could I have preserved the picturesque force of his style, and the humorous coloring which nature taught him how to throw over his descriptions, the result, I honestly believe, would have been something new in literature. Or I might readily have found a more serious task. It was a folly, with the materiality of this daily life pressing so intrusively upon me, to attempt to fling myself back into another age; or to insist on creating the semblance of a world out of airy matter, when, at every moment, the impalpable beauty of my soap-bubble was broken by the rude contact of some actual circumstance. The wiser effort would have been, to diffuse thought and imagination through the opaque substance of to-day, and thus to make it a bright transparency; to spiritualize the burden that began to weigh so heavily; to seek, resolutely, the true and indestructible value that lay hidden in the petty and wearisome incidents, and ordinary characters, with which I was now conversant. The fault was mine. The page of life that was spread out before me seemed dull and commonplace, only because I had not fathomed its deeper import. A better book than I shall ever write was there; leaf after leaf presenting itself to me, just as it was written out by the reality of the flitting hour, and vanishing as fast as written, only because my brain wanted the insight and my hand the cunning to transcribe it. At some future day, it may be, I shall remember a few scattered fragments and broken paragraphs, and write them down, and find the letters turn to gold upon the page.

These perceptions have come too late. At the instant, I was only conscious that what would have been a pleasure once was now a hopeless toil. There was no occasion to make much moan about this state of affairs. I had ceased to be a writer of tolerably poor tales and essays, and had become a tolerably good Surveyor of the Customs. That was all. But, nevertheless, it is any thing but agreeable to be haunted by a suspicion that one's intellect is dwindling away; or exhaling, without your consciousness, like ether out of a phial; so that, at every glance, you find a smaller and less volatile residuum. Of the fact, there could be no doubt; and, examining myself and others, I was led to conclusions in reference to the effect of public office on the character, not very favorable to the mode of life in question. In some other form, perhaps, I may hereafter develop these effects. Suffice it here to say, that a Custom-House officer, of long continuance, can hardly be a very praiseworthy or respectable personage, for many reasons; one of them, the tenure by which he holds his situation, and another, the very nature of his business, which—though, I trust, an honest one—is of such a sort that he does not share in the united effort of mankind.

An effect—which I believe to be observable, more or less, in every individual who has occupied the position—is, that, while he leans on the mighty arm of the Republic, his own proper strength departs from him. He loses, in an extent proportioned to the weakness or force of his original nature, the capability of self-support. If he possess an unusual share of native energy, or the enervating magic of place do not operate too long upon him, his forfeited powers may be redeemable. The ejected officer—fortunate in the unkindly shove that sends him forth betimes, to struggle amid a struggling world—may return to himself, and become all that he has ever been. But this seldom happens. He usually keeps his ground just long enough for his own ruin, and is then thrust out, with sinews all unstrung, to totter along the difficult footpath of life as he best may. Conscious of his own infirmity,—that his tempered steel and elasticity are lost,—he for ever afterwards looks wistfully about him in quest of support external to himself. His pervading and continual hope—a hallucination, which, in the face of all discouragement, and making light of impossibilities, haunts him while he lives, and, I fancy, like the convulsive throes of the cholera, torments him for a brief space after death—is, that, finally, and in no long time, by some happy coincidence of circumstances, he shall be restored to office. This faith, more than any thing else, steals the pith and availability out of whatever enterprise he may dream of undertaking. Why should he toil and moil, and be at so much trouble to pick himself up out of the mud, when, in a little while hence, the strong arm of his Uncle will raise and support him? Why should he work for his living here, or go to dig gold in California,[3] when he is so soon to be made happy, at monthly intervals, with a little pile of glittering coin out of his Uncle's pocket? It is sadly curious to observe how slight a taste of office suffices to infect a poor fellow with this singular disease. Uncle Sam's gold—meaning no disrespect to the worthy old gentleman—has, in this respect, a quality of enchantment like that of the Devil's wages. Whoever touches it should look well to himself, or he may find the bargain to go hard against him, involving, if not his soul, yet many of its better attributes; its sturdy force, its courage and constancy, its truth, its self-reliance, and all that gives the emphasis to manly character.

Here was a fine prospect in the distance! Not that the Surveyor brought the lesson home to himself, or admitted that he could be so utterly undone, either by continuance in office, or ejectment. Yet my reflections were not the most comfortable. I began to grow

3. The California gold rush had begun the year before, in 1849.

melancholy and restless; continually prying into my mind, to discover which of its poor properties were gone, and what degree of detriment had already accrued to the remainder. I endeavoured to calculate how much longer I could stay in the Custom-House, and yet go forth a man. To confess the truth, it was my greatest apprehension,—as it would never be a measure of policy to turn out so quiet an individual as myself, and it being hardly in the nature of a public officer to resign,—it was my chief trouble, therefore, that I was likely to grow gray and decrepit in the Surveyorship, and become much such another animal as the old Inspector. Might it not, in the tedious lapse of official life that lay before me, finally be with me as it was with this venerable friend,—to make the dinner-hour the nucleus of the day, and to spend the rest of it, as an old dog spends it, asleep in the sunshine or the shade? A dreary look-forward this, for a man who felt it to be the best definition of happiness to live throughout the whole range of his faculties and sensibilities! But, all this while, I was giving myself very unnecessary alarm. Providence had meditated better things for me than I could possibly imagine for myself.

A remarkable event of the third year of my Surveyorship—to adopt the tone of "P.P."—was the election of General Taylor to the Presidency.[4] It is essential, in order to [form] a complete estimate of the advantages of official life, to view the incumbent at the incoming of a hostile administration. His position is then one of the most singularly irksome, and, in every contingency, disagreeable, that a wretched mortal can possibly occupy; with seldom an alternative of good, on either hand, although what presents itself to him as the worst event may very probably be the best. But it is a strange experience, to a man of pride and sensibility, to know that his interests are within the control of individuals who neither love nor understand him, and by whom, since one or the other must needs happen, he would rather be injured than obliged. Strange, too, for one who has kept his calmness throughout the contest, to observe the bloodthirstiness that is developed in the hour of triumph, and to be conscious that he is himself among its objects! There are few uglier traits of human nature than this tendency—which I now witnessed in men no worse than their neighbours—to grow cruel, merely because they possessed the power of inflicting harm. If the guillotine, as applied to office-holders, were a literal fact, instead of one of the most apt of metaphors, it is my sincere belief, that the active members of the victorious party were sufficiently excited to have chopped off all our heads, and have thanked Heaven for the opportunity! It appears to me—who have been a calm and curious observer, as well in victory as defeat—that this fierce and

4. Zachary Taylor, elected on the Whig ticket in 1848.

bitter spirit of malice and revenge has never distinguished the many triumphs of my own party as it now did that of the Whigs. The Democrats take the offices, as a general rule, because they need them, and because the practice of many years has made it the law of political warfare, which, unless a different system be proclaimed, it were weakness and cowardice to murmur at. But the long habit of victory has made them generous. They know how to spare, when they see occasion; and when they strike, the axe may be sharp, indeed, but its edge is seldom poisoned with ill-will; nor is it their custom ignominiously to kick the head which they have just struck off.

In short, unpleasant as was my predicament, at best, I saw much reason to congratulate myself that I was on the losing side, rather than the triumphant one. If, heretofore, I had been none of the warmest of partisans, I began now, at this season of peril and adversity, to be pretty acutely sensible with which party my predilections lay; nor was it without something like regret and shame, that, according to a reasonable calculation of chances, I saw my own prospect of retaining office to be better than those of my Democratic brethren. But who can see an inch into futurity, beyond his nose? My own head was the first that fell!

The moment when a man's head drops off is seldom or never, I am inclined to think, precisely the most agreeable of his life. Nevertheless, like the greater part of our misfortunes, even so serious a contingency brings its remedy and consolation with it, if the sufferer will but make the best, rather than the worst, of the accident which has befallen him. In my particular case, the consolatory topics were close at hand, and, indeed, had suggested themselves to my meditations a considerable time before it was requisite to use them. In view of my previous weariness of office, and vague thoughts of resignation, my fortune somewhat resembled that of a person who should entertain an idea of committing suicide, and, altogether beyond his hopes, meet with the good hap to be murdered. In the Custom-House, as before in the Old Manse, I had spent three years; a term long enough to rest a weary brain; long enough to break off old intellectual habits, and make room for new ones; long enough, and too long, to have lived in an unnatural state, doing what was really of no advantage nor delight to any human being, and withholding myself from toil that would, at least, have stilled an unquiet impulse in me. Then, moreover, as regarded his unceremonious ejectment, the late Surveyor was not altogether ill-pleased to be recognized by the Whigs as an enemy; since his inactivity in political affairs,—his tendency to roam, at will, in that broad and quiet field where all mankind may meet, rather than confine himself to those narrow paths where brethren of the same household must diverge from one another,—had sometimes made it questionable with his brother Democrats whether he was a friend. Now, after he had won the crown of martyrdom, (though with no longer a head to wear it on,) the point might be looked upon as settled. Finally, little heroic as he was, it seemed more decorous to be overthrown in the downfall of the party with which he had been content to stand, than to remain a forlorn survivor, when so many worthier men were falling; and, at last, after subsisting for four years on the mercy of a hostile administration, to be compelled then to define his position anew, and claim the yet more humiliating mercy of a friendly one.

Meanwhile, the press had taken up my affair, and kept me, for a week or two, careering through the public prints, in my decapitated state, like Irving's Headless Horseman;[5] ghastly and grim, and longing to be buried, as a politically dead man ought. So much for my figurative self. The real human being, all this time, with his head safely on his shoulders, had brought himself to the comfortable conclusion, that every thing was for the best; and, making an investment in ink, paper, and steel-pens, had opened his long-disused writing-desk, and was again a literary man.

Now it was, that the lucubrations of my ancient predecessor, Mr. Surveyor Pue, came into play. Rusty through long idleness, some little space was requisite before my intellectual machinery could be brought to work upon the tale, with an effect in any degree satisfactory. Even yet, though my thoughts were ultimately much absorbed in the task, it wears, to my eye, a stern and sombre aspect; too much ungladdened by genial sunshine; too little relieved by the tender and familiar influences which soften almost every scene of nature and real life, and, undoubtedly, should soften every picture of them. This uncaptivating effect is perhaps due to the period of hardly accomplished revolution, and still seething turmoil, in which the story shaped itself. It is no indication, however, of a lack of cheerfulness in the writer's mind; for he was happier, while straying through the gloom of these sunless fantasies, than at any time since he had quitted the Old Manse. Some of the briefer articles, which contribute to make up the volume, have likewise been written since my involuntary withdrawal from the toils and honors of public life, and the remainder are gleaned from annuals and magazines, of such antique date that they have gone round the circle, and come back to novelty again.[6] Keeping up the metaphor of the political guillotine, the whole may be considered as the "Posthumous Papers of a Decapitated Surveyor"; and the sketch which I

5. *Cf.* Irving's story, "The Legend of Sleepy Hollow."
6. "At the time of writing this article, the author intended to publish, along with *The Scarlet Letter*, several shorter tales and sketches. These it has been thought advisable to defer." [*Hawthorne's note.*]

am now bringing to a close, if too autobiographical for a modest person to publish in his lifetime, will readily be excused in a gentleman who writes from beyond the grave. Peace be with all the world! My blessing on my friends! My forgiveness to my enemies! For I am in the realm of quiet!

The life of the Custom-House lies like a dream behind me. The old Inspector,—who, by the by, I regret to say, was overthrown and killed by a horse, some time ago; else he would certainly have lived for ever,—he, and all those other venerable personages who sat with him at the receipt of custom, are but shadows in my view; white-headed and wrinkled images, which my fancy used to sport with, and has now flung aside for ever. The merchants,—Pingree, Phillips, Shepard, Upton, Kimball, Bertram, Hunt,—these, and many other names, which had such a classic familiarity for my ear six months ago,—these men of traffic, who seemed to occupy so important a position in the world,—how little time has it required to disconnect me from them all, not merely in act, but recollection! It is with an effort that I recall the figures and appellations of these few. Soon, likewise, my old native town will loom upon me through the haze of memory, a mist brooding over and around it; as if it were no portion of the real earth, but an overgrown village in cloud-land, with only imaginary inhabitants to people its wooden houses, and walk its homely lanes, and the unpicturesque prolixity of its main street. Henceforth, it ceases to be a reality of my life. I am a citizen of somewhere else. My good townspeople will not much regret me; for—though it has been as dear an object as any, in my literary efforts, to be of some importance in their eyes, and to win myself a pleasant memory in this abode and burial-place of so many of my forefathers—there has never been, for me, the genial atmosphere which a literary man requires, in order to ripen the best harvest of his mind. I shall do better amongst other faces; and these familiar ones, it need hardly be said, will do just as well without me.

It may be, however,—O, transporting and triumphant thought! —that the great-grandchildren of the present race may sometimes think kindly of the scribbler of bygone days, when the antiquary of days to come, among the sites memorable in the town's history, shall point out the locality of THE TOWN-PUMP![7]

---

7. "A Rill from the Town Pump," in Hawthorne's *Twice-Told Tales* (1837), is a monologue describing the life of Salem during one day, as viewed from a central vantage point.

The Scarlet Letter

I. The Prison-Door

A throng of bearded men, in sad-colored garments and gray, steeple-crowned hats, intermixed with women, some wearing hoods, and others bareheaded, was assembled in front of a wooden edifice, the door of which was heavily timbered with oak, and studded with iron spikes.

The founders of a new colony, whatever Utopia[1] of human virtue and happiness they might originally project, have invariably recognized it among their earliest practical necessities to allot a portion of the virgin soil as a cemetery, and another portion as the site of a prison. In accordance with this rule, it may safely be assumed that the forefathers of Boston had built the first prison-house, somewhere in the vicinity of Corn-hill, almost as seasonably as they marked out the first burial-ground, on Isaac Johnson's lot,[2] and round about his grave, which subsequently became the nucleus of all the congregated sepulchres in the old church-yard of King's Chapel. Certain it is, that, some fifteen or twenty years after the settlement of the town, the wooden jail was already marked with weather-stains and other indications of age, which gave a yet darker aspect to its beetle-browed and gloomy front. The rust on the ponderous iron-work of its oaken door looked more antique than anything else in the new world. Like all that pertains to crime, it seemed never to have known a youthful era. Before this ugly edifice, and between it and the wheel-track of the street, was a grass-plot, much overgrown with burdock, pig-weed, apple-peru, and such unsightly vegetation, which evidently found something congenial in the soil that had so early borne the black flower of civilized society, a prison. But, on one side of the portal, and rooted almost at the threshold, was a wild rose-bush, covered, in this month of June, with

1. Sir Thomas More's *Utopia* (translated "nowhere"), written in Latin in 1515, was, in various translations, long familiar to the early settlers as a satiric contrast of England with an ideal society.
2. Johnson died in the year of his arrival with the first settlers of Boston (1630); his land provided the site for prison, graveyard, and church, epitomizing the Puritan drama of sin, death, and salvation.

Although Hawthorne suggests that the novel starts "some fifteen or twenty years" later than 1630, it actually begins in 1642 and ends in 1649, as established by other internal evidence. The best-established historical date is March 26, 1649, the date of Governor Winthrop's death, in Chapter XII, although Hawthorne changes it to "early May"; he further says that this is "seven long years later" than the opening scene, which therefore must have occurred in the spring of 1642. Also Richard Bellingham addresses Hester on the pillory in his capacity as governor, and his term ended in 1642. In Chapters VII and VIII Pearl's age is three, hence the date is 1645. The final scene of the novel, portrayed in Chapters XXI to XXIII, occurred on a single day still "seven years" after the opening scene, or in 1649, and by internal evidence in the late spring or early summer.

its delicate gems, which might be imagined to offer their fragrance and fragile beauty to the prisoner as he went in, and to the condemned criminal as he came forth to his doom, in token that the deep heart of Nature could pity and be kind to him.

This rose-bush, by a strange chance, has been kept alive in history; but whether it had merely survived out of the stern old wilderness, so long after the fall of the gigantic pines and oaks that originally overshadowed it,—or whether, as there is fair authority for believing, it had sprung up under the footsteps of the sainted Ann Hutchinson,[1] as she entered the prison-door,—we shall not take upon us to determine. Finding it so directly on the threshold of our narrative, which is now about to issue from that inauspicious portal, we could hardly do otherwise than pluck one of its flowers and present it to the reader. It may serve, let us hope, to symbolize some sweet moral blossom, that may be found along the track, or relieve the darkening close of a tale of human frailty and sorrow.

II. *The Market-Place*

The grass-plot before the jail, in Prison Lane, on a certain summer morning, not less than two centuries ago, was occupied by a pretty large number of the inhabitants of Boston; all with their eyes intently fastened on the iron-clamped oaken door. Amongst any other population, or at a later period in the history of New England, the grim rigidity that petrified the bearded physiognomies of these good people would have augured some awful business in hand. It could have betokened nothing short of the anticipated execution of some noted culprit, on whom the sentence of a legal tribunal had but confirmed the verdict of public sentiment. But, in that early severity of the Puritan character, an inference of this kind could not so indubitably be drawn. It might be that a sluggish bond-servant, or an undutiful child, whom his parents had given over to the civil authority, was to be corrected at the whipping-post. It might be, that an Antinomian, a Quaker, or other heterodox religionist, was to be scourged out of the town, or an idle and vagrant Indian, whom the white man's fire-water had made riotous about the streets, was to be driven with stripes into the shadow of the forest. It might be, too, that a witch, like old Mistress Hibbins,

1. Anne Hutchinson (1590–1643) preached Antinominianism. This, like the later transcendentalism, which influenced Hawthorne, extolled salvation by faith, the intuitive revelation of God's indwelling "grace," a concept resembling the transcendentalists' "oversoul." Mrs. Hutchinson was banished from Massachusetts in 1638 for her beliefs.

the bitter-tempered widow of the magistrate, was to die upon the gallows.[2] In either case, there was very much the same solemnity of demeanour on the part of the spectators; as befitted a people amongst whom religion and law were almost identical, and in whose character both were so thoroughly interfused, that the mildest and the severest acts of public discipline were alike made venerable and awful. Meagre, indeed, and cold, was the sympathy that a transgressor might look for, from such bystanders at the scaffold. On the other hand, a penalty which, in our days, would infer a degree of mocking infamy and ridicule, might then be invested with almost as stern a dignity as the punishment of death itself.

It was a circumstance to be noted, on the summer morning when our story begins its course, that the women, of whom there were several in the crowd, appeared to take a peculiar interest in whatever penal infliction might be expected to ensue. The age had not so much refinement, that any sense of impropriety restrained the wearers of petticoat and farthingale from stepping forth into the public ways, and wedging their not unsubstantial persons, if occasion were, into the throng nearest to the scaffold at an execution. Morally, as well as materially, there was a coarser fibre in those wives and maidens of old English birth and breeding, than in their fair descendants, separated from them by a series of six or seven generations; for, throughout that chain of ancestry, every successive mother has transmitted to her child a fainter bloom, a more delicate and briefer beauty, and a slighter physical frame, if not a character of less force and solidity, than her own. The women, who were now standing about the prison-door, stood within less than half a century of the period when the man-like Elizabeth had been the not altogether unsuitable representative of the sex.[3] They were her countrywomen; and the beef and ale of their native land, with a moral diet not a whit more refined, entered largely into their composition. The bright morning sun, therefore, shone on broad shoulders and well-developed busts, and on round and ruddy cheeks, that had ripened in the far-off island, and had hardly yet grown paler or thinner in the atmosphere of New England. There was, moreover, a boldness and rotundity of speech among these matrons, as most of them seemed to be, that would startle us at the present day, whether in respect to its purport or its volume of tone.

"Goodwives," said a hard-featured dame of fifty, "I'll tell ye a piece of my mind. It would be greatly for the public behoof, if we women, being of mature age and church-members in good repute, should have the handling of such malefactresses as this Hester

2. Ann Hibbins, who appears periodically in the novel, was put to death as a witch in 1656.

3. Queen Elizabeth I of England, 1558–1603.

Prynne. What think ye, gossips?[4] If the hussy stood up for judgment before us five, that are now here in a knot together, would she come off with such a sentence as the worshipful magistrates have awarded? Marry, I trow not!"

"People say," said another, "that the Reverend Master Dimmesdale, her godly pastor, takes it very grievously to heart that such a scandal should have come upon his congregation."

"The magistrates are God-fearing gentlemen, but merciful overmuch,—that is a truth," added a third autumnal matron. "At the very least, they should have put the brand of a hot iron on Hester Prynne's forehead. Madam Hester would have winced at that, I warrant me. But she,—the naughty baggage,—little will she care what they put upon the bodice of her gown! Why, look you, she may cover it with a brooch, or such like heathenish adornment, and so walk the streets as brave as ever!"

"Ah, but," interposed, more softly, a young wife, holding a child by the hand, "let her cover the mark as she will, the pang of it will be always in her heart."

"What do we talk of marks and brands, whether on the bodice of her gown, or the flesh of her forehead?" cried another female, the ugliest as well as the most pitiless of these self-constituted judges. "This woman has brought shame upon us all, and ought to die. Is there no law for it? Truly there is, both in the Scripture and the statute-book.[5] Then let the magistrates, who have made it of no effect, thank themselves if their own wives and daughters go astray!"

"Mercy on us, goodwife," exclaimed a man in the crowd, "is there no virtue in woman, save what springs from a wholesome fear of the gallows? That is the hardest word yet! Hush, now, gossips; for the lock is turning in the prison-door, and here comes Mistress Prynne herself."

The door of the jail being flung open from within, there appeared, in the first place, like a black shadow emerging into the

---

4. Friends, acquaintances (usually used of women).

5. The acceptance of such cruel punishments as whipping, branding, and execution was the Puritan response to "the Scripture": "Thou shalt not commit adultery" (Exodus 20 : 14). The "old colony" (Plymouth) law merely called for exposure of the cloth A on the gown. This statute was dated 1694. Earlier, during the period of this novel, public whipping was universal; at some towns, *e.g.*, Duxbury, the adulteress was condemned "to be whipt at a cart's tayle through the town's streets." Salem's earliest statute decreed death for fornication but never enforced it; but John Winthrop's *Journals* of 1644 record the execution of Mary Latham for adultery.

In the records of the Salem Quarterly Court for the 1688 term the punishment of a girl named Hester (but not Prynne) is set down; Hawthorne probably knew about her, since he had combed through records of this nature and because his first American ancestor is named executioner: "Hester Craford, for fornication with John Wadg, as she confessed, to be severely whipped * * * a month or six weeks after the birth of the child * * * and the Worshipful Major William Hathorne to see it executed on a lecture day" (the "lecture" would draw a maximum crowd). See Charles Boewe and Murray Murphey, "Hester Prynne in History," reprinted on pp. 219–221 of this book.

sunshine, the grim and grisly presence of the town-beadle, with a sword by his side and his staff of office in his hand. This personage prefigured and represented in his aspect the whole dismal severity of the Puritanic code of law, which it was his business to administer in its final and closest application to the offender. Stretching forth the official staff in his left hand, he laid his right upon the shoulder of a young woman, whom he thus drew forward; until, on the threshold of the prison-door, she repelled him, by an action marked with natural dignity and force of character, and stepped into the open air, as if by her own free-will. She bore in her arms a child, a baby of some three months old, who winked and turned aside its little face from the too vivid light of day; because its existence, heretofore, had brought it acquainted only with the gray twilight of a dungeon, or other darksome apartment of the prison.

When the young woman—the mother of this child—stood fully revealed before the crowd, it seemed to be her first impulse to clasp the infant closely to her bosom; not so much by an impulse of motherly affection, as that she might thereby conceal a certain token, which was wrought or fastened into her dress. In a moment, however, wisely judging that one token of her shame would but poorly serve to hide another, she took the baby on her arm, and, with a burning blush, and yet a haughty smile, and a glance that would not be abashed, looked around at her townspeople and neighbours. On the breast of her gown, in fine red cloth, surrounded with an elaborate embroidery and fantastic flourishes of gold thread, appeared the letter A. It was so artistically done, and with so much fertility and gorgeous luxuriance of fancy, that it had all the effect of a last and fitting decoration to the apparel which she wore; and which was of a splendor in accordance with the taste of the age, but greatly beyond what was allowed by the sumptuary regulations of the colony.

The young woman was tall, with a figure of perfect elegance, on a large scale. She had dark and abundant hair, so glossy that it threw off the sunshine with a gleam, and a face which, besides being beautiful from regularity of feature and richness of complexion, had the impressiveness belonging to a marked brow and deep black eyes. She was lady-like, too, after the manner of the feminine gentility of those days; characterized by a certain state and dignity, rather than by the delicate, evanescent, and indescribable grace, which is now recognized as its indication. And never had Hester Prynne appeared more lady-like, in the antique interpretation of the term, than as she issued from the prison. Those who had before known her, and had expected to behold her dimmed and obscured by a disastrous cloud, were astonished, and even startled, to perceive how her beauty shone out, and made a halo of the misfortune and ignominy in which she was enveloped. It may be true, that, to a sensitive observer, there was something exquisitely painful in it. Her attire, which, indeed, she had wrought for the occasion, in prison, and had modelled much after her own fancy, seemed to express the attitude of her spirit, the desperate recklessness of her mood, by its wild and picturesque peculiarity. But the point which drew all eyes, and, as it were, transfigured the wearer,—so that both men and women, who had been familiarly acquainted with Hester Prynne, were now impressed as if they beheld her for the first time,—was that SCARLET LETTER, so fantastically embroidered and illuminated upon her bosom. It had the effect of a spell, taking her out of the ordinary relations with humanity, and inclosing her in a sphere by herself.

"She hath good skill at her needle, that's certain," remarked one of the female spectators; "but did ever a woman, before this brazen hussy, contrive such a way of showing it! Why, gossips, what is it but to laugh in the faces of our godly magistrates, and make a pride out of what they, worthy gentlemen, meant for a punishment?"

"It were well," muttered the most iron-visaged of the old dames, "if we stripped Madam Hester's rich gown off her dainty shoulders; and as for the red letter, which she hath stitched so curiously, I'll bestow a rag of mine own rheumatic flannel, to make a fitter one!"

"O, peace, neighbours, peace!" whispered their youngest companion. "Do not let her hear you! Not a stitch in that embroidered letter, but she has felt it in her heart."

The grim beadle now made a gesture with his staff.

"Make way, good people, make way, in the King's name," cried he. "Open a passage; and, I promise ye, Mistress Prynne shall be set where man, woman, and child may have a fair sight of her brave apparel, from this time till an hour past meridian. A blessing on the righteous Colony of the Massachusetts, where iniquity is dragged out into the sunshine! Come along, Madame Hester, and show your scarlet letter in the market-place!"

A lane was forthwith opened through the crowd of spectators. Preceded by the beadle, and attended by an irregular procession of stern-browed men and unkindly-visaged women, Hester Prynne set forth towards the place appointed for her punishment. A crowd of eager and curious schoolboys, understanding little of the matter in hand, except that it gave them a half-holiday, ran before her progress, turning their heads continually to stare into her face, and at the winking baby in her arms, and at the ignominious letter on her breast. It was no great distance, in those days, from the prison-door to the market-place. Measured by the prisoner's experience, however, it might be reckoned a journey of some length; for, haughty as her demeanour was, she perchance underwent an agony from every footstep of those that thronged to see her, as if her heart had been flung into the street for them all to spurn and trample upon. In our nature, however, there is a provision, alike marvellous and merciful, that the sufferer should never know the intensity of what he endures by its present torture, but chiefly by the pang that rankles after it. With almost a serene deportment, therefore, Hester Prynne passed through this portion of her ordeal, and came to a sort of scaffold, at the western extremity of the market-place. It stood nearly beneath the eaves of Boston's earliest church, and appeared to be a fixture there.

In fact, this scaffold constituted a portion of a penal machine, which now, for two or three generations past, has been merely historical and traditionary among us, but was held, in the old time, to be as effectual an agent in the promotion of good citizenship, as ever was the guillotine among the terrorists of France. It was, in short, the platform of the pillory; and above it rose the framework of that instrument of discipline, so fashioned as to confine the human head in its tight grasp, and thus hold it up to the public gaze. The very ideal of ignominy was embodied and made manifest in this contrivance of wood and iron. There can be no outrage, methinks, against our common nature,—whatever be the delinquencies of the individual,—no outrage more flagrant than to forbid the culprit to hide his face for shame; as it was the essence of this punishment to do. In Hester Prynne's instance, however, as not unfrequently in other cases, her sentence bore, that she should stand a certain time upon the platform, but without undergoing that gripe about the neck and confinement of the head, the proneness to which was the most devilish characteristic of this ugly engine. Knowing well her part, she ascended a flight of wooden steps, and was thus displayed to the surrounding multitude, at about the height of a man's shoulders above the street.

Had there been a Papist among the crowd of Puritans, he might have seen in this beautiful woman, so picturesque in her attire and mien, and with the infant at her bosom, an object to remind him of the image of Divine Maternity, which so many illustrious painters have vied with one another to represent; something which should remind him, indeed, but only by contrast, of that sacred image of sinless motherhood, whose infant was to redeem the world. Here, there was the taint of deepest sin in the most sacred quality of human life, working such effect, that the world was only the darker for this woman's beauty, and the more lost for the infant that she had borne.

The scene was not without a mixture of awe, such as must always invest the spectacle of guilt and shame in a fellow-creature, before society shall have grown corrupt enough to smile, instead of shuddering, at it. The witnesses of Hester Prynne's disgrace had not yet passed beyond their simplicity. They were stern enough to look upon her death, had that been the sentence, without a murmur at its severity, but had none of the heartlessness of another social state, which would find only a theme for jest in an exhibition like the present. Even had there been a disposition to turn the matter into ridicule, it must have been repressed and overpowered by the solemn presence of men no less dignified than the Governor, and several of his counsellors, a judge, a general, and the ministers of the town; all of whom sat or stood in a balcony of the meeting-house, looking down upon the platform. When such personages could constitute a part of the spectacle, without risking the majesty or reverence of rank and office, it was safely to be inferred that the infliction of a legal sentence would have an earnest and effectual meaning. Accordingly, the crowd was sombre and grave. The unhappy culprit sustained herself as best a woman might, under the heavy weight of a thousand unrelenting eyes, all fastened upon her, and concentred at her bosom. It was almost intolerable to be borne. Of an impulsive and passionate nature, she had fortified herself to encounter the stings and venomous stabs of public contumely, wreaking itself in every variety of insult; but there was a quality so much more terrible in the solemn mood of the popular mind, that she longed rather to behold all those rigid countenances contorted with scornful merriment, and herself the object. Had a roar of laughter burst from the multitude,—each man, each woman, each little shrill-voiced child, contributing their individual parts,—Hester Prynne might have repaid them all with a bitter and disdainful smile. But, under the leaden infliction which it was her doom to endure, she felt, at moments, as if she must needs shriek out with the full power of her lungs, and cast herself from the scaffold down upon the ground, or else go mad at once.

Yet there were intervals when the whole scene, in which she was the most conspicuous object, seemed to vanish from her eyes, or, at least, glimmered indistinctly before them, like a mass of imperfectly shaped and spectral images. Her mind, and especially her memory, was preternaturally active, and kept bringing up other scenes than this roughly hewn street of a little town, on the edge of the Western wilderness; other faces than were lowering upon her from beneath the brims of those steeple-crowned hats. Reminiscences, the most trifling and immaterial, passages of infancy and school-days, sports, childish quarrels, and the little domestic traits of her maiden years, came swarming back upon her, intermingled with recollections of whatever was gravest in her subsequent life;

one picture precisely as vivid as another; as if all were of similar importance, or all alike a play. Possibly, it was an instinctive device of her spirit, to relieve itself, by the exhibition of these phantasmagoric forms, from the cruel weight and hardness of the reality.

Be that as it might, the scaffold of the pillory was a point of view that revealed to Hester Prynne the entire track along which she had been treading, since her happy infancy. Standing on that miserable eminence, she saw again her native village, in Old England, and her paternal home; a decayed house of gray stone, with a poverty-stricken aspect, but retaining a half-obliterated shield of arms over the portal, in token of antique gentility. She saw her father's face, with its bald brow, and reverend white beard, that flowed over the old-fashioned Elizabethan ruff; her mother's, too, with the look of heedful and anxious love which it always wore in her remembrance, and which, even since her death, had so often laid the impediment of a gentle remonstrance in her daughter's pathway. She saw her own face, glowing with girlish beauty, and illuminating all the interior of the dusky mirror in which she had been wont to gaze at it. There she beheld another countenance, of a man well stricken in years, a pale, thin, scholar-like visage, with eyes dim and bleared by the lamp-light that had served them to pore over many ponderous books. Yet those same bleared optics had a strange, penetrating power, when it was their owner's purpose to read the human soul. This figure of the study and the cloister, as Hester Prynne's womanly fancy failed not to recall, was slightly deformed, with the left shoulder a trifle higher than the right. Next rose before her, in memory's picture-gallery, the intricate and narrow thoroughfares, the tall, gray houses, the huge cathedrals, and the public edifices, ancient in date and quaint in architecture, of a Continental city; where a new life had awaited her, still in connection with the misshapen scholar; a new life, but feeding itself on time-worn materials, like a tuft of green moss on a crumbling wall. Lastly, in lieu of these shifting scenes, came back the rude market-place of the Puritan settlement, with all the townspeople assembled and levelling their stern regards at Hester Prynne, —yes, at herself,—who stood on the scaffold of the pillory, an infant on her arm, and the letter A, in scarlet, fantastically embroidered with gold thread, upon her bosom!

Could it be true? She clutched the child so fiercely to her breast, that it sent forth a cry; she turned her eyes downward at the scarlet letter, and even touched it with her finger, to assure herself that the infant and the shame were real. Yes!—these were her realities, —all else had vanished!

III. The Recognition

From this intense consciousness of being the object of severe and universal observation, the wearer of the scarlet letter was at length relieved by discerning, on the outskirts of the crowd, a figure which irresistibly took possession of her thoughts. An Indian, in his native garb, was standing there; but the red men were not so infrequent visitors of the English settlements, that one of them would have attracted any notice from Hester Prynne, at such a time; much less would he have excluded all other objects and ideas from her mind. By the Indian's side, and evidently sustaining a companionship with him, stood a white man, clad in a strange disarray of civilized and savage costume.

He was small in stature, with a furrowed visage, which, as yet, could hardly be termed aged. There was a remarkable intelligence in his features, as of a person who had so cultivated his mental part that it could not fail to mould the physical to itself, and become manifest by unmistakable tokens. Although, by a seemingly careless arrangement of his heterogeneous garb, he had endeavoured to conceal or abate the peculiarity, it was sufficiently evident to Hester Prynne, that one of this man's shoulders rose higher than the other. Again, at the first instant of perceiving that thin visage, and the slight deformity of the figure, she pressed her infant to her bosom, with so convulsive a force that the poor babe uttered another cry of pain. But the mother did not seem to hear it.

At his arrival in the market-place, and some time before she saw him, the stranger had bent his eyes on Hester Prynne. It was carelessly, at first, like a man chiefly accustomed to look inward, and to whom external matters are of little value and import, unless they bear relation to something within his mind. Very soon, however, his look became keen and penetrative. A writhing horror twisted itself across his features, like a snake gliding swiftly over them, and making one little pause, with all its wreathed intervolutions in open sight. His face darkened with some powerful emotion, which, nevertheless, he so instantaneously controlled by an effort of his will, that, save at a single moment, its expression might have passed for calmness. After a brief space, the convulsion grew almost imperceptible, and finally subsided into the depths of his nature. When he found the eyes of Hester Prynne fastened on his own, and saw that she appeared to recognize him, he slowly and calmly raised his finger, made a gesture with it in the air, and laid it on his lips.

Then, touching the shoulder of a townsman who stood next to him, he addressed him in a formal and courteous manner.

"I pray you, good Sir," said he, "who is this woman?—and wherefore is she here set up to public shame?"

"You must needs be a stranger in this region, friend," answered the townsman, looking curiously at the questioner and his savage companion; "else you would surely have heard of Mistress Hester Prynne, and her evil doings. She hath raised a great scandal, I promise you, in godly Master Dimmesdale's church."

"You say truly," replied the other. "I am a stranger, and have been a wanderer, sorely against my will. I have met with grievous mishaps by sea and land, and have been long held in bonds among the heathen-folk, to the southward; and am now brought hither by this Indian, to be redeemed out of my captivity. Will it please you, therefore, to tell me of Hester Prynne's,—have I her name rightly? —of this woman's offences, and what has brought her to yonder scaffold?"

"Truly, friend, and methinks it must gladden your heart, after your troubles and sojourn in the wilderness," said the townsman, "to find yourself, at length, in a land where iniquity is searched out, and punished in the sight of rulers and people; as here in our godly New England. Yonder woman, Sir, you must know, was the wife of a certain learned man, English by birth, but who had long dwelt in Amsterdam,[6] whence, some good time agone, he was minded to cross over and cast in his lot with us of the Massachusetts. To this purpose, he sent his wife before him, remaining himself to look after some necessary affairs. Marry, good Sir, in some two years, or less, that the woman has been a dweller here in Boston, no tidings have come of this learned gentleman, Master Prynne; and his young wife, look you, being left to her own misguidance——"

"Ah!—aha!—I conceive you," said the stranger, with a bitter smile. "So learned a man as you speak of should have learned this too in his books. And who, by your favor, Sir, may be the father of yonder babe—it is some three or four months old, I should judge—which Mistress Prynne is holding in her arms?"

"Of a truth, friend, that matter remaineth a riddle; and the Daniel who shall expound it is yet a-wanting,"[7] answered the townsman. "Madam Hester absolutely refuseth to speak, and the magistrates have laid their heads together in vain. Peradventure the guilty one stands looking on at this sad spectacle, unknown of man, and forgetting that God sees him."

"The learned man," observed the stranger, with another smile, "should come himself to look into the mystery."

6. Persecuted English Separatists and Puritans found refuge in liberal Amsterdam, Holland, whither the Pilgrims fled in 1608, and whence, like other groups, they sailed for America (1620).

7. The prophet Daniel interpreted the cryptic writing that appeared on the wall during Belshazzar's feast: "Thou art weighed in the balance and found wanting" (Daniel 5).

"It behooves him well, if he be still in life," responded the townsman. "Now, good Sir, our Massachusetts magistracy, bethinking themselves that this woman is youthful and fair, and doubtless was strongly tempted to her fall;—and that, moreover, as is most likely, her husband may be at the bottom of the sea;—they have not been bold to put in force the extremity of our righteous law against her. The penalty thereof is death. But, in their great mercy and tenderness of heart, they have doomed Mistress Prynne to stand only a space of three hours on the platform of the pillory, and then and thereafter, for the remainder of her natural life, to wear a mark of shame upon her bosom."

"A wise sentence!" remarked the stranger, gravely bowing his head. "Thus she will be a living sermon against sin, until the ignominious letter be engraved upon her tombstone. It irks, me, nevertheless, that the partner of her iniquity should not, at least, stand on the scaffold by her side. But he will be known!—he will be known!—he will be known!"

He bowed courteously to the communicative townsman, and, whispering a few words to his Indian attendant, they both made their way through the crowd.

While they passed, Hester Prynne had been standing on her pedestal, still with a fixed gaze towards the stranger; so fixed a gaze, that, at moments of intense absorption, all other objects in the visible world seemed to vanish, leaving only him and her. Such an interview, perhaps, would have been more terrible than even to meet him as she now did, with the hot, midday sun burning down upon her face, and lighting up its shame; with the scarlet token of infamy on her breast; with the sin-born infant in her arms; with a whole people, drawn forth as to a festival, staring at the features that should have been seen only in the quiet gleam of the fireside, in the happy shadow of a home, or beneath a matronly veil, at church. Dreadful as it was, she was conscious of a shelter in the presence of these thousand witnesses. It was better to stand thus, with so many betwixt him and her, than to greet him, face to face, they two alone. She fled for refuge, as it were, to the public exposure, and dreaded the moment when its protection should be withdrawn from her. Involved in these thoughts, she scarcely heard a voice behind her, until it had repeated her name more than once, in a loud and solemn tone, audible to the whole multitude.

"Hearken unto me, Hester Prynne!" said the voice.

It has already been noticed, that directly over the platform on which Hester Prynne stood was a kind of balcony, or open gallery, appended to the meeting-house. It was the place whence proclamations were wont to be made, amidst an assemblage of the magistracy, with all the ceremonial that attended such public observances in those days. Here, to witness the scene which we are describing, sat Governor Bellingham[8] himself, with four sergeants about his chair, bearing halberds, as a guard of honor. He wore a dark feather in his hat, a border of embroidery on his cloak, and a black velvet tunic beneath; a gentleman advanced in years, and with a hard experience written in his wrinkles. He was not ill fitted to be the head and representative of a community, which owed its origin and progress, and its present state of development, not to the impulses of youth, but to the stern and tempered energies of manhood, and the sombre sagacity of age; accomplishing so much, precisely because it imagined and hoped so little. The other eminent characters, by whom the chief ruler was surrounded, were distinguished by a dignity of mien, belonging to a period when the forms of authority were felt to possess the sacredness of divine institutions. They were, doubtless, good men, just, and sage. But, out of the whole human family, it would not have been easy to select the same number of wise and virtuous persons, who should be less capable of sitting in judgment on an erring woman's heart, and disentangling its mesh of good and evil, than the sages of rigid aspect towards whom Hester Prynne now turned her face. She seemed conscious, indeed, that whatever sympathy she might expect lay in the larger and warmer heart of the multitude; for, as she lifted her eyes towards the balcony, the unhappy woman grew pale and trembled.

The voice which had called her attention was that of the reverend and famous John Wilson,[9] the eldest clergyman of Boston, a great scholar, like most of his contemporaries in the profession, and withal a man of kind and genial spirit. This last attribute, however, had been less carefully developed than his intellectual gifts, and was, in truth, rather a matter of shame than self-congratulation with him. There he stood, with a border of grizzled locks beneath his skull-cap; while his gray eyes, accustomed to the shaded light of his study, were winking, like those of Hester's infant, in the unadulterated sunshine. He looked like the darkly engraved portraits which we see prefixed to old volumes of sermons; and had no more right than one of those portraits would have, to step forth, as he now did, and meddle with a question of human guilt, passion, and anguish.

8. Richard Bellingham (1592–1672), a lawyer born in Lincolnshire, came to Boston in 1634. He was governor of Massachusetts colony in 1641, 1654, and 1665–1672.
9. John Wilson (1588–1667), English Congregational minister, came to Boston with the first settlers (1630). Cotton Mather described him in the *Magnalia Christi* as having "great zeal with great love * * * joined with orthodoxy." He was Mrs. Hutchinson's chief clerical opponent.

"Hester Prynne," said the clergyman, "I have striven with my young brother here, under whose preaching of the word you have been privileged to sit,"—here Mr. Wilson laid his hand on the shoulder of a pale young man beside him,—"I have sought, I say, to persuade this godly youth, that he should deal with you, here in the face of Heaven, and before these wise and upright rulers, and in hearing of all the people, as touching the vileness and blackness of your sin. Knowing your natural temper better than I, he could the better judge what arguments to use, whether of tenderness or terror, such as might prevail over your hardness and obstinacy; insomuch that you should no longer hide the name of him who tempted you to this grievous fall. But he opposes to me, (with a young man's over-softness, albeit wise beyond his years,) that it were wronging the very nature of woman to force her to lay open her heart's secrets in such broad daylight, and in presence of so great a multitude. Truly, as I sought to convince him, the shame lay in the commission of the sin, and not in the showing of it forth. What say you to it, once again, brother Dimmesdale? Must it be thou or I that shall deal with this poor sinner's soul?"

There was a murmur among the dignified and reverend occupants of the balcony; and Governor Bellingham gave expression to its purport, speaking in an authoritative voice, although tempered with respect towards the youthful clergyman whom he addressed.

"Good Master Dimmesdale," said he, "the responsibility of this woman's soul lies greatly with you. It behooves you, therefore, to exhort her to repentance, and to confession, as a proof and consequence thereof."

The directness of this appeal drew the eyes of the whole crowd upon the Reverend Mr. Dimmesdale; a young clergyman, who had come from one of the great English universities, bringing all the learning of the age into our wild forest-land. His eloquence and religious fervor had already given the earnest of high eminence in his profession. He was a person of very striking aspect, with a white, lofty, and impending brow, large, brown, melancholy eyes, and a mouth which, unless when he forcibly compressed it, was apt to be tremulous, expressing both nervous sensibility and a vast power of self-restraint. Notwithstanding his high native gifts and scholar-like attainments, there was an air about this young minister,—an apprehensive, a startled, a half-frightened look,—as of a being who felt himself quite astray and at a loss in the pathway of human existence, and could only be at ease in some seclusion of his own. Therefore, so far as his duties would permit, he trode in the shadowy by-paths, and thus kept himself simple and childlike; coming forth, when occasion was, with a freshness, and fragrance, and dewy purity of thought, which, as many people said, affected them like the speech of an angel.

Such was the young man whom the Reverend Mr. Wilson and the Governor had introduced so openly to the public notice, bidding him speak, in the hearing of all men, to that mystery of a woman's soul, so sacred even in its pollution. The trying nature of his position drove the blood from his cheek, and made his lips tremulous.

"Speak to the woman, my brother," said Mr. Wilson. "It is of moment to her soul, and therefore, as the worshipful Governor says, momentous to thine own, in whose charge hers is. Exhort her to confess the truth!"

The Reverend Mr. Dimmesdale bent his head, in silent prayer, as it seemed, and then came forward.

"Hester Prynne," said he, leaning over the balcony, and looking down steadfastly into her eyes, "thou hearest what this good man says, and seest the accountability under which I labor. If thou feelest it to be for thy soul's peace, and that thy earthly punishment will thereby be made more effectual to salvation, I charge thee to speak out the name of thy fellow-sinner and fellow-sufferer! Be not silent from any mistaken pity and tenderness for him; for, believe me, Hester, though he were to step down from a high place, and stand there beside thee, on thy pedestal of shame, yet better were it so, than to hide a guilty heart through life. What can thy silence do for him, except it tempt him—yea, compel him, as it were—to add hypocrisy to sin? Heaven hath granted thee an open ignominy, that thereby thou mayest work out an open triumph over the evil within thee, and the sorrow without. Take heed how thou deniest to him—who, perchance, hath not the courage to grasp it for himself—the bitter, but wholesome, cup that is now presented to thy lips!"

The young pastor's voice was tremulously sweet, rich, deep, and broken. The feeling that it so evidently manifested, rather than the direct purport of the words, caused it to vibrate within all hearts, and brought the listeners into one accord of sympathy. Even the poor baby, at Hester's bosom, was affected by the same influence; for it directed its hitherto vacant gaze towards Mr. Dimmesdale, and help up its little arms, with a half pleased, half plaintive murmur. So powerful seemed the minister's appeal, that the people could not believe but that Hester Prynne would speak out the guilty name; or else that the guilty one himself, in whatever high or lowly place he stood, would be drawn forth by an inward and inevitable necessity, and compelled to ascend the scaffold.

Hester shook her head.

"Woman, transgress not beyond the limits of Heaven's mercy!" cried the Reverend Mr. Wilson, more harshly than before. "That little babe hath been gifted with a voice, to second and confirm the counsel which thou hast heard. Speak out the name! That, and thy repentance, may avail to take the scarlet letter off thy breast."

"Never!" replied Hester Prynne, looking, not at Mr. Wilson, but into the deep and troubled eyes of the younger clergyman. "It is too deeply branded. Ye cannot take it off. And would that I might endure his agony, as well as mine!"

"Speak, woman!" said another voice, coldly and sternly, proceeding from the crowd about the scaffold. "Speak; and give your child a father!"

"I will not speak!" answered Hester, turning pale as death, but responding to this voice, which she too surely recognized. "And my child must seek a heavenly Father; she shall never know an earthly one!"

"She will not speak!" murmured Mr. Dimmesdale, who leaning over the balcony, with his hand upon his heart, had awaited the result of his appeal. He now drew back, with a long respiration. "Wondrous strength and generosity of a woman's heart! She will not speak!"

Discerning the impracticable state of the poor culprit's mind, the elder clergyman, who had carefully prepared himself for the occasion, addressed to the multitude a discourse on sin, in all its branches, but with continual reference to the ignominious letter. So forcibly did he dwell upon this symbol, for the hour or more during which his periods were rolling over the people's heads, that it assumed new terrors in their imagination, and seemed to derive its scarlet hue from the flames of the infernal pit. Hester Prynne, meanwhile, kept her place upon the pedestal of shame, with glazed eyes, and an air of weary indifference. She had borne, that morning, all that nature could endure; and as her temperament was not of the order that escapes from too intense suffering by a swoon, her spirit could only shelter itself beneath a stony crust of insensibility, while the faculties of animal life remained entire. In this state, the voice of the preacher thundered remorselessly, but unavailingly, upon her ears. The infant, during the latter portion of her ordeal, pierced the air with its wailings and screams; she strove to hush it, mechanically, but seemed scarcely to sympathize with its trouble. With the same hard demeanour, she was led back to prison, and vanished from the public gaze within its iron-clamped portal. It was whispered, by those who peered after her, that the scarlet letter threw a lurid gleam along the dark passage-way of the interior.

IV. *The Interview*

After her return to the prison, Hester Prynne was found to be in a state of nervous excitement that demanded constant watchfulness, lest she should perpetrate violence on herself, or do some half-frenzied mischief to the poor babe. As night approached, it proving impossible to quell her insubordination by rebuke or threats of punishment, Master Brackett, the jailer, thought fit to introduce a physician. He described him as a man of skill in all Christian modes of physical science, and likewise familiar with whatever the savage people could teach, in respect to medicinal herbs and roots that grew in the forest. To say the truth, there was much need of professional assistance, not merely for Hester herself, but still more urgently for the child; who, drawing its sustenance from the maternal bosom, seemed to have drank in with it all the turmoil, the anguish, and despair, which pervaded the mother's system. It now writhed in convulsions of pain, and was a forcible type, in its little frame, of the moral agony which Hester Prynne had borne throughout the day.

Closely following the jailer into the dismal apartment, appeared that individual, of singular aspect, whose presence in the crowd had been of such deep interest to the wearer of the scarlet letter. He was lodged in the prison, not as suspected of any offence, but as the most convenient and suitable mode of disposing of him, until the magistrates should have conferred with the Indian sagamores respecting his ransom. His name was announced as Roger Chillingworth. The jailer, after ushering him into the room, remained a moment, marvelling at the comparative quiet that followed his entrance; for Hester Prynne had immediately become as still as death, although the child continued to moan.

"Prithee, friend, leave me alone with my patient," said the practitioner. "Trust me, good jailer, you shall briefly have peace in your house; and, I promise you, Mistress Prynne shall hereafter be more amenable to just authority than you may have found her heretofore."

"Nay, if your worship can accomplish that," answered Master Brackett, "I shall own you for a man of skill indeed! Verily, the woman hath been like a possessed one; and there lacks little, that I should take in hand to drive Satan out of her with stripes."

The stranger had entered the room with the characteristic quietude of the profession to which he announced himself as belonging. Nor did his demeanour change, when the withdrawal of the prison-keeper left him face to face with the woman, whose absorbed notice of him, in the crowd, had intimated so close a relation between himself and her. His first care was given to the child; whose cries, indeed, as she lay writhing on the trundle-bed, made it of peremptory necessity to postpone all other business to the task of soothing her. He examined the infant carefully, and then proceeded to unclasp a leathern case, which he took from beneath his dress. It appeared to contain certain medical preparations, one of which he mingled with a cup of water.

"My old studies in alchemy," observed he, "and my sojourn, for above a year past, among a people well versed in the kindly properties of simples, have made a better physician of me than many that claim the medical degree. Here, woman! The child is yours,—she is none of mine,—neither will she recognize my voice or aspect as a father's. Administer this draught, therefore, with thine own hand."

Hester repelled the offered medicine, at the same time gazing with strongly marked apprehension into his face.

"Wouldst thou avenge thyself on the innocent babe?" whispered she.

"Foolish woman!" responded the physician, half coldly, half soothingly. "What should ail me to harm this misbegotten and miserable babe? The medicine is potent for good; and were it my child,—yea, mine own, as well as thine!—I could do no better for it."

As she still hesitated, being, in fact, in no reasonable state of mind, he took the infant in his arms, and himself administered the draught. It soon proved its efficacy, and redeemed the leech's pledge. The moans of the little patient subsided; its convulsive tossings gradually ceased; and in a few moments, as is the custom of young children after relief from pain, it sank into a profound and dewy slumber. The physician, as he had a fair right to be termed, next bestowed his attention on the mother. With calm and intent scrutiny, he felt her pulse, looked into her eyes,—a gaze that made her heart shrink and shudder, because so familiar, and yet so strange and cold,—and, finally, satisfied with his investigation, proceeded to mingle another draught.

"I know not Lethe nor Nepenthe,"[1] remarked he; "but I have learned many new secrets in the wilderness, and here is one of them,—a recipe that an Indian taught me, in requital of some lessons of my own, that were as old as Paracelsus.[2] Drink it! It may be less soothing than a sinless conscience. That I cannot give thee.

---

1. Greek mythology held that a draught of the waters of Lethe, a river in Hades, would induce forgetfulness; nepenthe was a drug (possibly opium) used by the Egyptians and other ancients to induce forgetfulness of sorrow. 2. Swiss alchemist and physician (1493–1541).

But it will calm the swell and heaving of thy passion, like oil thrown on the waves of a tempestuous sea."

He presented the cup to Hester, who received it with a slow, earnest look into his face; not precisely a look of fear, yet full of doubt and questioning, as to what his purposes might be. She looked also at her slumbering child.

"I have thought of death," said she,—"have wished for it,— would even have prayed for it, were it fit that such as I should pray for any thing. Yet, if death be in this cup, I bid thee think again, ere thou beholdest me quaff it. See! It is even now at my lips."

"Drink, then," replied he, still with the same cold composure. "Dost thou know me so little, Hester Prynne? Are my purposes wont to be so shallow? Even if I imagine a scheme of vengeance, what could I do better for my object than to let thee live,—than to give thee medicines against all harm and peril of life,—so that this burning shame may still blaze upon thy bosom?"—As he spoke, he laid his long forefinger on the scarlet letter, which forthwith seemed to scorch into Hester's breast, as if it had been red-hot. He noticed her involuntary gesture, and smiled.—"Live, therefore, and bear about thy doom with thee, in the eyes of men and women, —in the eyes of him whom thou didst call thy husband,—in the eyes of yonder child! And, that thou mayest live, take off this draught."

Without further expostulation or delay, Hester Prynne drained the cup, and, at the motion of the man of skill, seated herself on the bed where the child was sleeping; while he drew the only chair which the room afforded, and took his own seat beside her. She could not but tremble at these preparations; for she felt that— having now done all that humanity, or principle, or, if so it were, a refined cruelty, impelled him to do, for the relief of physical suffering—he was next to treat with her as the man whom she had most deeply and irreparably injured.

"Hester," said he, "I ask not wherefore, nor how, thou hast fallen into the pit, or say rather, thou hast ascended to the pedestal of infamy, on which I found thee. The reason is not far to seek. It was my folly, and thy weakness. I,—a man of thought,—the bookworm of great libraries,—a man already in decay, having given my best years to feed the hungry dream of knowledge,—what had I to do with youth and beauty like thine own! Misshapen from my birth-hour, how could I delude myself with the idea that intellectual gifts might veil physical deformity in a young girl's fantasy! Men call me wise. If sages were ever wise in their own behoof, I might have foreseen all this. I might have known that, as I came out of the vast and dismal forest, and entered this settlement of Christian men, the very first object to meet my eyes would be thyself, Hester Prynne, standing up, a statue of ignominy, before the people. Nay, from the moment when we came down the old church-steps together, a married pair, I might have beheld the bale-fire of that scarlet letter blazing at the end of our path!"

"Thou knowest," said Hester,—for, depressed as she was, she could not endure this last quiet stab at the token of her shame,— "thou knowest that I was frank with thee. I felt no love, nor feigned any."

"True!" replied he. "It was my folly! I have said it. But, up to that epoch of my life, I had lived in vain. The world had been so cheerless! My heart was a habitation large enough for many guests, but lonely and chill, and without a household fire. I longed to kindle one! It seemed not so wild a dream,—old as I was, and sombre as I was, and misshapen as I was,—that the simple bliss, which is scattered far and wide, for all mankind to gather up, might yet be mine. And so, Hester, I drew thee into my heart, into its innermost chamber, and sought to warm thee by the warmth which thy presence made there!"

"I have greatly wronged thee," murmured Hester.

"We have wronged each other," answered he. "Mine was the first wrong, when I betrayed thy budding youth into a false and unnatural relation with my decay. Therefore, as a man who has not thought and philosophized in vain, I seek no vengeance, plot no evil against thee. Between thee and me, the scale hangs fairly balanced. But, Hester, the man lives who has wronged us both! Who is he?"

"Ask me not!" replied Hester Prynne, looking firmly into his face. "That thou shalt never know!"

"Never, sayest thou?" rejoined he, with a smile of dark and self-relying intelligence. "Never know him! Believe me, Hester, there are few things,—whether in the outward world, or, to a certain depth, in the invisible sphere of thought,—few things hidden from the man, who devotes himself earnestly and unreservedly to the solution of a mystery. Thou mayest cover up thy secret from the prying multitude. Thou mayest conceal it, too, from the ministers and magistrates, even as thou didst this day, when they sought to wrench the name out of thy heart, and give thee a partner on thy pedestal. But, as for me, I come to the inquest with other senses than they possess. I shall seek this man, as I have sought truth in books; as I have sought gold in alchemy. There is a sympathy that will make me conscious of him. I shall see him tremble. I shall feel myself shudder, suddenly and unawares. Sooner or later, he must needs be mine!"

The eyes of the wrinkled scholar glowed so intensely upon her, that Hester Prynne clasped her hands over her heart, dreading lest he should read the secret there at once.

"Thou wilt not reveal his name? Not the less he is mine," resumed he, with a look of confidence, as if destiny were at one with him. "He bears no letter of infamy wrought into his garment, as thou dost; but I shall read it on his heart. Yet fear not for him! Think not that I shall interfere with Heaven's own method of retribution, or, to my own loss, betray him to the gripe of human law. Neither do thou imagine that I shall contrive aught against his life, no, nor against his fame; if, as I judge, he be a man of fair repute. Let him live! Let him hide himself in outward honor, if he may! Not the less he shall be mine!"

"Thy acts are like mercy," said Hester, bewildered and appalled. "But thy words interpret thee as a terror!"

"One thing, thou that wast my wife, I would enjoin upon thee," continued the scholar. "Thou hast kept the secret of thy paramour. Keep, likewise, mine! There are none in this land that know me. Breathe not, to any human soul, that thou didst ever call me husband! Here, on this wild outskirt of the earth, I shall pitch my tent; for, elsewhere a wanderer, and isolated from human interests, I find here a woman, a man, a child, amongst whom and myself there exist the closest ligaments. No matter whether of love or hate; no matter whether of right or wrong! Thou and thine, Hester Prynne, belong to me. My home is where thou art, and where he is. But betray me not!"

"Wherefore dost thou desire it?" inquired Hester, shrinking, she hardly knew why, from this secret bond. "Why not announce thyself openly, and cast me off at once?"

"It may be," he replied, "because I will not encounter the dishonor that besmirches the husband of a faithless woman. It may be for other reasons. Enough, it is my purpose to live and die unknown. Let, therefore, thy husband be to the world as one already dead, and of whom no tidings shall ever come. Recognize me not, by word, by sign, by look! Breathe not the secret, above all, to the man thou wottest of. Shouldst thou fail me in this, beware! His fame, his position, his life, will be in my hands. Beware!"

"I will keep thy secret, as I have his," said Hester.

"Swear it!" rejoined he.

And she took the oath.

"And now, Mistress Prynne," said old Roger Chillingworth, as he was hereafter to be named, "I leave thee alone; alone with thy infant, and the scarlet letter! How is it, Hester? Doth thy sentence bind thee to wear the token in thy sleep? Art thou not afraid of nightmares and hideous dreams?"

"Why dost thou smile so at me?" inquired Hester, troubled at the expression of his eyes. "Art thou like the Black Man[3] that haunts the forest round about us? Hast thou enticed me into a bond that will prove the ruin of my soul?"

"Not thy soul," he answered, with another smile. "No, not thine!"

V. Hester at Her Needle

Hester Prynne's term of confinement was now at an end. Her prison-door was thrown open, and she came forth into the sunshine, which, falling on all alike, seemed, to her sick and morbid heart, as if meant for no other purpose than to reveal the scarlet letter on her breast. Perhaps there was a more real torture in her first unattended footsteps from the threshold of the prison, than even in the procession and spectacle that have been described, where she was made the common infamy, at which all mankind was summoned to point its finger. Then, she was supported by an unnatural tension of the nerves, and by all the combative energy of her character, which enabled her to convert the scene into a kind of lurid triumph. It was, moreover, a separate and insulated event, to occur but once in her lifetime, and to meet which, therefore, reckless of economy, she might call up the vital strength that would have sufficed for many quiet years. The very law that condemned her—a giant of stern features, but with vigor to support, as well as to annihilate, in his iron arm—had held her up, through the terrible ordeal of her ignominy. But now, with this unattended walk from her prison-door, began the daily custom, and she must either sustain and carry it forward by the ordinary resources of her nature, or sink beneath it. She could no longer borrow from the future, to help her through the present grief. To-morrow would bring its own trial with it; so would the next day, and so would the next; each its own trial, and yet the very same that was now so unutterably grievous to be borne. The days of the far-off future would toil onward, still with the same burden for her to take up, and bear along with her, but never to fling down; for the accumulating days, and added years, would pile up their misery upon the heap of shame. Throughout them all, giving up her individuality, she would become the general symbol at which the preacher and moralist might point, and in which they might vivify and embody their images of woman's frailty and sinful passion. Thus the young and pure would be taught to look at her, with the scarlet letter flaming on her

---

3. The Black Man, in folklore the devil or his emissary, is associated with the "witch sabbath" in the forest, where the witches gathered to worship evil. Hawthorne described such a witch sabbath in "Young Goodman Brown."

breast,—at her, the child of honorable parents,—at her, the mother of a babe, that would hereafter be a woman,—at her, who had once been innocent,—as the figure, the body, the reality of sin. And over her grave, the infamy that she must carry thither would be her only monument.

It may seem marvellous, that, with the world before her,—kept by no restrictive clause of her condemnation within the limits of the Puritan settlement, so remote and so obscure,—free to return to her birthplace, or to any other European land, and there hide her character and identity under a new exterior, as completely as if emerging into another state of being,—and having also the passes of the dark, inscrutable forest open to her, where the wildness of her nature might assimilate itself with a people whose customs and life were alien from the law that had condemned her,—it may seem marvellous, that this woman should still call that place her home, where, and where only, she must needs be the type of shame. But there is a fatality, a feeling so irresistible and inevitable that it has the force of doom, which almost invariably compels human beings to linger around and haunt, ghost-like, the spot where some great and marked event has given the color to their lifetime; and still the more irresistibly, the darker the tinge that saddens it. Her sin, her ignominy, were the roots which she had struck into the soil. It was as if a new birth, with stronger assimilations than the first, had converted the forest-land, still so uncongenial to every other pilgrim and wanderer, into Hester Prynne's wild and dreary, but life-long home. All other scenes of earth—even that village of rural England, where happy infancy and stainless maidenhood seemed yet to be in her mother's keeping, like garments put off long ago—were foreign to her, in comparison. The chain that bound her here was of iron links, and galling to her inmost soul, but never could be broken.

It might be, too,—doubtless it was so, although she hid the secret from herself, and grew pale whenever it struggled out of her heart, like a serpent from its hole,—it might be that another feeling kept her within the scene and pathway that had been so fatal. There dwelt, there trode the feet of one with whom she deemed herself connected in a union, that, unrecognized on earth, would bring them together before the bar of final judgment, and make that their marriage-altar, for a joint futurity of endless retribution. Over and over again, the tempter of souls had thrust this idea upon Hester's contemplation, and laughed at the passionate and desperate joy with which she seized, and then strove to cast it from her. She barely looked the idea in the face, and hastened to bar it in its dungeon. What she compelled herself to believe,—what, finally, she reasoned upon, as her motive for continuing a resident of New

England,—was half a truth, and half a self-delusion. Here, she said to herself, had been the scene of her guilt, and here should be the scene of her earthly punishment; and so, perchance, the torture of her daily shame would at length purge her soul, and work out another purity than that which she had lost; more saint-like, because the result of martyrdom.

Hester Prynne, therefore, did not flee. On the outskirts of the town, within the verge of the peninsula, but not in close vicinity to any other habitation, there was a small thatched cottage. It had been built by an earlier settler, and abandoned, because the soil about it was too sterile for cultivation, while its comparative remoteness put it out of the sphere of that social activity which already marked the habits of the emigrants. It stood on the shore, looking across a basin of the sea at the forest-covered hills, towards the west. A clump of scrubby trees, such as alone grew on the peninsula, did not so much conceal the cottage from view, as seem to denote that here was some object which would fain have been, or at least ought to be, concealed. In this little, lonesome dwelling, with some slender means that she possessed, and by the license of the magistrates, who still kept an inquisitorial watch over her, Hester established herself, with her infant child. A mystic shadow of suspicion immediately attached itself to the spot. Children, too young to comprehend wherefore this woman should be shut out from the sphere of human charities, would creep nigh enough to behold her plying her needle at the cottage-window, or standing in the doorway, or laboring in her little garden, or coming forth along the pathway that led townward; and, discerning the scarlet letter on her breast, would scamper off, with a strange, contagious fear.

Lonely as was Hester's situation, and without a friend on earth who dared to show himself, she, however, incurred no risk of want. She possessed an art that sufficed, even in a land that afforded comparatively little scope for its exercise, to supply food for her thriving infant and herself. It was the art—then, as now, almost the only one within a woman's grasp—of needle-work. She bore on her breast, in the curiously embroidered letter, a specimen of her delicate and imaginative skill, of which the dames of a court might gladly have availed themselves, to add the richer and more spiritual adornment of human ingenuity to their fabrics of silk and gold. Here, indeed, in the sable simplicity that generally characterized the Puritanic modes of dress, there might be an infrequent call for the finer productions of her handiwork. Yet the taste of the age, demanding whatever was elaborate in compositions of this kind, did not fail to extend its influence over our stern progenitors, who had cast behind them so many fashions which it might seem harder to dispense with. Public ceremonies, such as ordinations, the installation of magistrates, and all that could give majesty to the forms in which a new government manifested itself to the people, were, as a matter of policy, marked by a stately and well-conducted ceremonial, and a sombre, but yet a studied magnificence. Deep ruffs, painfully wrought bands, and gorgeously embroidered gloves, were all deemed necessary to the official state of men assuming the reins of power; and were readily allowed to individuals dignified by rank or wealth, even while sumptuary laws forbade these and similar extravagances to the plebeian order. In the array of funerals, too,—whether for the apparel of the dead body, or to typify, by manifold emblematic devices of sable cloth and snowy lawn, the sorrow of the survivors,—there was a frequent and characteristic demand for such labor as Hester Prynne could supply. Baby-linen—for babies then wore robes of state—afforded still another possibility of toil and emolument.

By degrees, nor very slowly, her handiwork became what would now be termed the fashion. Whether from commiseration for a woman of so miserable a destiny; or from the morbid curiosity that gives a fictitious value even to common or worthless things; or by whatever other intangible circumstance was then, as now, sufficient to bestow, on some persons, what others might seek in vain; or because Hester really filled a gap which must otherwise have remained vacant; it is certain that she had ready and fairly requited employment for as many hours as she saw fit to occupy with her needle. Vanity, it may be, chose to mortify itself, by putting on, for ceremonials of pomp and state, the garments that had been wrought by her sinful hands. Her needle-work was seen on the ruff of the Governor; military men wore it on their scarfs, and the minister on his band; it decked the baby's little cap; it was shut up, to be mildewed and moulder away, in the coffins of the dead. But it is not recorded that, in a single instance, her skill was called in aid to embroider the white veil which was to cover the pure blushes of a bride. The exception indicated the ever relentless vigor with which society frowned upon her sin.

Hester sought not to acquire any thing beyond a subsistence, of the plainest and most ascetic description, for herself, and a simple abundance for her child. Her own dress was of the coarsest materials and the most sombre hue; with only that one ornament, —the scarlet letter,—which it was her doom to wear. The child's attire, on the other hand, was distinguished by a fanciful, or, we might rather say, a fantastic ingenuity, which served, indeed, to heighten the airy charm that early began to develop itself in the little girl, but which appeared to have also a deeper meaning. We may speak further of it hereafter. Except for that small expenditure in the decoration of her infant, Hester bestowed all her superfluous means in charity, on wretches less miserable than herself, and who not unfrequently insulted the hand that fed them. Much of the time, which she might readily have applied to the better efforts of her art, she employed in making coarse garments for the poor. It is probable that there was an idea of penance in this mode of occupation, and that she offered up a real sacrifice of enjoyment, in devoting so many hours to such rude handiwork. She had in her nature a rich, voluptuous, Oriental characteristic,—a taste for the gorgeously beautiful, which, save in the exquisite productions of her needle, found nothing else, in all the possibilities of her life, to exercise itself upon. Women derive a pleasure, incomprehensible to the other sex, from the delicate toil of the needle. To Hester Prynne it might have been a mode of expressing, and therefore soothing, the passion of her life. Like all other joys, she rejected it as sin. This morbid meddling of conscience with an immaterial matter betokened, it is to be feared, no genuine and steadfast penitence, but something doubtful, something that might be deeply wrong, beneath.

In this manner, Hester Prynne came to have a part to perform in the world. With her native energy of character, and rare capacity, it could not entirely cast her off, although it had set a mark upon her, more intolerable to a woman's heart than that which branded the brow of Cain.[4] In all her intercourse with society, however, there was nothing that made her feel as if she belonged to it. Every gesture, every word, and even the silence of those with whom she came in contact, implied, and often expressed, that she was banished, and as much alone as if she inhabited another sphere, or communicated with the common nature by other organs and senses than the rest of human kind. She stood apart from mortal interests, yet close beside them, like a ghost that revisits the familiar fireside, and can no longer make itself seen or felt; no more smile with the household joy, nor mourn with the kindred sorrow; or, should it succeed in manifesting its forbidden sympathy, awakening only terror and horrible repugnance. These emotions, in fact, and its bitterest scorn besides, seemed to be the sole portion that she retained in the universal heart. It was not an age of delicacy; and her position, although she understood it well, and was in little danger of forgetting it, was often brought before her vivid self-perception, like a new anguish, by the rudest touch upon the tenderest spot. The poor, as we have already said, whom she sought out

4. See Genesis 4 : 1–16.

to be the objects of her bounty, often reviled the hand that was stretched forth to succor them. Dames of elevated rank, likewise, whose doors she entered in the way of her occupation, were accustomed to distil drops of bitterness into her heart; sometimes through that alchemy of quiet malice, by which women can concoct a subtile poison from ordinary trifles; and sometimes, also, by a coarser expression, that fell upon the sufferer's defenceless breast like a rough blow upon an ulcerated wound. Hester had schooled herself long and well; she never responded to these attacks, save by a flush of crimson that rose irrepressibly over her pale cheek, and again subsided into the depths of her bosom. She was patient,—a martyr, indeed,—but she forbore to pray for her enemies; lest, in spite of her forgiving aspirations, the words of the blessing should stubbornly twist themselves into a curse.

Continually, and in a thousand other ways, did she feel the innumerable throbs of anguish that had been so cunningly contrived for her by the undying, the ever-active sentence of the Puritan tribunal. Clergymen paused in the street to address words of exhortation, that brought a crowd, with its mingled grin and frown, around the poor, sinful woman. If she entered a church, trusting to share the Sabbath smile of the Universal Father, it was often her mishap to find herself the text of the discourse. She grew to have a dread of children; for they had imbibed from their parents a vague idea of something horrible in this dreary woman, gliding silently through the town, with never any companion but one only child. Therefore, first allowing her to pass, they pursued her at a distance with shrill cries, and the utterance of a word that had no distinct purport to their own minds, but was none the less terrible to her, as proceeding from lips that babbled it unconsciously. It seemed to argue so wide a diffusion of her shame, that all nature knew of it; it could have caused her no deeper pang, had the leaves of the trees whispered the dark story among themselves,—had the summer breeze murmured about it,—had the wintry blast shrieked it aloud! Another peculiar torture was felt in the gaze of a new eye. When strangers looked curiously at the scarlet letter,—and none ever failed to do so,—they branded it afresh into Hester's soul; so 'that, oftentimes, she could scarcely refrain, yet always did refrain, from covering the symbol with her hand. But then, again, an accustomed eye had likewise its own anguish to inflict. Its cool stare of familiarity was intolerable. From first to last, in short, Hester Prynne had always this dreadful agony in feeling a human eye upon the token; the spot never grew callous; it seemed, on the contrary, to grow more sensitive with daily torture.

But sometimes, once in many days, or perchance in many months, she felt an eye—a human eye—upon the ignominious brand, that seemed to give a momentary relief, as if half of her agony were shared. The next instant, back it all rushed again, with still a deeper throb of pain; for, in that brief interval, she had sinned anew. Had Hester sinned alone?

Her imagination was somewhat affected, and, had she been of a softer moral and intellectual fibre, would have been still more so, by the strange and solitary anguish of her life. Walking to and fro, with those lonely footsteps, in the little world with which she was outwardly connected, it now and then appeared to Hester,—if altogether fancy, it was nevertheless too potent to be resisted,—she felt or fancied, then, that the scarlet letter had endowed her with a new sense. She shuddered to believe, yet could not help believing, that it gave her a sympathetic knowledge of the hidden sin in other hearts. She was terror-stricken by the revelations that were thus made. What were they? Could they be other than the insidious whispers of the bad angel, who would fain have persuaded the struggling woman, as yet only half his victim, that the outward guise of purity was but a lie, and that, if truth were everywhere to be shown, a scarlet letter would blaze forth on many a bosom be- sides Hester Prynne's? Or, must she receive those intimations—so obscure, yet so distinct—as truth? In all her miserable experience, there was nothing else so awful and so loathsome as this sense. It perplexed, as well as shocked her, by the irreverent inopportuneness of the occasions that brought it into vivid action. Sometimes, the red infamy upon her breast would give a sympathetic throb, as she passed near a venerable minister or magistrate, the model of piety and justice, to whom that age of antique reverence looked up, as to a mortal man in fellowship with angels. "What evil thing is at hand?" would Hester say to herself. Lifting her reluctant eyes, there would be nothing human within the scope of view, save the form of this earthly saint! Again, a mystic sisterhood would contuma- ciously assert itself, as she met the sanctified frown of some matron, who, according to the rumor of all tongues, had kept cold snow within her bosom throughout life. That unsunned snow in the matron's bosom, and the burning shame on Hester Prynne's,—what had the two in common? Or, once more, the electric thrill would give her warning,—"Behold, Hester, here is a companion!"—and, looking up, she would detect the eyes of a young maiden glancing at the scarlet letter, shyly and aside, and quickly averted, with a faint, chill crimson in her cheeks; as if her purity were somewhat sullied by that momentary glance. O Fiend, whose talisman was that fatal symbol, wouldst thou leave nothing, whether in youth or age, for this poor sinner to revere?—Such loss of faith is ever one of the saddest results of sin. Be it accepted as a proof that all was not corrupt in this poor victim of her own frailty, and man's hard law, that Hester Prynne yet struggled to believe that no fellow-mortal was guilty like herself.

The vulgar, who, in those dreary old times, were always contributing a grotesque horror to what interested their imaginations, had a story about the scarlet letter which we might readily work up into a terrific legend. They averred, that the symbol was not mere scarlet cloth, tinged in an earthly dye-pot, but was red-hot with infernal fire, and could be seen glowing all alight, whenever Hester Prynne walked abroad in the night-time. And we must needs say, it seared Hester's bosom so deeply, that perhaps there was more truth in the rumor than our modern incredulity may be inclined to admit.

VI. *Pearl*

We have as yet hardly spoken of the infant; that little creature, whose innocent life had sprung, by the inscrutable decree of Providence, a lovely and immortal flower, out of the rank luxuriance of a guilty passion. How strange it seemed to the sad woman, as she watched the growth, and the beauty that became every day more brilliant, and the intelligence that threw its quivering sunshine over the tiny features of this child! Her Pearl!—For so had Hester called her; not as a name expressive of her aspect, which had nothing of the calm, white, unimpassioned lustre that would be indicated by the comparison. But she named the infant "Pearl," as being of great price,—purchased with all she had,[5]—her mother's only treasure! How strange, indeed! Man had marked this woman's sin by a scarlet letter, which had such potent and disastrous efficacy that no human sympathy could reach her, save it were sinful like herself. God, as a direct consequence of the sin which man thus punished, had given her a lovely child, whose place was on that same dishonored bosom, to connect her parent for ever with the race and descent of mortals, and to be finally a blessed soul in heaven! Yet these thoughts affected Hester Pyrnne less with hope than apprehension. She knew that her deed had been evil; she could have no faith, therefore, that its result would be for good. Day after day, she looked fearfully into the child's expanding nature;

5. Cf. Matthew 13 : 45–46, the parable of the merchant who sells all that he has to purchase "one pearl of great price." In the medieval allegory, "The Pearl," the grieving father beholds his lost daughter across the river of life, the radiant "bride of Christ the Lamb."

ever dreading to detect some dark and wild peculiarity, that should correspond with the guiltiness to which she owed her being.

Certainly, there was no physical defect. By its perfect shape, its vigor, and its natural dexterity in the use of all its untried limbs, the infant was worthy to have been brought forth in Eden; worthy to have been left there, to be the plaything of the angels, after the world's first parents were driven out. The child had a native grace which does not invariably coexist with faultless beauty; its attire, however simple, always impressed the beholder as if it were the very garb that precisely became it best. But little Pearl was not clad in rustic weeds. Her mother, with a morbid purpose that may be better understood hereafter, had bought the richest tissues that could be procured, and allowed her imaginative faculty its full play in the arrangement and decoration of the dresses which the child wore, before the public eye. So magnificent was the small figure, when thus arrayed, and such was the splendor of Pearl's own proper beauty, shining through the gorgeous robes which might have extinguished a paler loveliness, that there was an absolute circle of radiance around her, on the darksome cottage-floor. And yet a russet gown, torn and soiled with the child's rude play, made a picture of her just as perfect. Pearl's aspect was imbued with a spell of infinite variety; in this one child there were many children, comprehending the full scope between the wild-flower prettiness of a peasant-baby, and the pomp, in little, of an infant princess. Throughout all, however, there was a trait of passion, a certain depth of hue, which she never lost; and if, in any of her changes, she had grown fainter or paler, she would have ceased to be herself;—it would have been no longer Pearl!

This outward mutability indicated, and did not more than fairly express, the various properties of her inner life. Her nature appeared to possess depth, too, as well as variety; but—or else Hester's fears deceived her—it lacked reference and adaptation to the world into which she was born. The child could not be made amenable to rules. In giving her existence, a great law had been broken; and the result was a being, whose elements were perhaps beautiful and brilliant, but all in disorder; or with an order peculiar to themselves, amidst which the point of variety and arrangement was difficult or impossible to be discovered. Hester could only account for the child's character—and even then, most vaguely and imperfectly—by recalling what she herself had been, during that momentous period while Pearl was imbibing her soul from the spiritual world, and her bodily frame from its material of earth. The mother's impassioned state had been the medium through which were transmitted to the unborn infant the rays of its moral life; and, however white and clear originally, they had taken the deep stains of crimson and gold, the fiery lustre, the black shadow, and the untempered light, of the intervening substance. Above all, the warfare of Hester's spirit, at that epoch, was perpetuated in Pearl. She could recognize her wild, desperate, defiant mood, the flightiness of her temper, and even some of the very cloud-shapes of gloom and despondency that had brooded in her heart. They were now illuminated by the morning radiance of a young child's disposition, but, later in the day of earthly existence, might be prolific of the storm and whirlwind.

The discipline of the family, in those days, was of a far more rigid kind than now. The frown, the harsh rebuke, the frequent application of the rod, enjoined by Scriptural authority,[6] were used, not merely in the way of punishment for actual offences, but as a wholesome regimen for the growth and promotion of all childish virtues. Hester Prynne, nevertheless, the lonely mother of this one child, ran little risk of erring on the side of undue severity. Mindful, however, of her own errors and misfortunes, she early sought to impose a tender, but strict, control over the infant immortality that was committed to her charge. But the task was beyond her skill. After testing both smiles and frowns, and proving that neither mode of treatment possessed any calculable influence, Hester was ultimately compelled to stand aside, and permit the child to be swayed by her own impulses. Physical compulsion or restraint was effectual, of course, while it lasted. As to any other kind of discipline, whether addressed to her mind or heart, little Pearl might or might not be within its reach, in accordance with the caprice that ruled the moment. Her mother, while Pearl was yet an infant, grew acquainted with a certain peculiar look, that warned her when it would be labor thrown away to insist, persuade, or plead. It was a look so intelligent, yet inexplicable, so perverse, sometimes so malicious, but generally accompanied by a wild flow of spirits, that Hester could not help questioning, at such moments, whether Pearl was a human child. She seemed rather an airy sprite, which, after playing its fantastic sports for a little while upon the cottage-floor, would flit away with a mocking smile. Whenever that look appeared in her wild, bright, deeply black eyes, it invested her with a strange remoteness and intangibility; it was as if she were hovering in the air and might vanish, like a glimmering light that comes we know not whence, and goes we know not whither. Beholding it, Hester was constrained to rush towards the child,—to pursue the little elf in the flight which she invariably began,—to snatch her to her bosom, with a close pressure and earnest kisses,—not so much from overflowing love, as to assure herself that Pearl was flesh and blood, and not utterly delusive. But Pearl's laugh, when she was

6. "He that spareth his rod hateth his son: but he that loveth him chasteneth him betimes" (Proverbs 13 : 24).

caught, though full of merriment and music, made her mother more doubtful than before.

Heart-smitten at this bewildering and baffling spell, that so often came between herself and her sole treasure, whom she had bought so dear, and who was all her world, Hester sometimes burst into passionate tears. Then, perhaps,—for there was no foreseeing how it might affect her,—Pearl would frown, and clench her little fist, and harden her small features into a stern, unsympathizing look of discontent. Not seldom, she would laugh anew, and louder than before, like a thing incapable and unintelligent of human sorrow. Or—but this more rarely happened—she would be convulsed with a rage of grief, and sob out her love for her mother, in broken words, and seem intent on proving that she had a heart, by breaking it. Yet Hester was hardly safe in confiding herself to that gusty tenderness; it passed, as suddenly as it came. Brooding over all these matters, the mother felt like one who has evoked a spirit, but, by some irregularity in the process of conjuration, has failed to win the master-word that should control this new and incomprehensible intelligence. Her only real comfort was when the child lay in the placidity of sleep. Then she was sure of her, and tasted hours of quiet, sad, delicious happiness; until—perhaps with that perverse expression glimmering from beneath her opening lids—little Pearl awoke!

How soon—with what strange rapidity, indeed!—did Pearl arrive at an age that was capable of social intercourse, beyond the mother's ever-ready smile and nonsense-words! And then what a happiness would it have been, could Hester Prynne have heard her clear, bird-like voice mingling with the uproar of other childish voices, and have distinguished and unravelled her own darling's tones, amid all the entangled outcry of a group of sportive children! But this could never be. Pearl was a born outcast of the infantile world. An imp of evil, emblem and product of sin, she had no right among christened infants. Nothing was more remarkable than the instinct, as it seemed, with which the child comprehended her loneliness; the destiny that had drawn an inviolable circle round about her; the whole peculiarity, in short, of her position in respect to other children. Never, since her release from prison, had Hester met the public gaze without her. In all her walks about the town, Pearl, too, was there; first as the babe in arms, and afterwards as the little girl, small companion of her mother, holding a forefinger with her whole grasp, and tripping along at the rate of three or four footsteps to one of Hester's. She saw the children of the settlement, on the grassy margin of the street, or at the domestic thresholds, disporting themselves in such grim fashion as the Puritanic nurture would permit; playing at going to church, perchance; or at scourging Quakers; or taking scalps in a sham-fight with the Indians; or scaring one another with freaks of imitative witchcraft. Pearl saw, and gazed intently, but never sought to make acquaintance. If spoken to, she would not speak again. If the children gathered about her, as they sometimes did, Pearl would grow positively terrible in her puny wrath, snatching up stones to fling at them, with shrill, incoherent exclamations that made her mother tremble, because they had so much the sound of a witch's anathemas in some unknown tongue.

The truth was, that the little Puritans, being of the most intolerant brood that ever lived, had got a vague idea of something outlandish, unearthly, or at variance with ordinary fashions, in the mother and child; and therefore scorned them in their hearts, and not unfrequently reviled them with their tongues. Pearl felt the sentiment, and requited it with the bitterest hatred that can be supposed to rankle in a childish bosom. These outbreaks of a fierce temper had a kind of value, and even comfort, for her mother; because there was at least an intelligible earnestness in the mood, instead of the fitful caprice that so often thwarted her in the child's manifestations. It appalled her, nevertheless, to discern here, again, a shadowy reflection of the evil that had existed in herself. All this enmity and passion had Pearl inherited, by inalienable right, out of Hester's heart. Mother and daughter stood together in the same circle of seclusion from human society; and in the nature of the child seemed to be perpetuated those unquiet elements that had distracted Hester Prynne before Pearl's birth, but had since begun to be soothed away by the softening influences of maternity.

At home, within and around her mother's cottage, Pearl wanted not a wide and various circle of acquaintance. The spell of life went forth from her ever creative spirit, and communicated itself to a thousand objects, as a torch kindles a flame wherever it may be applied. The unlikeliest materials, a stick, a bunch of rags, a flower, were the puppets of Pearl's witchcraft, and, without undergoing any outward change, became spiritually adapted to whatever drama occupied the stage of her inner world. Her one baby-voice served a multitude of imaginary personages, old and young, to talk withal. The pine-trees, aged, black, and solemn, and flinging groans and other melancholy utterances on the breeze, needed little transformation to figure as Puritan elders; the ugliest weeds of the garden were their children, whom Pearl smote down and uprooted, most unmercifully. It was wonderful, the vast variety of forms into which she threw her intellect, with no continuity, indeed, but darting up and dancing, always in a state of preternatural activity,—soon sinking down, as if exhausted by so rapid and feverish a tide of life, —and succeeded by other shapes of a similar wild energy. It was like nothing so much as the phantasmagoric play of the northern lights. In the mere exercise of the fancy, however, and the sportiveness of a growing mind, there might be little more than was observable in other children of bright faculties; except as Pearl, in the dearth of human playmates, was thrown more upon the visionary throng which she created. The singularity lay in the hostile feelings with which the child regarded all these offspring of her own heart and mind. She never created a friend, but seemed always to be sowing broadcast the dragon's teeth, whence sprung a harvest of armed enemies, against whom she rushed to battle.[7] It was inexpressibly sad—then what depth of sorrow to a mother, who felt in her own heart the cause!—to observe, in one so young, this constant recognition of an adverse world, and so fierce a training of the energies that were to make good her cause, in the contest that must ensue.

Gazing at Pearl, Hester Prynne often dropped her work upon her knees, and cried out, with an agony which she would fain have hidden, but which made utterance for itself, betwixt speech and a groan,—"O Father in Heaven,—if Thou art still my Father,— what is this being which I have brought into the world!" And Pearl, overhearing the ejaculation, or aware, through some more subtle channel, of those throbs of anguish, would turn her vivid and beautiful little face upon her mother, smile with sprite-like intelligence, and resume her play.

One peculiarity of the child's deportment remains yet to be told. The very first thing which she had noticed, in her life, was—what? —not the mother's smile, responding to it, as other babies do, by that faint, embryo smile of the little mouth, remembered so doubtfully afterwards, and with such fond discussion whether it were indeed a smile. By no means! But that first object of which Pearl seemed to become aware was—shall we say it?—the scarlet letter on Hester's bosom! One day, as her mother stooped over the cradle, the infant's eyes had been caught by the glimmering of the gold embroidery about the letter; and, putting up her little hand, she grasped at it, smiling, not doubtfully, but with a decided gleam that gave her face the look of a much older child. Then, gasping for breath, did Hester Prynne clutch the fatal token, instinctively endeavouring to tear it away; so infinite was the torture inflicted by the intelligent touch of Pearl's baby-hand. Again, as if her mother's agonized gesture were meant only to make sport for her, did little Pearl look into her eyes, and smile! From that epoch, except when the child was asleep, Hester had never felt a moment's safety; not a moment's calm enjoyment of her. Weeks, it is true,

7. In the Greek myth, Cadmus sows the teeth of a dragon he has killed; they grow into armed men, who fight each other until only five are left.

would sometimes elapse, during which Pearl's gaze might never once be fixed upon the scarlet letter; but then, again, it would come at unawares, like the stroke of sudden death, and always with that peculiar smile, and odd expression of the eyes.

Once, this freakish, elvish cast came into the child's eyes, while Hester was looking at her own image in them, as mothers are fond of doing; and, suddenly,—for women in solitude, and with troubled hearts, are pestered with unaccountable delusions,—she fancied that she beheld, not her own miniature portrait, but another face in the small black mirror of Pearl's eye. It was a face, fiend-like, full of smiling malice, yet bearing the semblance of features that she had known full well, though seldom with a smile, and never with malice, in them. It was as if an evil spirit possessed the child, and had just then peeped forth in mockery. Many a time afterwards had Hester been tortured, though less vividly, by the same illusion.

In the afternoon of a certain summer's day, after Pearl grew big enough to run about, she amused herself with gathering handfuls of wild-flowers, and flinging them, one by one, at her mother's bosom; dancing up and down, like a little elf, whenever she hit the scarlet letter. Hester's first motion had been to cover her bosom with her clasped hands. But, whether from pride or resignation, or a feeling that her penance might best be wrought out by this unutterable pain, she resisted the impulse, and sat erect, pale as death, looking sadly into little Pearl's wild eyes. Still came the battery of flowers, almost invariably hitting the mark, and covering the mother's breast with hurts for which she could find no balm in this world, nor knew how to seek it in another. At last, her shot being all expended, the child stood still and gazed at Hester, with that little, laughing image of a fiend peeping out—or, whether it peeped or no, her mother so imagined it—from the unsearchable abyss of her black eyes.

"Child, what art thou?" cried the mother.

"O, I am your little Pearl!" answered the child.

But, while she said it, Pearl laughed and began to dance up and down, with the humorsome gesticulation of a little imp, whose next freak might be to fly up the chimney.

"Art thou my child, in very truth?" asked Hester.

Nor did she put the question altogether idly, but, for the moment, with a portion of genuine earnestness; for, such was Pearl's wonderful intelligence, that her mother half doubted whether she were not acquainted with the secret spell of her existence, and might not now reveal herself.

"Yes; I am little Pearl!" repeated the child, continuing her antics.

"Thou art not my child! Thou art no Pearl of mine!" said the mother, half playfully; for it was often the case that a sportive impulse came over her, in the midst of her deepest suffering. "Tell me, then, what thou art, and who sent thee hither?"

"Tell me, mother!" said the child, seriously, coming up to Hester, and pressing herself close to her knees. "Do thou tell me!"

"Thy Heavenly Father sent thee!" answered Hester Prynne.

But she said it with a hesitation that did not escape the acuteness of the child. Whether moved only by her ordinary freakishness, or because an evil spirit prompted her, she put up her small forefinger, and touched the scarlet letter.

"He did not send me!" cried she, positively. "I have no Heavenly Father!"

"Hush, Pearl, hush! Thou must not talk so!" answered the mother, suppressing a groan. "He sent us all into this world. He sent even me, thy mother. Then, much more, thee! Or, if not, thou strange and elfish child, whence didst thou come?"

"Tell me! Tell me!" repeated Pearl, no longer seriously, but laughing, and capering about the floor, "It is thou that must tell me!"

But Hester could not resolve the query, being herself in a dismal labyrinth of doubt. She remembered—betwixt a smile and a shudder—the talk of the neighbouring townspeople; who, seeking vainly elsewhere for the child's paternity, and observing some of her odd attributes, had given out that poor little Pearl was a demon offspring;[8] such as, ever since old Catholic times, had occasionally been seen on earth, through the agency of their mothers' sin, and to promote some foul and wicked purpose. Luther,[9] according to the scandal of his monkish enemies, was a brat of that hellish breed; nor was Pearl the only child to whom this inauspicious origin was assigned, among the New England Puritans.

VII. *The Governor's Hall*

Hester Prynne went, one day, to the mansion of Governor Bellingham, with a pair of gloves, which she had fringed and embroidered to his order, and which were to be worn on some great occasion of state; for, though the chances of a popular election had caused this former ruler to descend a step or two from the highest rank, he still held an honorable and influential place among the

8. One of the superstitions of witchcraft, briefly sanctioned by the medieval Church and by the Puritans, held that evil spirits, "incubi" and "succubi," begot, upon sleeping persons, children prone by nature to wildness.
9. Martin Luther (1483–1546), father of the Reformation in Germany, preached the doctrine of salvation by faith rather than by works.

colonial magistracy.[1]

Another and far more important reason than the delivery of a pair of embroidered gloves impelled Hester, at this time, to seek an interview with a personage of so much power and activity in the affairs of the settlement. It had reached her ears, that there was a design on the part of some of the leading inhabitants, cherishing the more rigid order of principles in religion and government, to deprive her of her child. On the supposition that Pearl, as already hinted, was of demon origin, these good people not unreasonably argued that a Christian interest in the mother's soul required them to remove such a stumbling-block from her path. If the child, on the other hand, were really capable of moral and religious growth, and possessed the elements of ultimate salvation, then, surely, it would enjoy all the fairer prospect of these advantages by being transferred to wiser and better guardianship than Hester Prynne's. Among those who promoted the design, Governor Bellingham was said to be one of the most busy. It may appear singular, and, indeed, not a little ludicrous, that an affair of this kind, which, in later days, would have been referred to no higher jurisdiction than that of the selectmen of the town, should then have been a question publicly discussed, and on which statesmen of eminence took sides. At that epoch of pristine simplicity, however, matters of even slighter public interest, and of far less intrinsic weight than the welfare of Hester and her child, were strangely mixed up with the deliberations of legislators and acts of state. The period was hardly, if at all, earlier than that of our story, when a dispute concerning the right of property in a pig, not only caused a fierce and bitter contest in the legislative body of the colony, but resulted in an important modification of the framework itself of the legislature.

Full of concern, therefore,—but so conscious of her own right, that it seemed scarcely an unequal match between the public, on the one side, and a lonely woman, backed by the sympathies of nature, on the other,—Hester Prynne set forth from her solitary cottage. Little Pearl, of course, was her companion. She was now of an age to run lightly along by her mother's side, and, constantly in motion from morn till sunset, could have accomplished a much longer journey than that before her. Often, nevertheless, more from caprice than necessity, she demanded to be taken up in arms, but was soon as imperious to be set down again, and frisked onward before Hester on the grassy pathway, with many a harmless trip

1. In the spring of 1642 Governor Bellingham was ending the term to which he had been elected in 1641. He was not reelected governor until 1654, meanwhile serving as magistrate or deputy governor. The date of the present episode is 1645, when Pearl was three.

and tumble. We have spoken of Pearl's rich and luxuriant beauty; a beauty that shone with deep and vivid tints; a bright complexion, eyes possessing intensity both of depth and glow, and hair already of a deep, glossy brown, and which, in after years, would be nearly akin to black. There was fire in her and throughout her; she seemed the unpremeditated offshoot of a passionate moment. Her mother, in contriving the child's garb, had allowed the gorgeous tendencies of her imagination their full play; arraying her in a crimson velvet tunic, of a peculiar cut, abundantly embroidered with fantasies and flourishes of gold thread. So much strength of coloring, which must have given a wan and pallid aspect to cheeks of a fainter bloom, was admirably adapted to Pearl's beauty, and made her the very brightest little jet of flame that ever danced upon the earth.

But it was a remarkable attribute of this garb, and, indeed, of the child's whole appearance, that it irresistibly and inevitably reminded the beholder of the token which Hester Prynne was doomed to wear upon her bosom. It was the scarlet letter in another form; the scarlet letter endowed with life! The mother herself—as if the red ignominy were so deeply scorched into her brain, that all her conceptions assumed its form—had carefully wrought out the similitude; lavishing many hours of morbid ingenuity, to create an analogy between the object of her affection, and the emblem of her guilt and torture. But, in truth, Pearl was the one, as well as the other; and only in consequence of that identity had Hester contrived so perfectly to represent the scarlet letter in her appearance.

As the two wayfarers came within the precincts of the town, the children of the Puritans looked up from their play,—or what passed for play with those sombre little urchins,—and spake gravely one to another:—

"Behold, verily, there is the woman of the scarlet letter; and, of a truth, moreover, there is the likeness of the scarlet letter running along by her side! Come, therefore, and let us fling mud at them!"

But Pearl, who was a dauntless child, after frowning, stamping her foot, and shaking her little hand with a variety of threatening gestures, suddenly made a rush at the knot of her enemies, and put them all to flight. She resembled, in her fierce pursuit of them, an infant pestilence,—the scarlet fever, or some such half-fledged angel of judgment,—whose mission was to punish the sins of the rising generation. She screamed and shouted, too, with a terrific volume of sound, which doubtless caused the hearts of the fugitives to quake within them. The victory accomplished, Pearl returned quietly to her mother, and looked up smiling into her face.

Without further adventure, they reached the dwelling of Governor Bellingham. This was a large wooden house, built in a fashion of which there are specimens still extant in the streets of our elder towns; now moss-grown, crumbling to decay, and melancholy at heart with the many sorrowful or joyful occurrences remembered or forgotten, that have happened, and passed away, within their dusky chambers. Then, however, there was the freshness of the passing year on its exterior, and the cheerfulness, gleaming forth from the sunny windows, of a human habitation into which death had never entered. It had indeed a very cheery aspect; the walls being overspread with a kind of stucco, in which fragments of broken glass were plentifully intermixed; so that, when the sunshine fell aslantwise over the front of the edifice, it glittered and sparkled as if diamonds had been flung against it by the double handful. The brilliancy might have befitted Aladdin's palace, rather than the mansion of a grave old Puritan ruler. It was further decorated with strange and seemingly cabalistic figures and diagrams, suitable to the quaint taste of the age, which had been drawn in the stucco when newly laid on, and had now grown hard and durable, for the admiration of after times.

Pearl, looking at this bright wonder of a house, began to caper and dance, and imperatively required that the whole breadth of sunshine should be stripped off its front, and given her to play with.

"No, my little Pearl!" said her mother. "Thou must gather thine own sunshine. I have none to give thee!"

They approached the door; which was of an arched form, and flanked on each side by a narrow tower or projection of the edifice, in both of which were lattice-windows, with wooden shutters to close over them at need. Lifting the iron hammer that hung at the portal, Hester Prynne gave a summons, which was answered by one of the Governor's bond-servants; a free-born Englishman, but now a seven years' slave. During that term he was to be the property of his master, and as much a commodity of bargain and sale as an ox, or a joint-stool. The serf wore the blue coat, which was the customary garb of serving-men at that period, and long before, in the old hereditary halls of England.

"Is the worshipful Governor Bellingham within?" inquired Hester.

"Yea, forsooth," replied the bond-servant, staring with wide-open eyes at the scarlet letter, which, being a new-comer in the country, he had never before seen. "Yea, his honorable worship is within. But he hath a godly minister or two with him, and likewise a leech. Ye may not see his worship now."

"Nevertheless, I will enter," answered Hester Prynne; and the bond-servant, perhaps judging from the decision of her air and the glittering symbol in her bosom, that she was a great lady in the land, offered no opposition.

So the mother and little Pearl were admitted into the hall of entrance. With many variations, suggested by the nature of his building-materials, diversity of climate, and a different mode of social life, Governor Bellingham had planned his new habitation after the residences of gentlemen of fair estate in his native land. Here, then, was a wide and reasonably lofty hall, extending through the whole depth of the house, and forming a medium of general communication, more or less directly, with all the other apartments. At one extremity, this spacious room was lighted by the windows of the two towers, which formed a small recess on either side of the portal. At the other end, though partly muffled by a curtain, it was more powerfully illuminated by one of those embowed hall-windows which we read of in old books, and which was provided with a deep and cushioned seat. Here, on the cushion, lay a folio tome, probably of the Chronicles of England,[2] or other such substantial literature; even as, in our own days, we scatter gilded volumes on the centre-table, to be turned over by the casual guest. The furniture of the hall consisted of some ponderous chairs, the backs of which were elaborately carved with wreaths of oaken flowers; and likewise a table in the same taste; the whole being of the Elizabethan age, or perhaps earlier, and heirlooms, transferred hither from the Governor's paternal home. On the table—in token that the sentiment of old English hospitality had not been left behind —stood a large pewter tankard, at the bottom of which, had Hester or Pearl peeped into it, they might have seen the frothy remnant of a recent draught of ale.

On the wall hung a row of portraits, representing the forefathers of the Bellingham lineage, some with armour on their breasts, and others with stately ruffs and robes of peace. All were characterized by the sternness and severity which old portraits so invariably put on; as if they were the ghosts, rather than the pictures, of departed worthies, and were gazing with harsh and intolerant criticism at the pursuits and enjoyments of living men.

At about the centre of the oaken panels, that lined the hall, was suspended a suit of mail, not, like the pictures, an ancestral relic, but of the most modern date; for it had been manufactured by a skilful armorer in London, the same year in which Governor Bellingham came over to New England. There was a steel head-piece, a cuirass, a gorget, and greaves, with a pair of gauntlets and a sword hanging beneath; all, and especially the helmet and breastplate, so highly burnished as to glow with white radiance, and scatter an illumination everywhere about upon the floor. This bright panoply was not meant for mere idle show, but had been worn by the Governor on many a solemn muster and training field, and had glit-

2. Raphael Holinshed's *Chronicles of England, Scotland, and Ireland* (1577), a popular historical compilation; Shakespeare used it as a source book.

tered, moreover, at the head of a regiment in the Pequod war.[3] For, though bred a lawyer, and accustomed to speak of Bacon, Coke, Noye, and Finch,[4] as his professional associates, the exigencies of this new country had transformed Governor Bellingham into a soldier, as well as a statesman and ruler.

Little Pearl—who was as greatly pleased with the gleaming armour as she had been with the glittering frontispiece of the house —spent some time looking into the polished mirror of the breast-plate.

"Mother," cried she she, "I see you here. Look! Look!"

Hester looked, by way of humoring the child; and she saw that, owing to the peculiar effect of this convex mirror, the scarlet letter was represented in exaggerated and gigantic proportions, so as to be greatly the most prominent feature of her appearance. In truth, she seemed absolutely hidden behind it. Pearl pointed upward, also, at a similar picture in the head-piece; smiling at her mother, with the elfish intelligence that was so familiar an expression on her small physiognomy. That look of naughty merriment was likewise reflected in the mirror, with so much breadth and intensity of effect, that it made Hester Prynne feel as if it could not be the image of her own child, but of an imp who was seeking to mould itself into Pearl's shape.

"Come along, Pearl!" said she, drawing her away. "Come and look into this fair garden. It may be, we shall see flowers there; more beautiful ones than we find in the woods."

Pearl, accordingly, ran to the bow-window, at the farther end of the hall, and looked along the vista of a garden-walk, carpeted with closely shaven grass, and bordered with some rude and immature attempt at shrubbery. But the proprietor appeared already to have relinquished, as hopeless, the effort to perpetuate on this side of the Atlantic, in a hard soil and amid the close struggle for subsistence, the native English taste for ornamental gardening. Cabbages grew in plain sight; and a pumpkin vine, rooted at some distance, had run across the intervening space, and deposited one of its gigantic products directly beneath the hall-windows; as if to warn the Governor that this great lump of vegetable gold was as rich an ornament as New England earth would offer him. There were a few

3. The Pequots, an Algonquian tribe of about 3,000 Indians, controlled eastern Connecticut, menaced British settlements, and were finally crushed by British forces in 1637, after Bellingham first arrived.
4. Francis Bacon (1561–1626), a lord chancellor of England, formulated the new inductive science. Sir Edward Coke (1552–1634), parliamentarian and jurist, strengthened the common law, served as lord chief justice, and published the classic *Reports and Institutes*. William Noye (1577–1634), writer of legal commentaries, was appointed attorney general in 1631. Sir John Finch (1584–1660), baron of Fordwich, in his stormy career served as king's counsel, as Speaker of the House of Commons, and as a chief justice.

rose-bushes, however, and a number of apple-trees, probably the descendants of those planted by the Reverend Mr. Blackstone,[5] the first settler of the peninsula; that half mythological personage who rides through our early annals, seated on the back of a bull.

Pearl, seeing the rose-bushes, began to cry for a red rose, and would not be pacified.

"Hush, child, hush!" said her mother earnestly. "Do not cry, dear little Pearl! I hear voices in the garden. The Governor is coming, and gentlemen along with him!"

In fact, adown the vista of the garden-avenue, a number of persons were seen approaching towards the house. Pearl, in utter scorn of her mother's attempt to quiet her, gave an eldritch scream, and then became silent; not from any notion of obedience, but because the quick and mobile curiosity of her disposition was excited by the appearance of these new personages.

VIII. *The Elf-child and the Minister*

Governor Bellingham, in a loose gown and easy cap,—such as elderly gentlemen loved to indue themselves with, in their domestic privacy,—walked foremost, and appeared to be showing off his estate, and expatiating on his projected improvements. The wide circumference of an elaborate ruff, beneath his gray beard, in the antiquated fashion of King James's reign, caused his head to look not a little like that of John the Baptist in a charger.[6] The impression made by his aspect, so rigid and severe, and frost-bitten with more than autumnal age, was hardly in keeping with the appliances of worldly enjoyment wherewith he had evidently done his utmost to surround himself. But it is an error to suppose that our grave forefathers—though accustomed to speak and think of human existence as a state merely of trial and warfare, and though unfeignedly prepared to sacrifice goods and life at the behest of duty—made it a matter of conscience to reject such means of comfort, or even luxury, as lay fairly within their grasp. This creed was never taught, for instance, by the venerable pastor, John Wilson,[7] whose beard, white as a snow-drift, was seen over Governor Bellingham's shoulder; while its wearer suggested that pears and peaches might yet be naturalized in the New England climate, and that purple grapes

---

5. Blackstone, reputedly the first white settler near Boston, an Anglican, rode off to join the Indians soon after the Puritans, whom he disliked, arrived. The allusion to Blackstone, who rode a pagan bull and planted apples and roses, contributes to a suggestion of the Garden of Eden in these last paragraphs. Pearl cries for "a red rose" (symbol of passion and recalling the for-

bidden fruit), but then her mother hears "voices in the garden," reminiscent of "the voice of the Lord God walking in the Garden." *Cf.* Genesis ii: 16–17 and iii: 6–8.

6. See Mark 6 : 6–28. A "charger" is a platter.

7. The following comment on Puritan social life, then unconventional, is now verified by scholarship.

might possibly be compelled to flourish, against the sunny garden-wall. The old clergyman, nurtured at the rich bosom of the English Church, had a long established and legitimate taste for all good and comfortable things; and however stern he might show himself in the pulpit, or in his public reproof of such transgressions as that of Hester Prynne, still, the genial benevolence of his private life had won him warmer affection than was accorded to any of his professional contemporaries.

Behind the Governor and Mr. Wilson came two other guests; one, the Reverend Arthur Dimmesdale, whom the reader may remember, as having taken a brief and reluctant part in the scene of Hester Prynne's disgrace; and, in close companionship with him, old Roger Chillingworth, a person of great skill in physic, who, for two or three years past, had been settled in the town. It was understood that this learned man was the physician as well as friend of the young minister, whose health had severely suffered, of late, by his too unreserved self-sacrifice to the labors and duties of the pastoral relation.

The Governor, in advance of his visitors, ascended one or two steps, and, throwing open the leaves of the great hall window, found himself close to little Pearl. The shadow of the curtain fell on Hester Prynne, and partially concealed her.

"What have we here?" said Governor Bellingham, looking with surprise at the scarlet little figure before him. "I profess, I have never seen the like, since my days of vanity, in old King James's time, when I was wont to esteem it a high favor to be admitted to a court mask! There used to be a swarm of these small apparitions, in holiday-time; and we called them children of the Lord of Misrule.[8] But how gat such a guest into my hall?"

"Ay, indeed!" cried good old Mr. Wilson. "What little bird of scarlet plumage may this be? Methinks I have seen just such figures, when the sun has been shining through a richly painted window, and tracing out the golden and crimson images across the floor. But that was in the old land.[9] Prithee, young one, who art thou, and what has ailed thy mother to bedizen thee in this strange fashion? Art thou a Christian child,—ha? Dost know thy catechism? Or art thou one of those naughty elfs or fairies, whom we thought to have left behind us, with other relics of Papistry, in merry old England?"

"I am mother's child," answered the scarlet vision, "and my name is Pearl!"

"Pearl?—Ruby, rather!—or Coral!—or Red Rose, at the very

8. The master of the revels in medieval Christmas celebrations, often abetted by juvenile pranksters.
9. That is, England, where the Puritans had found offense in the stained glass and "graven images" of churches and cathedrals.

least, judging from thy hue!" responded the old minister, putting forth his hand in a vain attempt to pat little Pearl on the cheek. "But where is this mother of thine? Ah! I see," he added; and, turning to Governor Bellingham, whispered,—"This is the self-same child of whom we have held speech together; and behold here the unhappy woman, Hester Prynne, her mother!"

"Sayest thou so?" cried the Governor. "Nay, we might have judged that such a child's mother must needs be a scarlet woman, and a worthy type of her of Babylon![1] But she comes at a good time; and we will look into this matter forthwith."

Governor Bellingham stepped through the window into the hall, followed by his three guests.

"Hester Prynne," said he, fixing his naturally stern regard on the wearer of the scarlet letter, "there hath been much question concerning thee, of late. The point hath been weightily discussed, whether we, that are of authority and influence, do well discharge our consciences by trusting an immortal soul, such as there is in yonder child, to the guidance of one who hath stumbled and fallen, amid the pitfalls of this world. Speak thou, the child's own mother! Were it not, thinkest thou, for thy little one's temporal and eternal welfare, that she be taken out of thy charge, and clad soberly, and disciplined strictly, and instructed in the truths of heaven and earth? What canst thou do for the child, in this kind?"

"I can teach my little Pearl what I have learned from this!" answered Hester Prynne, laying her finger on the red token.

"Woman, it is thy badge of shame!" replied the stern magistrate. "It is because of the stain which that letter indicates, that we would transfer thy child to other hands."

"Nevertheless," said the mother calmly, though growing more pale, "this badge hath taught me,—it daily teaches me,—it is teaching me at this moment,—lessons whereof my child may be the wiser and better, albeit they can profit nothing to myself."

"We will judge warily," said Bellingham, "and look well what we are about to do. Good Master Wilson, I pray you, examine this Pearl,—since that is her name,—and see whether she hath had such Christian nurture as befits a child of her age."

The old minister seated himself in an arm-chair, and made an effort to draw Pearl betwixt his knees. But the child, unaccustomed to the touch or familiarity of any but her mother, escaped through the open window and stood on the upper step, looking like a wild, tropical bird, of rich plumage, ready to take flight into the upper

---

1. The "scarlet woman" and "the whore of Babylon," terms of opprobrium for the Catholic Church during the Refor- mation, originated in Revelation 18 : 1–5, denouncing ancient Babylon for its dissipations and idolatry.

air. Mr. Wilson, not a little astonished at this outbreak,—for he was a grandfatherly sort of personage, and usually a vast favorite with children,—essayed, however, to proceed with the examination.

"Pearl," said he, with great solemnity, "thou must take heed to instruction, that so, in due season, thou mayest wear in thy bosom the pearl of great price. Canst thou tell me, my child, who made thee?"

Now Pearl knew well enough who made her; for Hester Prynne, the daughter of a pious home, very soon after her talk with the child about her Heavenly Father, had begun to inform her of those truths which the human spirit, at whatever stage of immaturity, imbibes with such eager interest. Pearl, therefore, so large were the attainments of her three years' lifetime, could have borne a fair examination in the New England Primer, or the first column of the Westminster Catechism,[2] although unacquainted with the outward form of either of those celebrated works. But that perversity, which all children have more or less of, and of which little Pearl had a tenfold portion, now, at the most inopportune moment, took thorough possession of her, and closed her lips, or impelled her to speak words amiss. After putting her finger in her mouth, with many ungracious refusals to answer good Mr. Wilson's question, the child finally announced that she had not been made at all, but had been plucked by her mother off the bush of wild roses, that grew by the prison-door.

This fantasy was probably suggested by the near proximity of the Governor's red roses, as Pearl stood outside of the window; together with her recollection of the prison rose-bush, which she had passed in coming hither.

Old Roger Chillingworth, with a smile on his face, whispered something in the young clergyman's ear. Hester Prynne looked at the man of skill, and even then, with her fate hanging in the balance, was startled to perceive what a change had come over his features,—how much uglier they were,—how his dark complexion seemed to have grown duskier, and his figure more misshapen,—since the days when she had familiarly known him. She met his eyes for an instant, but was immediately constrained to give all her attention to the scene now going forward.

"This is awful!" cried the Governor, slowly recovering from the

2. The *New England Primer* (*ca.* 1683) taught the alphabet by means of didactic woodcuts and rhymes on Biblical characters and doctrine. The "Longer" and "Shorter" *Westminster Catechism*, adopted at Edinburgh in 1648, taught by question and answer the theology of John Calvin (1509–1564) formulated by the Westminster Confession (1645–1647) for the English churches, principally Presbyterian and Congregational, but accepted by other Puritan sects.

astonishment into which Pearl's response had thrown him. "Here is a child of three years old, and she cannot tell who made her! Without question, she is equally in the dark as to her soul, its present depravity, and future destiny! Methinks, gentlemen, we need inquire no further."

Hester caught hold of Pearl, and drew her forcibly into her arms, confronting the old Puritan magistrate with almost a fierce expression. Alone in the world, cast off by it, and with this sole treasure to keep her heart alive, she felt that she possessed indefeasible rights against the world, and was ready to defend them to the death.

"God gave me the child!" cried she. "He gave her, in requital of all things else, which ye had taken from me. She is my happiness!—she is my torture, none the less! Pearl keeps me here in life! Pearl punishes me too! See ye not, she is the scarlet letter, only capable of being loved, and so endowed with a million-fold the power of retribution for my sin? Ye shall not take her! I will die first!"

"My poor woman," said the not unkind old minister, "the child shall be well cared for!—far better than thou canst do it."

"God gave her into my keeping," repeated Hester Prynne, raising her voice almost to a shriek. "I will not give her up!"—And here, by a sudden impulse, she turned to the young clergyman, Mr. Dimmesdale, at whom, up to this moment, she had seemed hardly so much as once to direct her eyes.—"Speak thou for me!" cried she. "Thou wast my pastor, and hadst charge of my soul, and knowest me better than these men can. I will not lose the child! Speak for me! Thou knowest,—for thou hast sympathies which these men lack!—thou knowest what is in my heart, and what are a mother's rights, and how much the stronger they are, when that mother has but her child and the scarlet letter! Look thou to it! I will not lose the child! Look to it!"

At this wild and singular appeal, which indicated that Hester Prynne's situation had provoked her to little less than madness, the young minister at once came forward, pale, and holding his hand over his heart, as was his custom whenever his peculiarly nervous temperament was thrown into agitation. He looked now more careworn and emaciated than as we described him at the scene of Hester's public ignominy; and whether it were his failing health, or whatever the cause might be, his large dark eyes had a world of pain in their troubled and melancholy depth.

"There is truth in what she says," began the minister, with a voice sweet, tremulous, but powerful, insomuch that the hall reëchoed, and the hollow armour rang with it.—"truth in what

Hester says, and in the feeling which inspires her! God gave her the child, and gave her, too, an instinctive knowledge of its nature and requirements,—both seemingly so peculiar,—which no other mortal being can possess. And, moreover, is there not a quality of awful sacredness in the relations between this mother and this child?"

"Ay!—how is that, good Master Dimmesdale?" interrupted the Governor. "Make that plain, I pray you!"

"It must be even so," resumed the minister. "For, if we deem it otherwise, do we not thereby say that the Heavenly Father, the Creator of all flesh, hath lightly recognized a deed of sin, and made of no account the distinction between unhallowed lust and holy love? This child of its father's guilt and its mother's shame hath come from the hand of God, to work in many ways upon her heart, who pleads so earnestly, and with such bitterness of spirit, the right to keep her. It was meant for a blessing; for the one blessing of her life! It was meant, doubtless, as the mother herself hath told us, for a retribution too; a torture, to be felt at many an unthought of moment; a pang, a sting, an ever-recurring agony, in the midst of a troubled joy! Hath she not expressed this thought in the garb of the poor child, so forcibly reminding us of that red symbol which sears her bosom?"

"Well said, again!" cried good Mr. Wilson. "I feared the woman had no better thought than to make a mountebank of her child!"

"O, not so!—not so!" continued Mr. Dimmesdale. "She recognizes, believe me, the solemn miracle which God hath wrought, in the existence of that child. And may she feel, too,—what, methinks, is the very truth,—that this boon was meant, above all things else, to keep the mother's soul alive, and to preserve her from blacker depths of sin into which Satan might else have sought to plunge her! Therefore it is good for this poor, sinful woman that she hath an infant immortality, a being capable of eternal joy or sorrow, confided to her care,—to be trained up by her to righteousness,—to remind her, at every moment, of her fall,—but yet to teach her, as it were by the Creator's sacred pledge, that, if she bring the child to heaven, the child also will bring its parent thither! Herein is the sinful mother happier than the sinful father. For Hester Prynne's sake, then, and no less for the poor child's sake, let us leave them as Providence hath seen fit to place them!"

"You speak, my friend, with a strange earnestness," said old Roger Chillingworth, smiling at him.

"And there is weighty import in what my young brother hath spoken," added the Reverend Mr. Wilson. "What say you, worshipful Master Bellingham? Hath he not pleaded well for the poor woman?"

"Indeed hath he," answered the magistrate, "and hath adduced such arguments, that we will even leave the matter as it now stands; so long, at least, as there shall be no further scandal in the woman. Care must be had, nevertheless, to put the child to due and stated examination in the catechism at thy hands or Master Dimmesdale's. Moreover, at a proper season, the tithing-men[3] must take heed that she go both to school and to meeting."

The young minister, on ceasing to speak, had withdrawn a few steps from the group, and stood with his face partially concealed in the heavy folds of the window-curtain; while the shadow of his figure, which the sunlight cast upon the floor, was tremulous with the vehemence of his appeal. Pearl, that wild and flighty little elf, stole softly towards him, and, taking his hand in the grasp of both her own, laid her cheek against it; a caress so tender, and withal so unobtrusive, that her mother, who was looking on, asked herself,— "Is that my Pearl?" Yet she knew that there was love in the child's heart, although it mostly revealed itself in passion, and hardly twice in her lifetime had been softened by such gentleness as now. The minister,—for, save the long-sought regards of woman, nothing is sweeter than these marks of childish preference, accorded spontaneously by a spiritual instinct, and therefore seeming to imply in us something truly worthy to be loved,—the minister looked round, laid his hand on the child's head, hesitated an instant, and then kissed her brow. Little Pearl's unwonted mood of sentiment lasted no longer; she laughed, and went capering down the hall, so airily, that old Mr. Wilson raised a question whether even her tiptoes touched the floor.

"The little baggage hath witchcraft in her, I profess," said he to Mr. Dimmesdale. "She needs no old woman's broomstick to fly withal!"

"A strange child!" remarked old Roger Chillingworth. "It is easy to see the mother's part in her. Would it be beyond a philosopher's research, think ye, gentlemen, to analyze that child's nature, and, from its make and mould, to give a shrewd guess at the father?"

"Nay; it would be sinful, in such a question, to follow the clew of profane philosophy," said Mr. Wilson. "Better to fast and pray upon it; and still better, it may be, to leave the mystery as we find it, unless Providence reveal it of its own accord. Thereby, every good Christian man hath a title to show a father's kindness towards the poor, deserted babe."

The affair being so satisfactorily concluded, Hester Prynne, with Pearl, departed from the house. As they descended the steps, it is

3. Parish officers responsible for maintaining order.

averred that the lattice of a chamber-window was thrown open, and forth into the sunny day was thrust the face of Mistress Hibbins, Governor Bellingham's bitter-tempered sister, and the same who, a few years later, was executed as a witch.

"Hist, hist!" said she, while her ill-omened physiognomy seemed to cast a shadow over the cheerful newness of the house. "Wilt thou go with us to-night? There will be a merry company in the forest; and I wellnigh promised the Black Man that comely Hester Prynne should make one."

"Make my excuse to him, so please you!" answered Hester, with a triumphant smile. "I must tarry at home, and keep watch over my little Pearl. Had they taken her from me, I would willingly have gone with thee into the forest, and signed my name in the Black Man's book too, and that with mine own blood!"

"We shall have thee there anon!" said the witch-lady, frowning, as she drew back her head.

But here—if we suppose this interview betwixt Mistress Hibbins and Hester Prynne to be authentic, and not a parable—was already an illustration of the young minister's argument against sundering the relation of a fallen mother to the offspring of her frailty. Even thus early had the child saved her from Satan's snare.

IX. The Leech

Under the appellation of Roger Chillingworth, the reader will remember, was hidden another name, which its former wearer had resolved should never more be spoken. It has been related, how, in the crowd that witnessed Hester Prynne's ignominious exposure, stood a man, elderly, travel-worn, who, just emerging from the perilous wilderness, beheld the woman, in whom he hoped to find embodied the warmth and cheerfulness of home, set up as a type of sin before the people. Her matronly fame was trodden under all men's feet. Infamy was babbling around her in the public market-place. For her kindred, should the tidings ever reach them, and for the companions of her unspotted life, there remained nothing but the contagion of her dishonor; which would not fail to be distributed in strict accordance and proportion with the intimacy and sacredness of their previous relationship. Then why—since the choice was with himself—should the individual, whose connection with the fallen woman had been the most intimate and sacred of them all, come forward to vindicate his claim to an inheritance so little desirable? He resolved not to be pilloried beside her on her pedestal of shame. Unknown to all but Hester Prynne, and possessing the lock and key of her silence, he chose to withdraw his name from the roll of mankind, and, as regarded his former ties and interests, to vanish out of life as completely as if he indeed lay at the bottom of the ocean, whither rumor had long ago consigned him. This purpose once effected, new interests would immediately spring up, and likewise a new purpose; dark, it is true, if not guilty, but of force enough to engage the full strength of his faculties.

In pursuance of this resolve, he took up his residence in the Puritan town, as Roger Chillingworth, without other introduction than the learning and intelligence of which he possesed more than a common measure. As his studies, at a previous period of his life, had made him extensively acquainted with the medical science of the day, it was as a physician that he presented himself, and as such was cordially received. Skilful men, of the medical and chirurgical profession, were of rare occurrence in the colony. They seldom, it would appear, partook of the religious zeal that brought other emigrants across the Atlantic. In their researches into the human frame, it may be that the higher and more subtile faculties of such men were materialized, and that they lost the spiritual view of existence amid the intricacies of that wondrous mechanism, which seemed to involve art enough to comprise all of life within itself. At all events, the health of the good town of Boston, so far as medicine had aught to do with it, had hitherto lain in the guardianship of an aged deacon and apothecary, whose piety and godly deportment were stronger testimonials in his favor, than any that he could have produced in the shape of a diploma. The only surgeon was one who combined the occasional exercise of that noble art with the daily and habitual flourish of a razor. To such a professional body Roger Chillingworth was a brilliant acquisition. He soon manifested his familiarity with the ponderous and imposing machinery of antique physic; in which every remedy contained a multitude of far-fetched and heterogeneous ingredients, as elaborately compounded as if the proposed result had been the Elixir of Life.[4] In his Indian captivity, moreover, he had gained much knowledge of the properties of native herbs and roots; nor did he conceal from his patients, that these simple medicines, Nature's boon to the untutored savage, had quite as large a share of his own confidence as the European pharmacopœia, which so many learned doctors had spent centuries in elaborating.

This learned stranger was exemplary, as regarded at least the outward forms of a religious life, and, early after his arrival, had

4. A substance thought capable both of transmuting base metals into gold and of curing all disease. In two of his tales Hawthorne employed variants of the elixir theme: comically in "Dr. Heidegger's Experiment" and tragically in "The Birthmark."

chosen for his spiritual guide the Reverend Mr. Dimmesdale. The young divine, whose scholar-like renown still lived in Oxford, was considered by his more fervent admirers as little less than a heaven-ordained apostle, destined, should he live and labor for the ordinary term of life, to do as great deeds for the now feeble New England Church, as the early Fathers had achieved for the infancy of the Christian faith. About this period, however, the health of Mr. Dimmesdale had evidently begun to fail. By those best acquainted with his habits, the paleness of the young minister's cheek was accounted for by his too earnest devotion to study, his scrupulous fulfilment of parochial duty, and, more than all, by the fasts and vigils of which he made a frequent practice, in order to keep the grossness of this earthly state from clogging and obscuring his spiritual lamp. Some declared, that, if Mr. Dimmesdale were really going to die, it was cause enough, that the world was not worthy to be any longer trodden by his feet. He himself, on the other hand, with characteristic humility, avowed his belief, that, if Providence should see fit to remove him, it would be because of his own unworthiness to perform its humblest mission here on earth. With all this difference of opinion as to the cause of his decline, there could be no question of the fact. His form grew emaciated; his voice, though still rich and sweet, had a certain melancholy prophecy of decay in it; he was often observed, on any slight alarm or other sudden accident, to put his hand over his heart, with first a flush and then a paleness, indicative of pain.

Such was the young clergyman's condition, and so imminent the prospect that his dawning light would be extinguished, all untimely, when Roger Chillingworth made his advent to the town. His first entry on the scene, few people could tell whence, dropping down, as it were, out of the sky, or starting from the nether earth, had an aspect of mystery, which was easily heightened to the miraculous. He was now known to be a man of skill; it was observed that he gathered herbs, and the blossoms of wild-flowers, and dug up roots and plucked off twigs from the forest-trees, like one acquainted with hidden virtues in what was valueless to common eyes. He was heard to speak of Sir Kenelm Digby,[5] and other famous men,—whose scientific attainments were esteemed hardly less than supernatural,—as having been his correspondents or associates. Why, with such rank in the learned world, had he come hither? What could he, whose sphere was in great cities, be seeking in the wilderness? In answer to this query, a rumor gained ground,

5. Sir Kenelm Digby (1603–65), fantastic adventurer and bombastic writer, nevertheless held serious appointments as naval commander, diplomat, and government officer. He dabbled in occult sciences, but also he discovered that oxygen was necessary to plant life.

—and, however absurd, was entertained by some very sensible people,—that Heaven had wrought an absolute miracle, by transporting an eminent Doctor of Physic, from a German university, bodily through the air, and setting him down at the door of Mr. Dimmesdale's study! Individuals of wiser faith, indeed, who knew that Heaven promotes its purposes without aiming at the stage-effect of what is called miraculous interposition, were inclined to see a providential hand[6] in Roger Chillingworth's so opportune arrival.

This idea was countenanced by the strong interest which the physician ever manifested in the young clergyman; he attached himself to him as a parishioner, and sought to win a friendly regard and confidence from his naturally reserved sensibility. He expressed great alarm at his pastor's state of health, but was anxious to attempt the cure, and, if early undertaken, seemed not despondent of a favorable result. The elders, the deacons, the motherly dames, and the young and fair maidens, of Mr. Dimmesdale's flock, were alike importunate that he should make trial of the physician's frankly offered skill. Mr. Dimmesdale gently repelled their entreaties.

"I need no medicine," said he.

But how could the young minister say so, when, with every successive Sabbath, his cheek was paler and thinner, and his voice more tremulous than before,—when it had now become a constant habit, rather than a casual gesture, to press his hand over his heart? Was he weary of his labors? Did he wish to die? These questions were solemnly propounded to Mr. Dimmesdale by the elder ministers of Boston and the deacons of his church, who, to use their own phrase, "dealt with him" on the sin of rejecting the aid which Providence so manifestly held out. He listened in silence, and finally promised to confer with the physician.

"Were it God's will," said the Reverend Mr. Dimmesdale, when, in fulfilment of this pledge, he requested old Roger Chillingworth's professional advice, "I could be well content, that my labors, and my sorrows, and my sins, and my pains, should shortly end with me, and what is earthly of them be buried in my grave, and the spiritual go with me to my eternal state, rather than that you should put your skill to the proof in my behalf."

"Ah," replied Roger Chillingworth, with that quietness which, whether imposed or natural, marked all his deportment, "it is thus that a young clergyman is apt to speak. Youthful men, not having taken a deep root, give up their hold of life so easily! And saintly

6. The belief in God's special providence for the Puritan colonies was reflected in Roger Williams' Rhode Island settlement, Providence, and in the title of numerous books, such as Increase Mather's *Essay for the Recording of Illustrious Providences* and his son's *Memorable Providences*.

men, who walk with God on earth, would fain be away, to walk with him on the golden pavements of the New Jerusalem."[7]

"Nay," rejoined the young minister, putting his hand to his heart, with a flush of pain flitting over his brow, "were I worthier to walk there, I could be better content to toil here."

"Good men ever interpret themselves too meanly," said the physician.

In this manner, the mysterious old Roger Chillingworth became the medical adviser of the Reverend Mr. Dimmesdale. As not only the disease interested the physician, but he was strongly moved to look into the character and qualities of the patient, these two men, so different in age, came gradually to spend much time together. For the sake of the minister's health, and to enable the leech to gather plants with healing balm in them, they took long walks on the seashore, or in the forest; mingling various talk with the plash and murmur of the waves, and the solemn wind-anthem among the tree-tops. Often, likewise, one was the guest of the other, in his place of study and retirement. There was a fascination for the minister in the company of the man of science, in whom he recognized an intellectual cultivation of no moderate depth or scope; together with a range and freedom of ideas, that he would have vainly looked for among the members of his own profession. In truth, he was startled, if not shocked, to find this attribute in the physician. Mr. Dimmesdale was a true priest, a true religionist, with the reverential sentiment largely developed, and an order of mind that impelled itself powerfully along the track of a creed, and wore its passage continually deeper with the lapse of time. In no state of society would he have been what is called a man of liberal views; it would always be essential to his peace to feel the pressure of a faith about him, supporting, while it confined him within its iron framework. Not the less, however, though with a tremulous enjoyment, did he feel the occasional relief of looking at the universe through the medium of another kind of intellect than those with which he habitually held converse. It was as if a window were thrown open, admitting a freer atmosphere into the close and stifled study, where his life was wasting itself away, amid lamp-light, or obstructed day-beams, and the musty fragrance, be it sensual or moral, that exhales from books. But the air was too fresh and chill to be long breathed, with comfort. So the minister, and the physician with him, withdrew again within the limits of what their church defined as orthodox.

Thus Roger Chillingworth scrutinized his patient carefully, both as he saw him in his ordinary life, keeping an accustomed pathway

---

7. The "Heavenly City" of the redeemed souls, prophesied in Revelation 21 : 2.

in the range of thoughts familiar to him, and as he appeared when thrown amidst other moral scenery, the novelty of which might call out something new to the surface of his character. He deemed it essential, it would seem, to know the man, before attempting to do him good. Wherever there is a heart and an intellect, the diseases of the physical frame are tinged with the peculiarities of these. In Arthur Dimmesdale, thought and imagination were so active, and sensibility so intense, that the bodily infirmity would be likely to have its groundwork there. So Roger Chillingworth—the man of skill, the kind and friendly physician—strove to go deep into his patient's bosom, delving among his principles, prying into his recollections, and probing every thing with a cautious touch, like a treasure-seeker in a dark cavern. Few secrets can escape an investigator, who has opportunity and license to undertake such a quest, and skill to follow it up. A man burdened with a secret should especially avoid the intimacy of his physician. If the latter possess native sagacity, and a nameless something more,—let us call it intuition; if he show no intrusive egotism, nor disagreeably prominent characteristics of his own; if he have the power, which must be born with him, to bring his mind into such affinity with his patient's, that this last shall unawares have spoken what he imagines himself only to have thought; if such revelations be received without tumult, and acknowledged not so often by an uttered sympathy, as by silence, an inarticulate breath, and here and there a word, to indicate that all is understood; if, to these qualifications of a confidant be joined the advantages afforded by his recognized character as a physician;—then, at some inevitable moment, will the soul of the sufferer be dissolved, and flow forth in a dark, but transparent stream, bringing all its mysteries into the daylight.

Roger Chillingworth possessed all, or most, of the attributes above enumerated. Nevertheless, time went on; a kind of intimacy, as we have said, grew up between these two cultivated minds, which had as wide a field as the whole sphere of human thought and study, to meet upon; they discussed every topic of ethics and religion, of public affairs, and private character;- they talked much, on both sides, of matters that seemed personal to themselves; and yet no secret, such as the physician fancied must exist there, ever stole out of the minister's consciousness into his companion's ear. The latter had his suspicions, indeed, that even the nature of Mr. Dimmesdale's bodily disease had never fairly been revealed to him. It was a strange reserve!

After a time, at a hint from Roger Chillingworth, the friends of Mr. Dimmesdale effected an arrangement by which the two were lodged in the same house; so that every ebb and flow of the minister's life-tide might pass under the eye of his anxious and attached physician. There was much joy throughout the town, when this greatly desirable object was attained. It was held to be the best possible measure for the young clergyman's welfare; unless, indeed, as often urged by such as felt authorized to do so, he had selected some one of the many blooming damsels, spiritually devoted to him, to become his devoted wife. This latter step, however, there was no present prospect that Arthur Dimmesdale would be prevailed upon to take; he rejected all suggestions of the kind, as if priestly celibacy were one of his articles of church-discipline. Doomed by his own choice, therefore, as Mr. Dimmesdale so evidently was, to eat his unsavory morsel always at another's board, and endure the life-long chill which must be his lot who seeks to warm himself only at another's fireside, it truly seemed that this sagacious, experienced, benevolent, old physician, with his concord of paternal and reverential love for the young pastor, was the very man, of all mankind, to be constantly within reach of his voice.

The new abode of the two friends was with a pious widow, of good social rank, who dwelt in a house covering pretty nearly the site on which the venerable structure of King's Chapel has since been built. It had the grave-yard, originally Isaac Johnson's home-field, on one side, and so was well adapted to call up serious reflections, suited to their respective employments, in both minister and man of physic. The motherly care of the good widow assigned to Mr. Dimmesdale a front apartment, with a sunny exposure, and heavy window-curtains to create a noontide shadow, when desirable. The walls were hung round with tapestry, said to be from the Gobelin looms,[8] and, at all events, representing the Scriptural story of David and Bathsheba, and Nathan the Prophet,[9] in colors still unfaded, but which made the fair woman of the scene almost as grimly picturesque as the woe-denouncing seer. Here, the pale clergyman piled up his library, rich with parchment-bound folios of the Fathers, and the lore of Rabbis, and monkish erudition, of which the Protestant divines, even while they vilified and decried that class of writers, were yet constrained often to avail themselves. On the other side of the house, old Roger Chillingworth arranged his study and laboratory; not such as a modern man of science would reckon even tolerably complete, but provided with a distilling apparatus, and the means of compounding drugs and chemicals, which the practised alchemist knew well how to turn to purpose. With such commodiousness of situation, these two learned persons

8. A Paris family of clothmakers from the mid-fifteenth century; in 1601 Henry IV set workers at the Gobelin "factory" to making tapestries, and since then the name has signified the acme of tapestry weaving.

9. See II Samuel 11 and 12. Chillingworth arranged that Arthur should constantly witness Nathan's terrible condemnation of King David, who had sent Uriah to certain death in battle in order to obtain his wife, Bathsheba.

sat themselves down, each in his own domain, yet familiarly passing from one apartment to the other, and bestowing a mutual and not incurious inspection into one another's business.

And the Reverend Arthur Dimmesdale's best discerning friends, as we have intimated, very reasonably imagined that the hand of Providence had done all this, for the purpose—besought in so many public, and domestic, and secret prayers—of restoring the young minister to health. But—it must now be said—another portion of the community had latterly begun to take its own view of the relation betwixt Mr. Dimmesdale and the mysterious old physician. When an uninstructed multitude attempts to see with its eyes, it is exceedingly apt to be deceived. When, however, it forms its judgment, as it usually does, on the intuitions of its great and warm heart, the conclusions thus attained are often so profound and so unerring, as to possess the character of truths supernaturally revealed. The people, in the case of which we speak, could justify its prejudice against Roger Chillingworth by no fact or argument worthy of serious refutation. There was an aged handscraftsman, it is true, who had been a citizen of London at the period of Sir Thomas Overbury's murder,[1] now some thirty years agone; he testified to having seen the physician, under some other name, which the narrator of the story had now forgotten, in company with Doctor Forman, the famous old conjurer, who was implicated in the affair of Overbury. Two or three individuals hinted, that the man of skill, during his Indian captivity, had enlarged his medical attainments by joining in the incantations of the savage priests; who were universally acknowledged to be powerful enchanters, often performing seemingly miraculous cures by their skill in the black art. A large number—and many of these were persons of such sober sense and practical observation, that their opinions would have been valuable, in other matters—affirmed that Roger Chillingworth's aspect had undergone a remarkable change while he had dwelt in town, and especially since his abode with Mr. Dimmesdale. At first, his expression had been calm, meditative, scholar-like. Now, there was something ugly and evil in his face, which they had not previously noticed, and which grew still the more obvious to sight, the oftener they looked upon him. According to the vulgar idea, the fire in his laboratory had been brought from the lower regions, and was fed with infernal fuel; and so, as might be expected, his visage was getting sooty with the smoke.

To sum up the matter, it grew to be a widely diffused opinion,

1. Sir Thomas Overbury (1581–1613), miscellaneous writer remembered for his *Characters* (1614), opposed the marriage of his patron, Viscount Rochester, to the profligate countess of Essex, by whose connivance he was poisoned in the Tower of London. Dr. Simon Forman (1552–1611), astrologer, necromancer, and vendor of love philters, was scandalously implicated in the affairs of the countess by the posthumous evidence of his letters.

that the Reverend Arthur Dimmesdale, like many other personages of especial sanctity, in all ages of the Christian world, was haunted either by Satan himself, or Satan's emissary, in the guise of old Roger Chillingworth. This diabolical agent had the Divine permission, for a season, to burrow into the clergyman's intimacy, and plot against his soul. No sensible man, it was confessed, could doubt on which side the victory would turn. The people looked, with an unshaken hope, to see the minister come forth out of the conflict, transfigured with the glory which he would unquestionably win. Meanwhile, nevertheless, it was sad to think of the perchance mortal agony through which he must struggle towards his triumph.

Alas, to judge from the gloom and terror in the depths of the poor minister's eyes, the battle was a sore one, and the victory any thing but secure!

X. *The Leech and His Patient*

Old Roger Chillingworth, throughout life, had been calm in temperament, kindly, though not of warm affections, but ever, and in all his relations with the world, a pure and upright man. He had begun an investigation, as he imagined, with the severe and equal integrity of a judge, desirous only of truth, even as if the question involved no more than the air-drawn lines and figures of a geometrical problem, instead of human passions, and wrongs inflicted on himself. But, as he proceeded, a terrible fascination, a kind of fierce, though still calm, necessity seized the old man within its gripe, and never set him free again, until he had done all its bidding. He now dug into the poor clergyman's heart, like a miner searching for gold; or, rather, like a sexton delving into a grave, possibly in quest of a jewel that had been buried on the dead man's bosom, but likely to find nothing save mortality and corruption. Alas for his own soul, if these were what he sought!

Sometimes, a light glimmered out of the physician's eyes, burning blue and ominous, like the reflection of a furnace, or, let us say, like one of those gleams of ghastly fire that darted from Bunyan's awful door-way in the hill-side,[2] and quivered on the pilgrim's face. The soil where this dark miner was working had perchance shown indications that encouraged him.

"This man," said he, at one such moment, to himself, "pure as they deem him,—all spiritual as he seems,—hath inherited a strong animal nature from his father or his mother. Let us dig a little farther in the direction of this vein!"

2. The gates of Hell flamed from the hillside across Christian's pathway toward the Celestial City in Bunyan's *Pilgrim's Progress*.

Then, after long search into the minister's dim interior, and turning over many precious materials, in the shape of high aspirations for the welfare of his race, warm love of souls, pure sentiments, natural piety, strengthened by thought and study, and illuminated by revelation,—all of which invaluable gold was perhaps no better than rubbish to the seeker,—he would turn back, discouraged, and begin his quest towards another point. He groped along as stealthily, with as cautious a tread, and as wary an outlook, as a thief entering a chamber where a man lies only half asleep,—or, it may be, broad awake,—with purpose to steal the very treasure which this man guards as the apple of his eye. In spite of his premeditated carefulness, the floor would now and then creak; his garments would rustle; the shadow of his presence, in a forbidden proximity, would be thrown across his victim. In other words, Mr. Dimmesdale, whose sensibility of nerve often produced the effect of spiritual intuition, would become vaguely aware that something inimical to his peace had thrust itself into relation with him. But old Roger Chillingworth, too, had perceptions that were almost intuitive; and when the minister threw his startled eyes towards him, there the physician sat; his kind, watchful, sympathizing, but never intrusive friend.

Yet Mr. Dimmesdale would perhaps have seen this individual's character more perfectly, if a certain morbidness, to which sick hearts are liable, had not rendered him suspicious of all mankind. Trusting no man as his friend, he could not recognize his enemy when the latter actually appeared. He therefore still kept up a familiar intercourse with him, daily receiving the old physician in his study; or visiting the laboratory, and, for recreation's sake, watching the processes by which weeds were converted into drugs of potency.

One day, leaning his forehead on his hand, and his elbow on the sill of the open window, that looked towards the grave-yard, he talked with Roger Chillingworth, while the old man was examining a bundle of unsightly plants.

"Where," asked he, with a look askance at them,—for it was the clergyman's peculiarity that he seldom, now-a-days, looked straightforth at any object, whether human or inanimate,— "where, my kind doctor, did you gather those herbs, with such a dark, flabby leaf?"

"Even in the grave-yard, here at hand," answered the physician, continuing his employment. "They are new to me. I found them growing on a grave, which bore no tombstone, nor other memorial of the dead man, save these ugly weeds that have taken upon themselves to keep him in remembrance. They grew out of his heart, and typify, it may be, some hideous secret that was buried with him, and which he had done better to confess during his lifetime."

"Perchance," said Mr. Dimmesdale, "he earnestly desired it, but could not."

"And wherefore?" rejoined the physician. "Wherefore not; since all the powers of nature call so earnestly for the confession of sin, that these black weeds have sprung up out of a buried heart, to make manifest an unspoken crime?"

"That, good Sir, is but a fantasy of yours," replied the minister. "There can be, if I forebode aright, no power, short of the Divine mercy, to disclose, whether by uttered words, or by type or emblem, the secrets that may be buried with a human heart. The heart, making itself guilty of such secrets, must perforce hold them, until the day when all hidden things shall be revealed. Nor have I so read or interpreted Holy Writ, as to understand that the disclosure of human thoughts and deeds, then to be made, is intended as a part of the retribution. That, surely, were a shallow view of it. No; these revelations, unless I greatly err, are meant merely to promote the intellectual satisfaction of all intelligent beings, who will stand waiting, on that day, to see the dark problem of this life made plain.[3] A knowledge of men's hearts will be needful to the completest solution of that problem. And I conceive, moreover, that the hearts holding such miserable secrets as you speak of will yield them up, at that last day, not with reluctance, but with a joy unutterable."

"Then why not reveal them here?" asked Roger Chillingworth, glancing quietly aside at the minister. "Why should not the guilty ones sooner avail themselves of this unutterable solace?"

"They mostly do," said the clergyman, griping hard at his breast, as if afflicted with an importunate throb of pain. "Many, many a poor soul hath given its confidence to me, not only on the deathbed, but while strong in life, and fair in reputation. And ever, after such an outpouring, O, what a relief have I witnessed in those sinful brethren! even as in one who at last draws free air, after long stifling with his own polluted breath. How can it be otherwise? Why should a wretched man, guilty, we will say, of murder, prefer to keep the dead corpse buried in his own heart, rather than fling it forth at once, and let the universe take care of it!"

"Yet some men bury their secrets thus," observed the calm physician.

"True; there are such men," answered Mr. Dimmesdale. "But, not to suggest more obvious reasons, it may be that they are kept silent

3. "That day" is Judgment Day, the clarification or revelation of all truth, the final stage in the salvation of the elect.

by the very constitution of their nature. Or,—can we not suppose it?—guilty as they may be, retaining, nevertheless, a zeal for God's glory and man's welfare, they shrink from displaying themselves black and filthy in the view of men; because, thenceforward, no good can be achieved by them; no evil of the past be redeemed by better service. So, to their own unutterable torment, they go about among their fellow-creatures, looking pure as new-fallen snow; while their hearts are all speckled and spotted with iniquity of which they cannot rid themselves."

"These men deceive themselves," said Roger Chillingworth, with somewhat more emphasis than usual, and making a slight gesture with his forefinger. "They fear to take up the shame that rightfully belongs to them. Their love for man, their zeal for God's service, —these holy impulses may or may not coexist in their hearts with the evil inmates to which their guilt has unbarred the door, and which must needs propagate a hellish breed within them. But, if they seek to glorify God, let them not lift heavenward their unclean hands! If they would serve their fellow-men, let them do it by making manifest the power and reality of conscience, in constraining them to penitential self-abasement! Wouldst thou have me to believe, O wise and pious friend, that a false show can be better— can be more for God's glory, or man's welfare—than God's own truth? Trust me, such men deceive themselves!"

"It may be so," said the young clergyman indifferently, as waiving a discussion that he considered irrelevant or unseasonable. He had a ready faculty, indeed, of escaping from any topic that agitated his too sensitive and nervous temperament.—"But, now, I would ask of my well-skilled physician, whether, in good sooth, he deems me to have profited by his kindly care of this weak frame of mine?"

Before Roger Chillingworth could answer, they heard the clear, wild laughter of a young child's voice, proceeding from the adjacent burial-ground. Looking instinctively from the open window,—for it was summer-time,—the minister beheld Hester Prynne and little Pearl passing along the footpath that traversed the inclosure. Pearl looked as beautiful as the day, but was in one of those moods of perverse merriment which, whenever they occurred, seemed to remove her entirely out of the sphere of sympathy or human contact. She now skipped irreverently from one grave to another; until, coming to the broad, flat, armorial tombstone of a departed worthy, —perhaps of Isaac Johnson himself,—she began to dance upon it. In reply to her mother's command and entreaty that she would behave more decorously, little Pearl paused to gather the prickly burrs from a tall burdock, which grew beside the tomb. Taking a handful of these, she arranged them along the lines of the scarlet letter that decorated the maternal bosom, to which the burrs, as their nature was, tenaciously adhered. Hester did not pluck them off.

Roger Chillingworth had by this time approached the window, and smiled grimly down.

"There is no law, nor reverence for authority, no regard for human ordinances or opinions, right or wrong, mixed up with that child's composition," remarked he, as much to himself as to his companion. "I saw her, the other day, bespatter the Governor himself with water, at the cattle-trough in Spring Lane. What, in Heaven's name, is she? Is the imp altogether evil? Hath she affections? Hath she any discoverable principle of being?"

"None,—save the freedom of a broken law," answered Mr. Dimmesdale, in a quiet way, as if he had been discussing the point within himself. "Whether capable of good, I know not."

The child probably overheard their voices; for, looking up to the window, with a bright, but naughty smile of mirth and intelligence, she threw one of the prickly burrs at the Reverend Mr. Dimmesdale. The sensitive clergyman shrunk, with nervous dread, from the light missile. Detecting his emotion, Pearl clapped her little hands in the most extravagant ecstasy. Hester Prynne, likewise, had involuntarily looked up; and all these four persons, old and young, regarded one another in silence, till the child laughed aloud, and shouted,— "Come away, mother! Come away, or yonder old Black Man will catch you! He hath got hold of the minister already. Come away, mother, or he will catch you! But he cannot catch little Pearl!"

So she drew her mother away, skipping, dancing, and frisking fantastically among the hillocks of the dead people, like a creature that had nothing in common with a bygone and buried generation, nor owned herself akin to it. It was as if she had been made afresh, out of new elements, and must perforce be permitted to live her own life, and be a law unto herself, without her eccentricities being reckoned to her for a crime.

"There goes a woman," resumed Roger Chillingworth, after a pause, "who, be her demerits what they may, hath none of that mystery of hidden sinfulness which you deem so grievous to be borne. Is Hester Prynne the less miserable, think you, for that scarlet letter on her breast?"

"I do verily believe it," answered the clergyman. "Nevertheless, I cannot answer for her. There was a look of pain in her face, which I would gladly have been spared the sight of. But still, methinks, it must needs be better for the sufferer to be free to show his pain, as this poor woman Hester is, than to cover it all up in his heart."

There was another pause; and the physician began anew to examine and arrange the plants which he had gathered.

"You inquired of me, a little time agone," said he, at length, "my judgment as touching your health."

"I did," answered the clergyman, "and would gladly learn it. Speak frankly, I pray you, be it for life or death."

"Freely, then, and plainly," said the physician, still busy with his plants, but keeping a wary eye on Mr. Dimmesdale, "the disorder is a strange one; not so much in itself, nor as outwardly manifested, —in so far, at least, as the symptoms have been laid open to my observation. Looking daily at you, my good Sir, and watching the tokens of your aspect, now for months gone by, I should deem you a man sore sick, it may be, yet not so sick but that an instructed and watchful physician might well hope to cure you. But—I know not what to say—the disease is what I seem to know, yet know it not."

"You speak in riddles, learned Sir," said the pale minister, glancing aside out of the window.

"Then, to speak more plainly," continued the physician, "and I crave pardon, Sir,—should it seem to require pardon,—for this needful plainness of my speech. Let me ask,—as your friend,—as one having charge, under Providence, of your life and physical well-being,—hath all the operation of this disorder been fairly laid open and recounted to me?"

"How can you question it?" asked the minister. "Surely, it were child's play to call in a physician, and then hide the sore!"

"You would tell me, then, that I know all?" said Roger Chilling-worth, deliberately, and fixing an eye, bright with intense and con-centrated intelligence, on the minister's face. "Be it so! But, again! He to whom only the outward and physical evil is laid open knoweth, oftentimes, but half the evil which he is called upon to cure. A bodily disease, which we look upon as whole and entire within itself, may, after all, be but a symptom of some ailment in the spiritual part. Your pardon, once again, good Sir, if my speech give the shadow of offence. You, Sir, of all men whom I have known, are he whose body is the closest conjoined, and imbued, and identified, so to speak, with the spirit whereof it is the instrument."

"Then I need ask no further," said the clergyman, somewhat hastily rising from his chair. "You deal not, I take it, in medicine for the soul!"

"Thus, a sickness," continued Roger Chillingworth, going on, in an unaltered tone, without heeding the interruption,—but stand-ing up, and confronting the emaciated and white-cheeked minister with his low, dark, and misshapen figure,—"a sickness, a sore place, if we may so call it, in your spirit, hath immediately its appropriate manifestation in your bodily frame. Would you, therefore, that your physician heal the bodily evil? How may this be, unless you first lay open to him the wound or trouble in your soul?"

"No!—not to thee!—not to an earthly physician!" cried Mr. Dimmesdale, passionately, and turning his eyes, full and bright, and with a kind of fierceness, on old Roger Chillingworth. "Not to thee! But, if it be the soul's disease, then do I commit myself to the one Physician of the soul! He, if it stand with his good pleasure, can cure; or he can kill! Let him do with me as, in his justice and wisdom, he shall see good. But who art thou, that meddlest in this matter?—that dares thrust himself between the sufferer and his God?"

With a frantic gesture, he rushed out of the room.

"It is as well to have made this step," said Roger Chillingworth to himself, looking after the minister with a grave smile. "There is nothing lost. We shall be friends again anon. But see, now, how passion takes hold upon this man, and hurrieth him out of himself! As with one passion, so with another! He hath done a wild thing ere now, this pious Master Dimmesdale, in the hot passion of his heart!"

It proved not difficult to reëstablish the intimacy of the two companions, on the same footing and in the same degree as heretofore. The young clergyman, after a few hours of privacy, was sensible that the disorder of his nerves had hurried him into an unseemly outbreak of temper, which there had been nothing in the physician's words to excuse or palliate. He marvelled, indeed, at the violence with which he had thrust back the kind old man, when merely proffering the advice which it was his duty to bestow, and which the minister himself had expressly sought. With these remorseful feelings, he lost no time in making the amplest apologies, and besought his friend still to continue the care, which, if not successful in restoring him to health, had, in all probability, been the means of prolonging his feeble existence to that hour. Roger Chillingworth readily assented, and went on with his medical supervision of the minister; doing his best for him, in all good faith, but always quitting the patient's apartment, at the close of a professional interview, with a mysterious and puzzled smile upon his lips. This expression was invisible in Mr. Dimmesdale's presence, but grew strongly evident as the physician crossed the threshold.

"A rare case!" he muttered. "I must needs look deeper into it. A strange sympathy betwixt soul and body! Were it only for the art's sake, I must search this matter to the bottom!"

It came to pass, not long after the scene above recorded, that the Reverend Mr. Dimmesdale, at noonday, and entirely unawares, fell into a deep, deep slumber, sitting in his chair, with a large blackletter[4] volume open before him on the table. It must have been

4. Printed in Old English or Gothic type.

a work of vast ability in the somniferous school of literature. The profound depth of the minister's repose was the more remarkable; inasmuch as he was one of those persons whose sleep, ordinarily, is as light, as fitful, and as easily scared away, as a small bird hopping on a twig. To such an unwonted remoteness, however, had his spirit now withdrawn into itself, that he stirred not in his chair, when old Roger Chillingworth, without any extraordinary precaution, came into the room. The physician advanced directly in front of his patient, laid his hand upon his bosom, and thrust aside the vestment, that, hitherto, had always covered it even from the professional eye.

Then, indeed, Mr. Dimmesdale shuddered, and slightly stirred.

After a brief pause, the physician turned away.

But with what a wild look of wonder, joy, and horror! With what a ghastly rapture, as it were, too mighty to be expressed only by the eye and features, and therefore bursting forth through the whole ugliness of his figure, and making itself even riotously manifest by the extravagant gestures with which he threw up his arms towards the ceiling, and stamped his foot upon the floor! Had a man seen old Roger Chillingworth, at that moment of his ecstasy, he would have had no need to ask how Satan comports himself, when a precious human soul is lost to heaven, and won into his kingdom.

But what distinguished the physician's ecstasy from Satan's was the trait of wonder in it!

XI. The Interior of a Heart

After the incident last described, the intercourse between the clergyman and the physician, though externally the same, was really of another character than it had previously been. The intellect of Roger Chillingworth had now a sufficiently plain path before it. It was not, indeed, precisely that which he had laid out for himself to tread. Calm, gentle, passionless, as he appeared, there was yet, we fear, a quiet depth of malice, hitherto latent, but active now, in this unfortunate old man, which led him to imagine a more intimate revenge than any mortal had ever wreaked upon an enemy. To make himself the one trusted friend, to whom should be confided all the fear, the remorse, the agony, the ineffectual repentance, the backward rush of sinful thoughts, expelled in vain! All that guilty sorrow, hidden from the world, whose great heart would have pitied and forgiven, to be revealed to him, the Pitiless, to him, the Unforgiving! All that dark treasure to be lavished on the very man, to whom nothing else could so adequately pay the debt of vengeance!

The clergyman's shy and sensitive reserve had balked this scheme. Roger Chillingworth, however, was inclined to be hardly, if at all, less satisfied with the aspect of affairs, which Providence—using the avenger and his victim for its own purposes, and, perchance, pardoning, where it seemed most to punish—had substituted for his black devices. A revelation, he could almost say, had been granted to him. It mattered little, for his object, whether celestial, or from what other region. By its aid, in all the subsequent relations betwixt him and Mr. Dimmesdale, not merely the external presence, but the very inmost soul of the latter seemed to be brought out before his eyes, so that he could see and comprehend its every movement. He became, thenceforth, not a spectator only, but a chief actor, in the poor minister's interior world. He could play upon him as he chose. Would he arouse him with a throb of agony? The victim was for ever on the rack; it needed only to know the spring that controlled the engine;—and the physician knew it well! Would he startle him with sudden fear? As at the waving of a magician's wand, uprose a grisly phantom,—uprose a thousand phantoms,—in many shapes, of death, or more awful shame, all flocking round about the clergyman, and pointing with their fingers at his breast!

All this was accomplished with a subtlety so perfect, that the minister, though he had constantly a dim perception of some evil influence watching over him, could never gain a knowledge of its actual nature. True, he looked doubtfully, fearfully,—even, at times, with horror and the bitterness of hatred,—at the deformed figure of the old physician. His gestures, his gait, his grizzled beard, his slightest and most indifferent acts, the very fashion of his garments, were odious in the clergyman's sight; a token, implicitly to be relied on, of a deeper antipathy in the breast of the latter than he was willing to acknowledge to himself. For, as it was impossible to assign a reason for such distrust and abhorrence, so Mr. Dimmesdale, conscious that the poison of one morbid spot was infecting his heart's entire substance, attributed all his presentiments to no other cause. He took himself to task for his bad sympathies in reference to Roger Chillingworth, disregarded the lesson that he should have drawn from them, and did his best to root them out. Unable to accomplish this, he nevertheless, as a matter of principle, continued his habits of social familiarity with the old man, and thus gave him constant opportunities for perfecting the purpose to which —poor, forlorn creature that he was, and more wretched than his victim—the avenger had devoted himself.

While thus suffering under bodily disease, and gnawed and tortured by some black trouble of the soul, and given over to the machinations of his deadliest enemy, the Reverend Mr. Dimmesdale had achieved a brilliant popularity in his sacred office. He won it, indeed, in great part, by his sorrows. His intellectual gifts, his moral perceptions, his power of experiencing and communicating emotion, were kept in a state of preternatural activity by the prick and anguish of his daily life. His fame, though still on its upward slope, already overshadowed the soberer reputations of his fellow-clergymen, eminent as several of them were. There were scholars among them, who had spent more years in acquiring abstruse lore, connected with the divine profession, than Mr. Dimmesdale had lived; and who might well, therefore, be more profoundly versed in such solid and valuable attainments than their youthful brother. There were men, too, of a sturdier texture of mind than his, and endowed with a far greater share of shrewd, hard, iron or granite understanding; which, duly mingled with a fair proportion of doctrinal ingredient, constitutes a highly respectable, efficacious, and unamiable variety of the clerical species. There were others, again, true saintly fathers, whose faculties had been elaborated by weary toil among their books, and by patient thought, and etherealized, moreover, by spiritual communications with the better world, into which their purity of life had almost introduced these holy personages, with their garments of mortality still clinging to them. All that they lacked was the gift that descended upon the chosen disciples, at Pentecost, in tongues of flame;[5] symbolizing, it would seem, not the power of speech in foreign and unknown languages, but that of addressing the whole human brotherhood in the heart's native language. These fathers, otherwise so apostolic, lacked Heaven's last and rarest attestation of their office, the Tongue of Flame. They would have vainly sought—had they ever dreamed of seeking—to express the highest truths through the humblest medium of familiar words and images. Their voices came down, afar and indistinctly, from the upper heights where they habitually dwelt.

Not improbably, it was to this latter class of men that Mr. Dimmesdale, by many of his traits of character, naturally belonged. To their high mountain-peaks of faith and sanctity he would have climbed, had not the tendency been thwarted by the burden, whatever it might be, of crime or anguish, beneath which it was his doom to totter. It kept him down, on a level with the lowest; him, the man of ethereal attributes, whose voice the angels might else have listened to and answered! But this very burden it was, that gave him sympathies so intimate with the sinful brotherhood of mankind; so that his heart vibrated in unison with theirs, and received their pain into itself, and sent its own throb of pain through a thousand other hearts, in gushes of sad, persuasive eloquence. Oftenest persuasive, but sometimes terrible! The people knew not the power that moved them thus. They deemed the young clergy-

5. See Acts 2 : 1–11. "The gift" was the Holy Spirit, which enabled the preaching of the apostles of Jesus to be understood by each listener in his own language.

man a miracle of holiness. They fancied him the mouth-piece of Heaven's messages of wisdom, and rebuke, and love. In their eyes, the very ground on which he trod was sanctified. The virgins of his church grew pale around him, victims of a passion so imbued with religious sentiment that they imagined it to be all religion, and brought it openly, in their white bosoms, as their most acceptable sacrifice before the altar. The aged members of his flock, beholding Mr. Dimmesdale's frame so feeble, while they were themselves so rugged in their infirmity, believed that he would go heavenward before them, and enjoined it upon their children, that their old bones should be buried close to their young pastor's holy grave. And, all this time, perchance, when poor Mr. Dimmesdale was thinking of his grave, he questioned with himself whether the grass would ever grow on it, because an accursed thing must there be buried!

It is inconceivable, the agony with which this public veneration tortured him! It was his genuine impulse to adore the truth, and to reckon all things shadow-like, and utterly devoid of weight or value, that had not its divine essence as the life within their life. Then, what was he?—a substance?—or the dimmest of all shadows? He longed to speak out, from his own pulpit, at the full height of his voice, and tell the people what he was. "I, whom you behold in these black garments of the priesthood,—I, who ascend the sacred desk, and turn my pale face heavenward, taking upon myself to hold communion, in your behalf, with the Most High Omniscience,—I, in whose daily life you discern the sanctity of Enoch,[6]—I, whose footsteps, as you suppose, leave a gleam along my earthly track, whereby the pilgrims that shall come after me may be guided to the regions of the blest,—I, who have laid the hand of baptism upon your children,—I, who have breathed the parting prayer over your dying friends, to whom the Amen sounded faintly from a world which they had quitted,—I, your pastor, whom you so reverence and trust, am utterly a pollution and a lie!"

More than once, Mr. Dimmesdale had gone into the pulpit, with a purpose never to come down its steps, until he should have spoken words like the above. More than once, he had cleared his throat, and drawn in the long, deep, and tremulous breath, which, when sent forth again, would come burdened with the black secret of his soul. More than once—nay, more than a hundred times—he had actually spoken! Spoken! But how? He had told his hearers that he was altogether vile, a viler companion of the vilest, the worst of sinners, an abomination, a thing of unimaginable iniquity; and that the only wonder was, that they did not see his wretched body shrivelled up before their eyes, by the burning wrath of the Al-

6. Enoch "walked with God" and "was translated" (without dying) to Heaven (Genesis 5 : 21–24; Hebrews 11 : 5).

mighty! Could there be plainer speech than this? Would not the people start up in their seats, by a simultaneous impulse, and tear him down out of the pulpit which he defiled? Not so, indeed! They heard it all, and did but reverence him the more. They little guessed what deadly purport lurked in those self-condemning words. "The godly youth!" said they among themselves. "The saint on earth! Alas, if he discern such sinfulness in his own white soul, what horrid spectacle would he behold in thine or mine!" The minister well knew—subtle, but remorseful hypocrite that he was!—the light in which his vague confession would be viewed. He had striven to put a cheat upon himself by making the avowal of a guilty conscience,[7] but had gained only one other sin, and a self-acknowledged shame, without the momentary relief of being self-deceived. He had spoken the very truth, and transformed it into the veriest falsehood. And yet, by the constitution of his nature, he loved the truth, and loathed the lie, as few men ever did. Therefore, above all things else, he loathed his miserable self!

His inward trouble drove him to practices, more in accordance with the old, corrupted faith in Rome, than with the better light of the church in which he had been born and bred. In Mr. Dimmesdale's secret closet, under lock and key, there was a bloody scourge.[8] Oftentimes, this Protestant and Puritan divine had plied it on his his own shoulders; laughing bitterly at himself the while, and smiting so much the more pitilessly, because of that bitter laugh. It was his custom, too, as it has been that of many other pious Puritans, to fast,—not, however, like them, in order to purify the body and render it the fitter medium of celestial illumination, —but rigorously, and until his knees trembled beneath him, as an act of penance. He kept vigils, likewise, night after night, sometimes in utter darkness; sometimes with a glimmering lamp; and sometimes, viewing his own face in a looking-glass, by the most powerful light which he could throw upon it. He thus typified the constant introspection wherewith he tortured, but could not purify, himself. In these lengthened vigils, his brain often reeled, and visions seemed to flit before him; perhaps seen doubtfully, and by a faint light of their own, in the remote dimness of the chamber, or more vividly, and close beside him, within the looking-glass. Now it was a herd of diabolic shapes, that grinned and mocked at the pale minister, and beckoned him away with them; now a group of shining angels, who flew upward heavily, as sorrow-laden, but grew more ethereal as they rose. Now came the dead friends of his youth, and his white-bearded father, with a saint-like frown, and his

7. *I.e.*, to delude himself into believing he made an honest confession.
8. A whip. Such extreme penitential practices occurred very seldom, even among the most ascetic Puritans. Cotton Mather reportedly observed sixty fasts and twenty vigils in one year.

mother, turning her face away as she passed by. Ghost of a mother, —thinnest fantasy of a mother,—methinks she might yet have thrown a pitying glance towards her son! And now, through the chamber which these spectral thoughts had made so ghastly, glided Hester Prynne, leading along little Pearl, in her scarlet garb, and pointing her forefinger, first, at the scarlet letter on her bosom, and then at the clergyman's own breast.

None of these visions ever quite deluded him. At any moment, by an effort of his will, he could discern substances through their misty lack of substance, and convince himself that they were not solid in their nature, like yonder table of carved oak, or that big, square, leathern-bound and brazen-clasped volume of divinity. But, for all that, they were, in one sense, the truest and most substantial things which the poor minister now dealt with. It is the unspeakable misery of a life so false as his, that it steals the pith and substance out of whatever realities there are around us, and which were meant by Heaven to be the spirit's joy and nutriment. To the untrue man, the whole universe is false,—it is impalpable,—it shrinks to nothing within his grasp. And he himself, in so far as he shows himself in a false light, becomes a shadow, or, indeed, ceases to exist. The only truth, that continued to give Mr. Dimmesdale a real existence on this earth, was the anguish in his inmost soul, and the undissembled expression of it in his aspect. Had he once found power to smile, and wear a face of gayety, there would have been no such man!

On one of those ugly nights, which we have faintly hinted at, but forborne to picture forth, the minister started from his chair. A new thought had struck him. There might be a moment's peace in it. Attiring himself with as much care as if it had been for public worship, and precisely in the same manner, he stole softly down the staircase, undid the door, and issued forth.

XII. *The Minister's Vigil*

Walking in the shadow of a dream, as it were, and perhaps actually under the influence of a species of somnambulism, Mr. Dimmesdale reached the spot, where, now so long since, Hester Prynne had lived through her first hour of public ignominy. The same platform or scaffold, black and weather-stained with the storm or sunshine of seven long years, and foot-worn, too, with the tread of many culprits who had since ascended it, remained standing beneath the balcony of the meeting-house. The minister went up the steps.

It was an obscure night of early May. An unvaried pall of cloud muffled the whole expanse of sky from zenith to horizon. If the same multitude which had stood as eyewitnesses while Hester

Prynne sustained her punishment could now have been summoned forth, they would have discerned no face above the platform, nor hardly the outline of a human shape, in the dark gray of the midnight. But the town was all asleep. There was no peril of discovery. The minister might stand there, if it so pleased him, until morning should redden in the east, without other risk than that the dank and chill night-air would creep into his frame, and stiffen his joints with rheumatism, and clog his throat with catarrh and cough; thereby defrauding the expectant audience of to-morrow's prayer and sermon. No eye could see him, save that ever-wakeful one which had seen him in his closet, wielding the bloody scourge. Why, then, had he come hither? Was it but the mockery of penitence? A mockery, indeed, but in which his soul trifled with itself! A mockery at which angels blushed and wept, while fiends rejoiced, with jeering laughter! He had been driven hither by the impulse of that Remorse which dogged him everywhere, and whose own sister and closely linked companion was that Cowardice which invariably drew him back, with her tremulous gripe, just when the other impulse had hurried him to the verge of a disclosure. Poor, miserable man! what right had infirmity like his to burden itself with crime? Crime is for the iron-nerved, who have their choice either to endure it, or, if it press too hard, to exert their fierce and savage strength for a good purpose, and fling it off at once! This feeble and most sensitive of spirits could do neither, yet continually did one thing or another, which intertwined, in the same inextricable knot, the agony of heaven-defying guilt and vain repentance.

And thus, while standing on the scaffold, in this vain show of expiation, Mr. Dimmesdale was overcome with a great horror of mind, as if the universe were gazing at a scarlet token on his naked breast, right over his heart. On that spot, in very truth, there was, and there had long been, the gnawing and poisonous tooth of bodily pain. Without any effort of his will, or power to restrain himself, he shrieked aloud; an outcry that went pealing through the night, and was beaten back from one house to another, and reverberated from the hills in the background; as if a company of devils, detecting so much misery and terror n it, had made a plaything of the sound, and were bandying it to and fro.

"It is done!" muttered the minister, covering his face with his hands. "The whole town will awake, and hurry forth, and find me here!"

But it was not so. The shriek had perhaps sounded with a far greater power, to his own startled ears, than it actually possessed. The town did not awake; or, if it did, the drowsy slumberers mistook the cry either for something frightful in a dream, or for the noise of witches; whose voices, at that period, were often heard to pass over the settlements or lonely cottages, as they rode with Satan through the air. The clergyman, therefore, hearing no symptoms of disturbance, uncovered his eyes and looked about him. At one of the chamber-windows of Governor Bellingham's mansion, which stood at some distance, on the line of another street, he beheld the appearance of the old magistrate himself, with a lamp in his hand, a white night-cap on his head, and a long white gown enveloping his figure. He looked like a ghost, evoked unseasonably from the grave. The cry had evidently startled him. At another window of the same house, moreover, appeared old Mistress Hibbins, the Governor's sister, also with a lamp, which, even thus far off, revealed the expression of her sour and discontented face. She thrust forth her head from the lattice, and looked anxiously upward. Beyond the shadow of a doubt, this venerable witch-lady had heard Mr. Dimmesdale's outcry, and interpreted it, with its multitudinous echoes and reverberations, as the clamor of the fiends and night-hags, with whom she was well known to make excursions into the forest.

Detecting the gleam of Governor Bellingham's lamp, the old lady quickly extinguished her own, and vanished. Possibly, she went up among the clouds. The minister saw nothing further of her motions. The magistrate, after a wary observation of the darkness—into which, nevertheless, he could see but little farther than he might into a mill-stone—retired from the window.

The minister grew comparatively calm. His eyes, however, were soon greeted by a little, glimmering light, which, at first a long way off was approaching up the street. It threw a gleam of recognition on here a post, and there a garden-fence, and here a latticed window-pane, and there a pump, with its full trough of water, and here, again, an arched door of oak, with an iron knocker, and a rough log for the door-step. The Reverend Mr. Dimmesdale noted all these minute particulars, even while firmly convinced that the doom of his existence was stealing onward, in the footsteps which he now heard; and that the gleam of the lantern would fall upon him, in a few moments more, and reveal his long-hidden secret. As the light drew nearer, he beheld, within its illuminated circle, his brother clergyman,—or, to speak more accurately, his professional father, as well as highly valued friend,—the Reverend Mr. Wilson; who, as Mr. Dimmesdale now conjectured, had been praying at the bedside of some dying man. And so he had. The good old minister came freshly from the death-chamber of Governor Winthrop,[9] who had passed from earth to heaven within that very

9. Governor John Winthrop, born in 1588, died on March 26, 1649, although Hawthorne set his scene on a night "in early May." University-bred, Winthrop forsook the law to become a founder of the Massachusetts Bay colony in 1630, and was almost continuously re-elected governor or deputy governor until his death. A valuable historical record of the colony is his *Journal* (1790), enlarged as *The History of New England, 1630-1649* (2 vols., 1825-26).

hour. And now, surrounded, like the saint-like personages of olden times, with a radiant halo, that glorified him amid this gloomy night of sin,—as if the departed Governor had left him an inheritance of his glory, or as if he had caught upon himself the distant shine of the celestial city, while looking thitherward to see the triumphant pilgrim pass within its gates,—now, in short, good Father Wilson was moving homeward, aiding his footsteps with a lighted lantern! The glimmer of this luminary suggested the above conceits to Mr. Dimmesdale, who smiled,—nay, almost laughed at them,—and then wondered if he were going mad.

As the Reverend Mr. Wilson passed beside the scaffold, closely muffling his Geneva cloak[1] about him with one arm, and holding the lantern before his breast with the other, the minister could hardly restrain himself from speaking.

"A good evening to you, venerable Father Wilson! Come up hither, I pray you, and pass a pleasant hour with me!"

Good heavens! Had Mr. Dimmesdale actually spoken? For one instant, he believed that these words had passed his lips. But they were uttered only within his imagination. The venerable Father Wilson continued to step slowly onward, looking carefully at the muddy pathway before his feet, and never once turning his head towards the guilty platform. When the light of the glimmering lantern had faded quite away, the minister discovered, by the faintness which came over him, that the last few moments had been a crisis of terrible anxiety; although his mind had made an involuntary effort to relieve itself by a kind of lurid playfulness.

Shortly afterwards, the like grisly sense of the humorous again stole in among the solemn phantoms of his thought. He felt his limbs growing stiff with the unaccustomed chilliness of the night, and doubted whether he should be able to descend the steps of the scaffold. Morning would break, and find him there. The neighbourhood would begin to rouse itself. The earliest riser, coming forth in the dim twilight, would perceive a vaguely defined figure aloft on the place of shame; and, half crazed betwixt alarm and curiosity, would go, knocking from door to door, summoning all the people to behold the ghost—as he needs must think it—of some defunct transgressor. A dusky tumult would flap its wings from one house to another. Then—the morning light still waxing stronger—old patriarchs would rise up in great haste, each in his flannel gown, and matronly dames, without pausing to put off their night-gear. The whole tribe of decorous personages, who had never heretofore been seen with a single hair of their heads awry, would start into public view, with the disorder of a nightmare in their aspects. Old Gov-

1. The black cloak then worn by Calvinist ministers, its name recalling the association of John Calvin with the city of Geneva.

ernor Bellingham would come grimly forth, with his King James's ruff fastened askew; and Mistress Hibbins, with some twigs of the forest clinging to her skirts, and looking sourer than ever, as having hardly got a wink of sleep after her night ride; and good Father Wilson, too, after spending half the night at a death-bed, and liking ill to be disturbed, thus early, out of his dreams about the glorified saints. Hither, likewise, would come the elders and deacons of Mr. Dimmesdale's church, and the young virgins who so idolized their minister, and had made a shrine for him in their white bosoms; which, now, by the by, in their hurry and confusion, they would scantly have given themselves time to cover with their kerchiefs. All people, in a word, would come stumbling over their thresholds, and turning up their amazed and horror-stricken visages around the scaffold. Whom would they discern there, with the red eastern light upon his brow? Whom, but the Reverend Arthur Dimmesdale, half frozen to death, overwhelmed with shame, and standing where Hester Prynne had stood!

Carried away by the grotesque horror of this picture, the minister, unawares, and to his own infinite alarm, burst into a great peal of laughter. It was immediately responded to by a light, airy, childish laugh, in which, with a thrill of the heart,—but he knew not whether of exquisite pain, or pleasure as acute,—he recognized the tones of little Pearl.

"Pearl! Little Pearl!" cried he, after a moment's pause; then, suppressing his voice,—"Hester! Hester Prynne! Are you there?"

"Yes; it is Hester Prynne!" she replied, in a tone of surprise; and the minister heard her footsteps approaching from the sidewalk, along which she had been passing.—"It is I, and my little Pearl."

"Whence come you, Hester?" asked the minister. "What sent you hither?"

"I have been watching at a death-bed," answered Hester Prynne; —"at Governor Winthrop's death-bed, and have taken his measure for a robe, and am now going homeward to my dwelling."

"Come up hither, Hester, thou and little Pearl," said the Reverend Mr. Dimmesdale. "Ye have both been here before, but I was not with you. Come up hither once again, and we will stand all three together!"

She silently ascended the steps, and stood on the platform, holding little Pearl by the hand. The minister felt for the child's other hand, and took it. The moment that he did so, there came what seemed a tumultuous rush of new life, other life than his own, pouring like a torrent into his heart, and hurrying through all his veins, as if the mother and the child were communicating their vital warmth to his half-torpid system. The three formed an electric chain.

"Minister!" whispered little Pearl.

"What wouldst thou say, child?" asked Mr. Dimmesdale.

"Wilt thou stand here with mother and me, to-morrow noon-tide?" inquired Pearl.

"Nay; not so, my little Pearl!" answered the minister; for, with the new energy of the moment, all the dread of public exposure, that had so long been the anguish of his life, had returned upon him; and he was already trembling at the conjunction in which—with a strange joy, nevertheless—he now found himself. "Not so, my child. I shall, indeed, stand with thy mother and thee one other day, but not to-morrow!"

Pearl laughed, and attempted to pull away her hand. But the minister held it fast.

"A moment longer, my child!" said he.

"But wilt thou promise," asked Pearl, "to take my hand, and mother's hand, to-morrow noontide?"

"Not then, Pearl," said the minister, "but another time!"

"And what other time?" persisted the child.

"At the great judgment day!" whispered the minister,—and, strangely enough, the sense that he was a professional teacher of the truth impelled him to answer the child so. "Then, and there, before the judgment-seat, thy mother, and thou, and I, must stand together! But the daylight of this world shall not see our meeting!"

Pearl laughed again.

But, before Mr. Dimmesdale had done speaking, a light gleamed far and wide over all the muffled sky. It was doubtless caused by one of those meteors, which the night-watcher may so often observe burning out to waste, in the vacant regions of the atmosphere. So powerful was its radiance, that it thoroughly illuminated the dense medium of cloud betwixt the sky and earth. The great vault brightened, like the dome of an immense lamp. It showed the familiar scene of the steet, with the distinctness of mid-day, but also with the awfulness that is always imparted to familiar objects by an unaccustomed light. The wooden houses, with their jutting stories and quaint gable-peaks; the door-steps and thresholds, with the early grass springing up about them; the garden-plots, black with freshly turned earth; the wheel-track, little worn, and, even in the market-place, margined with green on either side;—all were visible, but with a singularity of aspect that seemed to give another moral interpretation to the things of this world than they had ever borne before. And there stood the minister, with his hand over his heart; and Hester Prynne, with the embroidered letter glimmering on her bosom; and little Pearl, herself a symbol, and the connecting link between those two. They stood in the noon of that strange and solemn splendor, as if it were the light that is to reveal all secrets, and the daybreak that shall unite all who belong to one another.

There was witchcraft in little Pearl's eyes; and her face, as she glanced upward at the minister, wore that naughty smile which made its expression frequently so elvish. She withdrew her hand from Mr. Dimmesdale's, and pointed across the street. But he clasped both his hands over his breast, and cast his eyes towards the zenith.

Nothing was more common, in those days, than to interpret all meteoric appearances, and other natural phenomena, that occurred with less regularity than the rise and set of sun and moon, as so many revelations from a supernatural source. Thus, a blazing spear, a sword of flame, a bow, or a sheaf of arrows, seen in the midnight sky, prefigured Indian warfare. Pestilence was known to have been foreboded by a shower of crimson light. We doubt whether any marked event, for good or evil, ever befell New England, from its settlement down to Revolutionary times, of which the inhabitants had not been previously warned by some spectacle of this nature. Not seldom, it had been seen by multitudes. Oftener, however, its credibility rested on the faith of some lonely eyewitness, who beheld the wonder through the colored, magnifying, and distorting medium of his imagination, and shaped it more distinctly in his after-thought. It was, indeed, a majestic idea, that the destiny of nations should be revealed, in these awful hieroglyphics, on the cope of heaven. A scroll so wide might not be deemed too expansive for Providence to write a people's doom upon. The belief was a favorite one with our forefathers, as betokening that their infant commonwealth was under a celestial guardianship of peculiar intimacy and strictness. But what shall we say, when an individual discovers a revelation, addressed to himself alone, on the same vast sheet of record! In such a case, it could only be the symptom of a highly disordered mental state, when a man, rendered morbidly self-contemplative by long, intense, and secret pain, had extended his egotism over the whole expanse of nature, until the firmament itself should appear no more than a fitting page for his soul's history and fate.

We impute it, therefore, solely to the disease in his own eye and heart, that the minister, looking upward to the zenith, beheld there the appearance of an immense letter,—the letter A,—marked out in lines of dull red light. Not but the meteor may have shown itself at that point, burning duskily through a veil of cloud; but with no such shape as his guilty imagination gave it; or, at least, with so little definiteness, that another's guilt might have seen another symbol in it.

There was a singular circumstance that characterized Mr. Dimmesdale's psychological state, at this moment. All the time that he gazed upward to the zenith, he was, nevertheless, perfectly aware that little Pearl was pointing her finger towards old Roger Chillingworth, who stood at no great distance from the scaffold. The minister appeared to see him, with the same glance that discerned the miraculous letter. To his features, as to all other objects, the meteoric light imparted a new expression; or it might well be that the physician was not careful then, as at all other times, to hide the malevolence with which he looked upon his victim. Certainly, if the meteor kindled up the sky, and disclosed the earth, with an awfulness that admonished Hester Prynne and the clergyman of the day of judgment, then might Roger Chillingworth have passed with them for the arch-fiend, standing there, with a smile and scowl, to claim his own. So vivid was the expression, or so intense the minister's perception of it, that it seemed still to remain painted on the darkness, after the meteor had vanished, with an effect as if the street and all things else were at once annihilated.

"Who is that man, Hester?" gasped Mr. Dimmesdale, overcome with terror. "I shiver at him! Dost thou know the man? I hate him, Hester!"

She remembered her oath, and was silent.

"I tell thee, my soul shivers at him," muttered the minister again. "Who is he? Who is he? Canst thou do nothing for me? I have a nameless horror of the man."

"Minister," said little Pearl, "I can tell thee who he is!"

"Quickly, then, child!" said the minister, bending his ear close to her lips. "Quickly!—and as low as thou canst whisper."

Pearl mumbled something into his ear, that sounded, indeed, like human language, but was only such gibberish as children may be heard amusing themselves with, by the hour together. At all events, if it involved any secret information in regard to old Roger Chillingworth, it was in a tongue unknown to the erudite clergyman, and did but increase the bewilderment of his mind. The elvish child then laughed aloud.

"Dost thou mock me now?" said the minister.

"Thou wast not bold!—thou wast not true!" answered the child. "Thou wouldst not promise to take my hand, and mother's hand, to-morrow noontide!"

"Worthy Sir," said the physician, who had now advanced to the foot of the platform. "Pious Master Dimmesdale! can this be you? Well, well, indeed! We men of study, whose heads are in our books, have need to be straitly looked after! We dream in our waking moments, and walk in our sleep. Come, good Sir, and my dear friend, I pray you, let me lead you home!"

"How knewest thou that I was here?" asked the minister, fearfully.

"Verily, and in good faith," answered Roger Chillingworth, "I knew nothing of the matter. I had spent the better part of the night at the bedside of the worshipful Governor Winthrop, doing what my poor skill might to give him ease. He going home to a better world, I, likewise, was on my way homeward, when this strange light shone out. Come with me, I beseech you, Reverend Sir; else you will be poorly able to do Sabbath duty to-morrow. Aha! see now, how they trouble the brain,—these books!—these books! You should study less, good Sir, and take a little pastime; or these night-whimseys will grow upon you!"

"I will go home with you," said Mr. Dimmesdale.

With a chill despondency, like one awaking, all nerveless, from an ugly dream, he yielded himself to the physician, and was led away.

The next day, however, being the Sabbath, he preached a discourse which was held to be the richest and most powerful, and the most replete with heavenly influences, that had ever proceeded from his lips. Souls, it is said, more souls than one, were brought to the truth by the efficacy of that sermon, and vowed within themselves to cherish a holy gratitude towards Mr. Dimmesdale throughout the long hereafter. But, as he came down the pulpit-steps, the gray-bearded sexton met him, holding up a black glove, which the minister recognized as his own.

"It was found," said the sexton, "this morning, on the scaffold, where evil-doers are set up to public shame. Satan dropped it there, I take it, intending a scurrilous jest against your reverence. But, indeed, he was blind and foolish, as he ever and always is. A pure hand needs no glove to cover it!"

"Thank you, my good friend," said the minister gravely, but startled at heart; for, so confused was his remembrance, that he had almost brought himself to look at the events of the past night as visionary. "Yes, it seems to be my glove indeed!"

"And, since Satan saw fit to steal it, your reverence must needs handle him without gloves, henceforward," remarked the old sexton, grimly smiling. "But did your reverence hear of the portent that was seen last night? A great red letter in the sky,—the letter A,—which we interpret to stand for Angel. For, as our good Governor Winthrop was made an angel this past night, it was doubtless held fit that there should be some notice thereof!"

"No," answered the minister. "I had not heard of it."

XIII. Another View of Hester

In her late singular interview with Mr. Dimmesdale, Hester Prynne was shocked at the condition to which she found the clergyman reduced. His nerve seemed absolutely destroyed. His moral force was abased into more than childish weakness. It grovelled helpless on the ground, even while his intellectual faculties retained their pristine strength, or had perhaps acquired a morbid energy, which disease only could have given them. With her knowledge of a train of circumstances hidden from all others, she could readily infer, that, besides the legitimate action of his own conscience, a terrible machinery had been brought to bear, and was still operating, on Mr. Dimmesdale's well-being and repose. Knowing what this poor, fallen man had once been, her whole soul was moved by the shuddering terror with which he had appealed to her,—the outcast woman,—for support against his instinctively discovered enemy. She decided, moreover, that he had a right to her utmost aid. Little accustomed, in her long seclusion from society, to measure her ideas of right and wrong by any standard external to herself, Hester saw —or seemed to see—that there lay a responsibility upon her, in reference to the clergyman, which she owed to no other, nor to the whole world besides. The links that united her to the rest of human kind—links of flowers, or silk, or gold, or whatever the material—had all been broken. Here was the iron link of mutual crime, which neither he nor she could break. Like all other ties, it brought along with it its obligations.

Hester Prynne did not now occupy precisely the same position in which we beheld her during the earlier periods of her ignominy. Years had come, and gone. Pearl was now seven years old. Her mother, with the scarlet letter on her breast, glittering in its fantastic embroidery, had long been a familiar object to the townspeople. As is apt to be the case when a person stands out in any prominence before the community, and, at the same time, interferes neither with public nor individual interests and convenience, a species of general regard had ultimately grown up in reference to Hester Prynne. It is to the credit of human nature, that, except where its selfishness is brought into play, it loves more readily than it hates. Hatred, by a gradual and quiet process, will even be transformed to love, unless the change be impeded by a continually new irritation of the original feeling of hostility. In this matter of Hester Prynne, there was neither irritation nor irksomeness. She never battled with the public, but submitted uncomplainingly to its worst usage; she made no claim upon it, in requital for what she suffered; she did not weigh upon its sympathies. Then, also, the blameless purity of her life, during all these years in which she had been set apart to infamy, was reckoned largely in her favor. With nothing now to lose, in the sight of mankind, and with no hope, and seemingly no wish, of gaining any thing, it could only be a genuine regard for virtue that had brought back the poor wanderer to its paths.

It was perceived, too, that while Hester never put forward even the humblest title to share in the world's privileges,—farther than to breathe the common air, and earn daily bread for little Pearl and herself by the faithful labor of her hands,—she was quick to acknowledge her sisterhood with the race of man, whenever benefits were to be conferred. None so ready as she to give of her little substance to every demand of poverty; even though the bitter-hearted pauper threw back a gibe in requital of the food brought regularly to his door, or the garments wrought for him by the fingers that could have embroidered a monarch's robe. None so self-devoted as Hester, when pestilence stalked through the town. In all seasons of calamity, indeed, whether general or of individuals, the outcast of society at once found her place. She came, not as a guest, but as a rightful inmate, into the household that was darkened by trouble; as if its gloomy twilight were a medium in which she was entitled to hold intercourse with her fellow-creatures. There glimmered the embroidered letter, with comfort in its unearthly ray. Elsewhere the token of sin, it was the taper of the sick-chamber. It had even thrown its gleam, in the sufferer's hard extremity, across the verge of time. It had shown him where to set his foot, while the light of earth was fast becoming dim, and ere the light of futurity could reach him. In such emergencies, Hester's nature showed itself warm and rich; a well-spring of human tenderness, unfailing to every real demand, and inexhaustible by the largest. Her breast, with its badge of shame, was but the softer pillow for the head that needed one. She was self-ordained a Sister of Mercy; or, we may rather say, the world's heavy hand had so ordained her, when neither the world nor she looked forward to this result. The letter was the symbol of her calling. Such helpfulness was found in her,—so much power to do, and power to sympathize,—that many people refused to interpret the scarlet A by its original signification. They said that it meant Able; so strong was Hester Prynne, with a woman's strength.

It was only the darkened house that could contain her. When sunshine came again, she was not there. Her shadow had faded across the threshold. The helpful inmate had departed, without one backward glance to gather up the meed of gratitude, if any were in the hearts of those whom she had served so zealously. Meeting them in the street, she never raised her head to receive their greeting. If they were resolute to accost her, she laid her finger on the scarlet letter, and passed on. This might be pride, but was so like humility, that it produced all the softening influence of the latter quality on the public mind. The public is despotic in its temper; it is capable of denying common justice, when too strenuously demanded as a right; but quite as frequently it awards more than justice, when the appeal is made, as despots love to have it made, entirely to its generosity. Interpreting Hester Prynne's deportment as an appeal of this nature, society was inclined to show its former victim a more benign countenance than she cared to be favored with, or, perchance, than she deserved.

The rulers, and the wise learned men of the community, were longer in acknowledging the influence of Hester's good qualities than the people. The prejudices which they shared in common with the latter were fortified in themselves by an iron framework of reasoning, that made it a far tougher labor to expel them. Day by day, nevertheless, their sour and rigid wrinkles were relaxing into something which, in the due course of years, might grow to be an expression of almost benevolence. Thus it was with the men of rank, on whom their eminent position imposed the guardianship of the public morals. Individuals in private life, meanwhile, had quite forgiven Hester Prynne for her frailty; nay, more, they had begun to look upon the scarlet letter as the token, not of that one sin, for which she had borne so long and dreary a penance, but of her many good deeds since. "Do you see that woman with the embroidered badge?" they would say to strangers. "It is our Hester,—the town's own Hester,—who is so kind to the poor, so helpful to the sick, so comfortable to the afflicted!" Then, it is true, the propensity of human nature to tell the very worst of itself, when embodied in the person of another, would constrain them to whisper the black scandal of bygone years. It was none the less a fact, however, that, in the eyes of the very men who spoke thus, the scarlet letter had the effect of the cross on a nun's bosom. It imparted to the wearer a kind of sacredness, which enabled her to walk securely amid all peril. Had she fallen among thieves, it would have kept her safe. It was reported, and believed by many, that an Indian had drawn his arrow against the badge, and that the missile struck it, but fell harmless to the ground.

The effect of the symbol—or rather, of the position in respect to society that was indicated by it—on the mind of Hester Prynne herself, was powerful and peculiar. All the light and graceful foliage of her character had been withered up by this red-hot brand, and had long ago fallen away, leaving a bare and harsh outline, which might have been repulsive, had she possessed friends or companions to be repelled by it. Even the attractiveness of her person had undergone a similar change. It might be partly owing to the studied austerity of her dress, and partly to the lack of demonstration in her manners. It was a sad transformation, too, that her rich and luxuriant hair had either been cut off, or was so completely hidden by a cap, that not a shining lock of it ever once gushed into the sunshine. It was due in part to all these causes, but still more to something else, that there seemed to be no longer any thing in Hester's face for Love to dwell upon; nothing in Hester's form, though majestic and statue-like, that Passion would ever dream of clasping in its embrace; nothing in Hester's bosom, to make it ever again the pillow of Affection. Some attribute had departed from her, the permanence of which had been essential to keep her a woman. Such is frequently the fate, and such the stern development, of the feminine character and person, when the woman has encountered, and lived through, an experience of peculiar severity. If she be all tenderness, she will die. If she survive, the tenderness will either be crushed out of her, or—and the outward semblance is the same—crushed so deeply into her heart that it can never show itself more. The latter is perhaps the truest theory. She who has once been woman, and ceased to be so, might at any moment become a woman again, if there were only the magic touch to effect the transfiguration. We shall see whether Hester Prynne were ever afterwards so touched, and so transfigured.

Much of the marble coldness of Hester's impression was to be attributed to the circumstance that her life had turned, in a great measure, from passion and feeling, to thought. Standing alone in the world,—alone, as to any dependence on society, and with little Pearl to be guided and protected,—alone, and hopeless of retrieving her position, even had she not scorned to consider it desirable, —she cast away the fragments of a broken chain. The world's law was no law for her mind. It was an age in which the human intellect, newly emancipated, had taken a more active and a wider range than for many centuries before. Men of the sword had overthrown nobles and kings. Men bolder than these had overthrown and rearranged—not actually, but within the sphere of theory, which was their most real abode—the whole system of ancient prejudice, wherewith was linked much of ancient principle. Hester Prynne imbibed this spirit. She assumed a freedom of speculation, then common enough on the other side of the Atlantic, but which our forefathers, had they known of it, would have held to be a deadlier crime than that stigmatized by the scarlet letter. In her lonesome cottage, by the sea-shore, thoughts visited her, such as dared to enter no other dwelling in New England; shadowy guests, that would have been as perilous as demons to their entertainer, could they have been seen so much as knocking at her door.

It is remarkable, that persons who speculate the most boldly often conform with the most perfect quietude to the external regulations of society. The thought suffices them, without investing itself in the flesh and blood of action. So it seemed to be with Hester. Yet, had little Pearl never come to her from the spiritual world, it might have been far otherwise. Then, she might have come down to us in history, hand in hand with Ann Hutchinson, as the foundress of a religious sect. She might, in one of her phases, have been a prophetess. She might, and not improbably would, have suffered death from the stern tribunals of the period, for attempting to undermine the foundations of the Puritan establishment. But, in the education of her child, the mother's enthusiasm of thought had something to wreak itself upon. Providence, in the person of this little girl, had assigned to Hester's charge the germ and blossom of womanhood, to be cherished and developed amid a host of difficulties. Every thing was against her. The world was hostile. The child's own nature had something wrong in it, which continually betokened that she had been born amiss,—the effluence of her mother's lawless passion,—and often impelled Hester to ask, in bitterness of heart, whether it were for ill or good that the poor little creature had been born at all.

Indeed, the same dark question often rose into her mind, with reference to the whole race of womanhood. Was existence worth accepting, even to the happiest among them? As concerned her own individual existence, she had long ago decided in the negative, and dismissed the point as settled. A tendency to speculation, though it may keep woman quiet, as it does man, yet makes her sad. She discerns, it may be, such a hopeless task before her. As a first step, the whole system of society is to be torn down, and built up anew. Then, the very nature of the opposite sex, or its long hereditary habit, which has become like nature, is to be essentially modified, before woman can be allowed to assume what seems a fair and suitable position. Finally, all other difficulties being obviated, woman cannot take advantage of these preliminary reforms, until she herself shall have undergone a still mightier change; in which, perhaps, the ethereal essence, wherein she has her truest life, will be found to have evaporated. A woman never overcomes these problems by any exercise of thought. They are not to be solved, or only in one way. If her heart chance to come uppermost, they vanish. Thus, Hester Prynne, whose heart had lost its regular and healthy throb, wandered without a clew in the dark labyrinth of mind; now turned aside by an insurmountable precipice; now starting back from a deep chasm. There was wild and ghastly scenery all around her, and a home and comfort nowhere. At times, a fearful doubt strove to possess her soul, whether it were not better to send Pearl at once to heaven, and go herself to such futurity as Eternal Justice should provide.

The scarlet letter had not done its office.

Now, however, her interview with the Reverend Mr. Dimmesdale, on the night of his vigil, had given her a new theme of reflection, and held up to her an object that appeared worthy of any exertion and sacrifice for its attainment. She had witnessed the intense misery beneath which the minister struggled, or, to speak more accurately, had ceased to struggle. She saw that he stood on the verge of lunacy, if he had not already stepped across it. It was impossible to doubt, that, whatever painful efficacy there might be in the secret sting of remorse, a deadlier venom had been infused into it by the hand that proffered relief. A secret enemy had been continually by his side, under the semblance of a friend and helper, and had availed himself of the opportunities thus afforded for tampering with the delicate springs of Mr. Dimmesdale's nature. Hester could not but ask herself, whether there had not originally been a defect of truth, courage, and loyalty, on her own part, in allowing the minister to be thrown into a position where so much evil was to be foreboded, and nothing auspicious to be hoped. Her only justification lay in the fact, that she had been able to discern no method of rescuing him from a blacker ruin than had overwhelmed herself, except by acquiescing in Roger Chillingworth's scheme of disguise. Under that impulse, she had made her choice, and had chosen, as it now appeared, the more wretched alternative of the two. She determined to redeem her error, so far as it might yet be possible. Strengthened by years of hard and solemn trial, she felt herself no longer so inadequate to cope with Roger Chillingworth as on that night, abased by sin, and half maddened by the ignominy that was still new, when they had talked together in the prison-chamber. She had climbed her way, since then, to a higher point. The old man, on the other hand, had brought himself nearer to her level, or perhaps below it, by the revenge which he had stooped for.

In fine, Hester Prynne resolved to meet her former husband, and do what might be in her power for the rescue of the victim on whom he had so evidently set his gripe. The occasion was not long to seek. One afternoon, walking with Pearl in a retired part of the peninsula, she beheld the old physician, with a basket on one arm, and a staff in the other hand, stooping along the ground, in quest of roots and herbs to concoct his medicines withal.

XIV. *Hester and the Physician*

Hester bade little Pearl run down to the margin of the water, and play with the shells and tangled sea-weed, until she should have talked awhile with yonder gatherer of herbs. So the child flew away like a bird, and, making bare her small white feet, went pattering along the moist margin of the sea. Here and there, she came to a full stop, and peeped curiously into a pool, left by the retiring tide as a mirror for Pearl to see her face in. Forth peeped at her, out of the pool, with dark, glistening curls around her head, and an elf-smile in her eyes, the image of a little maid, whom Pearl, having no other playmate, invited to take her hand and run a race with her. But the visionary little maid, on her part, beckoned likewise, as if to say,—"This is a better place! Come thou into the pool!" And Pearl, stepping in, mid-leg deep, beheld her own white feet at the bottom; while, out of a still lower depth, came the gleam of a kind of fragmentary smile, floating to and fro in the agitated water.

Meanwhile, her mother had accosted the physician.

"I would speak a word with you," said she,—"a word that concerns us much."

"Aha! And is it Mistress Hester that has a word for old Roger Chillingworth?" answered he, raising himself from his stooping posture. "With all my heart! Why, Mistress, I hear good tidings of you on all hands! No longer ago than yester-eve, a magistrate, a wise and godly man, was discoursing of your affairs, Mistress Hester, and whispered me that there had been question concerning you in the council. It was debated whether or no, with safety to the commonweal, yonder scarlet letter might be taken off your bosom. On my life, Hester, I made my entreaty to the worshipful magistrate that it might be done forthwith!"

"It lies not in the pleasure of the magistrates to take off this badge," calmly replied Hester. "Were I worthy to be quit of it, it would fall away of its own nature, or be transformed into something that should speak a different purport."

"Nay, then, wear it, if it suit you better," rejoined he. "A woman must needs follow her own fancy, touching the adornment of her person. The letter is gayly embroidered, and shows right bravely on your bosom!"

All this while, Hester had been looking steadily at the old man, and was shocked, as well as wonder-smitten, to discern what a change had been wrought upon him within the past seven years. It was not so much that he had grown older; for though the traces of advancing life were visible, he bore his age well, and seemed to retain a wiry vigor and alertness. But the former aspect of an intellectual and studious man, calm and quiet, which was what she best remembered in him, had altogether vanished, and been succeeded by an eager, searching, almost fierce, yet carefully guarded look. It seemed to be his wish and purpose to mask this expression with a smile; but the latter played him false, and flickered over his visage so derisively, that the spectator could see his blackness all the better for it. Ever and anon, too, there came a glare of red light out of his eyes; as if the old man's soul were on fire, and kept on smouldering duskily within his breast, until, by some casual puff of passion, it was blown into a momentary flame. This he repressed as speedily as possible, and strove to look as if nothing of the kind had happened.

In a word, old Roger Chillingworth was a striking evidence of man's faculty of transforming himself into a devil, if he will only, for a reasonable space of time, undertake a devil's office. This unhappy person had effected such a transformation by devoting himself, for seven years, to the constant analysis of a heart full of torture, and deriving his enjoyment thence, and adding fuel to those fiery tortures which he analyzed and gloated over.

The scarlet letter burned on Hester Prynne's bosom. Here was another ruin, the responsibility of which came partly home to her.

"What see you in my face," asked the physician, "that you look at it so earnestly?"

"Something that would make me weep, if there were any tears bitter enough for it," answered she. "But let it pass! It is of yonder miserable man that I would speak."

"And what of him?" cried Roger Chillingworth eagerly, as if he loved the topic, and were glad of an opportunity to discuss it with the only person of whom he could make a confidant. "Not to hide the truth, Mistress Hester, my thoughts happen just now to be busy with the gentleman. So speak freely; and I will make answer."

"When we last spake together," said Hester, "now seven years ago, it was your pleasure to extort a promise of secrecy, as touching the former relation betwixt yourself and me. As the life and good fame of yonder man were in your hands, there seemed no choice to me, save to be silent, in accordance with your behest. Yet it was not without heavy misgivings that I thus bound myself; for, having cast off all duty towards other human beings, there remained a duty towards him; and something whispered me that I was betraying it, in pledging myself to keep your counsel. Since that day, no man is so near to him as you. You tread behind his every footstep. You are beside him, sleeping and waking. You search his thoughts. You burrow and rankle in his heart! Your clutch is on his life, and you cause him to die daily a living death; and still he knows you not. In permitting this, I have surely acted a false part by the only man to whom the power was left me to be true!"

"What choice had you?" asked Roger Chillingworth. "My finger, pointed at this man, would have hurled him from his pulpit into a dungeon,—thence, peradventure, to the gallows!"

"It had been better so!" said Hester Prynne.

"What evil have I done the man?" asked Roger Chillingworth again. "I tell thee, Hester Prynne, the richest fee that ever physician earned from monarch could not have bought such care as I have wasted on this miserable priest! But for my aid, his life would have burned away in torments, within the first two years after the perpetration of his crime and thine. For, Hester, his spirit lacked the strength that could have borne up, as thine has, beneath a burden like thy scarlet letter. O, I could reveal a goodly secret! But enough! What art can do, I have exhausted on him. That he now breathes, and creeps about on earth, is owing all to me!"

"Better he had died at once!" said Hester Prynne.

"Yea, woman, thou sayest truly!" cried old Roger Chillingworth, letting the lurid fire of his heart blaze out before her eyes. "Better had he died at once! Never did mortal suffer what this man has suffered. And all, all, in the sight of his worst enemy! He has been conscious of me. He has felt an influence dwelling always upon him like a curse. He knew, by some spiritual sense,—for the Creator never made another being so sensitive as this,—he knew that no friendly hand was pulling at his heart-strings, and that an eye was looking curiously into him, which sought only evil, and found it. But he knew not that the eye and hand were mine! With the superstition common to his brotherhood, he fancied himself given over to a fiend, to be tortured with frightful dreams, and desperate thoughts, the sting of remorse, and despair of pardon; as a foretaste of what awaits him beyond the grave. But it was the constant shadow of my presence!—the closest propinquity of the man whom he had most vilely wronged!—and who had grown to exist only by this perpetual poison of the direst revenge! Yea, indeed!—he did not err!—there was a fiend at his elbow! A mortal man, with once a human heart, has become a fiend for his especial torment!"

The unfortunate physician, while uttering these words, lifted his hands with a look of horror, as if he had beheld some frightful shape, which he could not recognize, usurping the place of his own image in a glass. It was one of those moments—which sometimes occur only at the interval of years—when a man's moral aspect is faithfully revealed to his mind's eye. Not improbably, he had never before viewed himself as he did now.

"Hast thou not tortured him enough?" said Hester, noticing the old man's look. "Has he not paid thee all?"

"No!—no!—He has but increased the debt!" answered the physician; and, as he proceeded, his manner lost its fiercer characteristics, and subsided into gloom. "Dost thou remember me, Hester, as I was nine years agone? Even then, I was in the autumn of my days, nor was it the early autumn. But all my life had been made up of earnest, studious, thoughtful, quiet years, bestowed faithfully for the increase of mine own knowledge, and faithfully, too, though this latter object was but casual to the other,—faithfully for the advancement of human welfare. No life had been more peaceful and innocent than mine; few lives so rich with benefits conferred. Dost thou remember me? Was I not, though you might deem me cold, nevertheless a man thoughtful for others, craving little for himself, —kind, true, just, and of constant, if not warm affections? Was I not all this?"

"All this, and more," said Hester.

"And what am I now?" demanded he, looking into her face, and permitting the whole evil within him to be written on his features. "I have already told thee what I am! A fiend! Who made me so?"

"It was myself!" cried Hester, shuddering. "It was I, not less than he. Why hast thou not avenged thyself on me?"

"I have left thee to the scarlet letter," replied Roger Chillingworth. "If that have not avenged me, I can do no more!"

He laid his finger on it, with a smile.

"It has avenged thee!" answered Hester Prynne.

"I judged no less," said the physician. "And now, what wouldst thou with me touching this man?"

"I must reveal the secret," answered Hester, firmly. "He must discern thee in thy true character. What may be the result, I know not. But this long debt of confidence, due from me to him, whose bane and ruin I have been, shall at length be paid. So far as concerns the overthrow or preservation of his fair fame and his earthly state, and perchance his life, he is in thy hands. Nor do I,—whom the scarlet letter has disciplined to truth, though it be the truth of red-hot iron, entering into the soul,—nor do I perceive such advantage in his living any longer a life of ghastly emptiness, that I shall stoop to implore thy mercy. Do with him as thou wilt! There is no good for him,—no good for me,—no good for thee! There is no good for little Pearl! There is no path to guide us out of this dismal maze!"

"Woman, I could wellnigh pity thee!" said Roger Chillingworth, unable to restrain a thrill of admiration too; for there was a quality almost majestic in the despair which she expressed. "Thou hadst great elements. Peradventure, hadst thou met earlier with a better love than mine, this evil had not been. I pity thee, for the good that has been wasted in thy nature!"

"And I thee," answered Hester Prynne, "for the hatred that has transformed a wise and just man to a fiend! Wilt thou yet purge it out of thee, and be once more human? If not for his sake, then doubly for thine own! Forgive, and leave his further retribution to the Power that claims it! I said, but now, that there could be no good event for him, or thee, or me, who are here wandering together in this gloomy maze of evil, and stumbling, at every step, over the guilt wherewith we have strewn our path. It is not so! There might be good for thee, and thee alone, since thou hast been deeply wronged, and hast it at thy will to pardon. Wilt thou give up that only privilege? Wilt thou reject that priceless benefit?"

"Peace, Hester, peace!" replied the old man, with gloomy sternness. "It is not granted me to pardon. I have no such power as thou tellest me of. My old faith, long forgotten, comes back to me, and explains all that we do, and all we suffer. By thy first step awry, thou didst plant the germ of evil; but, since that moment, it has all been a dark necessity. Ye that have wronged me are not sinful, save in a kind of typical illusion; neither am I fiend-like, who have snatched a fiend's office from his hands. It is our fate. Let the black flower blossom as it may! Now go thy ways, and deal as thou wilt with yonder man."

He waved his hand, and betook himself again to his employment of gathering herbs.

XV. *Hester and Pearl*

So Roger Chillingworth—a deformed old figure, with a face that haunted men's memories longer than they liked—took leave of Hester Prynne, and went stooping away along the earth. He gathered here and there an herb, or grubbed up a root, and put it into the basket on his arm. His gray beard almost touched the ground, as he crept onward. Hester gazed after him a little while, looking with a half-fantastic curiosity to see whether the tender grass of early spring would not be blighted beneath him, and show the wavering track of his footsteps, sere and brown, across its cheerful verdure. She wondered what sort of herbs they were, which the old man was so sedulous to gather. Would not the earth, quickened to an evil purpose by the sympathy of his eye, greet him with poisonous shrubs, of species hitherto unknown, that would start up under his fingers? Or might it suffice him, that every wholesome growth should be converted into something deleterious and malignant at his touch? Did the sun, which shone so brightly everywhere else, really fall upon him? Or was there, as it rather seemed, a circle of ominous shadow moving along with his deformity, whichever way he turned himself? And whither was he now going? Would he not suddenly sink into the earth, leaving a barren and blasted spot, where, in due course of time, would be seen deadly nightshade, dogwood, henbane,[2] and whatever else of vegetable wickedness the climate could produce, all flourishing with hideous luxuriance? Or would he spread bat's wings and flee away, looking so much the uglier, the higher he rose towards heaven?

2. Deadly nightshade (belladonna) and henbane produce poisons possessing magical powers in ancient folklore and necromancy; together with dogwood they occur in the pharmacopoeia of witchcraft.

"Be it sin or no," said Hester Prynne bitterly, as she still gazed after him, "I hate the man!"

She upbraided herself for the sentiment, but could not overcome or lessen it. Attempting to do so, she thought of those long-past days, in a distant land, when he used to emerge at eventide from the seclusion of his study, and sit down in the fire-light of their home, and in the light of her nuptial smile. He needed to bask himself in that smile, he said, in order that the chill of so many lonely hours among his books might be taken off the scholar's heart. Such scenes had once appeared not otherwise than happy, but now, as viewed through the dismal medium of her subsequent life, they classed themselves among her ugliest remembrances. She marvelled how such scenes could have been! She marvelled how she could ever have been wrought upon to marry him! She deemed it her crime most to be repented of, that she had ever endured, and reciprocated, the lukewarm grasp of his hand, and had suffered the smile of her lips and eyes to mingle and melt into his own. And it seemed a fouler offence committed by Roger Chillingworth, than any which had since been done him, that, in the time when her heart knew no better, he had persuaded her to fancy herself happy by his side.

"Yes, I hate him!" repeated Hester, more bitterly than before. "He betrayed me! He has done me worse wrong than I did him!"

Let men tremble to win the hand of woman, unless they win along with it the utmost passion of her heart! Else it may be their miserable fortune, as it was Roger Chillingworth's, when some mightier touch than their own may have awakened all her sensibilities, to be reproached even for the calm content, the marble image of happiness, which they will have imposed upon her as the warm reality. But Hester ought long ago to have done with this injustice. What did it betoken? Had seven long years, under the torture of the scarlet letter, inflicted so much of misery, and wrought out no repentance?

The emotions of that brief space, while she stood gazing after the crooked figure of old Roger Chillingworth, threw a dark light on Hester's state of mind, revealing much that she might not otherwise have acknowledged to herself.

He being gone, she summoned back her child.

"Pearl! Little Pearl! Where are you?"

Pearl, whose activity of spirit never flagged, had been at no loss for amusement while her mother talked with the old gatherer of herbs. At first, as already told, she had flirted fancifully with her own image in a pool of water, beckoning the phantom forth, and —as it declined to venture—seeking a passage for herself into its sphere of impalpable earth and unattainable sky. Soon finding, however, that either she or the image was unreal, she turned elsewhere for better pastime. She made little boats out of birch-bark, and freighted them with snail-shells, and sent out more ventures on the mighty deep that any merchant in New England; but the larger part of them foundered near the shore. She seized a live horse-shoe[3] by the tail, and made prize of several five-fingers,[4] and laid out a jelly-fish to melt in the warm sun. Then she took up the white foam, that streaked the line of the advancing tide, and threw it upon the breeze, scampering after it with winged footsteps, to catch the great snow-flakes ere they fell. Perceiving a flock of beach-birds, that fed and fluttered along the shore, the naughty child picked up her apron full of pebbles, and, creeping from rock to rock after these small sea-fowl, displayed remarkable dexterity in pelting them. One little gray bird, with a white breast, Pearl was almost sure, had been hit by a pebble, and fluttered away with a broken wing. But then the elf-child sighed, and gave up her sport; because it grieved her to have done harm to a little being that was as wild as the sea-breeze, or as wild as Pearl herself.

Her final employment was to gather sea-weed, of various kinds, and make herself a scarf, or mantle, and a head-dress, and thus assume the aspect of a little mermaid. She inherited her mother's gift for devising drapery and costume. As the last touch to her mermaid's garb, Pearl took some eel-grass, and imitated, as best she could, on her own bosom, the decoration with which she was so familiar on her mother's. A letter,—the letter A,—but freshly green, instead of scarlet! The child bent her chin upon her breast, and contemplated this device with strange interest; even as if the one only thing for which she had been sent into the world was to make out its hidden import.

"I wonder if mother will ask me what it means!" thought Pearl.

Just then, she heard her mother's voice, and, flitting along as lightly as one of the little sea-birds, appeared before Hester Prynne, dancing, laughing, and pointing her finger to the ornament upon her bosom.

"My little Pearl," said Hester, after a moment's silence, "the green letter, and on thy childish bosom, has no purport. But dost thou know, my child, what this letter means which thy mother is doomed to wear?"

"Yes, mother," said the child. "It is the great letter A. Thou hast taught it me in the horn-book."[5]

3. Horseshoe crab.
4. Starfish.
5. A tablet used to teach spelling: early examples usually consisted of a cover of transparent horn and a single sheet of parchment bearing the alphabet and, perhaps, a prayer.

Hester looked steadily into her little face; but, though there was that singular expression which she had so often remarked in her black eyes, she could not satisfy herself whether Pearl really attached any meaning to the symbol. She felt a morbid desire to ascertain the point.

"Dost thou know, child, wherefore thy mother wears this letter?"

"Truly do I!" answered Pearl, looking brightly into her mother's face. "It is for the same reason that the minister keeps his hand over his heart!"

"And what reason is that?" asked Hester, half smiling at the absurd incongruity of the child's observation; but, on second thoughts, turning pale. "What has the letter to do with any heart, save mine?"

"Nay, mother, I have told all I know," said Pearl, more seriously than she was wont to speak. "Ask yonder old man whom thou hast been talking with! It may be he can tell. But in good earnest now, mother dear, what does this scarlet letter mean?—and why dost thou wear it on thy bosom?—and why does the minister keep his hand over his heart?"

She took her mother's hand in both her own, and gazed into her eyes with an earnestness that was seldom seen in her wild and capricious character. The thought occurred to Hester, that the child might really be seeking to approach her with childlike confidence, and doing what she could, and as intelligently as she knew how, to establish a meeting-point of sympathy. It showed Pearl in an unwonted aspect. Heretofore, the mother, while loving her child with the intensity of a sole affection, had schooled herself to hope for little other return than the waywardness of an April breeze; which spends its time in airy sport, and has its gusts of inexplicable passion, and is petulant in its best of moods, and chills oftener than caresses you, when you take it to your bosom; in requital of which misdemeanours, it will sometimes, of its own vague purpose, kiss your cheek with a kind of doubtful tenderness, and play gently with your hair, and then begone about its other idle business, leaving a dreamy pleasure at your heart. And this, moreover, was a mother's estimate of the child's disposition. Any other observer might have seen few but unamiable traits, and have given them a far darker coloring. But now the idea came strongly into Hester's mind, that Pearl, with her remarkable precocity and acuteness, might already have approached the age when she could be made a friend, and intrusted with as much of her mother's sorrows as could be imparted, without irreverence either to the parent or the child. In the little chaos of Pearl's character, there might be seen emerging —and could have been, from the very first—the steadfast principles of an unflinching courage,—an uncontrollable will,—a sturdy pride, which might be disciplined into self-respect,—and a bitter scorn of many things, which, when examined, might be found to have the taint of falsehood in them. She possessed affections, too, though hitherto acrid and disagreeable, as are the richest flavors of unripe fruit. With all these sterling attributes, thought Hester, the evil which she inherited from her mother must be great indeed, if a noble woman do not grow out of this elfish child.

Pearl's inevitable tendency to hover about the enigma of the scarlet letter seemed an innate quality of her being. From the earliest epoch of her conscious life, she had entered upon this as her appointed mission. Hester had often fancied that Providence had a design of justice and retribution, in endowing the child with this marked propensity; but never, until now, had she bethought herself to ask, whether, linked with that design, there might not likewise be a purpose of mercy and beneficence. If little Pearl were entertained with faith and trust, as a spirit-messenger no less than an earthly child, might it not be her errand to soothe away the sorrow that lay cold in her mother's heart, and converted it into a tomb?—and to help her to overcome the passion, once so wild, and even yet neither dead nor asleep, but only imprisoned within the same tomb-like heart?

Such were some of the thoughts that now stirred in Hester's mind, with as much vivacity of impression as if they had actually been whispered into her ear. And there was little Pearl, all this while, holding her mother's hand in both her own, and turning her face upward, while she put these searching questions, once, and again, and still a third time.

"What does the letter mean, mother?—and why dost thou wear it?—and why does the minister keep his hand over his heart?"

"What shall I say?" thought Hester to herself.—"No! If this be the price of the child's sympathy, I cannot pay it!"

Then she spoke aloud.

"Silly Pearl," said she, "what questions are these? There are many things in this world that a child must not ask about. What know I of the minister's heart? And as for the scarlet letter, I wear it for the sake of its gold thread!"

In all the seven bygone years, Hester Prynne had never before been false to the symbol on her bosom. It may be that it was the talisman of a stern and severe, but yet a guardian spirit, who now forsook her; as recognizing that, in spite of his strict watch over her heart, some new evil had crept into it, or some old one had never been expelled. As for little Pearl, the earnestness soon passed out of her face.

But the child did not see fit to let the matter drop. Two or three times, as her mother and she went homeward, and as often at supper-time, and while Hester was putting her to bed, and once after she seemed to be fairly asleep, Pearl looked up, with mischief gleaming in her black eyes.

"Mother," said she, "what does the scarlet letter mean?"

And the next morning, the first indication the child gave of being awake was by popping up her head from the pillow, and making that other inquiry, which she had so unaccountably connected with her investigations about the scarlet letter:—

"Mother!—Mother!—Why does the minister keep his hand over his heart?"

"Hold thy tongue, naughty child!" answered her mother, with an asperity that she had never permitted to herself before. "Do not tease me; else I shall shut thee into the dark closet!"

XVI. A Forest Walk

Hester Prynne remained constant in her resolve to make known to Mr. Dimmesdale, at whatever risk of present pain or ulterior consequences, the true character of the man who had crept into his intimacy. For several days, however, she vainly sought an opportunity of addressing him in some of the meditative walks which she knew him to be in the habit of taking, along the shores of the peninsula, or on the wooded hills of the neighbouring country. There would have been no scandal, indeed, nor peril to the holy whiteness of the clergyman's good fame, had she visited him in his own study; where many a penitent, ere now, had confessed sins of perhaps as deep a dye as the one betokened by the scarlet letter. But, partly that she dreaded the secret or undisguised interference of old Roger Chillingworth, and partly that her conscious heart imputed suspicion where none could have been felt, and partly that both the minister and she would need the whole wide world to breathe in, while they talked together,—for all these reasons, Hester never thought of meeting him in any narrower privacy than beneath the open sky.

At last, while attending in a sick-chamber, whither the Reverend Mr. Dimmesdale had been summoned to make a prayer, she learnt that he had gone, the day before, to visit the Apostle Eliot,[6] among his Indian converts. He would probably return, by a certain hour, in the afternoon of the morrow. Betimes, therefore, the

6. John Eliot (1604–90), educated at Cambridge, England, emigrated to Boston in 1631, was the first to preach to the American Indians in their own dialects, and soon became known as "Apostle to the Indians."

next day, Hester took little Pearl,—who was necessarily the companion of all her mother's expeditions, however inconvenient her presence,—and set forth.

The road, after the two wayfarers had crossed from the peninsula to the mainland, was no other than a footpath. It straggled onward into the mystery of the primeval forest. This hemmed it in so narrowly, and stood so black and dense on either side, and disclosed such imperfect glimpses of the sky above, that, to Hester's mind, it imaged not amiss the moral wilderness in which she had so long been wandering. The day was chill and sombre. Overhead was a gray expanse of cloud, slightly stirred, however, by a breeze; so that a gleam of flickering sunshine might now and then be seen at its solitary play along the path. This flitting cheerfulness was always at the farther extremity of some long vista through the forest. The sportive sunlight—feebly sportive, at best, in the predominant pensiveness of the day and scene—withdrew itself as they came nigh, and left the spots where it had danced the drearier, because they had hoped to find them bright.

"Mother," said little Pearl, "the sunshine does not love you. It runs away and hides itself, because it is afraid of something on your bosom. Now, see! There it is, playing, a good way off. Stand you here, and let me run and catch it. I am but a child. It will not flee from me; for I wear nothing on my bosom yet!"

"Nor ever will, my child, I hope," said Hester.

"And why not, mother?" asked Pearl, stopping short, just at the beginning of her race. "Will not it come of its own accord, when I am a woman grown?"

"Run away, child," answered her mother, "and catch the sunshine! It will soon be gone."

Pearl set forth, at a great pace, and, as Hester smiled to perceive, did actually catch the sunshine, and stood laughing in the midst of it, all brightened by its splendor, and scintillating with the vivacity excited by rapid motion. The light lingered about the lonely child, as if glad of such a playmate, until her mother had drawn almost nigh enough to step into the magic circle too.

"It will go now!" said Pearl, shaking her head.

"See!" answered Hester, smiling. "Now I can stretch out my hand, and grasp some of it."

As she attempted to do so, the sunshine vanished; or, to judge from the bright expression that was dancing on Pearl's features, her mother could have fancied that the child had absorbed it into herself, and would give it forth again, with a gleam about her path, as they should plunge into some gloomier shade. There was no other attribute that so much impressed her with a sense of new and untransmitted vigor in Pearl's nature, as this never-failing vivacity of spirits; she had not the disease of sadness, which almost all children, in these latter days, inherit, with the scrofula,[7] from the troubles of their ancestors. Perhaps this too was a disease, and but the reflex of the wild energy with which Hester had fought against her sorrows, before Pearl's birth. It was certainly a doubtful charm, imparting a hard, metallic lustre to the child's character. She wanted —what some people want throughout life—a grief that should deeply touch her, and thus humanize and make her capable of sympathy. But there was time enough yet for little Pearl!

"Come, my child!" said Hester, looking about her, from the spot where Pearl had stood still in the sunshine. "We will sit down a little way within the wood, and rest ourselves."

"I am not aweary, mother," replied the little girl. "But you may sit down, if you will tell me a story meanwhile."

"A story, child!" said Hester. "And about what?"

"O, a story about the Black Man!" answered Pearl, taking hold of her mother's gown, and looking up, half earnestly, half mischievously, into her face. "How he haunts this forest, and carries a book with him,—a big, heavy book, with iron clasps; and how this ugly Black Man offers his book and an iron pen to every body that meets him here among the trees; and they are to write their names with their own blood. And then he sets his mark on their bosoms! Didst thou ever meet the Black Man, mother?"

"And who told you this story, Pearl?" asked her mother, recognizing a common superstition of the period.

"It was the old dame in the chimney-corner, at the house where you watched last night," said the child. "But she fancied me asleep while she was talking of it. She said that a thousand and a thousand people had met him here, and had written in his book, and have his mark on them. And that ugly-tempered lady, old Mistress Hibbins, was one. And, mother, the old dame said that this scarlet letter was the Black Man's mark on thee, and that it glows like a red flame when thou meetest him at midnight, here in the dark wood. Is it true, mother? And dost thou go to meet him in the night-time?"

"Didst thou ever awake, and find thy mother gone?" asked Hester.

"Not that I remember," said the child. "If thou fearest to leave me in our cottage, thou mightest take me along with thee. I would very gladly go! But, mother, tell me now! Is there such a Black Man? And didst thou ever meet him? And is this his mark?"

7. A tuberculous condition, most common in children, but not hereditary.

"Wilt thou let me be at peace, if I once tell thee?" asked her mother.

"Yes, if thou tellest me all," answered Pearl.

"Once in my life I met the Black Man!" said her mother. "This scarlet letter is his mark!"

Thus conversing, they entered sufficiently deep into the wood to secure themselves from the observation of any casual passenger along the forest-track. Here they sat down on a luxuriant heap of moss; which, at some epoch of the preceding century, had been a gigantic pine, with its roots and trunk in the darksome shade, and its head aloft in the upper atmosphere. It was a little dell where they had seated themselves, with a leaf-strewn bank rising gently on either side, and a brook flowing through the midst, over a bed of fallen and drowned leaves. The trees impending over it had flung down great branches, from time to time, which choked up the current, and compelled it to form eddies and black depths at some points; while, in its swifter and livelier passages, there appeared a channel-way of pebbles, and brown, sparkling sand. Letting the eyes follow along the course of the stream, they could catch the reflected light from its water, at some short distance within the forest, but soon lost all traces of it amid the bewilderment of tree-trunks and underbrush, and here and there a huge rock, covered over with gray lichens. All these giant trees and boulders of granite seemed intent on making a mystery of the course of this small brook; fearing, perhaps, that, with its never-ceasing loquacity, it should whisper tales out of the heart of the old forest whence it flowed, or mirror its revelations on the smooth surface of a pool. Continually, indeed, as it stole onward, the streamlet kept up a babble, kind, quiet, soothing, but melancholy, like the voice of a young child that was spending its infancy without playfulness, and knew not how to be merry among sad acquaintance and events of sombre hue.

"O brook! O foolish and tiresome little brook!" cried Pearl, after listening awhile to its talk. "Why art thou so sad? Pluck up a spirit, and do not be all the time sighing and murmuring!"

But the brook, in the course of its little lifetime among the forest-trees, had gone through so solemn an experience that it could not help talking about it, and seemed to have nothing else to say. Pearl resembled the brook, inasmuch as the current of her life gushed from a well-spring as mysterious, and had flowed through scenes shadowed as heavily with gloom. But, unlike the little stream, she danced and sparkled, and prattled airily along her course.

"What does this sad little brook say, mother?" inquired she.

"If thou hadst a sorrow of thine own, the brook might tell thee of it," answered her mother, "even as it is telling me of mine! But now, Pearl, I hear a footstep along the path, and the noise of one putting aside the branches. I would have thee betake thyself to play, and leave me to speak with him that comes yonder."

"Is it the Black Man?" asked Pearl.

"Wilt thou go and play, child?" repeated her mother. "But do not stray far into the wood. And take heed that thou come at my first call."

"Yes, mother," answered Pearl. "But, if it be the Black Man, wilt thou not let me stay a moment, and look at him, with his big book under his arm?"

"Go, silly child!" said her mother, impatiently. "It is no Black Man! Thou canst see him now through the trees. It is the minister!"

"And so it is!" said the child. "And, mother, he has his hand over his heart! Is it because, when the minister wrote his name in the book, the Black Man set his mark in that place? But why does he not wear it outside his bosom, as thou dost, mother?"

"Go now, child, and thou shalt tease me as thou wilt another time," cried Hester Prynne. "But do not stray far. Keep where thou canst hear the babble of the brook."

The child went singing away, following up the current of the brook, and striving to mingle a more lightsome cadence with its melancholy voice. But the little stream would not be comforted, and still kept telling its unintelligible secret of some very mournful mystery that had happened—or making a prophetic lamentation about something that was yet to happen—within the verge of the dismal forest. So Pearl, who had enough of shadow in her own little life, chose to break off all acquaintance with this repining brook. She set herself, therefore, to gathering violets and wood-anemones, and some scarlet columbines that she found growing in the crevices of a high rock.

When her elf-child had departed, Hester Prynne made a step or two towards the track that led through the forest, but still remained under the deep shadow of the trees. She beheld the minister advancing along the path, entirely alone, and leaning on a staff which he had cut by the way-side. He looked haggard and feeble, and betrayed a nerveless despondency in his air, which had never so remarkably characterized him in his walks about the settlement, nor in any other situation where he deemed himself liable to notice. Here it was wofully visible, in this intense seclusion of the forest, which of itself would have been a heavy trial to the spirits. There was a listlessness in his gait; as if he saw no reason for taking one step farther, nor felt any desire to do so, but would have been glad, could he be glad of any thing, to fling himself down at the root of the nearest tree, and lie there passive for evermore. The leaves might bestrew him, and the soil gradually accumulate and form a little hillock over his frame, no matter whether there were life in it or no. Death was too definite an object to be wished for, or avoided.

To Hester's eye, the Reverend Mr. Dimmesdale exhibited no symptom of positive and vivacious suffering, except that, as little Pearl had remarked, he kept his hand over his heart.

XVII. *The Pastor and His Parishioner*

Slowly as the minister walked, he had almost gone by, before Hester Prynne could gather voice enough to attract his observation. At length, she succeeded.

"Arthur Dimmesdale!" she said, faintly at first; then louder, but hoarsely. "Arthur Dimmesdale!"

"Who speaks?" answered the minister.

Gathering himself quickly up, he stood more erect, like a man taken by surprise in a mood to which he was reluctant to have witnesses. Throwing his eyes anxiously in the direction of the voice, he indistinctly beheld a form under the trees, clad in garments so sombre, and so little relieved from the gray twilight into which the clouded sky and the heavy foliage had darkened the noontide, that he knew not whether it were a woman or a shadow. It may be, that his pathway through life was haunted thus, by a spectre that had stolen out from among his thoughts.

He made a step nigher, and discovered the scarlet letter.

"Hester! Hester Prynne!" said he. "Is it thou? Art thou in life?"

"Even so!" she answered. "In such life as has been mine these seven years past! And thou, Arthur Dimmesdale, dost thou yet live?"

It was no wonder that they thus questioned one another's actual and bodily existence, and even doubted of their own. So strangely did they meet, in the dim wood, that it was like the first encounter, in the world beyond the grave, of two spirits who had been intimately connected in their former life, but now stood coldly shuddering, in mutual dread; as not yet familiar with their state, nor wonted to the companionship of disembodied beings. Each a ghost, and awe-stricken at the other ghost! They were awe-stricken likewise at themselves; because the crisis flung back to them their consciousness, and revealed to each heart its history and experience, as life never does, except at such breathless epochs. The soul beheld its features in the mirror of the passing moment. It was with fear, and tremulously, and, as it were, by a slow, reluctant necessity, that Arthur Dimmesdale put forth his hand, chill as death, and touched the chill hand of Hester Prynne. The grasp, cold as it was, took away what was dreariest in the interview. They now felt themselves, at least, inhabitants of the same sphere.

Without a word more spoken,—neither he nor she assuming the guidance, but with an unexpressed consent,—they glided back into the shadow of the woods, whence Hester had emerged, and sat down on the heap of moss where she and Pearl had before been sitting. When they found voice to speak, it was, at first, only to utter remarks and inquiries such as any two acquaintance might have made, about the gloomy sky, the threatening storm, and, next, the health of each. Thus they went onward, not boldly, but step by step, into the themes that were brooding deepest in their hearts. So long estranged by fate and circumstances, they needed something slight and casual to run before, and throw open the doors of intercourse, so that their real thoughts might be led across the threshold.

After a while, the minister fixed his eyes on Hester Prynne's.

"Hester," said he, "hast thou found peace?"

She smiled drearily, looking down upon her bosom.

"Hast thou?" she asked.

"None!—nothing but despair!" he answered. "What else could I look for, being what I am, and leading such a life as mine? Were I an atheist,—a man devoid of conscience,—a wretch with coarse and brutal instincts,—I might have found peace, long ere now. Nay, I never should have lost it! But, as matters stand with my soul, whatever of good capacity there originally was in me, all of God's gifts that were the choicest have become the ministers of spiritual torment. Hester, I am most miserable!"

"The people reverence thee," said Hester. "And surely thou workest good among them! Doth this bring thee no comfort?"

"More misery, Hester!—only the more misery!" answered the clergyman, with a bitter smile. "As concerns the good which I may appear to do, I have no faith in it. It must needs be a delusion. What can a ruined soul, like mine, effect towards the redemption of other souls?—or a polluted soul, towards their purification? And as for the people's reverence, would that it were turned to scorn and hatred! Canst thou deem it, Hester, a consolation, that I must stand up in my pulpit, and meet so many eyes turned upward to my face, as if the light of heaven were beaming from it!—must see my flock hungry for the truth, and listening to my words as if a tongue of Pentecost were speaking!—and then look inward, and discern the black reality of what they idolize? I have laughed, in bitterness and agony of heart, at the contrast between what I seem and what I am! And Satan laughs at it!"

"You wrong yourself in this," said Hester, gently. "You have deeply and sorely repented. Your sin is left behind you, in the days long past. Your present life is not less holy, in very truth, than it seems in people's eyes. Is there no reality in the penitence thus sealed and witnessed by good works? And wherefore should it not bring you peace?"

"No, Hester, no!" replied the clergyman. "There is no substance in it! It is cold and dead, and can do nothing for me! Of penance I have had enough! Of penitence there has been none! Else, I should long ago have thrown off these garments of mock holiness, and have shown myself to mankind as they will see me at the judgment-seat. Happy are you, Hester, that wear the scarlet letter openly upon your bosom! Mine burns in secret! Thou little knowest what a relief it is, after the torment of a seven years' cheat, to look into an eye that recognizes me for what I am! Had I one friend,—or were it my worst enemy!—to whom, when sickened with the praises of all other men, I could daily betake myself, and be known as the vilest of all sinners, methinks my soul might keep itself alive thereby. Even thus much of truth would save me! But now, it is all falsehood!—all emptiness!—all death!"

Hester Prynne looked into his face, but hesitated to speak. Yet, uttering his long-restrained emotions so vehemently as he did, his words here offered her the very point of circumstances in which to interpose what she came to say. She conquered her fears, and spoke.

"Such a friend as thou hast even now wished for," said she, "with whom to weep over thy sin, thou hast in me, the partner of it!"— Again she hesitated, but brought out the words with an effort.— "Thou hast long had such an enemy, and dwellest with him under the same roof!"

The minister started to his feet, gasping for breath, and clutching at his heart as if he would have torn it out of his bosom.

"Ha! What sayest thou?" cried he. "An enemy! And under mine own roof! What mean you?"

Hester Prynne was now fully sensible of the deep injury for which she was responsible to this unhappy man, in permitting him to lie for so many years, or, indeed, for a single moment, at the mercy of one, whose purposes could not be other than malevolent. The very contiguity of his enemy, beneath whatever mask the latter might conceal himself, was enough to disturb the magnetic sphere of a being so sensitive as Arthur Dimmesdale. There had been a period when Hester was less alive to this consideration; or, perhaps, in the misanthropy of her own trouble, she left the minister to bear what she might picture to herself as a more tolerable doom. But of late, since the night of his vigil, all her sympathies towards him had been both softened and invigorated. She now read his heart more accurately. She doubted not, that the continual presence of Roger Chillingworth,—the secret poison of his malignity, infecting all the air about him,—and his authorized interference, as a physician, with the minister's physical and spiritual infirmities,—that these bad opportunities had been turned to a cruel purpose. By means of them, the sufferer's conscience had been kept in an irritated state, the tendency of which was, not to cure by wholesome pain, but to disorganize and corrupt his spiritual being. Its result, on earth, could hardly fail to be insanity, and hereafter, that eternal alienation from the Good and True, of which madness is perhaps the earthly type.

Such was the ruin to which she had brought the man, once,—nay, why should we not speak it?—still so passionately loved! Hester felt that the sacrifice of the clergyman's good name, and death itself, as she had already told Roger Chillingworth, would have been infinitely preferable to the alternative which she had taken upon herself to choose. And now, rather than have had this grievous wrong to confess, she would gladly have lain down on the forest-leaves, and died there, at Arthur Dimmesdale's feet.

"O Arthur," cried she, "forgive me! In all things else, I have striven to be true! Truth was the one virtue which I might have held fast, and did hold fast through all extremity; save when thy good,—thy life,—thy fame,—were put in question! Then I consented to a deception. But a lie is never good, even though death threaten on the other side! Dost thou not see what I would say? That old man!—the physician!—he whom they call Roger Chillingworth!—he was my husband!"

The minister looked at her, for an instant, with all that violence of passion, which—intermixed, in more shapes than one, with his higher, purer, softer qualities—was, in fact, the portion of him which the Devil claimed, and through which he sought to win the rest. Never was there a blacker or a fiercer frown, than Hester now encountered. For the brief space that it lasted, it was a dark transfiguration. But his character had been so much enfeebled by suffering, that even its lower energies were incapable of more than a temporary struggle. He sank down on the ground, and buried his face in his hands.

"I might have known it!" murmured he. "I did know it! Was not the secret told me in the natural recoil of my heart, at the first sight of him, and as often as I have seen him since? Why did I not understand? O Hester Prynne, thou little, little knowest all the horror of this thing! And the shame!—the indelicacy!—the horrible ugliness of this exposure of a sick and guilty heart to the very eye that would gloat over it! Woman, woman, thou art accountable for this! I cannot forgive thee!"

"Thou shalt forgive me!" cried Hester, flinging herself on the fallen leaves beside him. "Let God punish! Thou shalt forgive!"

With sudden and desperate tenderness, she threw her arms around him, and pressed his head against her bosom; little caring though his cheek rested on the scarlet letter. He would have released himself, but strove in vain to do so. Hester would not set him free, lest he should look her sternly in the face. All the world had frowned on her,—for seven long years had it frowned upon this lonely woman,—and still she bore it all, nor ever once turned away her firm, sad eyes. Heaven, likewise, had frowned upon her, and she had not died. But the frown of this pale, weak, sinful, and sorrow-stricken man was what Hester could not bear, and live!

"Wilt thou yet forgive me?" she repeated, over and over again. "Wilt thou not frown? Wilt thou forgive?"

"I do forgive you, Hester," replied the minister, at length, with a deep utterance out of an abyss of sadness, but no anger. "I freely forgive you now. May God forgive us both! We are not, Hester, the worst sinners in the world. There is one worse than even the polluted priest! That old man's revenge has been blacker than my sin. He has violated, in cold blood, the sanctity of a human heart. Thou and I, Hester, never did so!"

"Never, never!" whispered she. "What we did had a consecration of its own. We felt it so! We said so to each other! Hast thou forgotten it?"

"Hush, Hester!" said Arthur Dimmesdale, rising from the ground. "No; I have not forgotten!"

They sat down again, side by side, and hand clasped in hand, on the mossy trunk of the fallen tree. Life had never brought them a gloomier hour; it was the point whither their pathway had so long been tending, and darkening ever, as it stole along;—and yet it inclosed a charm that made them linger upon it, and claim another, and another, and, after all, another moment. The forest was obscure around them, and creaked with a blast that was passing through it. The boughs were tossing heavily above their heads; while one solemn old tree groaned dolefully to another, as if telling the sad story of the pair that sat beneath, or constrained to forebode evil to come.

And yet they lingered. How dreary looked the forest-track that led backward to the settlement, where Hester Prynne must take up again the burden of her ignominy, and the minister the hollow mockery of his good name! So they lingered an instant longer. No golden light had ever been so precious as the gloom of this dark forest. Here, seen only by his eyes, the scarlet letter need not burn into the bosom of the fallen woman! Here, seen only by her eyes, Arthur Dimmesdale, false to God and man, might be, for one moment, true!

He started at a thought that suddenly occurred to him.

"Hester," cried he, "here is a new horror! Roger Chillingworth knows your purpose to reveal his true character. Will he continue, then, to keep our secret? What will now be the course of his revenge?"

"There is a strange secrecy in his nature," replied Hester, thoughtfully; "and it has grown upon him by the hidden practices of his revenge. I deem it not likely that he will betray the secret. He will doubtless seek other means of satiating his dark passion."

"And I!—how am I to live longer, breathing the same air with this deadly enemy?" exclaimed Arthur Dimmesdale, shrinking within himself, and pressing his hand nervously against his heart,— a gesture that had grown involuntary with him. "Think for me, Hester! Thou art strong. Resolve for me!"

"Thou must dwell no longer with this man," said Hester, slowly and firmly. "Thy heart must be no longer under his evil eye!"

"It were far worse than death!" replied the minister. "But how to avoid it? What choice remains to me? Shall I lie down again on these withered leaves, where I cast myself when thou didst tell me what he was? Must I sink down there, and die at once?"

"Alas, what a ruin has befallen thee!" said Hester, with the tears gushing into her eyes. "Wilt thou die for very weakness? There is no other cause!"

"The judgment of God is on me," answered the conscience-stricken priest. "It is too mighty for me to struggle with!"

"Heaven would show mercy," rejoined Hester, "hadst thou but the strength to take advantage of it."

"Be thou strong for me!" answered he. "Advise me what to do."

"Is the world then so narrow?" exclaimed Hester Prynne, fixing her deep eyes on the minister's, and instinctively exercising a magnetic power over a spirit so shattered and subdued, that it could hardly hold itself erect. "Doth the universe lie within the compass of yonder town, which only a little time ago was but a leaf-strewn desert, as lonely as this around us? Whither leads yonder forest-track? Backward to the settlement, thou sayest! Yes; but onward, too! Deeper it goes, and deeper, into the wilderness, less plainly to be seen at every step; until, some few miles hence, the yellow leaves will show no vestige of the white man's tread. There thou art free! So brief a journey would bring thee from a world where thou hast been most wretched, to one where thou mayest still be happy! Is there not shade enough in all this boundless forest to hide thy heart from the gaze of Roger Chillingworth?"

"Yes, Hester; but only under the fallen leaves!" replied the minister, with a sad smile.

"Then there is the broad pathway of the sea!" continued Hester. "It brought thee hither. If thou so choose, it will bear thee back again. In our native land, whether in some remote rural village or in vast London,—or, surely, in Germany, in France, in pleasant Italy,—thou wouldst be beyond his power and knowledge! And what hast thou to do with all these iron men, and their opinions? They have kept thy better part in bondage too long already!"

"It cannot be!" answered the minister, listening as if he were called upon to realize a dream. "I am powerless to go. Wretched and sinful as I am, I have had no other thought than to drag on my earthly existence in the sphere where Providence hath placed me. Lost as my own soul is, I would still do what I may for other human souls! I dare not quit my post, though an unfaithful sentinel, whose sure reward is death and dishonor, when his dreary watch shall come to an end!"

"Thou are crushed under this seven years' weight of misery," replied Hester, fervently resolved to buoy him up with her own energy. "But thou shalt leave it all behind thee! It shall not cumber thy steps, as thou treadest along the forest-path; neither shalt thou freight the ship with it, if thou prefer to cross the sea. Leave this wreck and ruin here where it hath happened! Meddle no more with it! Begin all anew! Hast thou exhausted possibility in the failure of this one trial? Not so! The future is yet full of trial and success. There is happiness to be enjoyed! There is good to be done! Exchange this false life of thine for a true one. Be, if thy spirit summon thee to such a mission, the teacher and apostle of the red men. Or,—as is more thy nature,—be a scholar and a sage among the wisest and the most renowned of the cultivated world. Preach! Write! Act! Do anything, save to lie down and die! Give up this name of Arthur Dimmesdale, and make thyself another, and a high one, such as thou canst wear without fear or shame. Why shouldst thou tarry so much as one other day in the torments that have so gnawed into thy life!—that have made thee feeble to will and to do!—that will leave thee powerless even to repent! Up, and away!"

"O Hester!" cried Arthur Dimmesdale, in whose eyes a fitful light, kindled by her enthusiasm, flashed up and died away, "thou tellest of running a race to a man whose knees are tottering beneath him! I must die here. There is not the strength or courage left me to venture into the wide, strange, difficult world, alone!"

It was the last expression of the despondency of a broken spirit. He lacked energy to grasp the better fortune that seemed within his reach.

He repeated the word.

"Alone, Hester!"

"Thou shalt not go alone!" answered she, in a deep whisper.

Then, all was spoken!

XVIII. *A Flood of Sunshine*

Arthur Dimmesdale gazed into Hester's face with a look in which hope and joy shone out, indeed, but with fear betwixt them, and a kind of horror at her boldness, who had spoken what he vaguely hinted at, but dared not speak.

But Hester Prynne, with a mind of native courage and activity, and for so long a period not merely estranged, but outlawed, from society, had habituated herself to such latitude of speculation as was altogether foreign to the clergyman. She had wandered, without rule or guidance, in a moral wilderness; as vast, as intricate and shadowy, as the untamed forest, amid the gloom of which they were now holding a colloquy that was to decide their fate. Her intellect and heart had their home, as it were, in desert places, where she roamed as freely as the wild Indian in his woods. For years past she had looked from this estranged point of view at human institutions, and whatever priests or legislators had established; criticizing all with hardly more reverence than the Indian would feel for the clerical band, the judicial robe, the pillory, the gallows, the fireside, or the church. The tendency of her fate and fortunes had been to set her free. The scarlet letter was her passport into regions where other women dared not tread. Shame, Despair, Solitude! These had been her teachers,—stern and wild ones,— and they had made her strong, but taught her much amiss.

The minister, on the other hand, had never gone through an experience calculated to lead him beyond the scope of generally received laws; although, in a single instance, he had so fearfully transgressed one of the most sacred of them. But this had been a sin of passion, not of principle, nor even purpose. Since that wretched epoch, he had watched, with morbid zeal and minuteness, not his acts,—for those it was easy to arrange,—but each breath of emotion, and his every thought. At the head of the social system, as the clergymen of that day stood, he was only the more trammelled by its regulations, its principles, and even its prejudices. As a priest, the framework of his order inevitably hemmed him in. As a man who had once sinned, but who kept his conscience all alive and painfully sensitive by the fretting of an unhealed wound, he might have been supposed safer within the line of virtue, than if he had never sinned at all.

Thus, we seem to see that, as regarded Hester Prynne, the whole seven years of outlaw and ignominy had been little other than a preparation for this very hour. But Arthur Dimmesdale! Were such a man once more to fall, what plea could be urged in extenuation of his crime? None; unless it avail him somewhat, that he was broken down by long and exquisite suffering; that his mind was darkened and confused by the very remorse which harrowed it; that, between fleeing as an avowed criminal, and remaining as a hypocrite, conscience might find it hard to strike the balance; that it was human to avoid the peril of death and infamy, and the inscrutable machinations of an enemy; that, finally, to this poor pilgrim, on his dreary and desert path, faint, sick, miserable, there appeared a glimpse of human affection and sympathy, a new life, and a true one, in exchange for the heavy doom which he was now expiating. And be the stern and sad truth spoken, that the breach which guilt has once made into the human soul is never, in this mortal state, repaired. It may be watched and guarded; so that the enemy shall not force his way again into the citadel, and might even, in his subsequent assaults, select some other avenue, in preference to that where he had formerly succeeded. But there is still the ruined wall, and, near it, the stealthy tread of the foe that would win over again his unforgotten triumph.

The struggle, if there were one, need not be described. Let it suffice, that the clergyman resolved to flee, and not alone.

"If, in all these past seven years," thought he, "I could recall one instant of peace or hope, I would yet endure, for the sake of that earnest of Heaven's mercy. But now,—since I am irrevocably doomed,—wherefore should I not snatch the solace allowed to the condemned culprit before his execution? Or, if this be the path to a better life, as Hester would persuade me, I surely give up no fairer prospect by pursuing it! Neither can I any longer live without her companionship; so powerful is she to sustain,—so tender to soothe! O Thou to whom I dare not lift mine eyes, wilt Thou yet pardon me!"

"Thou wilt go!" said Hester calmly, as he met her glance.

The decision once made, a glow of strange enjoyment threw its flickering brightness over the trouble of his breast. It was the exhilarating effect—upon a prisoner just escaped from the dungeon of his own heart—of breathing the wild, free atmosphere of an unredeemed, unchristianized, lawless region. His spirit rose, as it were, with a bound, and attained a nearer prospect of the sky, than throughout all the misery which had kept him grovelling on the earth. Of a deeply religious temperament, there was inevitably a tinge of the devotional in his mood.

"Do I feel joy again?" cried he, wondering at himself. "Methought the germ of it was dead in me! O Hester, thou art my better angel! I seem to have flung myself—sick, sin-stained, and sorrow-blackened—down upon these forest-leaves, and to have risen up all made anew, and with new powers to glorify Him that hath been merciful! This is already the better life! Why did we not find it sooner?"

"Let us not look back," answered Hester Prynne. "The past is gone! Wherefore should we linger upon it now? See! With this symbol, I undo it all, and make it as it had never been!"

So speaking, she undid the clasp that fastened the scarlet letter, and, taking it from her bosom, threw it to a distance among the withered leaves. The mystic token alighted on the hither verge of the stream. With a hand's breadth farther flight it would have fallen into the water, and have given the little brook another woe to carry onward, besides the unintelligible tale which it still kept murmuring about. But there lay the embroidered letter, glittering like a lost jewel, which some ill-fated wanderer might pick up, and thenceforth be haunted by strange phantoms of guilt, sinkings of the heart, and unaccountable misfortune.

The stigma gone, Hester heaved a long, deep sigh, in which the burden of shame and anguish departed from her spirit. O exquisite relief! She had not known the weight, until she felt the freedom! By another impulse, she took off the formal cap that confined her hair; and down it fell upon her shoulders, dark and rich, with at once a shadow and a light in its abundance, and imparting the charm of softness to her features. There played around her mouth, and beamed out of her eyes, a radiant and tender smile, that seemed gushing from the very heart of womanhood. A crimson flush was glowing on her cheek, that had been long so pale. Her sex, her youth, and the whole richness of her beauty, came back from what men call the irrevocable past, and clustered themselves, with her maiden hope, and a happiness before unknown, within the magic circle of this hour. And, as if the gloom of the earth and sky had been but the effluence of these two mortal hearts, it vanished with their sorrow. All at once, as with a sudden smile of heaven, forth burst the sunshine, pouring a very flood into the obscure forest, gladdening each green leaf, transmuting the yellow fallen ones to gold, and gleaming adown the gray trunks of the solemn trees. The objects that had made a shadow hitherto, embodied the brightness now. The course of the little brook might be traced by its merry gleam afar into the wood's heart of mystery, which had become a mystery of joy.

Such was the sympathy of Nature—that wild, heathen Nature

of the forest, never subjugated by human law, nor illumined by higher truth—with the bliss of these two spirits! Love, whether newly born, or aroused from a deathlike slumber, must always create a sunshine, filling the heart so full of radiance, that it overflows upon the outward world. Had the forest still kept its gloom, it would have been bright in Hester's eyes, and bright in Arthur Dimmesdale's!

Hester looked at him with the thrill of another joy.

"Thou must know Pearl!" said she. "Our little Pearl! Thou hast seen her,—yes, I know it!—but thou wilt see her now with other eyes. She is a strange child! I hardly comprehend her! But thou wilt love her dearly, as I do, and wilt advise me how to deal with her."

"Dost thou think the child will be glad to know me?" asked the minister, somewhat uneasily. "I have long shrunk from children, because they often show a distrust,—a backwardness to be familiar with me. I have even been afraid of little Pearl!"

"Ah, that was sad!" answered the mother. "But she will love thee dearly, and thou her. She is not far off. I will call her! Pearl! Pearl!"

"I see the child," observed the minister. "Yonder she is, standing in a streak of sunshine, a good way off, on the other side of the brook. So thou thinkest the child will love me?"

Hester smiled, and again called to Pearl, who was visible, at some distance, as the minister had described her, like a bright-apparelled vision, in a sunbeam, which fell down upon her through an arch of boughs. The ray quivered to and fro, making her figure dim or distinct,—now like a real child, now like a child's spirit,—as the splendor went and came again. She heard her mother's voice, and approached slowly through the forest.

Pearl had not found the hour pass wearisomely, while her mother sat talking with the clergyman. The great black forest—stern as it showed itself to those who brought the guilt and troubles of the world into its bosom—became the playmate of the lonely infant, as well as it knew how. Sombre as it was, it put on the kindest of its moods to welcome her. It offered her the partridge-berries, the growth of the preceding autumn, but ripening only in the spring, and now red as drops of blood upon the withered leaves. These Pearl gathered, and was pleased with their wild flavor. The small denizens of the wilderness hardly took pains to move out of her path. A partridge, indeed, with a brood of ten behind her, ran forward threateningly, but soon repented of her fierceness, and clucked to her young ones not to be afraid. A pigeon, alone on a low branch, allowed Pearl to come beneath, and uttered a sound as much of greeting as alarm. A squirrel, from the lofty depths of his domestic tree, chattered either in anger or merriment,—for a squirrel is such a choleric and humorous little personage that it is hard to distinguish between his moods,—so he chattered at the child, and flung down a nut upon her head. It was a last year's nut, and already gnawed by his sharp tooth. A fox, startled from his sleep by her light footstep on the leaves, looked inquisitively at Pearl, as doubting whether it were better to steal off, or renew his nap on the same spot. A wolf, it is said,—but here the tale has surely lapsed into the improbable,—came up, and smelt of Pearl's robe, and offered his savage head to be patted by her hand. The truth seems to be, however, that the mother-forest, and these wild things which it nourished, all recognized a kindred wildness in the human child.

And she was gentler here than in the grassy-margined streets of the settlement, or in her mother's cottage. The flowers appeared to know it; and one and another whispered, as she passed, "Adorn thyself with me, thou beautiful child, adorn thyself with me!"— and, to please them, Pearl gathered the violets, and anemones, and columbines, and some twigs of the freshest green, which the old trees held down before her eyes. With these she decorated her hair, and her young waist, and became a nymph-child, or an infant dryad, or whatever else was in closest sympathy with the antique wood. In such guise had Pearl adorned herself, when she heard her mother's voice, and came slowly back.

Slowly; for she saw the clergyman!

XIX. *The Child at the Brook-Side*

"Thou wilt love her dearly," repeated Hester Prynne, as she and the minister sat watching little Pearl. "Dost thou not think her beautiful? And see with what natural skill she has made those simple flowers adorn her! Had she gathered pearls, and diamonds, and rubies, in the wood, they could not have become her better. She is a splendid child! But I know whose brow she has!"

"Dost thou know, Hester," said Arthur Dimmesdale, with an unquiet smile, "that this dear child, tripping about always at thy side, hath caused me many an alarm? Methought—O Hester, what a thought is that, and how terrible to dread it!—that my own features were partly repeated in her face, and so strikingly that the world might see them! But she is mostly thine!"

"No, no! Not mostly!" answered the mother with a tender smile. "A little longer, and thou needest not to be afraid to trace whose child she is. But how strangely beautiful she looks, with those wild flowers in her hair! It is as if one of the fairies, whom we left in our dear old England, had decked her out to meet us."

It was with a feeling which neither of them had ever before experienced, that they sat and watched Pearl's slow advance. In her was visible the tie that united them. She had been offered to the world, these seven years past, as the living hieroglyphic, in which was revealed the secret they so darkly sought to hide,—all written in this symbol,—all plainly manifest,—had there been a prophet or magician skilled to read the character of flame! And Pearl was the oneness of their being. Be the foregone evil what it might, how could they doubt that their earthly lives and future destinies were conjoined, when they beheld at once the material union, and the spiritual idea, in whom they met, and were to dwell immortally together? Thoughts like these—and perhaps other thoughts, which they did not acknowledge or define—threw an awe about the child, as she came onward.

"Let her see nothing strange—no passion nor eagerness—in thy way of accosting her," whispered Hester. "Our Pearl is a fitful and fantastic little elf, sometimes. Especially, she is seldom tolerant of emotion, when she does not fully comprehend the why and wherefore. But the child hath strong affections! She loves me, and will love thee!"

"Thou canst not think," said the minister, glancing aside at Hester Prynne, "how my heart dreads this interview, and yearns for it! But, in truth, as I already told thee, children are not readily won to be familiar with me. They will not climb my knee, nor prattle in my ear, nor answer to my smile; but stand apart, and eye me strangely. Even little babes, when I take them in my arms, weep bitterly. Yet Pearl, twice in her little lifetime, hath been kind to me! The first time,—thou knowest it well! The last was when thou ledst her with thee to the house of yonder stern old Governor."

"And thou didst plead so bravely in her behalf and mine!" answered the mother. "I remember it; and so shall little Pearl. Fear nothing! She may be strange and shy at first, but will soon learn to love thee!"

By this time Pearl had reached the margin of the brook, and stood on the farther side, gazing silently at Hester and the clergyman, who still sat together on the mossy tree-trunk, waiting to receive her. Just where she had paused the brook chanced to form a pool, so smooth and quiet that it reflected a perfect image of her little figure, with all the brilliant picturesqueness of her beauty, in its adornment of flowers and wreathed foliage, but more refined and spiritualized than the reality. This image, so nearly identical with the living Pearl, seemed to communicate somewhat of its own shadowy and intangible quality to the child herself. It was strange, the way in which Pearl stood, looking so steadfastly at them through the dim medium of the forest-gloom; herself, meanwhile, all glorified with a ray of sunshine, that was attracted thitherward as by a certain sympathy. In the brook beneath stood another child,—another and the same,—with likewise its ray of golden light. Hester felt herself, in some indistinct and tantalizing manner, estranged from Pearl; as if the child, in her lonely ramble through the forest, had strayed out of the sphere in which she and her mother dwelt together, and was now vainly seeking to return to it.

There was both truth and error in the impression; the child and mother were estranged, but through Hester's fault, not Pearl's. Since the latter rambled from her side, another inmate had been admitted within the circle of the mother's feelings, and so modified the aspect of them all, that Pearl, the returning wanderer, could not find her wonted place, and hardly knew where she was.

"I have a strange fancy," observed the sensitive minister, "that this brook is the boundary between two worlds, and that thou canst never meet thy Pearl again. Or is she an elfish spirit, who, as the legends of our childhood taught us, is forbidden to cross a running stream? Pray hasten her; for this delay has already imparted a tremor to my nerves."

"Come, dearest child!" said Hester encouragingly, and stretching out both her arms. "How slow thou art! When hast thou been so sluggish before now? Here is a friend of mine, who must be thy friend also. Thou wilt have twice as much love, henceforward, as thy mother alone could give thee! Leap across the brook and come to us. Thou canst leap like a young deer!"

Pearl, without responding in any manner to these honey-sweet expressions, remained on the other side of the brook. Now she fixed her bright, wild eyes on her mother, now on the minister, and now included them both in the same glance; as if to detect and explain to herself the relation which they bore to one another. For some unaccountable reason, as Arthur Dimmesdale felt the child's eyes upon himself, his hand—with that gesture so habitual as to have become involuntary—stole over his heart. At length, assuming a singular air of authority, Pearl stretched out her hand, with the small forefinger extended, and pointing evidently towards her mother's breast. And beneath, in the mirror of the brook, there was the flower-girdled and sunny image of little Pearl, pointing her small forefinger too.

"Thou strange child, why dost thou not come to me?" exclaimed Hester.

Pearl still pointed with her forefinger; and a frown gathered on her brow; the more impressive from the childish, the almost baby-like aspect of the features that conveyed it. As her mother still kept beckoning to her, and arraying her face in a holiday suit of unaccustomed smiles, the child stamped her foot with a yet more imperious look and gesture. In the brook, again, was the fantastic beauty of the image, with its reflected frown, its pointed finger, and imperious gesture, giving emphasis to the aspect of little Pearl.

"Hasten, Pearl; or I shall be angry with thee!" cried Hester Prynne, who, however inured to such behaviour on the elf-child's part at other seasons, was naturally anxious for a more seemly deportment now. "Leap across the brook, naughty child, and run hither! Else I must come to thee!"

But Pearl, not a whit startled at her mother's threats, any more than mollified by her entreaties, now suddenly burst into a fit of passion, gesticulating violently, and throwing her small figure into the most extravagant contortions. She accompanied this wild outbreak with piercing shrieks, which the woods reverberated on all sides; so that, alone as she was in her childish and unreasonable wrath, it seemed as if a hidden multitude were lending her their sympathy and encouragement. Seen in the brook, once more, was the shadowy wrath of Pearl's image, crowned and girdled with flowers, but stamping its foot, wildly gesticulating, and, in the midst of all, still pointing its small forefinger at Hester's bosom!

"I see what ails the child," whispered Hester to the clergyman, and turning pale in spite of a strong effort to conceal her trouble and annoyance. "Children will not abide any, the slightest, change in the accustomed aspect of things that are daily before their eyes. Pearl misses something which she has always seen me wear!"

"I pray you," answered the minister, "if thou hast any means of pacifying the child, do it forthwith! Save it were the cankered wrath of an old witch, like Mistress Hibbins," added he, attempting to smile, "I know nothing that I would not sooner encounter than this passion in a child. In Pearl's young beauty, as in the wrinkled witch, it has a preternatural effect. Pacify her, if thou lovest me!"

Hester turned again towards Pearl, with a crimson blush upon her cheek, a conscious glance aside at the clergyman, and then a heavy sigh; while, even before she had time to speak, the blush yielded to a deadly pallor.

"Pearl," said she, sadly, "look down at thy feet! There!—before thee!—on the hither side of the brook!"

The child turned her eyes to the point indicated; and there lay the scarlet letter, so close upon the margin of the stream, that the gold embroidery was reflected in it.

"Bring it hither!" said Hester.

"Come thou and take it up!" answered Pearl.

"Was ever such a child!" observed Hester aside to the minister. "O, I have much to tell thee about her. But, in very truth, she is right as regards this hateful token. I must bear its torture yet a little longer,—only a few days longer,—until we shall have left this region, and look back hither as to a land which we have dreamed of. The forest cannot hide it! The mid-ocean shall take it from my hand, and swallow it up for ever!"

With these words, she advanced to the margin of the brook, took up the scarlet letter, and fastened it again into her bosom. Hopefully, but a moment ago, as Hester had spoken of drowning it in the deep sea, there was a sense of inevitable doom upon her, as she thus received back this deadly symbol from the hand of fate. She had flung it into infinite space!—she had drawn an hour's free breath!—and here again was the scarlet misery, glittering on the old spot! So it ever is, whether thus typified or no, that an evil deed invests itself with the character of doom. Hester next gathered up the heavy tresses of her hair, and confined them beneath her cap. As if there were a withering spell in the sad letter, her beauty, the warmth and richness of her womanhood, departed, like fading sunshine; and a gray shadow seemed to fall across her.

When the dreary change was wrought, she extended her hand to Pearl.

"Dost thou know thy mother now, child?" asked she, reproachfully, but with a subdued tone. "Wilt thou come across the brook, and own thy mother, now that she has her shame upon her,—now that she is sad?"

"Yes; now I will!" answered the child, bounding across the brook, and clasping Hester in her arms. "Now thou art my mother indeed! And I am thy little Pearl!"

In a mood of tenderness that was not usual with her, she drew down her mother's head, and kissed her brow and both her cheeks. But then- -by a kind of necessity that always impelled this child to alloy whatever comfort she might chance to give with a throb of anguish—Pearl put up her mouth, and kissed the scarlet letter too!

"That was not kind!" said Hester. "When thou hast shown me a little love, thou mockest me!"

"Why doth the minister sit yonder?" asked Pearl.

"He waits to welcome thee," replied her mother. "Come thou, and entreat his blessing! He loves thee, my little Pearl, and loves thy mother too. Wilt thou not love him? Come! he longs to greet thee!"

"Doth he love us?" said Pearl, looking up with acute intelligence into her mother's face. "Will he go back with us, hand in hand, we three together, into the town?"

"Not now, dear child," answered Hester. "But in days to come he will walk hand in hand with us. We will have a home and fireside of our own; and thou shalt sit upon his knee; and he will teach thee many things, and love thee dearly. Thou wilt love him; wilt thou not?"

"And will he always keep his hand over his heart?" inquired Pearl.

"Foolish child, what a question is that!" exclaimed her mother. "Come and ask his blessing!"

But, whether influenced by the jealousy that seems instinctive with every petted child towards a dangerous rival, or from whatever caprice of her freakish nature, Pearl would show no favor to the clergyman. It was only by an exertion of force that her mother brought her up to him, hanging back, and manifesting her reluctance by odd grimaces; of which, ever since her babyhood, she had possessed a singular variety, and could transform her mobile physiognomy into a series of different aspects, with a new mischief in them, each and all. The minister—painfully embarrassed, but hoping that a kiss might prove a talisman to admit him into the child's kindlier regards—bent forward, and impressed one on her brow. Hereupon, Pearl broke away from her mother, and, running to the brook, stooped over it, and bathed her forehead, until the unwelcome kiss was quite washed off, and diffused through a long lapse of the gliding water. She then remained apart, silently watching Hester and the clergyman; while they talked together, and made such arrangements as were suggested by their new position, and the purposes soon to be fulfilled.

And now this fateful interview had come to a close. The dell was to be left a solitude among its dark, old trees, which, with their multitudinous tongues, would whisper long of what had passed there, and no mortal be the wiser. And the melancholy brook would add this other tale to the mystery with which its little heart was already overburdened, and whereof it still kept up a murmuring babble, with not a whit more cheerfulness of tone than for ages heretofore.

XX. *The Minister in a Maze*

As the minister departed, in advance of Hester Prynne and little Pearl, he threw a backward glance; half expecting that he should discover only some faintly traced features or outline of the mother and the child, slowly fading into the twilight of the woods. So great a vicissitude in his life could not at once be received as real. But there was Hester, clad in her gray robe, still standing beside the tree-trunk, which some blast had overthrown a long antiquity ago, and which time had ever since been covering with moss, so that these two fated ones, with earth's heaviest burden on them, might there sit down together, and find a single hour's rest and solace. And there was Pearl, too, lightly dancing from the margin of the brook,—now that the intrusive third person was gone,—and taking her old place by her mother's side. So the minister had not fallen asleep, and dreamed!

In order to free his mind from this indistinctness and duplicity of impression, which vexed it with a strange disquietude, he recalled and more thoroughly defined the plans which Hester and himself had sketched for their departure. It had been determined between them, that the Old World, with its crowds and cities, offered them a more eligible shelter and concealment than the wilds of New England, or all America, with its alternatives of an Indian wigwam, or the few settlements of Europeans, scattered thinly along the seaboard. Not to speak of the clergyman's health, so inadequate to sustain the hardships of a forest life, his native gifts, his culture, and his entire development would secure him a home only in the midst of civilization and refinement; the higher the state, the more delicately adapted to it the man. In furtherance of this choice, it so happened that a ship lay in the harbour; one of those questionable cruisers, frequent at that day, which, without being absolutely outlaws of the deep, yet roamed over its surface with a remarkable irresponsibility of character. This vessel had recently arrived from the Spanish Main, and, within three days' time, would sail for Bristol. Hester Prynne—whose vocation, as a self-enlisted Sister of Charity, had brought her acquainted wth the captain and crew—could take upon herself to secure the passage of two individuals and a child, with all the secrecy which circumstances rendered more than desirable.

The minister had inquired of Hester, with no little interest, the precise time at which the vessel might be expected to depart. It would probably be on the fourth day from the present. "That is most fortunate!" he had then said to himself. Now, why the Reverend Mr. Dimmesdale considered it so very fortunate, we hesitate to reveal. Nevertheless,—to hold nothing back from the reader,—it was because, on the third day from the present, he was to preach the Election Sermon;[8] and, as such an occasion formed an honorable epoch in the life of a New England clergyman, he could not have chanced upon a more suitable mode and time of terminating his professional career. "At least, they shall say of me," thought this exemplary man, "that I leave no public duty unperformed, nor

8. The Election Sermon was preached on the inauguration day of the newly elected governor, a customary observ- ance coinciding also with the opening session of the legislature. It was the highest honor accorded a clergyman.

ill performed!" Sad, indeed, that an introspection so profound and acute as this poor minister's should be so miserably deceived! We have had, and may still have, worse things to tell of him; but none, we apprehend, so pitiably weak; no evidence, at once so slight and irrefragable, of a subtle disease, that had long since begun to eat into the real substance of his character. No man, for any considerable period, can wear one face to himself, and another to the multitude, without finally getting bewildered as to which may be the true.

The excitement of Mr. Dimmesdale's feelings, as he returned from his interview with Hester, lent him unaccustomed physical energy, and hurried him townward at a rapid pace. The pathway among the woods seemed wilder, more uncouth with its rude natural obstacles, and less trodden by the foot of man, than he remembered it on his outward journey. But he leaped across the plashy places, thrust himself through the clinging underbrush, climbed the ascent, plunged into the hollow, and overcame, in short, all the difficulties of the track, with an unweariable activity that astonished him. He could not but recall how feebly, and with what frequent pauses for breath, he had toiled over the same ground only two days before. As he drew near the town, he took an impression of change from the series of familiar objects that presented themselves. It seemed not yesterday, not one, nor two, but many days, or even years ago, since he had quitted them. There, indeed, was each former trace of the street, as he remembered it, and all the peculiarities of the houses, with the due multitude of gable-peaks, and a weathercock at every point where his memory suggested one. Not the less, however, came this importunately obtrusive sense of change. The same was true as regarded the acquaintances whom he met, and all the well-known shapes of human life, about the little town. They looked neither older nor younger, now; the beards of the aged were no whiter, nor could the creeping babe of yesterday walk on his feet to-day; it was impossible to describe in what respect they differed from the individuals on whom he had so recently bestowed a parting glance; and yet the minister's deepest sense seemed to inform him of their mutability. A similar impression struck him most remarkably, as he passed under the walls of his own church. The edifice had so very strange, and yet so familiar, an aspect, that Mr. Dimmesdale's mind vibrated between two ideas; either that he had seen it only in a dream hitherto, or that he was merely dreaming about it now.

This phenomenon, in the various shapes which it assumed, indicated no external change, but so sudden and important a change in the spectator of the familiar scene, that the intervening space of a single day had operated on his consciousness like the lapse of years. The minister's own will, and Hester's will, and the fate that grew between them, had wrought this transformation. It was the same town as heretofore; but the same minister returned not from the forest. He might have said to the friends who greeted him,—"I am not the man for whom you take me! I left him yonder in the forest, withdrawn into a secret dell, by a mossy tree-trunk, and near a melancholy brook! Go, seek your minister, and see if his emaciated figure, his thin cheek, his white, heavy, pain-wrinkled brow, be not flung down there like a cast-off garment!" His friends, no doubt, would still have insisted with him,—"Thou art thyself the man!"—but the error would have been their own, not his.

Before Mr. Dimmesdale reached home, his inner man gave him other evidences of a revolution in the sphere of thought and feeling. In truth, nothing short of a total change of dynasty and moral code, in that interior kingdom, was adequate to account for the impulses now communicated to the unfortunate and startled minister. At every step he was incited to do some strange, wild, wicked thing or other, with a sense that it would be at once involuntary and intentional; in spite of himself, yet growing out of a profounder self than that which opposed the impulse. For instance, he met one of his own deacons. The good old man addressed him with the paternal affection and patriarchal privilege, which his venerable age, his upright and holy character, and his station in the Church, entitled him to use; and, conjoined with this, the deep, almost worshipping respect, which the minister's professional and private claims alike demanded. Never was there a more beautiful example of how the majesty of age and wisdom may comport with the obeisance and respect enjoined upon it, as from a lower social rank and inferior order of endowment, towards a higher. Now, during a conversation of some two or three moments between the Reverend Mr. Dimmesdale and this excellent and hoary-bearded deacon, it was only by the most careful self-control that the former could refrain from uttering certain blasphemous suggestions that rose into his mind, respecting the communion-supper. He absolutely trembled and turned pale as ashes, lest his tongue should wag itself, in utterance of these horrible matters, and plead his own consent for so doing, without his having fairly given it. And, even with this terror in his heart, he could hardly avoid laughing to imagine how the sanctified old patriarchal deacon would have been petrified by his minister's impiety!

Again, another incident of the same nature. Hurrying along the street, the Reverend Mr. Dimmesdale encountered the eldest female member of his church; a most pious and exemplary old dame; poor, widowed, lonely, and with a heart as full of reminiscences about her dead husband and children, and her dead friends of long ago, as a burial-ground is full of storied gravestones. Yet all this, which would else have been such heavy sorrow, was made almost a solemn joy to her devout old soul by religious consolations and the truths of Scripture, wherewith she had fed herself continually for more than thirty years. And, since Mr. Dimmesdale had taken her in charge, the good grandam's chief earthly comfort—which, unless it had been likewise a heavenly comfort, could have been none at all—was to meet her pastor, whether casually, or of set purpose, and be refreshed with a word of warm, fragrant, heaven-breathing Gospel truth from his beloved lips into her dulled, but rapturously attentive ear. But, on this occasion, up to the moment of putting his lips to the old woman's ear, Mr. Dimmesdale, as the great enemy of souls would have it, could recall no text of Scripture, nor aught else, except a brief, pithy, and, as it then appeared to him, unanswerable argument against the immortality of the human soul. The instilment thereof into her mind would probably have caused this aged sister to drop down dead, at once, as by the effect of an intensely poisonous infusion. What he really did whisper, the minister could never afterwards recollect. There was, perhaps, a fortunate disorder in his utterance, which failed to impart any distinct idea to the good widow's comprehension, or which Providence interpreted after a method of its own. Assuredly, as the minister looked back, he beheld an expression of divine gratitude and ecstasy that seemed like the shine of the celestial city on her face, so wrinkled and ashy pale.

Again, a third instance. After parting from the old church-member, he met the youngest sister of them all. It was a maiden newly won—and won by the Reverend Mr. Dimmesdale's own sermon, on the Sabbath after his vigil—to barter the transitory pleasures of the world for the heavenly hope, that was to assume brighter substance as life grew dark around her, and which would gild the utter gloom with final glory. She was fair and pure as a lily that had bloomed in Paradise. The minister knew well that he was himself enshrined within the stainless sanctity of her heart, which hung its snowy curtains about his image, imparting to religion the warmth of love, and to love a religious purity. Satan, that afternoon, had surely led the poor young girl away from her mother's side, and thrown her into the pathway of this sorely tempted, or—shall we not rather say?—this lost and desperate man. As she drew nigh, the arch-fiend whispered him to condense into small compass and drop into her tender bosom a germ of evil that would be sure to blossom darkly soon, and bear black fruit betimes. Such was his sense of power over this virgin soul, trusting him as she did, that the minister felt potent to blight all the field of innocence with but one wicked look, and develop all its opposite with but a word. So—with a mightier struggle than he had yet sustained—he held his Geneva cloak before his face, and hurried onward, making no sign of recognition, and leaving the young sister to digest his rudeness as she might. She ransacked her conscience,—which was full of harmless little matters, like her pocket or her work-bag,—and took herself to task, poor thing, for a thousand imaginary faults; and went about her household duties with swollen eyelids the next morning.

Before the minister had time to celebrate his victory over this last temptation, he was conscious of another impulse, more ludicrous, and almost as horrible. It was,—we blush to tell it,—it was to stop short in the road, and teach some very wicked words to a knot of little Puritan children who were playing there, and had just begun to talk. Denying himself this freak, as unworthy of his cloth, he met a drunken seaman, one of the ship's crew from the Spanish Main. And, here, since he had so valiantly forborne all other wickedness, poor Mr. Dimmesdale longed, at least, to shake hands with the tarry blackguard, and recreate himself with a few improper jests, such as dissolute sailors so abound with, and a volley of good, round, solid, satisfactory, and heaven-defying oaths! It was not so much a better principle, as partly his natural good taste, and still more his buckramed habit of clerical decorum, that carried him safely through the latter crisis.

"What is it that haunts and tempts me thus?" cried the minister to himself, at length, pausing in the street, and striking his hand against his forehead. "Am I mad? or am I given over utterly to the fiend? Did I make a contract with him in the forest, and sign it with my blood? And does he now summon me to its fulfilment, by suggesting the performance of ever wickedness which his most foul imagination can conceive?"

At the moment when the Reverend Mr. Dimmesdale thus communed with himself, and struck his forehead with his hand, old Mistress Hibbins, the reputed witch-lady, is said to have been passing by. She made a very grand appearance; having on a high head-dress, a rich gown of velvet, and a ruff done up with the famous yellow starch, of which Ann Turner, her especial friend, had taught her the secret, before this last good lady had been hanged for Sir Thomas Overbury's murder. Whether the witch had read the minister's thoughts, or no, she came to a full stop, looked shrewdly into his face, smiled craftily, and—though little given to converse with clergymen—began a conversation.

"So, reverend Sir, you have made a visit into the forest," observed the witch-lady, nodding her high head-dress at him. "The next time, I pray you to allow me only a fair warning, and I shall be proud to bear you company. Without taking overmuch upon myself, my good word will go far towards gaining any strange gentleman a fair reception from yonder potentate you wot of!"

"I profess madam," answered the clergyman, with a grave obeisance, such as the lady's rank demanded, and his own good-breeding made imperative,—"I profess, on my conscience and character, that I am utterly bewildered as touching the purport of your words! I went not into the forest to seek a potentate; neither do I, at any future time, design a visit thither, with a view to gaining the favor of such personage. My one sufficient object was to greet that pious friend of mine, the Apostle Eliot, and rejoice with him over the many precious souls he hath won from heathendom!"

"Ha, ha, ha!" cackled the old witch-lady, still nodding her high head-dress at the minister. "Well, well, we must needs talk thus in the daytime! You carry it off like an old hand! But at midnight, and in the forest, we shall have other talk together!"

She passed on with her aged stateliness, but often turning back her head and smiling at him, like one willing to recognize a secret intimacy of connection.

"Have I then sold myself," thought the minister, "to the fiend whom, if men say true, this yellow-starched and velveted old hag has chosen for her prince and master!"

The wretched minister! He had made a bargain very like it! Tempted by a dream of happiness, he had yielded himself with deliberate choice, as he had never done before, to what he knew was deadly sin. And the infectious poison of that sin had been thus rapidly diffused throughout his moral system. It had stupefied all blessed impulses, and awakened into vivid life the whole brotherhood of bad ones. Scorn, bitterness, unprovoked malignity, gratuitous desire of ill, ridicule of whatever was good and holy, all awoke, to tempt, even while they frightened him. And his encounter with old Mistress Hibbins, if it were a real incident, did but show his sympathy and fellowship with wicked mortals and the world of perverted spirits.

He had by this time reached his dwelling, on the edge of the burial-ground, and, hastening up the stairs, took refuge in his study. The minister was glad to have reached this shelter, without first betraying himself to the world by any of those strange and wicked eccentricities to which he had been continually impelled while passing through the streets. He entered the accustomed room, and looked around him on its books, its windows, its fireplace, and the tapestried comfort of the walls, with the same perception of strangeness that had haunted him throughout his walk from the forest-dell into the town, and thitherward. Here he had studied and written; here, gone through fast and vigil, and come forth half alive; here, striven to pray; here, borne a hundred thousand agonies! There was the Bible, in its rich old Hebrew, with Moses and the Prophets speaking to him, and God's voice through all! There, on the table, with the inky pen beside it, was an unfinished sermon, with a sentence broken in the midst, where his thoughts had ceased to gush out upon the page two days before. He knew that it was himself, the thin and white-cheeked minister, who had done and suffered these things, and written thus far into the Election Sermon! But he seemed to stand apart, and eye this former self with scornful, pitying, but half-envious curiosity. That self was gone! Another man had returned out of the forest; a wiser one; with a knowledge of hidden mysteries which the simplicity of the former never could have reached. A bitter kind of knowledge that!

While occupied with these reflections, a knock came at the door of the study, and the minister said, "Come in!"—not wholly devoid of an idea that he might behold an evil spirit. And so he did! It was old Roger Chillingworth that entered. The minister stood, white and speechless, with one hand on the Hebrew Scriptures, and the other spread upon his breast.

"Welcome home, reverend Sir!" said the physician. "And how found you that godly man, the Apostle Eliot? But methinks, dear Sir, you look pale; as if the travel through the wilderness had been too sore for you. Will not my aid be requisite to put you in heart and strength to preach your Election Sermon?"

"Nay, I think not so," rejoined the Reverend Mr. Dimmesdale. "My journey, and the sight of the holy Apostle yonder, and the free air which I have breathed, have done me good, after so long confinement in my study. I think to need no more of your drugs, my kind physician, good though they be, and administered by a friendly hand."

All this time, Roger Chillingworth was looking at the minister with the grave and intent regard of a physician towards his patient. But, in spite of this outward show, the latter was almost convinced of the old man's knowledge, or, at least, his confident suspicion, with respect to his own interview with Hester Prynne. The physician knew, then, that, in the minister's regard, he was no longer a trusted friend, but his bitterest enemy. So much being known, it would appear natural that a part of it should be expressed. It is singular, however, how long a time often passes before words embody things; and with what security two persons, who choose to avoid a certain subject, may approach its very verge, and retire without disturbing it. Thus, the minister felt no apprehension that

Roger Chillingworth would touch, in express words, upon the real position which they sustained towards one another. Yet did the physician, in his dark way, creep frightfully near the secret.

"Were it not better," said he, "that you use my poor skill tonight? Verily, dear Sir, we must take pains to make you strong and vigorous for this occasion of the Election discourse. The people look for great things from you; apprehending that another year may come about, and find their pastor gone."

"Yea, to another world," replied the minister, with pious resignation. "Heaven grant it be a better one; for, in good sooth, I hardly think to tarry with my flock through the flitting seasons of another year! But, touching your medicine, kind Sir, in my present frame of body I need it not."

"I joy to hear it," answered the physician. "It may be that my remedies, so long administered in vain, begin now to take due effect. Happy man were I, and well deserving of New England's gratitude, could I achieve this cure!"

"I thank you from my heart, most watchful friend," said the Reverend Mr. Dimmesdale, with a solemn smile. "I thank you, and can but requite your good deeds with my prayers."

"A good man's prayers are golden recompense!" rejoined old Roger Chillingworth, as he took his leave. "Yea, they are the current gold coin of the New Jerusalem, with the King's own mintmark on them!"

Left alone, the minister summoned a servant of the house, and requested food, which, being set before him, he ate with ravenous appetite. Then, flinging the already written pages of the Election Sermon into the fire, he forthwith began another, which he wrote with such an impulsive flow of thought and emotion, that he fancied himself inspired; and only wondered that Heaven should see fit to transmit the grand and solemn music of its oracles through so foul an organ-pipe as he. However, leaving that mystery to solve itself, or go unsolved for ever, he drove his task onward, with earnest haste and ecstasy. Thus the night fled away, as if it were a winged steed, and he careering on it; morning came, and peeped blushing through the curtains; and at last sunrise threw a golden beam into the study, and laid it right across the minister's bedazzled eyes. There he was, with the pen still between his fingers, and a vast, immeasurable tract of written space behind him!

XXI. *The New England Holiday*

Betimes in the morning of the day[9] on which the new Governor was to receive his office at the hands of the people, Hester

9. "The day" of the inauguration was three days after the meeting of Hester and Arthur in the forest. The concluding action of the novel occurs wholly on this day.

Prynne and little Pearl came into the market-place. It was already thronged with the craftsmen and other plebeian inhabitants of the town, in considerable numbers; among whom, likewise, were many rough figures, whose attire of deer-skins marked them as belonging to some of the forest settlements, which surrounded the little metropolis of the colony.

On this public holiday, as on all other occasions, for seven years past, Hester was clad in a garment of coarse gray cloth. Not more by its hue than by some indescribable peculiarity in its fashion, it had the effect of making her fade personally out of sight and outline; while, again, the scarlet letter brought her back from this twilight indistinctness, and revealed her under the moral aspect of its own illumination. Her face, so long familiar to the townspeople, showed the marble quietude which they were accustomed to behold there. It was like a mask; or rather, like the frozen calmness of a dead woman's features; owing this dreary resemblance to the fact that Hester was actually dead, in respect to any claim of sympathy, and had departed out of the world with which she still seemed to mingle.

It might be, on this one day, that there was an expression unseen before, nor, indeed, vivid enough to be detected now; unless some preternaturally gifted observer should have first read the heart, and have afterwards sought a corresponding development in the countenance and mien. Such a spiritual seer might have conceived, that, after sustaining the gaze of the multitude through seven miserable years as a necessity, a penance, and something which it was a stern religion to endure, she now, for one last time more, encountered it freely and voluntarily, in order to convert what had so long been agony into a kind of triumph. "Look your last on the scarlet letter and its wearer!"—the people's victim and life-long bond-slave, as they fancied her, might say to them. "Yet a little while, and she will be beyond your reach! A few hours longer, and the deep, mysterious ocean will quench and hide for ever the symbol which ye have caused to burn upon her bosom!" Nor were it an inconsistency too improbable to be assigned to human nature, should we suppose a feeling of regret in Hester's mind, at the moment when she was about to win her freedom from the pain which had been thus deeply incorporated with her being. Might there not be an irresistible desire to quaff a last, long, breathless draught of the cup of wormwood and aloes, with which nearly all her years of womanhood had been perpetually flavored? The wine of life, henceforth to be presented to her lips, must be indeed rich, delicious, and exhilarating, in its chased and golden beaker; or else leave an inevitable and weary languor, after the lees of bitterness wherewith she had been drugged, as with a cordial of intensest potency.

Pearl was decked out with airy gayety. It would have been impossible to guess that this bright and sunny apparition owed its existence to the shape of gloomy gray; or that a fancy, at once so gorgeous and so delicate as must have been requisite to contrive the child's apparel, was the same that had achieved a task perhaps more difficult, in imparting so distinct a peculiarity to Hester's simple robe. The dress, so proper was it to little Pearl, seemed an effluence, or inevitable development and outward manifestation of her character, no more to be separated from her than the many-hued brilliancy from a butterfly's wing, or the painted glory from the leaf of a bright flower. As with these, so with the child; her garb was all of one idea with her nature. On this eventful day, moreover, there was a certain singular inquietude and excitement in her mood, resembling nothing so much as the shimmer of a diamond, that sparkles and flashes with the varied throbbings of the breast on which it is displayed. Children have always a sympathy in the agitations of those connected with them; always, especially, a sense of any trouble or impending revolution, of whatever kind, in domestic circumstances; and therefore Pearl, who was the gem on her mother's unquiet bosom, betrayed, by the very dance of her spirits, the emotions which none could detect in the marble passiveness of Hester's brow.

This effervescence made her flit with a bird-like movement, rather than walk by her mother's side. She broke continually into shouts of a wild, inarticulate, and sometimes piercing music. When they reached the market-place, she became still more restless, on perceiving the stir and bustle that enlivened the spot; for it was usually more like the broad and lonesome green before a village meeting-house, than the centre of a town's business.

"Why, what is this, mother?" cried she. "Wherefore have all the people left their work to-day? Is it a play-day for the whole world? See, there is the blacksmith! He has washed his sooty face, and put on his Sabbath-day clothes, and looks, as if he would gladly be merry, if any kind body would only teach him how! And there is Master Brackett, the old jailer, nodding and smiling at me. Why does he do so, mother?"

"He remembers thee a little babe, my child," answered Hester.

"He should not nod and smile at me, for all that,—the black, grim, ugly-eyed old man!" said Pearl. "He may nod at thee if he will; for thou art clad in gray, and wearest the scarlet letter. But, see, mother, how many faces of strange people, and Indians among them, and sailors! What have they all come to do here in the market-place?"

"They wait to see the procession pass," said Hester. "For the Governor and the magistrates are to go by, and the ministers, and all the great people and good people, with the music, and the soldiers marching before them."

"And will the minister be there?" asked Pearl. "And will he hold out both his hands to me, as when thou ledst me to him from the brook-side?"

"He will be there, child," answered her mother. "But he will not greet thee to-day; nor must thou greet him."

"What a strange, sad man is he!" said the child, as if speaking partly to herself. "In the dark night-time, he calls us to him, and holds thy hand and mine, as when we stood with him on the scaffold yonder! And in the deep forest, where only the old trees can hear, and the strip of sky see it, he talks with thee, sitting on a heap of moss! And he kisses my forehead, too, so that the little brook would hardly wash it off! But here in the sunny day, and among all the people, he knows us not; nor must we know him! A strange, sad man is he, with his hand always over his heart!"

"Be quiet, Pearl! Thou understandest not these things," said her mother. "Think not now of the minister, but look about thee, and see how cheery is every body's face to-day. The children have come from their schools, and the grown people from their workshops and their fields, on purpose to be happy. For, to-day, a new man is beginning to rule over them; and so—as has been the custom of mankind ever since a nation was first gathered—they make merry and rejoice; as if a good and golden year were at length to pass over the poor old world!"

It was as Hester said, in regard to the unwonted jollity that brightened the faces of the people. Into this festal season of the year—as it already was, and continued to be during the greater part of two centuries—the Puritans compressed whatever mirth and public joy they deemed allowable to human infirmity; thereby so far dispelling the customary cloud, that, for the space of a single holiday, they appeared scarcely more grave than most other communities at a period of general affliction.

But we perhaps exaggerate the gray or sable tinge, which undoubtedly characterized the mood and manners of the age. The persons now in the market-place of Boston had not been born to an inheritance of Puritanic gloom. They were native Englishmen, whose fathers had lived in the sunny richness of the Elizabethan epoch; a time when the life of England, viewed as one great mass, would appear to have been as stately, magnificent, and joyous, as the world has ever witnessed. Had they followed their hereditary taste, the New England settlers would have illustrated all events of public importance by bonfires, banquets, pageantries, and processions. Nor would it have been impracticable, in the observance of majestic ceremonies, to combine mirthful recreation with solemnity, and give, as it were, a grotesque and brilliant embroidery to the great robe of state, which a nation, at such festivals, puts on. There was some shadow of an attempt of this kind in the mode of celebrating the day on which the political year of the colony commenced. The dim reflection of a remembered splendor, a colorless and manifold diluted repetition of what they had beheld in proud old London,—we will not say at a royal coronation, but at a Lord Mayor's show,[1]—might be traced in the customs which our forefathers instituted, with reference to the annual installation of magistrates. The fathers and founders of the commonwealth—the statesman, the priest, and the soldier—deemed it a duty to assume the outward state and majesty, which, in accordance with antique style, was looked upon as the proper garb of public or social eminence. All came forth, to move in procession, before the people's eye, and thus impart a needed dignity to the simple framework of a government so newly constructed.

Then, too, the people were countenanced, if not encouraged, in relaxing the severe and close application to their various modes of rugged industry, which, at all other times, seemed of the same piece and material with their religion. Here, it is true, were none of the appliances which popular merriment would so readily have found in the England of Elizabeth's time, or that of James;—no rude shows of a theatrical kind; no minstrel with his harp and legendary ballad, nor gleeman, with an ape dancing to his music; no juggler, with his tricks of mimic witchcraft; no Merry Andrew, to stir up the multitude with jests, perhaps hundreds of years old, but still effective, by their appeals to the very broadest sources of mirthful sympathy. All such professors of the several branches of jocularity would have been sternly repressed, not only by the rigid discipline of law, but by the general sentiment which gives law its vitality. Not the less, however, the great, honest face of the people smiled, grimly, perhaps, but widely too. Nor were sports wanting, such as the colonists had witnessed, and shared in, long ago, at the country fairs and on the village-greens of England; and which it was thought well to keep alive on this new soil, for the sake of the courage and manliness that were essential in them. Wrestling-matches, in the differing fashions of Cornwall and Devonshire, were seen here and there about the market-place; in one corner, there was a friendly bout at quarterstaff; and—what attracted most interest of all—on the platform of the pillory, already so noted in our pages, two masters of defence were commencing an exhibition with the buckler and broadsword. But, much to the disappointment of the crowd, this latter business was broken off by the interposition

1. The Lord Mayor's show, a function similar in significance, also included a "procession," on November 9, date of the annual inauguration of the Lord Mayor of London.

of the town beadle, who had no idea of permitting the majesty of the law to be violated by such an abuse of one of its consecrated places.

It may not be too much to affirm, on the whole, (the people being then in the first stages of joyless deportment, and the off-spring of sires who had known how to be merry, in their day,) that they would compare favorably, in point of holiday keeping, with their descendants, even at so long an interval as ourselves. Their immediate posterity, the generation next to the early emigrants, wore the blackest shade of Puritanism, and so darkened the national visage with it, that all the subsequent years have not sufficed to clear it up. We have yet to learn again the forgotten art of gayety.

The picture of human life in the market-place, though its general tint was the sad gray, brown, or black of the English emigrants, was yet enlivened by some diversity of hue. A party of Indians—in their savage finery of curiously embroidered deer-skin robes, wampum-belts, red and yellow ochre, and feathers, and armed with the bow and arrow and stone-headed spear—stood apart, with countenances of inflexible gravity, beyond what even the Puritan aspect could attain. Nor, wild as were these painted barbarians, were they the wildest feature of the scene. This distinction could more justly be claimed by some mariners,—a part of the crew of the vessel from the Spanish Main,—who had come ashore to see the humors of Election Day. They were rough-looking desperadoes, with sun-blackened faces, and an immensity of beard; their wide, short trousers were confined about the waist by belts, often clasped with a rough plate of gold, and sustaining always a long knife, and, in some instances, a sword. From beneath their broad-brimmed hats of palm-leaf, gleamed eyes which, even in good nature and merriment, had a kind of animal ferocity. They transgressed, without fear or scruple, the rules of behaviour that were binding on all others; smoking tobacco under the beadle's very nose, although each whiff would have cost a townsman a shilling; and quaffing, at their pleasure, draughts of wine or aqua-vitæ from pocket-flasks, which they freely tendered to the gaping crowd around them. It remarkably characterized the incomplete morality of the age, rigid as we call it, that a license was allowed the seafaring class, not merely for their freaks on shore, but for far more desperate deeds on their proper element. The sailor of that day would go near to be arraigned as a pirate in our own. There could be little doubt, for instance, that this very ship's crew, though no unfavorable specimens of the nautical brotherhood, had been guilty, as we should phrase it, of depredations on the Spanish commerce, such as would have perilled all their necks in a modern court of justice.

But the sea, in those old times, heaved, swelled, and foamed very much at its own will, or subject only to the tempestuous wind, with hardly any attempts at regulation by human law. The buccaneer on the wave might relinquish his calling, and become at once, if he chose, a man of probity and piety on land; nor, even in the full career of his reckless life, was he regarded as a personage with whom it was disreputable to traffic, or casually associate. Thus, the Puritan elders, in their black cloaks, starched bands, and steeple-crowned hats, smiled not unbenignantly at the clamor and rude deportment of these jolly seafaring men; and it excited neither surprise nor animadversion when so reputable a citizen as old Roger Chillingworth, the physician, was seen to enter the market-place, in close and familiar talk with the commander of the questionable vessel.

The latter was by far the most showy and gallant figure, so far as apparel went, anywhere to be seen among the multitude. He wore a profusion of ribbons on his garment, and gold lace on his hat, which was also encircled by a gold chain, and surmounted with a feather. There was a sword at his side, and a sword-cut on his forehead, which, by the arrangement of his hair, he seemed anxious rather to display than hide. A landsman could hardly have worn this garb and shown this face, and worn and shown them both with such a galliard air, without undergoing stern question before a magistrate, and probably incurring fine or imprisonment, or perhaps an exhibition in the stocks. As regarded the shipmaster, however, all was looked upon as pertaining to the character, as to a fish his glistening scales.

After parting from the physician, the commander of the Bristol ship strolled idly through the market-place; until, happening to approach the spot where Hester Prynne was standing, he appeared to recognize, and did not hesitate to address her. As was usually the case wherever Hester stood, a small, vacant area—a sort of magic circle—had formed itself about her, into which, though the people were elbowing one another at a little distance, none ventured, or felt disposed to intrude. It was a forcible type of the moral solitude in which the scarlet letter enveloped its fated wearer; partly by her own reserve, and partly by the instinctive, though no longer so unkindly, withdrawal of her fellow-creatures. Now, if never before, it answered a good purpose, by enabling Hester and the seaman to speak together without risk of being overheard; and so changed was Hester Prynne's repute before the public, that the matron in town most eminent for rigid morality could not have held such intercourse with less result of scandal than herself.

"So, mistress," said the mariner, "I must bid the steward make ready one more berth than you bargained for! No fear of scurvy or ship-fever, this voyage! What with the ship's surgeon and this other doctor, our only danger will be from drug or pill; more by token, as there is a lot of apothecary's stuff aboard, which I traded for with a Spanish vessel."

"What mean you?" inquired Hester, startled more than she permitted to appear. "Have you another passenger?"

"Why, know you not," cried the shipmaster, "that this physician here—Chillingworth, he calls himself—is minded to try my cabin-fare with you? Ay, ay, you must have known it; for he tells me he is of your party, and a close friend to the gentleman you spoke of,—he that is in peril from these sour old Puritan rulers!"

"They know each other well, indeed," replied Hester, with a mien of calmness, though in the utmost consternation. "They have long dwelt together."

Nothing further passed between the mariner and Hester Prynne. But, at that instant, she beheld old Roger Chillingworth himself, standing in the remotest corner of the market-place, and smiling on her; a smile which—across the wide and bustling square, and through all the talk and laughter, and various thoughts, moods, and interests of the crowd—conveyed secret and fearful meaning.

XXII. *The Procession*

Before Hester Prynne could call together her thoughts, and consider what was practicable to be done in this new and startling aspect of affairs, the sound of military music was heard approaching along a contiguous street. It denoted the advance of the procession of magistrates and citizens, on its way towards the meeting-house; where, in compliance with a custom thus early established, and ever since observed, the Reverend Mr. Dimmesdale was to deliver an Election Sermon.

Soon the head of the procession showed itself, with a slow and stately march, turning a corner, and making its way across the market-place. First came the music. It comprised a variety of instruments, perhaps imperfectly adapted to one another, and played with no great skill, but yet attaining the great object for which the harmony of drum and clarion addresses itself to the multitude,— that of imparting a higher and more heroic air to the scene of life that passes before the eye. Little Pearl at first clapped her hands, but then lost, for an instant, the restless agitation that had kept her in a continual effervescence throughout the morning; she gazed silently, and seemed to be borne upward, like a floating sea-bird, on the long heaves and swells of sound. But she was brought back to her former mood by the shimmer of the sunshine on the weapons and bright armour of the military company, which followed after the music, and formed the honorary escort of the procession. This body of soldiery—which still sustains a corporate existence, and marches down from past ages with an ancient and honorable fame —was composed of no mercenary materials.[2] Its ranks were filled with gentlemen, who felt the stirrings of martial impulse, and sought to establish a kind of College of Arms, where, as in an association of Knights Templars, they might learn the science, and, so far as peaceful exercise would teach them, the practices of war. The high estimation then placed upon the military character might be seen in the lofty port of each individual member of the company. Some of them, indeed, by their services in the Low Countries and on other fields of European warfare, had fairly won their title to assume the name and pomp of soldiership. The entire array, moreover, clad in burnished steel, and with plumage nodding over their bright morions,[3] had a brilliancy of effect which no modern display can aspire to equal.

And yet the men of civil eminence, who came immediately behind the military escort, were better worth a thoughtful observer's eye. Even in outward demeanour they showed a stamp of majesty that made the warrior's haughty stride look vulgar, if not absurd. It was an age when what we call talent had far less consideration than now, but the massive materials which produce stability and dignity of character a great deal more. The people possessed, by hereditary right, the quality of reverence; which, in their descendants, if it survive at all, exists in smaller proportion, and with a vastly diminished force in the selection and estimate of public men. The change may be for good or ill, and is partly, perhaps, for both. In that old day, the English settler on these rude shores,— having left king, nobles, and all degrees of awful rank behind, while still the faculty and necessity of reverence were strong in him,— bestowed it on the white hair and venerable brow of age; on long-tried integrity; on solid wisdom and sad-colored experience; on endowments of that grave and weighty order, which gives the idea of permanence, and comes under the general definition of respectability. These primitive statesmen, therefore,—Bradstreet, Endicott, Dudley, Bellingham,[4] and their compeers,—who were elevated to power by the early choice of the people, seem to have been not often brilliant, but distinguished by a ponderous sobriety,

---

2. The "body of soldiery" survived as The Ancient and Honorable Artillery Company of Massachusetts; they are whimsically compared with the College of Arms or Heralds' College, which since about 1460 has been custodian of the genealogies and armorial bearings of persons entitled to them, and with the Knights Templars, an order of twelfth-century crusaders suppressed by Papal authority in 1312.

3. High-crested helmets of Spanish origin.

4. Simon Bradstreet (1603–97), John Endicott (1588–1665), and Thomas Dudley (1576–1653) were all, like Richard Bellingham, early governors of New England colonies.

rather than activity of intellect. They had fortitude and self-reliance, and, in time of difficulty or peril, stood up for the welfare of the state like a line of cliffs against a tempestuous tide. The traits of character here indicated were well represented in the square cast of countenance and large physical development of the new colonial magistrates. So far as a demeanour of natural authority was concerned, the mother country need not have been ashamed to see these foremost men of an actual democracy adopted into the House of Peers, or made the Privy Council of the sovereign.

Next in order to the magistrates came the young and eminently distinguished divine, from whose lips the religious discourse of the anniversary was expected. His was the profession, at that era, in which intellectual ability displayed itself far more than in political life; for—leaving a higher motive out of the question—it offered inducements powerful enough, in the almost worshipping respect of the community, to win the most aspiring ambition into its service. Even political power—as in the case of Increase Mather—was within the grasp of a successful priest.[5]

It was the observation of those who beheld him now, that never, since Mr. Dimmesdale first set his foot on the New England shore, had he exhibited such energy as was seen in the gait and air with which he kept his pace in the procession. There was no feebleness of step, as at other times; his frame was not bent; nor did his hand rest ominously upon his heart. Yet, if the clergyman were rightly viewed, his strength seemed not of the body. It might be spiritual, and imparted to him by angelic ministrations. It might be the exhilaration of that potent cordial, which is distilled only in the furnace-glow of earnest and long-continued thought. Or, perchance, his sensitive temperament was invigorated by the loud and piercing music, that swelled heavenward, and uplifted him on its ascending wave. Nevertheless, so abstracted was his look, it might be questioned whether Mr. Dimmesdale even heard the music. There was his body, moving onward, and with an unaccustomed force. But where was his mind? Far and deep in its own region, busying itself, with preternatural activity, to marshal a procession of stately thoughts that were soon to issue thence; and so he saw nothing, heard nothing, knew nothing, of what was around him; but the spiritual element took up the feeble frame, and carried it along, unconscious of the burden, and converting it to spirit like itself. Men of uncommon intellect, who have grown morbid, possess this occasional power of mighty effort, into which they throw the life of many days, and then are lifeless for as many more.

5. Increase Mather (1639–1723) wielded political and ecclesiastical power even beyond that of his father, Richard, or his son, Cotton Mather. He has dubious fame as a persecutor of witches, but in general he was a creative leader, especially as president of Harvard College (1685–1701).

Hester Prynne, gazing steadfastly at the clergyman, felt a dreary influence come over her, but wherefore or whence she knew not; unless that he seemed so remote from her own sphere, and utterly beyond her reach. One glance of recognition, she had imagined, must needs pass between them. She thought of the dim forest, with its little dell of solitude, and love, and anguish, and the mossy tree-trunk, where, sitting hand in hand, they had mingled their sad and passionate talk with the melancholy murmur of the brook. How deeply had they known each other then! And was this the man? She hardly knew him now! He, moving proudly past, enveloped, as it were, in the rich music, with the procession of majestic and venerable fathers; he, so unattainable in his worldly position, and still more so in that far vista of his unsympathizing thoughts, through which she now beheld him! Her spirit sank with the idea that all must have been a delusion, and that, vividly as she had dreamed it, there could be no real bond betwixt the clergyman and herself. And thus much of woman was there in Hester, that she could scarcely forgive him,—least of all now, when the heavy footstep of their approaching Fate might be heard, nearer, nearer, nearer!—for being able so completely to withdraw himself from their mutual world; while she groped darkly, and stretched forth her cold hands, and found him not.

Pearl either saw and responded to her mother's feelings, or herself felt the remoteness and intangibility that had fallen around the minister. While the procession passed, the child was uneasy, fluttering up and down, like a bird on the point of taking flight. When the whole had gone by, she looked up into Hester's face.

"Mother," said she, "was that the same minister that kissed me by the brook?"

"Hold thy peace, dear little Pearl!" whispered her mother. "We must not always talk in the market-place of what happens to us in the forest."

"I could not be sure that it was he; so strange he looked," continued the child. "Else I would have run to him, and bid him kiss me now, before all the people; even as he did yonder among the dark old trees. What would the minister have said, mother? Would he have clapped his hand over his heart, and scowled on me, and bid me begone?"

"What should he say, Pearl," answered Hester, "save that it was no time to kiss, and that kisses are not to be given in the market-place? Well for thee, foolish child, that thou didst not speak to him!"

Another shade of the same sentiment, in reference to Mr. Dimmesdale, was expressed by a person whose eccentricities—or insanity, as we should term it—led her to do what few of the townspeople would have ventured on; to begin a conversation with the wearer of the scarlet letter, in public. It was Mistress Hibbins, who, arrayed in great magnificence, with a triple ruff, a broidered stomacher, a gown of rich velvet, and a gold-headed cane, had come forth to see the procession. As this ancient lady had the renown (which subsequently cost her no less a price than her life) of being a principal actor in all the works of necromancy that were continually going forward, the crowd gave way before her, and seemed to fear the touch of her garment, as if it carried the plague among its gorgeous folds. Seen in conjunction with Hester Prynne, —kindly as so many now felt towards the latter,—the dread inspired by Mistress Hibbins was doubled, and caused a general movement from that part of the market-place in which the two women stood.

"Now, what mortal imagination could conceive it!" whispered the old lady confidentially to Hester. "Yonder divine man! That saint on earth, as the people uphold him to be, and as—I must needs say—he really looks! Who, now, that saw him pass in the procession, would think how little while it is since he went forth out of his study,—chewing a Hebrew text of Scripture in his mouth, I warrant,—to take an airing in the forest! Aha! we know what that means, Hester Prynne! But, truly, forsooth, I find it hard to believe him the same man. Many a church-member saw I, walking behind the music, that has danced in the same measure with me, when Somebody was fiddler, and, it might be, an Indian powwow or a Lapland wizard changing hands with us! That is but a trifle, when a woman knows the world. But this minister! Couldst thou surely tell, Hester, whether he was the same man that encountered thee on the forest-path?"

"Madam, I know not of what you speak," answered Hester Prynne, feeling Mistress Hibbins to be of infirm mind; yet strangely startled and awe-stricken by the confidence with which she affirmed a personal connection between so many persons (herself among them) and the Evil One. "It is not for me to talk lightly of a learned and pious minister of the Word, like the Reverend Mr. Dimmesdale!"

"Fie, woman, fie!" cried the old lady, shaking her finger at Hester. "Dost thou think I have been to the forest so many times, and have yet no skill to judge who else has been there? Yea; though no leaf of the wild garlands, which they wore while they danced, be left in their hair! I know thee, Hester; for I behold the token. We may all see it in the sunshine; and it glows like a red flame in the dark. Thou wearest it openly; so there need be no question about that. But this minister! Let me tell thee in thine ear! When the Black Man sees one of his own servants, signed and scaled, so shy of owning to the bond as is the Reverend Mr. Dimmesdale, he hath a way of ordering matters so that the mark shall be disclosed in open daylight to the eyes of all the world! What is it that the minister seeks to hide, with his hand always over his heart? Ha, Hester Prynne!"

"What is it, good Mistress Hibbins?" eagerly asked little Pearl. "Hast thou seen it?"

"No matter, darling!" responded Mistress Hibbins, making Pearl a profound reverence. "Thou thyself wilt see it, one time or another. They say, child, thou art of the lineage of the Prince of the Air! Wilt thou ride with me, some fine night, to see thy father? Then thou shalt know wherefore the minister keeps his hand over his heart!"

Laughing so shrilly that all the market-place could hear her, the weird old gentlewoman took her departure.

By this time the preliminary prayer had been offered in the meeting-house, and the accents of the Reverend Mr. Dimmesdale were heard commencing his discourse. An irresistible feeling kept Hester near the spot. As the sacred edifice was too much thronged to adimt another auditor, she took up her position close beside the scaffold of the pillory. It was in sufficient proximity to bring the whole sermon to her ears, in the shape of an indistinct, but varied, murmur and flow of the minister's very peculiar voice.

This vocal organ was in itself a rich endowment; insomuch that a listener, comprehending nothing of the language in which the preacher spoke, might still have been swayed to and fro by the mere tone and cadence. Like all other music, it breathed passion and pathos, and emotions high or tender, in a tongue native to the human heart, wherever educated. Muffled as the sound was by its passage through the church-walls, Hester Prynne listened with such intentness, and sympathized so intimately, that the sermon had throughout a meaning for her, entirely apart from its indistinguishable words. These, perhaps, if more distinctly heard, might have been only a grosser medium, and have clogged the spiritual sense. Now she caught the low undertone, as of the wind sinking down to repose itself; then ascended with it, as it rose through progressive gradations of sweetness and power, until its volume seemed to envelop her with an atmosphere of awe and solemn grandeur. And yet, majestic as the voice sometimes became, there was for ever in it an essential character of plaintiveness. A loud or low expression of anguish,—the whisper, or the shriek, as it might be conceived, of suffering humanity, that touched a sensibility in every bosom! At times this deep strain of pathos was all that could be heard, and scarcely heard, sighing amid a desolate silence. But even when the minister's voice grew high and commanding,—when it gushed irrepressibly upward,—when it assumed its utmost breadth and power, so overfilling the church as to burst its way through the solid walls, and diffuse itself in the open air,—still, if the auditor listened intently, and for the purpose, he could detect the same cry of pain. What was it? The complaint of a human heart, sorrow-laden, perchance guilty, telling its secret, whether of guilt or sorrow, to the great heart of mankind; beseeching its sympathy or forgiveness,—at every moment,—in each accent,—and never in vain! It was this profound and continual undertone that gave the clergyman his most appropriate power.

During all this time Hester stood, statue-like, at the foot of the scaffold. If the minister's voice had not kept her there, there would nevertheless have been an inevitable magnetism in that spot, whence she dated the first hour of her life of ignominy. There was a sense within her,—too ill-defined to be made a thought, but weighing heavily on her mind,—that her whole orb of life, both before and after, was connected with this spot, as with the one point that gave it unity.

Little Pearl, meanwhile, had quitted her mother's side, and was playing at her own will about the market-place. She made the sombre crowd cheerful by her erratic and glistening ray; even as a bird of bright plumage illuminates a whole tree of dusky foliage by darting to and fro, half seen and half concealed, amid the twilight of the clustering leaves. She had an undulating, but, oftentimes, a sharp and irregular movement. It indicated the restless vivacity of her spirit, which to-day was doubly indefatigable in its tiptoe dance, because it was played upon and vibrated with her mother's disquietude. Whenever Pearl saw any thing to excite her ever active and wandering curiosity, she flew thitherward, and, as we might say, seized upon that man or thing as her own property, so far as she desired it; but without yielding the minutest degree of control over her motions in requital. The Puritans looked on, and, if they smiled, were none the less inclined to pronounce the child a demon offspring, from the indescribable charm of beauty and eccentricity that shone through her little figure, and sparkled with its activity. She ran and looked the wild Indian in the face; and he grew conscious of a nature wilder than his own. Thence, with native audacity, but still with a reserve as characteristic, she flew into the midst of a group of mariners, the swarthy-cheeked wild men of the ocean, as the Indians were of the land; and they gazed wonderingly and admiringly at Pearl, as if a flake of the sea-foam had taken the shape of a little maid, and were gifted with a soul of the sea-fire, that flashes beneath the prow in the night-time.

One of these seafaring men—the ship-master, indeed, who had

spoken to Hester Prynne—was so smitten with Pearl's aspect, that he attempted to lay hands upon her, with purpose to snatch a kiss. Finding it as impossible to touch her as to catch a humming-bird in the air, he took from his hat the gold chain that was twisted about it, and threw it to the child. Pearl immediately twined it around her neck and waist, with such happy skill, that, once seen there, it became a part of her, and it was difficult to imagine her without it.

"Thy mother is yonder woman with the scarlet letter," said the seaman. "Wilt thou carry her a message from me?"

"If the message pleases me I will," answered Pearl.

"Then tell her," rejoined he, "that I spake again with the black-a-visaged, hump-shouldered old doctor, and he engages to bring his friend, the gentleman she wots of, aboard with him. So let thy mother take no thought, save for herself and thee. Wilt thou tell her this, thou witch-baby?"

"Mistress Hibbins says my father is the Prince of the Air!" cried Pearl, with her naughty smile. "If thou callest me that ill name, I shall tell him of thee; and he will chase thy ship with a tempest!"

Pursuing a zigzag course across the market-place, the child returned to her mother, and communicated what the mariner had said. Hester's strong, calm, steadfastly enduring spirit almost sank, at last, on beholding this dark and grim countenance of an inevitable doom, which—at the moment when a passage seemed to open for the minister and herself out of their labyrinth of misery —showed itself, with an unrelenting smile, right in the midst of their path.

With her mind harassed by the terrible perplexity in which the shipmaster's intelligence involved her, she was also subjected to another trial. There were many people present, from the country roundabout, who had often heard of the scarlet letter, and to whom it had been made terrific by a hundred false or exaggerated rumors, but who had never beheld it with their own bodily eyes. These, after exhausting other modes of amusement, now thronged about Hester Prynne with rude and boorish intrusiveness. Unscrupulous as it was, however, it could not bring them nearer than a circuit of several yards. At that distance they accordingly stood, fixed there by the centrifugal force of the repugnance which the mystic symbol inspired. The whole gang of sailors, likewise, observing the press of spectators, and learning the purport of the scarlet letter, came and thrust their sunburnt and desperado-looking faces into the ring. Even the Indians were affected by a sort of cold shadow of the white man's curiosity, and, gliding through the crowd, fastened their snake-like black eyes on Hester's bosom; conceiving, perhaps, that the wearer of this brilliantly embroidered badge must needs be a personage of high dignity among her people. Lastly, the inhabitants of the town (their own interest in this worn-out subject languidly reviving itself, by sympathy with what they saw others feel) lounged idly to the same quarter, and tormented Hester Prynne, perhaps more than all the rest, with their cool, well-acquainted gaze at her familiar shame. Hester saw and recognized the self same faces of that group of matrons, who had awaited her forthcoming from the prison-door, seven years ago; all save one, the youngest and only compassionate among them, whose burial-robe she had since made. At the final hour, when she was so soon to fling aside the burning letter, it had strangely become the centre of more remark and excitement, and was thus made to sear her breast more painfully than at any time since the first day she put it on.

While Hester stood in that magic circle of ignominy, where the cunning cruelty of her sentence seemed to have fixed her for ever, the admirable preacher was looking down from the sacred pulpit upon an audience, whose very inmost spirits had yielded to his control. The sainted minister in the church! The woman of the scarlet letter in the market-place! What imagination would have been irreverent enough to surmise that the same scorching stigma was on them both?

XXIII. *The Revelation of the Scarlet Letter*

The eloquent voice, on which the souls of the listening audience had been borne aloft, as on the swelling waves of the sea, at length came to a pause. There was a momentary silence, profound as what should follow the utterance of oracles. Then ensued a murmur and half-hushed tumult; as if the auditors, released from the high spell that had transported them into the region of another's mind, were returning into themselves, with all their awe and wonder still heavy on them. In a moment more, the crowd began to gush forth from the doors of the church. Now that there was an end, they needed other breath, more fit to support the gross and earthly life into which they relapsed, than that atmosphere which the preacher had converted into words of flame, and had burdened with the rich fragrance of his thought.

In the open air their rapture broke into speech. The street and the market-place absolutely babbled, from side to side, with applauses of the minister. His hearers could not rest until they had told one another of what each knew better than he could tell or hear. According to their united testimony, never had man spoken in so wise, so high, and so holy a spirit, as he that spake this day; nor had inspiration ever breathed through mortal lips more evidently than it did through his. Its influence could be seen, as it were, descending upon him, and possessing him, and continually lifting him out of the written discourse that lay before him, and filling him with ideas that must have been as marvellous to himself as to his audience. His subject, it appeared, had been the relation between the Deity and the communities of mankind, with a special reference to the New England which they were here planting in the wilderness. And, as he drew towards the close, a spirit as of prophecy had come upon him, constraining him to its purpose as mightily as the old prophets of Israel were constrained; only with this difference, that, whereas the Jewish seers had denounced judgments and ruin on their country, it was his mission to foretell a high and glorious destiny for the newly gathered people of the Lord. But, throughout it all, and through the whole discourse, there had been a certain deep, sad undertone of pathos, which could not be interpreted otherwise than as the natural regret of one soon to pass away. Yes; their minister whom they so loved—and who so loved them all, that he could not depart heavenward without a sigh—had the foreboding of untimely death upon him, and would soon leave them in their tears! This idea of his transitory stay on earth gave the last emphasis to the effect which the preacher had produced; it was as if an angel, in his passage to the skies, had shaken his bright wings over the people for an instant,—at once a shadow and a splendor,—and had shed down a shower of golden truths upon them.

Thus, there had come to the Reverend Mr. Dimmesdale—as to most men, in their various spheres, though seldom recognized until they see it far behind them—an epoch of life more brilliant and full of triumph than any previous one, or than any which could hereafter be. He stood, at this moment, on the very proudest eminence of superiority, to which the gifts of intellect, rich lore, prevailing eloquence, and a reputation of whitest sanctity, could exalt a clergyman in New England's earliest days, when the professional character was of itself a lofty pedestal. Such was the position which the minister occupied, as he bowed his head forward on the cushions of the pulpit, at the close of his Election Sermon. Meanwhile, Hester Prynne was standing beside the scaffold of the pillory, with the scarlet letter still burning on her breast!

Now was heard again the clangor of the music, and the measured tramp of the military escort, issuing from the church-door. The procession was to be marshalled thence to the town-hall, where a solemn banquet would complete the ceremonies of the day.

Once more, therefore, the train of venerable and majestic fathers was seen moving through a broad pathway of the people, who drew back reverently, on either side, as the Governor and magistrates, the old and wise men; the holy ministers, and all that were eminent and renowned, advanced into the midst of them. When they were fairly in the market-place, their presence was greeted by a shout. This—though doubtless it might acquire additional force and volume from the childlike loyalty which the age awarded to its rulers—was felt to be an irrepressible outburst of the enthusiasm kindled in the auditors by that high strain of eloquence which was yet reverberating in their ears. Each felt the impulse in himself, and, in the same breath, caught it from his neighbour. Within the church, it had hardly been kept down; beneath the sky, it pealed upward to the zenith. There were human beings enough, and enough of highly wrought and symphonious feeling, to produce that more impressive sound than the organ-tones of the blast, or the thunder, or the roar of the sea; even that mighty swell of many voices, blended into one great voice by the universal impulse which makes likewise one vast heart out of the many. Never, from the soil of New England, had gone up such a shout! Never, on New England soil, had stood the man so honored by his mortal brethren as the preacher!

How fared it with him then? Were there not the brilliant particles of a halo in the air about his head? So etherealized by spirit as he was, and so apotheosized by worshipping admirers, did his footsteps in the procession really tread upon the dust of earth?

As the ranks of military men and civil fathers moved onward, all eyes were turned towards the point where the minister was seen to approach among them. The shout died into a murmur, as one portion of the crowd after another obtained a glimpse of him. How feeble and pale he looked amid all his triumph! The energy—or say, rather, the inspiration which had held him up, until he should have delivered the sacred message that brought its own strength along with it from heaven—was withdrawn, now that it had so faithfully performed its office. The glow, which they had just before beheld burning on his cheek, was extinguished, like a flame that sinks down hopelessly among the late-decaying embers. It seemed hardly the face of a man alive, with such a deathlike hue; it was hardly a man with life in him, that tottered on his path so nervelessly, yet tottered, and did not fall!

One of his clerical brethren,—it was the venerable John Wilson,—observing the state in which Mr. Dimmesdale was left by the retiring wave of intellect and sensibility, stepped forward hastily to offer his support. The minister tremulously, but decidedly, repelled the old man's arm. He still walked onward, if that movement could be so described, which rather resembled the wavering effort of an infant, with its mother's arms in view, outstretched to tempt him forward. And now, almost imperceptible as were the latter steps of his progress, he had come opposite the well-remembered and weather-darkened scaffold, where, long since, with all that dreary lapse of time between, Hester Prynne had encountered the world's ignominious stare. There stood Hester, holding little Pearl by the hand! And there was the scarlet letter on her breast! The minister here made a pause; although the music still played the stately and rejoicing march to which the procession moved. It summoned him onward,—onward to the festival!—but here he made a pause.

Bellingham, for the last few moments, had kept an anxious eye upon him. He now left his own place in the procession, and advanced to give assistance; judging from Mr. Dimmesdale's aspect that he must otherwise inevitably fall. But there was something in the latter's expression that warned back the magistrate, although a man not readily obeying the vague intimations that pass from one spirit to another. The crowd, meanwhile, looked on with awe and wonder. This earthly faintness was, in their view, only another phase of the minister's celestial strength; nor would it have seemed a miracle too high to be wrought for one so holy, had he ascended before their eyes, waxing dimmer and brighter, and fading at last into the light of heaven!

He turned towards the scaffold, and stretched forth his arms.

"Hester," said he, "come hither! Come, my little Pearl!"

It was a ghastly look with which he regarded them; but there was something at once tender and strangely triumphant in it. The child, with the bird-like motion which was one of her characteristics, flew to him, and clasped her arms about his knees. Hester Prynne—slowly, as if impelled by inevitable fate, and against her strongest will—likewise drew near, but paused before she reached him. At this instant old Roger Chillingworth thrust himself through the crowd,—or, perhaps, so dark, disturbed, and evil was his look, he rose up out of some nether region,—to snatch back his victim from what he sought to do! Be that as it might, the old man rushed forward and caught the minister by the arm.

"Madman, hold! What is your purpose?" whispered he. "Wave back that woman! Cast off this child! All shall be well! Do not blacken your fame, and perish in dishonor! I can yet save you! Would you bring infamy on your sacred profession?"

"Ha, tempter! Methinks thou art too late!" answered the minister, encountering his eye, fearfully, but firmly. "Thy power is not what it was! With God's help, I shall escape thee now!"

He again extended his hand to the woman of the scarlet letter.

"Hester Prynne," cried he, with a piercing earnestness, "in the name of Him, so terrible and so merciful, who gives me grace, at this last moment, to do what—for my own heavy sin and miserable agony—I withheld myself from doing seven years ago, come hither now, and twine thy strength about me! Thy strength, Hester; but let it be guided by the will which God hath granted me! This wretched and wronged old man is opposing it with all his might! —with all his own might and the fiend's! Come, Hester, come! Support me up yonder scaffold!"

The crowd was in a tumult. The men of rank and dignity, who stood more immediately around the clergyman, were so taken by surprise, and so perplexed as to the purport of what they saw,—unable to receive the explanation which most readily presented itself, or to imagine any other,—that they remained silent and inactive spectators of the judgment which Providence seemed about to work. They beheld the minister, leaning on Hester's shoulder and supported by her arm around him, approach the scaffold, and ascend its steps; while still the little hand of the sin-born child was clasped in his. Old Roger Chillingworth followed, as one intimately connected with the drama of guilt and sorrow in which they had all been actors, and well entitled, therefore, to be present at its closing scene.

"Hadst thou sought the whole earth over," said he, looking darkly at the clergyman, "there was no one place so secret,—no high place nor lowly place, where thou couldst have escaped me,—save on this very scaffold!"

"Thanks be to Him who hath led me hither!" answered the minister.

Yet he trembled, and turned to Hester with an expression of doubt and anxiety in his eyes, not the less evidently betrayed, that there was a feeble smile upon his lips.

"Is not this better," murmured he, "than what we dreamed of in the forest?"

"I know not! I know not!" she hurriedly replied. "Better? Yea; so we may both die, and little Pearl die with us!"

"For thee and Pearl, be it as God shall order," said the minister; "and God is merciful! Let me now do the will which he hath made plain before my sight. For, Hester, I am a dying man. So let me make haste to take my shame upon me."

Partly supported by Hester Prynne, and holding one hand of little Pearl's, the Reverend Mr. Dimmesdale turned to the dignified and venerable rulers; to the holy ministers, who were his brethren; to the people, whose great heart was thoroughly appalled, yet overflowing with tearful sympathy, as knowing that some deep life-matter—which, if full of sin, was full of anguish and repentance likewise—was now to be laid open to them. The sun, but little past its meridian, shone down upon the clergyman, and gave a distinctness to his figure, as he stood out from all the earth to put in his plea of guilty at the bar of Eternal Justice.

"People of New England!" cried he, with a voice that rose over them, high, solemn, and majestic,—yet had always a tremor through it, and sometimes a shriek, struggling up out of a fathomless depth of remorse and woe,—"ye, that have loved me!—ye, that have deemed me holy!—behold me here, the one sinner of the world! At last!—at last!—I stand upon the spot where, seven years since, I should have stood; here, with this woman, whose arm, more than the little strength wherewith I have crept hitherward, sustains me, at this dreadful moment, from grovelling down upon my face! Lo, the scarlet letter which Hester wears! Ye have all shuddered at it! Wherever her walk hath been,—wherever, so miserably burdened, she may have hoped to find repose,—it hath cast a lurid gleam of awe and horrible repugnance round about her. But there stood one in the midst of you, at whose brand of sin and infamy ye have not shuddered!"

It seemed, at this point, as if the minister must leave the remainder of his secret undisclosed. But he fought back the bodily weakness,—and, still more, the faintness of heart,—that was striving for the mastery with him. He threw off all assistance, and stepped passionately forward a pace before the woman and the child.

"It was on him!" he continued, with a kind of fierceness; so determined was he to speak out the whole. "God's eye beheld it! The angels were for ever pointing at it! The Devil knew it well, and fretted it continually with the touch of his burning finger! But he hid it cunningly from men, and walked among you with the mien of a spirit, mournful, because so pure in a sinful world!—and sad, because he missed his heavenly kindred! Now, at the death-hour, he stands up before you! He bids you look again at Hester's scarlet letter! He tells you, that, with all its mysterious horror, it is but the shadow of what he bears on his own breast, and that even this, his own red stigma, is no more than the type of what has seared his inmost heart! Stand any here that question God's judgment on a sinner? Behold! Behold a dreadful witness of it!"

With a convulsive motion he tore away the ministerial band from before his breast. It was revealed! But it were irreverent to describe that revelation. For an instant the gaze of the horror-stricken multitude was concentrated on the ghastly miracle; while the minister stood with a flush of triumph in his face, as one who, in the crisis of acutest pain, had won a victory. Then, down he sank upon the scaffold! Hester partly raised him, and supported his head against her bosom. Old Roger Chillingworth knelt down beside him, with a blank, dull countenance, out of which the life seemed to have departed.

"Thou hast escaped me!" he repeated more than once. "Thou hast escaped me!"

"May God forgive thee!" said the minister. "Thou, too, hast deeply sinned!"

He withdrew his dying eyes from the old man, and fixed them on the woman and the child.

"My little Pearl," said he feebly,—and there was a sweet and gentle smile over his face, as of a spirit sinking into deep repose; nay, now that the burden was removed, it seemed almost as if he would be sportive with the child,—"dear little Pearl, wilt thou kiss me now? Thou wouldst not yonder, in the forest! But now thou wilt?"

Pearl kissed his lips. A spell was broken. The great scene of grief, in which the wild infant bore a part, had developed all her sympathies; and as her tears fell upon her father's cheek, they were the pledge that she would grow up amid human joy and sorrow, nor for ever do battle with the world, but be a woman in it. Towards her mother, too, Pearl's errand as a messenger of anguish was all fulfilled.

"Hester," said the clergyman, "farewell!"

"Shall we not meet again?" whispered she, bending her face down close to his. "Shall we not spend our immortal life together? Surely, surely, we have ransomed one another, with all this woe! Thou lookest far into eternity, with those bright dying eyes! Then tell me what thou seest?"

"Hush, Hester, hush!" said he, with tremulous solemnity. "The law we broke!—the sin here so awfully revealed!—let these alone be in thy thoughts! I fear! I fear! It may be, that, when we forgot our God,—when we violated our reverence each for the other's soul,—it was thenceforth vain to hope that we could meet hereafter, in an everlasting and pure reunion. God knows; and He is merciful! He hath proved his mercy, most of all, in my afflictions. By giving me this burning torture to bear upon my breast! By sending yonder dark and terrible old man, to keep the torture always at red-heat! By bringing me hither, to die this death of triumphant ignominy before the people! Had either of these agonies been wanting, I had been lost for ever! Praised be his name! His will be done! Farewell!"

That final word came forth with the minister's expiring breath. The multitude, silent till then, broke out in a strange, deep voice of awe and wonder, which could not as yet find utterance, save in this murmur that rolled so heavily after the departed spirit.

XXIV. *Conclusion*

After many days, when time sufficed for the people to arrange their thoughts in reference to the foregoing scene, there was more than one account of what had been witnessed on the scaffold.

Most of the spectators testified to having seen, on the breast of the unhappy minister, a SCARLET LETTER—the very semblance of that worn by Hester Prynne—imprinted in the flesh. As regarded its origin, there were various explanations, all of which must necessarily have been conjectural. Some affirmed that the Reverend Mr. Dimmesdale, on the very day when Hester Prynne first wore her ignominious badge, had begun a course of penance,—which he afterwards, in so many futile methods, followed out,—by inflicting a hideous torture on himself. Others contended that the stigma had not been produced until a long time subsequent, when old Roger Chillingworth, being a potent necromancer, had caused it to appear, through the agency of magic and poisonous drugs. Others, again,—and those best able to appreciate the minister's peculiar sensibility, and the wonderful operation of his spirit upon the body, —whispered their belief, that the awful symbol was the effect of the ever active tooth of remorse, gnawing from the inmost heart outwardly, and at last manifesting Heaven's dreadful judgment by the visible presence of the letter. The reader may choose among these theories. We have thrown all the light we could acquire upon the portent, and would gladly, now that it has done its office, erase its deep print out of our own brain; where long meditation has fixed it in very undesirable distinctness.

It is singular, nevertheless, that certain persons, who were spectators of the whole scene, and professed never once to have removed their eyes from the Reverend Mr. Dimmesdale, denied that there was any mark whatever on his breast, more than on a new-born infant's. Neither, by their report, had his dying words acknowledged, nor even remotely implied, any, the slightest connection, on his part, with the guilt for which Hester Prynne had so long worn the scarlet letter. According to these highly respectable witnesses, the minister, conscious that he was dying,—conscious, also, that the reverence of the multitude placed him already among saints and angels,—had desired, by yielding up his breath in the arms of that fallen woman, to express to the world how utterly nugatory is the choicest of man's own righteousness. After exhausting life in his efforts for mankind's spiritual good, he had made the manner of his death a parable, in order to impress on his admirers the mighty and mournful lesson, that, in the view of Infinite Purity, we are sinners all alike. It was to teach them, that the holiest among us has but attained so far above his fellows as to discern more clearly the Mercy which looks down, and repudiate more utterly the phantom of human merit, which would look aspiringly upward. Without disputing a truth so momentous, we must be allowed to consider this version of Mr. Dimmesdale's story as only an instance of that stubborn fidelity with which a man's friends—and especially a clergyman's—will sometimes uphold his character; when proofs, clear as the mid-day sunshine on the scarlet letter, establish him a false and sin-stained creature of the dust.

The authority which we have chiefly followed—a manuscript of old date, drawn up from the verbal testimony of individuals, some of whom had known Hester Prynne, while others had heard the tale from contemporary witnesses—fully confirms the view taken in the foregoing pages. Among many morals which press upon us from the poor minister's miserable experience, we put only this into a sentence:—"Be true! Be true! Be true! Show freely to the world, if not your worst, yet some trait whereby the worst may be inferred!"

Nothing was more remarkable than the change which took place, almost immediately after Mr. Dimmesdale's death, in the appearance and demeanour of the old man known as Roger Chillingworth. All his strength and energy—all his vital and intellectual force— seemed at once to desert him; insomuch that he positively withered up, shrivelled away, and almost vanished from mortal sight, like an uprooted weed that lies wilting in the sun. This unhappy man had made the very principle of his life to consist in the pursuit and systematic exercise of revenge; and when, by its completest triumph and consummation, that evil principle was left with no further material to support it,—when, in short, there was no more devil's work on earth for him to do, it only remained for the unhumanized mortal to betake himself whither his Master would find him tasks enough, and pay him his wages duly. But, to all these shadowy beings, so long our near acquaintances,—as well Roger Chillingworth as his companions,—we would fain be merciful. It is a curious subject of observation and inquiry, whether hatred and love be not the same thing at bottom. Each, in its utmost development, supposes a high degree of intimacy and heart-knowledge; each renders one individual dependent for the food of his affections and spiritual life upon another; each leaves the passionate lover, or the no less passionate hater, forlorn and desolate by the withdrawal of his object. Philosophically considered, therefore, the two passions seem essentially the same, except that one happens to be seen in a celestial radiance, and the other in a dusky and lurid glow. In the spiritual world, the old physician and the minister—mutual victims as they have been—may, unawares, have found their earthly stock of hatred and antipathy transmuted into golden love.

Leaving this discussion apart, we have a matter of business to communicate to the reader. At old Roger Chillingworth's decease (which took place within the year), and by his last will and testament, of which Governor Bellingham and the Reverend Mr. Wilson were executors, he bequeathed a very considerable amount of property, both here and in England, to little Pearl, the daughter of Hester Prynne.

So Pearl—the elf-child,—the demon offspring, as some people, up to that epoch, persisted in considering her—became the richest heiress of her day, in the New World. Not improbably, this circumstance wrought a very material change in the public estimation; and, had the mother and child remained here, little Pearl, at a marriageable period of life, might have mingled her wild blood with the lineage of the devoutest Puritan among them all. But, in no long time after the physician's death, the wearer of the scarlet letter disappeared, and Pearl along with her. For many years, though a vague report would now and then find its way across the sea,—like a shapeless piece of driftwood tost ashore, with the initials of a name upon it,—yet no tidings of them unquestionably authentic were received. The story of the scarlet letter grew into a legend. Its spell, however, was still potent, and kept the scaffold awful where the poor minister had died, and likewise the cottage by the seashore, where Hester Prynne had dwelt. Near this latter spot, one afternoon, some children were at play, when they beheld a tall woman, in a gray robe, approach the cottage-door. In all those years it had never once been opened; but either she unlocked it, or the decaying wood and iron yielded to her hand, or she glided shadow-like through these impediments,—and, at all events, went in.

On the threshold she paused,—turned partly round,—for, perchance, the idea of entering, all alone, and all so changed, the home of so intense a former life, was more dreary and desolate than even she could bear. But her hesitation was only for an instant, though long enough to display a scarlet letter on her breast.

And Hester Prynne had returned, and taken up her long-forsaken shame. But where was little Pearl? If still alive, she must now have been in the flush and bloom of early womanhood. None knew—nor ever learned, with the fulness of perfect certainty—whether the elf-child had gone thus untimely to a maiden grave; or whether her wild, rich nature had been softened and subdued, and made capable of a woman's gentle happiness. But, through the remainder of Hester's life, there were indications that the recluse of the scarlet letter was the object of love and interest with some inhabitant of another land. Letters came, with armorial seals upon them, though of bearings unknown to English heraldry. In the cottage there were articles of comfort and luxury, such as Hester never cared to use, but which only wealth could have purchased, and affection have imagined for her. There were trifles, too, little ornaments, beautiful tokens of a continual remembrance, that must have been wrought by delicate fingers, at the impulse of a fond heart. And, once, Hester was seen embroidering a baby-garment, with such a lavish richness of golden fancy as would have raised a public tumult, had any infant, thus apparelled, been shown to our sobre-hued community.

In fine, the gossips of that day believed,—and Mr. Surveyor Pue, who made investigations a century later, believed,—and one of his recent successors in office, moreover, faithfully believes,—that Pearl was not only alive, but married, and happy, and mindful of her mother; and that she would most joyfully have entertained that sad and lonely mother at her fireside.

But there was a more real life for Hester Prynne, here, in New England, than in that unknown region where Pearl had found a home. Here had been her sin; here, her sorrow; and here was yet to be her penitence. She had returned, therefore, and resumed,—of her own free will, for not the sternest magistrate of that iron period would have imposed it,—resumed the symbol of which we have related so dark a tale. Never afterwards did it quit her bosom. But, in the lapse of the toilsome, thoughtful, and self-devoted years that made up Hester's life, the scarlet letter ceased to be a stigma which attracted the world's scorn and bitterness, and became a type of something to be sorrowed over, and looked upon with awe, yet with reverence too. And, as Hester Prynne had no selfish ends, nor lived in any measure for her own profit and enjoyment, people brought all their sorrows and perplexities, and besought her counsel, as one who had herself gone through a mighty trouble. Women, more especially,—in the continually recurring trials of wounded, wasted, wronged, misplaced, or erring and sinful passion,—or with the dreary burden of a heart unyielded, because unvalued and unsought,—came to Hester's cottage demanding why they were so wretched, and what the remedy! Hester comforted and counselled them, as best she might. She assured them, too, of her firm belief, that, at some brighter period, when the world should have grown ripe for it, in Heaven's own time, a new truth would be revealed, in order to establish the whole relation between man and woman on a surer ground of mutual happiness. Earlier in life, Hester had vainly imagined that she herself might be the destined prophetess, but had long since recognized the impossibility that any mission of divine and mysterious truth should be confided to a woman stained with sin, bowed down with shame, or even burdened with a life-long sorrow. The angel and apostle of the coming revelation must be a woman, indeed, but lofty, pure, and beautiful; and wise, moreover, not through dusky grief, but the ethereal medium of joy; and showing how sacred love should make us happy, by the truest test of a life successful to such an end!

So said Hester Prynne, and glanced her sad eyes downward at the scarlet letter. And, after many, many years, a new grave was delved, near an old and sunken one, in that burial-ground beside which King's Chapel has since been built. It was near that old and sunken grave, yet with a space between, as if the dust of the two sleepers had no right to mingle. Yet one tombstone served for both. All around, there were monuments carved with armorial bearings; and on this simple slab of slate—as the curious investigator may still discern, and perplex himself with the purport—there appeared the semblance of an engraved escutcheon. It bore a device, a herald's wording of which might serve for a motto and brief description of our now concluded legend; so sombre is it, and relieved only by one ever-glowing point of light gloomier than the shadow:—

"ON A FIELD, SABLE, THE LETTER A, GULES."[6]

1849   1850

6. Translated from heraldic terms this means: "On a black shield, the letter *A* in red."

Backgrounds and Sources

We reproduce on the following pages some representative source materials intended to facilitate the intrinsic study of this novel and to illustrate the method of such investigation.

The first group, "Records Based on Primary Sources," is documentary—selections from books which scrupulously reproduce and describe certain primary documents: Hawthorne's notebooks, and source histories such as those of Snow, Felt, and Mather.

The second section, "The Scholar and the Sources," presents works of scholarship based upon primary documents and source histories. The student may find that research publications of this character increase his understanding of the novel, of the creative process, and in some instances, of the artist himself. The reader of certain critical articles in this collection will perceive the indebtedness of some critics to primary research.

Records Based on Primary Sources

From Hawthorne's Notebooks and Journals†

NOTEBOOKS: SEEDS OF THE PLOT

To symbolize moral or spiritual disease by disease of the body;—thus, when a person committed any sin, it might cause a sore to appear on the body;—this to be wrought out.

[October 27, 1841]

[*In* The Scarlet Letter, *the suggestion of the flaming scarlet letter on Dimmesdale's breast is a striking use of this idea. Earlier, in "Lady Eleanore's Mantle" (1838), Eleanore's vanity and pride were symbolically correlated with the disfiguring and deadly smallpox.*]

One of my chief amusements is to see the boys sail their miniature vessels on the Frog Pond. There is a great variety of shipping owned among the young people; and they appear to have a considerable knowledge of the art of managing vessels.

[June 1, 1842]

[*An entire page of the notebook elaborates the description of boys and boats, the full-grown spectators, school-girls, and mariners from the dockside out for a sunset stroll. In* The Scarlet Letter, *"[Pearl] made little boats out of birch-bark, and freighted them with snail-shells, and sent out more ventures on the mighty deep than any merchant in New England."*]

† *The American Notebooks by Nathaniel Hawthorne: Based Upon the Original Manuscripts,* Randall Stewart, editor (1932); *The Heart of Hawthorne's Journals,* Newton Arvin, editor, (1929).

Numerous entries in Hawthorne's notebooks during the nine years from 1841 to 1850 show that the ideas of *The Scarlet Letter* suggested themselves to the novelist over and over again in his reading, his thought and his experience. Selected entries are reproduced here to illustrate Hawthorne's method of accreting his novel. They appear in the sequence of the original, with dates when known. Editorial comment on these entries is identified by italics.

A father confessor—his reflections on character, and the contrast of the inward man with the outward, as he looks round on his congregation—all whose secret sins are known to him.

[June 1, 1842]

[*Arthur Dimmesdale, as a minister, was "confessor" to many of the puritan colonists whose "secret sins" he knew; while his "inward man" was tortured by his own secret sin, which his "outward man" did not confess.*]

A person with an ice-cold hand—his right hand; which people ever afterward remember, when once they have grasped it.

[June 1, 1842]

[*In* The Scarlet Letter, *Chapter XVII, cf. the words of the lovers, meeting after the long separation: Arthur exclaims, " 'Hester Prynne! Art thou in life?' " She replied, " 'And thou, Arthur Dimmesdale, dost thou yet live?' * * * With fear, and tremulously, * * * Arthur put forth his hand, chill as death, and touched the chill hand of Hester Prynne."*]

Pearl—the English of Margaret—a pretty name for a girl in a story.

[1842?]

[*In naming her daughter (Chapter VI), Hester Prynne of course remembered the Biblical "pearl of great price," for which the owner sacrificed all others.*]

The baby, the other day, tried to grasp a handfull of sunshine. She also grasps at the shadows of things, in candle light.

[1844]

[*Cf.* Pearl, *in Chapter XVI, "A Forest Walk," catching the sunshine. The baby in Hawthorne's note—his daughter Una—served to some degree as his model for Hester's Pearl. In the entries for 1848 his journal became very detailed concerning Una's behavior, and a significant quantity of this reached the novel.*]

The Unpardonable Sin might consist in a want of love and reverence for the Human Soul; in consequence of which, the investigator pried into its dark depths, not with a hope or purpose of making it better, but from a cold philosophical curiosity,— content that it should be wicked in whatever kind or degree, and only desiring to study it out. Would not this, in other words, be the separation of the intellect from the heart?

[1844]

[*A revision of this passage was used in the tale of "Ethan Brand,"* *which appeared in a periodical in January, 1850. Undoubtedly the idea was simultaneously involved in the characterization of Chillingworth: see, for example, in Chapter XVII, Dimmesdale's exclamation, "We are not, Hester, the worst sinners in the world. * * * That old man's revenge * * * has violated, in cold blood, the sanctity of a human heart."]*

The life of a woman, who, by the old colony law, was condemned always to wear the letter A, sewed on her garment, in token of her having committed adultery.

[1845?]

[Hawthorne had depicted such a woman as one of a group of citizens in "Endicott and the Red Cross," published in 1837. Stewart (p. 229) gives the text of the law of Plymouth (1636) as follows: "* * * Whosoever shall comitt Adultery shalbee severely punished by whiping two severall times; viz. one whiles the Court is being att which they are convicted of the fact, and the second time as the Court shal order; and likewise to weare two Capitall letters viz. AD cut out in cloth and sewed on theire upermost Garments on their arme or back; and if att any time they shalbee taken without the said letters whiles they are in the Govrment soe worn to bee forthwith taken and publickly whipt."]

In the eyes of a young child, or other innocent person, the image of a cherub or an angel to be seen peeping out; in those of a vicious person, a devil.

[August 9, 1845]

[In The Scarlet Letter, especially in Chapter VI, Hawthorne made direct use of this device; for example: "[Suddenly, Hester] fancied that she beheld, not her own miniature portrait, but another face, in the small, black mirror of Pearl's eye. It was a face fiendlike, * * * as if an evil spirit possessed the child, and had just then peeped forth in mockery."]

It was believed by the Catholics that children might be begotten by intercourse between demons and witches. Luther was said to be a bastard of this hellish breed.

[October 11, 1845]

[Stewart (p. 301) notes that Hawthorne was recording statements derived from Richard Cumberland, The Observer, London, 1785, and quotes from that essay as follows: "Though heretics have obstinately denied the copulation of wizards with the female daemons called Succubae; and of witches with the males, or Incubi, yet the whole authority of the Catholic church, with the Bull of Pope Innocent VIII express it for a fact. * * * It is also an orthodox

opinion that children may be begotten by this diabolical commerce, and there is little doubt but that Luther was the son of an Incubus." In The Scarlet Letter, Chapter VI, Hester had to bear the slander "that poor little Pearl was a demon offspring * * * through the agency of [her] mother's sin."]

A story of the effects of revenge, in diabolizing him who indulges in it.

[November 17, 1847]

[Hawthorne obviously employed this idea in the characterization of Chillingworth. Hawthorne also connected the ideas of revenge and intellectual arrogance in the character of Ethan Brand. The latter, if not diabolized, was dehumanized, but Roger Chillingworth (Chapter XII), appearing to the minister in the light of the fiery "A" in the night sky, "might have passed for the archfiend, standing there with a smile and scowl, to claim his own * * * on the day of judgment.]

Ephraim told a story of a child who was lost, seventy or eighty years ago, among these [New Hampshire] woods and hills. He was about five years old, and had gone with some work-people to a clearing in the woods * * * He started for home alone, but did not arrive. They made what search for him they could [but] after a while, they gave up the search in despair. * * * Whether it was the next autumn, or a year or two after, some hunters came upon some trace of the child's wanderings among the hills. They found some little houses, such as children build of twigs and sticks of wood; and these the little fellow had probably built for amusement, in his lonesome travels. Nothing, it seems to me, was ever more strangely touching than * * * his finding time for childish play, while wandering to his death in these desolate woods, and then pursuing his way again, til at last he lay down to die on the dark mountain-side * * *

[September 17, 1849]

[Cf. Pearl, set apart from the village children, learning to play alone with the natural objects and creatures of the forest. Especially see Chapters VI, XV, XVI, XVIII.]

NOTEBOOKS: PEARL AND UNA

[The notebooks after 1847 show an increasing record of the novelist's study of the behavior of his own children, especially the older, his daughter Una, born in 1844. As the author of tales for children, Hawthorne had already demonstrated his understanding of juvenile behavior. However, *in his daughter, Una, he discerned certain special qualities of wildness, independence, and imagination that he attributed to Pearl in* The Scarlet Letter. *The following notes from his journal are a few of the numerous direct parallels between the novel and the notebooks.*]

Children always seem to like a very wide scope for imagination as respects their babies, or indeed, any playthings: this cushion, or a rolling pin, or a nine-pin, or any casual thing, seems to answer the purpose of a doll better than the nicest little wax figure that the art of man can contrive.

[January, 1849]

The Scarlet Letter: *The unlikeliest materials—a stick, a bunch of rags, a flower,—were the puppets of Pearl's witchcraft and, without undergoing any outward change, became spiritually adapted to whatever drama occupied the stage of her inner world. Chapter VI. Also cf. Chapter XVI.*

Una cannot at all bear to be laughed at * * * Her life at present is a tempestuous day, with blinks of sunshine gushing between the rifts of cloud; she is as full sometimes of acerbity as an unripe apple, that may be perfected to a mellow deliciousness hereafter.

[January, 1849]

The Scarlet Letter: "*[Pearl] possessed affections, too, though hitherto acrid and disagreeable, as are the richest flavors of unripe fruit.*" *Chapter XV.*

[Una] spends much of her time, in this summer weather, hanging on [the] gate, and peeping forth into the great, unknown world * * * Ever and anon, without giving us the slightest notice she is apt to take flight into the said unknown and * * * we find her surrounded by a knot of children with whom she has made acquaintance, and who gaze at her with a kind of wonder—recognizing that she is not altogether like themselves.

[July, 1849]

The Scarlet Letter, *Chapter VI: "What a happiness would it have been, could Hester have heard her clear, birdlike voice mingling with the uproar of other childish voices, and have distinguished and unravelled her own darling's tones * * * But this could never be. Pearl was a born outcast of the infantile world * * * Nothing was more remarkable than the instinct, as it seemed, with which the child comprehended her loneliness. * * *"*

To return to Una, there is something that almost frightens me about the child—I know not whether elfish or angelic, but, at all events, supernatural. She steps so boldly into the midst of everything, shrinks from nothing, * * * seems at times to have but little delicacy, and anon shows that she possesses the finest essence of it; now so hard, now so tender; now so perfectly unreasonable, soon again so wise. In short, I now and then catch an aspect of her, in which I cannot believe her to be my own human child, but a spirit strangely mingled with good and evil, haunting the house where I dwell.

[July, 1849]

The Scarlet Letter, *Chapter VI: "The infant [Pearl] was worthy to have been brought forth in Eden; worthy to have been left there, to be the plaything of the angels, after the world's first parents were driven out. * * * And yet * * * in this one child there were many children. * * * Throughout all, however, there was a trait of passion, a certain depth of hue, which she never lost. * * * In giving her existence, a great law had been broken, and the result was a being whose elements were perhaps beautiful and brilliant, but all in disorder. * * * Her mother * * * grew acquainted with a certain peculiar look * * * so intelligent, yet unexplicable, so perverse, sometimes so malicious, but generally accompanied by a wild flow of spirits, that Hester could not help questioning whether Pearl was a human child."*

THE HEART OF HAWTHORNE'S JOURNALS

To show the effect of gratified revenge. As an instance, merely, suppose a woman sues her lover for breach of promise, and gets the money by instalments, through a long series of years. At last, when the miserable victim were utterly trodden down, the triumpher would have become a very devil of evil passions—they having overgrown his whole nature; so that a far greater evil would have come upon himself than on his victim. [p. 16]

Insincerity in a man's own heart must make all his enjoyments, all that concerns him, unreal; so that his whole life must seem like a merely dramatic representation. And this would be the case, even though he were surrounded by true-hearted relatives and friends. [p. 31]

The situation of a man in the midst of a crowd, yet as completely in the power of another, life and all, as if they two were in the deepest solitude. [p. 35]

Character of a man who, in himself and his external circumstances, shall be equally and totally false; his fortune resting on baseless credit—his patriotism assumed—his domestic affections, his honor and honesty, all a sham. His own misery in the midst of it—it making the whole universe, heaven and earth alike an unsubstantial mockery to him. [p. 46]

CALEB H. SNOW

From A *History of Boston†*

On the death of John Cotton, 1652; cf. Dimmesdale's vigil the night Governor Winthrop died:
  "Strange and alarming signs appeared in the heavens, while his body lay, according to the custom of the times, till the Tuesday following, when it was most honourably interred. * * *" [p. 133]

Cf. Hawthorne's description of Governor Bellingham's residence:
  This * * * is perhaps the only wooden building now standing in the city to show what was considered elegance of architecture here, a century and a half ago. The peaks of the roof remain pre-cisely as they were first erected, the frame and external appearance never having been altered. The timber used in the building was principally oak, and, where it has been kept dry, is perfectly sound and intensely hard. The outside is covered with plastering or what is commonly called rough-cast. But instead of pebbles, which are generally used at the present day to make a hard surface on the mortar, broken glass was used. This glass appears like that of com-mon junk bottles, broken into pieces of about half an inch diameter, the sharp corners of which penetrate the cement in such a manner, that this great lapse of years had had no perceptible effect upon them . . . This surface was also variegated with ornamental squares, diamonds and flowers-de-luce. * * * [p. 167]

Cf. Hawthorne's account of Witch Hibbins:
  The most remarkable occurrence in the colony in the year 1655 was the trial and condemnation of Mrs. Ann Hibbins of Boston for witchcraft. Her husband, who died July 23, 1654, was an agent for the colony in England, several years one of the assistants, and a merchant of note in the town; but losses in the latter part of his life had reduced his estate, and increased the natural crabbedness of his wife's temper, which made her turbulent and quarrelsome, and brought her under church censures, and at length rendered her so odious to her neighbours as to cause some of them to accuse her

† *A History of Boston* (1825, 2nd ed., 1828).

of witchcraft. The jury brought her in guilty, but the magistrates refused to accept the verdict; so the cause came to the general court, where the popular clamour prevailed against her, and the miserable old lady was condemned and executed in June 1656. Search was made upon her body for tetts,[1] and in her chests and boxes for puppets or images, but there is no record of any thing of that sort being found. [p. 140]

JOSEPH B. FELT

Annals of Salem: [Laws Governing Adultery]†

May 5th, 1694. * * * A memorial was received, signed by many clergymen, desiring the Legislature to enact laws against prevailing iniquities. Among such laws, passed this session, were two against Adultery and Polygamy. Those guilty of the first crime, were to sit an hour on the gallows, with ropes about their necks,— be severely whipt not above 40 stripes; and forever after wear a capital A, two inches long, cut out of cloth coloured differently from their clothes, and sewed on the arms, or back parts of their garments so as always to be seen when they were about. The other crime, stated with suitable exceptions, was punishable with death.

COTTON MATHER

[Witches, the Black Man, and the Black Book]‡

Cf. Hawthorne's reference to the signing in the devil's book with an iron pen:

It was not long before M. L. Daughter of the said F. confess'd that *She* rode with her Mother to the said Witch-meeting, and confirm'd the Substance of her Mother's Confession. At another time M. L. *junior*, the Grand-daughter, aged about 17 Years, confesses the Substance of what her Grand-mother and Mother had related, and declares that when they, with E. C. rode on a Stick or Pole in the *Air*, *she* the said Grand-daughter, with R. C. rode upon another (and the said R. C. acknowledged the same) and that they set their Hands to the Devil's Book. * * * [Bk. VI, p. 81]

---

1. I.e., tufts of hair. [*Editors.*]
† *The Annals of Salem* * * * (Salem, 1827), p. 317.
‡ *Magnalia Christi Americana* (1702).

Cf. Pearl's telling her mother "a story about the Black Man":

These *Tormentors* tendred unto the afflicted a *Book*, requiring them to *Sign* it, or *Touch* it at least, in token of their consenting to be Li$ted in the Service of the *Devil*; which they refusing to do, the *Spectres* under the Command of that *Blackman*, as they called him, would apply themselves to Torture them with prodigious Molestations. The afflicted Wretches were horribly *Distorted* and Convulsed; they were *Pinched* Black and Blue: *Pins* would be run every where in their Flesh; they would be *Scalded* until they had *Blisters* raised on them; and a Thousand other things before Hundreds of Witnesses were done unto them, evidently preternatural. * * * [Bk. II, p. 60]

The Murder of Sir Thomas Overbury

This is a contemporary account based on court testimony and legal depositions affecting the principals in the murder of Sir Thomas Overbury in 1613. The original manuscript, known as "The Five Years of King James," was published in The Harleian Miscellany, *London, 1808. The following excerpts, in narrative sequence, are extracted from Alfred S. Reid's facsimile edition,* Sir Thomas Overbury's Vision * * * *and Other English Sources of the Scarlet Letter (1957).*

Hawthorne's interest in British historical antiquities and occult lore influenced his depiction of Roger Chillingworth and other characters in The Scarlet Letter. *In Chapter IX Chillingworth is gathering exotic herbs for his potent elixirs; it is said that his London friends included Sir Kenelm Digby (p. 88, note 5) a dabbler in "supernatural" science and "Dr. Forman (p. 93, note 1) the famous old conjurer, who was implicated in the affair of Overbury."*

The detection and trial of conspirators in the murder of Sir Thomas Overbury in 1613 resulted in scandalous revelations of the moral degradation and the evil superstitions of the Jacobean court. Thomas Overbury, author of the famous Characters, *a commoner and scholar of the laws, rose to knighthood along with his young friend, Robert Carr, who early won the favor of King James and became Viscount Rochester. The highborn Frances, child bride of the young Earl of Essex, loathed her husband after falling in love with Rochester, but her reputation for profligacy only inflamed his ardor without suggesting the extreme remedy of a legal marriage. The Countess thereupon arranged with two dingy denizens of court life, Anne Turner, a reputed mistress of black arts, and her "master," Dr. Forman, abortionist and necromancer, to employ witchcraft*

*upon Essex, to render him impotent (a legal ground for divorce),
and on Rochester, to enkindle him to regularize their passionate
intrigues by marriage. While Essex apparently sustained the attack,
he wearied of the vain effort to reform his wife, and agreed to a
divorce. Overbury vehemently denounced Rochester's obvious intention "to make her his wife whom he hath made his whore,"
and voiced this view too broadly for his own safety: Rochester
tricked him into offending the King, while Countess Essex influenced powerful friends to bring about his imprisonment in the
Tower, where he died. In this melodrama of actuality Dr. Forman
had also died, leaving letters unburned which suggested a plot to
kill Overbury in prison by the gradual administration of poison
through a chain of accomplices. After extended sensational trials,
several were executed including Anne Turner. The highborn
Rochester and his paramour, now married, were sentenced to imprisonment, but soon released on powerful intervention; they were
permanently exiled from the Court and courtly society. The records
suggest that the wronged husband, Essex, settled an inheritance
upon the daughter, born in prison. Cf. Chillingworth and Pearl.*

In such seventeenth-century records as the Loseley Manuscripts
and the Harleian Miscellany, *which Hawthorne withdrew from
the Salem Athenaeum, and in other records of the State Trials
available to him, the novelist found in the "Affair of Overbury"
the diabolism of the "Black Man" and witchcraft; the prototypes
of Chillingworth and Mistress Hibbins; details of such fictional
situations as the adulterous wife, the wronged or vengeful husband,
the inhibited lover, the woman exposed in public beneath the balcony of her judges, and the child born in prison. Among other
bewitchments he certainly found the yellow-starched ruff of Witch
Hibbins on Anne Turner, whose evil lore Mistress Hibbins transferred to the colonial forest.*

Now, the cares of the vulgar being filled with the fortunes of this
gentleman [Sir Robert Carr, Viscount Rochester] * * * some ex-
tol and laud his virtues, others the proportion of his personage,
many his outward courtship, and most, as they stood affected,
either praised or dispraised him, insomuch that, amongst the rest,
the Countess of Essex (a woman at this time not greatly affecting
her husband) and withal, being of a lustful appetite, prodigal of
expence, covetous of applause, ambitious of honour, and light of
behaviour, having taken notice of this young gentleman's prosperity, and great favour that was shewed towards him above others,
in hope to make some profit of him, most advances him to every
one, commending his worth, spirit, audacity, and agility of body,
so that her ancient, lawful, and accustomed love towards her lord
begins to be obscured, and those embraces, that seemed heretofore

pleasing, are turned into frowns, and harsh unseemly words usher her discontents unto her husband's ears. * * * Almost all men speak of the looseness of her carriage, and wonder that the earl will suffer her in those courses; whereupon he modestly tells her of it, giving her a check for her inordinate courses, shewing how much it both dishonoured him, and disparaged her, in persisting, in the eye of the world, after so loose and unseemly a sort; desiring her to be more civil at home, and not so often abroad; and thus they parted. * * *

Mr. Overbury (sometime a student of the law in the Middle-Temple) was newly arrived out of France, who having obtained some favour in court beforetimes, because of some discontents, got licence to travel, and now, at his return, was entertained into the favour of Sir Robert Carr; whether it proceeded of any love towards him or to the intent to make use of him, is not certain; yet, nevertheless, he puts him in trust with his most secret employments, * * * uniting him into friendship with himself, insomuch that, to the shew of the world, his bond was indisolvible, neither could there be more friendship used, since there was nothing so secret, nor any matter so private, but the knight imparted it to Mr. Overbury.

The Countess of Essex, having harboured in her heart envy towards her husband even until this time, makes her repair unto Mistress Turner, a gentlewoman that, from her youth, had been given over to a loose kind of life, being of a low stature, fair visage, for outward behaviour comely, but in prodigality and excess most riotous. * * * I say, having some familiarity with this woman, and now taking some discontent at her husband more than heretofore, by reason of her falling out with him, and his sharp answers, as she conceives, to her, repairs to her house, and there, amongst other discourses, disgorges herself against her husband, whereby the cause of her grief might easily be perceived. Mistress Turner, as feeling part of her pain, pities her, and in hope of profit, being now in necessity and want, is easily drawn to effect any thing that she requires; whereupon, by the report of some, it was concluded at this time between them to administer poison to the earl. * * * The earl having overpassed this evil, and continued still in his pristine estate, procured not any affection, but more hatred and loathsomeness; so that it burst forth daily to my lord's great discontent, and draws her headlong into her own destruction. * * *

The King taking great liking to this young gentleman [Robert Carr], to the intent that he might be no less eminent in honour, than he was powerful in wealth and substance, adorns him with the title of Viscount Rochester, and bestows the secretariship of state upon him, so that his honour and his wealth make him famous to foreign nations. * * * In these times the Countess of Essex being a spectator of those, and perceiving this viscount to be still raised up unto honours daily, in hope of greater, is the more fired with a lustful desire, and the greater are her endeavours by the instigation of some of her friends to accomplish what she determined. * * *

In these furious fits, she makes her repair to Mistress Turner, and begins a new complaint, whereby she makes manifest an extraordinary affection towards this young gentleman, so that she could not rest without his company; neither knew she any means to attain her ends, there being no relation nor acquaintance between them: Whereupon, Mistress Turner, being still her second, and ready to put an evil attempt into execution, concludes with the countess to inchant the viscount to affect her; and, for this purpose, they fall acquainted with one Doctor Forman, that dwelt at Lambeth, being an ancient gentleman, and thought to have skill in the magick art: This man by rewards and gifts was wont to join with Mistress Turner, who now, to the intent to prey upon the countess, endeavour, the best they may, to inchant the viscount's affection towards her: Much time is spent, many words of witchcraft, great cost of making pictures of wax, crosses of silver, and little babies for that use, yet all to small purpose: At length they, continuing in their sorcery, advised her to live at court, where she had free access without controul, though of small acquaintance with him, whom she most respected, nevertheless, shewing an affable countenance towards him, hoping, in process of time, to attain that she required. * * *

These things, having happened so well to her expectation, cause a great love towards this good couple, viz. Doctor Forman and Mistress Turner, solliciting them with letters, with money, and large promises, to continue still their friend; * * * for, a woman's hands being once entered into the act of sin, she runs headlong to her destruction, turning those evil acts to evil ends, and endeavouring to purchase by that means profit and commodity. * * * But from this time the countess and viscount continued their loose kind of life, and, as was commonly suspected, had further relation than was fitting, to the great disparagement of them both, and dishonour of so noble a house. * * *

After some continuance of time, Mr. Overbury grows eminent in court, as well by reason of the viscount's favour, as the good and careful diligence that he had in court employments; so, that now comparing his worth with his wealth, he is had in more respect, and the honour of knighthood bestowed upon him, with the hope of better things, * * * Overbury came acquainted with this intercourse between the viscount and the countess; for now they, having had some time of familiarity and intercourse in remote parts, shame not to commit the sin of venery in the court, and that to the privity of Sir Thomas, who both loaths and hates what he sees, avoiding rather than intruding himself to the knowledge of * * * places of meeting, which were appointed between them, by which means, comparing both actions together, he entered into the secrets of this mystery, and became acquainted with more things than the viscount would have had him, from whence a kind of jealousy was carried towards him. * * *

Now the Earl of Essex * * * enters into a new discourse with his lady, with many protestations both of his constancy and love towards her; but withal tells her of her looseness, of the report of the vulgar, and what a strange course of life she led, contrary to all piety and honesty, which stung the countess to the heart, and more increased and augmented her malice towards him, so that in a great fury she takes her coach, and repairs to her ancient acquaintance Mrs. Turner, who, according to her old custom, is ready to perform any evil act, and there they combine to bewitch the earl, and procure frigidity *quoad hanc*. For this purpose Dr. Forman is consulted, for the procuring of means. * * * Many attempts failed, and still the earl stood it out. * * * She [Countess of Essex] grew jealous of her art, and falls into a great fear, that all their labour was lost, whereupon she wrote a letter to Dr. Forman * * * and now he goes and inchants a nutmeg and a letter; one to be given to the viscount in his drink, the other to be sent unto him as a present; these things being accomplished, he [Dr. Forman], not long after, died, leaving behind him some of those letters, whereby the countess had intercourse with him, in his pocket, which gave some light into the business, amongst which this same was one. * * *

In the mean time, there is a motion between Rochester and her [the Countess] for a marriage; and, since it was so, that the world had taken notice of their business, now to make some satisfaction, they would consummate a wedding between them: This motion was well liked of, * * * whereupon, she grows the more eager of a divorce, that so she might have a new husband, for women of her disposition delight in change, and therefore renews her complaint [on grounds of impotence]; advice is taken in the business, * * * they grant a bill of divorce; and, now a separation being had between them, the earl in a great discontent, leaves the court, and repaired to his house in Warwickshire, and there lives a private life. * * *

Now might there be a lawful discourse of marriage, since there was a lawful divorce, had it nevertheless been kept private, and only some particular friends made privy on Rochester's side; but

Overbury's advice he requires amongst others, in this business, though to what end, it is unknown. Nevertheless, Overbury was utterly against it; and, being in serious discourse with him, concerning this subject, in the passage-gallery at Whitehall, entered into these or the like words, as was reported; * * * It is not the nature of a wise man to make her his wife, whom he hath made his whore. Lastly, he willed him to expect no better requital at her hands, than which she had shewed to her former husband, and withal, to weigh the present condition that he was in, and to compare it with the future; now he had, as it were, but an inclination unto such a thing, neither were those things made evident, that after ages would lay open; nevertheless, that he was taxed with incivility, levity, and indeed effeminateness; that, by the opinion of the wise, he was adjudged altogether unworthy of that honour, that was bestowed upon him. But, when these surmises should come by this his marriage to be made evident, what evils, before, were but suspected, should then be enlarged, and laid to his charge. * * * The countess having, before this, borne a deadly hate towards Overbury, because he had oftentimes before dissuaded the viscount, to abstain from her company; yet now, having disclosed unto her this speech, she becomes much more revengeful, especially, because he had taxed her, with the name of a whore; for truth is hateful to the evil, and what before she concealed, now breaks forth with fury. * * *

The countess thought it not enough to hear, nor to fret and fume, * * * but to Mrs. Turner she must go, and there renew her complaints with tears (hardly found in a woman of her disposition) protesting she was never so defamed, neither did she ever think, that any man durst to be so saucy, as to call her whore and base woman, and that to Rochester, her only hopes, and with an impudent face; but Overbury, that negro, that scum of men, that devil incarnate, he might do any thing, and pass either unregarded, or unpunished. This moves pity in this pitiful woman Mrs. Turner, who frets as fast to see her fret, so that there is such storming between them, as is incredible. At length, as we see two clouds, after long strife in the air, which shall have the priority in place, join in one; so these two women, after they had fulfilled their frantick humour, join in this, to be the death of him: That must be the end; there is no malice like the malice of a woman; no submission, no intreaty, no persuasion could prevail, but he must die. * * * Yet, for all this, coming to their right senses, they begin to weigh the matter, and that it was no small thing to kill a man, both in respect of conscience, and law; therefore they cast about which should be the best way to do it; at last they conclude, that to poison him was the only way, and that with least suspicion.

But then the party that should do it was to seek; for he must be no ordinary man, but an apothecary, or physician, that might temper the poison rightly to take effect, according to their mind, and of long study: One Weston was named, that had some time been servant to Dr. Turner, and thereby learned such experience, that none was so fitting to accomplish this exploit to him. * * * Two-hundred pounds are proffered him, and he of all men undertakes it. * * *

Weston, a man that had gotten the art of poisoning, entertained for the purpose, and with a resolute mind ready to effect it, made them neither suspect nor doubt any thing, only how they might get him to the Tower. * * * Whereupon my Lord of Rochester, amongst other things, at a time convenient, lets the King understand how insolent Overbury was grown; that he not only contemned him, but his Majesty also, estimating this employment to be sent ambassador either too light a preferment for his deserts, or else intended to procure him further evil, and that he utterly disliked it, and determined to refuse it. * * *

Sir Thomas Overbury and Rochester having, for some private occasion, fallen into a new breach at Newmarket, he returns very pensively to London; and now the time being come that he should give an answer, what he would do concerning this ambassage, he answered, that * * * he desired to be excused. It seeming something strange and harsh, that he should neglect his own good, and by this means incur the displeasure of the King, and lose his expectations, makes some of his friends to wonder, and others to stand in amaze.

But in the conclusion, as he had justly deserved, by reason of his contempt, he is committed to the Tower, but not to be kept as a close prisoner. * * *

One Franklin was entertained into these actions, a man of a reasonable stature, crook-shouldered, of a swarthy complexion, and thought to be no less a wizard than the two former, Gresham and Forman; this man was more employed to make poisons fit to be administered by Weston than otherwise; for he was excellent in that art, to mitigate or increase their strength, so that sometimes a poison should be a month before it worked. * * *

Weston, having received twenty-four pounds of his allowance, and yet nevertheless nothing accomplished according to the countess's expectation, is checked by Mistress Turner for delaying it; whereupon he gets into his hands certain poisons, viz. rosacre, white arsnick, mercury sublimate, cantharides, red mercury, with three or four more several poisons, tempering them with his broth and his meat, according as he saw them affected, increasing and diminishing their strength, as he was instructed by his ancient friend Master Franklin; besides these, tarts and jellies are sent by the viscount and countess * * * to Overbury, every of which tarts and jellies were poisoned with a several poison. * * * By this means he begins to grow extreme sickly, having been heretofore accustomed to very good health; insomuch that he can scarce stand or go, what with the pain of his body, and the heat: Yet, nevertheless, being a strong man, he stood it out a long time. * * *

Now Weston had found out an unknown apothecary, and with him concludes, for twenty pounds, to administer a clyster, wherein should be put mercury sublimate; the youth was to come to dye it; Weston prepares it, and persuades Sir Thomas that it will be much for his health; whereupon, about the fourteenth day of September, he brings the said apothecary, to execute his office, assists him therein, and, by the infusion thereof, he falls into a languishing disease, with a pain in his guts; the next day after, with extremity of pain, he gave up the ghost.[1]

1. The remainder of the account deals with the detection, trials, and punishment of the conspirators. [*Editors.*]

The Scholar and the Sources

CHARLES RYSKAMP

The New England Sources of *The Scarlet Letter*†

After all the careful studies of the origins of Hawthorne's tales
and the extensive inquiry into the English sources of *The Scarlet
Letter*,[1] it is surprising that the American sources for the factual
background of his most famous novel have been largely unnoticed.
As would seem only natural, Hawthorne used the most creditable
history of Boston available to him at that time, and one which
is still an important source for the identification of houses of the
early settlers and for landmarks in the city. The book is Dr. Caleb
H. Snow's *History of Boston*. Study and comparison of the many
histories read by Hawthorne reveal his repeated use of it for authen-
tication of the setting of *The Scarlet Letter*. Consequently, for the
most part this article will be concerned with Snow's book.

If we are to see the accurate background Hawthorne created,
some works other than Snow's must also be mentioned, and the
structure of time as well as place must be established. Then it will
become apparent that although Hawthorne usually demanded authentic details of colonial history, some small changes were necessary in his portrayal of New England in the 1640's. These were not
made because of lack of knowledge of the facts, nor merely by
whim, but according to definite purposes—so that the plot would
develop smoothly to produce the grand and simple balance of the
book as we know it.

During the "solitary years," 1825–37, Hawthorne was "deeply en-

† From *American Literature*, XXXI
(November 1959), pp. 257–272.

1. I shall make no reference to the
English sources of *The Scarlet Letter*
which have been investigated by Alfred
S. Reid in *The Yellow Ruff and The
Scarlet Letter* (Gainesville, 1955) and
in his edition of *Sir Thomas Overbury's
Vision . . . and Other English Sources
of Nathaniel Hawthorne's "The Scarlet

Letter" (Gainesville, 1957). Most of
this article was written before the publication of Reid's books. It may serve,
however, as a complement or corrective
to the central thesis put forth by Reid:
"that accounts of the murder of Sir
Thomas Overbury were Hawthorne's
principal sources in composing *The
Scarlet Letter*" (*The Yellow Ruff*, p.
112). * * *

gaged in reading everything he could lay his hands on. It was said in those days that he had read every book in the Athenaeum. . . ." [2] Yet no scholar has studied his notebooks without expressing surprise at the exceptionally few remarks there on his reading. Infrequently one will find a bit of "curious information, sometimes with, more often without, a notation of the source; and some of these passages find their way into his creative work."[3] But for the most part Hawthorne did not reveal clues concerning the books he read and used in his own stories. About half of his writings deal in some way with colonial American history, and Professor Turner believes that "Hawthorne's indebtedness to the history of New England was a good deal larger than has ordinarily been supposed."[4] Certainly in *The Scarlet Letter* the indebtedness was much more direct than has hitherto been known.

Any work on the exact sources would have been almost impossible if it had not been for Hawthorne's particular use of the New England annals. Most of these are similar in content. The later historian builds on those preceding, who, in turn, must inevitably base all history on the chronicles, diaries, and records of the first settlers. Occasionally an annalist turns up a hitherto unpublished fact, a new relationship, a fresh description. It is these that Hawthorne seizes upon for his stories, for they would, of course, strike the mind of one who had read almost all the histories, and who was intimate with the fundamentals of colonial New England government.

As a young bachelor in Salem Hawthorne, according to his future sister-in-law, Elizabeth Peabody, "made himself thoroughly acquainted with the ancient history of Salem, and especially with the witchcraft era."[5] This meant that he studied Increase Mather's *Illustrious Providences* and Cotton Mather's *Magnalia Christi Americana*. He read the local histories of all the important New England towns. He read—and mentioned in his works—Bancroft's *History of the United States*, Hutchinson's *History of Massachusetts*, Snow's *History of Boston*, Felt's *Annals of Salem*, and Winthrop's *Journal*.[6] His son reported that Hawthorne pored over the daily records of the past: newspapers, magazines, chronicles, English state trials, "all manner of lists of things. . . . The forgotten

2. James T. Fields, *Yesterdays with Authors* (Boston, 1900), p. 47. For a list of books which Hawthorne borrowed from the Salem Athenaeum, see Marion L. Kesselring, *Hawthorne's Reading 1828–1850* (New York, 1949). All of my sources are included in this list, except the second edition (1845) of Felt's *Annals of Salem*.
3. *The American Notebooks*, ed. Randall Stewart (New Haven, 1932), p. xxxii.

4. H. Arlin Turner, "Hawthorne's Literary Borrowings," *PMLA*, LI, 545 (June, 1936).
5. Moncure D. Conway, *Life of Nathaniel Hawthorne* (New York, 1890), p. 31.
6. Edward Dawson, *Hawthorne's Knowledge and Use of New England History: A Study of Sources* (Nashville, Tenn., 1939), pp. 5–6; Turner, p. 551.

volumes of the New England Annalists were favorites of his, and he drew not a little material from them."[7] He used these works to establish verisimilitude and greater materiality for his own books. His reading was perhaps most often chosen to help him—as he wrote to Longfellow—"give a life-like semblance to such shadowy stuff"[8] as formed his romances. Basically it was an old method of achieving reality, most successfully accomplished in his own day by Scott; but for Hawthorne the ultimate effects were quite different. Here and there Hawthorne reported actual places, incidents, and people—historical facts—and these were united with the creations of his mind. His explicitly stated aim in *The Scarlet Letter* was that "the Actual and the Imaginary may meet, and each imbue itself with the nature of the other." His audience should recognize "the authenticity of the outline" of the novel, and this would help them to accept the actuality of the passion and guilt which it contained. For the author himself, the strongest reality of outline or scene was in the past, especially the history of New England.

The time scheme of the plot of *The Scarlet Letter* may be dated definitely. In Chapter XII, "The Minister's Vigil," the event which brings the various characters together is the death of Governor Winthrop. From the records we know that the old magistrate died on March 26, 1649.[9] However, Hawthorne gives the occasion as Saturday, "an obscure night of early May." Some suggestions may be made as reasons for changing the date. It would be difficult to have a night-long vigil in the cold, blustery month of March without serious plot complications. The rigidly conceived last chapters of the book require a short period of time to be dramatically and psychologically effective. The mounting tension in the mind and heart of the Reverend Mr. Dimmesdale cries for release, for revelation of his secret sin. Hawthorne realized that for a powerful climax, not more than a week, or two weeks at the most, should elapse between the night of Winthrop's death, when Dimmesdale stood on the scaffold, and the public announcement of his sin to the crowd on Election Day. The Election Day and the Election Sermons (p. 257) were well-known and traditionally established in the early colony in the months of May or June.[1] (The election of 1649, at

7. Julian Hawthorne, *Hawthorne Reading* (Cleveland, 1902), pp. 107–108, 111, 132. Hawthorne's sister Elizabeth wrote to James T. Fields: "There was [at the Athenaeum] also much that related to the early History of New England . . . . I think if you looked over a file of old Colonial Newspapers you would not be surprised at the fascination my brother found in them. There were a few volumes in the Salem Athenaeum; he always complained because there were no more" (Randall Stewart, "Recollections of Hawthorne

by His Sister Elizabeth," *American Literature*, XVI, 324, 330, Jan., 1945).
8. *The American Notebooks*, p. xlii.
9. William Allen, *An American Biographical and Historical Dictionary* (Cambridge, Mass., 1809), p. 616; Caleb H. Snow, *A History of Boston* (Boston, 1825), p. 104; Thomas Hutchinson, *The History of Massachusetts* (Salem, 1795), I, 142.
1. John Winthrop, *The History of New England from 1630 to 1649* (Boston, 1825–1826), II, 31, 218 (a note on p. 31 states that the charter of

which John Endicott became governor, was held on May 2.) Consequently Hawthorne was forced to choose between two historical events, more than a month apart. He wisely selected May, rather than March, 1649, for the time of the action of the last half of the book (Chapters XII–XXIII).

The minister's expiatory watch on the scaffold is just seven years after Hester Prynne first faced the hostile Puritans on the same platform. Therefore, the first four chapters of *The Scarlet Letter* may be placed in June, 1642. Hawthorne says that at this time Bellingham was governor. Again one does not find perfect historical accuracy; if it were so, then Winthrop would have been governor, for Bellingham had finished his term of office just one month before.[2] A possible reason for Hawthorne's choice of Bellingham will be discussed later.

The next major scene—that in which Hester Prynne goes to the mansion of Bellingham—takes place three years later (1645).[3] Hawthorne correctly observes: "though the chances of a popular election had caused this former ruler to descend a step or two from the highest rank, he still held an honorable and influential place among the colonial magistracy."[4] From the description of the garden of Bellingham's house we know that the time of the year was late summer.

With these references to time, as Edward Dawson has suggested,[5] we can divide the major action of the novel as follows:

Act One

i. Chapters I–III. The Market-Place, Boston. A June morning, 1642.
ii. Chapter IV. The Prison, Boston. Afternoon of the same day.

1629 provided for a general election on "the last Wednesday in Easter term yearly"; after 1691, on the last Wednesday of May); also Daniel Neal, *The History of New-England . . . to . . . 1700* (London, 1747), II, 252. Speaking of New England festivals, Neal writes: "their Grand Festivals are the Day of the annual Election of Magistrates at Boston, which is the latter End of *May;* and the Commencement at *Cambridge,* which is the last *Wednesday* in *July,* when Business is pretty much laid aside, and the People are as chearful among their Friends and Neighbours, as the *English* are at *Christmas.*" Note Hawthorne's description of Election Day (*The Scarlet Letter,* p. 275): "Had they followed their hereditary taste, the New England settlers would have illustrated all events of public importance by bonfires, banquets, pageantries and processions . . . . There was some shadow of an attempt of this kind in the mode of celebrating the day on which the political year of the colony commenced.

The dim reflection of a remembered splendor, a colorless and manifold diluted repetition of what' they had beheld in proud old London . . . might be traced in the customs which our forefathers instituted, with reference to the annual installation of magistrates."
2. Winthrop, II, 31: June 2, 1641, Richard Bellingham elected governor. Winthrop, II, 63: May 18, 1642, John Winthrop elected governor.
3. *The Scarlet Letter,* p. 138: "Pearl, therefore, so large were the attainments of her three years' lifetime, could have borne a fair examination in the New England Primer, or the first column of the Westminster Catechisms, although unacquainted with the outward form of either of those celebrated works." The Westminster Catechisms were not formulated until 1647; the New England Primer was first brought out ca. 1690.
4. Winthrop, II, 220: on May 14, 1645, Thomas Dudley had been elected governor.
5. I am largely indebted to Dawson, p. 17, for this time scheme.

Act Two

Chapters VII–VIII. The home of Richard Bellingham, Boston. Late summer, 1645.

Act Three

i. Chapter XII. The Market-Place. Saturday night, early May, 1649.
ii. Chapters XIV–XV. The sea coast, "a retired part of the peninsula." Several days later.
iii. Chapters XVI–XIX. The forest. Several days later.

Act Four

Chapters XXI–XXIII. The Market-Place. Three days later.

The place of each action is just as carefully described as is the time. Hawthorne's picture of Boston is done with precise authentic-

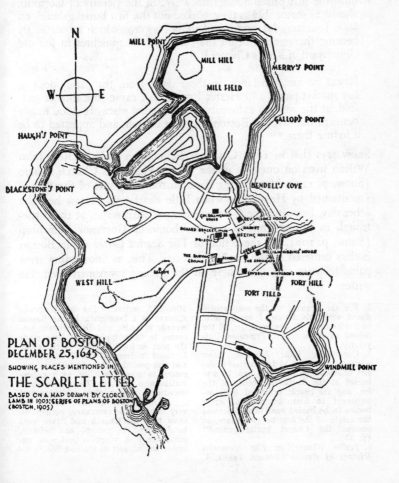

PLAN OF BOSTON,
DECEMBER 25, 1645

SHOWING PLACES MENTIONED IN

THE SCARLET LETTER

BASED ON A MAP DRAWN BY GEORGE
LAMB IN 1903; SERIES OF PLANS OF BOSTON
(BOSTON, 1905)

ity. A detailed street-by-street and house-by-house description of the city in 1650 is given by Snow in his *History of Boston*. It is certainly the most complete history of the early days in any work available to Hawthorne. Whether he had an early map of Boston cannot be known, but it is doubtful that any existed from the year 1650. However, the City of Boston Records, 1634–1660, and the "Book of Possessions" with the reconstructed maps (made in 1903–1905 by George Lamb, based on the original records)[6] prove conclusively the exactness of the descriptions written by Snow and Hawthorne.

Hawthorne locates the first scene of *The Scarlet Letter* in this way:

> . . . it may safely be assumed that the forefathers of Boston had built the first prison-house somewhere in the vicinity of Cornhill, almost as seasonably as they marked out the first burial-ground, on Isaac Johnson's lot, and round about his grave, which subsequently became the nucleus of all the congregated sepulchres in the old churchyard of King's Chapel.[7]

> It was no great distance, in those days, from the prison-door to the market-place. . . . Hester Prynne . . . came to a sort of scaffold, at the western extremity of the market-place. It stood nearly beneath the eaves of Boston's earliest church, and appeared to be a fixture there.[8]

Snow says that in 1650 Governor Bellingham and the Rev. John Wilson lived on one side of the Market-Place and Church Square (Snow, p. 117). Near Spring Lane on the other side of the Square (mentioned by Hawthorne when little Pearl says, "I saw her, the other day, bespatter the Governor himself with water, at the cattle-trough in Spring Lane") was the home of Governor Winthrop (Snow, p. 108). All the action of *The Scarlet Letter* set in Boston is thus centered in the heart of the city. This, as Snow takes great pains to point out, was where all the leading townsmen lived. He writes:

6. For the drawing of the map reproduced with this article, I am grateful to Professor W. F. Shellman, Jr., of the School of Architecture, Princeton University.

7. Concerning Isaac Johnson, Snow writes: "According to his particular desire expressed on his death bed, he was buried at the Southwest corner of the lot, and the people exhibited their attachment to him, by ordering their bodies to be buried near him. This was the origin of the first burying place, at present the Chapel burial ground" (p. 37).

8. Justin Winsor, in *The Memorial History of Boston* (Boston, 1881), I,

506, 539, writes: "The whipping-post appears as a land-mark in the Boston records in 1639, and the frequent sentences to be whipped must have made the post entirely familiar to the town. It stood in front of the First Church, and was probably thought to be as necessary to good discipline as a police-station now is . . . . The stocks stood sometimes near the whipping-post . . . . And here, at last, before the very door of the sanctuary, perhaps to show that the Church and State went hand-in-hand in precept and penalty, stood the first whipping-post,—no unimportant adjunct of Puritan life."

It has been so often repeated that it is now generally believed the north part of the town was at that period the most populous. We are convinced that the idea is erroneous. . . . The book of possessions records the estates of about 250, the number of their houses, barns, gardens, and sometimes the measurement of their lands. It seems to embrace the period from 1640 to 1650, and we conclude, gives us the names of almost, if not quite, all the freemen of Boston. They were settled through the whole length of the main street on both sides. . . . It is evident too, that most of the wealthy and influential characters lived in what is now the centre of the town. We discover only about thirty names of residents north of the creek.

A clear instance of Hawthorne's borrowing a fact from Snow is in the naming of "Master Brackett, the jailer." Few colonial historians mention a jailer in Boston at this time, and if they do, they give his name as Parker. But Snow, alone it would seem, gives this information about Brackett, after writing about the property of John Leverett: "His next neighbour on the south was Richard Parker or Brackett, whose name we find on the colony records as prison keeper so early as 1638. He had '*the market stead*' on the east, the prison yard west, and the meeting house on the south" (Snow, p. 116). This last sentence taken from Snow gives the exact location of the action of the early chapters of *The Scarlet Letter*.

Another example of Hawthorne's use of Snow is shown in the description of Governor Bellingham's house. Here Hawthorne builds a vivid image of the old mansion. He writes of Hester and Pearl:

> Without further adventure, they reached the dwelling of Governor Bellingham. This was a large wooden house, built in a fashion of which there are specimens still extant in the streets of our older towns. . . . It had, indeed, a very cheery aspect; the walls being overspread with a kind of stucco, in which fragments of broken glass were plentifully intermixed; so that, when the sunshine fell aslant-wise over the front of the edifice, it glittered and sparkled as if diamonds had been flung against it by the double handful. . . . It was further decorated with strange and seemingly cabalistic figures and diagrams, suitable to the quaint taste of the age, which had been drawn in the stucco when newly laid on, and had now grown hard and durable, for the admiration of after times.[9]

There are almost no representations of the first settlers' houses in the New England annals. But Snow on one occasion does print an old plate showing an "Ancient building at the corner of Ann-

9. Hawthorne also accurately noted that Governor Bellingham was "bred a lawyer." Snow writes of Bellingham: "He was by education a lawyer" (p. 159).

Street and Market-Square" (p. 166). And he describes the house in a way which bears a remarkable resemblance to the sketch written by Hawthorne twenty-five years later:

> This, says a description furnished by a friend, is perhaps the only wooden building now standing in the city to show what was considered elegance of architecture here, a century and a half ago. . . . The outside is covered with plastering, or what is commonly called rough-cast. But instead of pebbles, which are generally used at the present day to make a hard surface on the mortar, broken glass was used. This glass appears like that of common junk bottles, broken into pieces of about half an inch diameter. . . . This surface was also variegated with ornamental squares, diamonds and flowers-de-luce. (p. 167)[1]

Snow is also the only historian who tells the story of Mrs. Sherman's pig in order to bring out its effect upon the early Massachusetts government.[2] Hawthorne, with his characteristic interest in the unusual fact from the past, refers to this strange incident:

> At that epoch of pristine simplicity, however, matters of even slighter public interest, and of far less intrinsic weight, than the welfare of Hester and her child, were strangely mixed up with the deliberations of legislators and acts of state. The period was hardly, if at all, earlier than that of our story, when a dispute concerning the right of property in a pig not only caused a fierce and bitter contest in the legislative body of the colony, but resulted in an important modification of the framework itself of the legislature.

In his version of the story Snow said that the incident "gave rise to a change also in regard to the Assistants" (p. 95) and that because of the confusion and dissatisfaction over the decision of the court, "provision was made for some cases in which, if the two houses differed, it was agreed that the major vote of the whole should be decisive. This was the origin of our present Senate" (p. 96).

The characters named in *The Scarlet Letter*—other than Hester, Pearl, Chillingworth, and Dimmesdale, for whom we can find no real historical bases—were actual figures in history. The fictional protagonists of the action move and gain their being in part through their realistic meetings with well-known people of colonial Boston. Even the fantastic Pearl grows somewhat more substantial in the light of the legend and story of her primitive world. She is seen, for example, against the silhouette of the earlier Mr. Blackstone. When describing Bellingham's garden Hawthorne relates: "There

1. For a possible source for details concerning the interior of Bellingham's house, the front door, knocker, etc., see Joseph B. Felt, *Annals of Salem* (2nd ed.; Salem, 1845), I, 403–406.
2. Snow, pp. 95–96. Hutchinson, I, 135–136, also refers to the incident, but not in this particular way.

were a few rose-bushes, however, and a number of apple-trees, probably the descendants of those planted by the Reverend Mr. Blackstone, the first settler of the peninsula; that half-mythological personage, who rides through our early annals, seated on the back of
a bull." Snow had said:

> By right of previous possession, Mr. Blackstone had a title to
> proprietorship in the whole peninsula. It was in fact for a time
> called Blackstone's neck. . . . Mr. Blackstone was a very eccentrick
> character. He was a man of learning, and had received episcopal
> ordination in England. . . . It was not very long before Mr.
> Blackstone found that there might be more than one kind of non-
> conformity, and was virtually obliged to leave the remainder of
> his estate here. . . . Let the cause of his removal have been what
> it may, certain it is that he went and settled by the Pawtucket
> river. . . . At this his new plantation he lived uninterrupted for
> many years, and there raised an orchard, the first that ever bore
> apples in Rhode Island. He had the first of the sort called yellow
> sweetings, that were ever in the world, and is said to have planted
> the first orchard in Massachusetts also. . . . Though he was far
> from agreeing in opinion with Roger Williams, he used frequently
> to go to Providence to preach the gospel; and to encourage his
> younger hearers, while he gratified his own benevolent disposition,
> he would give them of his apples, which were the first they ever
> saw. It was said that when he grew old and unable to travel on
> foot, not having any horse, he used to ride on a bull, which he had
> tamed and tutored to that use. (pp. 50–53)

This account is taken virtually word for word from a series of
articles called "The Historical Account of the Planting and Growth
of Providence" published in the Providence *Gazette* (January 12
to March 30, 1765).[3] However, Snow adds to this narrative the
application to Boston, which would be of special interest to Hawthorne (the phrase, "and is said to have planted the first orchard
in Massachusetts also").

The only minor characters that are developed to such an extent
that they become in any way memorable figures are Mrs. Hibbins
and the Rev. John Wilson. Hawthorne's use of Mrs. Hibbins shows
again a precise interest in the byways of Boston history. He describes
the costume of the "reputed witch-lady" carefully. He refers to her
as "Governor Bellingham's bitter-tempered sister, . . . the same
who, a few years later, was executed as a witch." And again, during
the minister's vigil, Hawthorne writes that Dimmesdale beheld "at
one of the chamber-windows of Governor Bellingham's mansion
. . . the appearance of the old magistrate himself. . . . At another window of the same house, moreover, appeared old Mistress

3. These were reprinted in the Massachusetts Historical Society's *Collections*,
2nd Ser., IX, 166–203 (1820).

Hibbins, the Governor's sister . . ." In Snow's book there is this account of Mrs. Ann Hibbins:

> The most remarkable occurrence in the colony in the year 1655 was the trial and condemnation of Mrs. Ann Hibbins of Boston for witchcraft. Her husband, who died July 23, 1654, was an agent for the colony in England, several years one of the assistants, and a merchant of note in the town; but losses in the latter part of his life had reduced his estate, and increased the natural crabbedness of his wife's temper, which made her turbulent and quarrelsome, and brought her under church censures, and at length rendered her so odious to her neighbours as to cause some of them to accuse her of witchcraft. The jury brought her in guilty, but the magistrates refused to accept the verdict; so the cause came to the general court, where the popular clamour prevailed against her, and the miserable old lady was condemned and executed in June 1656. (p. 140)[4]

There seems to be only one source for Hawthorne's reference to Mrs. Hibbins as Bellingham's sister. That is in a footnote by James Savage in the 1825 edition of John Winthrop's *History of New England*, and it was this edition that Hawthorne borrowed from the Salem Athenaeum.[5] Savage writes that Mrs. Hibbins "suffered the punishment of death, for the ridiculous crime, the year after her husband's decease; her brother, Bellingham, not exerting, perhaps, his highest influence for her preservation."[6] Hawthorne leads the reader to assume that Mrs. Hibbins, nine years before the death of her husband, is living at the home of her brother. Hawthorne uses this relationship between Bellingham and Mrs. Hibbins in order to have fewer stage directions and explanations. It helps him to establish a more realistic unity in the tale. It partially explains the presence of the various people at the Market-Place the night of the minister's vigil, since Bellingham's house was just north of the scaffold. It also suggests why Bellingham is the governor chosen for the opening scenes of the novel, to prevent the plot from becoming encumbered with too many minor figures.

The Reverend John Wilson's description is sympathetically done, and it is for the most part historically accurate. Hawthorne presents him as "the reverend and famous John Wilson, the eldest clergyman of Boston, a great scholar, like most of his contemporaries in the profession, and withal a man of kind and genial spirit." Cotton Mather,[7] William Hubbard,[8] and Caleb Snow testify to his re-

4. This is almost a literal copy from Hutchinson, I, 173. See also William Hubbard, "A General History of New England," Massachusetts Historical Society *Collections*, 2nd Ser., V, 574 (1815); Winthrop, I, 321.
5. Kesselring, p. 64.
6. Winthrop, I, 321 n. This contradicts Julian Hawthorne's observation:

"As for Mistress Hibbins, history describes her as Bellingham's relative, but does not say that she was his sister, as is stated in the 'Romance'" ("Scenes of Hawthorne's Romances," *Century Magazine*, XXVIII, 391, July, 1884).
7. *Magnalia Christi Americana* (London, 1702), bk. III, p. 46.
8. Hubbard, p. 604.

markable "compassion for the distressed and . . . affection for all"
(Snow, p. 156). William Allen, in his *American Biographical and
Historical Dictionary*, writes that "Mr. Wilson was one of the most
humble, pious, and benevolent men of the age, in which he lived.
Kind affections and zeal were the prominent traits in his character.
. . . Every one loved him. . . ."[9] Hawthorne, to gain dramatic
opposition to Dimmesdale, makes the preacher seem older than he
really was. He pictures the man of fifty-seven as "the venerable
pastor, John Wilson . . . [with a] beard, white as a snow-drift";
and later, as the "good old minister."

Hawthorne's description of Puritan costuming has been substan-
tiated by twentieth-century research. Although the elders of the
colonial church dressed in "sad-colored garments, and gray, steeple-
crowned hats"[1] and preached simplicity of dress, Hawthorne recognized that "the church attendants never followed that preaching."[2]
"Lists of Apparell" left by the old colonists in their wills, inven-
tories of estates, ships' bills of lading, laws telling what must *not*
be worn, ministers' sermons denouncing excessive ornamentation
in dress, and portraits of the leaders prove that "little of the extreme
Puritan is found in the dress of the first Boston colonists."[3] Alice
Morse Earle, after going over the lists of clothing brought by the
Puritans, concludes:

> From all this cheerful and ample dress, this might well be a Cava-
> lier emigration; in truth, the apparel supplied as an outfit to the
> Virginia planters (who are generally supposed to be far more
> given over to rich dress) is not as full nor as costly as this apparel
> of Massachusetts Bay. In this as in every comparison I make, I
> find little to indicate any difference between Puritan and Cavalier
> in quantity of garments, in quality, or cost—or, indeed, in form.
> The differences in England were much exaggerated in print; in
> America they often existed wholly in men's notions of what a
> Puritan must be. (I, 34)

Hawthorne's descriptions agree with the early annals. The embroideries and bright colors worn by Pearl, the silks and velvets of
Mrs. Hibbins, Hester's needlework—the laces, "deep ruffs . . .

9. Allen, p. 613. The Reverend John Wilson was born in 1588; he died in 1667.
1. The phrase, "steeple-crowned hats," is used by Hawthorne each time he describes the dress of the Puritan elders (*The Scarlet Letter*, pp. 24, 67, 79, 278). The only source that I have been able to find for this particular phrase is in an essay on hats in a series of articles on clothing worn in former times: Joseph Moser, "Vestiges, Collected and Recollected, Number XXIV," *European Magazine*, XLV, 409–415 (1804). The Charge-Books of the Salem Athenaeum show that Hawthorne read the magazine in which this article appeared. Moser wrote about the "elevated and solemn beavers of the Puritans" (p. 414) and the "high and steeple-crowned hats, probably from an idea, that the conjunction of Church and State was necessary to exalt their archetype in the manner that it was exalted" (p. 411).
2. Alice Morse Earle, *Two Centuries of Costume in America* (New York, 1903), I, 8.
3. Earle, I, 13.

and gorgeously embroidered gloves"—were, as he said, "readily allowed to individuals dignified by rank or wealth, even while sumptuary laws forbade these and similar extravagances to the plebeian order." The Court in 1651 had recorded "its utter detestation and dislike that men or women of mean condition should take upon them the garb of Gentlemen, by wearing gold or silver lace . . . which, though allowable to persons of greater Estates or more liberal Education, yet we cannot but judge it intolerable in persons of such like condition."[4] Hawthorne's attempt to create an authentic picture of the seventeenth century is shown in *The American Notebooks* where he describes the "Dress of an old woman, 1656."[5] But all of Hawthorne's description is significant beyond the demands of verisimilitude. In *The Scarlet Letter* he is repeating the impressions which are characteristic of his tales: the portrayal of color contrasts for symbolic purposes, the play of light and dark, the rich color of red against black, the brilliant embroideries[6] on the sable background of the "sad-colored garments."

So far there has been slight mention of the influence of Cotton Mather's writings on *The Scarlet Letter*. These surely require our attention in any study such as this one. Professor Turner believes that certain elements of Mather's *Magnalia Christi Americana*, "and in particular the accounts of God's judgment on adulterers [in II, 397–398], may also have influenced *The Scarlet Letter*. Mather relates [II, 404–405] that a woman who had killed her illegitimate child was exhorted by John Wilson and John Cotton to repent while she was in prison awaiting execution. In like manner, as will be recalled, John Wilson joins with Governor Bellingham and Arthur Dimmesdale in admonishing Hester Prynne to reveal the father of her child."[7] It is possible that an echo of the witch tradition in the *Magnalia Christi Americana* may also be found in *The Scarlet Letter*. "The proposal by Mistress Hibbins that Hester accompany her to a witch meeting is typical of the Mather witch tradition, which included, in accordance with the well known passage in *The Scarlet Letter*, the signing in the devil's book with an iron pen and with blood for ink. . . ."[8] The Black Man mentioned so often by Hawthorne was familiar to the Puritan settlers of New England. Pearl tells her mother "a story about the Black

4. Winsor, I, 484–485. Hawthorne had read the *Acts and Laws . . . of the Massachusetts-Bay in New-England* (Boston, 1726)—see Kesselring, p. 56.
5. *The American Notebooks*, p. 109.
6. One of Hawthorne's favorite words —for example, see *The American Notebooks*, p. 97.
7. Turner, p. 550; Turner is using the Hartford (1855) edition of the *Magnalia Christi Americana*. See *The Scarlet Letter*, pp. 86–91.

8. Turner, p. 546—see *The Scarlet Letter*, pp. 143–144, and *Magnalia Christi Americana*, bk. VI, p. 81: "It was not long before *M. L.* . . . confess'd that *She* rode with her Mother to the said Witch-meeting . . . . At another time *M. L. junior*, the Granddaughter, aged about 17 Years . . . declares that . . . they . . . rode on a Stick or Pole in the *Air* . . . and that they set their Hands to the Devil's Book . . . ."

Man. . . . How he haunts this forest, and carries a book with him,—a big, heavy book, with iron clasps; and how this ugly Black Man offers his book and an iron pen to everybody that meets him here among the trees; and they are to write their names with their own blood." Concerning the Black Man, Cotton Mather had written: "These *Tormentors* tendred unto the afflicted a *Book*, requiring them to *Sign* it, or *Touch* it at least, in token of their consenting to be Listed in the Service of the *Devil*; which they refusing to do, the *Spectres* under the Command of that *Blackman*, as they called him, would apply themselves to Torture them with prodigious Molestations."[9]

Even the portent in the sky, the great red letter A, which was seen on the night of the revered John Winthrop's death (and Dimmesdale's vigil), would not have seemed too strange to Puritan historians. To them it would certainly not have been merely an indication of Hawthorne's gothic interests. Snow had related that when John Cotton had died on Thursday, December 23, 1652, "strange and alarming signs appeared in the heavens, while his body lay, according to the custom of the times, till the Tuesday following" (p. 133).

The idea of the scarlet A had been in Hawthorne's mind for some years before he wrote the novel. In 1844 he had made this comment in his notebooks as a suggestion for a story: "The life of a woman, who, by the old colony law, was condemned always to wear the letter A, sewed on her garment, in token of her having committed adultery."[1] Before that, in "Endicott and the Red Cross," he had told of a "woman with no mean share of beauty" who wore a scarlet A. It has commonly been accepted that the "old colony law" which he had referred to in his notebooks had been found in Felt's *Annals of Salem*, where we read under the date of May 5, 1694: "Among such laws, passed this session, were two against Adultery and Polygamy. Those guilty of the first crime, were to sit an hour on the gallows, with ropes about their necks,— be severely whipt not above 40 stripes; and forever after wear a capital A, two inches long, cut out of cloth coloured differently from their clothes, and sewed on the arms, or back parts of their garments so as always to be seen when they were about."[2]

Exactly when Hawthorne began writing *The Scarlet Letter* is not known, but by September 27, 1849, he was working on it throughout every day. It was finished by February 3, 1850.[3] In the novel there is the same rapid skill at composition which is typical of the note-

9. *Magnalia Christi Americana*, bk. II, p. 60; see also Massachusetts Historical Society *Collections*, V, 64 (1708); Neal, II, 131, 133–135, 144, 150, 158, 160, 169.
1. *The American Notebooks*, p. 107.

2. Joseph B. Felt, *The Annals of Salem, from Its First Settlement* (Salem, 1827), p. 317.
3. Randall Stewart, *Nathaniel Hawthorne* (New Haven, 1948), pp. 93–95.

books. From the multitude of historical facts he knew he could call forth with severe economy only a few to support the scenes of passion or punishment. Perhaps it does not seem good judgment to claim that Hawthorne wrote *The Scarlet Letter* with a copy of Snow's *History of Boston* on the desk. But it does not appear believable that all these incidental facts from New England histories, the exacting time scheme, the authentic description of Boston in the 1640's, should have remained so extremely clear and perfect in his mind when he was under the extraordinary strain of writing the story. Here the studies of Hawthorne's literary borrowings made by Dawson, Turner, and others must be taken into account. They have shown that in certain of his tales, he "seems to have written with his original open before him."[4] To claim a firm dependence upon certain New England histories for the background of *The Scarlet Letter* should therefore not seem unreasonable.

The incidents, places, and persons noticed in this article are the principal New England historical references in *The Scarlet Letter*. A study like this of Hawthorne's sources shows something of his thorough method of reading; it reveals especially his certain knowledge of colonial history and his interest in the unusual, obscure fact. But these are side lights of an author's mind. His steady determination was to make the romances of his imagination as real as the prison-house and the grave.

It would be unfair to leave the study of Hawthorne's historical approach here. His final concern in history was the attempt to find the "spiritual significance"[5] of the facts. As his sister Elizabeth had said of the young man: "He was not very fond of history in general."[6] Hawthorne stated concretely his conception of history and the novel in a review (1846) of W. G. Simms's *Views and Reviews in American History:*

> . . . we cannot help feeling that the real treasures of his subject have escaped the author's notice. The themes suggested by him, viewed as he views them, would produce nothing but historical novels, cast in the same worn out mould that has been in use these thirty years, and which it is time to break up and fling away. To be the prophet of Art requires almost as high a gift as to be a fulfiller of the prophecy. Mr. Simms has not this gift; he possesses nothing of the magic touch that should cause new intellectual and moral shapes to spring up in the reader's mind, peopling with varied life what had hitherto been a barren waste.[7]

With the evocation of the spirit of the colonial past, and with a realistic embodiment of scene, Hawthorne repeopled a landscape

4. Turner, p. 547.
5. Julian Hawthorne, *Hawthorne Reading*, p. 100.
6. "Recollections of Hawthorne by His Sister Elizabeth," p. 324.
7. Stewart, "Hawthorne's Contributions to *The Salem Advertiser*," *American Literature*, V, 331–332 (Jan., 1934).

wherein new intellectual and moral shapes could dwell. The new fiction of Hester Prynne and the old appearances of Mrs. Hibbins could not be separated. Time past and time present became explicable as they were identified in the same profound moral engagement.

CHARLES BOEWE *and* MURRAY G. MURPHEY

Hester Prynne in History†

A recent exhaustive examination by Charles Ryskamp of the contribution of Caleb H. Snow's *History of Boston* to the factual framework of *The Scarlet Letter*[1] goes far to justify Hawthorne's own claim for the historical "authenticity of the outline" of the story.[2] While no one supposes that an actual bundle of papers prepared by a Surveyor Jonathan Pue ever existed—like Defoe, Hawthorne loads on historicity in "The Custom House" to ballast his fancy—nevertheless it is far from certain that "no real historical bases" exist for Hester, as Mr. Ryskamp remarks in passing. It is not surprising that Hawthorne drew upon historical personages for minor characters and seemingly invented his major ones—that, after all, is standard practice in the historical novel. Yet, except in a strictly technical sense, Mr. Ryskamp's observation follows too literally another's assertion that "no Hester Prynne is to be discovered in the annals of Boston . . ."[3] and seems to imply that she is largely a fabrication.

If, literally, Hester is found neither in the annals of Boston nor in Snow's *History* compiled from those annals, perhaps the "real" Hester merely was relocated by Hawthorne's imagination. We believe she was.

Of course, the Hester Prynne of the novel was not drawn directly from a single seventeenth-century Puritan prototype in the way a minor character like Governor Bellingham was. In this sense she is not to be found in any of the annals. But already in print are most of the details necessary for one to conceive how Hawthorne built up her composite picture from historical scraps at hand. Most notable of them is the story of Goodwife Mendame of Duxbury, who was condemned "to be whipt at a cart's tayle through the town's streets,

† From *American Literature*, XXXII (May 1960), pp. 202–204.
1. Charles Ryskamp, "The New England Sources of *The Scarlet Letter*," *American Literature*, XXXI, 257–272 (Nov., 1959).
2. *Hawthorne's Works* (Boston, 1883), V, 52.
3. Austin Warren, "Introduction," *The Scarlet Letter*, Rinehart ed. (New York [1947]), p. vi.

and to weare a badge with the capital letters AD cut in cloth upon her left sleeve" when she was found guilty of adultery.[4] Duxbury was a satellite of Plymouth Colony, not of Massachusetts Bay, and Plymouth was traditionally referred to as the Old Colony. When Hawthorne jotted down the germ of his novel he wrote: "The life of a woman, who, by the *old colony* laws, was condemned always to wear the letter A, sewed on her garment, in token of her having committed adultery."[5]

If the idea of the symbolic letter may have come from Plymouth, the name of the character in the novel apparently derived from a source closer home. Hitherto unnoticed, we believe, is a rather striking item in the records of the Salem Quarterly Court which convened in November of 1668:

> Hester Craford, for fornication with John Wedg, as she confessed, was ordered to be severely whipped and that security be given to save the town from the charge of keeping the child. Mordecaie Craford [her father] bound. The judgment of her being whipped was respitted for a month or six weeks after the birth of the child, and it was left to the Worshipful Major William Hathorne to see it executed on a lecture day.[6]

Though Hawthorne recognized the careful distinction the Puritans made between fornication and adultery, this judgment would sufficiently account for the first name of his character, especially since his own stern ancestor was involved in the trial and punishment. While it cannot be proved with certainty from the known titles that Hawthorne read[7] that he happened across this passage, we are assured by the testimony of his son[8] that "forgotten volumes of the New England Annalists were favorites of his."

The outward details of the character Hester had to be a mosaic of bits and pieces. The action of the novel takes place between 1642 and 1649, as Mr. Ryskamp shows; even if the figure of the scarlet A did come from Joseph B. Felt's *Annals of Salem* as he suggests (p. 271), yet we must notice that the law establishing this peculiar punishment for adultery was passed only as late as 1694. Earlier, as the court record cited above shows, whipping was the standard punishment for fornication at Salem, while in 1644, in the middle of the very period the novel covers, the unfortunate Mary Latham, who was married to an old man whom she did not love and who committed adultery with "divers young men," was

4. Quoted by George F. Willison, *Saints and Strangers* (New York, 1945), p. 324; also quoted in Warren's Introduction.
5. *The American Notebooks*, ed. Randall Stewart (New Haven, 1932), p. 107. Italics ours.

6. *Records and Files of the Quarterly Courts of Essex County, Massachusetts* (Salem, 1914), IV, 84.
7. Marion L. Kesselring, *Hawthorne's Reading 1828–1850* (New York, 1949)
8. Quoted by Ryskamp, p. 259.

actually subjected to the statutory death penalty by the Massachusetts Bay court.[9] Hawthorne could not allow strict historical
accuracy to kill off his heroine in the first chapter.

Instead he simply exercised his novelist's prerogative of shifting
about the historical details to suit his purpose. He acknowledged
as much about the sketch "Main Street," the historical facts of
which he pretended came from one of Surveyor Pue's manuscripts,
as did those of *The Scarlet Letter*.[1] In "Main Street" an unnamed
critic of the mechanical panorama which exhibits Salem's history is
made to thunder: "you have fallen into anachronisms that I positively shudder to think of!" The showman Hawthorne calmly admits the charge, but mildly adds: "Sir, you break the illusion of
the scene. . . ."[2]

May the showman forgive us for sniffing out clues of the historical Hester.

ERNEST W. BAUGHMAN

Public Confession and *The Scarlet Letter*†

In *The Scarlet Letter,* Dimmesdale's story ends with the public
confession of his sin, the acknowledgement of Hester as his partner, and the recognition of Pearl as his child. The confession knits
up the story strands of the four major characters; and it further
affects the lives of the remaining characters. The psychological
necessity for Dimmesdale's confession has been established beyond
doubt long before it occurs. As the author has managed the plot, no
other ending is possible. However, Hester's treatment by colony
and church authorities in the first pillory scene implies that public
confession was customary for certain crimes in Massachusetts Bay
Colony, and it suggests that Hawthorne may have been using a
historical as well as psychological and dramatic necessity. If such
a tradition existed, the novel takes on an added dimension of fidelity to seventeenth-century theology, ethics, and law. If the tradition of public confession had a broader base than Massachusetts Bay
between 1642 and 1649 (the time of the story), this dimension
becomes even more important and adds greatly to the meanings of

---

9. Warren, p. vii, citing Winthrop's
Journals of 1644. Plymouth, too, had
the death penalty for adultery, but it
was never invoked.
1. *Works*, V, 49.

2. *Works*, III, 454.
† From *The New England Quarterly*,
40 (1967), 532–50. Footnotes have
been renumbered.

the actions of the major characters. The questions, then, are these. What was Puritan practice regarding public confession at the time of *The Scarlet Letter*? What authority for it existed in church discipline, traditional or written? Did it have a spiritual basis? Did it have legal as well as church enforcement? Had it been taken over from Plymouth Colony, or had it been developed because some kind of discipline was necessary after leaving Anglican forms behind? Did it have English roots? And was a person expected to confess secret crimes or sins to civil or church authorities? If we can find answers to these questions, we shall be better able to interpret Dimmesdale's need for confession and we shall be more able to place in perspective the effects of his confession on Hester, Pearl, and Chillingworth.

Literary evidence for required public confession is scant. In the novel both colony and church officers urge Hester to confess. And Dimmesdale and Chillingworth argue about whether one must confess an unknown sin during his lifetime. Samuel Sewall's *Diary* records that in January 1696–97 he publicly confessed his errors in the Salem witchcraft trials.[1] Sewall's confession, like Dimmesdale's, was voluntary; however it occurred about fifty years after Dimmesdale's; and it was a confession of error, not of a crime.

As a matter of record, public confession was required by both church and state for a variety of sins and crimes in the Massachusetts Bay Colony from the very beginning, in the Plymouth Colony at least as early as 1624, and—more surprising—in Virginia thirty years before Hester's humiliation on the pillory. Most surprising of all to those who have depended on literary sources for our history, the Puritans, the Pilgrims, and the Virginians were simply continuing a tradition as old as the England of Elizabeth (and for notorious crimes even older). Not only is the tradition old, it continued in fairly common use in New England into the nineteenth century and in Scotland until fairly late in that century. It is still in use today in some denominations in this country.[2] * * *

The American tradition had its beginnings at least by 1611. The *Lavves Diuine, Morall and Martiall*, etc., promulgated by Sir Thomas Dale as governor of Virginia, contains four items listing offenses for

1. Samuel Sewall (1652–1730), one of the most prominent figures in Puritan New England—chief justice of Massachusetts from 1718 to 1728—was one of the judges at the Salem witchcraft trials in 1692, which resulted in the execution of twenty persons. Five years later he stood before the congregation of the Old South Church to hear his confession of guilt read, in which he asked pardon of man and God for the "blame and shame" of his actions. [*Editor.*]

2. Alice Morse Earle, *Curious Punishments of Bygone Days* (New York, 1909), 106–108, 112. Her earliest case is 1534, her latest 1884, from Scotland. See also Charles Francis Adams, Jr., "Some Phases of Sexual Morality and Church Discipline in Colonial New England," *Proceedings of the Massachusetts Historical Society*, Second Series (1890–1891). VI 493. I know of similar cases in Indiana between 1934 and 1944.

which part of the punishment was confessing in church. The offenses include deriding the scriptures or ministers, detracting, slandering, calumniating, murmuring, mutinying, resisting, disobeying, or neglecting the commands of colony officers. For refusing to repair to the minister for religious instruction, one would be treated thus:

> The Gouernour shall cause the offender for his first time of refusall to be whipt, for the second time to be whipt twice, and to acknowledge his fault vpon the Saboth day, in the assembly of the congregation, and for the third time to be whipt euery day until he hath made the same acknowledgement, and asked forgiuenesse for the same, and shall repaire vnto the Minister, to be further instructed as aforesaid.[3] * * *

The first New England account I have found is from 1624. One John Lyford of Plymouth confessed that he had sent lying letters to the company officials in London and that he had used intemperate speech during his trial.[4]

The most abundant evidence for New England practice and for the overlapping of civil and church punishments between 1630 and 1650 comes from John Winthrop's *Journals*.[5] An account of 1640 presents a situation somewhat relevant to Dimmesdale's. Captain Underhill, like Dimmesdale guilty of adultery, returned to Boston after a long struggle with his conscience during his excommunication and banishment.

> The Lord after a long time and great afflictions, had broken his heart, and brought him to humble himself night and day with prayers and tears till his strength was wasted; and indeed he appeared as a man worn out with sorrow, and yet he could find no peace, therefore he was now come to seek it in this ordinance of God. (Winthrop, II, 12–14, September 3, 1640)

The *Journals* describe sixteen such cases handled by the courts, the church, or both. Adultery is central in four, contempt for authority in four, suspicion of heresy in two. Heresy, assault, overcharging for goods, disorderly conduct, and violent language appear in single cases. The accused make public confessions in all cases. The insistence on public confession is inescapable in these accounts;

3. *For the Colony of Virginea Brittania. Lavves Diuine, Morall and Martiall, etc.* (London, 1612), reprinted by Peter Force, editor, *Tracts and Other Papers Relating Principally to the Origin, Settlement and Progress of the Colonies of North America from the Discovery of the Country to the Year 1771* (New York, 1947), III, Tract No. 2, 17–18.
4. William Bradford, *History of Plymouth Plantation*, W. C. Ford, editor (Boston, 1912), I, 397.
5. John Winthrop, *Winthrop's Journal*, James K. Hosmer, ed. (New York, 1908). [Winthrop, 1588–1649, repeatedly elected governor of the Massachusetts Bay Colony, was the dominating influence on the life of the colony from its inception in 1630 to his death in 1649—*Editor*.]

however, the procedures and the lines of authority between the civil and church actions are vague. Some generalizations about these matters will appear later.

Because both the courts and the churches required public confession, we should expect to find statutes and church rules making the practice official. I have found no such statute; however, The Court of Assistants specified eight such penalties between 1632 and 1644.[6] Because this court had both judicial and legislative functions, a decision was quite probably the equivalent of a law. * * *

Before analyzing the importance of the practice of public confession in the novel, we should make what generalizations seem warrantable. (1) In most cases of the early seventeenth century, the court dealt with the offender first; it might or might not require public acknowledgement of error by the offender. (2) After the court had passed sentence, the congregation heard the evidence and dealt with the offender, determining whether to accept his confession or to cast him out. (3) After confessing in church, a member guilty of a civil or criminal offense was required to stand trial. He could be executed. He could not confess privately and receive absolution as an Anglican or Catholic could. (4) An erring member brought before the congregation for specific misconduct or suspected misconduct might be dealt with in four ways: he could be admonished to mend his ways; he could be suspended from participation in the Lord's Supper; he could be excommunicated; or he could be cleared either if he confessed or if adjudged innocent. (5) Confession was mandatory if one suspended from the privilege of the Lord's Supper or one excommunicated wished to be received back into the church. (6) Apparently confession was mandatory for all parents guilty of fornication before marriage if they were church members or if they later applied for church membership (the "seven-months' rule" affected both groups). (7) The dual jurisdiction of church and court was common in England and Scotland long before the seventeenth century; it was common in Massachusetts and Virginia during the seventeenth century. * * *

Because Hawthorne uses Dimmesdale's confession for the denouement of *The Scarlet Letter*, we should first consider his problem in light of the Puritan tradition. His being led to confession is the problem of the novel, the one dramatized; and because of the time and the place, the confession must be a public one.

Dimmesdale's guilt is known only to Hester and Chillingworth, neither of whom will disclose it. His defense for not confessing is his contention that public confession of sin is not required by Holy

6. *Records of the Court of Assistants of the Colony of the Massachusetts Bay*   *1630–1692* (Boston, 1904, 1928), II 24, 65, 92–93, 131; III, 74–75, 137.

Writ; he also argues that his capacity to do good (by serving God as a minister) would be lost if his guilt were known. He almost certainly knows that his position is false. Though the authority for mandatory confession of secret sin is less clear than that for known sin, he has no grounds for a distinction between secret and known sin.[7] Sin is sin and must be confessed. The Puritans took quite seriously the admonition of James: "Confess your faults to one another, and pray for one another, that ye may be healed." (James 5:16.) Dimmesdale is too weak to do what he knows is required of him. Today we would say that he rationalized; Hawthorne said, "He had a faculty, indeed, of escaping from any topic that agitated his too sensitive and nervous temperament." The fullest statement of his defense in the novel is addressed to Chillingworth:

> There can be . . . no power, short of Divine mercy, to disclose, whether by uttered words, or by type or emblem, the secrets that may be buried with a human heart. The heart, making itself guilty of such secrets, must perforce hold them, until the day when all hidden things shall be revealed. Nor have I so read or interpreted Holy Writ, as to understand that the disclosure of human thoughts and deeds, then to be made, is intended as a part of the retribution.

A little later in the same interview, pressed to reveal the source of his sickness of soul, he makes an impassioned refusal and rushes from the room:

> No!—not to thee!—not to an earthly physician . . . Not to thee! But, if it be the soul's disease, then do I commit myself to the one Physician of the soul! He, if it stand with his good pleasure, can cure; or he can kill! Let him do with me as, in his justice and wisdom, he shall see good. But who art thou, that meddlest in this matter?—that dares thrust himself between the sufferer and his God?

Dimmesdale could have made such statements to no one but Chillingworth (or Hester). "Thrusting oneself between the sufferer and his God" is exactly what a good Puritan was expected to do. Nevertheless he holds to his position until he is able to make the confession. During the seven years of silence he adds the sin of hypocrisy: in his sermons, in his plans to flee with Hester, and in refusing to admit that anyone besides Chillingworth has violated the sanctity of a human heart.

If we can assume that Dimmesdale completely believes his posi-

7. James Britton confessed voluntarily to guilt of adultery and was executed with his partner Mary Latham. Winthrop, II, 161–163 (March, 1644).

tion on confession (though if he did, he would have no problem; and there would be no novel), we may ask whether he is culpable in any other actions. One that should immediately come to mind is his complete disregard for the state of Hester's soul—or Pearl's—until the very end of his life. The words of Governor Bellingham remind us of this unconcern: ". . . the responsibility of this woman's soul lies greatly with you. It behooves you, therefore, to exhort her to repentance, and to confession, as a proof and consequence thereof."

A second source of cupability is Dimmesdale's receiving and administering the Lord's Supper during the seven-year hypocrisy. The main requirement of one engaging in the rite is that he be truly repentant. St. Paul is unequivocal: "Wherefore whosoever shall eat this bread, and drink this cup of the Lord unworthily, shall be guilty of the body and blood of the Lord. But let a man examine himself, and so let him eat of that bread and drink of that cup. For he that eateth and drinketh unworthily, eateth and drinketh damnation to himself, not discerning the Lord's body." (I Corinthians 12:27–29.) Dimmesdale has to know that he is unworthy of receiving the sacrament; he is probably even less worthy of administering the rite. He is guilty of a capital crime according to both colony and scriptural law. He has not made his "confession as a proof and consequence" of repentance.

Though he resolved to repent many times, as the chapter "The Interior of A Heart" attests, he could not. Several of Winthrop's cases shed light on Dimmesdale's problem: cases in which the confession is voluntary. That of Mr. Batchellor suggests Dimmesdale's problem with the Lord's Supper. A minister, he had attempted adultery with a parishioner and had slandered her when she accused him. "But soon after, when the Lord's Supper was to be administered, he did voluntarily confess the attempt, and that he did intend to have defiled her." (Winthrop, II, 45–46, November 12, 1641.) The weight of unconfessed sin is evident in three similar cases in which secret confession to God has been fruitless.[8] The case of one Turner who committed suicide because he could not bring himself to confess is perhaps applicable to Dimmesdale's situation. (Winthrop, II, 55, January 1642.) The whole chapter "The Minister in a Maze" indicates that he must do something desperate if he does not soon find release in confession.

Perhaps the most applicable case, after all, is that of Judge Sewall who rose to a tragic triumph when he confessed his errors in the witchcraft trials. The weight of tradition in both church and state demanded public confession. Hawthorne put the decision

8. Winthrop, II, 12–14, 29, 161–163.

squarely where he wanted it to rest: on the conscience of the guilty man. No outside agency forced it. When it finally came, it was complete and genuine. Gone were the rationalizations about his usefulness as a minister and his insistence that Chillingworth's crime was greater than that of Hester and himself. In fact, he acknowledged their guilt in the same terms he had earlier used to describe Chillingworth's crime. "It may be, that, when we forgot our God,—*when we violated our reverence each for the other's soul,*—it was thenceforth vain to hope that we could meet here-after, in an everlasting and pure reunion. God knows; and he is merciful!"[9] He asked for nothing but God's mercy, indicating the condition of the true penitent.

As the plot is handled there can be only one solution. If Dimmes-dale had confessed privately, to the Rev. John Wilson for example, he would need to confess publicly; he would be excommunicated, and he would stand trial for the crime of adultery. He could have been executed as Mary Latham and James Britton were in 1644. Although Hawthorne once considered having Dimmesdale confess to a Catholic priest, the difficulties of this ending are so obvious that we hardly need consider his rejection of it, though he was later able to use a somewhat similar confession in *The Marble Faun.*[1]***

MICHAEL J. COLACURCIO

Footsteps of Ann Hutchinson:
The Context of *The Scarlet Letter*†

* * *

In the first brief chapter of *The Scarlet Letter*, the narrator pays almost as much attention to a rose bush as he does to the appear-ance and moral significance of Puritan America's first prison. That "wild rose-bush, covered, in this month of June, with its delicate gems," contrasts with the "burdock, pig-weed, apple-peru" and other "unsightly vegetation"; yet all flourish together in the same

9. Italics mine. For the importance of violating the reverence for another's soul, see James E. Miller, Jr., "Haw-thorne and Melville: The Unpardonable Sin," *PMLA*, LXX, 91–114 (March, 1955).

1. In *The Marble Faun* (1860), Hilda, whose Puritan conscience is agonized by the knowledge that her two friends have committed a crime, finds a temporary relief from her "terrible secret" by con-fessing to a priest in St. Peter's in Rome. [*Editor.*]

† From *ELH*, 39 (1972). 459–94. Some footnotes have been deleted and the remainder renumbered.

"congenial" soil which has so early brought forth "the black flower of civilized society, a prison." And thus early are we introduced to the book's extremely complicated view of the natural and the social. Moreover, as the rose bush seems to offer Nature's sympathy to society's criminal, it becomes essentially associated with Hester Prynne, almost as *her* symbol. Accordingly, criticism has been lavish in its own attention to that rose bush: it has, out of perfect soundness of instinct, been made the starting point of more than one excellent reading of *The Scarlet Letter*; indeed the explication of this image and symbol is one of the triumphs of the "new" Hawthorne criticism."[1]

But if the "natural" and internal associations of this rose bush have been successfully elaborated, its external and "historic" implications have been largely ignored. And yet not for any fault of the narrator. This rose bush "has been kept alive in history," he assures us; and it may even be, as "there is fair authority for believing," that "it had sprung up under the footsteps of the sainted Ann Hutchinson, as she entered the prison-door."

We are, I suppose, free to ignore this critical invitation if we choose. Obviously we are being offered a saint's legend in which Hawthorne expects no reader literally to believe. Perhaps it is there only for the irony of "sainted" * * * for Hawthorne will have nearly as many reservations about Hester's sainthood as John Winthrop had about Mrs. Hutchinson's. Certainly the natural language of flowers is a more available and universal sort of literary knowledge than that overdetermined system of historical fixities and definites which laborers in the field of American studies call "Antinomianism."[2]
* * *

Still, a conscious decision *not* to look for and press a Hester Prynne–Ann Hutchinson analogy might be risky, the result of a critical bias. We should not, it seems to me, want to believe Hawthorne a casual name dropper unless he prove himself one. We should prefer a more rather than a less precise use of literary allusion, not only in this opening reference but also in a later one which suggests that, except for the existence of Pearl, Hester "might have come down to us in history, hand in hand with Ann Hutchinson, as the foundress of a religious sect." The references are, after all, pretty precise: Hester walks in the footsteps of (but not quite hand-in-hand with) Ann Hutchinson. And before we invest too heavily in Hawthorne's well

1. See, particularly, Hyatt H. Waggoner's *Hawthorne* (Cambridge, Mass., 1955, 1963) and Roy R. Male's "From the Innermost Germ," *ELH*, 20 (1953).
2. Antinomianism (literally: "against law") stressed the true believer's responsibility to the Holy Spirit within the individual, even to the point of disobeying biblical, clerical, or juridical laws. The Puritans naturally considered such a view tantamount to anarchy and moral license and Governor John Winthrop banished Mrs. Hutchinson from Massachusetts in 1638. See note 1, p. 40 of this book. [*Editor*]

known demurrer to Longfellow, we might remind ourselves that Hawthorne did write—near the outset of his career, in clear and close dependence on "a good many books"[3]—a well informed sketch called "Mrs. Hutchinson." He mentions her again, prominently, in those reviews of New England history entitled *Grandfather's Chair*[4] and "Main Street."[5] Now he seems to be apprising us of a relationship between Hester Prynne and that famous lady heretic. The man who created the one and memorialized the other ought to be in a position to know.

Clearly the relationship is not one of "identity": tempting as the view can be made to appear, *The Scarlet Letter* is probably not intended as an allegory of New England's Antinomian Crisis. Hawthorne's historical tales never work quite that simply: "The Gentle Boy," "Young Goodman Brown," and "The Minister's Black Veil" all have something quite precise and fundamental to say about the Puritan mind but, in spite of the precision with which they are set or "dated," they are not primarily "about" (respectively) the Quaker problem, the witchcraft delusion, or the great awakening. Their history is not quite that literalistic. And here, of course, the setting is "literally" Boston, 1642 to 1649—not 1636 and 1637. More importantly, but equally obviously, the career of Hawthorne's fictional Hester Prynne is far from identical with that of the historical Mrs. Hutchinson. However "antinomian" Hester becomes, it would be positively ludicrous to forget that her philosophical career is inseparable from adultery and illegitimate childbirth, events which have no very real counterpart in the life of that enthusiastic prophetess Hawthorne calls her prototype. '

But as important as are the simple differences, and as dangerous as it must always seem to turn away from the richness and particularity of Hester's own love story, Hawthorne himself seems to have invited us temporarily to do so. And if we follow his suggestion, a number of similarities come teasingly to mind.

Like Ann Hutchinson, Hester Prynne is an extraordinary woman who falls afoul of a theocratic and male-dominated society; and the problems which cause them to be singled out for exemplary punishment both begin in a special sort of relationship with a pastor who is one of the acknowledged intellectual and spiritual leaders of that society. No overt sexual irregularity seems to have been associated with Mrs. Hutchinson's denial that converted saints were under the

3. The critic must always be alert for tones of mock self-condescension in Hawthorne. In the famous letter to Longfellow (4 June 1837) Hawthorne calls his "studious life" at Salem a "desultory" one; but when he complains that his reading has not brought him "the fruits of study," he may well be remembering that it is *Longfellow* who went on from Bowdoin to become Professor of Modern Languages in Harvard University, rather than "the obscurest man of letters in America."

4. 1841. [*Editor.*]

5. 1849. [*Editor.*]

moral law, but * * * no one could read what seventeenth-century Puritan observers said about the "seductiveness" of her doctrines without sensing sexual implications everywhere. Evidently such implications were not lost on Hawthorne. Further, though with increasing complications, both of these remarkable and troublesome women have careers as nurses and counsellors to other women: Ann Hutchinson begins her prophetic career this way, whereas Hester Prynne moves in this direction as a result of her punishment. And most significantly—if most problematically—both make positive pronouncements about the inapplicability of what the majority of their contemporaries take to be inviolable moral law.[6]

To be sure, it takes Hester Prynne some time to catch up with Ann Hutchinson; but when Hawthorne says of Hester, in the full tide of her later speculative freedom, that "the world's law was no law to her mind," we may well suspect that he intends some conscious pun on the literal meaning of "antinomianism." If Hester's problems begin with sex more literally than do Ann Hutchinson's, her thinking eventually ranges far outward from that domestic subject. In some way, and for complicated reasons that need to be examined, Hester Prynne and sex are associated in Hawthorne's mind with Ann Hutchinson and spiritual freedom.

So teasing do Hawthorne's connections and analogies come to seem, that we are eventually led to wonder whether *The Scarlet Letter* shows only this one set of historical footprints. If Hester Prynne bears relation to Ann Hutchinson, would it be too outrageous to look for similarities between Arthur Dimmesdale and John Cotton, that high Calvinist who was variously asserted and denied to be the partner in heresy? And—granting that what is involved is neither allegory nor *roman à clef*—might there not be some fundamental relation between the deepest philosophical and theological "issues" raised by the Antinomian Controversy and the "themes" of Hawthorne's romance?

6. I have assumed a basic familiarity with the career and heresies, spoken and alleged, of Ann Hutchinson. A full study of her "influence," at least indirect, leads virtually everywhere in the seventeenth century. The following items seem most relevant: for primary sources beyond those *demonstrably* read by Hawthorne (Winthrop's *Journal*, Edward Johnson's *Wonder-Working Providence of Sion's Savior*, Cotton Mather's *Magnalia*, and Thomas Hutchinson's *History of Massachusetts Bay*), consult Charles Francis Adams' collection of material on *Antinomianism in the Colony of Massachusetts Bay, 1636–1638*, published as Volume 21 of the *Publications of the Prince Society* (Boston, 1894) and David D. Hall's *The Anti-nomian Controversy: A Documentary History* (Middletown, Conn., 1968). This last contains some sources which Hawthorne probably could *not* have seen; but both contain the crucial transcripts of her two "trials" as well as Winthrop's *Short Story of the Rise, Reign, and Ruine of the Antinomians, Familists, and Libertines* (1644). For modern commentary on the meaning of Mrs. Hutchinson's ideas and career, two works seem indispensable: Emery Battis, *Saints and Sectaries* (Chapel Hill, N. C., 1962) and Larzer Ziff, *John Cotton* (Princeton, N.J., 1962). Also useful is Part Two of C. F. Adams' *Three Episodes in Massachusetts History*, 2 vols. (Boston, 1893).

To the first of these questions, a certain kind of answer comes readily enough. Although the portrait of Dimmesdale is physically unlike the one Hawthorne gives of Cotton in his early sketch of "Mrs. Hutchinson," their positions are disturbingly similar: both are singled out from among distinguished colleagues as models of learning and piety; and both relate very ambiguously to a wayward woman on trial. It is impossible not to feel that John Cotton's drastic change of relation to Ann Hutchinson—a phenomenon as fascinating to scholars now as it was momentous to Puritans then— lies somewhere behind Dimmesdale's movement from partner in to judge of Hester's adultery. Both men sit in public judgment of an outrage against public order in which there is reason to believe they bear equal responsibility with the criminal.

Although his sketch of "Mrs. Hutchinson" suggests in one place that her enthusiasm had earlier been restrained from public manifestation by the influence of her favorite pastor, Hawthorne actually takes a rather harsh view of Cotton's role in her trial: "Mr. Cotton began to have that light in regard to her errors, which will sometimes break in upon the wisest and most pious men, when their opinions are unhappily discordant with those of the powers that be" (XII, 222).[7] That is to say: Cotton and his female parishioner have been what their society calls "antinomians" together, both "deceived by the fire" (221): but the respected minister saves himself. Not all modern commentators would agree that Cotton's behavior is to be judged this harshly, but that is not the issue here. At some point Cotton did clearly reverse his relationship to Ann Hutchinson, reproving doctrines she thought were his own offspring; and clearly Hawthorne's view of Cotton has influenced his treatment of Dimmesdale.[8] Except for the rather too delicate question of who first lit the strange fires, both Mrs. Hutchinson's treatment by Cotton and Hester's by Dimmesdale might almost be subtitled "Seduced and Abandoned in Old Boston."

Although the significance is completely ironic in *The Scarlet Letter*, both pastors are reminded by their colleagues that "the responsibility of [the] woman's soul" is largely within their sphere; Wilson's urging Dimmesdale to press repentence and confession upon Hester sounds a good deal like an ironic version of the ministerial pleas which Cotton, because of his doctrinal affinities with Ann Hutch-

7. "Mrs. Hutchinson" first appeared in the *Salem Gazette* for 7 December 1830. Quotations in this essay are from the "Riverside Edition" of *Hawthorne's Works*, Vol. 12 (Boston, 1882–83).
8. The harshest modern judgment is that of Perry Miller: "Cotton tried hard to adhere to the Protestant line until his colleagues forced him to recognize that he, for all his great position, would be sacrificed along with Mistress Hutchinson unless he yielded. As many another man in a similar predicament, Cotton bent" (*The New England Mind: From Colony to Province* [Cambridge, Mass., 1953], pp. 59–60). For a view which emphasizes Cotton's "idealistic" naiveté see Ziff, *Cotton*, pp. 106–118.

inson, so long refused to heed. And to the end, both men are spared from denunciation by their partners. Although Puritan defenders of Cotton's doctrinal reputation (like Cotton Mather) insisted he had been slandered by even being named in the same breath with the seductive Mrs. Hutchinson, there is no evidence to suggest that the "abandoned" one ever pointed a finger of public accusation at Cotton, or reproached him for infidelity to what she continued to believe were their shared experiences and beliefs. Cotton alone, Hawthorne reports, is excepted from her final denunciations. And in spite of Dimmesdale's false and unfaithful position on the balcony overlooking her scaffold, of his own part in her troubles, Hester "will not speak."

The Cotton-Dimmesdale analogy may seem treacherous on these internal grounds alone. After all, Cotton is not named by Hawthorne and Mrs. Hutchinson is. But there are also arguments which "implicate" Cotton in Dimmesdale—external reasons for believing that John Cotton could not be far from Hawthorne's mind when he wrote of the Reverend Mr. Dimmesdale. And in the light of these, the very omission of the name of Cotton seems glaringly to call attention to itself. The historically alert reader of *The Scarlet Letter* comes to sense the presence of Cotton's absence on almost every page.

First of all, in the public judgment of Hester, Dimmesdale stands as the partner of John Wilson, at the head of the Boston church of which Hester is a member: Wilson is the fervent, Dimmesdale the reluctant enforcer of discipline. Now it seems to me inconceivable that the man who wrote about the Hutchinson situation explicitly three separate times, using highly detailed contemporary sources as well as later histories (and who built into *The Scarlet Letter* certain colonial details so minutely accurate as to convince one recent critic that he wrote the romance with a number of books open before him) would *not* know that the famous partnership at Boston throughout the 1630's and 1640's was Wilson and Cotton. It might be too much to suggest that Dimmesdale is conceived and dramatized as a younger version of Cotton, one whose pastoral involvement with Hester Prynne amounted to a less metaphorical seduction than Cotton's relationship with Ann Hutchinson; but it is hard to believe Hawthorne could pair Wilson with *Dimmesdale* without thinking *Cotton*.

Several other, more curious "displacements" also implicate Cotton. Hawthorne had certainly read in Mather's *Magnalia* of a case in which John Wilson and John Cotton joined together publicly to urge public repentance upon a woman who had killed an illegitimate child; Mather's account surely lies somewhere behind Hawthorne's first scaffold scene. Also he could scarcely have *not* known that it was with Cotton's death in 1652 that the fiery signs in the sky were associated—not with Winthrop's in 1649. One could argue, of course, that this points *away* from Cotton; but just as cogently one can say that Hawthorne cannot *make* the transference without having Cotton in mind; and that the reader who knows the facts will make the application, especially when, standing on his midnight scaffold, Dimmesdale applies "Cotton's" sign to himself. And finally, it was not exactly a secret (despite Mather's silence) that Cotton's son, John Cotton, *Junior*, was deprived of his pastorship and excommunicated from church membership at Plymouth for adultery. Perhaps Dimmesdale is to be thought of— metaphorically, and with a certain irony—as a sort of offspring of Cotton's principles.

Now all of this may not add up to a completely rational calculus of "influence," but it does suggest that, at some level, *The Scarlet Letter* reflects a complicated response to more in the historic Puritan world than Ann Hutchinson alone. * * *

The place to begin an exploration of the inner similarities between Hester Prynne and Ann Hutchinson is with a closer look at Hawthorne's early sketch. In many ways a puzzling piece of historical fiction, the sketch does clear up one fundamental point immediately: Hester's sexual problems can be related to those of Mrs. Hutchinson because the latter are, in Hawthorne's view, themselves flagrantly sexual.

The sketch introduces itself, too heavily, as a lesson in that forlorn subject we used to call the nature and place of women. Mrs. Hutchinson is first presented as "the female"; she is offered as a forerunner of certain nameless public ladies of 1830, and the line from Hawthorne's remark here about "how much of the texture and body of cisatlantic literature is the work of those slender fingers" (XII, 217) to the more famous but equally sexist one later about "the damned mob of scribbling women" seems to run direct. * * *

If we glance again at the early sketch, we can notice that, embattled and argumentative as it is, it is yet about sex in some more elemental way than our discussion about "feminism" has so far indicated. With structural intention (and not, clearly, by obsession), the sketch tries hard to focus on several scenes in which Mrs. Hutchinson is the center of all male attention, prophesying doctrines that astound the male intellect. Most of the "historical" facts are there, but only a fairly well informed reader can feel assured of this; and except for an initial, one-paragraph reminder, the facts seem to fall out incidentally, so as not to distract from the dramatic confrontation. The implications, in turn, are not in the ordinary sense "theological": there is no mention of the famous eighty-two errors Mrs. Hutchinson is said to have spawned—as there is, self-consciously, in *Grandfather's Chair*; we are, historically and psychologically, beyond that sort of consideration. The issue is not sanctification as an evidence of justification, but the woman's own prophetic abilities. Having formerly cast aspersions on legal doctrines of salvation, the enthusiast now claims the spiritual "power of distinguishing between the chosen of man and the sealed of heaven" (XII, 224). What further need of witnesses? Clearly the progress of the strange fire of her enthusiasm is far advanced.

Nor is there any significant ambiguity about the source and significance of that fire: Mrs. Hutchinson's spiritual openings and leadings are inseparable from her female sexuality. Although her "dark enthusiasm" has deceived the impetuous Vane and the learned but mildly illuministic Cotton, it is clearly her own "strange fire now laid upon the altar" (XII, 221). The men, variously affected, must make of it whatever they can. Hawthorne does not quite identify enthusiasm with "the female," but we do not distort his intentions if—supplying our own italics—we take as the very heart of the sketch the following sentence: "In the midst, and in the center of all eyes, we see *the woman*" (XII, 224).

This may still be sexist, but it is no longer petty or carping. Mrs. Hutchinson's influence is indeed profound. Even the male chauvinist is compelled to admit it. The impulse to challenge the Puritan theocracy's dominant (and socially conservative) assumptions about "visible sanctity" evidently comes from a fairly deep and powerful source. It seems to be coming from—"the woman."

Evidently, in Hawthorne's view, fully awakened women accept the inevitability of a given legal order far less easily than their male counterparts. And clearly this is the central issue. What caused a state of near civil war in Boston and what creates the crackling tension in Hawthorne's sketch is Mrs. Hutchinson's proclamation—variously worded at various times, but always as far beyond the reach of the "trained and sharpened intellects" of the most scholastic Puritan controversialists as are Hester Prynne's sexual secrets—that "the chosen of man" are not necessarily "the sealed of heaven." Here, in her last, most devastating, and for Hawthorne most insupportable formulation, Mrs. Hutchinson is claiming that sort of direct inspiration and divine guidance necessary to distinguish between true and false, spiritual and legal teachers. But she has been forced to this last claim by the pressure of investigation and over-response; this, presumably, is what you are made bold to say when facing the legalistic integrity of John Winthrop—not to mention the holy wrath of Hugh Peters, the satiric antifeminism of Nathaniel Ward, and the sheer adamant intolerance of John Endicott.[9] Behind her last claim—as Hawthorne well knows—lies a series of far less drastic attempts to affirm that the Spirit does not always obey the laws of ordinary moral appearance. And even though she has moved from the dangerous to the intolerable, the weight of Hawthorne's subtlest moral judgment falls no more heavily on her head than on those of her judges.

In simple ironic fact, she is their natural opposite—induced into individualistic heresy by their organized, legalistic intolerance in much the same way as Hester's later denials are induced by the violence of the community's over-response. Beginning, apparently, with only a purer sort of Calvanism than was customarily preached in New England, Mrs. Hutchinson's ultimate claim to a totally self-sufficient private illumination seems the inevitable response to an emerging Puritan orthodoxy which, in its undeniable tendency to conflate the visible with the invisible church, was really claiming that for nearly all valid human purposes the "chosen of men" *were* the "sealed of heaven."[1] If the community overextends and mystifies its authority, the individual will trust the deepest passional self to nullify it all. Or at least "the woman" will.

What Hawthorne's figure of Mrs. Hutchinson suggests is that "the woman" is not by essence the safe and conserving social force the seventeenth and the nineteenth century (and much Hawthorne criticism) decreed her to be.[2] On the contrary female sexuality seems, in its concentration and power, both a source for and a type of individualistic nullification of social restraint. Obviously Hawthorne's feelings about this are not without ambivalence. Personally, of course, he would always prefer some less powerful, more submissive "Phoebe";[3] and in one way or another he would continue

9. Hugh Peter (or Peters) (1598–1660), a Salem minister from 1635 to 1841, was a hot-tempered and pugnacious defender of the Puritan faith; Nathaniel Ward (1578–1652), lawyer and minister, exhibited his low opinion of woman's intellect in an energetically witty attack on female fashions in his *The Simple Cobler of Aggawam* (1647); John Endicott (1589–1665), governor and magistrate, was a Puritan of the sternest and most uncompromising stamp, most remembered for his cutting down of the maypole at Merry Mount and his persecution of Quakers. [*Editor.*]
1. For an authoritative discussion of the way Puritan theory made the visible church *nearly* identical with the *invisible* (i.e., mystified the prime agent of "discipline") see Edmund Morgan, *Visible Saints* (New York, 1963). Some strong

sense of the process seems implied everywhere in Hawthorne's writings about the Puritans; and, indeed, one could scarcely read Mather's *Magnalia* without grasping that it was with the Ann Hutchinson affair that the mystified public achieved precedence, in the Puritan world, over the mystical private.
2. This point is made very effectively in a recent article by Nina Baym, in spite of an ill-informed and logically inconclusive "negative" argument about the lack of meaningful Puritan categories in *The Scarlet Letter.* See "Passion and Authority in *The Scarlet Letter*," *NEQ*, 43 (1970).
3. The conservative, conventional, order-loving heroine of Hawthorne's *The House of the Seven Gables* (1851). [*Editor.*]

to protest that "Woman's intellect should never give the tone to that of man," that her "morality is not exactly the material for masculine virtue" (XII, 217–18). But his clear recognition of the antisocial meaning of self-conscious female sexuality, first formulated in the theological context of Puritan heresy, goes a long way toward explaining the power and the pathos of Hester Prynne.

Hawthorne reformulates his insight in "The Gentle Boy."[4] Despite the complexities introduced by a "calm" male enthusiast and by the presence of the "rational piety" of that unreconstructed lover of home and children named Dorothy Pearson, we can hardly miss the elemental clash between "the female," Quaker Catherine, and the entire legalistic, repressive Puritan establishment. Against that male system of enforced rationlistic uniformity, she extravagantly testifies to the reality of an inspired and pluralistic freedom. Her response is, of course, extreme; Hawthorne is no more than faithful to history in judging it so (even though he does not have her walk naked through the streets of the Puritan capital). But, in a terrifying and elemental way, her response is effective. Tobias Pearson can only puzzle over and feel guilty about his drift toward the sect whose doctrines he thinks quite irresponsible; but this "muffled female" *must* stand up in the midst of a Puritan congregation (authoritatively and symbolically divided, by a wide aisle, into male and female) and denounce the minister's cruel and sterile formulation of the Puritan way.

The relevance of Quaker Catherine for Hester Prynne is simple and evident: here is the woman who has *not* been prevented from joining hands with Ann Hutchinson; her enthusiasm (and her sufferings) are such that not even little Ilbrahim can hold her back from a career of public testimony to the autonomous authority of conscience itself. Quaker Catherine does "come down to us *in history*, hand in hand with Ann Hutchinson." No doubt several historical women lie behind Hawthorne's figural portrait of Quaker Catherine, but surely none more powerfully than Mary Dyer, Ann Hutchinson's strongest female ally—who literally took her hand and accompanied her out of Cotton's church after her excommunication, went with her into exile, and (years after Mrs. Hutchinson had been providentially slaughtered by the Indians) went on to become notorious in the Quaker invasion of Massachusetts.[5]

Accordingly, another level of history is also involved: virtually all commentators have recognized that in New England, in dialectic

4. 1832. [*Editor.*]
5. There is no satisfactory reading of "The Gentle Boy" in print. The basic, old-fashioned "source" study—which includes some relevant material on Mary Dyer—is G. H. Orians. "Sources and Themes of 'The Gentle Boy,'" *NEQ*, 14 (1941).

with the Puritan Way, Ann Hutchinson and the Quakers go together; that the latter represent, chiefly a more organized and self-consciously sectarian espousal of the values of individualistic (or "spiritual") freedom which is the essence of Ann Hutchinson's doctrine. If one is committed and hostile, the cry against both is simply devilish and seductive enthusiasm, unregenerate impulse breaking all bonds of restraint and decorum. If one is committed and sympathetic, the cry is just as simple: the martyrdom of human dignity and divine freedom by aggressive repression. If one is a cautious modern commentator, one can only pity the victims and worry that both the Hutchinsonian and the (seventeenth-century) Quaker doctrines do rather tend to elevate the "individual conscience above all authority"; that both promote a "monistic egotism" which tends to dissolve "all those psychological distinctions man had invented to 'check, circumscribe, and surpass himself.' "[6]

None of these formulations would have been unfamiliar to Hawthorne. And neither would his knowledge or speculation be significantly advanced by the modern historian who, after discussing the Ann Hutchinson question as a "Pre-Quaker Movement," begins his chapters on Quakerism proper with the observation that as in London and at the great Universities of England, "so too, the first Quakers to reach the American hemisphere were women."[7] In every way it comes to seem the reverse of surprising that radical freedom and awakened female sexuality are inextricably linked in Hawthorne's most obviously historical romance. History itself had forged the link.

What is perhaps surprising is that Hawthorne is as sympathetic to a sex-related understanding of freedom as he is. His "Mrs. Hutchinson" is a profoundly troubled and dangerous woman; his Quaker Catherine becomes, in her "unbridled fanaticism," guilty of violating her most sacred duties (even if Ilbrahim is *not* a Christ-figure); even his Hester Prynne is far from the "Saint" she has occasionally been made out to be. But Hawthorne sympathizes with the problems as deeply as he fears the dangers; his compulsion to record warnings is no stronger than his desire to discover the laws by which powerful half truths generate their opposites or to feel the pain

6. The larger quotation is from Battis (p. 287); he, in turn, is quoting from Gertrude Huehns' *Antinomianism in English History* (London, 1951). The same sentiments can be found in many modern treatments of any of the more individualistic or "spiritual" forms of religious experience in the seventeenth century.

7. Rufus Jones, *The Quakers in the*

American Colonies (London, 1911), p. 26. See also Geoffrey Nuttall, *The Holy Spirit in Puritan Experience* (London, 1946). Nuttall treats early Quakerism as a "limit" of one sort of Puritan logic and experience; though he does not argue the case, one cannot help being struck by the prominence of women in his accounts of early Quaker prophecy.

of those being destroyed by that implacable dialectic. The context of the sex-freedom link in *The Scarlet Letter* is not adequately sensed, therefore, until we are in a position to measure Hawthorne's emotional distance from his seventeenth-century sources who first raised the issue of sex in connection with Ann Hutchinson's law-denying theology.

The measurement is swiftly made. It begins with Cotton Mather and runs backward directly to John Winthrop and Edward Johnson.[8] All three are, through the typology of Ann Hutchinson, important sources for *The Scarlet Letter*. And except that they are all highly scornful in tone, it might almost be said that these Puritan historians began the tranformation of Ann Hutchinson into Hester Prynne. Certainly they reduced Ann Hutchinson to a sexual phenomenon far more egregiously than did Hawthorne.

The emphasis of Cotton Mather's treatment of the Hutchinson controversy is double—but not very complex or subtle. On the one hand he utterly rejects the charge that his grandfather John Cotton was hypocritical in declining to espouse Ann Hutchinson as his partner in heresy: it is not, he pedantically insists, a case of a Montanus refusing to stand by the side of his Maxilla;[9] rather, obviously, of a notorious woman whom an infamous calumny connected with the name of an Athanasius.[1] (One thinks, perhaps, of certain obdurate refusals to believe Dimmesdale's final confession.) On the other hand, more expansively and with more literary flair, he is determined to treat the sectaries themselves in a frankly sexual way.

The following reflection—from a special sub-section titled "Dux Faemina Facta"[2]—may stand for Mather's theological antifeminism:

> It is the *mark of seducers* that *they lead captive silly women*; but what will you say, when you hear *subtil women* becoming the most *remarkable* of the *seducers*? . . . Arius[3] promoted his blasphemies
>
> by first proselyting seven hundred *virgins* thereunto. Indeed, a *poyson* does never insinuate so quickly, nor operate so strongly, as

8. Thomas Hutchinson's masterful, three-volume *History of Massachusetts Bay* probably provided Hawthorne with his most judicious account of the Hutchinson affair; certainly it was used in providing the transcript of Mrs. Hutchinson before the General Court at Newtown in November, 1637—where she gave a far better account of herself than would appear from Winthrop's *Short Story*. But the account given by *this* Hutchinson contains no hint of sexual language.

9. Montanus, a second-century Christian zealot, led a movement in the Church which advocated a radical re-nunciation of the world; Maximilla (not "Maxilla") was his most devoted woman disciple. [*Editor.*]

1. Athanasius (c. 298–371), known as "the Great," was bishop of Alexandria; his most lasting contribution to Christianity was his successful fight against theological opponents who denied the unity of God and the divinity of Christ. [*Editor.*]

2. "The leader has become a woman." [*Editor.*]

3. Arius (d. 336), a deacon in Alexandria, argued that Christ was essentially neither human nor divine, but rather a kind of semi-God. [*Editor.*]

when *women's milk* is the *vehicle* wherein 'tis given. Whereas the prime seducer of the whole faction which now began to threaten the country with something like a Munster tragedy,[4] was a woman, a gentlewoman, of "an haughty carriage, busie spirit, competent wit, and a voluble tongue."[5]

The quotation marks around the final descriptive phrase point back, of course, to a contemporary phase of anti-feminist response to Ann Hutchinson. As usual Mather is only elaborating what has come down to him.

But equally important in the "Wonderbook" which so pervasively influenced Hawthorne is the primary sexual language which informs Mather's account. Far more memorable than any formulation concerning the self-evidence of justification is a bastardy metaphor which helped to shape *The Scarlet Letter*: the doctrines of the Antinomians are "brats" whose "true parents" are to be discovered by the guardians of orthodoxy. And related to this basic concept is the whole grotesque business of the "very surprising *prodigies*" which were looked upon as testimonies from heaven against the ways of the arch-heretic: "The erroneous gentlewoman herself, convicted of holding about *thirty* monstrous opinions, growing big with child . . . was delivered of about *thirty* monstrous births at once." Or—behold the Puritan wit—perhaps "these were no more *monstrous births* than what is frequent for women, laboring with *false conceptions*, to produce."

Again, none of this is strictly original with Cotton Mather: the heretical-idea-as-illegitimate-child conceit is in the windy pages of Edward Johnson, and Winthrop himself labors the ugly details of monstrous births—which are at least the providential consequence of her criminal heresies. But the full "literary" elaboration of this sort of talk is Mather's, and his account seems most to have influenced Hawthorne.[6]

The influence is very curious. On the one hand, Hawthorne specifically declines to repeat the story of monstrous births in his "Mrs. Hutchinson"; such details are fitter for the "old and homely narrative than for modern repetition" (XII, 225). And the sketch makes

4. This is a reference to a bizarre chapter in the history of the Reformation. Münster, Germany, was the center of the Anabaptists, an extreme left-wing Protestant sect which denied the validity of infant baptism. In 1534, while the town was under seige by an army of orthodox Lutherans, John of Leyden, proclaiming himself the successor of David, became the ruler of the city. Justifying his measures by visions from heaven, he legalized polygamy (taking four wives himself and publicly beheading one) and turned Münster into a scene of unbridled profligacy for a year. [*Editor*.]

5. Of necessity I quote from a nineteenth-century edition: *Magnalia Christi Americana* (Hartford, Conn., 1855), II, 516.

6. The heresy-bastard conceit is also in Thomas Weld's "Preface" to Winthrop's *Short Story* (reprinted in Adams and Hall); the *Short Story*, is, in turn, the main source of Mather's account. It is not certain, but it seems likely, that Hawthorne saw Winthrop's book independently.

no use of any bastardy metaphor. On the other hand, however, in a rather startling display of creative process, it all comes back in the story of Ann Hutchinson's typic sister, Hester Prynne. Not only does Hester conceive a very real, natural child to accompany (and in some measure embody) her quasi-Hutchinsonian conception of spiritual freedom; but she finds it almost impossible to convince herself that Pearl is not in some sense a monstrous birth. Along with many other characters in *The Scarlet Letter* (and not a few critics) Hester daily stares at the child, waiting "to detect some dark and wild peculiarity," unable to believe that a sinful conception can come to any valid issue. This *might* be no more than the too-simply Puritan inability ever to separate the moral order from the physical (like looking for "A's" in the midnight sky), but with Mather's elaboration of Johnson and Winthrop behind it, it is evidently a bit more. As almost everywhere, Hawthorne seems to be making Hester Prynne literally what orthodox Puritan metaphor said Ann Hutchinson was "really" or spiritually.

One more telling detail from Mather—to which we can only imagine Hawthorne's convoluted reaction. Not quite faithful to the wording of Winthrop, Mather has John Cotton express the opinion that Mrs. Hutchinson ought "to be cast out with them that 'love and make a lie.' "[7]

Except for this peculiar formulation—which is not really related to Mather's basic set of sexual equivalences, but which just happens to read like an epitome of Dimmesdale's career—nearly all of Mather's basic vocabulary is second-hand. Mather's own debts are tedious to detail, and clearly Hawthorne could have got all he needed from the *Magnalia* (though it is certain he read most of Mather's sources independently). The basic antifeminist construction seems to originate with Winthrop—not only with his specific characterization of Mrs. Hutchinson as "a woman of a haughty and fierce carriage, of a nimble wit and active spirit, and a very voluble tongue" but also with the clear implication in his whole account that one very deep issue is Mrs. Hutchinson's female invasion of male "literary" prerogative. Mrs. Hutchinson insists, out of *Titus*, that "elder women should instruct the younger"; Winthrop might admit, under exegetical duress, that "elder women must instruct the younger about their business, and to love their husbands and not to make them to clash," but his deeper feeling is rationalized in *Timothy*: "I permit not a woman to teach."[8]

7. *Magnalia*, II, 518. Probably this is only Mather's pedantry at work—retranslating from Revelations. In Winthrop's *Short Story* Cotton says "make and maintaine a lye" (see Hall, *Antinomian Controversy*, p. 307).

8. Quoted from Hall, *Antinomian Con-*troversy, pp. 315–316 and p. 267. Hawthorne would have found all he needed in the "Appendix" to Thomas Hutchinson's second volume; see his *History* (Cambridge, Mass., 1936), II, 366–91, esp. 368–69.

This last makes the sexual politics of Hawthorne's remark about women's intellect not giving the tone to men's seem liberal. It also enables us to imagine, by simple contraries, what new and surer "relation between man and woman" Hester is teaching at the end of *The Scarlet Letter*. But, again, this is too easy.

If there is one formulation behind those of Cotton Mather's worth savoring on its own, it is something from Edward Johnson. His impassioned account of the seductive appeal of Mrs. Hutchinson's doctrines gives us the clearest sense that Puritans themselves feared sexual implications more profound than those involving ordinary decorum. Upon Johnson's return to New England, he was alarmed to discover that a "Masterpiece of Woman's wit" had been set up by her own sex as a "Priest"; and Johnson was invited to join the cult:

> There was a little nimble tongued Woman among them, who said she could bring me acquainted with one of her own Sex that would shew me a way, if I could attaine it, even Revelations, full of such ravishing joy that I should never have cause to be sorry for sinne, so long as I live.

Here, as clearly as we need, is the simply hostile version of Hawthorne's suggestion that "woman's morality is not quite the standard for masculine virtue"—as well as the perception, registered in anger and in fear, that antinomian doctrine is not separable from the tone and from the unsettling consequences of awakened female sexuality.[9]

To write *The Scarlet Letter* out of Hutchinsonian materials Hawthorne would have to feel that tone, but he would have to feel others as well. Fear "the woman" as he might, he would yet feel the justice of setting her—in reality, and as a symbol of radical and self-contained moral freedom—against the omnivorous legalism of the Puritan establishment. If he would reduce Ann Hutchinson to a female "case," his reduction would be less drastic than that of his ancestors. And he would preserve, amplify, and revalue certain deeper hints. *The Scarlet Letter* might not be "about" Ann Hutchinson, but it would be consciously and emphatically, about antinomianism and "the woman." * * *

The Scarlet Letter is about the reasons why "the woman" Hester Prynne reaches certain antinomian conclusions not unlike those of Ann Hutchinson; and why, though her progress seems somehow necessary, and though personally she enlists our deepest sympathies,

9. *Wonder-Working Providence of Sion's Saviour*, ed. by Franklin L. Jameson (New York, 1910), p. 134. Note also that Winthrop, besides his relentless pursuit of "monstrous" evidences against both Ann Hutchinson and Mary Dyer, does not overlook instances of irregular sexual practice resulting from Hutchinsonian principles; see his *Journal*, ed. by James Kendall Hosmer, 2 Vols. (New York, 1908), esp. II, 28.

both the tale and the teller force her to abandon those conclusions. More elliptically, it is also about Dimmesdale's lesser portion of the "strange fire"; about the failure of his Cottonesque, semi-antinomian theology; and, in the end, about his much-misunderstood "neonomian" emphasis on "the law" and "the sin." If we understand Hawthorne's relation to Mather, Johnson, and Winthrop properly, we can profitably view *The Scarlet Letter* as Hawthorne's own *Short Story of the Rise, Reign and Ruine of the Antinomians, Familists, and Libertines.*

In these terms, Hester's career is fairly easy to plot. At the outset she is not unambiguously antinomian. But she is conceived, like Hawthorne's Ann Hutchinson, as a woman who bears "trouble in her own bosom" (XII, 219); and her "desperate recklessness" on the scaffold, symbolized by the flagrancy of her embroidered "A," and issuing in "a haughty smile, and a glance that would not be abashed," seems deliberately to recall Mrs. Hutchinson's courtroom defiance:

> She stands loftily before her judges with a determined brow; and, unknown to herself, there is a flash of carnal pride half hidden in her eye, as she surveys the many learned and famous men whom her doctrines have put in fear. (XII, 224)

That might describe Hester easily enough. She begins, let us say, in a not very repentant spirit. Strong hints of her later denials and unorthodox affirmations are already there.

To be sure, Hester feels a deep sense of shame, and we scarcely need the still, small quasi-authorial voice of a young-woman spectator to tell us so; the "reduction" of Ann Hutchinson's doctrinal bastard to a living illegitimate child must, in a Puritan community, at least, count for something. And yet even here Hester feels little enough of what we should call "guilt."[1] Just after the trauma of public exposure, she does confess a real wrong done to Chillingworth; but defiance of hopelessly unqualified and painfully uncomprehending male judges seems clearly the dominant element in her early characterization. It is probably true to say that (ignoring the "epilogue") Hester is nearer to "repentance" at the very opening of *The Scarlet Letter* than she ever is again. But she is not very near it. And by the time she finds herself in the forest with Dimmesdale, she has evidently found that she "should never have cause to be sorry for sinne" again.

For that antinomian moment, the narrator severely instructs us, Hesters "whole seven years of outlaw and ignomy had been little

---

1. My Cornell colleague Michael Kammen first suggested to me that the modern sociological and anthropological distinction between "guilt" and the more primitive, less rational and internalized "shame" was useful in distinguishing Dimmesdale's from Hester's response to their adultery.

other than a preparation." The moment includes not only the decision to cast by all outward pretence of living by the Puritan "world's law" and run away with Dimmesdale but also, and even more radically, her attempt to convince that unreconstructed Puritan theologian that what they earlier did "had a consecration of its own"—they having felt it so and said so to each other. The painfulness of Hester's development toward this moment in no way lessens our sense of its inevitability. From the first she has seemed perilously close to defying her judges with the affirmation that her spirit posits and obeys its own law.

The narrator seems convinced that Hester has indeed sinned—deeply, and "in the most sacred quality of human life"; at one level of our response, the seventh commandment remains real enough. But what he urges far more strongly is the outrage to both human privacy and human conscience perpetrated by the "unpardonable" Puritan practice of exposure and enforced confession.[2] And he also feels—with Hester—that her adultery was, in quality, not entirely evil: the sacred is present along with the sinful; or, less paradoxically, that Hester has fulfilled her passionate self for the first time in her life.

But of course there are no Puritan categories for this ambiguity. There is no way for Hester to say to herself that her action had been naturally perfect and yet had introduced an element of profound social disharmony. And no way for the Puritan mind to treat her evident unwillingness *fully* to disown and un-will the affections and natural motions which caused the disorder as anything but evidence of unregenerated natural depravity. She evidently loves her sin, and theocrats in the business of inferring the ultimate moral quality of the self from the prevailing outward signs can reach only one conclusion. And, thus, when the Puritan establishment moves from the *fact* that Hester *has sinned* to the *conclusion* that she in essence *is sinful*, her rich and ambiguous personality has no life-saving resource but to begin a career of antinomian speculation, of internal resistance to all Puritan categories.

If Society must treat the negative implications of one mixed act as the symbol of the natural depravity of the Self, that Self is likely to respond with a simple affirmation of all its own profound impulses. If the Puritans begin by turning Hester into a sermon, a type, and an allegory of "Sin," she will end by nullifying their entire world of external law and interference with her own pure freedom. Ideally we might wish for Hester to cease feeling shame and to discover the real though limited extent of her guilt. But this, in the

2. For the Puritan doctrine and practice of confession—and for a very useful approach to *The Scarlet Letter*, which I regard as supplementary to my own—see Baughman, "Public Confession and *The Scarlet Letter*." [Ernest Baughman in *NEQ*, 40 (1967)—*Editor*.]

Puritan mental and social world seems impossible. Extremes of public legalism seem to breed their antinomian opposite by natural law.[3] At any rate, Hester finds no way to affirm the legitimacy of her powerful sexual nature without also affirming total, anarchic spiritual freedom.

Of course she begins in outward conformity, playing the game of "sanctification"—the single rule of which is that the true Self is the sum of all its outward works; indeed, by the time we see her in the chapter called "Another View of Hester," she has learned the game so well as to have covered her undestroyed inner pride with an external appearance "so like humility, that it produced all the soft-ening influence of that latter quality on the public mind." But all the while she is "preparing," moving toward the moment when she announces a doctrine of personal freedom which every orthodox Puritan sensed would lead directly to passionate license and judged a more serious threat to public order than adultery itself.

Her own version of the antinomian heresy does not, obviously, express itself in theological jargon; for the most part Hawthorne eschewed it even in treating Mrs. Hutchinson. No dogmatist, Haw-thorne is looking for differences that *make* a difference; and the anti-nomian difference is identically expressed in Mrs. Hutchinson and Hester Prynne, in association with but not quite reduced to a dis-covery and affirmation of the legitimacy of their female sexuality. Call it Spirit with the seventeenth, or Passional Self with a later century, one's affirmation is not very different: the significance of a life is *not* the sum of its legally regulated outward works; or, more radically, what one does has a consecration of its own provided the quality of deep inner feeling is right—i.e., authentic.

Now plainly this is all too partial a truth for Hawthorne; we are not wrong in hearing his own advice when Dimmesdale twice bids Hester's revolutionary voice to "Hush." And yet he understands how it all comes about. He even presents it as necessary for Hester

3. Through John Winthrop is only a background figure in *The Scarlet Letter*, his moral presence is strongly felt. It is surely the famous "little speech" on liberty of this most energetic oppo-nent of Ann Hutchinson that Haw-thorne had in mind when he wrote in "Main Street" that what the Puritans "called Liberty" was very much "like an iron cage" (III, 449). In fact, it is Winthrop's doctrine of liberty as holy obedience which sinews the clerical doctrines of visible sanctity, prepa-ration, and sanctification, to make the Puritan world the massive and unitary legal construct Hawthorne represents it to be in the opening pages of *The Scarlet Letter*. Hawthorne gives us that world as of the 1640's: one could argue that rigidification was not complete by that point and that Hawthorne is really describing a later stage of development, when "one generation had bequeathed . . . the counterfeit of its religious ardor to the next" (III, 460); for this view see E. H. Davidson, "The Question of History in *The Scarlet Letter*," *ESQ*, 25 (1951); but one can also argue that, though Hawthorne does indeed "encapsulate" a long historical sequence into the mo-ments of its beginning, he clearly in-tends to point us to the banishment of Ann Hutchinson (1636–1638) as the crucial defeat of spiritual libertarianism in the Puritan world.

to reach this stage of self-affirmation and release from shame before she can settle into anything approaching final peace.

While she cannot affirm her adultery, she cannot truly accept Pearl as a valid human person. It is probably too much to ask her to accept a good-out-of-evil doctrine all at once. Certainly it is better to affirm the natural order than to treat Pearl chiefly as a living sermon; clearly nothing good can happen as long as the mother is allegorizing the child even as the community has allegorized the mother; and surely a parent who is watching for a child to become a moral monster will not be disappointed.

And then there is the simple matter of Hester's integrity. Speculating so boldly and conforming so relentlessly, she has become—no less than Dimmesdale himself—two people. At one primal level, the whole antinomian controversy is about the inner and the outer, the private and the public person: what do our outward works, positive and negative, really reveal about our salvation status, or, in naturalized form, about our selves? Hawthorne's romance is, of course, busy denying total autonomous validity to the private or "spiritual" self; and the explicit "moral" about freely "showing forth" some inferential "token" clearly embodies the authorial realization that inner and outer can never be completely congruent.* * * And yet Hester must stop living a life so completely double. Quite like Dimmesdale, she must heal the wide and deep, "hypocritical" split between her outer and inner self. She may never realize as clearly as Dimmesdale finally does the extent to which (or the profound reasons why) the Self must accept the demystified implications of the visible, and dwell—though not as the great body of Puritans do—among moral surfaces.[4] But in the terms of her own developing theory of spiritual self-reliance, she must be, as fully as possible, whatever she truly is.

And we sense her self-acceptance and self-affirmation coming. She may seem to wander in confusion—thinking the sun of universal benevolence shines only to illuminate her scarlet letter, and deceiving herself about why she remains in New England; but from time to time, when a human eye (presumably Dimmesdale's) falls upon her "ignominious brand," she wills her old passion anew. She may worry about the condition and quality of Pearl's right to existence; but when the watchful theocratic government considers removing her natural child to some more socialized context of Christian nurture, Hester is simply defiant: "I will not lose the child!" She may argue from Pearl's moral use, but she is also affirming the validity of her sexual nature.

4. The lesson of the ultimate autonomy of the spiritual self, along with the coordinate subjection of the outward man to civil authority, is (presumably) the lesson Hawthorne learned from the career of Roger Williams—of whom Hawthorne seems a true spiritual disciple.

We can say—if we wish to maintain a *modern only* reading of *The Scarlet Letter*—that this is *all* Hester is affirming when she argues, finally, that her adultery had "a consecration of its own"; that Hawthorne has engaged Hester *entirely* in an *overt* struggle with the unruly and unsatisfied sexual emotions which the Puritans obscurely felt to lie unsublimated behind Mrs. Hutchinson's public career, and which they clearly felt would be unleashed upon their community by a public acceptance of her doctrine. (Male self-control being difficult enough when all women are passive or frigid.) But if our conclusions concern only Hester's movement from sexual shame to sexual affirmation, then Hawthorne has wasted a good deal of historic understanding and surmise as mere costume and color. It seems far more adequate to say—as we have already said—that Hawthorne regards awakened and not conventionally invested female sexual power as a source and type of individualistic nullification of social restraint.

Waiving the problem of vehicle and tenor, we may validly conclude that in *The Scarlet Letter* "the woman's" discovery of an authentic, valid, and not shameful sexual nature is not unlike the Self's discovery of its own interior, "spiritual" sanction. The *donnée* of Hawthorne's romance is such that Hester discover both together, and each reinforces the other. * * *

Criticism

Early Reviews

EVERT A. DUYCKINCK

[Great Feeling and Discrimination]†

* * *

The Scarlet Letter is a psychological romance. The hardiest Mrs. Malaprop[1] would never venture to call it a novel. It is a tale of remorse, a study of character in which the human heart is anatomized, carefully, elaborately, and with striking poetic and dramatic power. Its incidents are simply these. A woman in the early days of Boston becomes the subject of the discipline of the court of those times, and is condemned to stand in the pillory and wear henceforth, in token of her shame, the scarlet letter A attached to her bosom. She carries her child with her to the pillory. Its other parent is unknown. At this opening scene her husband from whom she had been separated in Europe, preceding him by ship across the Atlantic, reappears from the forest, whither he had been thrown by shipwreck on his arrival. He was a man of cold intellectual temperament, and devotes his life thereafter to search for his wife's guilty partner and a fiendish revenge. The young clergyman of the town, a man of a devout sensibility and warmth of heart, is the victim, as this Mephistophilean old physician fixes himself by his side to watch over him and protect his health, an object of great solicitude to his parishioners, and, in reality, to detect his suspected secret and gloat over his tortures. This slow, cool, devilish purpose, like the concoction of some sublimated hell broth, is perfected gradually and inevitably. The wayward, elfish child, a concentration of guilt and passion, binds the interests of the parties together, but throws little sunshine over the scene. These are all the characters, with some casual introductions of the grim personages and manners of the period, unless we add the scarlet letter, which, in Hawthorne's hands, skilled to these allegorical, typical semblances, becomes vital-

† From a review in the New York *Literary World*, 6 (March 30, 1850), 323–25.

1. A character in Richard Sheridan's *The Rivals* (1775) who mistakenly substitutes one word for another. [*Editor*.]

ized as the rest. It is the hero of the volume. The denouement is the death of the clergyman on a day of public festivity, after a public confession in the arms of the pilloried, branded woman. But few as are these main incidents thus briefly told, the action of the story, or its passion, is "long, obscure, and infinite." It is a drama in which thoughts are acts. The material has been thoroughly fused in the writer's mind, and springs forth an entire, perfect creation. * * * Nothing is slurred over, superfluous, or defective. The story is grouped in scenes simply arranged, but with artistic power, yet without any of those painful impressions which the use of the words, as it is the fashion to use them, "grouping" and "artistic" excite, suggesting artifice and effort at the expense of nature and ease.

Mr. Hawthorne has, in fine, shown extraordinary power in this volume, great feeling and discrimination, a subtle knowledge of character in its secret springs and outer manifestations. He blends, too, a delicate fancy with this metaphysical insight. We would instance the chapter towards the close, entitled "The Minister in a Maze," where the effects of a diabolic temptation are curiously depicted, or "The Minister's Vigil," the night scene in the pillory. The atmosphere of the piece also is perfect. It has the mystic element, the weird forest influences of the old Puritan discipline and era. Yet there is no affrightment which belongs purely to history, which has not its echo even in the unlike and perversely commonplace custom-house of Salem. Then for the moral. Though severe, it is wholesome, and is a sounder bit of Puritan divinity than we have been of late accustomed to hear from the degenerate successors of Cotton Mather. We hardly know another writer who has lived so much among the new school who would have handled this delicate subject without an infusion of George Sand.[2] The spirit of his old Puritan ancestors, to whom he refers in the preface, lives in Nathaniel Hawthorne.

* * *

EDWIN PERCY WHIPPLE

[Tragic Power][†]

* * *

With regard to "The Scarlet Letter," the readers of Hawthorne might have expected an exquisitely written story, expansive in sentiment, and suggestive in characterization, but they will hardly be prepared for a novel of so much tragic interest and tragic power, so

2. The pseudonymn of Amandine Aurore Dupin (1804–76), French woman novelist whose name came to stand for the immorally liberal depiction of sex in literature. [*Editor.*]
† From a review in *Graham's Magazine*, 36 (May 1850), 345–46.

deep in thought and so condensed in style, as is here presented to
them. It evinces equal genius in the region of great passions and
elusive emotions, and bears on every page the evidence of a mind
thoroughly alive, watching patiently the movements of morbid
hearts when stirred by strange experiences, and piercing, by its
imaginative power, directly through all the externals to the core of
things. The fault of the book, if fault it have, is the almost morbid
intensity with which the characters are realized, and the consequent
lack of sufficient geniality in the delineation. A portion of the pain
of the author's own heart is communicated to the reader, and
although there is great pleasure received while reading the volume,
the general impression left by it is not satisfying to the artistic
sense. Beauty bends to power throughout the work, and therefore
the power displayed is not always beautiful. There is a strange fascination to a man of contemplative genius in the psychological details
of a strange crime like that which forms the plot of "The Scarlet
Letter," and he is therefore apt to become like Hawthorne, too
painfully anatomical in his exhibition of them.

If there be, however, a comparative lack of relief to the painful
emotions which the novel excites, owing to the intensity with which
the author concentrates attention on the working of dark passions,
it must be confessed that the moral purpose of the book is made
more definite by this very deficiency. The most abandoned libertine
could not read the volume without being thrilled into something
like virtuous resolution, and the roué would find that the deep-
seeing eye of the novelist had mastered the whole philosophy of
that guilt of which practical roués are but childish disciples. To
another class of readers, those who have theories of seduction and
adultery modeled after the French school of novelists, and whom
libertinism is of the brain, the volume may afford matter for very
instructive and edifying contemplation; for, in truth, Hawthorne, in
"The Scarlet Letter," has utterly undermined the whole philosophy
on which the French novels rest, by seeing farther and deeper into
the essence both of conventional and moral laws; and he has given
the results of his insight, not in disquisitions and criticisms, but in
representations more powerful even than those of Sue, Dumas, or
George Sand.[1] He has made his guilty parties end, not as his own
fancy or his own benevolent sympathies might dictate, but as the
spiritual laws, lying back of all persons, dictated to him. In this
respect there is hardly a novel in English literature more purely
objective.

* * *

1. Eugene Sue (1804–57), Alexandre
Dumas (1824–95), George Sand (Aurore Dupin) (1804–76)—three examples of "the French school of novelists" whose handling of adultery in fiction Whipple considers inferior to Hawthorne's. [*Editor*.]

HENRY F. CHORLEY

[Severity, Purity, and Sympathy]†

This is a most powerful but painful story. Mr. Hawthorne must be well known to our readers as a favourite with the *Athenaeum*. We rate him as among the most original and peculiar writers of American fiction. There is in his works a mixture of Puritan reserve and wild imagination, of passion and description, of the allegorical and the real, which some will fail to understand, and which others will positively reject—but which, to ourselves, is fascinating, and which entitles him to be placed on a level with Brockden Brown[1] and the author of 'Rip Van Winkle.' 'The Scarlet Letter' will increase his reputation with all who do not shrink from the invention of the tale; but this, as we have said, is more than ordinarily painful. When we have announced that the three characters are a guilty wife, openly punished for her guilt,—her tempter, whom she refuses to unmask, and who during the entire story carries a fair front and an unblemished name among his congregation,—and her husband, who, returning from a long absence at the moment of her sentence, sits himself down betwixt the two in the midst of a small and severe community to work out his slow vengeance on both under the pretext of magnanimous forgiveness,—when we have explained that "The Scarlet Letter' is the badge of Hester Prynne's shame, we ought to add that we recollect no tale dealing with crime so sad and revenge so subtly diabolical, that is at the same time so clear of fever and of prurient excitement. The misery of the woman is as present in every page as the heading which in the title of the romance symbolizes her punishment. Her terrors concerning her strange elvish child present retribution in a form which is new and natural:—her slow and painful purification through repentance is crowned by no perfect happiness, such as awaits the decline of those who have no dark and bitter past to remember. Then, the gradual corrosion of [the] heart of Dimmesdale, the faithless priest, under the insidious care of the husband, (whose relationship to Hester is a secret known only to themselves,) is appalling; and his final confession and expiation are merely a relief, not a reconciliation.—We are by no means satisfied that passions and tragedies like these are the legitimate subjects for fiction; we are satisfied that

---

† From a review in the London *Athenaeum*, no. 1181 (June 15, 1850), 634.
1. Charles Brockden Brown (1771–1810), America's first professional nov-

elist, author of *Wieland* (1798), *Arthur Mervyn* (1799), and *Ormond* 1799), Gothic romances with a social and moral purpose. [*Editor.*]

novels such as 'Adam Blair'[2] and plays such as 'The Stranger'[3] may be justly charged with attracting more persons than they warn by their excitement. But if Sin and Sorrow in their most fearful forms are to be presented in any work of art, they have rarely been treated with a loftier severity, purity, and sympathy than in Mr. Hawthorne's 'Scarlet Letter.' The touch of the fantastic befitting a period of society in which ignorant and excitable human creatures conceived each other and themselves to be under the direct "rule and govern-ance" of the Wicked One, is most skilfully administered. The supernatural here never becomes grossly palpable:—the thrill is all the deeper for its action being indefinite, and its source vague and distant.

GEORGE BAILEY LORING

[Hester versus Dimmesdale]†

* * *

It would be hard to conceive of a greater outrage upon the freez-ing and self-denying doctrines of that day, than the sin for which Hester Prynne was damned by society, and for which Arthur Dim-mesdale damned himself. For centuries, the devoted and supersti-tious Catholic had made it a part of his creed to cast disgrace upon the passions, and the cold and rigid Puritan, with less fervor, and consequently with less beauty, had driven them out of his paradise, as the parents of all sin. * * * The state of society which this grizzly form of humanity created, probably served as little to purify men as any court of voluptuousness; and, while we recognize with compressed lip that heroism which braved seas and unknown shores, for opinion's sake, we remember, with a warm glow, the elegances and intrepid courage and tropical luxuriance of the cavaliers whom they left behind them. Asceticism and voluptuarism on either hand, neither fruitful of the finer and truer virtues, were all that men had arrived at in the great work of sensuous life.

It was the former which fixed the scarlet letter to the breast of Hester Prynne, and which drove Arthur Dimmesdale into a life of cowardly and selfish meanness, that added tenfold disgrace and ignominy to his original crime. * * * It was as heir of these virtues,

2. An 1822 novel by John Gibson Lock-hart which concerns an adulterous min-ister who makes a public confession of his sin. [*Editor*.]
3. A 1798 translation of *Menschenhass und Reue* (1789), a play by August

von Kotzebue about a wife who com-mits adultery. [*Editor*.]
† From a review in the *Massachusetts Quarterly Review*, 3 (September 30, 1850), 484–500.

and impressed with this education, that Arthur Dimmesdale, a clergyman, believing in and applying all the moral remedies of the
times, found himself a criminal. We learn nothing of his experience
during the seven long years in which his guilt was secretly gnawing
at his breast, unless it be the experience of pain and remorse. He
speaks no word of wisdom. He lurks and skulks behind the protection of his profession and his social position, neither growing wiser
nor stronger, but, day after day, paler and paler, more and more
abject. We do not find that, out of his sin, came any revelation of
virtue. No doubt exists of his repentance,—of that repentance
which is made up of sorrow for sin, and which grows out of fear of
consequences; but we learn nowhere that his enlightened conscience, rising above the dogmas and catechistic creeds of the day,
by dint of his own deep and solemn spiritual experiences, taught
him what obligations had gathered around him, children of his
crime, which he was bound to acknowledge before men, as they
stood revealed to God. Why had his religious wisdom brought him
no more heroism? He loved Hester Prynne—he had bound himself
to her by an indissoluble bond, and yet he had neither moral courage nor moral honesty, with all his impressive piety, to come forth
and assert their sins and their mutual obligations. He was, evidently, a man of powerful nature. His delicate sensibility, his fervor,
his influence upon those about him, and above all, his sin, committed when the tides of his heart rushed in and swept away all the
bulrush barriers he had heaped up against them, through years of
studious self-discipline,—show what a spirit, what forces, he had.
Against none of these forces had he sinned. And yet he was halting,
and wavering, and becoming more and more perplexed and worn
down with woe, because he had violated the dignity of his position,
and had broken a law which his education had made more prominent than any law in his own soul. In this way, he presented the
twofold nature which belongs to us as members of society;—
a nature born from ourselves and our associations, and comprehending all the diversity and all the harmony of our individual and social
duties. Violation of either destroys our fitness for both. And when
we remember that, in this development, no truth comes except
from harmony, no beauty except from a fit conjunction of the individual with society, and of society with the individual, can we
wonder that the great elements of Arthur Dimmesdale's character
should have been overbalanced by a detestable crowd of mean and
grovelling qualities, warmed into life by the hot antagonism he felt
radiating upon himself and all his fellow-men—from the society in
which he moved, and from which he received his engrafted moral
nature? He sinned in the arms of society, and fell almost beyond
redemption; his companion in guilt became an outcast, and a flood

of heroic qualities gathered around her. Was this the work of social influences?

This law of our nature, which applies to the well-directed and honest efforts of good progressive intentions, applies also to misguided and sinful actions. The stormy life of the erring mother affords no rest for the healthy development of her embryonic child. It amounts to but little for her to say, with Hester Prynne, "what we did had a consecration of its own," unless that consecration produces a heavenly calm, as if all nature joined in harmony. Pearl, that wild and fiery little elf, born of love, was also born of conflict; and had the accountability of its parents extended no farther than the confines of this world, the prospective debt due this offspring involved fearful responsibilities. How vividly this little child typified all their startled instincts, their convulsive efforts in life and thought, their isolation, and their self-inflicted contest with and distrust of all mankind. Arthur Dimmesdale, shrinking from intimate contact and intercourse with his child, shrunk from a visible and tangible representation of the actual life which his guilty love had created for himself and Hester Prynne;—love, guilty, because, secured as it may have been to them, it drove them violently from the moral centre around which they revolved.

We have seen that this was most especially the case with the man who was bound the labelled the puritan clergyman; that he had raised a storm in his own heavens which he could not quell, and had cast the whirlwind over the life of his own child. How was it with Hester Prynne?

On this beautiful and luxuriant woman, we see the effect of open conviction of sin, and the continued galling punishment. The heroic traits awakened in her character by her position were the great self-sustaining properties of woman, which, in tribulation and perplexity, elevate her so far above man. The sullen defiance in her, was imparted to her by society. Without, she met only ignominy, scorn, banishment, a shameful brand. Within, the deep and sacred love for which she was suffering martyrdom,—for her crime was thus sanctified in her own apprehension,—was turned into a store of perplexity, distrust, and madness, which darkened all her heavens. Little Pearl was a token more scarlet than the scarlet letter of her guilt; for the child, with a birth presided over by the most intense conflict of love and fear in the mother's heart, nourished at a breast swelling with anguish, and surrounded with burning marks of its mother's shame in its daily life, developed day by day into a void little demon perched upon the most sacred horn of the mother's altar. Even this child, whose young, plastic nature caught the impress which surrounding circumstances most naturally gave, bewildered and maddened her. The pledge of love which God had given her, seemed perverted into an emblem of hate. And yet how patiently and courageously she labored on, bearing her burthen the more firmly, because, in its infliction, she recognized no higher hand than that of civil authority! In her earnest appeal to be allowed to retain her child, she swept away all external influences, and seems to have inspired the young clergyman, even now fainting with his own sense of meaner guilt, to speak words of truth, which in those days must have seemed born of heaven.

* * *

Her social ignominy forced her back upon the true basis of her life. She alone, of all the world, knew the length and breadth of her own secret. Her lawful husband no more pretended to hold a claim, which may always have been a pretence; the father of her child, her own relation to both, and the tragic life which was going on beneath that surface which all men saw, were known to her alone. How poor and miserable must have seemed the punishment which society had inflicted! The scarlet letter was a poor type of the awful truth which she carried within her heart. Without deceit before the world, she stands forth the most heroic person in all that drama. When, from the platform of shame, she bade farewell to that world, she retired to a holier, and sought for such peace as a soul cast out by men may always find. This was her right. No lie hung over her head. Society had heard her story, and had done its worst. And while Arthur Dimmesdale, cherished in the arms of that society which he had outraged, glossing his life with a false coloring which made it beautiful to all beholders, was dying of an inward anguish, Hester stood upon her true ground, denied by this world, and learning that true wisdom which comes through honesty and self-justification. In casting her out, the world had torn from her all the support of its dogmatic teachings, with which it sustains its disciples in their inevitable sufferings, and had compelled her to rely upon that great religious truth which flows instinctively around a life of agony, with its daring freedom. How far behind her in moral and religious excellence was the accredited religious teacher, who was her companion in guilt!

* * *

ARTHUR CLEVELAND COXE

[The Nauseous Amour of a Puritan Pastor]†

* * *

Why has our author selected such a theme? Why, amid all the suggestive incidents of life in a wilderness; of a retreat from civilization to which, in every individual case, a thousand circumstances must have concurred to reconcile human nature with estrangement from home and country; or amid the historical connections of our history with Jesuit adventure, savage invasion, regicide outlawry, and French aggression, should the taste of Mr. Hawthorne have preferred as the proper material for romance, the nauseous amour of a Puritan pastor, with a frail creature of his charge, whose mind is represented as far more debauched than her body? Is it, in short, because a running undertide of filth has become as requisite to a romance, as death in the fifth act to a tragedy? Is the French era actually begun in our literature? And is the flesh, as well as the world and the devil, to be henceforth dished up in fashionable novels, and discussed at parties, by spinsters and their beaux, with as unconcealed a relish as they give to the vanilla in their ice cream? We would be slow to believe it, and we hope our author would not willingly have it so, yet we honestly believe that "the Scarlet Letter" has already done not a little to degrade our literature, and to encourage social licentiousness: it has started other pens on like enterprises, and has loosed the restraint of many tongues, that have made it an apology for "the evil communications which corrupt good manners." We are painfully tempted to believe that it is a book made for the market, and that the market has made it merchantable, as they do game, by letting everybody understand that the commodity is in high condition, and smells strongly of incipient putrefaction.

We shall entirely mislead our reader if we give him to suppose that "the Scarlet Letter" is coarse in its details, or indecent in its phraseology. This very article of our own, is far less suited to ears polite, than any page of the romance before us; and the reason is, we call things by their right names, while the romance never hints the shocking words that belong to its things, but, like Mephistophiles, insinuates that the arch-fiend himself is a very tolerable sort of person, if nobody would call him Mr. Devil. We have heard of persons who could not bear the reading of some Old Testament Lessons in the service of the Church: such persons would be delighted with our author's story; and damsels who shrink at the

† From "The Writings of Hawthorne," *Church Review,* 3 (January 1851), 489–511.

reading of the Decalogue, would probably luxuriate in bathing their imagination in the crystal of its delicate sensuality. The language of our author, like patent blacking, "would not soil the whitest linen," and yet the composition itself, would suffice, if well laid on, to Ethiopize the snowiest conscience that ever sat like a swan upon that mirror of heaven, a Christian maiden's imagination. We are not sure we speak quite strong enough, when we say, that we would much rather listen to the coarest scene of Goldsmith's "Vicar," read aloud by a sister or daughter, than to hear from such lips, the perfectly chaste language of a scene in "the Scarlet Letter," in which a married wife and her reverend paramour, with their unfortunate offspring, are introduced as the actors, and in which the whole tendency of the conversation is to suggest a sympathy for their sin, and an anxiety that they may be able to accomplish a successful escape beyond the seas, to some country where their shameful commerce may be perpetuated. Now, in Goldsmith's story there are very coarse words, but we do not remember anything that saps the foundations of the moral sense, or that goes to create unavoidable sympathy with unrepenting sorrow, and deliberate, premeditated sin. The "Vicar of Wakefield" is sometimes coarsely virtuous, but "the Scarlet Letter" is delicately immoral. * * *

But in Hawthorne's tale, the lady's frailty is philosophized into a natural and necessary result of the Scriptural law of marriage, which, by holding her irrevocably to her vows, as plighted to a dried up old book-worm, in her silly girlhood, is viewed as making her heart an easy victim to the adulterer. The sin of her seducer too, seems to be considered as lying not so much in the deed itself, as in his long concealment of it, and, in fact, the whole moral of the tale is given in the words—"Be true—be true," as if sincerity in sin were virtue, and as if "Be clean—be clean," were not the more fitting conclusion. "The untrue man" is, in short, the hang-dog of the narrative, and the unclean one is made a very interesting sort of a person, and as the two qualities are united in the hero, their composition creates the interest of his character. Shelley himself never imagined a more dissolute conversation than that in which the polluted minister comforts himself with the thought, that the revenge of the injured husband is worse than his own sin in instigating it. "Thou and I never did so, Hester"—he suggests: and she responds—"never, never! What we did had *a consecration of its own*, we felt it so —we said so to each other!" This is a little too much—it carries the Bay-theory a little too far for our stomach! "Hush, Hester!" is the sickish rejoinder; and fie, Mr. Hawthorne! is the weakest token of our disgust that we can utter. The poor bemired hero and heroine of the story should not have been seen wallowing in their filth, at such a rate as this.

* * *

The Custom-House

SAM S. BASKETT

The (Complete) *Scarlet Letter*†

* * *

In the two parts of his book Hawthorne weaves a pattern of repeated comparisons and contrasts which connect him with his ancestors, the present with the past, the world of the Custom House with the world of the New England theocracy. Most obviously, Salem and Boston are essentially the same setting; and the characters of "The Custom House" are the descendants of the Puritans. The soil of Salem is mingled with the "earthly substance" of his forefathers, Hawthorne remarks early in the sketch, and he goes on to describe in some detail the characteristics of his Puritan ancestors and their putative attitudes toward him. These allusions are reinforced by a number of less personal references which reflect Hawthorne's continuing concern with the connections between the Puritan past and his own era. When he describes "finding" the physical objects on which the Hester Prynne story is based, he adds that he also uncovered the "facts" upon which he constructed "Main Street." In this sketch written a few months *before The Scarlet Letter*, Hawthorne chronicles the growth of his native town "from infancy upward." "Main Street" is focussed on the past, for the machine which the author fancies as projecting the pictures of Salem breaks down just as the present is reached. "Alas," he comments ironically, "you know not the extent of your misfortune. The scenes to come were far better than the past." Written the year *after The Scarlet Letter*, *The House of the Seven Gables* compensates for this "misfortune" by concentrating mostly on the present. *Between* these two works Hawthorne wrote the two parts of *The Scarlet Letter* which even more emphatically illustrate his preoccupation with the theme of the relation of the past and present.

The insistence with which Hawthorne presents this theme is seen in the number of time shifts which occur in both "The Custom

† From *College English*, 22 (1961), 321–28.

House" and *The Scarlet Letter*. In the former, Hawthorne purportedly sets out to tell about his mid-nineteenth-century present.
Actually the past invades this present with Faulknerian persistence.
In the early pages while discussing his ancestors, Hawthorne
switches back and forth from 1850 to various points in the past at
least a dozen times. The lives of the Custom House denizens, significantly, are not so deeply rooted in the past, but there is a continual flow of references to times twenty, forty, sixty, seventy years earlier. In approaching the Hester Prynne materials, Hawthorne leads
the reader back to the immediate past, then to the Revolution and
eventually to the mid-seventeenth century via the Custom House
records; and while Hawthorne discusses these materials, his mind
alternately considers them in their supposed historical context and
as they impinge on and even define his own present predicament.
The Scarlet Letter, of course, is ostensibly set in the seventeenth
century. On a score of occasions, however, the author halts his story
and draws an explicit contrast between seventeenth- and nineteenth-century New England life. Hawthorne thus does not allow
the reader of *The Scarlet Letter* to forget the 1850 "present" just as
he does not allow the reader of "The Custom House" to forget the
past. * * *

This sharp contrast between the two societies, however, is really
secondary to Hawthorne's main concern throughout the book.
Actually, "The Custom House" and *The Scarlet Letter* are coupled
more by an underlying similarity than by the external ironic contrast. For Hawthorne himself in a sense is the major character in
the romance as well as in the sketch; and in both parts of the book
the theme is the same: the relation of the individual to whatever
the society, irrespective of its nature, in which he finds himself.

At the beginning of "The Custom House" Hawthorne states that
an author must establish "some true relation with his audience,"
"the few who will understand him," even though he keeps the
"inmost Me" behind the veil of native reserve. But once in his
account, as he describes finding the scarlet letter, Hawthorne for a
moment drops his detached, ironic manner and allows the reader a
glimpse behind the veil. Looking at the faded rag of scarlet cloth
and musing over the meaning of the "mystic symbol," he says,

> I happened to place it on my breast. It seemed to me,—the
> reader may smile, but he must not doubt my word,—it seemed to
> me, then, that I experienced a sensation not altogether physical,
> yet almost so, as of burning heat; and as if the letter were not
> of red cloth, but red-hot iron. I shuddered, and involuntarily let
> it fall upon the floor.

The reader "may smile," but Hawthorne is not merely indulging his
romantic fancy; his tone is deadly serious. Why is Hawthorne so

affected by the letter of guilt which Hester, Dimmesdale, and in a sense even Chillingworth, also wear? What is he trying to confess? Both "The Custom House" and *The Scarlet Letter* supply the answer—the same answer. In this scene Hawthorne at once expresses his alienation from his contemporaries—from both the transcendentalists who ignore guilt and the materialists who subsist on the subhuman level—and acknowledges his desire to end that alienation. In his actions as well as his writing, Hawthorne repeatedly made evident his strong sense of being at cross purposes with his age. He did live a mainly solitary twelve years as a young man in Salem. He did frequently mention his "home-feeling" for the past. His sense of isolation had not been lessened by his "grievous thralldom" at the Boston Custom House, nor by his failure to achieve a feeling of community with the transcendentalists at Brook Farm; and this sense was further aggravated by his experience with the workaday world at the Salem Custom House. Hawthorne's predicament, so apparent throughout "The Custom House," is also partly the result of his self-consciousness about his role as a writer. Of his writing, the core of his existence, his associates are unaware. "None of them, I presume, had ever read a page of my inditing, or would have cared a fig the more for me if they had read them all." In addition, he is certain that his Puritan forebears would have strongly disapproved of his vocation.

> "What is he?" murmurs one gray shadow of my forefathers to the other. "A writer of story-books! What kind of business in life,—what mode of glorifying God, or being serviceable to mankind in his day and generation,—may that be? Why the degenerate fellow might as well have been a fiddler." Such are the compliments bandied between my great-grandsires and myself, across the gulf of time!

Contemptuous of the values of his associates, ambivalent in his attitude toward the past, unsure of his place in society as a writer, the Hawthorne who condemns the Custom-House officer for not participating in the main stream of human endeavor stands fearfully alone in an unused room of the Custom House with the faded letter on his breast—the figure of the Alienated Artist. We can say "fearfully," for Hawthorne frequently reiterated his horror of isolation, his belief that man is a naturally sociable being whose mental energies are fully aroused only in society; and this was a time of crisis for Hawthorne as he was making the effort that led to his fuller involvement with his fellow man in the 1850's. * * *

Hawthorne's growing, if unwilling, understanding that, despite his desire for withdrawal from an uncongenial "system," he must somehow establish a significant, self-nurturing relation with it, is intensely signified when he places the scarlet letter on his breast.

His expiation has begun, albeit furtively; the letter has started to do its work. He relates that he achieved partial relief from "this incident": it recalled his mind, "in some degree, to the old track." Moreover, Hawthrone undertook a more public, if still somewhat veiled, expiation. This expiation is *The Scarlet Letter* and, for "the few who will understand him" "The Custom House." In the characterizations of Hester, Dimmesdale and Chillingworth, Hawthorne objectifies the several facets of his problem. Charles O'Donnell has analyzed the similar situations of Hawthorne and Dimmesdale; equally significant is the parallel between Hawthorne's predicament and that of each of the other major characters in *The Scarlet Letter*. Like Chillingworth, the Custom-House Hawthorne is capable of arrogant detachment from the entire community; and like him he can probe coldly and analytically into his associates and then sit in icy judgment on them. It is easy to see in "The Custom House" that the sin of intellectual and moral pride is one of the reasons for Hawthorne's alienation from his fellow man: he comes close to violating the sanctity of the human heart—at least so thought those who had sat unwittingly for his scapel-like pen. Like Dimmesdale and Hester, the Custom-House Hawthorne has an ambivalent attitude toward his alienation from his community and a possible expiation leading to reunion. As they are products of the Puritan way of life, so Hawthorne is a man of the nineteenth-century; as they violate the rules of that way of life and are thus rendered less effective members of the community, so Hawthorne denies many of the values of his age (here he is closer to Hester than to Dimmesdale), and thereby places himself outside its pale. Like Dimmesdale, Hawthorne has lived a hypocritical life among his associates; and, like Dimmesdale, after having scourged himself for years with his sensitivity, Hawthorne finally brings himself to a two-fold expiation, in the darkness of a romance purportedly dealing with the dim past, and in the ambiguous daylight of "The Custom House." Like Hester, whom Hawthorne repeatedly describes as an artist and who feels that what she had done had a consecration of its own, so Hawthorne tends to believe that as an artist he also is above the judgment of *his* society. And, like Hester, Hawthorne finally brings himself to the recognition that though he remains somewhat apart from his contemporaries, he must learn to live in some sort of relation with them. In other words, the similarity of Dimmesdale's situation with Hawthorne's own is but one of the many significant links between the two parts of Hawthorne's book. O'Donnell has observed that the action after Dimmesdale begins his confession "takes on all the qualities of a formal drama," that in effect Dimmesdale creates a form to express his experience, and

"through this form he finds his own victory, his own salvation."
The Scarlet Letter, Hawthorne's entire Puritan story, may be said
to bear exactly this relation to the author's "confession" scene in
"The Custom House."

* * *

MARSHALL VAN DEUSEN

Narrative Tone in "The Custom-House" and *The Scarlet Letter*†

* * *

The mood of romance is set in "The Custom House," and it is
not set simply by the famous passage there about moonlight. It is
felt throughout the preface, and perhaps especially in the paragraphs that include the mention of those curiously circumstantial
measurements of the scarlet letter. Those details, in context, are not
in the service of literary verisimilitude but of a symbolic ambiguity which centers for the moment on the problem of the meaning
of historical authenticity. "The Ancient Surveyor" seems to have
been "a local antiquarian"; yet some of "his facts" have found their
way into Hawthorne's fictionalized article on "Main Street." Hawthorne's ironic tone is surely unmistakable when he remarks that
"As a final disposition" of the "remainder" of Pue's facts, "I contemplate depositing them with the Essex Historical Society." And
his pun is surely intended when he contends that "the main facts" of
The Scarlet Letter "are *authorized* [my italics] and authenticated
by the document of Mr. Surveyor Pue," for two sentences later he
admits that in some places "I have allowed myself . . . nearly or
altogether as much license as if the facts had been entirely of my
own invention."

Nearly or altogether! In the second paragraph of his preface Hawthorne had introduced the ironic note by claiming to offer "proofs
of the authenticity of [his] narrative" and claiming for himself only
"my true position as editor, or very little more." Solemnly he
asserted that "this and no other is my true reason for assuming a
personal relation with the public"! He wished to offer his "proofs"
and to justify the "few extra touches" he had allowed himself.

Now, thirty pages later, it turns out that all Hawthorne contends

† From *Nineteenth-Century Fiction*, 21 (1966), 61–71.

for "is the authenticity of the outline"! The story of the scarlet letter is his story, not Mr. Surveyor Pue's. For, "I must not be understood," he writes, "as affirming, that, in the dressing up of the tale, and imagining the motives and modes of passion that influenced the characters who figure in it, I have invariably confined myself within the limits of the old Surveyor's half a dozen sheets of foolscap." It also develops that these sheets of foolscap "were documents . . . not official, but of a private nature," even though Jonathan Pue had been a historian. And Hawthorne's own name, imprinted "with a stencil and black paint, on pepper bags, and baskets of anatto, and cigar-boxes, and bales of all kinds of dutiable merchandise," had authorized and authenticated official governmental acts, though he was a writer of romances. Finally, by a kind of ironic *dédoublement*[1] of perspective Hawthorne speculates that his fictional writings rather than his official acts may perhaps become "materials of local history."

Hawthorne's tone in these remarks—and its manifold variations throughout the preface—is important. He is mocking the easy belief that a historian can penetrate truth by a simple disposition of his little hoard of "facts." But in these passages—and throughout the preface, especially in his account of his responses to his dismissal from the Custom House—he is also mocking himself; and in the ironic intensity of his hypnotic fascination with the letter itself, as well as in the long passage which culminates in his vision of fire and moonlight within the "haunted verge" of the looking glass, he is even mocking his mockery. "The Custom House" reflects not simply the wit and urbanity of the accomplished essayist; rather the urbanity exists to qualify and ameliorate the haunting and otherwise haunted reflections of the imaginative amateur of epistemology. The complication of tones defines more than doubt; it defines also a person; and that person is, by his own admission, the narrator of the whole *Scarlet Letter*, as well as of "The Custom House"; he is everywhere present in the whole book; it is his voice that interprets (creates?) Hester's and Dimmesdale's story. It is in this sense that the tone of "The Custom House" begins to define the content of *The Scarlet Letter*. In this sense Hawthorne, or more properly, the Surveyor of Customs who was also a sometime writer of tales and sketches and who is now the "editor" of a historical romance, is a character in that romance, and his voice, with its complication of tones, echoes throughout the book. Not to know the Surveyor is, thus, to miss some of the thematic concerns (*his* concerns) of *The Scarlet Letter* and to miss the characteristic interpretation which his voice gives them as he explores and tests their implications. * * *

1. Splitting into two. [*Editor.*]

The "Custom House" does more than introduce themes to be developed in the romance that follows. As I have suggested, it introduces also the character and voice of the narrator, that is of the "DECAPITATED SURVEYOR." And it is the echoing of that voice, sometimes querulous, sometimes self-doubting, throughout *The Scarlet Letter* that binds the two parts of the book into an indissoluble whole. We may notice, for example, that "the external ironic contrast" Baskett mentions between seventeenth- and nineteenth-century New England society becomes quite characteristically internal for Hawthorne in his praise and accusation of his ancestors (their "dim and dusky grandeur" coexisting with their "persecuting spirit") and in his defense and accusation of their descendant ("an idler like myself" who is a "writer of story books!"). This contrast at least is a matter of personal tension that serves to characterize the narrator as well as the societies of which he speaks. And it is this personal tension that "explains" and prepares us for the notorious doubleness of judgment which pervades the story of Hester's persecution.

The doubleness is enforced upon our attention very early in that story. Hester is characterized at the outset as possessed of "natural dignity," but she is also "haughty" and displays "a desperate recklessness of . . . mood." And there is a curious mixture of ironic diffidence and plaintive wishfulness in the narrator's quasi-blasphemous "Papist" comparison of her appearance to "the image of Divine Maternity, . . . whose infant was to redeem the world." And what of Hester's judges? In the first scene the narrator speaks with the enlightened assurance of the nineteenth-century progressive of "the whole dismal severity of the Puritanic code of law"; but he speaks also as the historical relativist in noting a "solemnity of demeanor on the part of the spectators" which "befitted a people amongst whom religion and law were almost identical, and in whose character both were so thoroughly interfused, that the mildest and severest acts of public discipline were alike made venerable and awful." And finally the personal reminiscene of his own experience in the Custom House surely lies behind his judgment that "The scene [before the jail] was not without a mixture of awe, such as must always invest the spectacle of guilt and shame in a fellow creature, before society shall have grown corrupt enough to smile, instead of shuddering, at it." For despite the stern severity of Hester's judges, there was in them "none of the heartlessness of another social state, which would find only a theme of jest in an exhibiton like the present."

I have suggested that in "The Custom House" Hawthorne, through his dramatic representation of himself, confronts the problem of historical knowledge, and by clear implication more general epistemological problems. In the first few pages of the romance proper he reminds us insistently and, if we remember his voice in "The Custom House," characteristically, that Hester Prynne's story is itself a historical problem that involves at once an understanding of *autre temps, autre moeurs*,[2] and a recognition of persistent patterns of human behavior. "The founders," he says, "of a new colony, whatever Utopia of human virtue and happiness they might originally project, have invariably recognized it among their earliest practical necessities to allot a portion of the virgin soil as a cemetery, and another portion as the site of a prison." And although the Puritan New England colony is, Hawthorne recalls, in its infancy, the door of the jail to which our attention is fixed on the very first page of the historical narrative, seems "Like all that pertains to crime . . . never to have known a youthful era." As for the rose bush, we cannot say whether it is rumor and legend or historical fact that connects it with "the sainted Anne Hutchinson." But "It may serve, let us hope, to symbolize some sweet moral blossom, that may be found along the track, or relieve the darkening close of a tale of human frailty and sorrow." That "let us hope," taken together with the defensive humor of the narrator's remarks about death and crime, is a way of combining the moralistic optimism of the nineteenth-century civil servant with the ironic skepticism of the sometime author of romances whose experience in the real word has made him unsure of that world and also of himself. We hear, thus, the echo of a voice as much as the echo of a theme. We hear perhaps the dramatic definition of a theme, and thus we understand its complexity in a way we could not were it presented "straight."

In these opening pages of Hester's story Hawthorne, the historical editor, even permits himself some of the same sort of musing digressions practiced in the preface by Hawthorne, the informal essayist. He describes the "not unsubstantial persons" of the women in the crowd by the prison door with their "broad shoulders and well-developed busts . . . and round and ruddy cheeks, that had ripened in the far-off island [England], and had hardly yet grown paler or thinner in the atmosphere of New England." In the best manner of the informal essayist, he wryly spins out his genetic explanation: "Morally, as well as materially, there was a coarser fibre in those wives and maidens of old English birth and breeding, than in their fair descendants, separated from them by a series of six or seven generations; for, throughout that chain of ancestry, every successive mother has transmitted to her child a fainter bloom, a more delicate and briefer beauty, and a slighter physical frame, if not a character of less force and solidity, then her own." Such a digression

2. Different times, different customs. [*Editor.*]

reminds us not simply of the contrast between two ages, for that contrast is hardly very objective, nor is it meant to be. We hear instead the voice of a particular narrator, speaking from the de-feminized, yet vaguely effeminate, world of the Custom House, offering a very proper, yet strangely envious, criticism of the decidely female, yet curiously masculine, women of his imagination. We hear a voice that plays urbanely with paradox as the only instrument adequate for controlling its own doubts, and which is yet a means of releasing them and giving them a dangerous license. We recognize the voice because we have met the speaker in "The Custom House."

Without such a recognition early in the game (for this romance is a kind of game, albeit a very serious one), we are likely to misestimate the import of many of the auctorial comments at crucial points. One passage will perhaps suffice to indicate what I mean. When Dimmesdale is returning home from the crucial interview with Hester (and Pearl) in the forest, he feels a strong urge to blaspheme and to address the most shocking crudities and impurities to the people he meets on the way. The narrator comments:

> Tempted by a dream of happiness, he had yielded himself with deliberate choice, as he had never done before, to what he knew was deadly sin. And the infectious poison of that sin had been thus rapidly diffused throughout his moral system. It had stupefied all blessed impulses, and awakened into vivid life the whole brotherhood of bad ones.

Ernest Sandeen has cited this passage in his persuasive article on *"The Scarlet Letter* as a Love Story" (*PMLA* LXXVII [Sept., 1962], 425–435) and has rightly sensed the inportance of its tone. The tone, he says, is one of "solemn moralism" and "pious pontificating," which Hawthorne "has made a part of (the narrator's) character." But Sandeen nowhere identifies the narrator, nor does he really seem to have any genuine sense of his "character," certainly not of him *as* a character. In another reference to a tone of "gloomy moralistic exaggeration," he speaks simply of Hawthorne's "narrative voice," and he suggests that "most, if not all," of the narrator's sermonizings are "Hawthorne's concession to his reader's prejudices"; yet he insists that "they serve simultaneously to keep clearly in view the moral distinctions which form the basic structure of the novel." Apparently they can be used in this way because the concession is ironic: "Some of the pious lectures which this narrative voice delivers are so plainly out of key with what is going on that we may suspect they are pieces of calculated irony." But Sandeen is uneasy with such an explanation and seems finally to wish to evade the problem by noting simply that the "tone of the narrative comments" sometimes runs "against the grain" and sometimes "with the grain of the narrative context."

Sandeen's sensitiveness to tone seems to me to invite such questions as, "Whose tone?" and "Why is there a special 'narrative voice' at all?" The failure to identify the narrator not only leaves him a rather puzzling technical complication, but also leaves the tone of such a passage as the one cited a kind of simple, unconscious irony which the reader and, presumably, Hawthorne too see through from a superior vantage point of amused condescension. Thus, the religious and ethical perspectives urged by the narrator's vocabulary are reduced in seriousness and *The Scarlet Letter* tends to be simplified into an "attack" on outmoded ideas from the point of view of progressive, enlightened liberalism. Such a result is clearly far from Sandeen's intention, and certainly it is false to the pervasive ambivalence of attitude which persists throughout the story of Hester's "persecution" and Dimmesdale's "salvation." But to forget the narrator we have met in the Custom House makes it difficult to understand and account for the complexity of perspective which Sandeen himself seems to feel in the development of the narrative proper, and difficult to understand and account for the variety of tones which we have heard this unsimple voice encompass at the very outset of that narrative.

To hear only or principally a tone of unconscious irony in the narrative of *The Scarlet Letter* suggests that the narrator, whoever he is, is a kind of fool, a figure of fun, whose viewpoint is simply rejected, and who is from our superior viewpoint not a part of the issues he bumblingly describes. He becomes a figure outside the drama, at best a mild kind of comic relief. But if we think of him as integrally related to the narrative through the Hawthorne of the preface, the historical, epistemological, and ethical themes of the whole book will be recognized as more serious and more subtle by virtue of their dramatic relationship to a character of genuinely complex intelligence and delicate sensibility. Even if we should imagine that in some passages we are hearing the voice, not of the "DECAPITATED SURVEYOR," but of "Mr. Surveyor Pue," we are taken back to the Custom House and we remember that Hawthorne has as much admiration as condescension for that worthy. We cannot be condescending even toward *his* voice. The "moralism" in *The Scarlet Letter* is not simple-minded; it is part of a range of tones of considerable variety, and though it may occasionally sound plaintive or nostalgic, there is an appeal in its winning simplicity that is almost as compelling as our sense of its final inadequacy. If we remember the sophisticated doubts about sophistication expressed by the author of the preface, the naive tone of parts of the narrative proper may be seen as a part of a dramatic testing of attitudes which defines a central epistemological issue that qualifies our understanding of all the themes of the book. In this sense, if in no other, "The Custom House" and our acquaintance with the mind and sensibility of its central character are an essential and indispensable part of our experience of *The Scarlet Letter*. * * *

DAVID STOUCK

The Surveyor of "The Custom-House": A Narrator for *The Scarlet Letter*†

* * *

I

"The Custom-House" opens with two preliminary paragraphs wherein the narrator introduces the problems of alienation and responsibility central both to the introduction and the romance. In the first paragraph the narrator describes himself as a man reluctant to talk about himself, even to his personal friends, and he says that in this somewhat alienated state he finds writing a means of self-expression and true communication. He extends this observation to suggest that writing is ultimately a means of self-discovery; that the printed word has the power to seek out and find "the divided segment of the writer's own nature," and "complete his circle of existence by bringing him into communion with it." The narrator defines himself then as an "alien seeking to integrate his own being, but in the same paragraph he says that even in his writing he will "keep the inmost Me behind its veil." The image of the veil reflects the ambiguity of the narrator's position throughout the romance. This ambiguity is referred to again in the second paragraph where the narrator states that his purpose in writing the introductory sketch is to put himself in his true position as "editor" of the romance, as an observer rather than the creator of the story. While this refusal of responsible authority absolves the narrator on a formal level from making value judgments on the characters in the story, thematically it anticipates that central concern in the romance with the individual's responsibility in relation to society.

The body of the Custom-House essay divides roughly into three parts which might be described as "the return to Salem," "the customs officers" and "the writing of the romance." In the first section the narrator describes the complexity of his emotions on returning to his birthplace. The town of Salem, and particularly its Custom-

†From *The Centennial Review*, 15 (1971), 309–29. Footnotes have been omitted.

House, is described as a place haunted by a sense of the past. The once powerful seaport has become a sleepy backwater town. The main office of the Custom-House is "cobwebbed and dingy with old paint" and its floor is covered with sand, a practice which has "elsewhere fallen into long disuse." The contrast between former activity and the stasis of the present is at once attractive to the narrator's imagination, for it reflects his own passive and "haunted" nature in relation to his family and the past. He tells us that he has lived much of the time away from Salem, but, while away, he was aware of the strong hold on his affections that the town possessed. It is an irrational sentiment that he is at a loss to explain, because he sees the town as an austere and joyless place and confesses that invariably he has been happier living elsewhere. The root of this affection he assigns to his ancestral tie, a "sensuous sympathy of dust for dust" in a place where his ancestors "have mingled their earthly substance with the soil." But the ancestral link is more complex than simply a sentiment of family loyalty, and he pursues his attempt to understand the attachment by evoking his ancestors from the past.

It has been customary to view Hawthorne's description of his earliest Puritan forefathers (the persecutor of the Quakers and the witch trial judge) as explaining his preoccupation with the past in both "The Custom-House" and The Scarlet Letter. Generally it is argued that Hawthorne has inherited a strong sense of guilt as a result of their deeds, and that his purpose in the romance is to expose the harsh, inhuman nature of Puritan society, thereby expiating the family sin. The narrator does in fact say that he takes shame upon himself for his forefathers' deeds and prays "that any curse incurred by them . . . may be now and henceforth removed." But the context in which he makes this statement is a very complex one, and to see the narrator as being motivated simply by a sense of ancestral guilt is to ignore a number of subtle innuendos surrounding his explanation. The narrator describes his ancestors as having "a dim and dusky grandeur . . . to my boyish imagination." The feeling is one of awe and oppressive reverence, yet it gives him a "home-feeling with the past, which [he] can scarcely claim in reference to the present phase of the town." This seems to suggest that the narrator, alienated from his contemporaries in the present, turns to the past and to his ancestors for some source of personal identification. This suggestion is made concrete when he says that he has a stronger claim to residence in Salem through his first ancestors than through himself "whose name is seldom heard and . . . face hardly known." Here is the first strong hint of the narrator's preoccupation with his own sense of inadequacy and insignificance; this echoes his earlier reference to a need for self-discovery through writing. Thus when he says that he will take the sins of his family on his own head in this book, the concept of expiation is clearly very personal and complex. One might reflect further on the emotional texture of this statement: when the narrator, feeling himself to be inferior to his ancestors, casts himself in the role of martyr and intercessor for their sins, we may see him as subtly undermining them and putting himself in a position of authority and control over them.

Everything thus far suggested in the sketch is confirmed in the ensuing paragraph where the narrator evokes his ancestors' ghosts. Here he says that his own presence on the family tree as an "idler" would be, to his ancestors, sufficient retribution for their sins. He feels that they would view him as a disgrace to the family and imagines their scorn expressed by such epithets as "writer of story-books" and "degenerate fellow." His sense of impotence is compounded when he reflects that, except for himself, the men in his family have been sea-farers, men of action, whose lives were characterized by a "tempestuous manhood." The narrator then comes to recognize that his attachment to Salem is not love or family pride, but an instinct. In spite of "the chillest of social atmospheres" a spell exists for the narrator "as if the natal spot were an earthly paradise." This metaphor suggests a kind of pastoral retreat to childhood. The return, he says, is a necessary one: "I felt it almost as a *destiny* to make Salem my home." But at the same time he recognizes the sentiment as an unhealthy one; too many generations wear out the soil, he says, and "my *doom* was on me." The narrator had left Salem several times, but always returned "as if Salem were . . . the *inevitable centre* of the universe" (my italics in the above quotations). The image clearly suggests the deep-seated necessity of returning to the scene of childhood, of putting right the past before living meaningfully in the present. The narrator's feelings of guilt and isolation (the two are mutually supporting) have their source in the childhood setting of the past.

This is as far as the narrator goes in "The Custom-House" in attempting to understand his emotions about Salem, but the exploration of this "feeling" is continued in the romance. The three central characters in *The Scarlet Letter* stand in the same relation to Boston as the narrator of the Custom-House does to Salem: they cannot leave the town that is the scene of their guilty drama, nor can they live there in a meaningful relationship to the larger community. The narrator's sense of shame in the eyes of his ancestors emerges again at the beginning of the romance when Hester faces the solemn crowd at the pillory. The Boston community is described as not characterized by "the impulses of youth," but by "the stern and tempered energies of manhood, and the sombre sagacity of age." Like the narrator, Hester feels herself under the weight of a "leaden infliction which it was her doom to endure." She feels that she cannot leave Boston:

> . . . it may seem marvellous, that this woman should still call that place her home, where, and where only, she must needs be the type of shame. But there is a fatality, a feeling so irresistible and inevitable that it has the force of doom, which almost invariably compels human beings to linger around and haunt, ghost-like, the spot where some great and marked event has given the color to their lifetime; and still the more irresistibly, the darker the tinge that saddens it. Her sin, her ignominy, were the roots which she had struck into the soil.

For the narrator this emotion was identified with his birthplace, and we hear an echo of that association again when he continues by saying: "It was as if a new birth, with stronger assimilations than the first, had converted the forest-land, still so uncongenial to every other pilgrim and wanderer, into Hester Prynne's wild and dreary, but lifelong home." After raising Pearl away from the Puritan community, Hester returns to "a more real life" in Boston because it is the scene of her guilt, just as the narrator returns to Salem, the source of his guilt feelings and alienation. Hester must remain there to be reintegrated into the community from which she has been cut off. The narrator says: "Here had been her sin; here, her sorrow; and here was yet to be her penitence."

Similarly Dimmesdale and Chillingworth are "destined" to remain in Boston. Hester says to Arthur in the forest: "Doth the universe lie within the compass of yonder town . . . ?" and he admits: "I am powerless to go. Wretched and sinful as I am, I have had no thought than to drag on my earthly existence in the sphere where Providence hath placed me." The community to which he belongs is the source of all his conscious values. His "doom" fails to provide any genuine alternatives: if he left Boston for a life of freedom with Hester, his religious conscience, the very essence of his being, would destroy him through remorse; remaining in Boston he is slowly destroyed by his own hypocrisy. For Chillingworth, too, Boston has become the whole of his world, and when Dimmesdale dies there, the European scholar also shrivels away and dies there within another year.

II

In the second section of the introductory sketch the narrator describes his employment as Surveyor of the Salem Custom-House. Of special interest here is his description of the customs officers and his relationship to them. He tells us first of all that they are nearly all old men, but more interesting is the fact that, like the narrator's ancestors, nearly all of them were once sea-captains. Throughout this section the narrator's sense of inadequacy in the eyes of his ancestors is significantly reversed. In dealing with the old customs officers, "a patriarchal body of veterans," the narrator takes a curious pleasure in his position of power over them. This feeling of power is clearly related to his oppressive sense of his forefathers and the fact that he did not go to sea himself:

> It pained and at the same time amused me, to behold the terrors that attended my advent; to see a furrowed cheek, weather-beaten by half a century of storms, turn ashy pale at the glance of so harmless an individual as myself; to detect, as one or another addressed me, the tremor of a voice, which, in long-past days, had been wont to bellow through a speaking trumpet, hoarsely enough to frighten Boreas himself.

The old men know that "they ought to have given place to younger men" and the narrator enjoys their sense of insecurity. He constantly views the old men humorously in the first part of this section and treats them in a patronizing manner. He describes them as loitering and sleeping about the place, making a great fuss over little matters and allowing significant ones to slip through their fingers. The old officers are presented comically because their physical reality does not threaten the narrator. A reversal has taken place; the narrator feels himself "paternal and protective" in relation to these old men and compares their jollity to "the mirth of children." The narrator's treatment of the old men suggests a vicarious form of revenge for the sense of unworthiness evoked by his ancestors. His quasi-sadistic pleasure in the old men's insecurity looks forward to Chillingworth's prolonged torture of Dimmesdale. Both revenge their sense of personal failure by exercising arbitrary and capricious power over the lives of others. However, when the narrator singles out three of the officers to describe in detail, his tone again changes significantly. He is no longer concerned with making them look senile and childish. Understood and within his control, they are restored and idealized as venerable figures. This heightens the importance of his control over them.

My reading of this section of "The Custom-House" rejects entirely the conventional view that Hawthorne deliberately presents these three men as wearisome eccentrics and that he is particularly offended by the animality of the old Inspector. This latter view is based on the assumption that a "man of letters" would naturally be offended by grossness in human nature, but this is to ignore the text itself. The narrator certainly recognizes that the Inspector possesses nothing more than a few basic instincts, and that from one point of view he is a "shallow . . . nonentity." But at the same time he marvels at "the rare perfection of his animal nature" and says he experiences "an entire contentment with what I found in him." He admits that he used to watch and study the old Inspector with "livelier curiosity than any other form of humanity there presented to my notice." He seems to envy the old man's spontaneity and easy acceptance of life. The Inspector is eighty years old and his three wives and twenty children are all dead, but he does not sorrow over the loss of his family. His preoccupation with the past is limited simply to recollecting good meals he has eaten:

> It was marvellous to observe how the ghosts of bygone meals were continually rising up before him; not in anger or retribution, but as if grateful for his former appreciation, and seeking to reduplicate an endless series of enjoyment, at once shadowy and sensual.

One cannot help but contrast this to the narrator's "ghosts." The chief tragic event of the old Inspector's life was a mishap with a certain goose which proved tough. The narrator, however, finds the Inspector's gourmandism "a highly agreeable trait": ". . . it always pleased and satisfied me to hear him expatiate on fish, poultry, and butcher's meat. . . ."

The portrait of the Collector—a former general in the War of 1812—is also idealized. In contrast to the animal vigor of the Inspector, the Collector's calm demeanor is always suggestive of contemplation and inner serenity. He has been an efficient soldier, yet the narrator feels that there is no cruelty in his heart and is instead attracted to an innate kindness in him, suggested perhaps by the Collector's feminine appreciation of flowers. Just as the Inspector is unique for his animal spirits, so the Collector in his spiritual repose seems "remote" from the others. A third officer is singled out for the perspicacity of his intellect. He is described as "prompt, acute, clear-minded; with an eye that saw through all perplexities . . . ." We are told that 'he stood as the ideal of his class." This is further elaborated in terms similar to those used to describe the perfection of the Inspector and the Collector:

> His integrity was perfect; it was a *law of nature* with him, rather than a choice or principle; nor can it be otherwise than the main condition of an intellect so remarkably clear and accurate as his, to be honest and regular in the administration of affairs. (my italics)

In all three of these men the narrator perceives a natural harmony, and though he recognizes them as individually representing only "faculties" of human nature, he feels himself better "balanced" for knowing them.

In the Custom-House sketch the narrator has idealized the qualities of these paternal figures, but in the romance these same qualities reappear in the major characters as eccentricities, or as dominant traits which destroy the ideal balance of human nature. Outside the restrictive Puritan community Hester is characterized by a natural, sensual vitality: "a rich, voluptuous, Oriental characteristic." She has deep black eyes, abundant glossy hair and a rich complexion. Dimmesdale, like the Collector, is remote and contemplative "with a white, lofty and impending brow, large brown, melancholy eyes. . . ." And like the customs officer remarkable for his intellect, Chillingworth is a man of intellectual pursuits, a scholar and necromancer. But whereas the customs officers are remarkable for the natural perfection of their traits, the dominant faculties in the characters of the romance are distorted and perverted. Living in a Puritan community Hester's sensuality is the cause of her isolation and misery. Dimmesdale, in cultivating only the life of the spirit, represses his physical and emotional desires and ultimately destroys himself. And Chillingworth, unlike the customs officer of intellect who "waves an enchanter's wand" and makes "the incomprehensible . . . clear as daylight," devotes his intellectual powers to chaotic and destructive ends.

In this section then the narrator is given power over a group of old men, and this helps him overcome his feelings of inadequacy in relation to his ancestors. As paternal forces which have been mastered, the three customs officers are viewed positively, as idealized "types" of the sensual, spiritual and intellectual man respectively. They come together in the perception of the narrator who experiences a sense of balance or wholeness from knowing and mastering them. But then as his thoughts turn inevitably to literature and he thinks of himself again in terms of his true vocation as a writer, he reflects that these old men do not really know him for what he is. He realizes they are responding to him in terms of his public role as the surveyor, and as he sees through this comfortable illusion his sense of "balance" is lost. Now he seems to recognize that control over a few old men does not constitute a genuine proof of his ability as a man, and he turns his troubled thoughts once again to books, his real sphere of endeavor. Yet the integration of those dominant forces in human nature remains the ideal for which is striving, for only the whole or balanced man can relate meaningfully to the larger society.

III

In the third section of "The Custom-House" the narrator finally arrives at his professed purpose in the essay, which is to tell the reader how he came to write the romance. He approaches the subject obliquely so that again we learn much about the emotional context surrounding the issue. A number of significant reflections occupy his mind. While working in the Custom-House the narrator feels his imagination to be "suspended and inanimate," but at the same time he feels he can revive it if he chooses. His occupation dulls his imagination, but to protect himself he does not look upon his position as permanent. A feeling of detachment is very important to him; he must yet remain free in order to explore further his own personal preoccupations. When he begins to look through the old documents on the second-story of the Custom-House, it is with a "saddened, weary, half-reluctant interest." The reluctance he feels about delving into the past suggests that he fears something lurking there. With the discovery of the cloth letter, he begins to focus on the idea of a meaning in the past; but it eludes analysis, and affects rather his "sensibilities." When he holds the letter to his breast, it becomes a physical sensation. This argues strongly that the meaning of the tale is not contained in a moral to be schematized allegorically—"be true"—, but that it has a deeper emotional import that even the narrator himself does not fully comprehend. This is also suggested by the strong sense of duty that the narrator feels toward Surveyor Pue (a personification of the past). He describes this obligation in curious father-son terms. He feels exhorted by Pue "on the *sacred* consideration of . . . *filial duty* and *reverence* towards him" (my italics) to bring the tale to the public. Significantly, our first hint of the story to be told is a glimpse of Hester Prynne as the Sister of Mercy, doing good deeds—an extension of the motif of duty and reverence.

With the manuscript at hand the narrator tries to write, but he finds the mundane atmosphere of the Custom-House inimical to his imagination. He finds moonlight an atmosphere conducive for writing the romance, for there "a form beloved, but gone hence" might appear. The suggestion again is that the world of the narrator's imagination is peopled with family ghosts. He continues to express fears that he is losing his imagination by working in the Custom-House; he feels he has ceased to be a writer of tales and instead has become a good surveyor. He finds it easy to relax and drift along with the customs work, leaning "on the mighty arm of the Republic"; but this natural inclination is challenged from time to time by his ambition as a writer and by his need to prove himself: "A dreary look-forward this, for a man who felt it to be the best definition of happiness to live throughout the whole range of his faculties and sensibilities!" He says that he is afraid he will become "such another animal as the old Inspector." But the ambivalence of his feelings becomes clear when we remember the admiration that he expressed for the Inspector's nature. The narrator's dilemma here looks forward to Dimmesdale's position wherein his conscious moral values are at war with his natural instincts towards Hester. Similarly the falseness of his position of power over the old men—they fear and respect him only in terms of his authority—is parallel to Dimmesdale's false position as the virtuous pastor in the Puritan community.

The tension grows for the narrator; he becomes "melancholy and restless." Then the shift of political power brings his dismissal from office and he is suddenly left free to write the romance. At first he reacts to the dismissal as if it were a death by execution. In *The Scarlet Letter* the only release for Dimmesdale *is* in his death. But the "decapitated" narrator lives on and his role then becomes comparable to that of Hester's. After his dismissal the narrator feels injured and overwhelmed by a sense of injustice. He observes wryly:

> . . . it is a strange experience, to a man of pride and sensibility, to know that his interests are within the control of individuals who neither love nor understand him, and by whom, since one or the other must needs happen, he would rather be injured than obliged.

This picture of a worthy individual unjustly treated by society is exactly the first glimpse we get of Hester. The narrator's passive acceptance of the situation is closely akin to the dignity of Hester's martyrdom; they have their source in the same complex of emotions. The narrator consoles himself that he is now free to devote his time to writing. Like Hester's penance through good works, his work is described as "toil that would . . . still an unquiet impulse in me." As in Hester's life-long martyrdom there is a quasi-masochistic pleasure in the narrator's description of his work. He says of himself "that he was happier, while straying through the gloom of these sunless fantasies, than at any time since he had quitted the Old Manse." The happiness here is related to the "affection" he feels for joyless Salem (an "earthly paradise") and would seem to derive from a release of overpowering feelings of guilt through penance. The inadequacy and guilt that the narrator feels are being assuaged by his attempts to communicate through art. In the same way Hester is described as an artist, expressing herself by means of her needle.

* * *

v

But the question must still be asked: in what ways does the identification of the narrator of *The Scarlet Letter* as the Surveyor of the Custom-House advance our understanding and appreciation of the book? Most obviously it explains the narrator's reluctance to pass judgment on his characters. Seldom in the romance does the narrator view the characters allegorically (as manifesting traits which mark them as good or evil); rather it is the characters within the Puritan community itself, who view each other this way. For example, it is through Hester's eyes that we are made to see Chilling-worth as a demonic character, and it is in the eyes of the Boston community at the end of the book that Hester herself assumes something of a saintly character. The narrator, who identifies with all three of his major characters, passes judgment only on the community as a whole—on its prejudices and on its actions. This I would argue is where the real dialectic of the novel lies: not in the insoluble relationships of the characters to each other, but in the alienation from the community that they each experience. Here lies the "felt experience," the motive force behind the book. For, those emotions which are central to the dilemma of each character are emotions which have been experienced first by the Surveyor of the Custom-House, and in each instance they had their source in the Surveyor's sense of isolation from the community. Thus at the root of Hester's need to do penance is her experience of guilt and shame in the eyes of the people in Boston. Dimmesdale's agony, though secret, also derives from his guilty inability to be an honest member of the community. And Chillingworth's desire for revenge, while occasioned by Hester's betrayal, is in fact the final gesture of a man whose life has been devoted to the lonely pursuit of knowledge.

In Hawthorne criticism there has been considerable debate over the relationship of the characters in The Scarlet Letter. But if, in fact, the novel's mode of subjectivity (the central consciousness) is shared by all three major characters, then it would never be possible to fully understand or explain the relationships of the characters to each other. Thus, while Hester at the beginning of the novel is clearly identified as the "heroine" and elicits our complete sympathy, further on in the book her nature may seem to change because we are now looking at the story from Dimmesdale's or Chilling-worth's perspective and Hester may be "felt" to be a corrupting force. In reverse fashion we may feel a measure of sympathy and understanding for Chillingworth who is otherwise a vengeful and negative figure. The narrator clearly identifies with Chillingworth as much as with the other two, for it is Chillingworth who is in control of the situation (like the author) and who recognizes that it is all a "dark necessity" and "our fate." There is no resolution possible, save death, for the relationship which binds the three together because ultimately they are each locked within a dilemma which is self-engendered and self-perpetuating. Why do Hester and Arthur not leave Boston and its Puritan values which are destroying their lives? Why does Hester not reveal Chillingworth's identity to Dimmesdale and release the latter from the protracted torture he endures? Why does Hester come back to live out her life in Boston, the scene of her ignominy and shame? To ask these questions is futile because if the three characters are all projections of the narra-

tor (three facets of his dilemma of isolation) then a "realistic" relationship among the three as separate entities is ultimately not possible. If this analysis of the relationship of the sketch to the romance
is correct, then we must finally view *The Scarlet Letter* not as a love
story or historical romance, nor as a dramatization of a moral idea,
but as a story about isolation whose characters are symbolic, dream-
like projections of the author's alienated state of mind.

NINA BAYM

The Romantic *Malgré Lui:*[1]
Hawthorne in "The Custom-House"†

The Scarlet Letter was partially written when Hawthorne composed "The Custom-House."[2] Some biographers believe that,
unable to rid his romance of its pervasive gloom, he composed the
preface as a cheerful counterbalance; others see it as revenge on the
political enemies who engineered his humiliating dismissal from the
custom house. These views find the essay a tangential afterthought
or corrective to *The Scarlet Letter*, as does the observation that
Hawthorne expected "The Custom-House" to preface a collection
of tales among which *The Scarlet Letter* was to be only one.
Accordingly, the essay until recently was generally omitted from edi-
tions of the romance and ignored in the criticism. Yet the circumstances of its composition argue as strongly for its relatedness to
The Scarlet Letter (written as it was in *The Scarlet Letter's* very
midst) as they do for the reverse, and now criticism has begun to
note parallel themes, symbols, and situations. Scholars have seen
similarities in Hawthorne's custom house experience to aspects of
Hester's, Dimmesdale's, and Chillingworth's histories; they have
identified as a key connective scene the "discovery" of the scarlet
letter in the custom house when Hawthorne puts it on his breast.
But only a few quite recent articles have seen more than an inter-

---

1. Despite himself. [*Editor*.]
† From *ESQ: A Journal of the American Renaissance*, 19 (1973), 14–25.
Footnotes have been renumbered.
2. William Charvat, in his introduction
to the Centenary Edition of *The Scarlet
Letter*, cites evidence to show that it
was completed by 15 January 1850, before the romance was finished (Columbus: Ohio State Univ. Press, 1962),
pp. xxi-xxiii. In order to avoid ambiguities I shall, when speaking of *The Scarlet Letter*, always be referring to the
romance alone, and not to the book
which includes both the romance and
"The Custom-House." For the external
circumstances surrounding Hawthorne's
tenure in the custom house, among
which his poverty figures in a very real
fashion, see Hubert H. Hoeltje, "The
Writing of *The Scarlet Letter*," *New
England Quarterly*, 27 (1954), 326–346.

mittent pertinence to the essay, or found it to be a coherent narrative in itself.[3]

I propose, instead of asking how "The Custom-House" fits *The Scarlet Letter*, to observe rather how *The Scarlet Letter* fits "The Custom-House." I also hope to demonstrate that it coheres as a narrative in its own right; the "discovery" is the turning point in a story that begins when Hawthorne leaves his idyllic existence among the Transcendentalists, and culminates when he leaves the custom house and writes *The Scarlet Letter*. In this narrative, "Hawthorne" is the main character, for its source is an "autobiographical impulse" which he had felt—or at least admitted to—only once before. Although "The Custom-House" was intended for a volume which would contain other tales besides *The Scarlet Letter*, this is the work which, represented by its symbol, stands for Hawthorne's art, and it is to this work, accordingly, that "The Custom-House" is specifically directed. The sequence of events in the essay chronicles Hawthorne's vain attempt to escape his destiny as a romancer, an attempt which culminates in his commitment—or recommitment —to this vocation about which he felt so ambivalently.

The introduction is not, to be sure, a matter-of-fact, externally accurate autobiography; in the manner of a Transcendentalist journal, the quotidian, the contingent, the economic have been expunged. It is a psychological autobiography, and since Hawthorne uses the methods of romance to project the drama of his inner life, it may perhaps most accurately be called an autobiographical romance. Within this romance, *The Scarlet Letter* figures both as an autobiographical event and as an example of Hawthorne's art. The scarlet letter that Hawthorne puts to his breast symbolizes that romance and stands to Hawthorne in the same relation that the letter A, in the romance, stands to Hester. Like Hester's letter, Hawthorne's is the rebellious beautifying of a socially inadmissible, and therefore sinful, impulse. But Hester is forced to wear her letter by authorities whose judgment she cannot accept; Hawthorne, more

3. See Larzer Ziff, "The Ethical Dimension of 'The Custom House,'" *Modern Language Notes*, 73 (1958), 338–344; Charles R. O'Donnell, "Hawthorne and Dimmesdale: The Search for the Realm of Quiet," *Nineteenth-Century Fiction*, 14 (1960), 317–332; Sam S. Baskett, "The (Complete) Scarlet Letter," *College English*, 22 (1961), 321–328; Frank McShane, "The House of the Dead: Hawthorne's Custom House and *The Scarlet Letter*," *New England Quarterly*, 35 (1962), 93–101; Marshall Van Deusen, "Narrative Tone in 'The Custom-House' and *The Scarlet Letter*," *Nineteenth-Century Fiction*, 21 (1967), 349–358; Joel Porte, *The Romance in America* (Middleton, Conn.: Wesleyan Univ. Press, 1969), pp. 98–102. David Stouck. "The Surveyor of the Custom-House: A Narrator for *The Scarlet Letter*," *Centennial Review*, 15 (1971). 309–329, examines the essay as an integral part of the novel. John Paul Eakin, "Hawthorne's Imagination and the Structure of 'The Custom-House,'" *American Literature*, 43 (1971), 346–358, considers it as a unified essay-fiction. Eakin's article, though quite different in interpretive detail, takes much the same approach to "The Custom-House" as does the present article.

complexly, feels that judgment but puts the letter on, out of an internal necessity, even so.[4]

In "The Custom-House" Hawthorne represents himself, by dint of much omission, as having returned to Salem and taken a position as a customs officer in response to *psychological* imperatives. The conflict that develops is, therefore, a psychological one, and it is symbolized by imagined events and figures—Surveyor Pue, the Puritan ancestor, Hester. The retreat from the ground floor to the upper story of the custom house signifies Hawthorne's withdrawal from external reality into the private reality of his own mind. Surveyor Pue, the presiding genius of the upper story, represents a part of Hawthorne—the fancy or imagination—suppressed by life in the custom house, and his manuscript which Hawthorne elaborates into *The Scarlet Letter* with "nearly or altogether as much license as if the facts had been entirely of my own invention" represents the core fantasy from which the book derives. Placing the letter on his own breast, Hawthorne identifies himself with Hester. This scene, of course, is a "fiction." Surveyor Pue and the Puritan ancestor have been appropriated by the imagination and turned into denizens of Hawthorne's mind, whose qualities they embody. The mind is both the generator and subject of this episode, and, inevitably, romantic techniques are used to render it.

On the other hand, for the events—or non-events—of the custom house day, Hawthorne uses the mode of surface representation, or "realism"; for mental events, the technique is that of symbolic narrative. There are, that is, two literary modes operating in the essay, each decorously matched to its subject matter. The shift in tone which accompanies a shift from the inner to outer world helps to demarcate the mental life from the outside world which surrounds it. Though this outside world causes Hawthorne's predicament, the *story* remains entirely an inner one. The fact that events of the imagination must be expressed through imaginary events does not, however, mean that they are "unreal." On the contrary they are more real than anything that happens in the custom house, as Hawthorne is careful to show in the essay. So long, however, as the internal and external function side by side, the internal has a kind of dim insubstantiality that seems to invalidate it. But so soon as the pressure of the mundane is removed, the internal fantasy expands to fill all the available space, and in its completeness as well as its concentration creates a reality far more powerful than that of the quotidian.

The Scarlet Letter is Hawthorne's fantasy embodied in a fable

---

4. For a full analysis of Hester along these lines, as well as a discussion of Hawthorne's characteristic uses of the Puritans, see my "Passion and Authority in *The Scarlet Letter*," *New England Quarterly*, 43 (1970), 206–230.

which, freed from the constraints of irrelevant contingency, makes its own world. This fantasy deals in part with Hawthorne's dilemma concerning the question of the force and value of the imagination. An important stage in his development as an artist is marked when he adopts Surveyor Pue, his "official ancestor," as his spiritual forefather, thereby replacing—or displacing—"the figure of that first ancestor," the "bitter persecutor," who had been present to his boyhood imagination as far back as he could remember. The sense of that ancestor's scorn and disapproval has borne heavily on his mental and emotional life, especially in regard to his feelings about authorship. Now, however, he accepts Surveyor Pue's injunction— "I charge you, in this matter of Old Mistress Prynne, give to your predecessor's memory the credit which will be rightfully its due"— even though he realizes that to carry it out will set him irreversibly against his ancestor.

This is so because, for one thing, the Puritan disapproves of art. "What is he? . . . A writer of story-books! What kind of a business in life,—what mode of glorifying God, or being serviceable to mankind in his day and generation,—may that be? Why, the degenerate fellow might as well have been a fiddler!" Moreover, the Puritan had been particularly characterized by "an incident of hard severity" towards a Quaker woman, and Hawthorne's book defending a woman condemned by the Puritans must necessarily be not merely an idle book, but an evil one, implicating its author in whatever judgment the Puritan passed on the woman.[5] Hawthorne symbolizes his awareness of this implication by the act of wearing her letter.

The reader may well wonder how, given the connotations of guilt associated with the letter, as well as the notorious ambiguities of *The Scarlet Letter* and the critical controversy that surrounds its interpretation, it can be so categorically asserted that Hawthorne picks up his pen in Hester's defense. Might he not, on the contrary, be defending the judgment of his ancestors? All interpretations of the book—and they are numerous—which see Hawthorne as condemning her, do in effect identify Hawthorne with his Puritan forebears. But in "The Custom-House" Hawthorne openly condemns his ancestors for the act against the woman; he does not hesitate to consign them to hell for it. Further, he treats the letter and Hester

5. The Quakers are represented by Hawthorne as being persecuted by the Puritans for two reasons. First, they adhere to the doctrine of the "inner light" which leads them to defy authority and trust themselves. Second, and not unrelatedly, they give unrestrained expression to their feelings and emotions; this, in an authoritarian society that stresses rule and order, is just another form of defiance. Hester, of course, has no doctrinal preoccupations, is not a religious woman, and is not given to verbalization of her feelings; after her one great "sin," she is a model of self-restraint. Nevertheless, her whole inner life exemplifies these Quaker "sins," as her speech in the forest scene makes clear.

with extreme disingenuousness, concealing and emphasizing in a manner that forces the reader to judge both favorably. The letter, for example, is described as "a certain affair of fine red cloth" wrought "with wonderful skill of needlework. . . . It had been intended, there could be no doubt, as an ornamental article of dress." As for Hester, we are told that

> it had been her habit, from an almost immemorial date, to go about the country as a kind of voluntary nurse, and doing whatever miscellaneous good she might; taking upon herself, likewise, to give advice in all matters, especially those of the heart; by which means, as a person of such propensities inevitably must, she gained from many people the reverence due to an angel, but, I should imagine, was looked upon by others as an intruder and a nuisance. Prying further into the manuscript, I found the record of other doings and sufferings of this singular woman.

Description of this sort, coupled with Surveyor Pue's certainty that Hester's story will bring him reflected glory, creates an image of Hester as an unambiguous heroine. This image precedes the reader's acquaintance with her. Even more deviously, Hawthorne presents Hester in "The Custom-House" as an old woman (though not decrepit), and thus diverts us from the true or primary meaning of her scarlet letter. Many critics have pointed out that "Ad" rather than "A" is the sign the historical Puritans used to label adultery. Hawthorne simplified the symbol in order to permit multiple readings of it; in "The Custom-House" the simplification serves the further purpose of keeping us ignorant of its meaning in the romance.

Furthermore, "The Custom-House" has meanings of its own for the letter. Since the title of Hawthorne's romance is *The Scarlet Letter*, the letter symbolizes that tale, which in turn stands as a representative of Romantic art. (A number of critics have suggested that the letter means "art" in *The Scarlet Letter*.) As the "wrapper" for the surveyor's manuscript, the letter conceptualizes art as a finished product, the form or container given to a fantasy—in this case a verbal form, since "A" is a letter. At the same time, the "A" is not only a letter but a "mystic symbol" which operates outside of the rational faculties, its meanings subtly communicated to the sensibilities but "evading the analysis of [the] mind." Yet again, the letter stands for an object in the real world which, for reasons not understood, acts like an electric charge upon the artist's imagination. "I experienced a sensation not altogether physical, yet almost so, as of burning heat; and as if the letter were not of red cloth, but red-hot iron." This sensation is not guilt alone, but also the terrifying excitement an artist feels when he finds his subject. Thus the letter stands all at once for art as inspiration, art as transcendental symbol, and art as verbal construct or form. And beyond that, of course, it stands for a range of ideas about art in its social context, including the idea of the artist as a branded man, and the idea that art when it is the expression of an artist's private fantasies (as in Hawthorne's case it must always be) represents an act of civil disobedience which will, if its nature is recognized, be condemned by authority.

The theme of the individual in conflict with authority runs obsessively through all of Hawthorne's long romances, and it is of great interest to find it here, in this essay which memorializes his commitment to romance, so firmly embedded in his own life. In "The Custom-House," as I have noted, the conflict is entirely within Hawthorne's mind, and the authority is therefore internalized authority, the conscience. The conflict is polarized between Surveyor Pue and "Uncle Sam," that seemingly benevolent yet secretly castrating parent:

> While [the custom-house officer] leans on the mighty arm of the Republic, his own proper strength departs from him. He loses, in an extent proportioned to the weakness or force of his original nature, the capability of self-support. . . . Uncle Sam's gold—meaning no disrespect to the worthy old gentleman—has, in this respect, a quality of enchantment like that of the Devil's wages. Whoever touches it should look well to himself, or he may find the bargain go hard against him, involving, if not his soul, yet many of its better attributes; its sturdy force, its courage and constancy, its truth, its self-reliance, and all that gives the emphasis to manly character.

The ejected officer, thrust out "to totter along the difficult footpath of life as best he may," is one who "forever afterwards looks wistfully about him in quest of support external to himself." This language anticipates Dimmesdale, that apprehensive, tottering soul for whose peace the pressure of a faith would always be essential, "supporting while it confined him within its iron framework."

Uncle Sam, the "worthy old gentleman," and Surveyor Pue with his "wig of majestic frizzle" are both handled somewhat in the comic mode; in *The Scarlet Letter* all the symbols of the conflict in the custom house are transformed, under the power of the Romantic imagination, into symbols of great seriousness and intensity. The Surveyor is replaced by Hester, Uncle Sam by the Puritan magistrates. The custom house, representing incarceration in the forms of a commercial democracy, becomes the prison house from which Hester (like Hawthorne only a few pages before her) issues with the letter on her breast. And, finally, Hawthorne's place is taken by Dimmesdale, caught like him in a conflict between social norms and imperatives on the one hand, private fulfillment and desires on the other. Like Dimmesdale, Hawthorne aspires for the approval of, and even membership in, the establishment. "It has been as dear an object as any, in my literary efforts, to be of some importance in [my good townspeople's] eyes, and to win myself a pleasant memory in this abode and burial-place of so many of my forefathers." Moreover, like Dimmesdale, he seems really to have wanted to produce works of moral edification, to be, if not quite a holy man, at least a sage. In his preface to *Mosses from an Old Manse*, the first autobiographical excursion, he had written:

> Nor, in truth, had the Old Manse ever been profaned by a lay occupant until that memorable summer afternoon when I entered it as my home. A priest had built it; a priest had succeeded to it; other priestly men from time to time had dwelt in it; and children born in its chambers had grown up to assume the priestly character. . . . I took shame to myself for having been so long a writer of idle stories, and ventured to hope that wisdom would descend upon me with the falling leaves of the avenue and that I should light upon an intellectual treasure in the Old Manse. . . . Profound treatises on morality . . . views of religion; histories . . . ; in the humblest event, I resolved at least to achieve a novel that should evolve some deep lesson, and should possess physical substance enough to stand alone.[6]

But such a "treasure of intellectual good" never came to light in the Old Manse. The impetus to dig and mine for it was lacking in the mood of Arcadian bliss Hawthorne felt in this "spot so sheltered from the turmoil of life's ocean." All he had to show when he left were "a few tales and essays, which had blossomed out like flowers in the calm summer of my heart and mind." The combined influences of Nature and the Transcendentalists acted like a narcotic on Hawthorne's spirit, and "three years hastened away with a noiseless flight, as the breezy sunshine chases the cloud shadows across the depths of a still valley." Hawthorne concludes "The Old Manse" with mention of his impending transference into the custom house; he contemplates this "strange vicissitude" with a mixture of regret and anticipation. In this new life he may achieve those things that he left undone in the drowsy atmosphere of Concord. This mood continues into "The Custom-House."

> After my fellowship of toil and impracticable schemes, with the dreamy brethren of Brook Farm; after living for three years within the subtle influence of an intellect like Emerson's; after those wild, free days on the Assabeth, indulging fantastic speculations beside our fire of fallen boughs, with Ellery Channing; after talk-

6. "The Old Manse," in *Mosses from an Old Manse* (1846), many times reprinted, and frequently authologized separately. The ranking of literary works in a moral order which places the novel at the bottom and omits the romance altogether indicates Hawthorne's dilemma as a romancer very fully, and foreshadows the conflict that comes to a head in "The Custom-House."

ing with Thoreau about pine-trees and Indian relics, in his hermitage at Walden; . . . it was time, at length, that I should exercise other faculties of my nature, and nourish myself with food for which I had hitherto had little appetite. Even the Old Inspector was desirable, as a change of diet, to a man who had known Alcott.

If one may continue Hawthorne's food metaphor, he imagines that life in the custom house will supplement an ambrosial diet with the hearty fare of the everyday; if there is no nature, no literature, and no intellect in the stew, there is plenty of the meat and potatoes of mundane materiality, and "human nature" in abundance.[7] Although Hawthorne resigns himself at first (until he discovers a subject) to giving up authorship for the duration,[8] he seems to have expected that he might gather there substance for a novel— which he still thought of as a better or at any rate as a more respectable literary product than a romance and continued to hope might be possible for him to write.

* * *

7. Human nature seems to mean external eccentricity—human nature in a crudely Dickensian sense. Dickens would unavoidably be much in Hawthorne's mind when he talked about the novel.
8. Hawthorne's ambivalences about what he was doing in the custom house lead to contradictory statements about how long he hopes or fears he will be there. He fears he will grow grey at his post but also never doubts that his custom-house existence will be transitory.

Modern Criticism

HENRY JAMES

[Densely Dark, with a Spot of Vivid Colour]†

* * * *The Scarlet Letter* contains little enough of gaiety or of hopefulness. It is densely dark, with a single spot of vivid colour in it; and it will probably long remain the most consistently gloomy of English novels of the first order. But I just now called it the author's masterpiece, and I imagine it will continue to be, for other generations than ours, his most substantial title to fame. The subject had probably lain a long time in his mind, as his subjects were apt to do; so that he appears completely to possess it, to know it and feel it. It is simpler and more complete than his other novels; it achieves more perfectly what it attempts, and it has about it that charm, very hard to express, which we find in an artist's work the first time he has touched his highest mark—a sort of straightness and naturalness of execution, an unconsciousness of his public, and freshness of interest in his theme. It was a great success, and he immediately found himself famous. * * * Hawthorne himself was very modest about it; he wrote to his publisher, when there was a question of his undertaking another novel, that what had given the history of Hester Prynne its "vogue" was simply the introductory chapter. In fact, the publication of *The Scarlet Letter* was in the United States a literary event of the first importance. The book was the finest piece of imaginative writing yet put forth in the country. There was a consciousness of this in the welcome that was given it—a satisfaction in the idea of America having produced a novel that belonged to literature, and to the forefront of it. Something might at last be sent to Europe as exquisite in quality as anything that had been received, and the best of it was that the thing was absolutely American; it belonged to the soil, to the air; it came out of the very heart of New England.

It is beautiful, admirable, extraordinary; it has in the highest degree that merit which I have spoken of as the mark of Hawthorne's best things—an indefinable purity and lightness of concep-

† From *Hawthorne* (London, 1879), pp. 87–92.

tion, a quality which in a work of art affects one in the same way as the absence of grossness does in a human being. His fancy, as I just now said, had evidently brooded over the subject for a long time; the situation to be represented had disclosed itself to him in all its phases. When I say in all its phases, the sentence demands modification; for it is to be remembered that if Hawthorne laid his hand upon the well-worn theme, upon the familiar combination of the wife, the lover, and the husband, it was, after all, but to one period of the history of these three persons that he attached himself. The situation is the situation after the woman's fault has been committed, and the current of expiation and repentance has set in. In spite of the relation between Hester Prynne and Arthur Dimmesdale, no story of love was surely ever less of a "love-story." To Hawthorne's imagination the fact that these two persons had loved each other too well was of an interest comparatively vulgar; what appealed to him was the idea of their moral situation in the long years that were to follow. The story, indeed, is in a secondary degree that of Hester Prynne; she becomes, really, after the first scene, an accessory figure; it is not upon her the *dénoûement* depends. It is upon her guilty lover that the author projects most frequently the cold, thin rays of his fitfully-moving lantern, which makes here and there a little luminous circle, on the edge of which hovers the livid and sinister figure of the injured and retributive husband. The story goes on, for the most part, between the lover and the husband—the tormented young Puritan minister, who carries the secret of his own lapse from pastoral purity locked up beneath an exterior that commends itself to the reverence of his flock, while he sees the softer partner of his guilt standing in the full glare of exposure and humbling herself to the misery of atonement—between this more wretched and pitiable culprit, to whom dishonour would come as a comfort and the pillory as a relief, and the older, keener, wiser man, who, to obtain satisfaction for the wrong he has suffered, devises the infernally ingenious plan of conjoining himself with his wronger, living with him, living upon him; and while he pretends to minister to his hidden ailment and to sympathise with his pain, revels in his unsuspected knowledge of these things, and stimulates them by malignant arts. The attitude of Roger Chillingworth, and the means he takes to compensate himself—these are the highly original elements in the situation that Hawthorne so ingeniously treats. None of his works are so impregnated with that after-sense of the old Puritan consciousness of life to which allusion has so often been made. If, as M. Montégut[1] says, the qualities of his an-

---

1. Emile Montégut (1825–95), an influential French critic; James is referring to Montégut's essay on Hawthorne, "A Social Novelist in America," published in the *Revue des Deux Mondes* (December 1, 1852). [*Editor.*]

cestors *filtered* down through generations into his composition, *The Scarlet Letter* was, as it were, the vessel that gathered up the last of the precious drops. And I say this not because the story happens to be of so-called historical cast, to be told of the early days of Massachusetts, and of people in steeple-crowned hats and sad-coloured garments. The historical colouring is rather weak than otherwise; there is little elaboration of detail, of the modern realism of research; and the author has made no great point of causing his figures to speak the English of their period. Nevertheless, the book is full of the moral presence of the race that invented Hester's penance—diluted and complicated with other things, but still perfectly recognisable. Puritanism, in a word, is there, not only objectively, as Hawthorne tried to place it there, but subjectively as well. Not, I mean, in his judgment of his characters in any harshness of prejudice, or in the obtrusion of a moral lesson; but in the very quality of his own vision, in the tone of the picture, in a certain coldness and exclusiveness of treatment.

The faults of the book are, to my sense, a want of reality and an abuse of the fanciful element—of a certain superficial symbolism. The people strike me not as characters, but as representatives, very picturesquely arranged, of a single state of mind; and the interest of the story lies, not in them, but in the situation, which is insistently kept before us, with little progression, though with a great deal, as I have said, of a certain stable variation; and to which they, out of their reality, contribute little that helps it to live and move. * * *

In *The Scarlet Letter* there is a great deal of symbolism; there is, I think, too much. It is overdone at times, and becomes mechanical; it ceases to be impressive, and grazes triviality. The idea of the mystic A which the young minister finds imprinted upon his breast and eating into his flesh, in sympathy with the embroidered badge that Hester is condemned to wear, appears to me to be a case in point. This suggestion should, I think, have been just made and dropped; to insist upon it and return to it, is to exaggerate the weak side of the subject. Hawthorne returns to it constantly, plays with it, and seems charmed by it; until at last the reader feels tempted to declare that his enjoyment of it is puerile. In the admirable scene, so superbly conceived and beautifully executed, in which Mr. Dimmesdale, in the stillness of the night, in the middle of the sleeping town, feels impelled to go and stand upon the scaffold where his mistress had formerly enacted her dreadful penance, and then, seeing Hester pass along the street, from watching at a sick-bed, with little Pearl at her side, calls them both to come and stand there beside him—in this masterly episode the effect is almost spoiled by the introduction of one of these superficial conceits. What leads up to it is very fine—so fine that I cannot do better than quote it as a specimen of one of the striking pages of the book.

> "But before Mr. Dimmesdale had done speaking, a light gleamed far and wide over all the muffled sky. It was doubtless caused by one of those meteors which the night-watcher may so often observe burning out to waste in the vacant regions of the atmosphere. So powerful with its radiance that it thoroughly illuminated the dense medium of cloud betwixt the sky and earth. The great vault brightened, like the dome of an immense lamp. It showed the familiar scene of the street with the distinctness of mid-day, but also with the awfulness that is always imparted to familiar objects by an unaccustomed light. The wooden houses, with their jutting stories and quaint gablepeaks; the doorsteps and thresholds, with the early grass springing up about them; the garden-plots, black with freshly-turned earth; the wheel-track, little worn, and, even in the market-place, margined with green on either side;—all were visible, but with a singularity of aspect that seemed to give another moral interpretation to the things of this world than they had ever borne before. And there stood the minister, with his hand over his heart; and Hester Prynne, with the embroidered letter glimmering on her bosom; and little Pearl, herself a symbol, and the connecting link between these two. They stood in the noon of that strange and solemn splendour, as if it were the light that is to reveal all secrets, and the daybreak that shall unite all that belong to one another."

That is imaginative, impressive, poetic; but when, almost immediately afterwards, the author goes on to say that "the minister looking upward to the zenith, beheld there the appearance of an immense letter—the letter A—marked out in lines of dull red light," we feel that he goes too far, and is in danger of crossing the line that separates the sublime from its intimate neighbour. We are tempted to say that this is not moral tragedy, but physical comedy. In the same way, too much is made of the intimation that Hester's badge had a scorching property, and that if one touched it one would immediately withdraw one's hand. Hawthorne is perpetually looking for images which shall place themselves in picturesque correspondence with the spiritual facts with which he is concerned, and of course the search is of the very essence of poetry. But in such a process discretion is everything, and when the image becomes importunate it is in danger of seeming to stand for nothing more serious than itself. When Hester meets the minister by appointment in the forest, and sits talking with him while little Pearl wanders away and plays by the edge of the brook, the child is represented as at last making her way over to the other side of the woodland stream, and disporting herself there in a manner which makes her mother feel herself, "in some indistinct and tantalising manner, estranged from Pearl; as if the child, in her lonely ramble through the forest, had strayed out of the sphere in which she and her mother dwelt together, and was now vainly seeking to return to it." And Hawthorne devotes a chapter to this idea of the child's having, by putting the brook between Hester and herself, established a kind of spiritual gulf, on the verge of which her little fantastic person innocently mocks at her mother's sense of bereavement. This conception belongs, one would say, quite to the lighter order of a story-teller's devices, and the reader hardly goes with Hawthorne in the large development he gives to it. He hardly goes with him either, I think, in his extreme predilection for a small number of vague ideas which are represented by such terms as "sphere" and "sympathies." Hawthorne makes too liberal a use of these two substantives; it is the solitary defect of his style; and it counts as a defect partly because the words in question are a sort of specialty with certain writers immeasurably inferior to himself.

I had not meant, however, to expatiate upon his defects, which are of the slenderest and most venial kind. *The Scarlet Letter* has the beauty and harmony of all original and complete conceptions, and its weaker spots, whatever they are, are not of its essence; they are mere light flaws and inequalities of surface. One can often return to it; it supports familiarity, and has the inexhaustible charm and mystery of great works of art. * * *

W. C. BROWNELL

[This New England Faust]†

The Scarlet Letter is not merely a masterpiece, it is a unique book. It does not belong in the populous category with which its title superficially associates it, and the way in which Hawthorne lifts it out of this and—without losing his hold of a theme that from the beginnings of literature has, in the work of the greatest masters as well as in that of the most sordid practitioners, demonstrated its vitality and significance—nevertheless, conducts its development in a perfectly original way, is indisputable witness of the imaginative power he possessed but so rarely exercised. So multifariously has the general theme that the scarlet letter symbolizes been treated in all literature and by all "schools" from the earliest to the latest, that however its inexhaustibility may be thus attested—an inexhaustibility paralleled by that of the perennial instinct with

† This selection, originally titled "Hawthorne: The Scarlet Letter," is reprinted from *American Prose Masters* by W. C. Brownell. (New York: Charles Scribner's Sons, 1909), pp. 96–103.

which it deals—any further treatment of it must forego, one would have said, the element of novelty, at least. Hawthorne's genius is thus to be credited even in this respect with a remarkable triumph. But that it should not only have thus won a triumph of originality by eluding instead of conquering the banality of the theme—by taking it in a wholly novel way, that is to say—but have produced, in its new departure, a masterpiece of beauty and power, is an accomplishment of accumulated distinction. *The Scarlet Letter*, in short, is not only an original work in a field where originality is the next thing to a miracle, but a work whose originality is in no wise more marked than its intrinsic substance.

It is not a story of adultery. The word does not, I think, occur in the book—a circumstance in itself typifying the detachment of the conception and the delicate art of its execution. But in spite of its detachment and delicacy, the inherent energy of the theme takes possession of the author's imagination and warms it into exalted exercise, making it in consequence at once the most real and the most imaginative of his works. It is essentially a story neither of the sin nor of the situation of illicit love—presents neither its psychology nor its social effects; neither excuses nor condemns nor even depicts, from this specific point of view. The love of Hester and Dimmesdale is a postulate, not a presentment. Incidentally, of course, the sin colors the narrative, and the situation is its particular result. But, essentially, the book is a story of concealment. Its psychology is that of the concealment of sin amid circumstances that make a sin of concealment itself. The sin itself might, one may almost say, be almost any other. And this constitutes no small part of the book's formal originality. To fail to perceive this is quite to misconceive it. As a story of illicit love its omissions are too great, its significance is not definite enough, its detail has not enough richness; the successive scenes of which it is composed have not an effective enough cohesion. From this point of view, but for the sacred profession of the minister and the conduct this imposes, it would be neither moving nor profound. Its moral would not be convincing. Above all, Chillingworth is a mistake, or at most a wasted opportunity. For he is specialized into a mere function of malignity, and withdrawn from the reader's sympathies, whereas what completes, if it does not constitute, the tragedy of adultery, is the sharing by the innocent of the punishment of the guilty. This inherent element of the situation, absolutely necessary to a complete presentment of it, the crumbling of the innocent person's inner existence, is absolutely neglected in "The Scarlet Letter," and the element of a malevolent persecution of the culpable substituted for it. The innocent person thereby becomes, as I have already said, a device, and though in this way Hawthorne is enabled to vivify the effect of remorse upon the minister by personifying its furies, in this way, too, he sacrifices at once the completeness of his picture and its depth of truth by disregarding one of its most important elements.

He atones for this by concentration on the culpable. It is *their* psychology alone that he exhibits. And though in this way he has necessarily failed to write the *chef-d'œuvre* of the general subject that in the field of art has been classic since monogamy established itself in society, he has produced a perfect masterpiece in the more detached and withdrawn sphere more in harmony with his genius. In narrowing his range and observing its limits he has perhaps even increased the poignancy of his effect. And his effect *is* poignant and true as reality itself. In confining himself to the concealment of sin rather than depicting its phenomena and its results, he has indeed brought out, as has never been done elsewhere, the importance of this fatal increment of falsity among the factors of the whole chaotic and unstable moral equilibrium. Concealment in *The Scarlet Letter*, to be sure, is painted in very dark colors. In similar cases it may be a duty, and is, at all events, the mere working of a natural instinct—at worst a choice of the lesser evil. But surely there is no exaggeration or essential loss of truth in the suggestion of its potentialities for torture conveyed by the agony of the preacher's double life. It is true his concealment condemned another to solitary obloquy. But if that be untypically infrequent and also not inherent in the situation as such, it is fairly counterbalanced by consolatory thought of the exceptional havoc confession would have wrought in his case. That is to say, if his remorse is exceptionally acute it is also exceptionally alleviated. On the whole the potential torture of remorse for a life that is flagrantly an acted lie is not misrepresented, either in truth or art, by the fate of Dimmesdale, though it is treated in the heightened way appropriate to the typical. * * *

F. O. MATTHIESSEN

[From Allegory to Symbolism]†

* * *

No art that sprang from American roots in this period could fail to show the marks of abstraction. * * * The tendency of American idealism to see a spiritual significance in every natural fact was far more broadly diffused than transcendentalism. Loosely Platonic, it came specifically from the common background that lay behind Emerson and Hawthorne, from the Christian habit of mind that saw

† From *American Renaissance: Art and Expression in the Age of Emerson and Whitman*, by F. O. Matthiessen. (New York: Oxford University Press, 1941), pp. 242–82. Footnotes have been renumbered.

the hand of God in all manifestations of life, and which, in the intensity of the New England seventeenth century, had gone to the extreme of finding "remarkable providences" even in the smallest phenomena, tokens of divine displeasure in every capsized dory or runaway cow.

Hawthorne was never inclined to the metaphysical speculation that absorbed Melville in his efforts to express the human tragedy involved in the doctrine of "innate depravity" that he had inherited from his Presbyterian youth. Nevertheless, Hawthorne could not help being interested in ideas, if only on the level of meditation. He typified the process from which his art arose by describing what he found in the symbolical letter A. His attention had first fixed upon its possibilities when giving an account of various punishments inflicted in "Endicott and the Red Cross" (1837). But a dozen years later when he purported to have found an actual letter of scarlet cloth among some old documents in the custom-house, his imagination pressed further: "Certainly, there was some deep meaning in it, most worthy of interpretation, and which, as it were, streamed forth from the mystic symbol, subtly communicating itself to my sensibilities, but evading the analysis of my mind."

With all the forces conditioning his art that we have noted—the scantiness of material and atmosphere, his lack of plastic experience, his steady moral preoccupation—it is no wonder that the favorites of his childhood, Spenser and Bunyan,[1] rose again to the surface when he began to write, and helped determine his bias to allegory. In working out his allegorical patterns, he seems sometimes to have started from a physical object, the minister's black veil, the Faun of Praxiteles, and to have worried it for implications. On the other hand, he could also start with noting an idea— "The Unpardonable Sin might consist in a want of love and reverence for the Human Soul"—and then work up an embodiment to fit it. In either case the method could very readily lose proportion. His idea might be promising enough, as in several of the processional sketches, but then the illustrations it suggested to him could be as ingeniously trivial as the crowd of impossible guests, the Oldest Inhabitant, Monsieur On-Dit, the Clerk of the Weather, Nobody, who clutter the party of the Man of Fancy, and obscure the telling portrait of the Master Genius of the age.[2] Or again, his idea might

1. Edmund Spenser's *The Faerie Queene* (1590, 1596) and John Bunyan's *The Pilgrim's Progress* (1678, 1684) are among the great allegorical works in English literature. [*Editor*.]
2. Yet even here Melville was greatly stimulated by this description of "a young man in poor attire, with no insignia of rank or acknowledged eminence," who learned that the only way to reach posterity "is to live truly and wisely for your own age." This is the man "for whom our country is looking anxiously into the mist of Time, as destined to fulfil the great mission of creating an American literature, hewing it, as it were, out of the unwrought granite of our intellectual quarries. From him, whether moulded in the form of an epic poem or assuming a guise altogether new as the spirit itself may determine, we are to receive our first great original work." These thoughts led directly into Melville's own hopes, and caused him to think that the sustained fancy of this sketch, "A Select Party," was surpassed by "nothing in Spenser."

itself be hardly more than a nervous *tic,* some freakish notion that possessed him in his solitude: "To personify If—But—And—Though, etc." To be sure, this proved too unsubstantial even for Hawthorne, and got no further than his notebook, but some of the themes on which he spent his talents were hardly more rewarding, as when he determined "to make a story of all strange and impossible things,—as the Salamander, the Phoenix," and the result was "A Virtuoso's Collection," a prolonged enumeration of such oddities.

* * *

Coleridge, as we might expect, distinguished the symbolical from the allegorical by calling it a part of some whole that it represents. Allegory "cannot be other than spoken consciously," whereas in the symbol "it is very possible that the general truth represented may be working unconsciously in the writer's mind . . . The advantage of symbolical writing over allegory is, that it presumes no disjunction of faculties, but simple predominance." This emphasis on how the imagination operates beneath conscious levels is apposite to Hawthorne's remark concerning the way that "the mystic symbol" of the scarlet letter had struck him, "communicating itself to my sensibilities, but evading the analysis of my mind."

* * *

The differentiation between symbolism and allegory, between Melville and Hawthorne at their most typical, is thus seen to be allied to Coleridge's fundamental distinction between imagination and fancy. Using some of Coleridge's terms, it may be said that symbolism is esemplastic, since it shapes new wholes; whereas allegory deals with fixities and definites that it does not basically modify. As a result *Moby-Dick* is, in its main sweep, an example of the reconcilement of the general with the concrete, of the fusion of idea and image; whereas, even in *The Scarlet Letter,* the abstract, the idea, is often of greater interest than its concrete expression.

* * *

The Scarlet Letter

Why Hawthorne came nearest to achieving that wholeness [of imaginative composition] in *The Scarlet Letter* may be accounted for in various ways. The grounds on which, according to Trollope,[3] its superiority was "plain to anyone who had himself been concerned in the writing of novels" were that here Hawthorne had developed his most coherent plot. Its symmetrical design is built around the three scenes on the scaffold of the pillory. There Hester endures her

3. Anthony Trollope (1815–82), the English novelist, wrote a laudatory essay on Hawthorne entitled "The Genius of Nathaniel Hawthorne" (*North American Review,* September 1879). [*Editor.*]

public shaming in the opening chapter. There, midway through the book, the minister, who has been driven almost crazy by his guilt but has lacked the resolution to confess it, ascends one midnight for self-torture, and is joined by Hester, on her way home from watching at a deathbed, and there they are overseen by Chillingworth. There, also, at the end, just after his own knowledge of suffering has endowed his tongue with eloquence in his great election sermon, the exhausted and death-stricken Dimmesdale totters to confess his sin at last to the incredulous and only half-comprehending crowd, and to die in Hester's arms.

Moreover, Hawthorne has also managed here his utmost approach to the inseparability of elements that James insisted on when he said that "character, in any sense in which we can get at it, is action, and action is plot." Of his four romances, this one grows most organically out of the interactions between the characters, depends least on the backdrops of scenery that so often impede the action in *The Marble Faun*.[4] Furthermore, his integrity of effect is due in part to the incisive contrasts among the human types he is presenting. The sin of Hester and the minister, a sin of passion not of principle, is not the worst in the world, as they are aware, even in the depths of their misery. She feels that what they did "had a consecration of its own"; he knows that at least they have never "violated, in cold blood, the sanctity of a human heart." They are distinguished from the wronged husband in accordance with the theological doctrine that excessive love for things which should take only a secondary place in the affections, though leading to the sin of lust, is less grave than love distorted, love turned from God and from his creatures, into self-consuming envy and vengeful pride. The courses that these three run are also in natural accord with their characters as worked upon by circumstance. The physician's native power in reading the human soul, when unsupported by any moral sympathies, leaves him open to degradation, step by step, from a man into a fiend. Dimmesdale, in his indecisive waverings, filled as he is with penance but no penitence, remains in touch with reality only in proportion to his anguish. The slower, richer movement of Hester is harder to characterize in a sentence. Even Chillingworth, who had married her as a young girl in the knowledge that she responded with no love for his old and slightly deformed frame, even he, after all that has happened, can still almost pity her "for the good that has been wasted" in her nature. Her purgatorial course through the book is from desperate recklessness to a strong, placid acceptance of her suffering and retribution.

4. Hawthorne's last completed novel (1860). [*Editor.*]

But beyond any interest in ordering of plot or in lucid discrimination between characters, Hawthorne's imaginative energy seems to have been called out to the full here by the continual correspondences that his theme allowed him to make between external events and inner significances. Once again his version of this transcendental habit took it straight back to the seventeenth century, and made it something more complex than the harmony between sunrise and a young poet's soul. In the realm of natural phenomena, Hawthorne examined the older world's common belief that great events were foreboded by supernatural omens, and remarked how "it was, indeed, a majestic idea, that the destiny of nations should be revealed, in these awful hieroglyphics, on the cope of heaven." But when Dimmesdale, in his vigil on the scaffold, beholds an immense dull red letter in the zenith, Hawthorne attributes it solely to his diseased imagination, which sees in everything his own morbid concerns. Hawthorne remarks that the strange light was "doubtless caused" by a meteor "burning out to waste"; and yet he also allows the sexton to ask the minister the next morning if he had heard of the portent, which had been interpreted to stand for Angel, since Governor Winthrop had died during the night.

Out of such variety of symbolical reference Hawthorne developed one of his most fertile resources, the device of multiple choice, which James was to carry so much further in his desire to present a sense of the intricacy of any situation for a perceptive being. One main source of Hawthorne's method lay in these remarkable providences, which his imagination felt challenged to search for the amount of emblematic truth that might lie hidden among their superstitions. He spoke at one point in this story of how "individuals of wiser faith" in the colony, while recognizing God's Providence in human affairs, knew that it "promotes its purposes without aiming at the stage-effect of what is called miraculous interposition." But he could not resist experimenting with this dramatic value, and his imagination had become so accustomed to the weirdly lighted world of Cotton Mather[5] that even the fanciful possibilities of the growth of the stigma on Dimmesdale did not strike him as grotesque. But when the minister "unbreasts" his guilt at last, the literal correspondence of that metaphor to a scarlet letter in his flesh, in strict accord with medieval and Spenserian personifications, is apt to strike us as a mechanical delimitation of what would otherwise have freer symbolical range.

For Hawthorne its value consisted in the variety of explanations

5. Mather's "weirdly lighted world" is most evident in his *Wonders of the Invisible World* (1693), a narrative of the Salem witchcraft period, full of instances of "a thousand preternatural things [happening] every day before our eyes." [*Editor.*]

to which it gave rise. Some affirmed that the minister had begun a course of self-mortification on the very day on which Hester Prynne had first been compelled to wear her ignominious badge, and had thus inflicted this hideous scar. Others held that Roger Chillingworth, "being a potent necromancer, had caused it to appear, through the agency of magic and poisonous drugs." Still others, "those best able to appreciate the minister's peculiar sensibility, and the wonderful operation of his spirit upon the body," whispered that "the awful symbol was the effect of the ever-active tooth of remorse," gnawing from his inmost heart outward. With that Hawthorne leaves his reader to choose among these theories. He does not literally accept his own allegory, and yet he finds it symbolically valid because of its psychological exactitude. His most telling stroke comes when he adds that certain spectators of the whole scene denied that there was any mark whatever on Dimmesdale's breast. These witnesses were among the most respectable in the community, including his fellow-ministers who were determined to defend his spotless character. These maintained also that his dying confession was to be taken only in its general significance, that he "had desired, by yielding up his breath in the arms of that fallen woman, to express to the world how utterly nugatory is the choicest of man's own righteousness." But for this interpretation, so revelatory of its influential proponents, Hawthorne leaves not one shred of evidence.

It should not be thought that his deeply ingrained habit of apprehending truth through emblems needed any sign of miraculous intervention to set it into action. Another aspect of the intricate correspondences that absorbed him is provided by Pearl. She is worth dissecting as the purest type of Spenserian characterization, which starts with abstract qualities and hunts for their proper embodiment; worth murdering, most modern readers of fiction would hold, since the tedious reiteration of what she stands for betrays Hawthorne at his most barren.

When Hester returned to the prison after standing her time on the scaffold, the infant she had clasped so tightly to her breast suddenly writhed in convulsions of pain, "a forcible type, in its little frame, of the moral agony" that its mother had borne throughout the day. As the story advances, Hawthorne sees in this child "the freedom of a broken law." In the perverseness of some of her antics, in the heartless mockery that can shine from her bright black eyes, she sometimes seems to her harassed mother almost a witch-baby. But Hester clings to the hope that her girl has capacity for strong affection, which needs only to be awakened by sympathy; and when there is some talk by the authorities of taking the wilful child's rearing into their own hands, Hester also clings to her possession of it as both her torture and happiness, her blessing and retribution, the one thing that has kept her soul alive in its hours of desperation.

Hawthorne's range of intention in this characterization comes out most fully in the scene where Hester and the minister have met in the woods, and are alone for the first time after so many years. Her resolution to save him from Chillingworth's spying, by flight together back to England, now sweeps his undermined spirit before it. In their moment of reunion, the one moment of released passion in the book, the beauty that has been hidden behind the frozen mask of her isolation reasserts itself. She takes off the formal cap that has confined the dark radiance of her hair and lets it stream down on her shoulders; she impulsively unfastens the badge of her shame and throws it to the ground. At that moment the minister sees Pearl, who has been playing by the brook, returning along the other side of it. Picked out by a beam of sunlight, with some wild flowers in her hair, she reminds Hester of "one of the fairies, whom we left in our dear old England," a sad reflection on the rich folklore that had been banished by the Puritans along with the maypoles. But as the two parents stand watching their child for the first time together, the graver thought comes to them that she is "the living hieroglyphic" of all they have sought to hide, of their inseparably intertwined fate.

As Pearl sees her mother, she stops by a pool, and her reflected image seems to communicate to her something "of its own shadowy and intangible quality." Confronted with this double vision, dissevered from her by the brook, Hester feels, "in some indistinct and tantalizing manner," suddenly estranged from the child, who now fixes her eyes on her mother's breast. She refuses Hester's bidding to come to her. Instead she points her finger, and stamps her foot, and becomes all at once a little demon of extravagant protest, all of whose wild gestures are redoubled at her feet. Hester understands what the matter is, that the child is outraged by the unaccustomed change in her appearance. So she wearily picks up the letter, which had fallen just short of the brook, and hides her luxuriant hair once more beneath her cap. At that Pearl is mollified and bounds across to them. During the weeks leading up to this scene, she had begun to show an increasing curiosity about the letter, and had tormented her mother with questions. Now she asks whether the minister will walk back with them, hand in hand, to the village, and when he declines, she flings away from his kiss, because he is not "bold" and "true." The question is increasingly raised for the reader, just how much of the situation this strange child understands.

Thus, when the stiff layers of allegory have been peeled away, even Hawthorne's conception of Pearl is seen to be based on exact psychological notation. She suggests something of the terrifying precocity which Edwards' acute dialectic of the feelings revealed in the children who came under his observation during the emotional strain of the Great Awakening.[6] She suggests, even more directly, James' *What Maisie Knew*, though it is typical of the later writer's refinement of skill and sophistication that he would set himself the complicated problem of having both parents divorced and married again, of making the child the innocent meeting ground for a liaison between the step-parents, and of confining his report on the situation entirely to what could be glimpsed through the child's inscrutable eyes.

* * *

JOHN C. GERBER

Form and Content in *The Scarlet Letter*†

* * *

Form in *The Scarlet Letter* rises out of a basic division of the whole into four parts, each of which gains its distinctiveness from the character that precipitates or is responsible for the action that takes place within its limits. Furthermore, the order of the parts is determined by the desires and capabilities of the characters. Thus the community, aside from the four main characters, is responsible for the action in the first part (Chapter I–VIII); Chillingworth for that in the second (XI–XII); Hester for that in the third (XIII–XX); and Dimmesdale for that in the fourth (XXI–XXIV). Within each part, moreover, there is a noticeable division between cause and effect, between material dealing primarily with the activating agent and material dealing primarily with the person or persons acted upon. * * *

It is not surprising that Hawthorne should have the community directing events as the story opens. Indeed, once he has selected his main characters he can do little else, since none of them can logically create the social situation which is the necessary antecedent to

6. The "Great Awakening" is the name given to a period of tremendous religious enthusiasm begun by Jonathan Edwards (1703–58) in 1734; his *Narrative of Surprising Conversions* (1736, 1737) includes an account of the astonishing conduct of a converted four-year-old girl. [*Editor.*]
† From *The New England Quarterly*, 17 (1944), 25–55. Footnotes have been omitted.

the spiritual complication. Hester is indifferent to what the people think of her baby, Dimmesdale is afraid of what they think, and Chillingworth is too recent a newcomer to affect their thought. Hence, in no case can a social situation be forced unless the community forces it. When the story opens, therefore, the people of the town of Boston are the logical and necessary activators, and they remain such throughout the first eight chapters of the book.

It is not entirely proper, however, to conceive of the community during this time as directly forcing the main characters into further sin. It does force isolation upon Hester. Otherwise, its function is to place the characters into such juxtaposition that new choices between good and evil must be made by each of them. If in every case the character chooses evil, the town can hardly be blamed except as an accessory before the fact. The rich irony of the situation is that the community while in the very act of abetting the spread of sin is complacently certain that it is stemming it.

Specifically, Boston places Hester upon the scaffold where she is seen and recognized by Chillingworth; it compels Dimmesdale to speak about Hester before the entire town, thereby forcing the issue of confession; it throws Hester and Chillingworth together in prison, where Chillingworth, because of his wife's distraught condition, is able to extract a vow to conceal his identity; it requires Hester to wear the scarlet letter; and through a threat against Pearl it brings the main characters together in a scene at the Governor's hall in which Dimmesdale unwittingly betrays his feelings to Chillingworth. * * *

The transition from the first to the second part of *The Scarlet Letter* is so sound in motivation and so subtle in presentation that the reader is likely to be unaware until pages later that a fundamental break in the book has been passed. It occurs in this way. At the conclusion of Chapter VIII, the Reverend Mr. Wilson, as spokesman for the community, closes the case of Boston *versus* the unknown lover of Hester Prynne. In turning down Chillingworth's request for further investigation he says:

> "Nay; it would be sinful, in such a question, to follow the clew of profane philosophy. Better to fast and pray upon it; and still better, it may be, to leave the mystery as we find it, unless Providence reveal it of its own accord. Thereby, every good Christian man hath a title to show a father's kindness towards the poor, deserted babe."

It is abundantly clear, however, that so charitable a disposition of the case is not acceptable to Chillingworth. Not only has he vowed to discover the identity of Hester's lover, but already his mind has been kindled by the possibilities of "a philosopher's research" into the mystery. Confronted with this double urge to investigation on the one hand and the community's withdrawal from the case on the other, the old doctor is placed in a position where he must force the action or give up all but the slenderest hope of revenge. By this time, however, the reader knows enough about Chillingworth to realize that the second alternative is for him not really an alternative at all. The reader, therefore, is not at all surprised that in Chapter IX the responsibility for the main action of the story shifts from the community to him.

The happenings which Chillingworth precipitates in this second part of the book can be quickly summarized. At first by frequent consultations and then by effecting an arrangement whereby he can live in the same house with Dimmesdale, the physician succeeds in becoming a daily and often hourly irritant to Dimmesdale's already sensitive conscience. Cautiously but surely, he succeeds in wearing down the young minister's defenses until in desperation Dimmesdale resorts to flagellation, fasts, and long vigils to ease the increasing torture. Generally, this section is a study of psychological cause and effect, with the victim frantically but ineffectively trying to deal with the effects rather than eliminating the cause. More particularly, it is a rich study in guilt and isolation. Before it is over, Chillingworth forces Dimmesdale into so deep a consciousness of sin that to the distracted minister it seems as if all the bonds which have held him to the forces for right have frayed beyond repair. But in so doing Chillingworth breaks all his own connections with what [Newton] Arvin calls "the redemptive force of normal human relations," and substitutes for them an ineluctable union with evil.

* * *

The depths into which Dimmesdale has been thrust by Chillingworth are best demonstrated in the final chapter of this section, the midnight vigil scene on the scaffold. Here, Hawthorne makes it plain that the minister is not only incapable of changing his sinful course by the action of his own will but has been so weakened that he is incapable of right action even when assistance is offered by outside agents. The vigil itself is another of Dimmesdale's attempts at penance. There might, he feels, be a moment's peace in it. Once on the scaffold, the realization of his isolation sweeps across him, and he involuntarily shrieks aloud. In the moments that follow, three persons appear: Governor Bellingham, Mistress Hibbins, and the venerable Father Wilson. Here are three opportunities for him to break his loneliness and to establish connection with one of the great societies—earthly, hellish, or heavenly. But an involuntary shriek is not enough; before Dimmesdale can be admitted to one of these great companies, a voluntary confession or commitment must be made. One of these three persons must be hailed. For a man of average moral strength, the problem would be to choose among the three. For him the problem is whether he shall choose any. In the end, he cowers silent upon the scaffold and the figures disappear. Thus does Arthur Dimmesdale reach the extreme of his isolation. For the time being, seemingly, earth, hell, and heaven are all closed to him. Had he chosen hell, his eventual fate would have been more terrible, but his immediate suffering could not have been greater.

When his mind begins to give way under the impact of this new sense of alienation, he again reacts involuntarily, this time to burst into a peal of insane laughter. What follows is a series of four rapid occurrences, each of which serves to remind the distracted minister of a source of power which is denied him only because of his failure to expiate his guilt. But in each case, Dimmesdale fails to grasp the opportunity and succeeds only in sinning further. Hester and Pearl, first of all, bring a rush of new life to the collapsing man. Here, presumably, is the perfect reminder of that bond of human affection which strengthens the human heart and enables it to find the path to truth. But when Pearl reminds her father of the expiation which is necessary before the bond can be strong and lasting, he dodges her question by giving it an impersonal and stereotyped answer. Secondly, the meteoric flash across the sky should remind him of strength through union with the tremendous yet wholesome forces of nature Instead, his diseased mind, extending its "egotism over the whole expanse of nature," sees only a large A, symbol of his guilt. In the third place, the appearance of Chillingworth should remind him of the horror of union with evil and, by contrast, the glory of a courageous stand before God. But though his "soul shivers" at the old physician, he obediently follows him home. Finally, the following morning, his own rich and powerful discourse to his congregation should by its own "heavenly influences" catapult him into giving expression to the truth, that quality which by his nature he loves most of all. Yet when the sexton asks him so simple a question as whether he has heard of the A in the sky the preceding night, Dimmesdale answers, "No, I had not heard of it."

Four decisions are thus forced upon Dimmesdale: he must assert his position in relation to man, to nature, to God, and to his own original and better self. In each case, from sheer weakness and despair of spirit he only adds new falsity to that which already exists. Chillingworth has worked better than he knows. If Dimmesdale is to be saved, aid must come from some outside source.

In the transition from part two to part three of *The Scarlet Letter*, content has again created form. Hawthorne once more has brought his story to a point where only one character is in a position to force the action. The community has been provided no reason for reentering the story as an activating force; Chillingworth has rather obviously run his course; and Dimmesdale is clearly lacking in both physical and moral vigor. Only Hester is capable of action. It is Hester, moreover, who wants action. For the first time she has fully comprehended the result of her vow to Chillingworth, and her sense of responsibility for Dimmesdale's condition has thrust all thoughts of her own temporarily from her mind. It is not surprising, therefore, that Chapter XIII should begin with a summary of Hester's activities during the seven years since the scaffold scene and that the following pages should reveal her as the source of whatever action takes place.

The third part of *The Scarlet Letter* extends from Chapter XIII to Chapter XX. In form, it is almost an exact duplication of the second part. Each sketches the immediate past of the main character, details the present action initiated by that character, and describes the results of that action upon another character. In each case, the other character is Dimmesdale.

Hester is sketched as independent and disillusioned. In some ways her isolation has been almost as complete as Dimmesdale's. For seven years now, heaven and earth "have frowned on her." Even though society has grown more benignant, it has never really accepted her save in time of sickness or death; God, never really a great influence in her life, seems to have become less real; nature's sunlight vanishes on her approach; and her own personality has lost its womanly charm. In brief, shame, despair, and solitude have been her teachers just as they have for Dimmesdale.

Two elements, however, have strengthened her while Dimmesdale weakened: her intellectual speculation and her daughter Pearl. The former has been possible only because her sin has been public and her mind hence not cramped by fears of exposure. It has resulted in a latitude of thought which allows her to picture herself as the prophetess of a new order and which causes her to scorn the institutions of the old: "the clerical band, the judicial robe, the pillory, the gallows, the fireside, or the church." In the second place, Pearl has kept a sense of moral direction in Hester, even though Hester has never fully acted upon it. Once, Pearl saved her mother from the devil in the guise of Mistress Hibbins; constantly, she has saved her from complete surrender to her own cynicism. In a loose sense, Pearl performs the same service for Hester that Chillingworth does for Dimmesdale, since both serve as pricks to the conscience. When their functions are examined more closely, however, it can be observed that these services have opposite effects. For Dimmesdale, if let alone, might eventually get his spiritual house in order. His natural gravitation is heavenward, and he continues to move toward evil simply because Chillingworth keeps nudging him in that direction. But Hester's inclination is not so dominantly heavenward, and she is kept from an alliance with the Devil largely because Pearl keeps hold of her. Intellectual speculation, stimulating as it has been, has led Hester into moral confusion. It is Pearl who has kept this confusion from collapsing into surrender. This she has done by keeping alive the spark of human affection and by standing rigidly against falsity wherever in her precocious way she has sensed it. Given these complementary sources of power, Hester is easily the strongest character in the book at this point. Even Chillingworth can recognize a quality "almost majestic" which shines through her despair. * * *

That Hester is able to win release from her vow to Chillingworth is due primarily to his admiration for his wife's cynical independence and to his own surrender to the course of events. The latter is the more important and represents the difference between the second and third parts of the book. In the second part the vow of secrecy was necessary so that he could direct events; now he is content merely to "let the black flower blossom as it may."

Hester's actions from this point break loosely into two lines, that directed toward expiation of her sin of hypocrisy and that directed toward escape from the consequences of her act of adultery. The two lines form an illuminating contrast between the proper and improper methods of dealing with guilt, the one leading to moral triumph and the other to moral failure. Fundamentally, the success of the first line is due to the fact that it arises out of a keen sense of responsibility for wrongdoing. To Hester this sense comes first when she sees Dimmesdale's emaciated figure upon the scaffold at midnight. Her later self-analysis is cuttingly honest. In all things else she has striven to be true. Truth has been the one virtue to which she might have held fast, and did hold fast "in all extremity" save in that one moment of weakness when she consented to deception. But now she finds that "a lie is never good, even though death threatens on the other side." In short, she has been false to her own nature, with the result that Dimmesdale has suffered possibly beyond repair. Realizing all this and recognizing at last the obligation which she owes Dimmesdale because of her love and her share in his crime, Hester becomes deeply and earnestly repentant.

Sincere repentance brings proper action. First, Hester obtains her release from Chillingworth, for any other procedure would merely have substituted one dishonesty for another. Then she waylays Dimmesdale in the forest in order to confess and implore his forgiveness. Confession can rectify the false relation which her silence has created, but only forgiveness from the one who has suffered can bring her peace. "Wilt thou yet forgive me!" she repeats over and over again until her lover at length replies, "I do forgive you, Hester." * * *

Hester's second line of action is related to her sin of adultery and her attempt to overcome the isolation imposed by it. Ironically, the very element which led her to repent for her sin of hypocrisy—truth to her own nature—now provides her with a justification for her act of adultery. When Dimmesdale observes sadly that Chillingworth's sin has been blacker than theirs, Hester is quick to whisper, "What we did had a consecration of its own! We felt it so! We said so to each other!" Confident in this belief, she proposes that they dispel their sense of moral isolation by translating it into physical terms. She and Dimmesdale and Pearl must flee to Europe. And her insistence that Dimmesdale agree represents the highest point in her activities as a directing force in the story.* * *

When Hester suggests a solution involving an easier means and an alternative end—temporal happiness—the solution appears so simple and so breathtaking to Dimmesdale that he wonders why they had never thought of it before. It offers a whole new realm of action, unchristianized and lawless but free and exciting. So exciting is it, in fact, that he is quick to put down any temporary misgivings. Reunion with God? He is irrevocably doomed anyway. Reunion with his people? Hester is all that he needs to sustain him. Union with his own spirit? Already he can feel life coursing through his veins without it. And so for the first time he consents with purpose and deliberation to something that basically he knows to be wrong. The immediate result is a sudden plunge into moral confusion. Like Hester before him, he has sinned against his own better nature. * * *

The fourth part of *The Scarlet Letter* offers an interesting variation from the other three parts. Whereas each of these gives immediate attention to the character which is to direct its action, the fourth part withholds such attention for almost two chapters. Indeed, these chapters, "The New England Holiday" and "The Procession," might with some justice be considered a final section of the third part inasmuch as they deal chiefly with the results of Hester's activities as they operate upon Hester herself. There are other and more cogent reasons, however, for considering them as belonging to the fourth part of the book and as a kind of introduction for Dimmesdale's final act. The most obvious is that the background ties these chapters with Chapter XXIII, in which he takes control. Hawthorne is carefully setting the stage for his climax. In terms of content there are other elements to be considered. Dimmesdale's final action must not appear as something opposing Hester's desires but as something evolving from them and sublimating them. Hence, it must be made clear to the reader that Hester has lost confidence in her own scheme and will ultimately be favorably affected by Dimmesdale's expiation rather than antagonized by his seeming disregard for her plans and wishes. Another element is the character of his action. Whereas the community, Chillingworth, and Hester needed days, months, and even years to accomplish their purposes, Dimmesdale needs only moments. Theirs was a series of actions, each carefully plotted and integrated with every other; his is one bold stroke. Their actions created complexities; his removes them. Hence, his can be encompassed and should be encompassed in a much smaller space. But it is equally true that the setting must be carefully prepared, or the action will pass before the reader is prepared to comprehend its full significance. It seems useful and understandable, therefore, that Hawthorne should devote Chapters XXI and XXII to introductory material, Chapter XXIII to Dimmesdale's expiatory action, and Chapter XXIV to the consequences of that action.

By contrast with her previous aggressiveness, Hester's mood in the market place sinks from one of loneliness to one of almost complete despair. Seldom has she seemed so completely isolated. Her frozen calmness, we are told, is due to the fact that she is "actually dead, in respect to any claim of sympathy" and has "departed out of the world, with which she still seems to mingle." The good people of the town sidle away from her and strangers openly gawk. Nor has she come any closer to Pearl. When Pearl keeps asking about the minister, Hester shuts her off with "Be quiet, Pearl! thou understandest not these things." Even Dimmesdale she sees moodily as existing in a sphere remote and "utterly beyond her reach." Indeed, she can hardly find it in her heart to forgive him for "being able so completely to withdraw himself from their mutual world; while she groped darkly, and stretched forth her cold hands, and found him not." Finally, the news that Chillingworth is to take passage on the same ship transforms her loneliness into consternation and despair. "Hester's strong, calm, steadfastly enduring spirit almost sank, at last, on beholding this dark and grim countenance of an inevitable doom, which . . . showed itself, with an unrelenting smile, right in the midst of their path."

Once Dimmesdale begins to direct the action, however, any effort of either Hester or Chillingworth becomes incidental. With a fine sense for dramatic contrast, Hawthorne has Dimmesdale reach his greatest success as a minister a few short minut fesses his crime. Never has he been more upliftin spiritually inclined. Already we know the Election thing born of new awareness and a sudden stiffen Since the world is no longer illusory or his own Dimmesdale apparently has made his peace with t

ce.
You
omitte
1. Jean

and with himself. But he still feels estranged from God and from the community because of his sins of adultery and hypocrisy. His confession on the scaffold, therefore, is necessary as penance for both these sins, and its dual character Dimmesdale himself makes clear:

> "God knows; and He is merciful; He hath proved his mercy, most of all, in my afflictions. By giving me this burning torture to bear upon my breast! By sending yonder dark and terrible old man, to keep the torture always at red heat! By bringing me hither, to die this death of triumphant ignominy before the people! Had either of these agonies been wanting, I had been lost forever! Praised be his name! His will be done! Farewell!"

In such a manner does Dimmesdale perform true penance and emerge finally at the moment of his death into a true relation with all the elements against which he has sinned. It is vain for him to hope for "an everlasting and pure reunion," but he has made himself worthy of whatever reunion God grants to those who repent.

FREDERIC I. CARPENTER

Scarlet A Minus†

From the first *The Scarlet Letter* has been considered a classic. It has appealed not only to the critics but to the reading public as well. The young Henry James described the feeling of mystery and terror which it aroused in his childish mind—a feeling not easily definable, but reaching to the depths of his nature. The scarlet letter has seemed the very symbol of all sin, translating into living terms the eternal problem of evil. And in 1850 the book was timely as well as timeless: it specifically suggested the nineteenth-century answer to the eternal problem. "Sin" might sometimes be noble, and "virtue" ignoble. Rousseau himself might have defined the scarlet letter as the stigma which society puts upon the natural instincts of man.[1]

But in modern times *The Scarlet Letter* has come to seem less

† From *College English*, V (January 1944), pp. 173–80. This essay was re-printed in the author's volume. *Ameri-* *Literature and the Dream*, New , 1955. Some footnotes have been d and the remainder renumbered. Jacques Rousseau (1712–78), French author whose belief in the superiority of "the noble savage" to civilized man has made his name synonymous with the view that man's natural passions are good and their suppression by society bad. [*Editor*.]

than perfect. Other novels, like *Anna Karenina,* have treated the same problem with a richer humanity and a greater realism. If the book remains a classic, it is of a minor order. Indeed, it now seems not quite perfect even of its own kind. Its logic is ambiguous, and its conclusion moralistic. The ambiguity is interesting, of course, and the moralizing slight, but the imperfection persists.

In one sense the very imperfection of *The Scarlet Letter* makes it classic: its ambiguity illustrates a fundamental confusion in modern thought. To the question "Was the action symbolized by the scarlet letter wholly sinful?" it suggests a variety of answers: "Yes," reply the traditional moralists; "Hester Prynne broke the Commandments." But the romantic enthusiasts answer: "No; Hester merely acted according to the deepest of human instincts." And the transcendental idealists reply: "In part; Hester truly sinned against the morality which her lover believed in, but did not sin against her own morality, because she believed in a 'higher law.' To her own self, Hester Prynne remained true."

From the perspective of a hundred years we shall reconsider these three answers to the problem of evil suggested by *The Scarlet Letter.* The traditional answer remains clear, but the romantic and the idealistic have usually been confused. Perhaps the imperfection of the novel arises from Hawthorne's own confusion between his heroine's transcendental morality and mere immorality. Explicitly, he condemned Hester Prynne as immoral; but implicitly, he glorified her as courageously idealistic. And this confusion between romantic immorality and transcendental idealism has been typical of the genteel tradition in America.

I

According to the traditional moralists, Hester Prynne was truly a sinful woman. Although she sinned less than her hypocritical lover and her vengeful husband, she nevertheless sinned; and, from her sin, death and tragedy resulted. At the end of the novel, Hawthorne himself positively affirmed this interpretation:

> Earlier in life, Hester had vainly imagined that she herself might be the destined prophetess, but had long since recognized the impossibility that any mission of divine and mysterious truth should be confided to a woman stained with sin.

And so the traditional critics have been well justified. *The Scarlet Letter* explicitly approves the tragic punishment of Hester's sin and explicitly declares the impossibility of salvation for the sinner.

But for the traditionalists there are many kinds and degrees of sin, and *The Scarlet Letter,* like Dante's *Inferno,* describes more than one. According to the orthodox, Hester Prynne belongs with the romantic lovers of the *Inferno,* in the highest circle of Hell. For

Hester sinned only through passion, but her lover through passion and concealment, and her husband through "violating, in cold blood, the sanctity of the human heart." Therefore, Hester's sin was the least, and her punishment the lightest.

But Hester sinned, and, according to traditional Puritanism, this act shut her off forever from paradise. Indeed, this archetypal sin and its consequent tragedy have been taken to symbolize the eternal failure of the American dream. Hester suggests "the awakening of the mind to 'moral gloom' after its childish dreams of natural bliss are dissipated."[2] Thus her lover, standing upon the scaffold, exclaimed: "Is this not better than we dreamed of in the forest?" And Hawthorne repeated that Hester recognized the eternal justice of her own damnation. The romantic dream of natural freedom has seemed empty to the traditionalists, because sin and its punishment are eternal and immutable.

That Hester's sin was certain, and her dream of freedom impossible, traditional Catholicism has also agreed. But the Catholic critics object that Hawthorne's Puritanism denies the Christian doctrine of the forgiveness of sin. They believe that Hester expiated her evil by means of repentance and a virtuous later life: "Hester represents the repentant sinner, Dimmesdale the half-repentant sinner, and Chillingworth the unrepentant sinner."[3] Therefore, Hester individually achieved salvation, even though her sin was clear and her dream of universal freedom impossible.

But all the traditionalists agree that Hester's action was wholly sinful. That Hester herself never admitted this accusation and that Hester is never represented as acting blindly in a fit of passion and that Hester never repented of her "sin" are facts which the traditionalists overlook. Moreover, they forget that Hawthorne's condemnation of Hester's sin is never verified by Hester's own words. But of this more later.

Meanwhile, other faults in Hester's character are admitted by the traditional and the liberal alike. Even if she did not do what *she* believed to be evil, Hester nevertheless did tempt her lover to do what *he* believed to be evil and thus caused his death. And because she wished to protect her lover, she consented to a life of deception and concealment which she herself knew to be false. But for the traditional moralists neither her temptation of her lover nor her deception of him was a cardinal sin. Only her act of passion was.

Therefore Hester's passion was the fatal flaw which caused the tragedy. Either because of some womanly weakness which made her unable to resist evil, or because of some pride which made her oppose her own will to the eternal law, she did evil. Her sin was

2. H. W. Schneider, *The Puritan Mind* (New York, 1930), p. 259. 3. Yvor Winters, *Maule's Curse* (Norfolk, Conn., 1938), p. 16.

certain, the law she broke was immutable, and the human tragedy was inevitable—according to the traditional moralists.

II

But, according to the romantic enthusiasts, *The Scarlet Letter* points a very difficult moral. The followers of Rousseau have said that Hester did not sin at all; or that, if she did, she transformed her sin into a virtue. Did not Hawthorne himself describe the radiance of the scarlet letter, shining upon her breast like a symbol of victory? "The tendency of her fate had been to set her free. The scarlet letter was her passport into regions where other women dared not tread." Hester—if we discount Hawthorne's moralistic conclusion—never repented of her "sin" of passion, because she never recognized it as such.

In absolute contrast to the traditionalists, the romantics have described *The Scarlet Letter* as a masterpiece of "Hawthorne's immoralism." Not only Hester but even the Puritan minister becomes "an amoralist and a Nietzschean."[4] "In truth," wrote Hawthorne, "nothing short of a total change of dynasty and moral code in that interior kingdom was adequate to account for the impulses now communicated to the . . . . minister." But Hester alone became perfectly immoral, for "the world's law was no law for her mind." She alone dared renounce utterly the dead forms of tradition and dared follow the natural laws of her own instinctive nature to the end.

Therefore, the romantics have praised *The Scarlet Letter* for preaching "*la mystique de l'Amour.*" And especially the French critics, following D. H. Lawrence, have spoken of Hawthorne's "gospel of love."[5] "Hester gave everything to love," they have repeated:

> Give all to love;
> Obey thy heart;
> Friends, kindred, days,
> Estate, good-fame,
> Plans, credit and the Muse,—
> Nothing refuse.[6]

As Emerson counseled, so Hester acted. In spite of Hawthorne's moralistic disclaimer, his heroine has seemed to renounce traditional

---

4. Regis Michaud, *The American Novel Today* (Boston, 1928), pp. 36, 44. [Friedrich Nietzsche, 1844–1900, a German philosopher, emphasized the superiority of intense emotion to thought in both life and art—*Editor.*]

5. D. H. Lawrence (1885–1930), English novelist whose works emphasized the centrality of the erotic in life ("The body is the soul"); his "Nathaniel Hawthorne and *The Scarlet Letter*" in *Studies in Classic American Literature* (1923) sees Hester as the destructive female principle that delights in making of Dimmesdale a fallen saint—hardly a "gospel of love." [*Editor.*]

6. The first stanza of Ralph Waldo Emerson's "Give All to Love" (1847); another section of the poem is quoted further on in the essay. [*Editor.*]

morality and to proclaim the new morality of nature and the human heart.

Therefore, according to the romantics, the tragedy of *The Scarlet Letter* does not result from any tragic flaw in the heroine, for she is romantically without sin. It results, rather, from the intrinsic evil of society. Because the moral law imposes tyrannical restraints upon the natural instincts of man, human happiness is impossible in civilization. *The Scarlet Letter,* therefore, becomes the tragedy of perfection, in which the ideal woman is doomed to defeat by an inflexible moral tradition. Because Hester Prynne was so perfectly loyal and loving that she would never abandon her lover, she was condemned by the Puritans. Not human frailty, therefore, or any tragic imperfection of character, but only the inevitable forces of social determinism caused the disaster described by *The Scarlet Letter*—according to the romantic enthusiasts.

III

Between the orthodox belief that Hester Prynne sinned utterly and the opposite romantic belief that she did not sin at all, the transcendental idealists seek to mediate. Because they deny the authority of the traditional morality, these idealists have sometimes seemed merely romantic. But because they seek to describe a new moral law, they have also seemed moralistic. The confusion of answers to the question of evil suggested by *The Scarlet Letter* arises, in part, from a failure to understand the transcendental ideal.

With the romantics, the transcendentalists[7] agree that Hester did wisely to "give all to love." But they insist that Hester's love was neither blindly passionate nor purposeless. "What we did," Hester exclaims to her lover, "had a consecration of its own." To the transcendental, her love was not sinful because it was not disloyal to her evil husband (whom she had never loved) or to the traditional morality (in which she had never believed). Rather her love was purposefully aimed at a permanent union with her lover— witness the fact that it had already endured through seven years of separation and disgrace. Hester did well to "obey her heart," because she felt no conflict between her heart and her head. She was neither romantically immoral nor blindly rebellious against society and its laws.

This element of conscious purpose distinguishes the transcendental Hester Prynne from other, merely romantic heroines. Because she did not deny "the moral law" but went beyond it to a "higher law," Hester transcended both romance and tradition. As if to

7. Critics suggesting this "transcendental" point of view include the following: Moncure D. Conway, *Life of Nathaniel Hawthorne* (London, 1870); John Erskine, "Hawthorne," in *CHAL,* II, 16–31; and Stuart P. Sherman, "Hawthorne," in *Americans,* pp. 122–52.

emphasize this fact, Hawthorne himself declared that she "assumed a freedom of speculation which our forefathers, had they known it, would have held to be a deadlier crime than that stigmatized by the scarlet letter." Unlike her lover, she had explicitly been led "beyond the scope of generally received laws." She had consciously wished to become "the prophetess" of a more liberal morality.

According to the transcendentalists, therefore, Hester's "sin" was not that she broke the Commandments—for, in the sight of God, she had never truly been married. Nor was Hester the blameless victim of society, as the romantics believed. She had sinned in that she had deceived her lover concerning the identity of her husband. And she admitted this clearly:

> "O Arthur," cried she, "forgive me! In all things else, I have striven to be true! Truth was the one virtue to which I might have held fast, and did hold fast, through all extremity; save when thy good . . . were put in question! Then I consented to a deception. But a lie is never good, even though death threaten on the other side."

Not traditional morality, but transcendental truth, governed the conscience of Hester Prynne. But she had a conscience, and she had sinned against it.

Indeed, Hester Prynne had "sinned," exactly *because* she put romantic "love" ahead of ideal "truth." She had done evil in allowing the "good" of her lover to outweigh the higher law. She had sacrificed her own integrity by giving absolutely everything to her loved one. For Emerson had added a transcendental postscript to his seemingly romantic poem:

> Leave all for love;
> Yet, hear me, yet
>
> . . . .
>
> Keep thee to-day,
> To-morrow, forever,
> Free as an Arab
> Of thy beloved.
>
> Heartily know
> When half-gods go,
> The gods arrive.

That is to say: True love is a higher law than merely traditional morality, but, even at best, human love is "daemonic." The highest law of "celestial love" is the law of divine truth.

According to the transcendental idealists, Hester Prynne sinned in that she did not go beyond human love. In seeking to protect her lover by deception, she sinned both against her own "integrity" and against God. If she had told the whole truth in the beginning, she would have been blameless. But she lacked this perfect self-reliance.

Nevertheless, tragedy would have resulted even if Hester Prynne had been transcendentally perfect. For the transcendental ideal implies tragedy. Traditionally, tragedy results from the individual imperfection of some hero. Romantically, it results from the evil of society. But, ideally, it results from a conflict of moral standards or values. The tragedy of *The Scarlet Letter* resulted from the conflict of the orthodox morality of the minister with the transcendental morality of the heroine. For Arthur Dimmesdale, unlike Hester Prynne, did sin blindly through passion, committing an act which he felt to be wrong. And because he sinned against his own morality, he felt himself unable to grasp the freedom which Hester urged. If, on the contrary, he had conscientiously been able to flee with her to a new life on the western frontier, there would have been no tragedy. But:

> "It cannot be!" answered the minister, listening as if he were called upon to realize a dream. "I am powerless to go. Wretched and sinful as I am, I have had no other thought than to drag on my earthly existence where Providence hath placed me."

To those who have never believed in it, the American dream of freedom has always seemed utopian and impossible of realization. Tragedy results from this conflict of moralities and this unbelief.

IV

According to the orthodox, Hester Prynne sinned through blind passion, and her sin caused the tragedy. According to the romantic, Hester Prynne heroically "gave all to love," and tragedy resulted from the evil of society. According to the transcendentalists, Hester Prynne sinned through deception, but tragedy resulted from the conflict of her dream of freedom with the traditional creed of her lover. Dramatically, each of these interpretations is possible: *The Scarlet Letter* is rich in suggestion. But Hawthorne the moralist sought to destroy this richness.

The Scarlet Letter achieves greatness in its dramatic, objective presentation of conflicting moralities in action: each character seems at once symbolic, yet real. But this dramatic perfection is flawed by the author's moralistic, subjective criticism of Hester Prynne. And this contradiction results from Hawthorne's apparent confusion between the romantic and the transcendental moralities. While the characters of the novel objectively act out the tragic conflict between the traditional morality and the transcendental dream, Hawthorne subjectively damns the transcendental for being romantically immoral.

Most obviously, Hawthorne imposed a moralistic "Conclusion" upon the drama which his characters had acted. But the artistic and moral falsity of this does not lie in its didacticism or in the personal intrusion of the author, for these were the literary conventions of the age. Rather it lies in the contradiction between the author's moralistic comments and the earlier words and actions of his characters. Having created living protagonists, Hawthorne sought to impose his own will and judgment upon them from the outside. Thus he described Hester as admitting her "sin" of passion and as renouncing her "selfish ends" and as seeking to "expiate" her crime. But Hester herself had never admitted to any sin other than deception and had never acted "selfishly" and had worn her scarlet letter triumphantly, rather than penitently. In his "Conclusion," therefore, Hawthorne did violence to the living character whom he had created.

His artificial and moralistic criticism is concentrated in the "Conclusion." But it also appears in other chapters of the novel. In the scene between Hester and Arthur in the forest, Hawthorne had asserted:

> She had wandered, without rule or guidance, in a moral wilderness. . . . Shame, Despair, Solitude! These had been her teachers,—stern and wild ones,—and they had made her strong, but taught her much amiss.

And again Hawthorne imputed "Shame" to Hester, and declared that her "strength" was immoral.

This scene between Hester and her lover in the forest also suggests the root of Hawthorne's confusion. To the traditional moralists, the "forest," or "wilderness," or "uncivilized Nature" was the symbolic abode of evil—the very negation of moral law. But to the romantics, wild nature had become the very symbol of freedom. In this scene, Hawthorne explicitly condemned Hester for her wildness—for "breathing the wild, free atmosphere of an unredeemed, unchristianized, lawless region." And again he damned her "sympathy" with "that wild, heathen Nature of the forest, never subjugated by human law, nor illumined by higher truth." Clearly he hated moral romanticism. And this hatred would have been harmless, if his heroine had merely been romantic, or immoral.

But Hester Prynne, as revealed in speech and in action, was not romantic but transcendental. And Hawthorne failed utterly to distinguish, in his moralistic criticism, between the romantic and the transcendental. For example, he never described the "speculations" of Hester concerning "freedom" as anything but negative, "wild," "lawless," and "heathen." All "higher truth" for him seemed to reside exclusively in traditional, "civilized" morality. But Hawthorne's contemporaries, Emerson and Thoreau, had specifically described the "wilderness" (*Life in the* Woods)[8] as the precondition of the new morality of freedom; and "Nature" as the very abode of "higher truth": all those transcendental "speculations" which Hawthorne imputed to his heroine conceived of "Nature" as offering the opportunity for the realization of the higher moral law and for the development of a "Christianized" society more perfectly illumined by the divine truth.

Therefore, Hawthorne's moralistic passages never remotely admitted the possible truth of the transcendental ideal which he had objectively described Hester Prynne as realizing. Having allowed his imagination to create an idealistic heroine, he did not allow his conscious mind to justify—or even to describe fairly—her ideal morality. Rather, he damned the transcendental character whom he had created, for being romantic and immoral. But the words and deeds by means of which he had created her contradicted his own moralistic criticisms.

V

In the last analysis, the greatness of *The Scarlet Letter* lies in the character of Hester Prynne. Because she dared to trust herself and to believe in the possibility of a new morality in the new world, she achieved spiritual greatness in spite of her own human weakness, in spite of the prejudices of her Puritan society, and, finally, in spite of the prejudices of her creator himself. For the human weakness which made her deceive her lover in order to protect him makes her seem only the more real. The calm steadfastness with which she endures the ostracism of society makes her heroic. And the clear purpose which she follows, despite the denigrations of Hawthorne, makes her almost ideal!

Hester, almost in spite of Hawthorne, envisions the transcendental ideal of positive freedom, instead of the romantic ideal of mere escape. She urges her lover to create a new life with her in the wilderness: "Doth the universe lie within the compass of yonder town? Whither leads yonder forest track?" And she seeks to arouse him to a pragmatic idealism equal to the task: "Exchange this false life of thine for a true one! . . . . Preach! Write! Act! Do anything save to lie down and die!"

Thus Hester Prynne embodies the authentic American dream of a new life in the wilderness of the new world, and of self-reliant action to realize that ideal. In the Puritan age in which he lived, and in Hawthorne's own nineteenth century, this ideal was actually being realized in practice. Even in our modern society with its more liberal laws, Hester Prynne might hope to live happily with her lover, after winning divorce from her cruel and vengeful husband.

8. The subtitle of the first edition of   [*Editor.*]
Henry David Thoreau's *Walden* (1854).

But in every century her tragedy would still be the same. It would result from her own deception and from the conflicting moral belief of her lover. But it would not result from her own sense of guilt or shame.

In *The Scarlet Letter* alone among his novels, Hawthorne succeeded in realizing a character embodying the authentic American dream of freedom and independence in the new world. But he succeeded in realizing this ideal emotionally rather than intellectually. And, having completed the novel, he wondered at his work: "I think I have never overcome my adamant in any other instance," he said. Perhaps he added the moralistic "Conclusion" and the various criticisms of Hester, in order to placate his conscience. In any case, he never permitted himself such freedom—or such greatness—again.

Where *The Scarlet Letter* described the greatness as well as the human tragedy which lies implicit in the American dream of freedom, Hawthorne's later novels describe only the romantic delusion which often vitiates it. *The Blithedale Romance* emphasizes the delusion of utopianism, and *The Marble Faun* preaches the falsity of the ideal of "nature" (Donatello). Where Hester Prynne was heroically self-reliant, Zenobia becomes pathetically deluded, and Miriam romantically blind. Hawthorne, rejecting the transcendental idealism which Hester Prynne seems to have realized almost in spite of his own "adamant," piously recanted in his "Conclusion" and took good care that his later "dark" heroines should be romantic, unsympathetic, and (comparatively) unimportant.

DARREL ABEL

Hawthorne's Hester†

Hester Prynne, the heroine of *The Scarlet Letter*, typifies romantic individualism, and in her story Hawthorne endeavored to exhibit the inadequacy of such a philosophy. The romantic individualist repudiates the doctrine of a supernatural ethical absolute. He rejects both the authority of God, which sanctions a pietistic ethic, and the authority of society, which sanctions a utilitarian ethic, to affirm the sole authority of Nature. Hester, violating piety and decorum, lived a life of nature and attempted to rationalize her romantic self-indulgence; but, although she broke the laws of God and man, she failed to secure even the natural satisfactions she sought.

Many modern critics, however, who see her as a heroine *à la*

† From *College English*, 13 (1952), 303–9. Footnotes have been renumbered.

George Sand,[1] accept her philosophy and regard her as the central figure of the romance—the spokesman of Hawthorne's views favoring "a larger liberty." Hawthorne's women are usually more sympathetic and impressive than his men; because Hester is more appealing than either her husband or her lover, it is easy to disregard their more central roles in the story.[2] Furthermore, the title of the romance is commonly taken to refer mainly to the letter on Hester's dress and thus somehow to designate her as the central figure; but, in fact, the ideal letter, not any particular material manifestation of it, is referred to in the title. Actually its most emphatic particular manifestation is the stigma revealed on Dimmesdale's breast in the climaxing chapter of the book, "The Revelation of the Scarlet Letter."

Hester's apologists unduly emphasize circumstances which seem to make her the engaging central figure of the romance, and they ignore or even decry the larger tendency of the book, which subordinates her and exposes her moral inadequacy. "She is a free spirit liberated in a moral wilderness."[3]

> She has sinned, but the sin leads her straightway to a larger life. . . . Hawthorne . . . lets the sin elaborate itself, so far as Hester's nature is concerned, into nothing but beauty. . . . since her love for Dimmesdale was the one sincere passion of her life, she obeyed it utterly, though a conventional judgment would have said that she was stepping out of the moral order. There is nothing in the story to suggest condemnation of her or of the minister in their sin. . . . The passion itself, as the two lovers still agree at the close of their hard experience, was sacred and never caused them repentance.[4]

This opinion sublimely disregards Hawthorne's elaborate exposition of the progressive moral dereliction of Hester, during which "all the light and graceful foliage of her character [was] withered up by this red-hot brand" of sinful passion. It even more remarkably ignores her paramour's seven-year-long travail of conscience for (in his own dying words) "the sin here so awfully revealed."

The most recent and immoderate advocate of Hester as the prepossessing exponent of a wider freedom in sexual relations is Professor Frederic I. Carpenter:

1. The pseudonym of Amandine Aurore Dupin (1804–76), French woman novelist whose works exalted the sexually liberated woman. [*Editor.*]

2. "Hester Prynne . . . becomes, really, after the first scene, an accessory figure; it is not upon her the denouement depends" (Henry James, *Hawthorne* [New York, 1879], p. 109). James had a virtue excellent and rare among readers: he attended to his author's *total* intention and exposition. Apparently Hester's modern champions are misled by their prepossessions; they share the general tendency of our time to believe more strongly in the reality and value of natural instincts than in the truth and accessibility of supernatural absolutes.

3. Stuart P. Sherman, "Hawthorne: A Puritan Critic of Puritans," *Americans* (New York, 1922), p. 148.

4. John Erskine, *CHAL*, II, 26–27.

In the last analysis, the greatness of *The Scarlet Letter* lies in the character of Hester Prynne. Because she dared to trust herself to believe in the possibility of a new morality in the new world, she achieved spiritual greatness in spite of her own human weakness, in spite of the prejudices of her Puritan society, . . . in spite of the prejudices of her creator himself.[5]

It is a tribute to Hawthorne's art that Hester's champion believes in her so strongly that he presumes to rebuke her creator for abusing her and rejoices in his conviction that she triumphs over the author's "denigrations."

In fact, Hawthorne does feel moral compassion for Hester, but her role in the story is to demonstrate that persons who engage our moral compassion may nevertheless merit moral censure. We sympathize with Hester at first because of her personal attraction, and our sympathy deepens throughout the story because we see that she is more sinned against than sinning.

The prime offender against her is Roger Chillingworth, who married her before she was mature enough to know the needs of her nature. There is a tincture of Godwinism—even of Fourierism—in Hawthorne's treatment of Hester's breach of her marriage obligations. Godwin held that marriage was "the most odious of all monopolies" and that it was everyone's duty to love the worthiest. After her lapse, Hester told her husband, "Thou knowest I was frank with thee. I felt no love, nor feigned any." According to Godwinian principles, then, her duty to him was slight, especially if a man came along whom she could love. Chillingworth freely acknowledged that he had wronged her in marrying her before she was aware of the needs of her nature: "Mine was the first wrong, when I betrayed they budding youth into a false and unnatural relation with my decay." His second, less heinous, offense was his neglectfully absenting himself from her after their marriage. His experience understood what her innocence could not foresee, that the awakening passion in her might take a forbidden way: "If sages were ever wise in their own behoof, I might have foreseen all this." His third and culminating offense was his lack of charity toward her after her disgrace. Although he admitted his initial culpability in betraying her into "a false and unnatural relation," he refused to share the odium brought upon her in consequence of the situation he had created. True, he plotted no revenge against her, but cold forbearance was not enough. He was motivated not by love but by self-love; in his marriage and in his vengeance he cherished and pursued his private objects, to the exclusion of the claims of others, whose lives were involved with his own. He regarded his wife jealously, as a chattel,[6] not as a person with needs and rights of her own. Her error touched his compassion only perfunctorily, but it gave a mortal wound to his *amour-propre*.[7] Hester's adulterous passion was nobler, for she wished that she might bear her paramour's shame and anguish as well as her own. Thus Chillingworth triply offended against her: he drew her into a relationship which made her liable to sin, did not duly defend her from the peril in which he had placed her, and cast her off when she succumbed.

The nature of Dimmesdale's offense against Hester is too obvious to require specification, but both Hester's conduct and his own deserve whatever extenuation may be due to the passionate and impulsive errors of inexperience: "This had been a sin of passion, not of principle, nor even purpose." The minister's conduct toward Hester, then, is less blameworthy than her husband's, who had knowingly and deliberately jeopardized her happiness and moral security; Dimmesdale tells Hester: "We are not, Hester, the worst sinners in the world. There is one worse than even the polluted priest!" A distinction must be made, however, between Dimmesdale's moral responsibility and Hester's; her sin was contingent upon his, and her conduct is therefore more deserving of palliation than his. Besides, he had moral defenses and moral duties which she did not have. He had a pastoral duty toward her and a professional duty to lead an exemplary life. Also, according to Hawthorne's view of the distinctive endowments of the sexes, Hester depended upon her womanly feeling, but he had the guidance of masculine intellect and moral erudition. Above all, he was free to marry to satisfy "the strong animal nature" in him, but Hester met her happiest choice too late, when she was "already linked and wedlock bound to a fell adversary." But the minister's really abominable fault was not his fornication; it was his unwillingness to confess his error, his hypocrisy. Hester wished she might bear his shame as well as her own, but he shrank from assuming his place beside her because his perilous pride in his reputation for sanctity was dearer to him than truth. Like Chillingworth, he wronged Hester and left her to bear the punishment alone.

Society wronged Hester as grievously as, though less invidiously than, particular persons wronged her. Hawthorne distinguished between society under its instinctively human aspect and society under its institutional aspect. Society as collective humanity sympathized and was charitable: "It is to the credit of human nature, that, except where its selfishness is brought into play, it loves more readily than it hates." But society under its institutional aspect pur-

---

6. "Woman is born for love, and it is impossible to turn her from seeking it. Men should deserve her love as an inheritance, rather than seize and guard it like a prey" (Margaret Fuller, *Woman in the Nineteenth Century* [Boston, 1893], p. 337).

7. Vanity. [*Editor.*]

sued an abstraction, conceived as the general good, which disposed it vindictively toward errant individuals. Hawthorne remarked in "The New Adam and Eve": "[The] Judgment Seat [is] the very symbol of man's perverted state." A scheme of social justice supplants the essential law of love which is grounded in human hearts; any system of expedient regulations tends to become sacrosanct eventually, so that instead of serving humanity it becomes a tyrannical instrument for coercing nonconformists.

Harsh legalism has been remarked as a characteristic of the Puritan theocracy by social historians: "The effect of inhumane punishments on officials and the popular mind generally . . . [was apparently] a brutalizing effect . . . , rendering them more callous to human sufferings."[8] "To make the people good became the supreme task of the churches, and legalism followed as a matter of course."[9] "The theory was that Jehovah was the primary law-giver, the Bible a statute-book, the ministers and magistrates stewards of the divine will."[1] Hester, then, Hawthorne tells us, suffered "the whole dismal severity of the Puritanic code of law" in "a period when the forms of authority were felt to possess the sacredness of Divine institutions." Her punishment shows how society had set aside the humane injunction that men should love one another, to make a religion of the office of vengeance, which in the Scriptures is exclusively appropriated to God. The wild-rose bush, with "its delicate gems," which stood by the prison door, and "the burdock, pigweed, apple-peru, and other such unsightly vegetation" which grew with such appropriate luxuriance in the prison yard symbolize the mingled moral elements in "the dim, awful, mysterious, grotesque, intricate nature of man."[2] Puritan society, unfortunately, had cultivated the weeds and neglected the flowers of human nature and attached more significance to "the black flower of civilized life, a prison," than to the rose bush, "which, by a strange chance, has been kept alive in history" "to symbolize some sweet moral blossom." There is powerful irony in Hawthorne's picture of the harsh matrons who crowded around the pillory to demand that Hester be put to death: "Is there not law for it? Truly, there is, both in Scripture and the statute-book." Surely Hawthorne was here mindful of the question which the scribes and Pharisees put to Jesus concerning the woman taken in adultery: "Now Moses in the law com-

8. L. T. Merrill, "The Puritan Policeman," *American Sociological Review*, X (December, 1945), 768.
9. Joseph Haroutunian, *Piety Versus Moralism: The Passing of the New England Theology* (New York, 1932), p. 90.
1. Merrill, op. cit., p. 766.
2. Hawthorne remarked, in the *American Notebooks*, that "there is an unmistakeable analogy between the wicked weeds and the bad habits and sinful propensities which have overrun the moral world." There is an excellent explication of the symbolism of *The Scarlet Letter* in H. H. Waggoner's "Nathaniel Hawthorne: The Cemetery, the Prison, and the Rose" *University of Kansas City Review*, XIV (spring, 1948), 175–90.

manded us that such should be stoned: but what sayest thou?" The harshness of this tirade reflects the perversion of womanliness which has been wrought among this "people amongst whom religion and law were almost identical." A man in the crowd offered timely reproof to the chider: "Is there no virtue in woman, save what springs from a wholesome fear of the gallows?"—a reminder that virtue must be voluntary, an expression of character, and that there is little worth in a virtue that is compulsory, an imposition of society.

The ostracism called too lenient a punishment by the perhaps envious matrons of the town was almost fatal to Hester's sanity and moral sense, for it almost severed "the many ties, that, so long as we breathe the common air . . . , unite us to our kind." "Man had marked this woman's sin by a scarlet letter, which had such potent and disastrous efficacy that no human sympathy could reach her, save it were sinful like herself." Even children "too young to comprehend wherefore this woman should be shut out from the sphere of human charities" learned to abhor the woman upon whom society had set the stigma of the moral outcast. The universal duty of "acknowledging brotherhood even with the guiltiest" was abrogated in the treatment of Hester:

> In all her intercourse with society, . . . there was nothing which made her feel as if she belonged to it. . . . She was banished, and as much alone as if she inhabited another sphere, or communicated with the common nature by other organs and senses than the rest of human kind. She stood apart from moral interests, yet close beside them, like a ghost that revisits the familiar fireside, and can no longer make itself seen or felt.

The peculiar moral danger to Hester in her isolation was that it gave her too little opportunity for affectionate intercourse with other persons. Hawthorne regarded a woman's essential life as consisting in the right exercise of her emotions. His attitude toward women is that of Victorian liberalism; he looked upon them as equal to men, but differently endowed. To him, the distinctive feminine virtues were those characteristic of ideal wifehood and motherhood: instinctive purity and passionate devotion. His prescription for the happiest regulation of society was "Man's intellect, moderated by Woman's tenderness and moral sense." Dimmesdale's history shows the corruption of the masculine virtues of reason and authority in a sinner who has cut himself off from the divine source of those virtues; Hester's history shows the corruption of the feminine virtues of passion and submission in a sinner who has been thrust out from the human community on which those virtues depend for their reality and function. In this essential feminine attribute, the working of her moral sensibility through her feelings rather than her thought, she bears a strong general resemblance to Milton's Eve (who is, however, more delicately conceived).[3] She is * * * a charmingly real woman whose abundant sexuality, "whatever hypocrites austerely talk," was the characteristic and valuable endowment of her sex.

In consequence of her ostracism, Hester's life turned, "in a great measure, from passion and feeling, to thought"; she "wandered without a clew in the dark labyrinth of mind." Reflecting bitterly upon her own experience, she was convinced equally of the injustice and the hopelessness of a woman's position in society:

> Was existence worth accepting, even to the happiest among them? As concerned her own individual existence, she had long ago decided in the negative. . . . [A woman who considers what reforms are desirable discerns] a hopeless task before her. As a first step, the whole system of society is to be torn down, and built up anew. Then, the very nature of the opposite sex, or its long hereditary habit, which has become like nature, is to be essentially modified, before woman can be allowed to assume what seems a fair and suitable position. Finally, all other difficulties being obviated, woman cannot take advantage of these preliminary reforms, until she herself shall have undergone a still mightier change; in which, perhaps, the ethereal essence, wherein she has her truest life, will be found to have evaporated.

Although Hawthorne to some degree sympathized with Hester's rebellious mood, he did not, as Stuart P. Sherman averred, represent her as "a free spirit liberated in a moral wilderness," but as a human derelict who "wandered, without rule or guidance, in a moral wilderness." "A woman never overcomes these problems by any exercise of thought," and Hester's teachers—"Shame, Despair, Solitude!"—had "taught her much amiss." Thus, unfitted by her intense femininity for intellectual speculations, as well as by her isolation from the common experience of mankind, which rectifies aberrant thought, she unwomaned herself and deluded herself with mistaken notions.

The pathetic moral interdependence of persons is strikingly illustrated in the relations of Hester, Dimmesdale, and little Pearl. Dimmesdale acceded to Hester's plan of elopement because his will was enfeebled and he needed her resolution and affection to support him, but he was well aware that her proposals would be spiritually fatal to them. He evaded this death of the soul by the grace of God, who granted him in his death hour the strength to confess and deliver himself from the untruth which threatened his spiritual

3. In John Milton's great epic poem, *Paradise Lost* (1667). [*Editor.*]

extinction. His dramatic escape fortuitously prevented Hester from surrendering her soul to mere nature in flight from her unhappiness. The rescue of her soul is as much a matter of accident as the shipwreck of her happiness had been. It is one of the truest touches of Hawthorne's art that Hester was not reclaimed to piety by the edifying spectacle of Dimmesdale's death in the Lord but that persistent in error, even as he expired in her arms breathing hosannas, she frantically insisted that her sole hope of happiness lay in personal reunion with him—in heaven, if not on earth.

One channel of moral affection in her life, however, had never been clogged—her love for little Pearl. This had sustained her in her long solitude by affording a partial outlet for her emotions, and Hawthorne's rather perfunctory and improbable "Conclusion" informs us that, when she had abated her resentment at being frustrated of worldly happiness, the affection between her and little Pearl drew her into a state of pious resignation and thus served as a means of positive redemption.

In the last analysis, the error for which Hester suffered was her too-obstinate supposition that human beings had a right to happiness. "Hester's tragedy came upon her in consequence of excessive yielding to her own heart."[4] Hawthorne remarked in his notebooks that "happiness in this world, if it comes at all, comes incidentally. Make it the object of pursuit, and it leads us a wild-goose chase, and is never attained." The proper pursuit of man, he thought, was not happiness but a virtuous life; he inherited the Puritan conviction that

> the good which God seeks and accomplishes is the display of infinite being, a good which transcends the good of finite existence. If the misery of the sinner is conducive to such a display, which it must be because sinners are in fact miserable, then it is just and good that sinners should be punished with misery.[5]

Although we are expected to love and pity Hester, we are not invited to condone her fault or to construe it as a virtue. More a victim of circumstances than a wilful wrongdoer, she is nevertheless to be held morally responsible. In her story Hawthorne intimates that, tangled as human relationships are and must be, no sin ever issues solely from the intent and deed of the individual sinner, but that it issues instead from a complicated interplay of motives of which he is the more or less willing instrument. Even so, however strong, insidious, and unforeseeable the influences and compulsions which prompted his sin, in any practicable system of ethics the sinner must be held individually accountable for it. This is harsh

4. F. O. Matthiessen, *American Renaissance* (New York, 1941), p. 348.   5. Haroutunian, p. 144.

doctrine, but there is no escape from it short of unflinching repudiation of the moral ideas which give man his tragic and lonely dignity in a world in which all things except himself seem insensate and all actions except his own seem mechanical. The Puritans were no more illogical in coupling the assumption of moral determinism with the doctrine of individual responsibility to God than is our own age in conjoining theories of biological and economic determinism with the doctrine of individual responsibility to society. The Puritan escaped from his inconsistency by remarking that God moves in a mysterious way; we justify ours by the plea of expediency. Hawthorne, however, was content merely to pose the problem forcibly in the history of Hester Prynne.

RICHARD HARTER FOGLE

[Realms of Being and Dramatic Irony]†

* * *

The problem of *The Scarlet Letter* can be solved only by introducing the supernatural level of heaven, the sphere of absolute knowledge and justice and—hesitantly—of complete fulfillment. This may seem to be another paradox, and perhaps a disappointing one. Without doubt *The Scarlet Letter* pushes *towards* the limit of moral judgment, suggesting many possible conclusions. It is even relentless in its search in the depths of its characters. There is yet, however, a point beyond which Hawthorne will not go; ultimate solutions are not appropriate in the merely human world.* * *

There are four states of being in Hawthorne: one subhuman, two human, and one superhuman. The first is Nature, which comes to our attention in *The Scarlet Letter* twice. It appears first in the opening chapter, in the wild rosebush which stands outside the blackbrowed Puritan jail, and whose blossoms "might be imagined to offer their fragrance and fragile beauty to the prisoner as he went in, and to the condemned criminal as he came forth to his doom, in token that the deep heart of Nature could pity and be kind to him." The second entrance of Nature comes in the forest scene, where it sympathizes with the forlorn lovers and gives them hope. "Such was the sympathy of Nature—that wild, heathen Nature of the forest, never subjugated by human law, nor illumined by higher truth. . . ." The sentence epitomizes both the virtues of Nature and its

† From *Hawthorne's Fiction: The Light and the Dark* by Richard Harter Fogle   (Norman: University of Oklahoma Press, 1952), pp. 106–18.

inadequacy. In itself good, Nature is not a sufficient support for human beings.

The human levels are represented by Hawthorne's distinction between Heart and Head. The heart is closer to nature, the head to the supernatural. The heart may err by lapsing into nature, which means, since it has not the innocence of nature, into corruption. The danger of the head lies in the opposite direction. It aspires to be superhuman, and is likely to dehumanize itself in the attempt by violating the human limit. Dimmesdale, despite his considerable intellect, is predominantly a heart character, and it is through the heart that sin has assailed him, in a burst of passion which overpowered both religion and reason. The demoniac Chillingworth is of the head, a cold experimenter and thinker. It is fully representative of Hawthorne's general emphasis that Chillingworth's spiritual ruin is complete. Hester Prynne is a combination of head and heart, with a preponderance of head. Her original sin is of passion, but its consequences expose her to the danger of absolute mental isolation. The centrifugal urge of the intellect is counteracted in her by her duty to her daughter Pearl, the product of the sin, and by her latent love for Dimmesdale. Pearl herself is a creature of nature, most at home in the wild forest: ". . . the mother-forest, and these wild things which it nourished, all recognized a kindred wildness in the human child." She is made human by Dimmesdale's confession and death: "The great scene of grief, in which the wild infant bore a part, had developed all her sympathies. . . ."

The fourth level, the superhuman or heavenly, will perhaps merely be confused by elaborate definition. It is the sphere of absolute insight, justice, and mercy. Few of Hawthorne's tales and romances can be adequately considered without taking it into account. As Mark Van Doren has recently emphasized, it is well to remember Hawthorne's belief in immortality. It is because of the very presence of the superhuman in Hawthorne's thinking that the destinies of his chief characters are finally veiled in ambiguity. He respects them as he would have respected any real person by refusing to pass the last judgment, by leaving a residue of mysterious individuality untouched. The whole truth is not for a fellow human to declare.

These four states are not mutually exclusive. Without the touch of nature human life would be too bleak. The Puritans of The Scarlet Letter are deficient in nature, and they are consequently dour and overrighteous. Something of the part that nature might play in the best human life is suggested in the early chapters of The Marble Faun, particularly through the character Donatello.[1]

1. One of the four chief characters in the novel, characterized before he murders his lover's tormenter as a child of nature who both resembles and acts like a simple, carefree faun. [Editor.]

The defects of either Heart or Head in a state of isolation have already been mentioned. And without some infusion of superhuman meaning into the spheres of the human, life would be worse than bestial. Perhaps only one important character in all of Hawthorne's works finds it possible to dispense completely with heaven— Westervelt, of *The Blithedale Romance*—and he is essentially diabolic. In some respects the highest and the lowest of these levels are most closely akin, as if their relationship were as points of a circle. The innocence of nature is like the innocence of heaven. It is at times, when compared to the human, like the Garden before the serpent, like heaven free of the taint of evil. Like infancy, however, nature is a stage which man must pass through, whereas his destination is heaven. The juxtaposition of highest and lowest nevertheless involves difficulties, when perfect goodness seems equivalent to mere deprivation and virtue seems less a matter of choosing than of being untempted.

The intensity of *The Scarlet Letter*, at which Hawthorne himself was dismayed, comes from concentration, selection, and dramatic irony. The concentration upon the central theme is unremitting. The tension is lessened only once, in the scene in the forest, and then only delusively, since the hope of freedom which brings it about is quickly shown to be false and even sinful. The characters play out their tragic action against a background in itself oppressive —the somber atmosphere of Puritanism. Hawthorne calls the progression of the story "the darkening close of a tale of human frailty and sorrow." Dark to begin with, it grows steadily deeper in gloom. The method is almost unprecedentedly selective. Almost every image has a symbolic function; no scene is superfluous. One would perhaps at times welcome a loosening of the structure, a moment of wandering from the path. The weedy grassplot in front of the prison; the distorting reflection of Hester in a breastplate, where the Scarlet Letter appears gigantic; the tapestry of David and Bathsheba on the wall of the minister's chamber; the little brook in the forest; the slight malformation of Chillingworth's shoulder; the ceremonial procession on election day—in every instance more is meant than meets the eye.

The intensity of *The Scarlet Letter* comes in part from a sustained and rigorous dramatic irony, or irony of situation. This irony arises naturally from the theme of "secret sin," or concealment. "Show freely of your worst," says Hawthorne; the action of *The Scarlet Letter* arises from the failure of Dimmesdale and Chillingworth to do so. The minister hides his sin, and Chillingworth hides his identity. This concealment affords a constant drama. There is the irony of Chapter III, "The Recognition," in which Chillingworth's ignorance is suddenly and blindingly reversed. Separated from his wife by many vicissitudes, he comes upon her as she is dramatically exposed to public infamy. From his instantaneous decision, symbolized by the lifting of his finger to his lips to hide his tie to her, he precipitates the further irony of his sustained hypocrisy.

In the same chapter Hester is confronted with her fellow-adulterer, who is publicly called upon to persuade her as her spiritual guide to reveal his identity. Under the circumstances the situation is highly charged, and his words have a double meaning—one to the onlookers, another far different to Hester and the speaker himself. " 'If thou feelest it to be for thy soul's peace, and that thy earthly punishment will therefore be made more effectual to salvation, I charge thee to speak out the name of thy fellow-sinner and fellow-sufferer!' "

From this scene onward Chillingworth, by living a lie, arouses a constant irony, which is also an ambiguity. With a slight shift in emphasis all his actions can be given a very different interpretation. Seen purely from without, it would be possible to regard him as completely blameless. Hester expresses this ambiguity in Chapter IV, after he has ministered to her sick baby, the product of her faithlessness, with tenderness and skill. " 'Thy acts are like mercy,' " said Hester, bewildered and appalled. 'But thy words interpret thee as a terror!' " Masquerading as a physician, he becomes to Dimmesdale a kind of attendant fiend, racking the minister's soul with constant anguish. Yet outwardly he has done him nothing but good. " 'What evil have I done the man?' asked Roger Chillingworth again. 'I tell thee, Hester Prynne, the richest fee that ever physician earned from monarch could not have bought such care as I have wasted on this miserable priest!' " Even when he closes the way to escape by proposing to take passage on the same ship with the fleeing lovers, it is possible to consider the action merely friendly. His endeavor at the end to hold Dimmesdale back from the saving scaffold is from one point of view reasonable and friend-like, although he is a devil struggling to snatch back an escaping soul. " 'All shall be well! Do not blacken your fame, and perish in dishonor! I can yet save you! Would you bring infamy on your sacred profession?' " Only when Dimmesdale has successfully resisted does Chillingworth openly reveal his purposes. With the physician the culminating irony is that in seeking to damn Dimmesdale he has himself fallen into damnation. As he says in a moment of terrible self-knowledge, " 'A mortal man, with once a human heart, has become a fiend for his especial torment!' " The effect is of an Aristotelian reversal, where a conscious and deep-laid purpose brings about totally unforeseen and opposite results. Chillingworth's relations with Dimmesdale have the persistent fascination of an almost absolute knowledge and power working their will with a helpless victim, a fascination which is heightened by the minister's awareness of an evil close beside him which he cannot place. "All this was accomplished with a subtlety so perfect that the minister, though he had constantly a dim perception of some evil influence watching over him, could never gain a knowledge of its actual nature." It is a classic situation wrought out to its fullest potentialities, in which the reader cannot help sharing the perverse pleasure of the villain.

From the victim's point of view the irony is still deeper, perhaps because we can participate still more fully in his response to it. Dimmesdale, a "remorseful hypocrite," is forced to live a perpetual lie in public. His own considerable talents for self-torture are supplemented by the situation as well as by the devoted efforts of Chillingworth. His knowledge is an agony. His conviction of sin is in exact relationship to the reverence in which his parishioners hold him. He grows pale and meager—it is the asceticism of a saint on earth; his effectiveness as a minister grows with his despair; he confesses the truth in his sermons, but transforms it "into the veriest falsehood" by the generality of his avowal and merely increases the adoration of his flock; every effort deepens his plight, since he will not—until the end—make the effort of complete self-revelation. His great election-day sermon prevails through anguish of heart; to his listeners divinely inspired, its power comes from its undertone of suffering, "the complaint of a human heart, sorrowladen, perchance guilty, telling its secret, whether of guilt or sorrow, to the great heart of mankind. . . ." While Chillingworth at last reveals himself fully, Dimmesdale's secret is too great to be wholly laid bare. His utmost efforts are still partially misunderstood, and "highly respectable witnesses" interpret his death as a culminating act of holiness and humility.

Along with this steady irony of situation there is the omnipresent irony of the hidden meaning. The author and the reader know what the characters do not. Hawthorne consistently pretends that the coincidence of the action or the image with its significance is merely fortuitous, not planned, lest the effect be spoiled by overinsistence. In other words, he attempts to combine the sufficiently probable with the maximum of arrangement. Thus the waxing and waning of sunlight in the forest scene symbolize the emotions of Hester and Dimmesdale, but we accept this coincidence most easily if we can receive it as chance. Hawthorne's own almost amused awareness of his problem helps us to do so. Yet despite the element of play and the deliberate self-deception demanded, the total effect is one of intensity. Hawthorne is performing a difficult feat with sustained virtuosity in reconciling a constant stress between naturally divergent qualities.

The character of Pearl illuminates this point. Pearl is pure symbol, the living emblem of the sin, a human embodiment of the Scarlet Letter. Her mission is to keep Hester's adultery always before her eyes, to prevent her from attempting to escape its moral consequences. Pearl's childish questions are fiendishly apt; in speech and in action she never strays from the control of her symbolic function; her dress and her looks are related to the letter. When Hester casts the letter away in the forest, Pearl forces her to reassume it by flying into an uncontrollable rage. Yet despite the undeviating arrangement of every circumstance which surrounds her, no single action of hers is ever incredible or inconsistent with the conceivable actions of any child under the same conditions. Given the central improbability of her undeviating purposiveness, she is as lifelike as the brilliantly drawn children of Richard Hughes's *The Innocent Voyage.*[2]

These qualities of concentration, selectivity, and irony, which are responsible for the intensity of *The Scarlet Letter*, tend at their extreme toward excessive regularity and a sense of over-manipulation, although irony is also a counteragent against them. This tendency toward regularity is balanced by Hawthorne's use of ambiguity. The distancing of the story in the past has the effect of ambiguity. Hawthorne so employs the element of time as to warn us that he cannot guarantee the literal truth of his narrative and at the same time to suggest that the essential truth is the clearer; as facts shade off into the background, meaning is left in the foreground unshadowed and disencumbered. The years, he pretends, have winnowed his material, leaving only what is enduring. Tradition and superstition, while he disclaims belief in them, have a way of pointing to truth.

Thus the imagery of hell-fire which occurs throughout *The Scarlet Letter* is dramatically proper to the Puritan background and is attributed to the influence of superstitious legend. It works as relief from more serious concerns and still functions as a symbol of psychological and religious truth. In Chapter III, as Hester is returned from the scaffold to the prison, "It was whispered, by those who peered after her, that the scarlet letter threw a lurid gleam along the dark passage-way of the interior." The imagery of the letter may be summarized by quoting a later passage:

> The vulgar, who, in those dreary old times, were always contributing a grotesque horror to what interested their imaginations, had a story about the scarlet letter which we might readily work up into a terrific legend. They averred, that the symbol was not mere

2. This 1929 novel, better known by its second title, *A High Wind in Jamaica*, is a psychological study of the profound changes in a group of children lost in the Caribbean. [*Editor.*]

scarlet cloth, tinged in an earthly dye-pot, but was red-hot with infernal fire, and could be seen glowing all alight, whenever Hester Prynne walked abroad in the nighttime. And we must needs say, it seared Hester's bosom so deeply, that perhaps there was more truth in the rumor than our modern incredulity may be inclined to admit.

The lightness of Hawthorne's tone lends relief and variety, while it nevertheless reveals the function of the superstition. "The vulgar," "dreary old times," "grotesque horror," "work up into a terrific legend"—his scorn is so heavily accented that it discounts itself and satirizes the "modern incredulity" of his affected attitude. The playful extravagance of "red-hot with infernal fire" has the same effect. And the apparent begrudging of the concession in the final sentence—"And we must needs say"—lends weight to a truth so reluctantly admitted.

Puritan demonology is in general used with the same effect. It has the pathos and simplicity of an old wives' tale and yet contains a deep subterranean power which reaches into daylight from the dark caverns of the mind. The Black Man of the unhallowed forest —a useful counterbalance to any too-optimistic picture of nature— and the witchwoman Mistress Hibbins are cases in point. The latter is a concrete example of the mingled elements of the superstitious legend. Matter-of-factly, she is a Puritan lady of high rank, whose ominous reputation is accounted for by bad temper combined with insanity. As a witch, she is a figure from a child's storybook, an object of delighted fear and mockery. Yet her fanciful extravagance covers a real malignity, and because of it she has an insight into the secret of the letter. With one stroke she lays bare the disease in Dimmesdale, as one who sees evil alone but sees it with unmatched acuteness: "'When the Black Man sees one of his own servants, signed and sealed, so shy of owning to the bond as is the Reverend Mr. Dimmesdale, he hath a way of ordering matters so that the mark shall be disclosed to the eyes of all the world.'"

This use of the past merges into a deep-seated ambiguity of moral meaning. Moral complexity and freedom of speculation, like the lighter ambiguity of literal fact, temper the almost excessive unity and symmetry of *The Scarlet Letter* and avoid a directed verdict. In my opinion the judgment of Hawthorne upon his characters is entirely clear, although deliberately limited in its jurisdiction. But he permits the possibility of other interpretations to appear, so that the consistent clarity of his own emphasis is disguised. Let us take for example the consideration of the heroine in Chapter XIII, "Another View of Hester." After seven years of disgrace, Hester has won the unwilling respect of her fellow-townsmen by her good works and respectability of conduct. From one point of view she is clearly their moral superior: she has met rigorous cruelty with kindness, arrogance with humility. Furthermore, living as she has in enforced isolation has greatly developed her mind. In her breadth of intellectual speculation she has freed herself from any dependence upon the laws of Puritan society. "She cast away the fragments of a broken chain." She pays outward obedience to a system which has no further power upon her spirit. Under other conditions, Hawthorne suggests, she might at this juncture have become another Anne Hutchinson, the foundress of a religious sect, or a great early feminist. The author's conclusions about these possibilities, however, are specifically stated: "The scarlet letter had not done its office." Hester is wounded and led astray, not improved, by her situation. Hawthorne permits his reader, if he wishes, to take his character from his control, to say that Hester Prynne is a great woman unhappily born before her time, or that she is a good woman wronged by her fellow men. But Hawthorne is less confident.

* * *

HYATT HOWE WAGGONER

[Three Orders: Natural, Moral, and Symbolic]†

* * *

In the three paragraphs of his opening chapter Hawthorne introduces the three chief symbols that will serve to give structure to the story on the thematic level, hints at the fourth, and starts two of the chief lines of imagery. The opening sentence suggests the darkness ("sad-colored," "gray"), the rigidity ("oak," "iron"), and the aspiration ("steeple-crowned") of the people "amongst whom religion and law were almost identical." Later sentences add "weatherstains," "a yet darker aspect," and "gloomy" to the suggestions already begun through color imagery. The closing words of the chapter make the metaphorical use of color explicit: Hawthorne hopes that a wild rose beside the prison door may serve "to symbolize some sweet moral blossom, that may be found along the

† From *Hawthorne: A Critical Study* by Hyatt H. Waggoner (Cambridge, Mass.: The Belknap Press of Harvard University Press, 1955).

track, or relieve the darkening close of a tale of human frailty and sorrow."

* * *

Finally, in addition to the Puritans themselves, the jail before which they stand, and the weeds and the rose, one other object, and only one, is mentioned in this first chapter. In the only generalized comment in a chapter otherwise devoted to objective description, Hawthorne tells us that "The founders of a new colony, whatever Utopia of human virtue and happiness they might originally project, have invariably recognized it among their earliest practical necessities to allot a portion of the virgin soil as a cemetery, and another as the site of a prison." The three climactic scenes of the novel take place before the scaffold in front of the prison. The cemetery, by contrast, remains in the background. We are not allowed to forget it, we learn that Chillingworth has a special interest in it, but we are not encouraged to make it the center of our attention until the end, when it moves into the foreground as the site of the tombstone with the strange inscription.

The cemetery, the prison, and the rose, with their associated values and the extensions of suggestion given them by the image patterns that intersect them, as the ugliest weeds are later discovered growing out of graves, suggest a symbolic pattern within which nearly everything that is most important in the novel may be placed. The cemetery and the prison are negative values, in some sense evils. The rose is a positive value, beautiful, in some sense a good. But the cemetery and the prison are not negative in the same sense: death, "the last great enemy," is a natural evil, resulting as some theologies would have it from moral evil but distinguished by coming to saint and sinner alike; the prison is a reminder of the present actuality of moral evil. Natural and moral evil, then, death and sin, are here suggested. The rose is "good" in the same sense in which the cemetery is an "evil": its beauty is neither moral nor immoral but is certainly a positive value. Like the beauty of a healthy child or an animal, it is the product not of choice but of necessity, of the laws of its being, so that it can be admired but not judged. Pearl, later in the story, is similarly immune from judgment. There is no strong suggestion of moral goodness in this first chapter, nor will there be in what is to follow. The cemetery and the weeds contrast with the rose, but only the suggestions of worship in the shape of the hats of the Puritans contrast with the prison, and those steeple-crowned hats are gray, a color which later takes on strongly negative associations.

Among the ideas implicit in the opening chapter, then, are, first, that the novel is to be concerned with the relationships of good and evil; second, that it will distinguish between two types of good and evil; and, third, that moral good will be less strongly felt than moral and natural evil. A symmetrical pattern is theoretically suggested here, and as we shall see, in the rest of the novel. But what is actually felt is an asymmetrical pattern, an imbalance, in which the shapes of moral and natural evil loom so large as to make it difficult to discern, or to "believe in" once we have discerned, the reality of moral goodness or redemption. The rose, in short, is finally not sufficient to relieve "the darkening close of a tale of human frailty and sorrow." The celestial radiance later seen gleaming from the white hair of Mr. Wilson is not sufficient either, nor the snowy innocence said to exist in the bosoms of certain maidens. In writing *The Scarlet Letter* Hawthorne let his genius take its course, and death and sin turned out to be more convincing than life and goodness.

* * *

The "burdock, pigweed, apple-peru, and such unsightly vegetation" growing beside the prison, that "black flower of civilized society," where grass should have been, begin the flower and weed imagery, which, in some thirty images and extended analogies, reinforces and extends the implications of the imagery of color and light. Since these implications have already been drawn out, I shall simply call attention briefly to four relationships Hawthorne has set up.

First, and most clearly, the unnatural flowers and unsightly vegetation are aligned with moral evil, and with Chillingworth in particular. He too with his deformity is "unsightly." Low, dark, and ugly, he suggests to some people the notion that his step must wither the grass wherever he walks. The sun seems not to fall on him but to create "a circle of ominous shadow moving along with his deformity." It is natural enough then to find him explicitly associated with "deadly nightshade" and other types of "vegetable wickedness," to see him displaying a "dark, flabby leaf" found growing out of a grave, and to hear that prominent among the herbs he has gathered are some "black weeds" that have "sprung up out of a buried heart." When his evil work was done "he positively withered up, shriveled away . . . like an uprooted weed that lies wilting in the sun." Flower and weed imagery unites with light and color imagery to define Chillingworth's position as that of the chief sinner.

But Chillingworth is not the only one so aligned. Less emphatically, the Puritans themselves are associated with weeds and black flowers. The implications of color imagery first set up the association: as their "Puritanic gloom" increases in the second generation to "the blackest shade of Puritanism," we begin to see them as cousins to the "nightshade" and so are prepared for Pearl's pretense that the weeds she attacks in her solitary games are Puritan children. Accustomed to her apparently infallible instinct for the truth, we see in her game something more than childish imagination.

The second relationship deserving of note also starts in the first chapter. We recall Hawthorne's saying of the wild rose-bush in bloom beside the prison that he hoped it might "relieve the darkening close" of his tale. No "sweet moral blossom" plays any significant part in the main story, but the happy fortune of Pearl, related in the concluding chapter, does offer a contrast with the "frailty and sorrow" of the tale proper. Thus Pearl's final role is foreshadowed in the first chapter. But Hawthorne does not wait until the end to make this apparent. He constantly associates her not only with the scarlet letter on her mother's dress but with the red rose. The rose bears "delicate gems" and Pearl is the red-clad "gem" of her mother's bosom. Her flowerlike beauty is frequently underscored. And naturally so, for we are told that she had sprung, "a lovely and immortal flower," out of the "rank luxuriance" of a guilty passion.

The position thus defined is repeatedly emphasized. Pearl cries for a red rose in the governor's garden. She answers the catechetical question who made her by declaring that she had not been made at all but "had been plucked by her mother off the bush of wild roses that grew by the prison door." She decorates her hair with flowers, which are said to become her perfectly. She is reflected in the pool in "all the brilliant picturesqueness of her beauty, in its adornment of flowers." Her "flower-girdled and sunny image" has all the glory of a "bright flower." Pearl is a difficult child, capricious, unintentionally cruel, unfeeling in her demand for truth, but she has both the "naturalness" and the beauty of the rose, and like the rose she is a symbol of love and promise.

These are the associations Hawthorne most carefully elaborates, but there are two others worth noting briefly. Weeds or "black flowers" are on several occasions associated with Hester. The most striking instance of this occurs when Pearl pauses in the graveyard to pick "burrs" and arrange them "along the lines of the scarlet letter that decorated the maternal bosom, to which the burrs, as their nature was, tenaciously adhered." The burrs are like Pearl in acting according to nature, and what they suggest in their clinging cannot be wholly false. Hester implicitly acknowledges the truth of what the burrs have revealed when she suggests to Dimmesdale that they let the "black flower" of their love "blossom as it may."

But a more frequent and impressive association is set up between Hester and normal flowers. Even the badge of her shame, the token of her "guilty" love, is thus associated with natural beauty. The scarlet letter is related to the red rose from the very beginning. As Hester stands before her judges in the opening scenes, the sun shines on just two spots of vivid color in all that massed black, brown, and gray: on the rose and the letter, both red. The embroidery with which she decorates the letter further emphasizes the likeness, so that when Pearl throws flowers at her mother's badge and they hit the mark, we share her sense that this is appropriate. Burrs and flowers seem to have an affinity for Hester's letter. Hawthorne was too much of a Protestant to share the Catholic attitude toward "natural law": the imagery here suggests that moral law and nature's ways do not perfectly coincide, or run parallel on different levels; they cross, perhaps at something less than a right angle. At the point of their crossing the lovers' fate is determined. No reversal of the implied moral judgment is suggested when nature seems to rejoice at the reaffirmed love of the pair in the forest: "Such was the sympathy of Nature—that wild, heathen Nature of the forest, never subjugated to human law, nor illumined by higher truth—with the bliss of these two spirits! Love, whether newly born, or aroused from a death-like slumber, must always create a sunshine."

Hester's emblem, then, points to a love both good and bad. The ambiguity of her gray robes and dark glistening hair, her black eyes and bright complexion, is thus emphasized by the flower and weed imagery. As Chillingworth is associated with weeds, Pearl with flowers, and Dimmesdale with no natural growing thing at all, so Hester walks her ambiguous way between burdock and rose, neither of which is alone sufficient to define her nature and her position.

* * *

The Scarlet Letter is the most nearly static of all Hawthorne's novels. There is very little external action. We can see one of the evidences for this, and perhaps also one of the reasons for it, when we compare the amount of space Hawthorne devotes to exposition and description with the amount he devotes to narration. It is likewise true, in a sense not yet fully explored, that on the deepest level of meaning the novel has only an ambiguous movement. But in between the surface and the depths movement is constant and complex, and it is in this middle area that the principal value of the work lies.

The movement may be conceived as being up and down the lines of natural and moral value, lines which, if they were to be represented in a diagram, should be conceived as crossing to form an X. Thus, most obviously, Hester's rise takes her from low on the line of moral value, a "scarlet woman" guilty of a sin black in the eyes of the Puritans, to a position not too remote from Mr. Wilson's, as she becomes a sister of mercy and the light of the sickroom: this when we measure by the yardstick of community approval. When we apply a standard of measurement less relativistic—and all but the most consistent ethical relativists will do so, consciously or unconsciously, thoughtfully or unthoughtfully—we are also likely to find that there has been a "rise." I suppose most of us will agree, whatever our religion or philosophy may be, that Hester has gained in stature and dignity by enduring and transcending suffering, and that she has grown in awareness of social responsibility. Like all tragic protagonists, she has demonstrated the dignity and potentialities of man, even in her defeat.

Dimmesdale is a more complicated, though less admirable and sympathetic, figure. He first descends from his original position as the saintly guide and inspiration of the godly to the position he occupies during the greater part of the novel as very nearly the worst of the sinners in his hypocrisy and cowardice, then reascends by his final act of courageous honesty to a position somewhere in between his reputation for light and his reality of darkness. He emerges at last, that is, into the light of day, if only dubiously into that shining from the celestial city. We cannot help feeling, I think, that if he had had any help he might have emerged from the darkness much sooner.

As for Chillingworth, he of course descends, but not to reascend. As in his injured pride and inhuman curiosity he devotes himself to prying into the minister's heart, whatever goodness had been his—which had always been negative, the mere absence of overt evil—disappears and pride moves into what had been a merely cold heart, prompting to revenge and displacing intellectual curiosity, which continues only as a rationalization, a "good" reason serving to distract attention from the real one. He becomes a moral monster who feeds only on another's torment, divorced wholly from the sources of life and goodness. He is eloquent testimony to the belief that Hawthorne shared with Shakespeare and Melville, among others: that it is possible for man to make evil his good.

Thus the three principal characters move up and down the scale of moral values in a kind of counterpoint: Chillingworth clearly down, Hester ambiguously up, Dimmesdale in both directions, first down, then up, to end somewhere in the center. But this is not the end of the matter. Because there are obscure but real relationships, if only of analogy, between the moral and the natural (I am using "natural" in the sense of those aspects of existence studied by the natural sciences, which do not include the concept of freedom of

choice among their working principles or their assumptions), because there are relations between the moral and the natural, the
movements of the characters up and down the scale of moral values
involve them in symbolic movements on the scale of natural values.
The moral journeys are, in fact, as we have abundantly seen, largely
suggested by physical imagery. Chillingworth becomes blacker and
more twisted as he becomes more evil. Hester's beauty withers under
the scorching brand, then momentarily reasserts itself in the forest
scene, then disappears again. Dimmesdale becomes paler and walks
more frequently in the shadow as his torment increases and his sin
is multiplied.

But the moral changes are not simply made visible by the changes
in the imagery: in their turn they require the visible changes and
determine their direction. The outstanding example of this is of
course Chillingworth's transformation. As we infer the potential
evil in him from the snake imagery, the deformity, and the darkness
associated with him when we first see him, so later his dedication
to evil as his good suggests the "fancy" of the lurid flame in his
eyes and the "notion" that it would be appropriate if he blasted the
beauty of nature wherever he walked. So too the minister's moral
journey suggests to the minds of the people both the red stigma
which some think they see over his heart and the red A in the sky,
with its ambiguous significance of angel or adultery. The total
structure of the novel implies that the relation between fact and
value is never simple: that neither is reducible to the other, yet
that they are never wholly distinct.

All three of the chief characters, in short, exist on both of our
crossed lines, the moral and the natural. They are seen in two
perspectives, not identical but obscurely related. Pearl's situation,
however, is somewhat different. She seems not to exist on the moral
line at all. She is an object of natural beauty, a flower, a gem, instinctively trusted by the wild creatures of the forest. She is as incapable of deceit or dishonesty as nature itself, and at times as unsympathetic. She is not good or bad, because she is not responsible. Like the letter on her mother's breast, she is an emblem of
sin. Like the red spot over the minister's heart, she is also a result
of sin. But she is not herself a moral agent. Even when she torments her mother with her demands for the truth, or refuses to
acknowledge the minister until he acknowledges them, she is not
bad, she is merely natural. She is capricious with an animal's, or
a small child's, lack of understanding of the human situation and
consequent lack of responsiveness to emotions which it cannot
understand.

Pearl is more than a picture of an intelligent and willful child
drawn in part from Hawthorne's observations of his daughter Una:

she is a symbol of what the human being would be if his situation were simplified by his existing on the natural plane only, as a creature. Hawthorne tells us that Pearl is potentially an immortal soul, but actually, at least before the "Conclusion," she seems more nearly a bird, a flower, or a ray of sunlight. Because of this "naturalness," this simplification, she can reach the patches of sunlight in the forest when Hester cannot: she is first cousin to the sunlight in moral neutrality as well as in brightness. From one point of view it seems curious that most readers find it harder to "believe in" Pearl than in any other major character in the book except perhaps in Chillingworth in his last stages, for Pearl is the only character drawn from Hawthorne's immediate experience with a living person. If the naturalistic aesthetic of the late nineteenth century were a correct description of the nature and processes of art, we should expect to find Pearl Hawthorne's most "real" character. That she is not (though it is easy to exaggerate her "unreality") is I suspect partly the result of the drastic simplification of life Hawthorne has here indulged in, in giving Pearl existence only on the natural plane. He has surely exaggerated a child's incapacity for moral action, its lack of involvement in the demands of right and wrong, and so has produced in Pearl the only important character in the book who constantly comes close to being an abstraction. In creating Pearl, Hawthorne wrote partly out of the currents of primitivism of his age, suppressing or refusing to extend his normal insights, much as he made an exception to his convictions about the nature of the human heart when he created his blonde maidens, who are equally hard to "believe in," and for rather similar reasons. Oversimplified conceptions of experience cannot be made convincing.

Since "history" is created by the interaction of natural conditions and human choice, there is a significant sense in which Pearl has no history in the story. She moves in and out of the foreground, a bright spot of color in a gloomy scene, serving to remind Hester of her sin and the reader of the human condition by the absence of one of its two poles in her being, but never becoming herself fully human. In the final scaffold scene Hawthorne shows us Pearl weeping for the first time and tells us that her tears "were the pledge that she would grow up amid human joy and sorrow, nor forever do battle with the world, but be a woman in it." In the "Conclusion," when Hawthorne gives us a glimpse of the years following the real end of his tale in the minister's confession, he suggests that Pearl grew to happy womanhood abroad. If so, she must have taken her place with Hester and Dimmesdale and Chillingworth in the realm of moral values, making her history and being made by it.

But the others, including the Puritan populace, have histories and are involved in the larger movements of history created by all of them together existing in nature as creatures and moral beings. Hester might not have committed adultery had Chillingworth had a warmer heart, or perhaps even had he been younger or less deformed. He might not have fallen from a decent moral neutrality to positive vice had she not first fallen. Hester is forced to become stronger because the minister is so weak, and he gains strength by contact with her strength when they meet again in the forest. Chillingworth is stimulated by his victim's helplessness to greater excesses of torment and sin, and the Puritan women around the scaffold are stirred by Hester's youth and beauty to greater cruelty than was implicit in their inquisition anyway. History as conceived in *The Scarlet Letter* is complex, dynamic, ambiguous; it is never static or abstractly linear, as both simple materialism and simple moralism tend to picture it. St. Paul's "We are members one of another" could be taken as a text to be illustrated by the histories of human hearts recounted in the novel.

Yet with all this complex movement on two planes, with all this richness, this density, of history, when we ask ourselves the final questions of meaning and value we find the movement indecisive or arrested in one direction, continuing clearly only in the other. The Puritan people and Chillingworth are condemned, but are Hester and Dimmesdale redeemed? It is significant in this connection that Pearl's growth into womanhood takes place after the end of the story proper. It is also significant that though Hester bore her suffering nobly, it is not clear that she ever repented; and that, though he indulged in several kinds of penance, it is possible to doubt that the minister ever did. * * *

There is, then, despite Hester's rise, no certainty of final release from evil or of the kind of meaning to be found in tragedy, no well-grounded hope of escape from their sin for the sinners. The minister's dying words and the legend engraved on the tombstone both seem to me to make this clear. We recall the scene of the dance on the graves in "Alice Doane's Appeal."[1] Here is a vision of history containing judgment but not mercy, condemnation but not forgiveness, sin and suffering but no remission, no "newness of life." If, as someone has suggested, the heraldic wording of the gravestone's inscription contains the possible suggestion that, just as the stigma of bastardy was wiped out by being emblazoned as the bar sinister on the noble escutcheon, so the sinfulness of the adultery was removed by being thus permanently acknowledged, the suggestion is surely not strongly supported by what has pre-

---

1. In this tale, published in 1835 but written several years earlier, Hawthorne presents a vision of the dead solely as "a miserable multitude" of sinful souls wracked by "intolerable pain and hellish passion." [*Editor.*]

ceded. Hawthorne, in this respect a man of his age, never formulated his religious feelings and attitudes into any clear-cut theology. If he had done so, he might have been puzzled by the question of how central and significant a place to give to the Atonement.

In this final theological sense then the work is static. On the natural plane, beauty and ugliness, red rose and pigweed, equally exist with indisputable reality. But on the moral plane, only evil and suffering are really vivid and indisputable. Hawthorne's constant exception to his ordinary characterization of the human heart, the spotless, lily-like hearts of pure maidens, will hardly bear looking into. The light around Mr. Wilson's head shines too weakly to penetrate far into the surrounding gloom. And the only light into which Dimmesdale certainly emerges is the light of common day. The novel is structured around the metaphor of bringing the guilty secret from the black depths of the heart out into the light. But it is suggestive not only of what went on in his own heart but of the poverty both of the Puritanism of which he wrote and of the Unitarianism which Puritanism became and which Hawthorne knew at first hand that Hawthorne could conceive of the need but not the existence or the nature of any further step. After confession, what then? "No great wrong is ever undone." Surely being "true," the one moral among many, as Hawthorne tells us, that he chose to underscore, is not enough. *The Scarlet Letter* sprang from Hawthorne's heart, not from his head.

The dominant symbols, to return to the first chapter once more, are the cemetery, the prison, and the rose. The religious idealism suggested by the steeple-crowned hats is ineffective, positively perverted even, as the man of adamant's sincere piety was perverted by his fanaticism. The clearest tones in the book are the black of the prison and the weeds and the grave, and the redness of the letter and the rose, suggesting moral and natural evil and natural goodness, but not moral goodness. "On a field, sable, the letter A, gules." Of the literal and figurative light, one, the sunlight, is strong and positive, while the other, shining, as St. John tells us, from the Light of the World, falls fitfully and dimly over minor characters or is posited in mere speculative possibility.

The Scarlet Letter, then, like the majority of the best tales, suggests that Hawthorne's vision of death was a good deal stronger and more constant than his vision of life.[2] This is indeed, as Hawthorne calls it, a dark tale, and its mesh of good and evil is not

2. W. Stacey Johnson has marshaled considerable evidence for the contrary view in his "Sin and Salvation in Hawthorne," *The Hibbert Journal*, October 1951. My comment on the argument of a part of this excellent article is that, while it is true that Hawthorne believed in the possibility of redemption, he did not "believe in it" in the same way, with the same kind of conviction, that he believed in sin and death.

equally strong in all its parts. Hawthorne was right in not wanting to be judged as a man solely by it, though I think he must have known, as we do, that it is his greatest book. For in it there is perfect charity, and a real, though defective, faith, but almost no hope. Unlike most of us today, Hawthorne was close enough to historic Christianity to know its main dogmas, even those he did not fully share. He preferred not to seem to be denying so central a part of the Christian Gospel as that men can be saved from their sins.

R. W. B. LEWIS

The Return into Time: Hawthorne†

* * *

The isolated hero "alone in a hostile, or at best a neutral, universe" begins to replace the Adamic personality in the New World Eden. The essential continuity of American fiction explains itself through this historic transformation whereby the Adamic fable yielded to what I take to be the authentic American narrative. For much of that fable remained in the later narrative: the individual going forth toward experience, the inventor of his own character and creator of his personal history; the self-moving individual who is made to confront that "other"—the world or society, the element which provides experience. But as we move from Cooper to Hawthorne, the situation very notably darkens; qualities of evil and fear and destructiveness have entered; self-sufficiency is questioned through terrible trials; and the stage is set for tragedy. The solitary hero and the alien tribe; "the simple genuine self against the whole world"—this is still the given, for the American novelist. The variable is this: the novelist's sense of the initial tension—whether it is comforting, or whether it is potentially tragic; whether the tribe promises love, or whether it promises death.

Hawthorne was perhaps the first American writer to detect the inevitable doubleness in the tribal promise. For he was able by temperament to give full and fair play to both parties in the agon:[1] to the hero and to the tribe as well. And, having done so, he penetrated to the pattern of action—a pattern of escape and return, at once tragic and hopeful—which was likely to flow from the

† From *The American Adam: Innocence, Tragedy, and Tradition in the Nineteenth Century*, by R.W.B. Lewis (Chicago: University of Chicago Press, 1955), pp. 111–16.

1. The conflict between the chief characters. [*Editor.*]

situation as given. In addition, Hawthorne felt very deeply the intimacy between experience and art, and he enacted a change as well in the resources and methods of the narrative art: something which mirrored, even while it articulated, his heroes' and heroines' adventures. Finally, it was Hawthorne who saw in American experience the re-creation of the story of Adam and who, more than any other contemporary, exploited the active metaphor of the American as Adam—before and during and after the Fall. These are the three aspects of Hawthorne that I shall consider.

I

The opening scene of *The Scarlet Letter* is the paradigm dramatic image in American literature. With that scene and that novel, New World fiction arrived at its first fulfilment, and Hawthorne at his. And with that scene, all that was dark and treacherous in the American situation became exposed. Hawthorne said later that the writing of *The Scarlet Letter* had been oddly simple, since all he had to do was to get his "pitch" and then to let it carry him along. He found his pitch in an opening tableau fairly humming with tension—with coiled and covert relationships that contained a force perfectly calculated to propel the action thereafter in a direct line to its tragic climax.

It was the tableau of the solitary figure set over against the inimical society, in a village which hovers on the edge of the inviting and perilous wilderness; a handsome young woman standing on a raised platform, confronting in silence and pride a hostile crowd whose menace is deepened by its order and dignity; a young woman who has come alone to the New World, where circumstances have divided her from the community now gathered to oppose her; standing alone, but vitally aware of the private enemy and the private lover—one on the far verges of the crowd, one at the place of honor within it, and neither conscious of the other— who must affect her destiny and who will assist at each other's destruction. Here the situation inherent in the American scene was seized entire and without damage to it by an imagination both moral and visual of the highest quality: seized and located, not any longer on the margins of the plot, but at its very center.

The conflict is central because it is total; because Hawthorne makes us respect each element in it. Hawthorne felt, as Brown and Cooper and Bird[2] had felt, that the stuff of narrative (in so far as it was drawn from local experience) consisted in the imaginable brushes between the deracinated and solitary individual and the society or world awaiting him. But Hawthorne had learned the

2. Three earlier American novelists: Charles Brockden Brown (1771–1810); James Fenimore Cooper (1789–1851); Robert Montgomery Bird (1806–54). [*Editor.*]

lesson only fitfully apprehended by Cooper. In *The Scarlet Letter* not only do the individual and the world, the conduct and the institutions, measure each other: the measurement and its consequences are precisely and centrally what the novel is about. Hester Prynne has been wounded by an unfriendly world; but the society facing her is invested by Hawthorne with assurance and authority, its opposition is defensible and even valid. Hester's misdeed appears as a disturbance of the moral structure of the universe; and the society continues to insist in its joyless way that certain acts deserve the honor of punishment. But if Hester has sinned, she has done so as an affirmation of life, and her sin is the source of life; she incarnates those rights of personality that society is inclined to trample upon. The action of the novel springs from the enormous but improbable suggestion that the society's estimate of the moral structure of the universe may be tested and found inaccurate.

The Scarlet Letter, like all very great fiction, is the product of a controlled division of sympathies; and we must avoid the temptation to read it heretically. It has always been possible to remark, about Hawthorne, his fondness for the dusky places, his images of the slow movement of sad, shut-in souls in the half-light. But it has also been possible to read *The Scarlet Letter* (not to mention "The New Adam and Eve" and "Earth's Holocaust") as an indorsement of hopefulness: to read it as a hopeful critic named Loring read it (writing for Theodore Parker's forward-looking *Massachusetts Quarterly Review*) as a party plea for self-reliance and an attack upon the sterile conventions of institutionalized society.[3] One version of him would align Hawthorne with the secular residue of Jonathan Edwards; the other would bring him closer to Emerson.[4] But Hawthorne was neither Emersonian nor Edwardsean; or rather he was both. The characteristic situation in his fiction is that of the Emersonian figure, the man of hope, who by some frightful mischance has stumbled into the time-burdened world of Jonathan Edwards. And this grim picture is given us by a writer who was skeptically cordial toward Emerson, but for whom the vision of Edwards, filtered through a haze of hope, remained a wonderfully useful metaphor.[5] The situation, in the form which Hawthorne's ambivalence gave it, regularly led in his fiction to a moment of crucial choice; an invitation to the lost Emersonian, the thunder-struck Adam, to make up his mind—whether to accept the world he had fallen into, or

3. An excerpt from Loring's essay (1850) is reprinted on pp. 253–256 of this book. [*Editor.*]

4. Jonathan Edwards (1703–58), the Calvinist theologian, and Ralph Waldo Emerson (1803–82), the chief oracle of Transcendentalism, here represent opposing views of man as a radically limited creature versus man as a creature of un-limited spiritual possibilities. [*Editor.*]

5. Cf. the fine observation and the accompanying discussion of Mark Van Doren, in *Nathaniel Hawthorne* (1949), p. 162: "Hawthorne did not need to believe in Puritanism in order to write a great novel about it. He had only to understand it, which for a man of his time was harder."

whether to flee it, taking his chances in the allegedly free wilderness to the west. It is a decision about ethical reality, and most of Hawthorne's heroes and heroines eventually have to confront it.

That is why we have the frantic shuttling, in novel after novel, between the village and the forest, the city and the country; for these are the symbols between which the choice must be made and the means by which moral inference is converted into dramatic action. Unlike Thoreau or Cooper, Hawthorne never suggested that the choice was an easy one. Even Arthur Mervyn[6] had been made to reflect on "the contrariety that exists between the city and the country"; in the age of hope the contrariety was taken more or less simply to lie between the restraints of custom and the fresh expansiveness of freedom. Hawthorne perceived greater complexities. He acknowledged the dependence of the individual, for nourishment, upon organized society (the city), and he believed that it was imperative "to open an intercourse with the world." But he knew that the city could destroy as well as nourish and was apt to destroy the person most in need of nourishment. And while he was responsive to the attractions of the open air and to the appeal of the forest, he also understood the grounds for the Puritan distrust of the forest. He retained that distrust as a part of the symbol. In the forest, possibility was unbounded; but just because of that, evil inclination was unchecked, and witches could flourish there.

For Hawthorne, the forest was neither the proper home of the admirable Adam, as with Cooper; nor was it the hideout of the malevolent adversary, as with Bird. It was the ambiguous setting of moral choice, the scene of reversal and discovery in his characteristic tragic drama. The forest was the pivot in Hawthorne's grand recurring pattern of escape and return.

It is in the forest, for example, that *The Scarlet Letter* version of the pattern begins to disclose itself: in the forest meeting between Hester and Dimmesdale, their first private meeting in seven years. During those years, Hester has been living "on the outskirts of the town," attempting to cling to the community by performing small services for it, though there had been nothing "in all her intercourse with society . . . that made her feel as if she belonged to it." And the minister has been contemplating the death of his innocence in a house fronting the village graveyard. The two meet now to join in an exertion of the will and the passion for freedom. They very nearly persuade themselves that they can escape along the forest track, which, though in one direction it goes "backward to the settlement," in another goes onward—"deeper it goes, and deeper into the wilderness, until . . . the yellow leaves will show

6. *Arthur Mervyn* (1799), by Charles Brockden Brown, is a novel of intrigue and horror set in Philadelphia during the Yellow Fever epidemic of 1793. [*Editor.*]

no vestiges of the white man's tread." But the energy aroused by their encounter drives them back instead, at the end, to the heart of the society, to the penitential platform which is also the heart of the book's structure.

In no other novel is the *agon* so sharp, the agony so intense. But the pattern is there again in *The Marble Faun*, as Miriam and Donatello flee separately from the city to the wooded Apennines to waste their illicit exultation in the discovery that they must return to Rome and the responsibility for their crime. It is true that Zenobia, in *The Blithedale Romance*, never does return from her flight: because her escape consummates itself in suicide, and she drowns in the river running through the woods near the utopian colony. Zenobia, who is often associated in the narrator's fancy with the figure of Eve, is too much of an Eve to survive her private calamity. * * *

Many things are being *tested* as well as exemplified in these circular journeys, in the pattern of escape and return. Among them, the doctrine inherited from Edwards that "an evil taint, in consequence of a crime committed twenty or forty years ago, remain[s] still, and even to the end of the world and forever." Among them, too, the proposition, implicit in much American writing from Poe and Cooper to Anderson and Hemingway, that the valid rite of initiation for the individual in the new world is not an initiation *into* society, but, given the character of society, an initiation *away from it*: something I wish it were legitimate to call "*de*nitiation." The true nature of human wickedness is also in question. Hawthorne's heroes and heroines are almost always criminals, according to the positive laws of the land, but Hawthorne presumed all men and women to be somehow criminals, and himself not the least so. The elder James reported to Emerson how Hawthorne had looked to him at a Saturday Club meeting in Boston: "like a rogue who finds himself in the company of detectives"; we can imagine him there: furtive, uneasy, out of place, half-guilty and half-defiant, poised for instant flight. No doubt it was because he appraised his personal condition this way that Hawthorne so frequently put his characters in the same dilemma: James's comment is a droll version of the opening glimpse of Hester Prynne. And no doubt also this was why Hawthorne so obviously sympathized with what he nevertheless regarded as an impossible enterprise—the effort to escape.

But if he customarily brought his sufferers back *into* the community; if he submitted most of his rogues to ultimate arrest; if the "evil taint" does turn out to be ineradicable, it was not because Hawthorne yielded in the end to the gloomy doctrine of Edwards. It was much rather because, for all his ambivalence, Hawthorne had made a daring guess about the entire rhythm of experience and so was willing to risk the whole of it. His qualifications as a novelist were at stake; for if the guess had been less comprehensive, he would have been a novelist of a very different kind: an inferior Melville, perhaps, exhausting himself in an excess of response to every tragic, new, unguessed-at collision. But if the guess had been any more certain, he might scarcely have been a novelist at all, but some sort of imperturbable tractarian. As it was, he could share some part of the hope motivating the flight; he could always see beyond the hope to the inevitable return; and he could even see a little distance beyond the outcome of surrender to the light and strength it perhaps assured.

* * *

ROY R. MALE

[Transformations: Hester and Arthur]†

* * * Vision alone is insufficient as a means of conversion. To "be true," as [*The Scarlet Letter's*] moral indicates, one must also "utter," make plain, "show freely" to others the secret of his identity. As the spirit is clothed in flesh and the flesh is clothed in garments, so ideas are clothed in words. The outer garments may be true to the inner reality: Hester's ascension is a mute utterance made manifest by the letter which society has vested upon her and which she has embroidered. Or they may be false covering: Dimmesdale's ascension at the close depends upon his willingness to divest himself of the priestly robe. Most of the garments in the book are accurate reflections of character. The massive women in the first pillory scene are swathed in petticoats and farthingales that match their "boldness and rotundity of speech"; Governor Bellingham's rigid devotion to outward forms may be seen in the hollow suit of armor, and his head and heart are separated by an imposing ruff; Mistress Hibbins wears a triple ruff for the same reason; the sea captain, the sailors, and the Indians express their individuality in their garb of scarlet and gold.

The Light is a process of seeing and disclosing; the Word is a process of uttering and investing; the Act is the intuitive union of both. Truth comes as a reward for intellectual discipline and human sympathy, but the ultimate incarnation that unites light and letter, spirit and flesh can only *be*. This intuition may be simply a sign, like Pearl's gestures, or a facial expression, like Chillingworth's when he discovers the letter on Dimmesdale's breast. More sig-

† From Roy R. Male, *Hawthorne's Tragic Vision* (Austin: University of Texas Press, 1957), pp. 102–17.

nificant expression is achieved in art: Hester's needlework, Chilling-worth's psychiatric alchemy, and Dimmesdale's Election Sermon. The highest form of intuitive truth, however, is the life that is pat-terned as a work of art. To make one's life a parable is to be the word incarnate; from one perspective, Dimmesdale's final symbolic gesture approaches this saintly level.

The action of the book shows how the two major characters are transformed when they join the Word and the Light in their actions and their art. Pearl, of course, does not change except at the end when she loses her allegorical function and becomes humanized. To know her in full context is the object of the quest; as a living hieroglyphic, a "character of flame," she unites language and vision in symbol. In so far as he is a character, Roger Chillingworth seeks to learn her origin and identity. He succeeds by inhumanely uniting his dim but penetrating gaze with amoral lore, both Indian and civilized, to perfect his art. But he is more significant in his alle-gorical relation to Hester and Arthur than he is as a character.

The main action concerns Hester Prynne and Arthur Dimmes-dale as they seek transformation. Hester attains her most nearly complete vision in the first third of the book. She is seen: the object of "universal observation," she feels the "heavy weight of a thousand unrelenting eyes upon her" as she presents a living sermon to those who witness the spectacle. "Transfigured" by the scarlet letter, she discovers that the platform offers perspective in every direction. It enables her to look inward and backward to her parents, her former home, and her guilt; downward to the living realities of her present, the infant and the letter; and, for the only time in the book, upward, to the balcony where authority is seated.

The clarity of her vision at this point in the book is emphasized by the "recognition" scene. Though forced upon her by the com-munity, it is an open recognition of guilt. Standing on her pedestal, Hester squarely faces the stranger who could not be buried in the sea or the wilderness and fixes her gaze upon him—"so fixed a gaze, that, at moments of intense absorption, all other objects in the visible world seemed to vanish, leaving only him and her. Such an interview, perhaps would have been more terrible than even to meet him as she now did, with the hot, mid-day sun burning down upon her face, and lighting up its shame." This lucid "interview" between Hester and Roger Chillingworth is interrupted by one of the preachers of the word, John Wilson, who urges her to "hearken," though he is poorly qualified to "step forth, as he now did, and meddle with a question of human guilt."

Nevertheless, Hester's ascension is limited. She sees the truth, but she will not utter the word. Heeding Chillingworth's gesture of secrecy, she does not publicly identify him. She has been educated under Dimmesdale's "preaching of the word"; she listens to his eloquent appeal for her to reveal her fellow-sinner's identity—an appeal that prompts a half-pleased, half-plaintive murmur from Pearl; but Hester will not utter the name. "She will not speak." And when her actual interview with Roger Chillingworth occurs, not in the mid-day sun but in the dark prison, we have the first clue to what will eventually develop into merely superficial penance. In this "dismal apartment" of her heart, she is confronted by her guilt, who lays his long forefinger on the scarlet letter and makes it his symbolic representative. Chillingworth then enjoins her to keep his identity secret, especially from Dimmesdale. "Recognize me not, by word, by sign, by look!" She determines to recognize only the letter and not the living embodiment of her guilt; and her release from confinement immediately follows.

Hester has thus gained only a partial insight from her plunge into the pit and her consequent ascent. She decides to stay in Boston, reasoning that the scene of her sin should become the scene of her penance. Since her deepest motive, however, is to remain close to her lover, her ideas about expiating the sin are partly rationalization. Nevertheless, she does resist a retreat into space—eastward to Europe or westward into the wilderness. Uniting the perspective gained from the pillory with the word, the letter branded upon her, she puts off the old garments and finds a new self in her art.

Only in her art does Hester begin to find grace and to grasp the truth; that is, only in her art does she come to know Pearl. Her needlework is an "act of penance," a product of delicate imaginative skill, and under other circumstances it might have been the "passion of her life." Through it she becomes involved with birth and death, with the social hierarchy, with all phases of community life (save marriage), adding the hidden sins and wounds of mankind to her own burden. Allowing her imagination full play, she has wrought better than she knew in creating Pearl's attire, and she has been imaginatively right in naming the child.

Unsatisfied with the intuitive vision of her art, however, Hester is tortured by her inability to understand Pearl in any rational medium. Her offspring is fanciful, spritelike, inscrutable; in her wild, bright, deep-black eyes she reflects the truth; but reflection can also foster diabolical illusion. "Brooding over all these matters, the mother felt like one who has evoked a spirit, but, by some irregularity in the process of conjuration, has *failed to win the master-word* that should control this new and incomprehensible intelligence." At the end of Chapter VII she makes an abortive effort to grasp the truth intellectually, putting the child through a half-earnest, half-playful catechism. "Art thou my child, in very truth?" she asks. "Tell me, then, what thou art, and who sent thee hither." (We notice, again, how Hawthorne suggests Pearl's fusion of art and truth in the archaisms of the dialogue.) But Pearl is not to be apprehended in this manner, and she further punishes Hester by refusing to admit a heavenly Father so long as the earthly father is concealed.

The superiority of Hester's artistic insight over the hollow rigidity of the orthodox is made clear when she and Pearl educate the highest members of the local hierarchy in the Governor's hall. She goes there to deliver a pair of embroidered gloves—we later learn that "a pure hand needs no glove to cover it"—and to argue for her right to keep Pearl. Bellingham's personality is neatly expressed in his stuccoed house, his gilded volumes, and the suit of armor. His views toward Hester and Pearl reveal themselves in the grotesque, inhuman distortions reflected by the armor. Cut off like Prufrock from spontaneity and fruitful emotion, he appears in an elaborate ruff that causes his head "to look not a little like that of John the Baptist in a charger." His astonishment at seeing the truth incarnate in his house is quite understandable. "I have never seen the like," he says, in unwitting self-criticism. "How gat such a guest into my hall?"

It soon becomes clear that the "truths of heaven and earth" cannot be seen through the catechism. Pearl, though unacquainted with the "outward form" of the New England Primer or the Westminster Catechism,[1] could have undergone a fair examination in these works. But she naturally evades the question of the clergyman John Wilson about her origin, finally informing him that she had been plucked from the wild rose bush. The stunned Governor asserts that she is "in the dark," thereby provoking Hester into a heated illumination of his own blindness. "See ye not, she is the scarlet letter, only capable of being loved, and so endowed with a millionfold the power of retribution for my sin?" Turning to Dimmesdale, she cries: "Speak for me . . . thou knowest what is in my heart, and what are a mother's rights, and how much the stronger they are, when that mother has but her child and the scarlet letter! Look thou to it!" "There is truth in what she says," answers the minister, who has always been more responsive to the word than to the vision. Upon the Governor's request that he "make that plain," Dimmesdale teaches him what is expressed by Hester's art—namely that Pearl is both burden and blessing.

During the first third of the book, therefore, Hester, her glowing letter, and Pearl are as lights shining in the darkness of the community. The minister, meanwhile, fasts and vigils in the darkness and preaches words that place him in a false light. He attains a new

1. The New England Primer (c. 1683) was a Puritan schoolbook which illustrated the letters of the alphabet with moral and theological precepts ("In Adam's fall / We sinned all"); The Westminister Confession (1646) was the basic platform of Calvinist theological beliefs. [Editor.]

perspective, however, when he begins to live with his guilt. When Chillingworth moves in with him, Dimmesdale finds in the physician's mind a remarkable depth and scope. "It was as if a window were thrown open," but "the air was too fresh and chill to be long breathed with comfort." Later, as Chillingworth keeps probing for "God's own truth," both men hear Pearl's laughter outside. "Looking instinctively from the open window," the minister sees Hester and Pearl in the adjacent burial ground. Here, seen from the new perspective and clearly outlined in the bright sunlight of the summer day, is the very truth that Chillingworth is seeking, but neither man can perceive it. Chillingworth looks at Pearl and asks, "What, in Heaven's name, is she?" And Dimmesdale is unable to explain her "principle of being."

The comprehension and communication of religious truth demands an intuitive fusion of language and vision. Hawthorne suggests that if Dimmesdale had not sinned, his native gifts would have placed him among the group of true saintly fathers whose only fault was their failure to communicate the highest truths to the populace. "All that they lacked was the gift that descended upon the chosen disciples at Pentecost, in tongues of flames; symbolizing, it would seem, not the power of speech in foreign and unknown languages, but that of addressing the whole human brotherhood in the heart's native language. These fathers, otherwise so apostolic, lacked Heaven's last and rarest attestation of their office, The Tongue of Flame. They would have vainly sought—had they ever dreamed of seeking—to express the highest truths through the humblest medium of familiar words and images." But Dimmesdale's burden keeps him on a level with the lowest. His congregation worships him; their adoration intensifies his guilty anguish; and his suffering heightens his fervor. Yet before he can truly speak with the Tongue of Flame, he must not only relate but reveal. He has already *spoken* the truth—confessed his sin—but in such abstract terms that he well knew "*the light* in which his vague confession would be viewed."

So long as they are covert, the minister's gestures are but a mockery of penitence, and his cloistral flagellations, fasts, and vigils are unavailing. The magnificent midnight scaffold scene dramatizes the various degrees of moral blindness in the community and throws the falsity of the minister's rationalizations into sharp relief. Clothed as if he were going to attend public worship, he ascends the platform, which is cloaked in darkness. Much more perceptive than the Governor, who can "see but little further than a mill-stone" in the darkness, he also has a more exalted perspective than John Wilson's. That elderly clergyman approaches the platform, but his glimmering lantern reveals only "the muddy pathway" beneath his feet.

Dimmesdale still persists in his argument, eternally true perhaps, but humanly false, that revelation must wait until judgment day. Hester and Pearl have joined him on the platform; he has been infused with new life as he takes Pearl's hand; but the tableau that follows is a visualization of his argument. For the awesome light of the meteor provides a kind of noon, "as if it were the light that is to reveal all secrets." It is like the day of doom, and in this lurid light the minister sees the ambiguity of his argument without being consciously aware of it. Though he gazes toward the zenith he is at the same time perfectly aware that Pearl is pointing toward Roger Chillingworth, his earthly guilt. He is close to perceiving the relation between the woman, their mutual guilt and their possible salvation; but when he asks Pearl to translate this vision into rational terms, he is unable to understand her natural or intuitive language. She speaks "in a tongue unknown to the erudite clergyman." Nevertheless, his revelation has unconsciously begun. He has divested himself of part of his hollow armor—the black glove.

The middle third of the book is perfectly and ironically balanced, for as the minister is struggling toward outsight and disclosure, Hester is seeking insight and utterance. Her moral predicament during the past few years has been just the reverse of his. Outwardly she has been a penitent sinner, and by her good works she has transmuted the letter into a badge of mercy. To many, the letter has "the effect of a cross on a nun's bosom." But her nominal penance is just as incomplete as Dimmesdale's closeted flagellations. Since the "interview" of Chapter IV she has not acknowledged her connection with Roger Chillingworth, and his symbol, the letter, has ceased being a vital one for her. Without the spirit, the letter killeth: the A may now stand for "Able," but there is "nothing in Hester's bosom, to make it ever again the pillow of Affection," unless another transfiguration occurs. She has become a mannish vagrant, speculating in the gloomy labyrinth of the mind. It is a kind of dissipation in which her natural role as woman has evaporated into space. The Word, outwardly imposed and outwardly worn, has failed in its traditional rhetorical discipline. "The scarlet letter had not done its office."

Thus the midnight scaffold scene has been a dark night of the soul for her as well as for the minister. But as a result of Dimmesdale's changed aspect, she has been given a "new theme for reflection." She resolves to confront her guilt and confess it to the minister. "I would speak a word with you," she says to Chillingworth, "a word that concerns us much." The word amounts to a new acceptance of her responsibility in the sin; and her emotions as she watches Chillingworth depart throw "a dark light" on her state of mind, "revealing much that she might not otherwise have acknowledged to herself." Pearl seems much closer and more earnest than ever before. But Hester is not yet ready for the utterance of the whole truth. To Pearl's relentless questions, Hester can only reply, "Hold thy tongue," and threaten to shut the child in *her* dark closet.

The complex interweaving of utterance and vision, investment and speculation, time and space reaches a peak in the forest interview. Dimmesdale tells Hester of his torture, which has been augmented by his native gifts: "Canst thou deem it, Hester, a consolation, that I must stand up in my pulpit, and meet so many eyes turned upward to my face, as if the *light of heaven* were beaming from it!—must see my flock hungry for the truth, and listening to my words *as if a tongue of Pentecost were speaking!* and then look inward, and discern the black reality of what they idolize?" Hester gently suggests that the sin has been left behind, that penitence is sealed and witnessed by good works. But the pastor knows better. Then she conquers her fears and utters her responsibility for the guilt that now resides with him. "Dost thou not *see* what I would *say?* That old man!—the physician!—he whom they call Roger Chillingworth! he was my husband." Like Milton's Adam, Arthur sternly repels her; and then his heart relents.

At this point Hester offers a way of lightening the burden in their share of woe. Never—not even in the exhortations of Emerson and Thoreau—has the vision of dawn, the promise of America, the dream of a second chance found more deeply felt utterance than in her appeal, as she urges the time-drenched man to recover himself, to put on a new name and leave the ruin behind him. "Preach! Write! Act! Do anything save to lie down and die!" The closing formula of her brief but eloquent sermon is "Up and away!" The fact that this phrase is likely to call up for some modern readers a vision of the gaudily vested Superman may seem unfortunate. But this association is not entirely irrelevant: as we know, one consequence of the doctrine of self-reliance, was its distortion into a grossly materialized version of the superman. And the modern connotations of the phrase, voiced as it is by the woman, simply point up the inversion of roles that climaxes the forest scene. She has grown eloquent while he is now silent; she has lost insight while he is gaining outsight. The parishioner is now preaching to the pastor. Dimmesdale, on the other hand, in whose eyes "a fitful light" has been kindled by Hester's enthusiasm, now gazes upon her with a "look in which hope and joy shone out." She has spoken "what he vaguely hinted at but dared not speak."

As the succeeding events reveal, Hester has preached a half-truth. She has rightly told him to be a man, to exert his protestant function of penetrating into space and conquering new fields. All this he could do—alone. What Hester does not see is that if she is to go with him, he must accept the catholic involvement in guilt-stained time that is the essence of her womanhood. She has usurped the masculine prerogative of speculation, and her intellectual wanderings have been so undisciplined that they have become obscure. In the gloom of the wilderness or the blankness of space, nothing of temporal or moral significance can be seen.

That her proposal is only half valid may be discerned from her symbolic relation to Pearl and the stream of time. Hester would like to retain only the pleasant aspects of the past. She throws off the scarlet letter (it lands, however, on the "hither verge" of the stream of time); she removes the formal cap that confines her hair, resuming "her sex, her youth, and the whole richness of her beauty" from "what men call the irrevocable past." And she tells Arthur: "Thou must know Pearl. . . . Thou hast seen her,—yes, I know it!—but thou wilt see her now with other eyes. She is a strange child. I hardly comprehend her." With his newly discovered vision, the minister can see Pearl, standing a good way off on the other side of the brook. But neither he nor Hester is yet skilled to read "the character of flame," the "oneness of their being." Pearl will not join them, for wholeness is not achieved by drawing a sharp boundary between the worlds of past and present. Her symbolic gestures, reflected in the stream, indicate that their proposed escape from time into motion and space is an unrealizable dream—or at least can be effected only at the cost of leaving their salvation behind.

Though Hester desperately clings to the hope of drowning her guilt in the deep sea, she now recognizes that the forest cannot hide it. The moment of inspiration has passed. By flinging the letter "into infinite space" she had drawn "an hour's free breath," but now the burden must be resumed. The child rejoins her mother, but between Pearl and the minister there is no expression, no communion. He awkwardly impresses a kiss on her brow, which she hastily washes off in the brook.

The precise nature of the minister's transformation in the forest is once again worked out in terms of the Word and the Light. He has stripped away the old words; he has discarded his old self amid the decaying leaves "like a cast-off garment." The scales have dropped from his eyes; he has attained an Emersonian vision. But his old insight has been temporarily obliterated. His condition is indicated by Hawthorne's complex moral topography. The pathway in the woods seems "wilder, more uncouth with its rude natural obstacles, and less trodden by the foot of man, than he remembered it on his outward journey." On the one hand, he is closer to the freedom of individual growth, less hampered by the principles and prejudices of the social system; on the other, he is, as the chapter title indicates, "the minister in a maze"—more deeply involved in a moral wilderness with its "plashy places" and its "clinging underbrush."

In this mood, it is all that Dimmesdale can do to keep from mocking his old words. Intoxicated and unbalanced by the heady wine of the new, he runs into a series of delightfully wrought encounters that anticipate Clifford Pyncheon's escape from his past in *The House of the Seven Gables*.[2] He has temporarily substituted the undisciplined "vision" for communion; thus when he meets a hoary old deacon he has to forcibly restrain himself from "uttering certain blasphemous suggestions that entered his mind, respecting the communion supper. He absolutely trembled and turned pale as ashes, lest his tongue should wag itself, in utterance of these horrible matters." He resists the temptation to blight the innocence of a virgin with "but one wicked look" and the development of evil with "but a word." All his other misadventures stem from his rejection of the old rhetorical discipline. The sinister side of his revolt is cleverly shown by the pompous modern jargon of his conversation with Mistress Hibbins, the embodiment of ubiquitous evil. "I profess, madam," he says, with "a grave obeisance, such as the lady's rank" demands, "I profess, on my conscience and character, that I am utterly bewildered as touching the purport of your words! I went not into the forest to seek a potentate; neither do I, at any future time, design a visit thither, with a view to gaining the favor of such a personage."

After the vision of the forest interview, what Dimmesdale clearly needs now is to be nourished by a communion with the tomb-fed faith and the tome-fed wisdom of the past. In order to grasp the truth in his art form, he must return to the rich intellectual resources of the study, adjacent to the graveyard. "Here he had studied and written; here, gone through fast and vigil, and come forth half alive; here, striven to pray; here, borne a hundred thousand agonies! There was the Bible, in its rich old Hebrew, with Moses and the Prophets speaking to him, and God's voice through all!" White and speechless, he has been able to confront Roger Chillingworth squarely; he has withstood the travail of temptation in the wilderness; and now he is able to join the new vision with the rich utterances of the past. The long fast is over. Partaking of supper, he composes, as if divinely inspired, the flaming rhetoric of the Election Sermon. This is *his* new field; this is his true dawn; and as the golden sunrise beams in his study, he is seen with the pen still between his fingers and "a vast, immeasurable tract of written space behind him."

The Election Sermon itself cannot be rationally reproduced—it is heard and felt. To Hester, who is outside the church, it sounds like the great organ music of "a tongue native to the human heart,

2. In Hawthorne's next novel (1851), Clifford, who had been unjustly imprisoned for thirty years and has recently returned to the ancestral home (the symbol of his family's bondage to a ruinous past), flees into the streets of Salem and takes a train ride where he encounters various impressions of life which temporarily energize him. [*Editor.*]

wherever educated." In its undertone may be detected the deep ache at the heart of human life itself—a sense of atonement not only for the individual sin but for Original Sin. The crowd inside the church is spellbound at the close of the sermon, profoundly silent as if they had heard "the utterance of oracles." Then they gush forth from the doors, feeling the need of "other breath, more fit to support the gross and earthly life into which they relapsed, than that atmosphere which the preacher had converted into *words of flame*." The subject of the sermon, as it is later revealed, is akin to the theme of the book: "the relation between the Deity and the communities of mankind, with a special reference to the New England which they were planting here in the wilderness." The minister prophesies a high and glorious destiny for these communities, just as God has providentially transformed his own moral wilderness into glory.

The last ascension scene captures with terse, compelling inevitability the paradox that lies at the heart of tragedy and Christianity. Time and eternity intersect on the platform of the pillory as Dimmesdale, "in the name of Him, so terrible and so merciful, who gives me grace at this last moment," makes the final revelation and is at last united with Pearl. With his vision into eternity, he asks Hester, "Is not this better . . . than what we dreamed of in the forest?" Her answer is the temporal one: "I know not. . . . Better? Yea; so we may both die, and little Pearl die with us." Even her last hope—for a specific reunion in an afterlife—is clothed in earthly terms, and in his dying breath Dimmesdale offers her no encouragement.

The various reactions of the crowd to Dimmesdale's revelation are presented in ascending order from the crude to the spiritual. The first two conjectures about the origin of the letter on his breast— that it was self-imposed torture, or that Roger Chillingworth wrought it with his poisonous drugs—are the most naturalistic and the least valid. A third group—"those best able to appreciate the minister's peculiar sensibility and the wonderful operation of his spirit upon the body"—see the letter as a psychic cancer that gradually manifested itself physically. But the last group is the most interesting. These "highly respectable witnesses" are "spectators of the whole scene," and they see the minister as a saint. They associate his final action with Christ's sympathy for the adulteress, and they think Dimmesdale so shaped the manner of his death as to make of it a parable, illustrating "that in the view of Infinite Purity, we are sinners all alike."

Having stated this view in more detail than any of the others, Hawthorne then explicitly questions it in the light of common sense. A clue to the ambiguity here is offered by the meanings of the word *respectable*. In its usual sense, the adjective tells us that these witnesses were among the more pious and pompous members of the community, stubbornly refusing to see any evil in the high representatives of their society. Yet in a book where the language itself points back to the original—a book dealing with vision and language, where words like "spectator" and "speculation" are extremely significant—we begin to wonder about our easy rejection of these "respectable" witnesses. Etymologically, these are the spectators who *look back*; and from this point of view their version of the minister's life is the most original, the most spiritual of all.

Considerable evidence supporting their view may be found in Hawthorne's description of the New England holiday. Despite its sable tinge, there is an aura of hope. "For today," as Hester tells Pearl, "a new man is beginning to rule over them; and so—as has been the custom of mankind ever since a nation was first gathered—they make merry and rejoice; as if a good and golden year were at length to *pass over* the poor old world." The new man is really Arthur Dimmesdale. Having achieved individuation in the forest, he now returns to join the procession only to rise above it. "The spiritual element took up the feeble frame, and carried it along, unconscious of the burden and converting it to spirit like itself."

But the whole truth is not distilled in the refined perception of the respectable witnesses. Their view must be considered along with the crude ideas of the materialists; and the composite of the two is represented by those firmly grounded in the temporal life who nevertheless appreciate the minister's sensibility, the interaction of flesh and spirit. The "moral," which at first sight seems to be an oversimplification, should be read in this light. To "be true," one must not mean but be. The truth, that is to say, can only be grasped in its total living context; and since this comprehensive view is impossible from any single human perspective, the closest we can come to it is through "expression"—art, symbol, gesture, or parable—a showing "of some trait" from which the totality may be inferred.

At the end we are left with the symbol into which the whole meaning of the book has been distilled. Around the letter have gathered not only the explicit associations of Adultress, Able, Affection, and Angel but also the myriad subtle suggestions of art, atonement, ascension, and the Acts of the Apostles. Here is the A, each limb of which suggests an ascension, with Pearl the link between the two; here is the sable background of the Puritan community; and fused in the entire symbol are the flesh and the spirit, the word and the light, the letter A, gules. * * *

SEYMOUR GROSS

"Solitude, and Love, and Anguish": The Tragic Design of The Scarlet Letter†

* * *

I believe that The Scarlet Letter, like all great novels, en-
riches our sense of human experience and complicates and hu-
manizes our approach to it. It does not try to convince us—or at
least that is not its central or distinctive purpose—of the validity
of this or that particular moral precept. The inadequacy of a
didactic reading of The Scarlet Letter, whether it posits for Hawthorne an orthodox or romantic point of view, can be most clearly
seen in the fact that neither of these positions has been able to
take into account Hester's deep sense of having committed a sin
and her feelings of guilt, even though Hawthorne insists upon our
considering them. For example, of her continued stay in Boston
she thinks, "Here had been the scene of her guilt, and here should
be the scene of her earthly punishment . . ." (ch. V). And when
Pearl strikes her scarlet letter with flowers, Hester refrains from
covering her bosom "that her penance might be best wrought out
by this unutterable pain" (ch. VI). In answer to Pearl's persistent
questions about the significance of the letter, Hester finally tells
her that "once in my lifetime I met the Black Man [and] this
scarlet letter is his mark" (ch. XVI). Even more explicitly, we are
told that "she knew that her deed had been evil; she had no faith,
therefore, that its result [Pearl] would be good," and that "It
appalled her to discern in [Pearl] a shadowy reflection of the evil
that had existed in herself" (ch. VI). For obvious reasons the
critics have paid little or no attention to these remarks: they cannot be made to fit into any moralistic reading of the novel: for
whether Hester is seen as the glorious incarnation of the transcendental soul or as the damnable spirit of romantic self-indulgence,
these guilt-laden comments .are equally out of character. If, on the
other hand, these are the legitimate marks of an orthodox repentence, then how can Hester say after seven (supposedly) purgatorial
years that her adultery "had a consecration of its own"? John C.
Gerber, one of the best of the novel's critics, both presents the
problem of Hester's guilt feelings most clearly and indicates, without solving, the central difficulty. "From the first it is plain that
Hester does not consider her act of adultery as a sin against God

† From CLA Journal, III (March 1968), pp. 154–65.

or against any law of her own nature. Nor does she feel that she has sinned against the community. Yet clearly she knows that her deed has been wrong and that, somehow, the result cannot be good." It is the purpose of this paper to fix the nature of Professor Gerber's "somehow," and to show how this shapes the tragic design of the book.

The "A" which Hester wears on her bosom does not, of course, signify adultery in her eyes: its ornate embroidery (which Hawthorne mentions three times) is an implicit rejection of the community's view of her act; it is, in fact, a symbolic foreshadowing of her "consecration" assertion seven years later. But Hawthorne does not imply that Hester is therefore an irresponsible libertine: it is simply that she cannot imagine any law as taking precedence over the law of love between a man and a woman. For her, marriage *in se* is not a sacramental union—only love can truly sacramentalize it. In this she is not, like, say, Ivan Karamazov or Ahab,[1] posing her will against God's, as some recent critics assert; it is rather that she, like Anne Hutchinson, with whom she is twice linked in the novel, is convinced through an "Inner Light" that her way is not a violation of God's law. This, I take it, is what Hester means when in the "Conclusion" she tells the troubled women who come to her for counsel "of her firm belief, that, at some brighter period, when the world should have grown ripe for it, in Heaven's own time, a new truth would be revealed, in order to establish the whole relation between man and woman on a surer ground of mutual happiness." Having arrived at this conviction through the experience of love, Hester considers her marriage with Chillingworth as invalid, for, as she reminds him, "I felt no love [for you], nor feigned any" (ch. IV). Indeed, from the vantage point of a "consecrated" marriage, she looks back upon her loveless union with her legal husband with horror: "She deemed it her crime most to be repented of that she had ever endured, and reciprocated, the lukewarm grasp of his hand . . ." (ch. XV). Though she talks of hands, what sickens Hester is, I believe, clear. That Hawthorne does not present Hester's position as either romantically irresponsible or gloriously liberated is evidenced in Chillingworth's quiet reply: "We have wronged each other . . . Mine was the first wrong, when I betrayed thy budding youth into a false and unnatural relation with my decay" (ch. IV). This scene, like most of the novel, is the product of a deliberately controlled balance of sympathies—the balance that is tragic not didactic. I do not mean to imply that Hawthorne had no convictions personally about the responsibilities and nature of marriage—of course he did; it would not be difficult

1. Two of literature's most famous God rejecters, from Fyodor Dostoevsky's *The Brothers Karamazov* (1880) and Herman Melville's *Moby-Dick* (1851).

to isolate from his life and letters a body of doctrine to which we can be fairly certain he personally subscribed. The point is that abstract conviction does not represent his total attitude towards the problem, for it neglects the context of concrete experience, which for the artist, as opposed to the theologian, is an essential element in its definition. Therefore, what is significant in *The Scarlet Letter* is not that Hester is right or wrong in an absolute sense, but rather that she has integrity in her own terms, that she has fallen in love with a minister who has integrity in different terms, and that therefore their love is condemned to be mangled in the clash of their ultimately irreconcilable moralities.

It is this conflict of moralities which is the source of Hester's sense of sin: the guilt which she suffers can only be related to what Hester has done to her lover. In Hester's view, as we have already said, she has not sinned against community, husband, or God; but she *has* sinned against Dimmesdale (it is a convenient coincidence that the "A" she wears is the initial of her lover's first name). Although she has committed no evil in terms of her own morality, she has been, nevertheless, the instrument of Dimmesdale's having committed a horrible sin against his: it is she who has caused the physical and spiritual desiccation of her lover, and for this she suffers her sense of guilt. It is beside the point that she has destroyed him unwittingly: the knowledge of what she has done to him is her own form of "bloody scourge." It is this tragic paradox—that out of love she has violated love—which accounts for Hester's painful awareness that "her deed had been evil." Her "impulsive and passionate nature" is neither romantically exalted nor moralistically condemned: it is simply presented as tragic because it was its fate to intersect with Dimmesdale's equally passionate desire for renunciation. In the iron world of *The Scarlet Letter*, passion, whether human or divine, is its own cross.

Hester's refusal to leave Boston—which has confused some critics —and her withdrawal from Dimmesdale are the necessary results of this tragic conflict. Roy Male's assertion that Hester stays in Boston to be close to her lover and that this shows that "her ideas about expiating her guilt are partly rationalization" misses the point I believe. Hester cannot go into Dimmesdale's world, where both might find peace of soul in an orthodox submission to the Calvinistic God; and he cannot come into hers, where both might find joy in a free submission to human love. They are both doomed to their own private purgatories, their own parallel agonies. But their release from the "sin and sorrow" of their lives must come from different sources. For whereas Dimmesdale must struggle to make himself a fit receptacle for God's grace before his "A" can be purged, Hester's purgation can only be effected by Dimmesdale himself—only he can take the stigma from her breast. That Hester's absolution can come only from Dimmesdale is made quite clear early in the novel. When the Reverend Mr. Wilson offers Hester the removal of the letter in return for the name of Pearl's father, Hester answers, " 'Never!' . . . looking, not at Mr. Wilson, but into the deep and troubled eyes of the younger clergyman [Dimmesdale]. 'It is too deeply branded. Ye cannot take it off. And would that I might endure his agony as well as mine!' " (ch. III). Here, quite explicitly, we are shown that Hester feels that her sin is only against her lover and that, consequently, only he can ease her of her pain. In the same vein she later tells Chillingworth, when he assures her that the community will allow her to remove her stigma, "It lies not in the pleasure of the magistrates to take off this badge . . . Were I worthy to be quit of it, it would fall away of its own nature or be transformed into something which speaks a different purport" (ch. XIV). But it has *already* been transformed into something which speaks a different purport—the community now interprets the letter as standing for Able (ch. XIII). The point is that forgiveness has come from an irrelevant source. The theocratic society of seventeenth century Boston would have the right to remove the letter or transform its meaning only if Hester's sin were that of adultery; but since she herself conceives of her sin in different terms, the attitude of magistrate or minister (save one) is beside the point. Only Dimmesdale has the power to remove the letter—which is precisely what happens several chapters later in the forest scene.

It is the index of Hester's love for Dimmesdale and her consciousness of having violated him that at no time during the seven years leading up to the climactic forest scene does she try to save Dimmesdale (and herself) within the context of her own beliefs. She leaves him, instead, to try to work out his release in terms of his own orthodox world, even though such a release can bring her no happiness; that is, if Dimmesdale is able to resolve his spiritual agony with God, the painful image of what she had caused would dissolve. But there would be no radiant joy in its stead. Dimmesdale's peace would still leave Hester alone in her world. The absence of pain is not happiness, yet the absence of pain is all she allows herself to hope for. Hester accepts this life of "no hope, and seemingly no wish, of gaining anything" for herself because she loves the man she ruined.

It would be a mistake to minimize the extent of her ordeal. For all the moral and psychological toughness she has achieved in the seven years, her life has been as drab and grey as the garb she wears. When Dimmesdale asks her in the forest "Art thou in life?," she can only find it in herself to answer, "In such life as has been mine these seven years past!" But so deeply rooted is her sense of sin and her acceptance of its tragic consequences that even in the second scaffold scene, when years of unnatural asceticism have all but effaced the natural richness of her being, she still refrains from any attempt at intimate contact with the minister. It is Pearl who talks to him and it is she whose hand he holds. It is only when she has to face the "shuddering terror" of what was once her lover, with his "nerve . . . destroyed" and his "moral force abased" (ch. XIII), that she decides to break out of her penitential isolation; but her daring to intersect with Dimmesdale's life again has no personal element of hope in it. She is not going to attempt a resurrection of both their lives with the vitality of her love; she is merely going to rectify her error in judgment in having sworn to Chillingworth not to disclose his identity—an understandable concession when we remember that it was exacted from her when she had just undergone a mind-shattering experience.

Those critics who see the forest scene as the Second Temptation surely miss the fineness of Hawthorne's tragic vision. Hester is not a seventeenth century Sadie Thompson:[2] she goes into the forest only to give Dimmesdale information (his tormentor's identity) which will strengthen him in his private struggle with God, and then to return to her own isolated world. That it becomes for Dimmesdale a Second Temptation is a consequence of his own terrible sense of defeat, not of Hester's guile. Indeed, at the outset, Hester tries to lift the burden of Dimmesdale's miserable suffering and wretched despair with the comforting words of *religion*, not love:

> "You wrong yourself in this," said Hester, gently. "You have deeply and sorely repented. Your sin is left behind you, in the days long past. Your present life is not less holy, in very truth, than it seems in people's eyes. Is there no reality in the penitence thus sealed and witnessed by good works? And wherefore should it not bring you peace?" (ch. XVII)

This is hardly the language of a woman who has been accused by various critics of "desperate recklessness," "romantic self-indulgence," "unyokable paganism," "foolish and fatuous arrogance."

What is usually missed in the forest scene is that Hester's final offer to go away with Dimmesdale is the result of a gradual interaction of his agony and her love—*in that sequence*. It is only when a spiritually shattered Dimmesdale, "crushed under this seven years' weight of misery," begs her "Resolve for me . . . be strong for me," that Hester dares to advise him to run away to a new

2. The harlot in William Somerset Maugham's *Rain* (1921), who, after being converted to virtue by a Protestant minister, sleeps with him, which results in his suicide and her return to her old profession.

religious life ("Preach! Write! Act!") before "the torments that have so gnawed into thy life . . . leave thee powerless even to repent!" It is only then that she dares to intimate that his orthodoxy has enslaved him needlessly: "what hast thou to do with all these iron men, and their opinions? They have kept thy better part in bondage too long already." Malcolm Cowley's comment that Hester *urges* Dimmesdale to "flee with her to a foreign country" is not a fair description of what happens in the forest, and Hugh Maclean's assertion that "Hester's continual harping on the 'happiness' she can win for them both would be almost comic, were it not such a pathetic effort to escape the will of God" is a gross distortion of it. It is only when Dimmesdale himself (and this is always overlooked) covertly begs her to go with him with his pathetically repeated "Alone, Hester!" that she allows her deepest desire to escape from its self-imposed penitential prison into the joy of consent. Hawthorne makes it quite explicit that she has not seduced him—she has merely articulated "what he vaguely hinted at but dared not speak" (ch. XVIII). Orthodoxy in her view, and, for the moment, in his too, has had its chance—and failed! Now human love—exalted and consecrated—is to have its chance at resurrecting their shattered world.

And for a pathetically brief moment, in the appropriately entitled chapter, "A Flood of Sunshine," it does. But unlike the Graham Greene character who hopelessly and despondently gives himself over to human love when God seems gone, here human love is "transvalued" into religious exaltation. "Do I feel joy again?" Dimmesdale cries out ecstatically.

> "Methought the germ of it was dead in me! O Hester, thou art my better angel! I seem to have flung myself—sick, sin-stained, and sorrow-blackened—down upon these forest leaves, and to have risen up all made anew, *and with new powers to glorify Him that hath been merciful!* This is already the better life! Why did we not find it sooner?" (ch. XVIII; my italics)

It is at this moment, when Hester's love has freed Dimmesdale from the slough of despond into which it had cast him, that Hester can at last unclasp the scarlet letter from her bosom and cast it away "among the withered leaves." Dimmesdale's having "risen up all made anew" is the absolution of her sin: his rebirth is her forgiveness: *he* has taken off the letter. Free at last from her burden of "sin and sorrow," Hester, in a breath-taking movement, loosens her abundantly rich and dark hair from the nun-like cap in which she has encased it for seven years, releasing her "sex, her youth, and the whole richness of her beauty." This is not, however, an image of sexual potency to be admired or condemned according to the critic's point of view: it is a moment of fruition, a moment paid for with humiliation, isolation, forbearance, and pain.

But the "magic" of this hour in the forest is doomed to be dispelled in the resurgence of Dimmesdale's Puritan Christianity, as is symbolically foreshadowed in the failure of the brook (a baptismal image) to carry away the discarded letter and in Pearl's washing off of her father's kiss in the same brook. It is inevitable that Dimmesdale, being the kind of man he is, should shortly realize that, "Tempted by a dream of happiness, . . . he had yielded himself, with deliberate choice, as he had never done before, to what he knew was deadly sin," and should therefore renounce his human love. Customarily, Dimmesdale's final release in the spiritual embrace of his Orthodoxy is viewed either as a wretched betrayal of Hester's love or as an implicit condemnation of her misguided "presumption" which would have resulted in the loss of both their salvations. In its final effect it is neither. In the tragic conflict of moralities, it is inevitable that Hester should try—after Orthodoxy seemed to have failed—to save the man she loves and ruined in the only way she can; and it is equally inevitable that this "polluted priest" should ultimately save himself—even at the expense of his mortal lover—in the only way he can. Had Hawthorne wished for Hester to appear as erring romantic irresponsibility, he could have shown her as bitterly and frantically attempting to recall Dimmesdale from his beatific escape, in the manner of Paphnutius in Anatole France's *Thaïs*.[3] (It is the demonic Chillingworth, by the way, who plays this role in the novel; it is he who tries "to snatch back [Dimmesdale] from what he sought to do!") Or had he wished Hester to appear as the glowing spirit of romantic freedom and love, he would not have given to Dimmesdale's final moments the sincere accents of mystical joy. What Hawthorne has given us instead is a marvelously poised and powerful vision of tragic separation: an excruciating sense of division pervades the final scene from the moment of Dimmesdale's entry until his death. As the minister, energized by his spiritual resolve, arrives to give his Election Sermon, Hester suddenly realizes what she had allowed herself in the forest to forget—that their lives could never really mesh:

> She thought of the dim forest, with its little dell of solitude, and love, and anguish, and the mossy tree-trunk, where sitting hand in hand, they had mingled their sad and passionate talk with the melancholy murmur of the brook. How deeply had they known each other then! And was this the man? She hardly knew him now! He, moving proudly past . . . he, so unattainable in his . . . unsympathizing thoughts, through which she now beheld him!

3. In Anatole France's novel (1890), Paphnutius, a priest, converts the actress-courtesan Thaïs to Christianity, only to become consumed with sexual desire himself; on her death bed he pleads with her to live so that he can love her, for "Nothing is true but life on earth, and carnal love."

Her spirit sank with the idea that all must have been a delusion, and that . . . there could be no real bond betwixt the clergyman and herself.

Though it is Hester's strength that Dimmesdale asks for in his ascent to the public confessional, though it is in her arms that he dies, both pursue their separate destinies to the end. When the clergyman asks her the rhetorical question, "Is this not better . . . than what we dreamed of in the forest?," she can only answer, "I know not! I know not! . . . Better? Yea; so we may both die. . . ." And when Hester pleadingly asks Dimmesdale, "Shall we not meet again? . . . Shall we not spend our immortal life together? Surely, surely, we have ransomed one another with all this woe!," all he can say is "Hush, Hester, hush. . . . The law we broke—the sin here so awfully revealed—let these alone be in thy thoughts!"

Hawthorne tells us that he suffered a "great diversity and severity of emotion" while writing *The Scarlet Letter* and that when he finished it he was in a "very nervous state." I find it difficult to believe that such emotional upset could have come from an intention that was merely moralistic or didactic. But the novel itself, as I have tried to show, is the best proof of Hawthorne's tragic design. As I read the novel, it does not matter who was "right." What matters is that Dimmesdale is dead and that Hester is alone; that a love that should have flourished in the sunlight had but one moment of stolen light and seven years of darkness. What matters is that in *The Scarlet Letter* the color of adultery was the color of roses *and* the color of death.

DANIEL G. HOFFMAN

Hester's Double Providence: The Scarlet Letter and the Green†

* * *

It is apparent that the Puritans badly bungled the case of Hester Prynne. The scarlet letter they condemned her to wear was a self-evident judgment: A for Adultery. "Giving up her individuality, she would become a general symbol at which the preacher and moralist might point, and in which they might vivify and embody their

† From *Form and Fable in American Fiction* by Daniel G. Hoffman (New York: Oxford University Press, 1961), pp. 177–86. Some footnotes have been omitted and the remainder renumbered.

images of woman's frailty and sinful passion." Hester would cease to be a woman, and be henceforth a living emblem in a morality play: guilt without redemption, suffering without end.

Yet in her first appearance the child at her breast made her, "A" and all, resemble "the image of Divine Maternity." By midpoint in the tale we can be told that "The scarlet letter had not done its office," for her "A" has taken on significations unintended by the judges. After some years of tending the sick as a "self-ordained Sister of Mercy," it was said that "The letter was the symbol of her calling. . . . They said it meant Able, so strong was Hester Prynne, with a woman's strength." Stranger still, it "had the effect of the cross on a nun's bosom," endowing Hester with "a kind of sacredness." Yet she herself tells Pearl that the "A" is "The Black Man's mark," and when, in her forest rendezvous with Dimmesdale, she removed the scarlet letter, and shook loose her hair, she was at once transformed. "Her sex, her youth, and the whole richness of her beauty, came back," as sunshine flooded down in token of the sympathy of Nature—"that wild, heathen Nature of the forest, never subjugated by human law, or illumined by higher truth."

But now Pearl does not recognize her mother.

Many modern readers find Hester's elf-child intolerably arch, with her pranks and preternatural knowledge. She is indeed a remarkable infant, distinguished as much for her fidelity to the actual psychology of a three-year-old child as for the allegorism with which Hawthorne manipulates her strange behavior. Her fixation upon the "A" might seem completely arbitrary, yet children of that age do indeed become attached to familiar objects in just such a fashion. Pearl was closely modelled on Hawthorne's own little daughter Una. And if Una was named for Spenser's allegorical heroine, Pearl, as Mr. Male remarks, takes her name from the passage in Matthew which signifies truth and grace. When Hester strips herself of the scarlet letter she regains her pagan sexuality in the heathen world of Nature, beyond human law and divine truth. She has also taken off a token familiar to Pearl since earliest infancy. Both literally and figuratively, her child must resent her changed appearance until the familiar badge of discipline is resumed.

At one point Pearl amuses herself by mimicking her mother. She has been gazing into a pool in the woods, "seeking a passage for herself into its [reflected] sphere of impalpable earth and unattainable sky." Her attempt to merge herself into the elements is unavailing, and she turns to other tricks. She makes herself a mantle of seaweed, and, "As the last touch to her mermaid's garb, Pearl took some eel-grass, and imitated, as best she could, on her own bosom . . . the letter A,—but freshly green instead of scarlet!" When Hester beholds her handiwork she says, "My little Pearl, the green letter, on thy childish bosom, has no purport. But dost thou know, my child, what this letter means which thy mother is doomed to wear?" Pearl, with her preternatural intuition, answers "Truly do I! It is for the same reason that the minister keeps his hand over his heart!" But Hester cannot bear to tell her what she seems already to know, and breaks off, saying, "I wear it for the sake of its gold thread."

This scene perhaps seems a digression which fails to advance our understanding of either Hester or Pearl. But in fact it comprises a metaphoric recapitulation and explanation of the nature of Hester's offense. Pearl's allegorical function brings into *The Scarlet Letter* the pagan values which Hawthorne had synthesized in "The May-pole of Merry Mount."[1] But in *The Scarlet Letter* the amoral free-dom of the green natural world is viewed with yet greater reservations than was true of his story, written fifteen years earlier. We have al-ready noticed that the forest is described, in Hester's rendezvous with Dimmesdale, as "wild, heathen Nature." The child will not let her mother cast the scarlet letter aside because Pearl herself is emblem of a passion which partook of that same heathen, natural wildness. "What we did had a consecration of its own," Hester assures Arthur, but that consecration was not a Christian or a moral sanctity. It was an acknowledgment of the life force itself. Consequently Pearl is endowed with the morally undirected energies of life. "The spell of life went forth from her ever creative spirit, and communicated itself to a thousand objects, as a torch kindles a flame wherever it may be applied." This spell is the power of fecundity, and its derivative power, that of imagination. "The un-likeliest materials—a stick, a bunch of rags, a flower—were the puppets of Pearl's witchcraft . . ."[2] These she brings to life, and she feels in herself kinship with life in every form. Although the forest is a place of dread and evil, the haunt of witches and of heathen Indian sorcerers, Pearl is at home among its creatures. It "became the playmate of the lonely infant" and "put on the kindest of moods to welcome her." Squirrels fling their treasured nuts to Pearl, while even wolves and foxes take caresses from her hand. "The mother-forest, and those wild things which it nourished, all recog-nized a kindred wildness in the human child."

It was in this mother-forest that Hester had had her tryst with Dimmesdale, beyond human law and divine truth. Hester herself sees that "The child could not be made amenable to rules. In

1. In this story (1836), Hawthorne de-picts the conflict between the natural joyousness of Merry Mount and the gloomy moral seriousness of Salem, with reservations about each and a possible reconciliation of the two in the "trou-bled joy" of human love. [*Editor.*]

2. Compare the passage on imagination in "The Custom-House" chapter: "Nothing is too small or too trifling to undergo this change [from material-ity into things of intellect], and ac-quire dignity thereby. A child's shoe; the doll . . . the hobby-horse. . . ."

giving her existence, a great law had been broken; and the result was a being whose elements were perhaps beautiful and brilliant, but all in disorder."

What is lacking in Pearl of course is the imposition of that transcendent ordering principle which man, through grace, imposes upon Nature. Lacking this, she seems to the Puritans a "demon offspring." Mr. Wilson, the most humane among them, asks her, "Art thou a Christian child, ha? Dost know thy catechism? Or art thou one of those naughty elfs or fairies, whom we thought to have left behind us, with other relics of Papistry, in merry old England?" Pearl is indeed an elf, a pre-Christian Nature-spirit in human form, whose soul must be made whole by submission to divinely ordered morality before it can be saved. Mistress Hibbins, the witch, is eager to attach Pearl to her legion, and tells her that her father is the Prince of the Air, just as she tells Dimmesdale to let her know when he goes again into the forest, for "My good word will go far towards gaining any strange gentleman a fair reception from yonder potentate you wot of." When Dimmesdale protests that he was only on his way to greet the Apostle Eliot,

> "Ha, ha, ha!" cackled the old witch-lady. . . . "Well, well, we must needs talk thus in the daytime! You carry it off like an old hand! But at midnight, and in the forest, we shall have other talk together!"

Dimmesdale, however, has not yet sold his soul to the devil, as had Young Goodman Brown—who was lawfully wedded at that. Dimmesdale's intuitive knowledge of the sin that sears all human hearts has made him more compassionate, not less so, and his sufferings result from his moral cowardice rather than from the presumptive sin of loving Hester. In the exposition of Dimmesdale's spiritual progress Mistress Hibbins plays a considerable role, though she remains a minor character. We find her present, for instance, on that midnight when Dimmesdale mounted the scaffold but could not bring himself publicly to confess his sin. He shrieks aloud, but no one awakes, or, if they did, "the drowsy slumberers mistook the cry either for something frightful in a dream, or for the noises of witches . . . as they rode with Satan through the air." Besides the family group (Hester, Pearl, and Chillingworth) there are but three observers of Dimmesdale's self-torment. One is Governor Bellingham, who comes to his window, startled by the cry. He is the surrogate of earthly power, the ranking representative of civil government. Dimmesdale could confess to him, but he does not do so. A second observer appears at the window of the same house— Mistress Hibbins, who is Governor Bellingham's sister. In historical fact one Mrs. Ann Hibbins, "widow of one of the foremost

men in Boston and said to have been a sister of Governor Bellingham," was executed for a witch in 1656. This account fitted Hawthorne's schematic purposes perfectly, to have the figurehead of
Earthly Power aligned by blood and residence with the Mistress of
Darkness. The third passerby is the Reverend Mr. Wilson, who
"came freshly from the death-chamber of Governor Winthrop."
Thus Dimmesdale's abortive confession is made at the moment of
the reception into Heaven of a Puritan saint. Wilson represents the
power of Heavenly succour. These are the three realms of power
in Puritan New England—civil, daimonic, and divine. Dimmesdale
is thus given opportunities to ally himself with each, and allay or
compound his guilt. But his isolation is so complete that none of
these links with man, the devil, or God, can comfort him.

I would suggest that Mistress Hibbins's role as a witch should be
taken as seriously in *The Scarlet Letter* as was the use of witchcraft in "Young Goodman Brown."[3] Indeed, she brings into the
moral universe of *The Scarlet Letter* all of the associations which
are so fully developed in the earlier story. Like Young Goodman
Brown, like Mr. Hooper,[4] like Dimmesdale himself, she, who has
experienced sin herself, has intuitive knowledge of the sinful nature
of her fellow-mortals:

> "Many a church-member saw I, walking behind the music, that
> has danced in the same measure with me, when Somebody was
> fiddler . . . But this minister! Couldst thou surely tell, Hester,
> whether he was the same man that encountered thee on the forest-
> path?"

Hester, startled, protests that she knows nothing of this. But
Mistress Hibbins takes the scarlet letter to be Hester's badge in her
own sorority of sin:

> "I know thee, Hester; for I behold the token. . . . But this minis-
> ter! Let me tell thee, in thine ear! When the Black Man sees one
> of his own servants, signed and sealed, so shy of owning to the
> bond as is the Reverend Mr. Dimmesdale, he hath a way of order-
> ing matters so that the mark shall be disclosed in open daylight to
> the eyes of all the world!"

Who could say that the demonic prophecy failed of fulfillment?

Mistress Hibbins had already set her cap for Hester's soul. Like a
good witch she is always on the look-out for acolytes, and so she had
whispered "Hist! . . . wilt thou go with us tonight? There will be a
merry company in the forest; and I well-nigh promised the Black

---

3. Witchcraft in this story (1835) is
taken seriously in the sense that the
Witches' Sabbath, which constitutes the
climactic part of the story and is the
cause of the main character's loss of
faith in mankind, is not presented as
mere seventeenth-century superstition,
but, rather, as an historically credible
image of human sinfulness. [*Editor*.]
4. Parson Hooper, the central figure in
"The Minister's Black Veil" (1836),
wears a veil over his face as a token
of human sin and sorrow. [*Editor*.]

Man that comely Hester Prynne should make one." What saved Hester from this temptation, if such it would otherwise have been to her, was Mr. Wilson's Christian charity in granting her custody of Pearl. "Had they taken her from me, I would willingly have gone with thee into the forest, and signed my name in the Black Man's book too, and that with mine own blood," says Hester. As long as Hester is responsible for Pearl—who represents both the emblem of her sin and, as grace, the possibility of her own redemption, she will be proof against the blandishments of the Black Man's coven.

The salvation of Pearl depends upon Dimmesdale. Until he acknowledges himself her father she can have no human patrimony, and must remain a Nature-spirit, untouched by the redemptive order that was broken in her conception. For Hawthorne, Nature is amoral but not malign. Witchcraft is not the forest's nature; it comes into being when man repudiates God and chooses Satan. The forest, having no moral will, can shelter either the spirit of the Maypole or the self-damned coven of the Prince of Air. Hence Pearl, like the Maypole mummers, is not yet damned, because unfallen; but, like them, she is not yet wholly human either. Dimmesdale's confession wrenches her first kiss for him from Pearl, and her first tears. "As her tears fell upon her father's cheek, they were the pledge that she would grow up amid human joy and sorrow, nor forever do battle with the world, but be a woman in it. Towards her mother, too, Pearl's errand as a messenger of anguish was all fulfilled."

If Mistress Hibbins be the devil's servant, the Prince of Darkness has yet a closer liegeman in *The Scarlet Letter*. From his first appearance Roger Chillingworth is described in demonic terms. He steps forth from the forest accompanied by a heathen sachem, and later avows that he has learned more of his medical arts from "a people well versed in the kindly properties of simples" than from the universities of Europe. Indeed, the townsfolk, who had at first welcomed him as Mr. Dimmesdale's companion and saviour, by the end of chapter IX have begun to suspect that his medicine was learned from those "powerful enchanters" skilled "in the black arts." And many persons of "sober sense and practical observation" note the change that has overtaken Chillingworth. "Now there was something ugly and evil in his face. . . . According to the vulgar idea, the fire in his laboratory had been brought from the lower regions, and was fed with infernal fuel; and so, as might be expected, his visage was getting sooty with smoke." Here again the superstition is offered half-mockingly; yet the image, which links Chillingworth with the base, demonic alter ego of the alchemist Aylmer in "The Birthmark"—a monster stained with soot—is indeed appropriate to Chillingworth; like Aylmer himself, Chillingworth too is guilty of an unforgivable sin of intellect, and much less forgivably so. Hawthorne goes on to aver that "it grew to be a widely diffused opinion, that the Reverend Arthur Dimmesdale, like many other personages of especial sanctity, in all ages of the Christian world, was haunted either by Satan himself, or Satan's emissary in the guise of old Roger Chillingworth. . . . The people looked, with an unshaken hope, to see the minister come forth out of the conflict, transfigured with the glory which he would unquestionably win." Public opinion is now unanimous in reading Chillingworth's role aright, but at the beginning of that chapter it had concurred in seeing his presence in its obscure community in a different light: it was believed "that Heaven had wrought an absolute miracle, by transporting an eminent Doctor of Physic, from a German university, bodily through the air, and setting him down at the door of Mr. Dimmesdale's study." At the doctor's suggestion, Dimmesdale's friends arrange for them to lodge in the same house. Not until much later do the people recognize that their German doctor may well be a Faust. Yet in the end it is popular rumor and fireside tradition which does see the truth about Chillingworth. The force of popular belief is stronger, in the end, than even the force of religious law which branded Hester, for she long outlives the censure with which her letter was to have forever marked her. The same people who reviled her at the scaffold live to seek her counsel in their own trials.

Hawthorne rather heavily underscores Chillingworth's demonism in the eleventh chapter, calling him "the Pitiless . . . the Unforgiving." There it is made plain that Dimmesdale's sufferings are purgatorial, but that those of his leech have no cessation in prospect since he has broken both the natural ties that bind and the natural barriers that separate men. Chillingworth's demonism is closely associated with his metamorphic power: indeed, he is the only character in this book who holds that power. From the beginning he appears in disguise, hiding his true name and his relationship to Hester, as he will later mask his vengeful hatred of Dimmesdale. Neither the minister, on his way toward repentance, nor Hester, on hers toward stoical resignation and reintegration with society, can avail themselves of such slippery tricks. Dimmesdale's seeming purity wracks him with inward torture, while Hester is bound by Chillingworth's will, not her own, to conceal his relationship to her. The lovers' desperate plan of escaping from New England to assume new identities among the anonymous multitudes of London is still-born, and not only because Roger would prevent it. Just as Hester realizes that she cannot flee, so is Dimmesdale drawn again and again to the scaffold, the scene of her public and his secret shame. They can struggle toward grace, they can know their own true identities, only in their own persons. And they are what their histories have made them be. * * *

ERNEST SANDEEN

The Scarlet Letter as a Love Story†

The Scarlet Letter has been interpreted as a story of sins and sinners for so long that this perspective has hardened into a convention. In Hester, Dimmesdale, and Pearl the sin of adultery and its consequences are seen; to Dimmesdale is added the further, less sympathetic sin of hypocrisy; and beyond the pale stands Chillingworth in his isolating sin of pride and self-consuming revenge. Once this standard point of view is assumed, it can be supported by what is incontrovertibly in the text, but if the angle of attention is shifted so that the novel is seen as a love story, that is, as a tragedy of the grand passion rather than as a tale of sinful passion, then certain features in our picture of the novel, obscure before, will leap into prominence and some of the previously more emphatic features will change their value in relation to the whole composition. Hawthorne's masterpiece may remain for us a haunted book, but it will be haunted by a mystery which we can identify as the mystery of erotic passion itself. It will be seen, in this perspective, that passion is the fixed reality throughout the novel and that it is "sin" which is the shifting, ambiguous term, as it is refracted in the many-sided ironies of the plot and of the narrative commentary. Further, from this point of view it becomes clear that the passion of the lovers is entering its most interesting phase when the story opens instead of being over and done with, except for its consequences, as is tacitly assumed in the conventional approach.

* * *

Hester Prynne can never honestly bring herself to regard her relations with Arthur Dimmesdale as "sinful." It is true that she submits to the harsh, life-long penance of the scarlet letter and suffers with patience the various agonies which it daily imposes on her. Because she knows what the letter means to the townspeople, she also feels the shame which was intended to be her punishment. But there is no reason to conclude that she regrets her passion. The narrator observes that her capacity to regard as sin the joy she took in fine needle work—work which "might have been a mode of expressing, and therefore soothing, the passion of her life"—"betokened . . . no genuine and steadfast repentance, but something . . . that might be deeply wrong, beneath." Again, after her second interview with her husband, Hester concludes quite simply that she hates

† From *PMLA*, 77 (1962), 425–35. Footnotes have been omitted.

him; he has wronged her more deeply than she ever wronged him. "But Hester," comments the narrator, "ought long ago to have done with this injustice. What did it betoken? Had seven long years, under the torture of the scarlet letter, inflicted so much of misery, and wrought out no repentance?" As she watches Chillingworth walk away, Hester wonders how she could have been persuaded to marry him. "She deemed it her crime most to be repented of, that she had ever endured, and reciprocated, the lukewarm grasp of his hand, and had suffered the smile of her lips and eyes to mingle and melt into his own." True passion, even though adulterous, may not be a sin to be repented of, but a loveless marriage is.

If Hester is willing to endure "the torture of the scarlet letter," it is because she is still in love, not because she is penitent. Her suffering is not the price she has agreed to pay for her guilt but the cost she is glad to bear for her love. Her apparent humility and patience conceal her inner subversion of the penance imposed upon her at the same time that they express her devotion to her lover. Intimations of her true feelings are provided from the first scaffold scene on, but in her meeting with Arthur in the forest her secret is fully revealed. Here it is confessed that Arthur is for her the man "once —nay, why should we not speak it?—still so passionately loved!"

When, a moment later, she has disclosed that Chillingworth is her husband, and Arthur has reacted as she feared he might, declaring that he cannot forgive her for her part in the conspiracy of silence, her passion breaks through the quiet, intimate decorum which they have preserved up to this point in their meeting. She clasps him desperately to her and simply demands his forgiveness. "All the world had frowned on her,—for seven long years had it frowned upon this lonely woman,—and still she bore it all . . . Heaven, likewise, had frowned upon her, and she had not died. But the frown of this pale, weak, sinful, and sorrow-stricken man was what Hester could not bear, and live!" It is the most moving passage in the book, a moment prepared for with careful dramatic calculation, in which Hester's life in all its tragic simplicity is illuminated.

Arthur, like Hester, can regard the guilt of the vengeful husband as greater than that of their adultery: Chillingworth has deliberately violated "the sanctity of a human heart," something which they never did. But Hester's vehement confirmation goes further: "Never, never! . . . What we did had a consecration of its own. We felt it so! We said so to each other!" Such an ardent belief in the self-sufficiency and self-justification of love shows the advantage Hester has over Arthur in their present crisis. For as soon as Arthur grants her the forgiveness she must have, Hester takes control of the situation, and Arthur, all at sea as to what should be done, readily submits. Tenderly but firmly, with a lover's calculation, she leads him step by step to consider and finally to accept her simple plan of their running away from this community of "iron men" to live together in Europe.

As the meeting in the forest flowers into a love scene, there is a disclosure of Hester's physical beauty which accompanies the revelation of her soul's secret. She casts the scarlet letter from her first; then she removes the cap which confines her hair, "and down it fell upon her shoulders, dark and rich, with at once a shadow and a light in its abundance, and imparting the charm of softness to her features." Her face is lighted with a new radiance which flushes her cheek, glows in her eyes and in her smile. Hester in this moment becomes, in effect, the very goddess of love who rules her life, just as the flood of sunshine which now pours into the forest is another outer manifestation of the same inner divinity. "Love, whether newly born, or aroused from a deathlike slumber, must always create a sunshine, filling the heart so full of radiance, that it overflows upon the outward world. Had the forest still kept its gloom, it would have been bright in Hester's eyes, and bright in Arthur Dimmesdale's!" Here the deep force which moves through the story is at last called by its proper name—not sin, not guilty passion, not shame, not hypocrisy, but "love."

Hester's transfiguration in this scene gives substance to a mysterious quality associated with her from the beginning, a quality which suggests that the role she plays has a generic, communal significance. Something of the commanding radiance of the goddess, fully revealed in the forest, is evoked in Hester's very first appearance. The description given of her as she steps through the prison door into the sunshine emphasizes her beauty and dignity of bearing, but what is brought out most forcefully by her statuesque yet elegant figure, her abundance of dark, glossy hair, her regular features and rich complexion, her "marked brow and deep black eyes," is an impression of great erotic power. It is this power which comes to a focus in the scarlet letter she is wearing. Through her skill in embroidery she has converted the shameful "A" into such an arresting work of art that it makes a mockery of the punitive intention of her judges. In short, her whole appearance—significantly resented by the matrons in the crowd—seems to glorify the very passion for which she is supposedly being exposed to public shame.

In the years that follow, Hester comes gradually to play a part in the community which expresses in sublimated form the love that she is prevented from expressing directly. But at the same time it is a part which stresses the representative character of her role in the novel. Necessarily, she finds her place in those neglected areas of communal life where impulses for good are called for which cannot be commanded by force, and where mercy, sympathy, and pity are more appropriate than justice or legislated goodness. She fashions clothes for the poor and even feeds them from her meager supply, although frequently the only thanks she gets is a jibe. In the more prosperous families, indeed in the best families, she comes to have a welcome and intimate place in times of pestilence, sickness, and death. "In such emergencies, Hester's nature showed itself warm and rich; a well-spring of human tenderness. . . ." As a lover she has been ostracized but as a "self-ordained Sister of Mercy" she is warmly accepted, although her works of charity spring from the same fertile depths of her being as the passion which has made her an outcast. She is the pariah that the human family takes to its heart in times of affliction; she bears the burden of man's affective nature, including outlawed passion, which the Puritan society is trying to suppress but which it cannot do without. Again, the capacity which her scarlet letter gives her to detect the presence of others, no matter how respectable or venerable, who are guilty of the same sinful passion as she, serves to emphasize her scapegoat role. Openly branded with the offense which many others share with her in secret, she purges the public conscience.

* * *

Seven years after its imposition there are many townspeople who read the scarlet letter as meaning "Able" or "Admirable" rather than the word it was originally intended to stand for. To the reader, however, who has the advantage of witnessing the lovers' meeting in the forest, another word occurs which the scarlet "A" might appropriately signify but which the pious citizens could not be expected to think of. That word is "Amor."

It has been observed again and again that Arthur Dimmesdale suffers more from the guilt of his hypocrisy than from the guilt of his passion, and it has been generally assumed that he is prevented from making a public confession by his weakness and lack of courage. Yet despite his physical frailty the impression he conveys throughout the novel is that of a man of exceptionally powerful character and personality.

If his sin were a matter of a single impulsive act which belonged to the past, it ought to have been over and done with. Hester states the case with uncanny precision in the course of their conversation in the forest. "You have deeply and sorely repented. Your sin is left behind you, in the days long past. Your present life is not less holy, in very truth, than it seems in people's eyes. Is there no reality in the penitence thus sealed and witnessed by good works?" If this is a lover's question on Hester's part, posed in the hope of a negative response, she is not disappointed. " 'No, Hester, no!' replied the clergyman. 'There is no substance in it! It is cold and dead, and can do nothing for me! Of penance I have had enough! Of penitence there has been none!' " What horrifies Arthur is not his feeling of guilt but his inability to feel the guilt which he believes he ought to feel.

He has prayed long and earnestly; he has subjected himself to fasts, vigils, and even flagellations. Why, then, has there been no repentance? The obvious explanation would seem to be that in some unacknowledged depth of his psyche he is still in love and can no more regret his passion than Hester can regret hers. If he is weak, it is only because he is, unlike Hester, obscurely but fatally at war with himself. Hester gives the impression of strength because of the complete self-knowledge and self-command she displays, but Arthur is presented, up to the last few chapters of the book, as a person the reader can know better than Arthur can know himself. The very orthodoxy of his mind prevents him from recognizing the heresy of passion in which he is entangled and which nullifies the remorse he tries so hard to suffer.

* * *

Arthur's night vigil on the scaffold is not altogether the hollow, ineffectual miming which it would seem to be at the time. It turns out to be a rehearsal for the final climactic scene in his life's drama in which he will act out the part of his conscience in the clear, public light of day. Before he can achieve this triumph, however, he must deal with the inner obstruction which blocks his way to repentance.

His opportunity comes during his meeting with Hester in the forest, but it is an opportunity disguised at first as utter despair. He must arrive, it seems, at the very end of his moral strength before his salvation can begin. Exhausted by his long, fruitless struggle with his conscience and horrified at the prospects opened up by what Hester has told him of Chillingworth, Arthur turns to her in a state of abject helplessness. "Think for me, Hester! Thou art strong. Resolve for me!" Again, a moment later, "Be thou strong for me! . . . Advise me what to do." As we have seen, Hester responds to his need, and with a tender but shrewd regard for his moral predicament she gradually leads him to her own bold solution of his difficulties—and of hers.

Clearly, Arthur is not a disciple of true love; he is not a typical initiate into the mysteries of the grand passion. Nevertheless he has been touched in some hidden recess of his soul with the divine—or, from his point of view—diabolical Eros. As was noted earlier, passion is the basic principle and purpose of Hester's life, and in her secret heart she wears the scarlet "A," not as a shameful badge of sin, but as a proud banner of love. She has scarcely more reverence for "whatever priests or legislators [have] established" than has "the wild Indian in his woods." Arthur, on the other hand, is sincerely and wholly dedicated to a social and religious code which condemns the passion joining him to Hester. He has never been able to assimilate this passion into the orthodoxy which forms his view of life and his image of himself, except as sin. His love for Hester continues to smolder in him on a submerged level where it effectually frustrates all his attempts to feel fully penitent, but it remains something not dreamt of in his philosophy. Whenever it flares up momentarily as it did that night when he, Pearl, and Hester stood with joined hands on the scaffold, he can only wonder at it. He feels it as a force which flows into him from outside, a "rush of new life, *other life than his own*" [italics added]; he cannot or will not recognize it as part of himself.

However, when he consents to escape with Hester to Europe he also consents, by implication, to make of their love a primary principle of life, as she has done from the first. He agrees to base his future, as she is willing to base hers, on the passion which has united them. In short, the clergyman becomes the lover. For the first time Arthur Dimmesdale has accepted his passion and made it his own.

Once he has assented to Hester's plan, Arthur feels an invigorating sense of relief and liberation. "His spirit rose, as it were, with a bound, and attained a nearer prospect of the sky, than throughout all the misery which had kept him grovelling on the earth. Of a deeply religious temperament, there was inevitably a tinge of the devotional in his mood." He is experiencing the joy of the convert to the Church of Love and he feels deeply grateful to the priestess who converted him. "O Hester, thou art my better angel! I seem to have flung myself—sick, sin-stained, and sorrow-blackened—down upon these forest-leaves, and to have risen up all made anew, and with new powers to glorify Him that hath been merciful! This is already the better life! Why did we not find it sooner?"

Arthur's backward glance and his confusing his new enthusiasm with his former worship of the Puritan Deity strike the ominous note of a possible relapse which Hester is quick to detect and to squelch, as well she might. "Let us not look back, . . . The past is gone! Wherefore should we linger upon it now? See! With this symbol, I undo it all, and make it as it had never been!" Whereupon Hester removes the scarlet letter and flings it from her. It is, as she has said, a symbolic act involving both of them, and it means that their passion has redeemed them from the law which would damn them. Here in the wildwood true love has cast off guilt.

On his way home from the forest Arthur continues to feel the transforming effects of his conversion. He moves along with an unwonted abundance of energy, but as he comes into the town and hurries through the streets, there appear "other evidences of a revolution in the sphere of [his] thought and feeling" which are more painful than exhilarating. They take the form of almost uncontrollable impulses to utter heresies, impieties, blasphemies, and impurities to the various people he meets. If he were to give way to these impulses, he feels "that it would be at once involuntary and intentional; in spite of himself, yet growing out of a profounder self than that which opposed the impulse." The two selves of Arthur Dimmesdale are now more nearly on equal terms than they have ever been before. The "profounder self"—the asocial, "natural," uncivilized self—has at last been released and his first inclination is to take revenge on the other, orthodox self who has kept him so long confined and submerged.

The narrator, with the solemn moralism which Hawthorne has made a part of his character, "explains" Dimmesdale's psychological state: "Tempted by a dream of happiness, he had yielded himself with deliberate choice, as he had never done before, to what he knew was deadly sin. And the infectious poison of that sin had been thus rapidly diffused throughout his moral system. It had stupefied all blessed impulses, and awakened into vivid life the whole brotherhood of bad ones." What is being emphasized under this pious pontificating is that Arthur has chosen something *which he has never chosen before*. For the first time in his life he has taken into account his "profounder self," the submerged affective self of desire, feeling, and passion.

As the sequel shows, the narrator's moralizing is Hawthorne's ironic *mock*-moralizing. The events which follow prove that the narrator's analysis is wrong, that the choice Arthur made in the forest has *not* stupefied all his good impulses and awakened all his bad ones. On the contrary, if he had never chosen to accept his passion as he did, he might well have died in his sins. To be sure, he has not, with this choice, achieved his moral redemption in one stroke, as Hester believes he has. But he has taken what will prove to have been the decisive and necessary first step.

Arriving home, Dimmesdale finds that in the intimacy of his study where he has spent so many hours of anguish his sense of having come from the forest a new man is, if anything, intensified; "he seemed to stand apart, and eye this former self with scornful, pitying, but half-envious curiosity. That self was gone! Another man had returned out of the forest; a wiser one; with a knowledge of hidden mysteries which the simplicity of the former never could have reached. A bitter kind of knowledge that!" Here, as before, Hawthorne is using his narrative voice to make an important observation at the same time that he distorts it with gloomy moralistic exaggeration. It is true that Arthur's new self, the self he chose in the forest, is now dominant but the disappearance of the old self is more apparent than real. For it is hardly "in character" for the newly liberated "self" alone, after flinging the already written pages of the Election sermon into the fire, to sit down to the task of writing a new one. Surely it is more accurate to say that the *two* selves of Arthur Dimmesdale sit down together. The minister, having finally accepted the lover, has found an ally where before he had found an enemy.

With the power of passion now working with him and not against him, he writes "with such an impulsive flow of thought and emotion, that he [fancies] himself inspired." A trace of his habitual scrupulosity lingers on as he wonders "that Heaven should see fit to transmit the grand and solemn music of its oracles through so foul an organ-pipe as he." But in a moment he has recklessly dismissed "that mystery to solve itself, or go unsolved forever . . ." Clergyman and lover work together in a fruitful, ecstatic harmony which speeds the night away. At sunrise there sits Dimmesdale "with the pen still between his fingers, and a vast, immeasurable. tract of written space behind him!"

* * *

In the moral dilemma which he represents Arthur Dimmesdale brings to a focus the conflict which runs through the novel between the demands of primitive nature and the demands of civilized society. He is implicated in the passion which makes him one with Hester but he is even more deeply implicated in the Puritan theocracy. His bad conscience causes him to believe his role as a leader in the affairs of the community is a hollow sham but actually it is less a deception than is Hester's apparently humble acceptance of the public will. For most of the story we see him in his associations with the town, but when he leaves the forest after his meeting with Hester, he has oscillated for the moment, in his conflicting double commitment, toward passion and the lawless wilderness.

In the climactic scene which has for its setting the Puritan Election Day, color images are used to heighten the contrast between the theocratic town and its primitive surroundings, the forest and the sea. Election Day may be a Puritan festival but it is the barbarian outsiders and not the citizens who furnish the festive hues. Highlighted against the soberly dressed crowd, for example, stand "a party of Indians—in their savage finery." But these are not "the wildest feature of the scene." This distinction is reserved for "some mariners,—a part of the crew of the vessel from the Spanish Main . . . rough-looking desperadoes" who violate with impunity "the rules of behavior . . . binding on all others," smoking tobacco in public, for instance, and imbibing from their pocket-flasks. All of them are colorful in their dress but their master is "by far the most showy and gallant figure" in the whole crowd, with "a profusion of ribbons on his garment," a sword at his side, gold lace and a gold chain on a hat which is topped with a feather. The symbolic relation of sailors to Red Men is specified; the mariners were "the swarthy-cheeked wild men of the ocean, as the Indians were of the land," for "the sea, in those old times, heaved, swelled, and foamed very much at its own will, . . . with hardly any attempts at regulation by human law."

Hester Prynne's attire embodies the contrast in color between the citizens' and the outlanders' dress. Her garment is of "coarse gray cloth" and "by some indescribable peculiarity in its fashion" has "the effect of making her fade personally out of sight and outline." At the same time, however, her "scarlet letter [brings] her back from this twilight indistinctness, and [reveals] her under the moral aspect of its own illumination." Her costume, that is, would serve as a camouflage causing her to blend deceptively into the crowd as if she were one of them, were it not that it fails to conceal the brilliant letter and, in fact, makes it stand out more prominently. The total impression is of a woman who is all scarlet letter. The garish "A" sets her off from the multitude and associates her allegorically with the Indians and Mariners, and with the same "wilderness" that they belong to. Dressed as always in the brilliant hues that make her a living projection of the scarlet letter, Pearl links Hester even more closely to the colorful outsiders. Darting here and there through the multitude, "she ran and looked the wild Indian in the face; and he grew conscious of a nature wilder than his own." The shipmaster, having failed to catch her and steal a kiss from her, flings her his gold chain which she "immediately twined . . . around her neck and waist, with such happy skill, that, once seen there, it became a part of her, and it was difficult to imagine her without it."

It is left to Arthur Dimmesdale to bring together the two antagonistic moral worlds represented by the color imagery: the somberly attired Puritan crowd, and those set apart from the crowd by their symbolically primitive gaudiness of dress—the Indians, the semi-piratical mariners, Hester, and Pearl. Yet no one could appear more completely partisan in his allegiance than Arthur does in the first part of the holiday scene. The appointed preacher of the Election Day sermon, he walks in the procession to the church with an unusually energetic step, and once in the pulpit he inspires his listeners as they have seldom if ever been inspired before. Speaking of the theme of God's relation to certain "communities of mankind" and especially to that of New England, he breaks into a visionary strain and predicts for these "newly gathered people of the Lord" a "high and glorious destiny." Afterward, his listeners declare that "never had man spoken in so wise, so high, and so holy a spirit" as the minister.

The heavy emphasis on this public image of Dimmesdale as the idealized Puritan Everyman who vindicates the whole theocratic idea is obviously intended to strike the reader as ironic. For the reader knows, as the people cannot, that the creative energy which produced the sermon and sustained Dimmesdale in the pulpit had its source in the lovers' meeting in the forest. To put it bluntly, the inspiration which breathed through the preacher's apologia for the Puritan system is simply, from the Puritan point of view, "outlawed passion." * * *

During the seven years between Hester's public humiliation and his meeting with her in the forest Arthur tries valiantly to give himself up entirely to his conscience as his loyalty to the theocracy would demand. But it proves impossible to be rid of his passion merely by running away from it and trying to ignore it. It is ever with him, frustrating his every attempt to arrive at the state of penitence his conscience requires. Then, in his private meeting with Hester, he resolves to try the opposite alternative; he will become wholly the lover and flee from all his obligations to the community. We can only speculate as to the consequences, had he and Hester been allowed to proceed with their plan to escape, but, in view of his character, it is unlikely that Arthur would have been any more successful in trying to run away from his conscience than he had been before in trying to run away from his passion.

Hester's dismay at Arthur's apparent withdrawal from their secret world when she sees him in the Election Day procession is well founded. She has believed that under her influence he has been converted to her own credo of love and thereby freed of his obligations as a man of God. But what she has done instead is to help him to reconcile the warring motivations in his soul. Through her the minister has been enabled to recognize and accept as the lover the self he had regarded before only as the sinner. Far from being destroyed in the process, the minister has found access to fresh inspiration and unsuspected energies which he has made use of in writing his sermon. Arthur has indeed become a new man but this new man is a synthesis of two selves, not a conversion from one self into the other. The new Arthur Dimmesdale has not at all shut Hester out of his world as she fears he has, but he has assumed a position of leadership in their relations. A dying man though he is, Arthur dominates the confession scene as Hester dominated the forest scene.

Arthur's near attainment of inner wholeness not only makes possible a public "confession," but makes it imperative. Conscience and passion both demand a hearing. If Arthur in the final scaffold scene confesses his adulterous passion as a sin, he also bears witness to it as a power. A sinner, he feels shame before his fellowman and fear before his God. But he also conveys a feeling which could be called spiritual pride if it were expressed by the sinner and not by the lover. When he bares his breast to reveal his own scarlet "A," he stands before the people "with a flush of triumph in his face, as one who, in the crisis of acutest pain, had won a victory." Even with his dying breath he thanks God for having granted him "this death of triumphant ignominy" before the people. We are reminded that Hester, in her ordeal on the scaffold, also managed to expose her guilt to the public gaze with an air of pride. * * *

Hester Prynne is scrupulously kept "in character" through the confession scene. Since her view of their love is the traditional one of all true lovers, in which the grand passion is its own excuse for being, she accedes to Arthur's resolution of their dilemma only with the greatest reluctance. She does not sympathize with him in his anxious concern about their social and religious obligations, nor does she share his elation at having reconciled passion and conscience. When he calls to her at the foot of the scaffold, she must intuit his intention at once, for she responds "slowly, as if impelled by inevitable fate, and against her strongest will." Later, when they have ascended the scaffold and his purpose is clear, he asks her, "Is not this better, . . . than what we dreamed of in the forest?" Her answer is confused but is characteristic of her romantic desire for simple escape. "I know not! I know not! . . . Better? Yea; so we may both die, and little Pearl die with us!"

Such a forthright expression of the "death wish" is typical among lovers who think and feel in the grand style. Arthur, however, makes it clear that such an ideal suicidal consummation is far from his thought, though he himself is about to die. "For thee and Pearl, be it as God shall order . . . and God is merciful! Let me now do the will which he hath made plain before my sight. For, Hester, I am a dying man."

Hester's last speech to her lover is also characteristic. " 'Shall we not meet again?' whispered she, bending her face down close to his. 'Shall we not spend our immortal life together? Surely, surely, we have ransomed one another, with all this woe!' " In her view, love like theirs earns its own way even in the life beyond the grave. We recall that in the forest meeting she had insisted, "What we did had a consecration of its own." But Arthur will not leave her with even this last consolation of the religion of love. He reminds her, instead, of the law they broke when they "violated [their] reverence each for the other's soul." As a consequence he fears it may be "vain to hope that we could meet hereafter, in an everlasting and pure union. God knows and He is merciful." Thus Arthur consigns Hester's immortal, as he has consigned her mortal, life to a merciful God, but not to the god of romantic love.

* * *

FREDERICK C. CREWS

The Ruined Wall†

"The golden sands that may sometimes be gathered (always, perhaps, if we know how to seek for them) along the dry bed of a torrent, adown which passion and feeling have foamed, and past away. It is good, therefore, in mature life, to trace back such torrents to their source."
—HAWTHORNE, *American Notebooks*

Hester Prynne and Arthur Dimmesdale, in the protective gloom of the forest surrounding Boston, have had their fateful reunion. While little Pearl, sent discreetly out of hearing range, has been romping about in her unrestrained way, the martyred lovers have unburdened themselves. Hester has revealed the identity of Chillingworth and has succeeded in winning Dimmesdale's forgiveness for her previous secrecy. Dimmesdale has explained the agony of his seven years' torment. Self-pity and compassion have led unexpectedly to a revival of desire; "what we did," as Hester boldly remembers, "had a consecration of its own," and Arthur Dimmesdale cannot deny it. In his state of helpless longing he allows himself to be swayed by Hester's insistence that the past can be forgotten, that deep in the wilderness or across the ocean, accompanied and sustained by Hester, he can free himself from the revengeful gaze of Roger Chillingworth.

Hester's argument is of course a superficial one; the ultimate source of Dimmesdale's anguish is not Chillingworth but his own remorse, and this cannot be left behind in Boston. The closing chapters of *The Scarlet Letter* demonstrate this clearly enough, but Hawthorne, with characteristic license, tells us at once that Hester is wrong. "And be the stern and sad truth spoken," he says, "that the breach which guilt has once made into the human soul is never, in this mortal state, repaired. It may be watched and guarded; so that the enemy shall not force his way again into the citadel, and might even, in his subsequent assaults, select some other avenue, in

† From *The Sins of the Fathers: Hawthorne's Psychological Themes* by Frederick C. Crews. (New York: Oxford University Press, 1966), pp. 136–53.

preference to that where he had formerly succeeded. But there is still the ruined wall, and, near it, the stealthy tread of the foe that would win over again his unforgotten triumph."

This metaphor is too striking to be passed over quickly. Like Melville's famous comparison of the unconscious mind to a subterranean captive king in Chapter XLI of *Moby-Dick*, it provides us with a theoretical understanding of behavior we might otherwise judge to be poorly motivated. Arthur Dimmesdale, like Ahab, is "gnawed within and scorched without, with the infixed, unrelenting fangs of some incurable idea," and Hawthorne's metaphor, inserted at a crucial moment in the plot, enables us to see the inner mechanism of Dimmesdale's torment.

At first, admittedly, we do not seem entitled to draw broad psychological conclusions from these few sentences. Indeed, we may even say that the metaphor reveals a fruitless confusion of terms. Does Hawthorne mean to describe the soul's precautions against the repetition of overt sin? Apparently not, since the "stealthy foe" is identified as *guilt* rather than as the forbidden urge to sin. But if the metaphor means what it says, how are we to reduce it to common sense? It is plainly inappropriate to see "guilt" as the original assailant of the citadel, for feelings of guilt arise only in *reaction against* condemned acts or thoughts. The metaphor would seem to be plausible only in different terms from those that Hawthorne selected.

We may resolve this confusion by appealing to Arthur Dimmesdale's literal situation. In committing adultery he has succumbed to an urge which, because of his ascetic beliefs, he has been unprepared to find in himself. Nor, given the high development of his conscience and the sincerity of his wish to be holy, could he have done otherwise than to have violently expelled and denied the sensual impulse, once gratified. It was at this point, we may say—the point at which one element of Dimmesdale's nature passed a sentence of exile on another—that the true psychological damage was done. The original foe of his tranquility *was* guilt, but guilt for this thoughtless surrender to passion. In this light we see that Hawthorne's metaphor has condensed two ideas that are intimately related. Dimmesdale's moral enemy is the forbidden impulse, while his psychological enemy is guilt; but there is no practical difference between the two, for they always appear together. We may understand Hawthorne's full meaning if we identify the potential invader of the citadel as a libidinal impulse, *now necessarily bearing a charge of guilt*.

This hypothesis helps us to understand the sophisticated view of Dimmesdale's psychology that Hawthorne's metaphor implies. Dimmesdale's conscience (the watchful guard) has been delegated to prevent repetition of the temptation's "unforgotten triumph." The deterrent weapon of conscience is its capacity to generate feelings of guilt, which are of course painful to the soul. Though the temptation retains all its strength (its demand for gratification), this is counterbalanced by its burden of guilt. To readmit the libidinal impulse through the guarded breach (to gratify it in the original way) would be to admit insupportable quantities of guilt. The soul thus keeps temptation at bay by meeting it with an equal and opposite force of condemnation.

But let us consider the most arresting feature of Hawthorne's metaphor. The banished impulse, thwarted in one direction, "might even, in his subsequent assaults, select some other avenue, in preference to that where he had formerly succeeded." Indeed, the logic of Hawthorne's figure seems to assure success to the temptation in finding another means of entrance, since conscience is massing all its defenses at the breach. This devious invasion would evidently be less gratifying than the direct one, for we are told that the stealthy foe would stay in readiness to attack the breach again. Some entry, nevertheless, is preferable to none, especially when it can be effectuated with a minimum resistance on the part of conscience. Hawthorne has set up a strong likelihood that the libidinal impulse will change or disguise its true object, slip past the guard of conscience with relative ease, and take up a secret dwelling in the soul.

In seeking to explain what Hawthorne means by this "other avenue" of invasion, we must bear in mind the double reference of his metaphor. It describes the soul's means of combating both sin and guilt—that is, both *gratification* of the guilty impulse and *consciousness* of it. For Dimmesdale the greatest torment is to acknowledge that his libidinous wishes are really his, and not a temptation from the Devil. His mental energy is directed, not simply to avoiding sin, but to expelling it from consciousness—in a word, to repressing it. The "other avenue" is the means his libido chooses, given the fact of repression, to gratify itself surreptitiously. In psychoanalytic terms this is the avenue of compromise that issues in a neurotic symptom.

Hawthorne's metaphor of the besieged citadel cuts beneath the theological and moral explanations in which Dimmesdale puts his faith, and shows us instead an inner world of unconscious compulsion. Guilt will continue to threaten the timid minister in spite of his resolution to escape it, and indeed (as the fusion of "temptation" and "guilt" in the metaphor implies) this resolution will only serve to upset the balance of power and enable guilt to conquer the soul once more. Hawthorne's metaphor demands that we see Dimmesdale not as a free mortal agent but as a victim of feelings he can neither understand nor control. And the point can be extended to include Chillingworth and even Hester, whose minds have been likewise altered by the consequences of the unforgotten act, the permanent breach in the wall. If, as Chillingworth asserts, the awful course of events has been "a dark necessity" from the beginning, it is not because Hawthorne believes in Calvinistic predestination or wants to imitate Greek tragedy, but because all three of the central characters have been ruled by motives inaccessible to their conscious will.

The implications we have drawn, perhaps over-subtly, from Hawthorne's metaphor begin to take on substance as we examine Arthur Dimmesdale in the forest scene. His nervousness, his mental exhaustion, and his compulsive gesture of placing his hand on his heart reveal a state that we would now call neurotic inhibition. His lack of energy for any of the outward demands of life indicates how all-absorbing is his internal trouble, and the stigma on his chest, though a rather crass piece of symbolism on Hawthorne's part, must also be interpreted psychosomatically. Nor can we avoid observing that Dimmesdale shows the neurotic's reluctance to give up his symptoms. How else can we account for his obtuseness in not having recognized Chillingworth's character? "I might have known it!" he murmurs when Hester forces the revelation upon him. "I did know it! Was not the secret told me in the natural recoil of my heart, at the first sight of him, and as often as I have seen him since? Why did I not understand?" The answer, hidden from Dimmesdale's surface reasoning, is that his relationship with Chillingworth, taken together with the change in mental economy that has accompanied it, has offered perverse satisfactions which he is even now powerless to renounce. Hester, whose will is relatively independent and strong, is the one who makes the decision to break with the past.

We can understand the nature of Dimmesdale's illness by defining the state of mind that has possessed him for seven years. It is of course his concealed act of adultery that lies at the bottom of his self-torment. But why does he lack the courage to make his humiliation public? Dimmesdale himself offers us the clue in a cry of agony: "Of penance I have had enough! Of penitence there has been none! Else, I should long ago have thrown off these garments of mock holiness, and have shown myself to mankind as they will see me at the judgment-seat." The plain meaning of this outburst is that Dimmesdale has never surmounted the libidinal urge that produced his sin. His "penance," including self-flagellation and the more refined torment of submitting to Chillingworth's influence, has failed to purify him because it has been unaccompanied by the feeling of penitence, the resolution to sin no more. Indeed, I submit, Dimmesdale's penance has incorporated and embodied the very urge it has been punishing. If, as he says, he has kept his garments of mock holiness *because* he has not repented, he must mean that in some way or another the forbidden impulse has found gratification in the existing circumstances, in the existing state of his soul. And this state is one of morbid remorse. The stealthy foe has re-entered the citadel through the avenue of remorse.

This conclusion may seem less paradoxical if we bear in mind a distinction between remorse and true repentance. In both states the sinful act is condemned morally, but in strict repentance the soul abandons the sin and turns to holier thoughts. Remorse of Dimmesdale's type, on the other hand, is attached to a continual re-enacting of the sin in fantasy and hence a continual renewal of the need for self-punishment. Roger Chillingworth, the psychoanalyst *manqué*, understands the process perfectly: "the fear, the remorse, the agony, the ineffectual repentance, the backward rush of sinful thoughts, expelled in vain!" As Hawthorne explains, Dimmesdale's cowardice is the "sister and closely linked companion" of his remorse.

Thus Dimmesdale is helpless to reform himself at this stage because the passional side of his nature has found an outlet, albeit a self-destructive one, in his present miserable situation. The original sexual desire has been granted recognition *on the condition of being punished*, and the punishment itself is a form of gratification. Not only the overt masochism of fasts, vigils, and self-scourging (the last of these makes him laugh, by the way), but also Dimmesdale's emaciation and weariness attest to the spending of his energy against himself. It is important to recognize that this is the same energy previously devoted to passion for Hester. We do not exaggerate the facts of the romance in saying that the question of Dimmesdale's fate, for all its religious decoration, amounts essentially to the question of what use is to be made of his libido.

We are now prepared to understand the choice that the poor minister faces when Hester holds out the idea of escape. It is not a choice between a totally unattractive life and a happy one (not even Dimmesdale could feel hesitation in that case), but rather a choice of satisfactions, of avenues into the citadel. The seemingly worthless alternative of continuing to admit the morally condemned impulse by the way of remorse has the advantage, appreciated by all neurotics, of preserving the status quo. Still, the other course naturally seems more attractive. If only repression can be weakened—and this is just the task of Hester's rhetoric about freedom—Dimmesdale can hope to return to the previous "breach" of adultery.

In reality, however, these alternatives offer no chance for happiness or even survival. The masochistic course leads straight to death, while the other, which Dimmesdale allows Hester to choose for him, is by now so foreign to his withered, guilt-ridden nature that it can never be put into effect. The resolution to sin will, instead, necessarily redouble the opposing force of conscience, which will be stronger in proportion to the overtness of the libidinal threat. As the concluding chapters of *The Scarlet Letter* prove, the only possible result of Dimmesdale's attempt to impose, in Hawthorne's phrase, "a total change of dynasty and moral code, in that interior kingdom" will be a counter-revolution so violent that it will slay Dimmesdale himself along with his upstart libido. We thus see that in the forest, while Hester is prating of escape renewal, and success, Arthur Dimmesdale unknowingly faces a choice of two paths to suicide.

Now, this psychological impasse is sufficient in itself to refute the most "liberal" critics of *The Scarlet Letter*—those who take Hester's proposal of escape as Hawthorne's own advice. However much we may admire Hester and prefer her boldness to Dimmesdale's self-pity, we cannot agree that she understands human nature very deeply. Her shame, despair, and solitude "had made her strong," says Hawthorne, "but taught her much amiss." What she principally ignores is the truth embodied in the metaphor of the ruined wall, that men are altered irreparably by their violations of conscience. Hester herself is only an apparent exception to this rule. She handles her guilt more successfully than Dimmesdale because, in the first place, her conscience is less highly developed than his; and secondly because, as he tells her, "Heaven hath granted thee an open ignominy, that thereby thou mayest work out an open triumph over the evil within thee, and the sorrow without." Those who believe that Hawthorne is an advocate of free love, that adultery has no ill effects on a "normal" nature like Hester's, have failed to observe that Hester, too, undergoes self-inflicted punishment. Though permitted to leave, she has remained in Boston not simply because she wants to be near Arthur Dimmesdale, but because this has been the scene of her humiliation. "Her sin, her ignominy, were the roots which she had struck into the soil," says Hawthorne. "The chain that bound her here was of iron links, and galling to her inmost soul, but never could be broken."

We need not dwell on this argument, for the liberal critics of *The Scarlet Letter* have been in retreat for many years. Their place has been taken by subtler readers who say that Hawthorne brings us from sin to redemption, from materialistic error to pure spiritual truth. The moral heart of the novel, in this view, is contained in Dimmesdale's Election Sermon, and Dimmesdale himself is pictured as Christ-like in his holy death. Hester, in comparison, degenerates spiritually after the first few chapters; the fact that her thoughts are still on earthly love while Dimmesdale is looking toward heaven is a serious mark against her.

This redemptive scheme, which rests on the uncriticized assumption that Hawthorne's point of view is identical with Dimmesdale's at the end, seems to me to misrepresent the "felt life" of *The Scarlet Letter* more drastically than the liberal reading. Both take for granted the erroneous belief that the novel consists essentially of the dramatization of a moral idea. The tale of human frailty and sorrow, as Hawthorne calls it in his opening chapter, is treated merely as the fictionalization of an article of faith. Hawthorne himself, we might repeat, did not share this ability of his critics to shrug off the psychological reality of his work. *The Scarlet Letter* is, he said, "positively a hell fired story, into which I found it almost impossible to throw any cheering light."

* * *

Dimmesdale's sexual energy has temporarily found a new alternative to its battle with repression—namely, sublimation. In sublimation, we are told, the libido is not repressed but redirected to aims that are acceptable to conscience. The writing of the Election Sermon is just such an aim, and readers who are familiar with psychoanalysis will not be puzzled to find that Dimmesdale has passed without hesitation from the greatest blasphemy to fervent religious rhetoric.

There is little doubt that Dimmesdale has somehow recovered his piety in the three days that intervene between the writing of the sermon and its delivery. Both Hester and Mistress Hibbins "find it hard to believe him the same man" who emerged from the forest. Though he is preoccupied with his imminent sermon as he marches past Hester, his energy seems greater than ever and his nervous mannerism is absent. We could say, if we liked, that at this point God's grace has already begun to sustain Dimmesdale, but there is nothing in Hawthorne's description to warrant a resort to supernatural explanations. It seems likely that Dimmesdale has by now felt the full weight of his conscience's case against adultery, has already determined to confess his previous sin publicly, and so is no longer suffering from repression. His libido is now free, not to attach itself to Hester, but to be sublimated into the passion of delivering his sermon and then expelled forever.

The ironies in Dimmesdale's situation as he leaves the church, having preached with magnificent power, are extremely subtle. His career, as Hawthorne tells us, has touched the proudest eminence that any clergyman could hope to attain, yet this eminence is due, among other things, to "a reputation of whitest sanctity." Furthermore, Hester has been silently tormented by an inquisitive mob while Dimmesdale has been preaching, and we feel the injustice of the contrast. And yet Dimmesdale has already made the choice that will render him worthy of the praise he is now receiving. If his public hypocrisy has not yet been dissolved, his hypocrisy with himself is over. It would be small-minded not to recognize that Dimmesdale has, after all, achieved a point of heroic independence—an independence not only of his fawning congregation but also of Hester, who frankly resents it. If the Christian reading of *The Scarlet Letter* judges Hester too roughly on theological grounds, it is at least correct in seeing that she lacks the detachment to appreciate Dimmesdale's final act of courage. While she remains on the steady level of her womanly affections, Dimmesdale, who has previously stooped below his ordinary manhood, is now ready to act with the exalted fervor of a saint.

All the moral ambiguity of *The Scarlet Letter* makes itself felt in Dimmesdale's moment of confession. We may truly say that no one has a total view of what is happening. The citizens of Boston, for whom it would be an irreverent thought to connect their minister with Hester, turn to various rationalizations to avoid comprehending the scene. Hester is bewildered, and Pearl feels only a generalized sense of grief. But what about Arthur Dimmesdale? Is he really on his way to heaven as he proclaims God's mercy in his dying words?

> "He hath proved his mercy, most of all, in my afflictions. By giving me this burning torture to bear upon my breast! By sending yonder dark and terrible old man, to keep the torture always at red-heat! By bringing me hither, to die this death of triumphant ignominy before the people! Had either of these agonies been wanting, I had been lost for ever! Praised be his name! His will be done! Farewell!"

This reasoning, which sounds so cruel to the ear of rational humanism, has the logic of Christian doctrine behind it; it rests on the paradox that a man must lose his life to save it. The question that the neo-orthodox interpreters of *The Scarlet Letter* invariably ignore, however, is whether Hawthorne has prepared us to understand this scene only in doctrinal terms. Has he abandoned his usual irony and lost himself in religious transport?

The question ultimately amounts to a matter of critical method: whether we are to take the action of *The Scarlet Letter* in natural or supernatural terms. Hawthorne offers us naturalistic explanations for everything that happens, and though he also puts forth opposite theories—Pearl is an elf-child, Mistress Hibbins is a witch, and so on—this mode of thinking is discredited by the simplicity of the people who employ it. We cannot conscientiously say that Chillingworth *is* a devil, for example, when Hawthorne takes such care to show us how his devilishness has proceeded from his physical

deformity, his sense of inferiority and impotence, his sexual jealousy, and his perverted craving for knowledge. Hawthorne carries
symbolism to the border of allegory but does not cross over. As for
Dimmesdale's retrospective idea that God's mercy has been responsible for the whole chain of events, we cannot absolutely deny that
this may be true; but we can remark that if it *is* true, Hawthorne
has vitiated his otherwise brilliant study of motivation.

Nothing in Dimmesdale's behavior on the scaffold is incongruous
with his psychology as we first examined it in the forest scene. We
merely find ourselves at the conclusion to the breakdown of repression that began there, and' which has necessarily brought about a
renewal of opposition to the forbidden impulses. Dimmesdale has
been heroic in choosing to eradicate his libidinal self with one
stroke, but his heroism follows a sound principle of mental economy. Further repression, which is the only other alternative for his
conscience-ridden nature, would only lead to a slower and more
painful death through masochistic remorse. Nor can we help but see
that his confession passes beyond a humble admission of sinfulness
and touches the pathological. His stigma has become the central
object in the universe: "God's eye beheld it! The angels were for
ever pointing at it! The Devil knew it well, and fretted it continually with the touch of his burning finger!" Dimmesdale is so
obsessed with his own guilt that he negates the Christian dogma of
original sin: "behold me here, the one sinner of the world!" This
strain of egoism in his "triumphant ignominy" does not subtract
from his courage, but it casts doubt on his theory that all the preceding action has been staged by God for the purpose of saving his
soul.

However much we may admire Dimmesdale's final asceticism,
there are no grounds for taking it as Hawthorne's moral ideal. The
last developments of plot in *The Scarlet Letter* approach the
"mythic level" which redemption-minded critics love to discover,
but the myth is wholly secular and worldly. Pearl, who has hitherto
been a "messenger of anguish" to her mother, is emotionally transformed as she kisses Dimmesdale on the scaffold. "A spell was
broken. The great scene of grief, in which the wild infant bore a
part, had developed all her sympathies; and as her tears fell upon
her father's cheek, they were the pledge that she would grow up
amid human joy and sorrow, nor for ever do battle with the world,
but be a woman in it." Thanks to Chillingworth's bequest—for
Chillingworth, too, finds that a spell is broken when Dimmesdale
confesses, and he is capable of at least one generous act before he
dies—Pearl is made "the richest heiress of her day, in the New
World." At last report she has become the wife of a European
nobleman and is living very happily across the sea. This grandiose

and perhaps slightly whimsical epilogue has one undeniable effect on the reader: it takes him as far as possible from the scene and spirit of Dimmesdale's farewell. Pearl's immense wealth, her noble title, her lavish and impractical gifts to Hester, and of course her successful escape from Boston all serve to disparage the Puritan sense of reality. From this distance we look back to Dimmesdale's egocentric confession, not as a moral example which Hawthorne would like us to follow, but as the last link in a chain of compulsion that has now been relaxed.

To counterbalance this impression we have the case of Hester, for whom the drama on the scaffold can never be completely over. After raising Pearl in a more generous atmosphere she voluntarily returns to Boston to resume, or rather to begin, her state of penitence. We must note, however, that this penitence seems to be devoid of theological content; Hester has returned because Boston and the scarlet letter offer her "a more real life" than she could find elsewhere, even with Pearl. This simply confirms Hawthorne's emphasis on the irrevocability of guilty acts. And though Hester is now selfless and humble, it is not because she believes in Christian submissiveness but because all passion has been spent. To the women who seek her help "in the continually recurring trials of wounded, wasted, wronged, mispaced, or erring and sinful passion," Hester does not disguise her conviction that women are pathetically misunderstood in her society. She assures her wretched friends that at some later period "a new truth would be revealed, in order to establish the whole relation between man and woman on a surer ground of mutual happiness." Hawthorne may or may not believe the prediction, but it has a retrospective importance in *The Scarlet Letter*. Hawthorne's characters originally acted in ignorance of passion's strength and persistence, and so they became its slaves.

"It is a curious subject of observation and inquiry," says Hawthorne at the end, "whether hatred and love be not the same thing at bottom. Each, in its utmost development, supposes a high degree of intimacy and heart-knowledge; each renders one individual dependent for the food of his affections and spiritual life upon another; each leaves the passionate lover, or the no less passionate hater, forlorn and desolate by the withdrawal of his object." These penetrating words remind us that the tragedy of *The Scarlet Letter* has chiefly sprung, not from Puritan society's imposition of false social ideals on the three main characters, but from their own inner world of frustrated desires. Hester, Dimmesdale, and Chillingworth have been ruled by feelings only half perceived, much less understood and regulated by consciousness; and these feelings, as Hawthorne's bold equation of love and hatred implies, successfully resist translation into terms of good and evil. Hawthorne does not leave us simply with the Sunday-school lesson that we should "be true,"

but with a tale of passion through which we glimpse the ruined wall
—the terrible certainty that, as Freud put it, the ego is not master
in its own house. It is this intuition that enables Hawthorne to
reach a tragic vision worthy of the name: to see to the bottom of
his created characters, to understand the inner necessity of everything they do, and thus to pity and forgive them in the very act of
laying bare their weaknesses.

CHARLES FEIDELSON, JR.

[The People of Boston]†

* * *

The book begins with a vignette of the people of Boston—a
single sentence set off in a paragraph by itself: "A throng of
bearded men, in sad-colored garments and gray, steeple-crowned
hats, intermixed with women, some wearing hoods, and others bareheaded, was assembled in front of a wodden edifice, the door of
which was heavily timbered with oak, and studded with iron
spikes." Just as Hawthorne gazes at the symbolic letter, seeking the
meaning in it, they stand "with their eyes intently fastened on the
iron-clamped oaken door," out of which Hester Prynne will come
with the letter on her bosom. In effect, the prison door is their
avenue to the meaning of the symbol; and these colorless men and
women, though they stand outside the prison, have all the demeanor
of prisoners. Any Utopian colony, Hawthorne declares, will soon
find it necessary "to allot a portion of the virgin soil as a cemetery,
and another portion as the site of a prison"; but these people
embrace the necessity. Though they are "founders of a new
colony," they have based it upon the oldest facts of human experience—crime and death. Though they would cultivate "human
virtue and happiness," they have no faith in any direct approach to
this end. The jail and its companion place, the burial ground, are
their proper meeting houses; the scaffold, situated "nearly beneath
the eaves of Boston's earliest church," is the center of the society.
Not once in the book is a church physically described or a scene
actually staged within it. Their true religious exercise is the contemplation of Hester, their scapegoat and counterpart, set up before
them on the scaffold. Even as they denounce her, they are fascinated by her as an emblem of the world they inhabit.

The ceremony in the market place is genuinely religious, not

† From *"The Scarlet Letter,"* in *Hawthorne Centenary Essays*, ed. Roy Harvey Pearce (Columbus: Ohio State University Press, 1964), pp. 31–77.

merely perverse, but it is oblique. The ministers do not urge Hester to seek divine support but only to suffer her punishment, repent her transgression, and name another sinner. If there were some "Papist among the crowd of Puritans," this woman taken in adultery might recall to his mind the contrasting "image of Divine Maternity." But the Puritans invoke no such image to relieve the horror before them; on the contrary, their faith positively depends on discovering a "taint of deepest sin in the most sacred quality of human life." They would honor a transcendent God who enters this world mainly as law-giver and executioner. His mercy appears through his justice, his love through his power. His incarnation is the impress of his abstract supernatural code, which primarily reveals the evils of flesh and the universality of sin. As administrators of the code, the ministers and magistrates on the balcony have no concrete human existence for themselves or others, and they have no perception of the concrete reality of Hester on the scaffold. "Sages of rigid aspect," standing in God's holy fire, they are blind to the "mesh of good and evil" before them. They see only the abstract Adulteress. As when Hester later views her image in Governor Bellingham's breastplate, she is "absolutely hidden behind" the "exaggerated and gigantic" abstraction that engrosses her accusers.

If they were merely self-righteous and sadistic, these Bostonians would be much less formidable. They are impressive because their doctrinaire moralism has a metaphysical basis: they purge their town in token of a universe where only God is really pure and only purity is of any account. Hawthorne does full justice to the moral seriousness, the strength of character, and the practical ability that their way of thinking could foster. He affirms that the Puritan society "accomplish[ed] so much, precisely because it imagined and hoped so little." And in various ways his Puritans, though eccentric, are old-fashioned folk, not radical innovators. In comparison with the "heartlessness" of a later era of sophisticated moral tolerance, the punishment inflicted on Hester, however cruel, is dignified by moral principle. In comparison with later democratic irreverence, the respectfulness and loyalty of the Massachusetts citizens to their leaders are still close to the feudal virtues. In comparison with their genteel descendants, the merciless harpies of the market place still have a moral as well as physical substance, "a boldness and rotundity," that derives from the old England they have put behind them.

But in all fundamental respects Hawthorne's Puritans are both problematic and unprecedented. They are men responding to an extreme intellectual predicament by extreme measures, and their predicament is one with their disseverance from the old world. The pompous forms and dress of their great public occasions, like the aristocratic menage of Governor Bellingham, are nostalgic and imitative, not characteristic. The old order vaguely survives in their consciousness because they stand at the beginning of a new epoch, but it survives much as memories of King James' court flit through the mind of the Reverened Mr. Wilson. It is true that Europe sometimes figures in the book as "newer" than the Puritan colony: the "other side of the Atlantic" is a place of intellectual and social emancipation, to which Dimmesdale and Hester might flee and to which Pearl betakes herself at the end. But Europe is a refuge because, whether old or new, feudal or modern, it signifies no struggle of consciousness, no necessity to reckon with the foundations of the new era. New England is the place where men must confront the founding questions of their time, which are set forth in the topography, the intellectual landscape, of *The Scarlet Letter*.

Above them stretches the heaven of supernatural revelation, where "any marked event, for good or evil," is prefigured in "awful hieroglyphics." The physical heavens are also spiritual, a medium of the divine word. But no civilized society was ever so directly in contact with brute nature. The settlement is encircled by the teeming "Western wilderness" on one side and the open sea on the other. Though the townsmen studiously abjure this "wild, heathen Nature . . . , never subjugated by human law, nor illumined by higher truth," it invades their prison-fortress. Savage Indians and even more savage sailors are a familiar sight in their streets. And physical nature is equivocal in relation to man. While it reduces him to "animal ferocity," it also sanctions "human nature," the life of feeling, and the virtues of the heart. The possibility of a humanistic naturalism lurks in the wild rosebush growing out of "the deep heart of Nature" beside the prison door. The possibility becomes actual in the person of Hester Prynne on the scaffold and later in her cottage on the outskirts of the town between the sea and the forest. What is more, Hester represents a positive individualism, alien to Puritan society but capable of creating a human community of its own. By her refusal to play out her appointed role on the scaffold, she becomes doubly an outcast from Boston; and yet, standing there in all her concrete individuality, she seems to claim a general truth, a concrete universality. She tacitly challenges the abstract city of their abstract God.

The challenge is momentous because she activates problems that their rationale is designed to anticipate and lay to rest. And similar questions rise to the surface, make themselves manifest, in ironic turns of the Puritan mind and behavior. Hawthorne persistently describes the spiritual abstraction of these people in terms of inanimate physical nature. The "rigid aspect" of the sages on the balcony corresponds to "the grim rigidity that petrifie[s] the bearded physiognomies" of the congregation in the market place. These are "iron men," as Hester later says; their creed is an "iron framework," aptly reflected in the "iron-clamped oaken door" on which their eyes are fixed and in the "contrivance of wood and iron," the pillory, that stands on the scaffold. It is as though their aspiration toward abstract supernatural truth has ironically brought them around to an abstract natural automatism, a world of law that is closer to the inorganic forms of stone, metal, and dead timber than to the mind of God. On the other hand, the ferocity of the women in the market place is as lawless and as natural as the lust they denounce, and it complements the rigid natural law that dominates their men. For all of them, "civilized life" consists of putting nature into prison; but the prison itself, the "black flower" of their town, partakes of the subhuman nature they contemn and obsessively scrutinize. The black flower blossoms apace, as Chillingworth observes. Meanwhile, natural affection, the red flower, lives on, unwanted and disclaimed, in the heart of Mr. Wilson and in the potential "heart of the multitude." Two voices of that heart, one of personal sympathy and one of faith in natural virtue, arise unaccountably amidst the chorus of reprobation. They are barely individualized, simply a young wife with a child and "a man in the crowd," but they testify to a community of individuals within this authoritarian society. The official "community" depends on a consensus of power and submission, a free election of individuals chosen to suppress individuality. But the scene in the market place, with elevated individual dignitaries opposed to a shapeless "throng" below, intimates a latent failure within the Puritan social system. The way is open for the "multitude" to gain shape through respect for its own multiple individuality. Puritanism contains and secretly invites its opposite, as it contained Anne Hutchinson from whose footsteps the wild rose bush may have sprung.

In this sense, the Puritans of *The Scarlet Letter* are deeply involved in the dialectic of modern freedom. They themselves are creatures of the early modern era with which Hawthorne explicity associates Hester—that moment when "the human intellect, newly emancipated, . . . [took] a more active and a wider range than for many centuries before." In Europe, "men of the sword [have] overthrown nobles and kings," and "men bolder than these [have] overthrown and rearranged . . . the whole system of ancient prejudice, wherewith was linked much of ancient principle." The mind of Hawthorne's Puritans is a negative version of this same libertarianism, which has cut loose the secular world from God, mankind from nature, and individual men from universal Man. In them, freedom appears as *deprivation*: a world removed from God and definable only in terms of that distance—a mankind at war with nature and able to create value out of it only by denying its intrinsic value, as God denies the value of man—and an individual alienated from humanity, who can rehabilitate himself only by self-annihilation before an external public law. In their prison-worship, the Puritans define modern liberty as a fearful freedom, and they make the most of fear, the terror of deprivation, in order to regain an idea of universal law, however abstract, unnatural, and inhuman. What dogs them, and confronts them in the person of Hester, is the other face of freedom—an affirmative individualism, humanism, and naturalism. The proscribed individual regenerates their society; they unwittingly are moved, for good and evil, by the nature they vilify; and a multiform, emergent divinity speaks in the forest or shows his features in Hester's elf-child.

By and large, in the course of the book, the Puritan version of the modern consciousness gives way to this positive version. Hester comes to dominate the landscape not only as a character in the eyes of the reader but also as an agent of transvaluation for her contemporaries. The natural affections of the "multitude," oriented toward her, escape from the abstract law of the ministers and magistrates. The final scene in the market place is very different in tonality from that of the first three chapters. There is variety, color, and movement in the picture; the darting figure of the antinomian Pearl weaves through the crowd. And yet we are reminded that "the blackest shade of Puritanism" still lies in the future and that its effect will linger on for two centuries. The populace gathered for this New England holiday are intent on the sign of sin and once more condemn Hester to "moral solitude." The climactic death of Dimmesdale in utter self-negation recalls the basic negativity of the Puritan vision which underlies the solemn procession of dignitaries and his own eloquent sermon on God's work in Massachusetts. For, given Hawthorne's historical method, he can have no intellectual right, and indeed no desire, to represent a complete and irreversible transformation of Puritan orthodoxy. It is the Puritan mind that proposes his subject, postulates the scarlet letter; he can move beyond this negative frame of reference only by keeping it in view. If the letter were not potentially more than a doom and a sign of doom, he could not turn back upon it and repossess it; but if it did not continue to have power to burn, he would not be trying to discover its meaning.

* * *

LEO B. LEVY

The Landscape Modes of *The Scarlet Letter*†

The impact of the traditions of the sublime and the picturesque upon American painting and literature of the Romantic period has been frequently examined, but the importance of these traditions in determining the structure and meaning of *The Scarlet Letter*, the chief literary masterpiece of the age, has been little noticed. Two

† From *Nineteenth-Century Fiction*, 23 (1969), 377–92. Footnotes have been renumbered.

critics, however, have noted the general principles which such a study must follow. Leo Marx observes that in Hawthorne's romance "landscape . . . is inseparable from policy and action and meaning. . . . [Hawthorne] turns the whole landscape into a metaphor";[1] and Edward H. Davidson, in an earlier discussion, characterizes this landscape as "a symbolic abbreviation which is capable of an infinite extension beyond the mere spatiotemporal limitations of characters in a scene; they are in it, but it is never permissively subservient to them."[2] As these critics imply, the symbolic character of *The Scarlet Letter* originates in the analogical relationship between landscape style, the emotions of the characters, and the emergent themes of the work. The functions of landscape, however, and the way in which Hawthorne transcends landscape through an extension of the principles by which he visualizes it, can be described only by an analysis of the conventions that give his work its moral and aesthetic organization.

The compositional mode of the picturesque, with its interplay of light and shadow, uncertain brightness, and obscurely visualized outlines, determines the graphic form of the forest background against which Hester Prynne and Arthur Dimmesdale meet after their seven-year separation. The dimness, mystery, and pervasive gloom of this setting is in effect an evaluation of the plight of the lovers. In search of the minister, Hester and Pearl follow a footpath into a wilderness whose primeval qualities are free of any implication of the Edenic. As Dimmesdale passes by, Hester is standing in shadows; when she calls to him, "he indistinctly beheld a form under the trees, clad in garments so sombre, and so little relieved from the gray twilight into which the clouded sky and the heavy foliage had darkened the noontide, that he knew not whether it were a woman or a shadow." The practice of the Hudson River painters of representing human figures diminished or scarcely identifiable in a surrounding wilderness is paralleled here, but Hawthorne's motive is in part the psychological one of exhibiting the haunted state which causes the sight of Hester to resemble "a spectre that had stolen out from among [Dimmesdale's] thoughts." This union of psychic and pictorial intentions dominates the whole episode (Chap. XVI through part of XX) in its representation of flickering light and shadow emanating from a vast forest and reflecting every nuance of thought and mood of the characters.

Hawthorne tells us that the wilderness is unredeemed, lawless, and pagan—the place to which Mistress Hibbins retreats for her convocations with the Black Man—but this conception, essential in dramatizing the Puritan dread of man's sinfulness, is an abstraction

1. "Foreword," *The Scarlet Letter* (Signet ed.: New York, 1959), pp. viii, ix. 2. "Hawthorne and the Pathetic Fallacy," *JEGP*, 54 (1955), 493.

less forceful than the picturesque imagery which creates the actuality of the forest. The dominant visual impression is one of antiquity: as the lovers talk, they sit on "the mossy trunk of the fallen tree" where Hester and Pearl had waited, and where the moss "at some epoch of the preceding century, had been a gigantic pine, with its roots and trunk in the darksome shade, and its head aloft in the upper atmosphere." This setting, with a brook in the midst, a leaf-strewn bank on either side, and trees impending over it whose fallen branches have choked the current, fixes an impression of time inexorable in its action, ever tending toward decay and death. The impulses that stir the reunited lovers are in effect abrogated; the pathos of Hester's cry to the minister, "Begin all anew!" derives from this oppressive environment. Even as Hawthorne declares that Hester's womanhood "came back from what men call the irrevocable past," the logic of his landscape suggests that the past cannot be called back; his heroine fails to impart to her lover her own courage and boldness.

Landscape is also an index to the shifting and uncertain feelings of the minister as he walks back to the Puritan village; picturesque images project a condition resembling hallucination. He glances backward, "half expecting that he should discover only some faintly traced features or outline of the mother and the child, slowly fading into the twilight of the woods." He fears that what he sees may be illusory rather than real, but it is only what he saw at the beginning: "Hester, clad in her gray robe, still standing beside the tree-trunk, which some blast had overthrown a long antiquity ago. . . ." The "indistinctness and duplicity of impression" that perplexes him increases as he approaches the town: familiar objects are now strange (as they were in the meteor light of the scaffold scene in "The Minister's Vigil") and "this importunately obtrusive sense of change" overwhelms him. The ambiguity of objects cultivated in picturesque painting becomes a visual derangement symptomatic of the compulsion that tempts Dimmesdale to whisper obscenities and blasphemies. A very different rendering of landscape visualizes the hopes which the meeting has encouraged in Hester. When she joyfully casts off the scarlet letter, the forest background is transformed into an harmonious expression of her liberating gesture:

> The stigma gone, Hester heaved a long, deep sigh, in which the burden of shame and anguish departed from her spirit. O exquisite relief! She had not known the weight, until she felt the freedom! By another impulse, she took off the formal cap that confined her hair; and down it fell upon her shoulders, dark and rich. . . . There played around her mouth, and beamed out of her eyes, a radiant and tender smile, that seemed gushing from the very heart of womanhood. . . . Her sex, her youth, and the whole

richness of her beauty, came back from what men call the irrevocable past, and clustered themselves, with her maiden hope, and a happiness before unknown, within the magic circle of this hour. . . .

Hawthorne's identification with the moment of Hester's release from her long ordeal seems so obvious that this passage has become the mainstay of most transcendental and romantic readings of *The Scarlet Letter*. Beginning with George B. Loring's critique in *The Massachusetts Quarterly Review* in September 1850, a succession of critics has declared that Hawthorne assents in Hester's eloquent assertion to Dimmesdale, "What we did had a consecration of its own. We felt it so!" The Freudian critics have appropriated this view by transposing it into the terms of unconscious conflict over the claims of a suppressed sexuality. The images which are the correlatives of Hawthorne's meaning, however, suggest that the element of transcendence, though genuine, is not all-embracing. Dimmesdale's tendency has been to allow the negatively envisaged landscape to absorb him into its being. Hester reverses this process, but in both instances landscape is the visible form of an emotional crisis. In the continuation of the above passage, the simplest kind of pathetic fallacy establishes a positive correspondence between Hester's feelings and sunlight, drawing upon images outside the range of a picturesque admixture of shadow and light;

All at once, as with a sudden smile of heaven, forth burst the sunshine, pouring a very flood into the obscure forest, gladdening each green leaf, transmuting the yellow fallen ones to gold, and gleaming adown the gray trunks of the solemn trees. The objects that had made a shadow hitherto, embodied the brightness now. The course of the little brook might be traced by its merry gleam afar into the wood's heart of mystery, which had become a mystery of joy.

When sunlight encloses both lovers, this pattern is affirmed in Hawthorne's observation that "love, whether newly born, or aroused from a deathlike slumber, must always create a sunshine, filling the heart so full of radiance, that it overflows upon the outward world." But images of brightness in the outward world of *The Scarlet Letter* are predominantly negative in force: the punitive action of sunlight defines the extremity of Hester's offense at the opening of the book as the beadle cries, "A blessing on the righteous colony of the Massachusetts, where iniquity is dragged out into the sunshine!" Hester is shown with "the hot midday sun burning down upon her face, and lighting up its shame." The sun glitters mercilessly upon the scarlet letter, and it pursues the errant Pearl everywhere; in the forest it follows her as she stands on the farther side of the brook, drawn to her by what Hawthorne calls "a certain sympathy"—

clearly of a kind different from that which expresses reawakened love. The use of light to represent lawlessness and shame and alternately love indicates the protean nature of Hawthorne's symbols; no single appearance of an image carries an implication of finality or ultimate intention. The value of the picturesque, however, is that it moves in the opposite direction: it offers a group of images related to one another by a common aesthetic tradition that in Hawthorne's usage is indicative of a specific range of feelings. By virtue of its selectivity, the picturesque structures meaning at the analogical level. The brightness that envelops Hester in her hour of freedom is antithetical to the picturesque, but the picturesque is restored in the fading sunshine and gray shadow that return when she again wears the letter. Sunlight, synonymous in the passage cited with beauty, warmth, and richness, is a transient alteration in the intensity of light in an otherwise picturesque setting. Even in this scene, an undercurrent of qualification may be present: sunlight gleams "adown the gray trunks of the solemn trees," but the grayness and solemnity are there, and though the leaves are turned to gold, yellowness—the sign of their decline—is also part of the image.

The conventionally picturesque treatment prevails in "the sportive sunlight—feebly sportive at best, in the predominant pensiveness of the day and scene. . . ." The dense black trees hemming in the road and the dell, the light reflected from the brook, soon lost "amid the bewilderment of tree-trunks and underbrush, and here and there a huge rock, covered over with gray lichens," are details of a picture that William Gilpin[3] and his followers would have understood and admired, and any one of them might have sketched a small thatched cottage resembling Hester's, fronted by "a clump of scrubby trees, such as alone grew on the peninsula, [which] did not so much conceal the cottage from view, as seem to denote that here was some object which would fain have been, or at least ought to be, concealed." Hawthorne knew the value of seclusion in a picturesque landscape, and of the irregularity of prospect evident in the tree-covered hills which the house faces. These graphic resources make tangible Hester's spiritual isolation from the Puritan community. Examples of this kind illustrate the extent of Hawthorne's familiarity with the requirements of a mode; they also illustrate his capacity for turning a tradition that began as a fashionable amusement to the purposes of serious art. He discovers in the picturesque a style which his moral and religious sensibility converts into a mode of the historical imagination, through which he dramatizes the relationship of Puritan New England to prior time and to his

3. An English writer on esthetics whose "Upon Prints" (1768) is credited with being the first attempt to establish precisely the various factors which make up the picturesque; Hawthorne knew some of his work. [*Editor.*]

own age. The remoteness from Puritan experience that Hawthorne and his contemporaries felt was very great; the picturesque was the lens that reduced that distance, bringing past and present into meaningful contact. At first glance it appears that this contact is conceived wholly in negative terms: the procession of dying generations evoked by "all the congregated sepulchres in the old churchyard of King's Chapel"—where Hawthorne's lovers are buried before the chapel is built—puts before the reader a controlling image of mortality from which the succeeding images of decay and ruin logically follow, and which collectively define the power that overcomes the human emotions and aspirations that oppose it. It is the collision of these forces that the picturesque dramatizes.

Governor Bellingham's house is a specimen of a kind "now moss-grown, crumbling to decay, and melancholy at heart"; it once glittered and sparkled, a "bright wonder of a house" before which little Pearl capered and danced. This juxtaposition of past and present, infused with nostalgia and regret, is the essence of the picturesque response to history. Hawthorne's paradox is that any present, if it is to be conscious of the past at all, must be aware of the past as a ruin, and hence skeptical of the promise of its own beginnings. All beginnings are invested with antiquity: in seventeenth-century Boston the promise of the new world is subverted by picturesque evidences of the old, visible in the weather-stained and worn appearance of the wooden jail, "some fifteen or twenty years after the settlement of the town. . . ." We are informed that "the rust on the ponderous iron-work of its oaken door looked more antique than anything else in the new world." The primary agency in this process is nature, which Hawthorne in accord with picturesque canons envisages in its terminating cycle of unending luxuriance fallen into organic decay. The encroaching grass-plot before the prison, "much over-grown with burdock, pig-weed, apple-peru, and such unsightly vegetation," shares its connotations of ugliness with the prison, symbol of the restraint with which man incarcerates the evil that is his own. The most enigmatic of Hawthorne's symbols, the wild rose-bush growing beside the prison door, seems to represent a withdrawal from the unrelieved despair of this view. Hester's beauty and freshness, and in some sense the natural impulses of the lovers, are undoubtedly symbolized in the rose, but meanings contrary to these are also present.

In commemorating the rose, Hawthorne combines the realistic and sentimental attitudes that enter into his portrait of Hester. The rose-bush is part of "the stern old wilderness" that it may have survived, "so long after the fall of the gigantic pines and oaks that originally overshadowed it." It is a lyrical protest against the recognition that in a ruined forest everything is levelled. In associating Hester and the rose with "the sainted Ann Hutchinson," the sentimental impulse to regard Hester as a martyr prevails; but twenty years before, Hawthorne had roundly condemned Mrs. Hutchinson in a sketch in which her portrait bears a strong resemblance to Hester. The lady stands before her examiners in an attitude of defiant pride similar to that of his heroine on the platform in the market-place.[4] Since Hester's wanderings in a maze of speculative and unorthodox thought are reported in the cautionary tone with which Mrs. Hutchinson's heresies are described, one is uncertain how to characterize the change in Hawthorne's attitudes, and unsure that there is not an ironical tinge in the application of the adjective "sainted." Many critics have noted the difficulty of finding the "sweet moral blossom" that Hawthorne says the rose may symbolize; and it is not easy to discover in what sense the rose may be said to "relieve the darkening close of a tale of human frailty and sorrow." The suspicion grows that Hawthorne is in effect paying tribute to impulses, and to an action, of which he cannot approve.

But Hawthorne does not go as far as those who understand the rose to be emblematic of Hester's struggle for a new life, and who see in Hester the embodiment of the American dream—of individualism, self-reliance, and the search for freedom. A more complex judgment is implicit in the picturesque imagery that places Hester's early life in relationship to her present situation. Under the strain of her three-hour agony on the scaffold of the pillory, she relieves the violence and madness that press upon her by conjuring up "a mass of imperfectly shaped and spectral images." She recalls her past in picturesque terms, remembering her paternal home as a "decayed house of gray stone, with a poverty-stricken aspect, but retaining a half-obliterated shield of arms over the portal, in token of antique gentility." These images, conforming to Hawthorne's way of picturing aristocratic settings fallen into decline, link the exhaustion of the old world to Hester's marriage: "memory's picture-gallery" evokes the Continental city "where a new life had awaited her, still in connection with the misshapen scholar; a new life, but feeding itself on time-worn materials, like a tuft of green moss on a crumbling wall." Hawthorne's echoing of the phrase, "a

4. "Mrs. Hutchinson" appeared in *The Salem Gazette* in 1830. The resemblances between Mrs. Hutchinson and Hester Prynne are striking. Like Hester's, "her hair, complexion, and eyes are dark" (*Hawthorne's Works*, Vol. XII, ed. G. P. Lathrop [Boston and New York, 1892] p. 220); she too stands "in the midst and in the centre of all eyes . . . loftily before her judges with a determined brow, and unknown to herself, there is a flash of carnal pride half hidden in her eye . . ." (224). Hawthorne castigates Mrs. Hutchinson as a danger to public safety; that she becomes "sainted" in the romance indicates only the necessity of conforming Hester's rebelliousness to a sympathetic view. That this drastic revision corresponded to a change in the views Hawthorne held at the time he wrote his sketch has not been demonstrated by any student of Hawthorne's thought. Hawthorne may have been influenced by Thomas Hooker's view that the casting out of Mrs. Hutchinson "would be 'forever marvellous in the eyes of all the saints' " (cited by Perry Miller, "Thomas Hooker and the Democracy of Connecticut," in *Errand into the Wilderness* [New York, 1964], p. 29).

new life," is something more than a verbal harmony. Since the materials of the new world in which Hester seeks another life are themselves "time-worn," this parallel suggests the futility of her search. We are already familiar with the consequences of her second beginning, and her plea to Dimmesdale in the forest is for the opportunity of a third. The rose and the moss state the argument that Hawthorne refrains from making altogether explicit—that the quest for a life free of the past rests upon a miscalculation of the nature of reality.

* * *

JOEL PORTE

The Dark Blossom of Romance†

* * *

It is not Hawthorne's purpose in *The Scarlet Letter* to assign blame, but rather to illustrate the process by which past pain and secret suffering flower into moral truth. For individual figures, that process is always analogous to the growth of consciousness in the romance artist.

In a remarkable insight underlying much of his work and clearly anticipating Freud's notions, not only of the sources of art in general, but more particularly of those dreams and fantasies which are the type of romance, Hawthorne suggests that there is a connection between "sin" (by which he means sexual knowledge and passion) and artistic understanding and power. In our sexual past or present, Hawthorne seems to say, lies our artistic—indeed, our human—future. Of this proposition *The Scarlet Letter* is a continual illustration, as if the tale had been designed to symbolize the theory that lies behind it, both form *and* theme thus being "the romance."

Hester Prynne is clearly the type of the artist; and if her art is limited to needlework it is only because (as Hawthorne somewhat incredibly insists) "it was the art—then, as now, almost the only one within a woman's grasp." The main embodiment, of course, of Hester's "rich, voluptuous, Oriental characteristic,—a taste for the gorgeously beautiful," is that very scarlet letter, "so artistically done, and with so much fertility and gorgeous luxuriance of fancy," that becomes Hawthorne's "mystic symbol"—Hester's art of the needle turned art of the romance. Not only do Hawthorne's adjectives suggest that Hester's "voluptuousness" has issued in art; we are told explicitly that her needlework was "a mode of expressing, and there-

† From *The Romance in America* by Joel Porte (Middletown, Conn.: Wes-   leyan University Press, 1969), pp. 98–114. Footnotes have been renumbered.

fore soothing, the passion of her life." The letter itself, the talisman of art, "transfigured the wearer. . . . It had the effect of a spell, taking her out of the ordinary relations with humanity, and inclosing her in a sphere by herself." Thrown away in that moment in the forest when Hester attempts the impossible—to cast off the doom of being an artist and return to simple womanhood—the "mystic token" is described in terms suggestive of romance art itself: "some ill-fated wanderer might pick it up, and thenceforth be haunted by strange phantoms of guilt." By the end of Hester's life, the letter comes to be regarded with that "awe" and "reverence" ultimately due to the truth and power of art.

As a sinner Hester is set off from the rest of the world percisely as is the artist, and Hawthorne describes her in terms he often used for describing himself, confessionally or fictitiously:

> In all her intercourse with society . . . there was nothing that made her feel as if she belonged to it. Every gesture, every word, and even the silence of those with whom she came in contact, implied, and often expressed, that she was banished, and as much alone as if she inhabited another sphere, or communicated with the common nature by other organs and senses than the rest of human kind. She stood apart from mortal interests, yet close beside them.

The scarlet letter, symbol and embodiment of both her sin and her art, "endowed her with a new sense. . . . a sympathetic knowledge of the hidden sin in other hearts." The secret truth about venerable ministers and righteous magistrates, chaste matrons and virginal maidens, is known to Hester. And Hawthorne, leaning heavily on the archetypal associations of the dark lady's sexuality with intellect and ultimately with art, makes it clear that her sexual experiences have increased those speculative powers that are necessary for the true artist. To be sure, Hawthorne hints first at a theory of sublimation, insisting that it was *because* the normal expression of passion had for so long been denied her that she turned from feeling to thought, assuming "a freedom of speculation . . . which our forefathers, had they known of it, would have held to be a deadlier crime than that stigmatized by the scarlet letter." But Hester's two "crimes"—intellectual freedom and sexual experience—are necessarily stigmatized by the same symbol, as any New England forefather would have known, since Adam fell simultaneously into both sexual awareness and that burdensome knowledge which brought literature, as well as death, into the world.

Hawthorne finally makes manifest the vital connection between the initial release of Hester's sexuality and the subsequent flourishing of her artistic power and understanding. "The scarlet letter was her passport into regions where other women dared not tread." Hester's "lawless passion" has turned her into a kind of white Indian, and she becomes in Hawthorne's mind a focus for all those associations of knowledge with sexual power which we have already observed in Cooper's mythic red men and dark ladies:

> Her intellect and heart had their home, as it were, in desert places, where she roamed as freely as the wild Indian in his woods. For years past she had looked from this estranged point of view at human institutions, and whatever priests or legislators had established; criticizing all with hardly more reverence than the Indian would feel for the clerical band, the judicial robe, the pillory, the gallows, the fireside, or the church. The tendency of her fate and fortunes had been to set her free.

Like the Promethean[1] archetype of the artist, Hester uses her freedom to become the benefactor of mankind, through her offer of artistic skill and the sympathy and understanding of her "warm and rich" nature. Throughout, Hawthorne makes it plain that her "well-spring of human tenderness" is fed by the subterranean river of barely submerged sexual passion. Or, to return to our original figure, "her sin, her ignominy, were the roots which she had struck into the soil," and the valuable—if dark—fruit of that buried "evil" is *The Scarlet Letter*.

As a corollary to Hester's position, we should note that by metaphoric implication and symbolic suggestion Pearl—the object of great price purchased by her mother's sexuality—comes to stand for that romance art which has the truth of secret human passion as its basis. Plucked by her mother, as Pearl herself insists, from the wild-rose bush growing in front of the prison, the "little creature" is described by Hawthorne as "a lovely and immortal flower" which had sprung "out of the rank luxuriance of a guilty passion." Nevertheless—and Hawthorne here exposes his own ambivalent attitude toward the curious romance art he practices—she is also "an imp of evil, emblem and product of sin." As she grows, her mother watches her carefully, "ever dreading to detect some dark and wild peculiarity, that should correspond with the guiltiness to which she owed her being." But the romance rarely reflects directly the obscure emotions to which it owes its being; these are perhaps manifested only as that "spell of infinite variety" and "trait of passion, a certain depth of hue," characteristic of the art. Pearl is indeed *The Scarlet Letter* "endowed with life."

As Hawthorne protracts his description of the child, he seems to be commenting, to some extent consciously, on his own difficult art, observed from the viewpoint of that world of novelistic verisimilitude whose rules of decorum he was painfully aware of violating:

> Her nature appeared to possess depth . . . as well as variety; but . . . it lacked reference and adaptation to the world into which

---

1. Prometheus, in Greek mythology, stole fire from the gods and gave it to man. [*Editor*.]

she was born. The child could not be made amenable to rules. In giving her existence, a great law had been broken; and the result was a being, whose elements were perhaps beautiful and brilliant, but all in disorder; or with an order peculiar to themselves, amidst which the point of variety and arrangement was difficult or impossible to be discovered.

The point of suggesting that Hawthorne is here, at some level of awareness, talking about the art of romance is not to prove how cleverly he went about composing an aesthetic allegory under the guise of doing something else, but rather to instance once more how in writing *The Scarlet Letter* he was preoccupied generally with the very nature of his chosen fictional genre. That some such barely conscious process is operative throughout Hawthorne's treatment of Pearl seems clear enough (although to demonstrate this thoroughly it would be necessary to quote almost everything he says about the child). Speaking of Pearl in another context, Daniel Hoffman calls attention to one passage in particular:

> The spell of life went forth from her ever creative spirit, and communicated itself to a thousand objects, as a torch kindles a flame wherever it may be applied. The unlikeliest materials, a stick, a bunch of rags, a flower, were the puppets of Pearl's witchcraft, and, without undergoing any outward change, became spiritually adapted to whatever drama occupied the stage of her inner world

and observes that Hawthorne here writes of her in precisely the terms he uses to describe the romance imagination in "The Custom-House."[2] If Pearl has never seemed a convincing reality to readers and critics of Hawthorne's tale, it may simply be because she is essentially a complex symbolic representation of the sources and attributes of the romance itself[3]—an embodiment of that bond of sex and creativity linking the artist Hester and her lover, the would-be romancer Dimmesdale.

For the minister, too, has many of the characteristics of the kind of artist typified by Hester—his major limitation being a fear of exposing, even symbolically, that truth of the human heart which is the romancer's ultimate theme. Could he so expose his inner being, the minister would prove himself an exceptionally successful romancer. In Chapter XI ("The Interior of a Heart"), the first which is devoted entirely to Dimmesdale, Hawthorne compares him to his fellow divines—men of intellect and learning, "of a sturdier texture of mind than his, and endowed with a far greater share of shrewd

2. *Form and Fable in American Fiction* (New York, 1965), p. 180. Cf. Richard Chase, *The American Novel and Its Tradition* (New York, 1957), p. 78.
3. John E. Hart calls Pearl "the living symbol of both sin and art" ("*The Scarlet Letter:* One Hundred Years After," p. 392). Rudolph Von Abele sees Pearl "as a symbol of Hawthorne's own art-works, or rather as embodying his theory of art" (*The Death of the Artist*, p. 53).

hard, iron or granite understanding"—and to saintly fathers of great spiritual purity. What they lack, and what Dimmesdale has in tragic abundance, is artistic eloquence—"the Tongue of Flame," "not the power of speech in foreign and unknown languages, but that of addressing the whole human brotherhood in the heart's native language," the ability "to express the highest truths through the humblest medium of familiar words and images." This gift was "won . . . in great part, by his sorrows," for it was his burden of guilt "that gave him sympathies so intimate with the sinful brotherhood of mankind . . . that his heart vibrated in unison with theirs, and received their pain into itself, and sent its own throb of pain through a thousand other hearts, in gushes of sad, persuasive eloquence."

As with Hester, Dimmesdale's artistic power is based on sexual experience. And robed in the "black garments of the priesthood," turning his "pale face heavenward," he seems the living embodiment of that dark blossom of romance truth about the "pollution" in his secret soul that is struggling to express itself through his religious eloquence. (Much later, when Dimmesdale is finally about to unburden himself, Hawthorne's controlling metaphor returns in full force. On the way to writing his Election Sermon the minister is tempted to drop into the bosom of a virgin "fair and pure as a lily that had bloomed in Paradise . . . a germ of evil that would be sure to blossom darkly soon, and bear black fruit betimes.")

Alone in his chamber, sitting in "utter darkness" or with the light of a "glimmering lamp," Dimmesdale keeps secret vigils in which, "viewing his own face in a looking-glass," he "typified the constant introspection wherewith he tortured, but could not purify, himself." His glimpses into his own heart are still vague and obscure. Purification will come only when he manages to bring to clarity that vision which will embody the truth of his inner being. Dimmesdale is thus seen by Hawthorne as a romancer struggling to transform furtive emotions into glimpses of imaginative truth.[4] He is, we should notice, precisely in the position of the author in "The Custom-House," whose imagination had become "a tarnished mirror" which either "would not reflect, or only with miserable dimness," the "tribe of unrealities" that embody his art because he had sold his soul for Uncle Sam's gold. Freed from the Custom-House, Hawthorne would once again be able to sit in his "deserted parlour, lighted only by the glimmering coal-fire and the moon," and call up from within the "haunted verge" of the looking-glass those "strange things" that romance converts into truth.

---

4. "That Hawthorne had the artist in mind when he created Dimmesdale there is little doubt, especially if we recognize the parallel between the minister's situation and Hawthorne's own as he outlines it in 'The Custom House,'" observes Charles R. O'Donnell ("Hawthorne and Dimmesdale: The Quest for the Realm of Quiet," *Nineteenth-Century Fiction*, XIV [1960], 328–329).

The minister does in fact manage to scare up, both in the chamber and in the mirror, ghostlike images of the romance meaning that is eluding him. He sees "diabolic shapes" that grin and mock; then "his white-bearded father, with a saint-like frown, and his mother, turning her face away"; and finally "Hester Prynne, leading along little Pearl, in her scarlet garb, and pointing her forefinger, first, at the scarlet letter on her bosom, and then at the clergyman's own breast." Hester seems clearly to be offering herself as a paradigm for the minister's creative efforts, but at this point he can believe only in "the anguish in his inmost soul," not in the truth of his visions.

On just such a night and in such a mood, "walking in the shadow of a dream, as it were, and perhaps actually under the influence of a species of somnambulism," Dimmesdale does indeed act out—in effect, composes—just the kind of symbolic fantasy that goes by the name of romance. Forcing himself to mount the scaffold of his mistress's ignominy, he imagines the townspeople horror-stricken the next morning to discover him "half frozen to death, overwhelmed with shame, and standing where Hester Prynne had stood!" Before long Hester and Pearl arrive to help the minister perform his symbolic charade, which is lit by the eerie glow of a meteor that gives a singular "moral interpretation" to the scene through "the awfulness that is always imparted to familiar objects by an unaccustomed light." (The light, that is, of romance, for Hawthorne is again reminding us of "The Custom-House," where the "unusual" moonlight of romance is described as spiritualizing the familiar investing it "with a quality of strangeness and remoteness.") In this "light that is to reveal all secrets" the minister is also driven by his "long, intense, and secret pain" to paint an allegory of his secret on the firmament itself, turning the whole cosmos, with the fantastic imagination of the romancer, into "no more than a fitting page for his soul's history and fate." Soon the sinister Roger Chillingworth arrives to offer the minister a devil's definition of the work of the romance artist—"we dream in our waking moments, and walk in our sleep"—whereupon Dimmesdale seems to awake from his "ugly dream."

The culmination of Dimmesdale's apprenticeship in converting submerged sexual energy into imaginative expression is his composition and performance of his Election Sermon and the concomitant "Revelation of the Scarlet Letter."[5] And it is, of course, Hester who incites simultaneously his passion and his artistic impulse. "Begin all anew!" she exclaims headily, exhorting him to exchange guilt over the sexual past for present satisfaction and creative

5. The view I take of Dimmesdale here has been anticipated at many points by Frederick C. Crews in his brilliant chapter on *The Scarlet Letter* in *The Sins of the Fathers: Hawthorne's Psychological Themes* (New York, 1966), pp. 136–153.

energy. "Preach! Write! Act! Do any thing, save to lie down and die!" And to implement Dimmesdale's improved career as lover and artist, Hester releases her dark, luxuriant, abundant hair, whereupon "her sex, her youth, and the whole richness of her beauty, came back from what men call the irrevocable past." Dimmesdale returns to the village from his forest interview with Hester visibly excited, as Hawthorne tells us, with his hitherto repressed and still forbidden sexuality straining toward consciousness in odd ways. He thinks he is going mad as his erotic energy first displaces itself into an evil urge "to do some strange, wild, wicked thing or other, with a sense that it would be at once involuntary and intentional; in spite of himself, yet growing out of a profounder self than that which opposed the impulse."

Barely managing to suppress his impulse to whisper obscenities and blasphemies, the minister is aware that some internal change is taking place: "he had yielded himself with deliberate choice, as he had never done before, to what he knew was deadly sin. And the infectious poison of that sin had been thus rapidly diffused throughout his moral system." He now feels a true "sympathy and fellowship with wicked mortals and the world of perverted spirits" and is thus fully prepared for the role of artist. Reaching his study, he sees the unfinished Election Sermon on his desk and thinks with scorn and pity (and some slight envy: dark knowledge is a burden) of that relatively innocent self who had aspired to inspiration before: "Another man had returned out of the forest; a wiser one; with a knowledge of hidden mysteries which the simplicity of the former never could have reached." Now in full contact with his primitive self, Dimmesdale is ready to convert sexual guilt into imaginative power.[6] He eats "with ravenous appetite" the food he requests from a servant. Then:

> Flinging the already written pages of the Election Sermon into the fire, he forthwith began another, which he wrote with such an impulsive flow of thought and emotion, that he fancied himself inspired; and only wondered that Heaven should see fit to transmit the grand and solemn music of its oracles through so foul an organ-pipe as he.

But "leaving that mystery to solve itself, or go unsolved for ever, he drove his task onward, with earnest haste and ecstasy," finding in the morning in front of his "bedazzled eyes" a "vast, immeasurable tract of written space."

Hawthorne's attitude toward Dimmesdale's "inspiration" is noticeably dual, and we should not overlook his ironies. The "grand and solemn music" that is being transmitted through the foul

6. Concerning the composition of the Election Sermon, Ernest Sandeen writes: "Clergyman and lover work together in a fruitful, ecstatic harmony" ("*The Scarlet Letter* as a Love Story," *PMLA*, LXXVII [1962], 430).

organ-pipe of the minister's emotion is (no matter what Dimmesdale may delude himself into thinking) clearly not a heavenly oracle but the still, sad music of humanity. Guilty passion turns him into a romancer, not a religious prophet. The truth of Dimmesdale's achievement is exposed by the response of the artist Hester—at once his most appreciative audience, his best critic, and his only muse—to his performance. The power of romance art lies more in connotation than in denotation, and it is Dimmesdale's soul music, not his religious libretto, that signifies for Hester. His words are "indistinguishable," since the meaning resides in the plaintive undertone of his song:

> A loud or low expression of anguish,—the whisper, or the shriek, as it might be conceived, of suffering humanity, that touched a sensibility in every bosom! At times this deep strain of pathos was all that could be heard, and scarcely heard. . . . The complaint of a human heart, sorrow-laden, perchance guilty, telling its secret. . . . It was this profound and continual undertone that gave the clergyman his most appropriate power.

Romance art, we must remember, is oblique art, the true meaning often contradicting what apparently is being said. The prophetic message contained in Dimmesdale's sermon differed, we are told, from that of the Old Testament prophets because "whereas the Jewish seers had denounced judgments and ruin on their country, it was his mission to foretell a high and glorious destiny for the newly gathered people of the Lord." The minister's listeners can explain the "sad undertone of pathos" discernible in the sermon only by assuming that it signaled his approaching holy death. But Hester (and the reader) knows the truth: Dimmesdale's romance/sermon is really a song of human woe. Why, then, does the sermon's religious message seem to contradict its inner meaning? Herein lies Hawthorne's most telling irony. Dimmesdale's Election Sermon is not complete until he has performed the coda: the revelation of the scarlet letter and his final speech. What he actually—and incredibly—does in his last utterance is to apply the sermon's prophetic message of a high and glorious destiny for the people of New England to himself. Dimmesdale concludes his Election Sermon by claiming that he is one of the Elect! All of his "afflictions" (the "burning torture" on his breast, the "dark and terrible" old Chillingworth, his "death of triumphant ignominy") are signs of salvation: "Had either of these agonies been wanting, I had been lost for ever!" To say the least, Dimmesdale's reading of providential signs is curious: he is surely saved because he appears thoroughly damned. Why—we certainly are expected to ask—may not his suffering be the type of what, being indeed damned, he will undergo throughout eternity? Dimmesdale himself, in his moment of truth with Hester in the forest, had already said, "The judgment of God is on me. . . . I am irrevocably doomed"; and Hawthorne has echoed this judgment by calling the minister, when he returns to the village, a "lost and desperate man."[7]

The fantastic pride evinced by Dimmesdale's Election Sermon is the final sign of his utter damnation. Thus the *real* meaning of the minister's prophetic claims does not contradict at all the underlying tone of pathos. The romance truth conveyed through Dimmesdale's performance is the inevitable one: sin, suffering, and ineluctable human tragedy. And the "mystery" of why heaven should use the energy of dark passion to express religious truth has been solved—it does not. The truth of romance is a human one, and it is dark indeed.

* * *

JOHN CALDWELL STUBBS

The Scarlet Letter:
"A Tale of Human Frailty and Sorrow"†

* * *

As the romance begins, we are quickly made aware that the setting is not just a physical place, but also a moral landscape. We encounter an expanding series of opposing images. First our attention focuses on a prison door. It is dark, severe, and ugly. Hawthorne associates it with the civilized world that constructed it. It represents the harshness of society's laws. Beside it grows a wild rose

---

7. The question of Dimmesdale's salvation or damnation is hotly disputed. For a vigorous defense of the authenticity of Dimmesdale's regeneration, see Darrel Abel, "Hawthorne's Dimmesdale: Fugitive from Wrath," *Nineteenth-Century Fiction*, XI (1956), 81–105; also, Hugh N. Maclean, "Hawthorne's *Scarlet Letter*: 'The Dark Problem of This Life,'" *American Literature*, XXVII (1955), 12–24. Roy R. Male sees Dimmesdale's final performance as a kind of apotheosis (*Hawthorne's Tragic Vision*, pp. 115–117). Hyatt H. Waggoner speaks of Dimmesdale's "final act of courageous honesty" but points out that the possibility of his being saved is ambiguous (*Hawthorne: A Critical Study*, revised edition [Cambridge, Mass., 1963], pp. 149–150). Ernest Sandeen argues forcefully against Dimmesdale: the image "of Dimmesdale as the idealized Puritan Everyman who vindicates the whole theocratic idea is obviously intended to strike the reader as ironic. For the reader knows, as the people cannot, that

the creative energy which produced the sermon and sustained Dimmesdale in the pulpit had its source in the lovers' meeting in the forest. To put it bluntly, the inspiration which breathed through the preacher's apologia for the Puritan system is simply, from the Puritan point of view, 'outlawed passion' " (*"The Scarlet Letter* as a Love Story," p. 432). Edward H. Davidson also argues persuasively for Dimmesdale's damnation, both as a Puritan and as a nineteenth-century romantic, in "Dimmesdale's Fall," *New England Quarterly*, XXXVI (1963), 358–370. See, too, William H. Nolte, "Hawthorne's Dimmesdale: A Small Man Gone Wrong," *New England Quarterly*, XXXVIII (1965), 168–186; and cf. Crews, *The Sins of the Fathers*, pp. 149 ff.

† From *The Pursuit of Form: A Study of Hawthorne and the Romance* by John Caldwell Stubbs (Urbana: University of Illinois Press, 1970), pp. 81–102. Some footnotes have been omitted and the remainder renumbered.

bush, a representative of the unrestricted world of nature, in obvious contrast to the prison door. The rose bush is delicate and fragile. It seems to offer its beauty to the prisoner "in token that the deep heart of Nature could pity and be kind."

This contrasting set of images is developed in human terms in the next chapter. The Puritan women of "The Market-Place" are extensions of the prison. They are manlike in their aggressiveness and severity. One woman—called an "autumnal matron"—wants Hester branded on the forehead for her adultery, and another, described as "the ugliest as well as the most pitiless of the self-constituted judges," calls out, "This woman has brought shame upon us all, and ought to die. Is there no law for it?" In contrast to this grim chorus of matrons is the softly feminine young wife holding her child by the hand. She understands Hester's anguish and feels sympathy for her. "O, peace, neighbours, peace!" she whispers. "Do not let her hear you! Not a stitch in that embroidered letter, but she has felt it in her heart." We should note that the young wife stresses the word *heart*. We first encountered it in connection with the rose bush as a token of the "heart of nature." The heart will, of course, become a dominant image in the book when we see Dimmesdale continually covering his heart with his hand. For the moment, let it suffice to say that Hawthorne uses the heart as a metaphor in the standard nineteenth-century way as the seat of the emotions. The young wife opposed to the matrons illustrates the natural emotions as against severe social laws of behavior. But we cannot say the matrons represent the *head*, seat of reason in the standard dichotomy Hawthorne was fond of speculating on in his notebooks. The matrons in their pursuit of fulfilling the letter of the law go far beyond any sense of reasoned justice. They are as emotionally charged in their defense of the law as the young wife is in her sympathy.

In precisely this context are Hester and Chillingworth presented to us. They are part of the series of opposed images. Hester is almost literally an intensification of the young wife. She carries her child in her arms. The striking richness of her attire and her dark hair make her woman on the large scale. Hawthorne likens her to the madonna of Renaissance art. Her role as representative of unrestricted, natural emotions is made all the more clear by contrast with the beadle marching before her as an embodiment of "the whole dismal severity of the Puritan code of law." The role of the beadle is quickly subsumed by Chillingworth. Seeing himself as an aging husband who wronged Hester by bringing her to a loveless marriage, he can forgive her adultery as no more than a counterbalancing wrong. But he burns to make the escaped lover suffer. Here he becomes Hester's ultimate adversary. In his demoniacal drive, he embodies the severest aspects of the hard justice of the Puritans to which Hester stands irrevocably opposed.

The opening movement of *The Scarlet Letter*, then, unfolds in a series of contrasts that define the boundaries of opposition in the work. The series may be diagrammed for convenience this way:

ETHICAL AND MORAL CONFLICT

Prison (emblem of society's restrictive laws)	versus	*Rose Bush* (unrestricted nature)
Puritan Matrons (severe, manlike purveyors of society's laws)	versus	*Young Wife with Child* (feminine woman of natural, unrestricted emotion of sympathy)
Beadle (emblem of severity of society's laws)	versus	*Hester with Pearl* (woman guilty of sin of unrestricted emotion)
Chillingworth (severe purveyor of society's laws)	versus	*Hester* (woman guilty of sin of unrestricted emotion)

The conflict reduced to its simplest terms exists between the laws of behavior fundamental to an ordered, moral society and the ungoverned, natural emotions of the human heart. With the dark-visaged Chillingworth and the feminine, loving Hester representing the two forces, we see that Hawthorne confronts us with the conventional opposition of the black Puritan and the fair Puritan. Hawthorne even shares the bias of contemporary romancers, initially at least, in showing Puritan severity in the worst and Hester's loving nature in the best possible light (as for instance in her loyalty to Dimmesdale on the pillory). But Hester differs from her prototype. Visually she is dark rather than blond. Ethically she is guilty of a demonstrable social wrong. From the beginning the simple opposition suggests future complexities beyond the conventional. Similarly, the neatness of the dichotomy must be suspect, for as we have seen, the purveyors of the social law are not without their *emotion*, which might be termed *natural* and *unrestricted* as well as the young wife's and Hester's. Yet despite these objections, or warnings of future complications, it is the clear-cut extremities of the conflict that Hawthorne wants us to recognize at the outset of *The Scarlet Letter*. By means of the partial abstractions of the fair Puritan and the black Puritan, he establishes the limits of the dilemma he is going to treat. They define the area to be probed and call attention to the work's artifice. The conventional opposition launches Hawthorne.

Directly between the two forces stands Arthur Dimmesdale. He is the romance's most complex character, its most "real" character, for he encompasses in his personality both of the extremes Hester and

Chillingworth define.[1] He has participated in the unrestricted passion of Hester, and he has punished himself as severely as even Chillingworth could require. A certain psychological complexity is apparent in him from the first speech he makes to Hester on the scaffold. He commands her to name her lover, *if*, and *only if*, he implies, naming him will aid her salvation and bring peace to her soul. Since naming her lover can do no more than reduce Hester's period for wearing the letter, Dimmesdale is effectively asking her not to reveal him. As he continues his speech, however, he contradicts himself. Hester's silence can only tempt her lover to "add hypocrisy to sin," he reasons. Ironically, Hester has been the fortunate one. Heaven has marked her guilt with the child Pearl. Ought she to withhold the similar relief of identification from her lover, he asks. Now he is on the verge of asking her, truly, to do what he is too weak to do—reveal his sin. He wants to confess, and he does not want to confess. This is exactly his state of mind when he ascends the scaffold late at night and calls out neither long enough nor loud enough to be discovered, when he sermonizes on his imperfection, knowing his parishioners will not believe him, and when he allows Chillingworth to probe him with his cat-and-mouse tactics. Dimmesdale has committed what he and his society feel to be a sin of unrestricted emotion. The need to redeem himself weighs heavily on him. Public confession is the means he envisions.

That his confession needs to be public is a vexing problem.[2] It smacks of tawdry exhibitionism. Why can't Dimmesdale repent his moral sin to God in private and tacitly balance his social offense by good works, we might well ask. Of course, the most immediate answer must be that a public confession is irrevocable, whereas a private confession to God may be countermanded at will. Also, in psychological terms, public confession would be the most excruciating form of masochism open to Dimmesdale if we assume, as Frederick Crews suggests, that Dimmesdale has repressed his sexual drive and converted it through reaction formation to self-flagellation. Then, too, public confession would remove the stain of hypocrisy from Dimmesdale. All of these answers seem valid for Dimmesdale the man. But for Dimmesdale the character, in a world view ordered by

1. One of the amusing aspects of Hawthorne criticism is the way critics have fought over the notion of whose book *The Scarlet Letter* is, Hester's or Dimmesdale's. Indeed, most of the most recent articles are concerned with defending a camp. I would want to urge a return to a "relativistic" reading such as that undertaken by John C. Gerber, "Form and Content in *The Scarlet Letter*," *New England Quarterly*, XVII (March, 1944), 25–55, where we study the effect each has on

the other. While I consider Dimmesdale to be easily the most "complex" character in *The Scarlet Letter*, I do not necessarily call the book "his."
2. In particular, it vexes Edward Davidson, "Dimmesdale's Fall," *New England Quarterly*, XXXVI (September, 1963), 358–370, and William Nolte, "Hawthorne's Dimmesdale: A Small Man Gone Wrong," *New England Quarterly*, XXXVIII (June, 1965), 168–186, both of whom find the confession a kind of bribe for grace.

Hawthorne the artificer, we must go back to the fundamental idea of all of Hawthorne's fiction, the idea that the individual must affirm sympathetic ties with his fellow human beings, sin-stained though they may be. Public confession is for Dimmesdale an affirmation that he is one with his fellow mortals. * * *

The situation confronting Dimmesdale is treated by means of emblematic characters such as we saw established at the beginning of the book. Chillingworth continues to represent a severe purging force. His immediate effect on Dimmesdale is debilitating. Chillingworth keeps Dimmesdale alive only to prolong the tortuous game Chillingworth enjoys playing with the minister. Yet we need not be concerned with Chillingworth's motivation at the moment. Here we may consider him an externalized force in what is essentially Dimmesdale's own psychodrama. When Chillingworth is not present, we know from the bloody scourge that Dimmesdale himself plays Chillingworth's part. Indeed, it is easy to imagine Dimmesdale alone in the famous interrogation scene of "The Leech and His Patient" playing both the role of prosecutor and of defendant, presenting himself with the black roots from the dead man's heart, and putting Chillingworth's questions to himself in the hope that he can refute them. The ease with which Dimmesdale turns aside Chillingworth's first group of questions indicates that Dimmesdale has been over the questions before in his own mind. The scene is a dramatization of what Hawthorne calls Dimmesdale's "constant introspection wherewith he tortured, but could not purify, himself." Even Chillingworth's final thrust, which confounds Dimmesdale and ends the questioning at that point, is only an elaboration of Dimmesdale's plea on the scaffold to Hester to save him from hypocrisy. Chillingworth rejects Dimmesdale's claim that some men maintain the false appearance of innocence in order to have the opportunity to perform good works. "These men deceive themselves," answers Chillingworth. "They fear to take up the shame that rightfully belongs to them. Their love for man, their zeal for God's service,—these holy impulses may or may not coexist in their hearts with the evil inmates to which their guilt has unbarred the door, and which must needs propagate a hellish breed within them. But, if they seek to glorify God, let them not lift heavenward their unclean hands! If they would serve their fellow-men, let them do it by making manifest the power and reality of conscience, in constraining them to penitential self-abasement!" Chillingworth puts it nicely. Ironically, he almost brings Dimmesdale to the means for escaping his torture—public confession. But Chillingworth knows his man, in this instance. Dimmesdale is not able to confess yet, and so the torture may go on, draining Dimmesdale of his energy and his will to enter the human world. Chillingworth goads Dimmesdale toward destruction by playing on his self-loathing, his

horror at the base stains in himself. These Chillingwort˳
before him.

The life-giving aspects of Dimmesdale's sin are represe⟨
Pearl. Surely an unconvincing human character, she is, nevert˳
a very important and very complicated symbolic one. Literally s˳ ˳s
the result of Dimmesdale's sin. Hawthorne refers to her as the
"living hieroglyphic" of the sin. Dressed in scarlet, she is an embodiment of the letter A. For Dimmesdale to acknowledge her, of
course, is another way for Dimmesdale to confess his guilt. So on a
naturalistic level her very existence implies a means of escape from
Chillingworth's hold. (Indeed, Dimmesdale feared a hereditary
resemblance might give him away.) The biblical connotations of
her name—usually associated with purity attained through Christ or
baptism—and Hawthorne's phrase describing her as worthy of Eden
suggests that she stands for the human heart purified or the state of
grace. We do see her in this role at the brookside, when she stands
separated by the stream from Dimmesdale and wreathed in flowers,
almost a medieval icon for grace, a pearl maiden. But this is not her
most prominent role. Mainly she is a humanizing or life-giving force
for Dimmesdale. This role is best illustrated during the middle scaffold scene, when Dimmesdale partially claims her by taking her
hand and being joined by her to Hester during the night. "The
minister felt for the child's other hand, and took it. The moment
that he did so, there came what seemed a tumultuous rush of new
life, other life than his own, pouring like a torrent into his heart,
and hurrying through all his veins, as if the mother and the child
were communicating their vital warmth to his half-torpid system.
The three formed an electric chain." Taking Pearl's hand is perhaps
an image contrasted to Dimmesdale's usual pose of covering his
heart with his hand. The vignette on the pillory is strikingly like
Hawthorne's usual representations of the human condition in its
emphasis on energy. Dimmesdale feels a tremendous inflow of
energy from this movement toward the release of confession. This is
the end which Pearl chiefly signifies. She represents the strength-giv-
ing powers of the human heart. Therefore, we may extend our original diagram to describe Dimmesdale's conflict in this way:

Chillingworth, *the Black Puritan* (severe restrictions on social conduct)	*Dimmesdale* (the sinner)	*Hester,* *the Fair Puritan* (unrestricted human emotions)
Chillingworth (debilitating force through loathing of unrestricted human emotions)	*Dimmesdale* (the sinner)	*Pearl* (life-giving force through affirmation of human emotions)

The second step above grows logically out of the first. In order for Dimmesdale to gain self-knowledge and an understanding of other men, he must recognize that he has human emotions. Then he may enter into a sympathetic understanding of his fellow men. To do this he must affirm Pearl. That done, he may feel the rush of energy of being part of a vital life force. But at the same time Dimmesdale knows and never doubts that he has committed a social and moral wrong. Therefore he wishes to purge himself of the tendency to sin. This is another way of saying that Dimmesdale is blocked in gaining self-knowledge because he loathes what he must affirm. Like Hamlet, he shrinks back from the contamination of the world in which he has to act.

As was the case with the opposing forces we found at the beginning, the roles of Chillingworth and Pearl overlap. The diagram should only serve to hold them apart momentarily. Pearl, for example, is in her own way just as torturing as Chillingworth. When the physician probes Dimmesdale with his questions in their lodging, Pearl comes to the window not to save Dimmesdale but to add her taunts. The cruelty of the daughter strongly affects Dimmesdale. In his dreams he is haunted by the figure of Pearl pointing her forefinger first at Hester's letter and then at Dimmesdale's own breast. The dream gesture is repeated twice more in the flow of real events.[3] On the scaffold at night, Pearl points to the dark form of Chillingworth watching the scene, and in the forest she points at her mother's breast, now stripped of the letter. In both instances she reminds Dimmesdale of the torturing aspect of the sin. Similarly, she heightens his agony by asking on the scaffold and in the forest when will he take her hand in front of the other people of Boston. We may say that these acts will eventually be regenerative for Dimmesdale since they push him toward realization of his flawed human condition. Yet if we say this of Pearl's role, must we not say it of Chillingworth's? Certainly Dimmesdale comes to feel before his death that the torture inflicted by Chillingworth has served ultimately a positive function in the design of Providence. He thanks God for an avenger to keep the torture "always at red-heat." The answer to our question must be *yes.* Chillingworth ultimately serves a positive function too.

* * *

At the beginning of the work, Dimmesdale wishes to deny the existence of sinful emotions in his heart. His act of adultery has

3. See Anne Marie McNamara, "The Character of Flame: The Function of Pearl," *American Literature*, XXVII (January, 1956), 537–553. McNamara makes this point and examines at length Pearl's role as goad to Dimmesdale. However, she goes too far when she claims Pearl is the "motivation" for Dimmesdale's confession. I would prefer to put it that Pearl symbolizes the positive force which drives him to confession.

shown him that they do, in fact, exist there, but he wishes to see the adultery as an aberration he can rectify. He cannot confess publicly, or totally to himself, because he refuses to believe that the capacity to sin is fundamental to his human condition. Therefore he scourges himself and submits to Chillingworth's interrogations to purify himself. His refusal to accept the capacity to sin is directly contrary to Hawthorne's notion that the individual must see the world as it is in order to act in it. But the refusal has a nobility. It is founded on Dimmesdale's desperately held longing to rise to the highest level of human life, to move toward perfection, and to strive toward his God.

The true nature of his condition is revealed to him in the forest with Hester. After seven years of trying to purge himself of his longing for Hester, Dimmesdale encounters her alone and discovers that his emotion is exactly as it was. Now he is forced to admit to himself that such emotions are fundamental to his nature. No amount of penitence can drive them out. He recognizes his common mortality. The result is a flow of energy through his body, more intense and lasting than the energy he felt on the scaffold at night. Dimmesdale describes his feeling to Hester: "I seem to have flung myself—sick, sin-stained, and sorrow-blackened—down upon these forest-leaves, and to have risen up all made anew, and with new powers to glorify Him that hath been merciful! This is already the better life!" He feels a release from his self-torture in this new affirmation of the emotions of his heart.

But while such emotions may be freely indulged in the forest, the world of nature, they must be restricted and governed in the world of men. This Dimmesdale discovers during the six confrontations he has on his walk back to town. In the first five cases, he is tempted to follow his emotions, but recognizes a need to curb them. He is tempted to make blasphemous suggestions about the Last Supper to a deacon, destroy a lonely old woman's belief in an afterlife, make lecherous signs to a young virgin, tell dirty words to a group of children, and trade off-color jokes with a drunken sailor. Each emotion Dimmesdale finds either needlessly harmful to other human beings or degradingly self-indulgent. What he has done in affirming his emotions becomes clear when he meets Mistress Hibbins in the sixth confrontation. He has, in effect, given his soul momentarily to the Black Man of the Forest. That is, he has consigned himself to the pursuit of emotions that may often be evil. Importantly, Hawthorne puts this revelation mostly in ethical rather than moral terms. If Dimmesdale were to follow his emotions completely, he would, quite demonstrably, hurt other human beings.

Dimmesdale now enters his third phase. He admits the full range of his human heart and seeks to atone for its base aspects. The shift from his initial situation is subtle. By the end of the work, he rejects both of the extreme positions open to him at the start and moves toward a synthesis. First, he rejects the debilitating aspects of severe punishment by cutting off Chillingworth's attempts to question him after his return from the forest. In doing this Dimmesdale strikes the pose of synthesis, as Anne Marie McNamara has shown us, by standing with one hand on the Hebrew scriptures (severe justice) and the other on his heart (unrestricted emotion). Second, at some point between his return to the town and the delivery of his election sermon, he rejects Hester's plan to run off to follow their emotions completely. The intellectual pride of Dimmesdale, so obviously a negative aspect of Dimmesdale earlier, now saves him from a life of utter self-indulgence. With his new knowledge he can recognize his heart for what it is and enter the brotherhood of men; but he refuses to sink into a brutish indulgence of his heart; he still wishes to rise to the highest level of life and to lead his fellow men with him. This is pride in the best sense, for it is coupled with humble recognition of the evil of which he is capable.

Seen from this perspective, the final pillory scene is a moment of triumph for Dimmesdale. At the election sermon, Dimmesdale speaks out with the "tongue of flame" on the relationship between the human condition and the divine. Hawthorne describes the effect of his voice: "Like all other music, it breathed passion and pathos, and emotions high or tender, in a tongue native to the human heart, wherever educated." Dimmesdale can now speak fully in the heart's native tongue, because he recognizes the full range of his own heart. At the same time, however, he urges his audience not to despair of attaining the grace of God. The overriding effect of his sermon is the note of hope that comes from the "passion and pathos" in his voice. The confession that follows outside the meeting house is a dramatic re-enactment of the sermon. Dimmesdale confesses his sin and throws himself repentant before God with hope. His act is a message to the other sin-tainted mortals around him. His final moment is one of leadership. Here on the scaffold he claims Pearl and escapes Chillingworth's destruction.

The question of whether or not Dimmesdale has received grace cannot be answered. The answer lies beyond the scope of the book. All we can say is that he has done everything in his power to understand his human condition, to repent its base aspects, and to lead his fellow mortals well. By any human standards he has acquitted himself as nobly as possible, but divine grace is beyond his human comprehension. So when Hester asks if they will be together in an afterlife, he can give no definitive answer. He fears and he hopes. All we may see at the end of the work are the two separate graves with the single tombstone to answer our own wondering. What we may conclude positively about Dimmesdale is that he has brought himself to the point where grace may come to him, and this is the most positive statement we should expect from Hawthorne. Dimmesdale is as triumphant as a *human being* can be.

* * *

GABRIEL JOSIPOVICI

[Letter into Hieroglyph]†

* * *

The pattern of the book [is] clear. Seen from a Puritan standpoint Hester is guilty of a terrible sin and Pearl is the visible and living symbol of that sin. Seen from a 'natural' perspective Hester's adultery with the man she loves is normal, perhaps even laudable, and nature's approval of her action can be seen in the fruit of that union, a child completely untainted by the false code of the Puritans and thus able to fulfil all her natural instincts. The novel would then be the description of the psychological state of guilt, the tragedy of a woman who accepts the guilt others bestow upon her even though she herself has not really done anything to incur it. Yet this explanation, however attractive to our anti-Puritan age, does not seem able to account for enough in this mysterious book. Hester may be the central character, but both she and Pearl only function in relation to the two men, Dimmesdale the father and Chillingworth the husband. It is the conflict between these two which actually provides the force that propels the story forward and brings it to its end. Moreover there is clearly a connection between the revelation of Dimmesdale and the metamorphosis of Pearl into a sentient human being, as well as between that revelation and the ending of the book. Simply to substitute an interpretation of the book in terms of Natural/Unnatural in the place of the Puritan terms of Good/Evil is clearly not enough. It fails to account for its peculiarly elusive quality, the sense that there is always a meaning over and above what is said.

A clue may be provided by an episode that occupies a central place in the structure of the book though not in that of the narrative. This is the appearance in the sky of the mysterious sign, which is 'read' in such different ways by the different characters, and

† From *The World and the Book: A Study of Modern Fiction* by Gabriel Josipovici (Stanford, Calif.: Stanford University Press, 1971), pp. 155–78. Some footnotes have been omitted and the remainder renumbered.

whose significance is explained by the narrator in terms which should be familiar to us from similar discussions in earlier chapters:

> Nothing was more common, in those days, than to interpret all meteoric appearances, and other natural phenomena that occurred with less regularity than the rise and set of sun and moon, as so many revelations from a supernatural source. . . . The belief was a favourite one with our forefathers, as betokening that their infant commonwealth was under a celestial guardianship of peculiar intimacy and strictness. But what shall we say, when an individual discovers a revelation, addressed to himself alone, on the same vast sheet or record. In such a case it could only be the symptom of a highly disordered mental state, when a man, rendered morbidly self-contemplative by long, intense, and secret pain, had extended his egotism over the whole expanse of nature, until the firmament itself should appear no more than a fitting page for his soul's history and fate.

It can only be for this reason, says the narrator, that Dimmesdale 'read' the sign in the sky that night as showing forth a huge letter 'A'. To the citizens of Salem[1] what appeared was 'a great red letter in the sky—the letter A, which we interpret to stand for Angel', and which they connect with the passing into heaven of the angelic Governor Winthrop. A little later we are told that many people regarded Hester as a Sister of Mercy, and 'refused to interpret the scarlet A by its original signification. They said that it meant Abel, so strong was Hester Prynne, with a woman's strength.' It is even suggested that the letter on her breast is a sort of nun's cross, the sign of her good work in the town among the poor and the sick, and near the close of the book we learn of the Indians who have come out of the forest to look around the town and who 'fastened their snake-like eyes on Hester's bosom, conceiving, perhaps, that the wearer of this billiantly-embroidered badge must needs be a personage of high dignity among her people'. In other words the letter forms part of a conventional, not a natural, language, and how we read it depends on what assumptions we bring to it, what language-game we are playing. Our earlier discovery that the Puritan view of the world in terms of Good and Evil was only one way of looking at things, and did not correspond to reality should have warned us that our new description in terms of Natural/Unnatural was similarly relative. The different interpretations of the letter confirm us in this view. The letter is not branded by God into Hester's flesh, it is stuck on there by the community. Hester, in other words, is only an adulteress because she is named one by the community in which she lives. But it would be equally wrong to say that if she is not an adulteress than she *is* something else. Yet that is the natural response. If she is not this then what is she? we ask. And we come back to that ambiguity of which Winters so greatly disapproved. If Pearl is not an elf-child then what is she? Why does Hawthorne stall in this way? Why won't he tell us straight out?

The really surprising thing is not the nature of the ambiguity, but the fact of it. We don't usually feel the need to ask such questions of characters in novels—as Winters correctly intuited. Novelists usually tell us what a character is 'really' like when they first introduce him, and if they keep the answer back for a while then this too is part of the plot and we wait eagerly for the answer to come. But, as Proust noted, we cannot do this kind of thing in ordinary life. We don't ever know who or what people 'really' are. Are they 'really' anything? Proust's novel suggests that the question is meaningless as such, that it is wrongly phrased. What Hawthorne's novel suggests is that to ask a question like that in the expectation of an answer, or to give an answer and imagine it to be the 'truth', is to act like Hester's Puritan accusers. We take it as perfectly natural for a novelist to tell us that X is a thief, Y an adulteress, and Z a middle-aged man whose wife has deserted him. We are so used to the convention that we don't think about it. But if we transfer the situation from the book to life we see at once what it implies. It implies that there is an essence in a person which can be labelled, defined, spelt out. But can we really say of any of our friends that they *are* this or that and imagine that this tells us what is essential to them? Can we say it of ourselves?

One of the central features of the seventeenth-century intellectual revolution which we briefly examined in the last chapter was a desire to get to the *truth* of things combined with a desire to remove the troublesome factor of *persons* from the field of inquiry. Just as language came to be seen in essentialist terms, as secreting meaning inside individual words, so people came to be seen in terms of discoverable motives revealing essences. 'There can be no power, short of Divine Mercy, to disclose whether by uttered word, or by type or emblem, the secrets that may be buried in the human heart', writes the narrator in *The Scarlet Letter*, but Chillingworth, the leech, as the old doctor is punningly called, knows nothing of divine mercy yet will not rest until he has uncovered Dimmesdale's secret. Like the new scientist forcing nature to yield up her secrets or like the Puritans creating the genre of the autobiography in their efforts to find out what it is they really are, Chillingworth sets to work on Hester's lover. But it is not really that he wants to find out what he does not know; rather he knows that Dimmesdale is the father of Hester's child but wants the man himself to confess it to him. Why? Why this need to hear the other *say* what he already knows? And why, once the other has spoken, is he free and does he die? To find the answers to these questions is finally to understand the book.

The moment Chillingworth sets eyes on the priest he seems to grasp his secret, and, although the other is unaware of it, from that moment he begins to work on him. But he sees this work as no more than a way of helping nature with her task, for, as he says to Hester:

> By thy first step awry, thou didst plant the germ of evil; but since that moment it has all been a dark necessity. Ye that have wronged me are not sinful, save in a kind of typical illusion; neither am I fiend-like, who have snatched a fiend's office from his hands. It is our fate. Let the black flower blossom as it may!

Note the way Chillingworth demythologises Puritan theology: You are not objectively sinful, he says, and I am not the devil, but your sin led to your guilt and to you my role is that of the devil, even as your sense of guilt is proof enough of your real guilt. We saw earlier that it was possible to make better sense of Hawthorne in psychological than in theological terms. Now we see that Puritanism itself conceives theology in psychological terms: demythologising is a Protestant, not a Catholic pursuit. The only difference between Chillingworth's view of Hester and that of the critic who holds that she is not really sinful but only obsessed by guilt at what she has done, lies in the interpretation of the word 'really'. It would be self-evident to a Calvinist that if someone *feels* guilty then he must *be* guilty; there is, after all, no other information to go on apart from our feelings. And as for the Freudian critic, he would no doubt agree with the linking of imagining and being, though he would feel no need to bring God into it. But the main point of the passage, and the one I wish to stress here, is Chillingworth's sense of the inevitability of the whole action, given that first, decisive event. Hester, Dimmesdale and himself, he says, are only agents in an action which it lies beyond them to influence in any way. There is a dark necessity at work in all their lives, a compulsive logic which will carry them to their inevitable ends.

Chillingworth is almost right. There is a logic of compulsion at work here, but it *can* be broken, and it is. By acknowledging his guilt in public Dimmesdale escapes at last from the clutches of his enemy—as Chillingworth is the first to realise. When what had been secret, buried from the community, from the reader, and even, we feel, from Dimmesdale's own consciousness, is brought out into the light of day, is *verbalised*, Dimmesdale, for the first time since his original guilty act, is free. But this freedom, strangely, seems to go hand in hand with death, as though what had kept him alive so far was the very thing that caused his torment, his refusal to acknowledge his guilt. And this guilt, we can now see, is what drove the novel forward, gave it its necessary direction and impetus, for it to expire when what had been repressed at last comes out into the open. What is this relationship then between fiction and guilt, between Hawthorne, his characters, and the scarlet letter itself?

Pearl *is* what Dimmesdale would suppress—both literally and figuratively. She is the embodiment of the letter, the living sign of adultery. Yet she herself does not know what the letter is. 'What is the meaning of the scarlet letter?' she asks. 'Why does the Miniser hold his hand continually to his breast?' It is because she *is* the letter that she cannot know what it *means*; so that, at the very end, when she comes to understand what it means, she changes her nature completely:

> Pearl kissed [Dimmesdale's] lips. A spell was broken. The great scene of grief, in which the wild infant bore a part had developed all her sympathies; and as her tears fell upon her father's cheek, they were the pledge that she would grow up amid human joy and sorrow, nor forever do battle with the world, but be a woman in it. Towards her mother too, Pearl's errand as a messenger of anguish was fulfilled.

Thus there are really two deaths: the literal death of Dimmesdale and the spiritual death of the old Pearl, Pearl-as-letter. But the two are of course aspects of the same situation. Pearl is what Dimmesdale would suppress, the scarlet letter itself; but since she is there, alive, in front of him, he cannot do so and must eventually acknowledge her. When he does so, verbalising his unconscious thoughts, he is freed from his guilt, which means that he ceases to feel it. And we, the readers, understanding what has happened, also cease to experience. Meaning has been substituted for feeling. In the words of Thomas Hooker, the experience, once articulated, becomes history, becomes a map of sin, and we no longer feel its poison. Language is what frees us from the immediate present, it allows us to make sense of sheer occurrence, as the bard made sense of Odysseus' exploits. But this freedom involves a loss, symbolised here by the breaking of the spell and the death of a man.

Pearl, we have said, *is* the letter, and so not really human; her discovery of the meaning of the letter is the equivalent of Marcel's discovery of the fact that even his mother is not one with him. It turns her into an adult, free to make choices and forced to accept responsibility in the world. Dimmesdale tries to repress the letter and is forced compulsively towards his own destruction. When he has spoken he too is freed, but, because he was an adult and therefore always responsible for his decisions, that freedom is only the freedom to die in peace. As for Hester, she wears the letter on her bosom because, unlike her lover, she accepts the judgement of society while recognising its limited and conventional character.

Not even the forest can hide the letter, she says, only the ocean can swallow it—meaning that only death can remove it from its place on her bosom. But, because she accepts it, she is free of Chillingworth, who can do nothing to her which she has not already done to herself. Where Chillingworth and Dimmesdale are in agreement, accepting the same standards of right and wrong, true and false, Hester accepts the naturalness of her act. For her the letter is perhaps only a sign of her involvement in man's fallen condition, and by accepting its conventional non-natural character, she is able to transform it into the mark of Abel, a nun's cross, a sign of high worth.[2]

Chillingworth is of course one of Hawthorne's many scientist-figures. His task is to drag the secret out of nature, to turn the silence of the universe into human and meaningful discourse. In other words, to turn nature into allegory. Dimmesdale is what he works on, but Dimmesdale resists him. Out of this resistance art is born. For art exists in the moment between the silence of nature and the verbalisation of allegory. For the silence of nature could only be conveyed in a wholly natural language; a conventional language, the language of ordinary discourse, will inevitably fail to convey it. What is required then is a language which is both natural and conventional, which can both embody the experience and communicate it: the language of hieroglyphics. For the hieroglyph represents what it means, is that of which it is the sign. Unfortunately, for a language of genuine hieroglyphs to be possible the world itself would have to be absolutely meaningful. All that the writer who is concerned with truth can do, therefore, is to articulate the conditions for a hieroglyphic language, and this is what Hawthorne does in The Scarlet Letter.

The artist is both Chillingworth and Dimmesdale. Like the former, he wants to force nature to speak, but success in his enterprise is synonymous with failure, since meaning, as we have seen, destroys being. At the same time, like the latter, he will feel guilt at a primal fault but will not confess it; and, confessing it, will no longer feel the necessity to write. But what is the artist's primal fault? It is his decision to write, and to write this rather than that, his choice of one theme and one beginning, which rule out all the others. His initial action is unnatural, it is the cutting up of a seamless whole for the purposes of exploration. Like adultery, it is an unnatural action, the memory of which he wishes to suppress, but the fruit of which is there, like Pearl, in front of him. And once he acknowledges it there is nothing more to write, for the novel was built out of the suppression of its own origins: unlike Pearl it is

2. Compare the way Arthur, in Sir Gawain and the Green Knight, alters, by a public action, the symbolism of Gawain's green girdle: instead of the sign of Gawain's guilt it becomes the sign of his common humanity.

made up of words, and therefore can articulate the conflict and reveal the forces that led to its own composition.

Hawthorne, we can now see, is not primarily interested in either theology or abnormal psychology. He is interested in trying to convey the experience of the journey by means of a map of the journey, and he does this by dramatising the relations between them, between journey and map, world and book. Hawthorne is not like Dimmesdale or Chillingworth, or even like Pearl. His *book* is like Pearl, a living, irreducible symbol, but he himself is like Hester, who accepts her guilt because she recognises that all human beings are guilty—guilty, that is, of betraying 'life' to 'meaning' in order to make sense of experience. That is a condition of being human, and that is what Pearl herself experiences at the last.[3]

Hawthorne's book steers between the silence of Dimmesdale and the knowledge of Chillingworth, as does Pearl herself, but, accepting its original sin—that of existing at all, a book in the world—it wears its title as Hester does her badge. It can do this ultimately, only because it gains its full meaning by referring away from itself to its maker, its final significance lying in that implied relationship. For *The Scarlet Letter*, we must remember, is more than the story of Hester and her badge; it is also the story, related in the preface, of how Hawthorne himself came to settle on this subject. In the traditional novel a preface in which the author describes how he came to find the MS. which forms the main body of the work serves merely to give a spurious authenticity to what follows. In this book, however, what is found is not a MS. but the letter itself—a physical object. Hawthorne insists that the few sheets of writing that went with it only served as the basis for his imaginative reconstruction of a possible occurrence. In the preface we see him among a group of men who are described in great detail, as though Hawthorne wished to show us what he could have done had he wanted to write a novel of this kind. But he does not want to because the very freedom which he has here, and in which a Dickens or a Hardy revels, is, for Hawthorne, synonymous with irresponsibility. Language used in a non-compulsive way is a sign of man's freedom from the immediate, but this freedom to Hawthorne is meaningless unless it is set against a prior bondage. So now we see him discovering the letter, pondering on its significance, submitting himself to its reality. The letter is in a room, the room is in a building (the Custom-House), but there is nothing *in* the letter: it just is. And yet:

> My eyes fastened themselves upon the old scarlet letter, and would not be turned aside. Certainly there was some deep meaning in

3. Lévi-Strauss recounts that 'the Jesuit missionary Sanchez Larador has described the passionate seriousness with which the natives devoted whole days to letting themselves be painted. He who is not painted, they said, is "dumb".' (*Structural Anthropology*, trans. Jacobson and Schoepf [London, 1969] 257.)

it most worthy of interpretation, and which, as it were, streamed forth from the mystic symbol, subtly communicating itself to my sensibilities, but evading the analysis of my mind.

The book which grows from this meditation, then, is Hawthorne's scarlet letter, living, like Pearl, and evading the deadly probing of those who, like Chillingworth, would pluck out its secret. But it can only do this because, like Hester Prynne, it recognises that the letter is not a natural sign whose meaning must be unearthed. Yet it is more than the first letter of the alphabet. . . . Out of this contradiction Hawthorne creates his novel, which mimes his own attempt to understand and, in doing so, allows being and saying to co-exist, turns letter into hieroglyph.

* * *

JOHN E. BECKER

The Concluding Ritual†

Hester put on the letter at the end of the forest meeting and became again the gloomy figure she has been throughout the story. But Dimmesdale seems to be a new man. * * *

What there is in Dimmesdale, is a new kind of animal vitality that has lain dormant throughout the book, the animal vitality that must have been there when he sinned with Hester. It has since been repressed, but now it springs forth once more. Dimmesdale delights in his march through the rough forest, he delights in his verbal sparring with Chillingworth, he eats ravenously, he produces the election-day sermon furiously, but morally he is not transformed. He is what he was, false, only more viciously so. Hawthorne gives no evidence of any other judgment upon him. As Hester is the representative of the moral inadequacy of the heart, Dimmesdale remains the representative of the falsity, the moral ambiguity, of Puritan righteousness. Neither hero nor heroine have so far achieved any moral heroism.

Hawthorne, at the end of his book, reconstitutes by means of a ritual the unchanged social texture of the Puritan world. The opening description of the New England holiday gives us the sense of a return to the surface of Puritan life. The forest scene brought all of our long involvement with its depth of personal pain to its climax. Now Hester is once more the muted public allegory of sin. Her gray

† From *Hawthorne's Historical Allegory: An Examination of the American Conscience* by John E. Becker (Port Washington, N.Y.: Kennikat Press, 1971), pp. 88–154. Footnotes have been omitted.

clothing makes her personality recede so that the letter advances, revealing her "under the moral aspect of its own illumination." But only a "preternaturally gifted observer" would have been able to detect in her any anticipatory glow of new freedom. Pearl is what she has always been, the incarnation of the letter and of that richness of personal response in Hester which has been obscured. Hawthorne creates the Puritan holiday scene through the dialogue of Hester and Pearl, then interposes another of his historical essays on the paradoxical Puritan love of ritual festivity. In the midst of this bustle of color and high feeling Hawthorne stages an almost operatic entrance of the sea captain with Chillingworth. One can hear the chords of the orchestra and feel the strokes of doom on Hester's heart. But Hawthorne wastes little time building suspense. He had never really allowed us to believe in the escape. The problem of *The Scarlet Letter* cannot be solved by plot. Hawthorne hastens on to the moral resolution of his story. And so we end where we began, on the scaffold, where the problem of society and the individual human heart was first proposed. This time we are armed with a deeper and broader moral insight into the conflict.

The crowd takes its ritual form as the procession begins, a more solemn and magnificent procession than the one which took Hester to the scaffold. But Hawthorne makes us see, nevertheless, that it is the same Puritan world. Of this scene Marius Bewley says:

> This crisis is enacted against a solidly realized background of civil and military order, and at this crucial moment of the novel the background has the effect of powerfully personifying that society from which Hester's and Dimmesdale's sin has alienated them. It clearly represents much more than was suggested by the rude inquisitiveness of the boors who gathered around Hester in the market-place. Without the resonance provided by this richly communicated sense of a more-than-Puritan society which we are given in such passages, the whole tragedy would lose stature.

The authority-structure is based, not on the old value of nobility, nor on the modern estimation of individual achievement, but on "the massive materials which produce stability and dignity of character." The climactic order of the procession, music, soldiery, the civil government, is crowned by the appearance of Dimmesdale. The retiring, sensitive saint has given way to a new person of ambiguous vitality who seems more fitted for the high position which the ministry held among these people. Dimmesdale is every inch the role he plays. But it is experienced as a role by Hester, who sees him as out of her reach, not the man with whom she had shared such an intimacy as the intimacy of the forest. Is it a man playing a role that we see? All that we have seen of Dimmesdale up to that forest meeting would lead us to think so. But we are meant to be uncertain. The whole of the story now focuses on this man. Hester has had her moment and been defeated. The malignancy of evil in the person of Chillingworth has thwarted all hope of escape. For her all is over. We have still to learn about Dimmesdale.

Hester takes up her position near the scaffold for this decisive ritual. Through her ears we hear the sermon as music. The words of the sermon are undoubtedly the words of the Puritan allegory, but that allegory is of little interest to her. She has rejected it from the beginning. All that is important to her is the person of her lover.

> The sermon had throughout a meaning for her, entirely apart from its indistinguishable words. These perhaps, if more distinctly heard, might have been only a grosser medium, and have clogged the spiritual sense.

She hears the rise and fall of his voice as the anguish of suffering humanity.

Meanwhile, Hester becomes the center of vulgar attention. Once more Hawthorne ventures that some, in this case the Indians, may consider the letter the sign of a high dignity. That had been his own first reaction in the Custom-House. He has used it repeatedly to keep our view of Hester distinct from the Puritan view. Hester sees the same group of matrons who had been at her first exposure on the pillory.

> At the final hour, when she was so soon to fling aside the burning letter, it had strangely become the centre of more remark and excitement, and was thus made to sear her breast more painfully, than at any time since the first day she put it on.

Hawthorne binds up beginning and end, impressing us with the irrevocable quality of Hester's punishment in spite of any changes in the attitude among the Puritan people.

Hawthorne has built up his picture of the Puritan holiday through the eyes of Hester and Pearl, and we have heard Dimmesdale's sermon through Hester's ears. Now the narrative point of view shifts with finality away from the interior world of Hester and back onto the social surface of the Puritan world. The Puritans, of course, are interested in Dimmesdale's words because they are the words of the Puritan allegory. But Hawthorne's irony, though subtle, is unmistakable as he gives us those words. Whatever high and glorious destiny New England may have, it is not, from his standpoint in time, as a people of the Lord. Hawthorne does not say it is not, but the fact that he puts it into the mouth of Dimmesdale, who is at one and the same time the most admired of Puritan divines, and the most deeply sinful of the Puritan people, implies something about the validity of the message. The secret of Dimmesdale's appeal as a preacher, all these years, has been the secret canker of guilt eating away at him; and this sermon, we know, is the product of a climactic surrender to evil which released a vitality in Dimmesdale that had long been repressed. Dimmesdale's triumph is ambiguous, as Puritanism's must be. It is defeated by the undertow of personal guilt, as the rigid Puritan world is bound to be defeated by the imperious undertow of natural humanity.

After his triumphant sermon, the procession forms again amidst a massive shout of the people. But their shout is silenced by the appearance of the minister, feeble and pale. Predictably they misinterpret.

> This earthly faintness was, in their view, only another phase of the minister's celestial strength; nor would it have seemed a miracle too high to be wrought for one so holy, had he ascended before their eyes, waxing dimmer and brighter, and fading at last into the light of heaven!

As Dimmesdale ascends the scaffold, Chillingworth is defeated. But the Puritan hierarchy, too, is defeated. Its world of clear meanings is upset and at a loss.

> The men of rank and dignity, who stood more immediately around the clergyman, were so taken by surprise, and so perplexed as to the purport of what they saw,—unable to receive the explanation which most readily presented itself, or to imagine any other,—that they remained silent and inactive spectators of the judgment which Providence seemed about to work.

Still, even this triumph is a profoundly ambiguous one.

> "For thee and Pearl, be it as God shall order," said the minister; "and God is merciful! Let me now do the will which he hath made plain before my sight. For, Hester, I am a dying man. So let me make haste to take my shame upon me."

Is this the self-centered individualism so characteristic not only of Puritan material culture, but especially of Puritan spirituality? Or is it the psychological freedom of a man who realizes that the deepest and fullest love cannot intrude between God and another soul, that love has to recognize this limit inherent in the solitude of every human person? Does Dimmesdale, at the very moment when he has the courage to acknowledge his love for Hester and Pearl, renounce them out of fear for his own salvation, or stand free of them with the clear-sighted love of a man who knows the limits of love? It seems an unresolved question which leaves the meaning of Dimmesdale's character ambiguous with precisely the ambiguity that is at the heart of Puritan faith.

Dimmesdale turns:

> to the people, whose great heart was thoroughly appalled, yet overflowing with tearful sympathy, as knowing that some deep

life-matter—which, if full of sin, was full of anguish, and repentance likewise—was now to be laid open to them.

The confession of Dimmesdale is a confession about the scarlet
letter. It is a revelation of its depths, depths which the Puritan
people had failed to penetrate. But Hawthorne insists that these
people are different from the crude multitude which had first stared
at Hester. They are different as well from their rigid Puritan leaders.
They are a people in whom nature has won out over dogma. Hawthorne speaks of their great heart overflowing with tearful sympathy. Dimmesdale calls on this natural human sympathy as he takes
them with him beneath the legal symbol into the heart where the
letter really exists and where they had not been able to perceive it
before. The form of the confession is a step by step penetration of
the interior reality of the symbol.

> He tells you, that, with all its mysterious horror, it is but the
> shadow of what he bears on his own breast, and that even this,
> his own red stigma, is no more than the type of what has seared
> his inmost heart.

In such a climax which finally interprets a symbol that has
focused the attention of the reader throughout the book, the characters themselves too must change. This is both a demand of psychological realism and a demand of the allegorical form. We have
here another moment within the fiction when what it is that makes
a character demonic or real is at work.

We saw Chillingworth change from man to demon at the beginning of the book, a multivalent human life gradually became
demonic as his obsession reduced Chillingworth's existence to a
single dimension. He became an embodiment of revenge, distilled
to its most subtle and intense essence. But the object of revenge is
now gone and his existence no longer has any principle of reality.
Chillingworth disappears.

Pearl, on the other hand, has not had her chance at real humanity. The psychological distortion which has been twisted into her
personality by her mother's guilt and isolation, and reinforced by
the Puritan community, has inhibited the free development of love
and the capacity to suffer. Here she is freed.

> Pearl kissed his lips. A spell was broken. The great scene of grief,
> in which the wild infant bore a part, had developed all her sym-
> pathies; and as her tears fell upon her father's cheek, they were
> the pledge that she would grow up amid human joy and sorrow,
> nor for ever do battle with the world, but be a woman in it.
> Towards her mother, too, Pearl's errand as a messenger of anguish
> was all fulfilled.

Her father's confession has released her from the inhibiting allegorical role she has been forced to assume. She is the one character of

the book who changes from allegorical to real. This transformation has been called the operation of a mere *deus ex machina*.[1] But if there is a lapse in characterization here, it is but a partial one. The relationship with Hester has been profoundly real.

Dimmesdale remains the ambiguous representative of the Puritan world. The vitality which came to him in the forest was not, in terms of the book, a vitality rooted in freedom, Christian or pagan. Perhaps there is no mimetic, that is, psychological explanation for Dimmesdale's confession. It remains tained with ambiguity.

> The law we broke!—the sin here so awfully revealed; let these alone be in thy thoughts! I fear! I fear! It may be, that, when we forgot our God,—when we violated our reverence each for the other's soul,—it was thenceforth vain to hope that we could meet hereafter, in an everlasting and pure reunion. God knows; and He is merciful! He hath proved his mercy, and most of all, in my afflictions.

Perhaps the same fear which vitiated Dimmesdale's stance toward his people inspirits him as he stands before God. Dimmesdale remains, as he dies, the symbol of an ambiguity within the heart of Puritanism.

Only Hester is by-passed by this climactic event. Only her love for Dimmesdale is important to her. The revelation of the scarlet letter as well as its larger moral implications leave her untouched. For her, there has been much passion, but no fulness of perception. She only begs desperately for reassurance that they will be reunited in heaven, and Dimmesdale cannot give it to her. Hester remains unfulfilled, more a twisted and scarred relic of sin than a tragic heroine.

There is still one significant group of people within the Puritan populace which must be mentioned. There were spectators at Dimmesdale's confession who denied it all: there had been no mark, no confession, only a spectacular display of humility. These are the purest Puritans who failed to be a part of that great heart of humanity because they are so tied to their dogmas. They are slaves of the drive of the Puritan mind to maintain the validity of its simple allegory of human guilt. Membership in the Puritan community, after all, was based on the ability of that community to judge by external signs the interior consciences of men. To admit the reality of such a colossal deception as the minister's was to catch a glimpse of the precarious uncertainty of the whole Puritan social and religious system. There were bound to be some who sensed and reacted to the threat posed by the minister's confession. For these people the Puritan allegorical process went inexorably on:

---

1. Literally, "god from the machine": from Greek drama where when a god intervened to solve a mortal problem he was lowered onto the stage by a ma- chine; now used to characterize any forced solution to a literary problem. [*Editor.*]

According to these highly respectable witnesses, the minister, conscious that he was dying,—conscious, also, that the reverence of the multitude placed him already among saints and angels,—had desired, by yielding up his breath in the arms of that fallen woman, to express to the world how utterly nugatory is the choicest of man's own righteousness. After exhausting life in his efforts for mankind's spiritual good, he had made the manner of his death a parable, in order to impress on his admirers the mighty and mournful lesson, that, in the view of Infinite Purity, we are sinners all alike.

Hawthorne strikes the same subtly ironic note here that he struck in describing the sermon at the end of Hester's hours on the scaffold. In both moments it is possible to sense the depths of Hawthorne's understanding of Puritanism, but also his understanding of humanity itself, which is able to go on quietly but persistently driving the most profoundly complex agonies of the individual conscience into the simple ethical patterns of a social code.

Hawthorne steps forward once more at the story's end, though his presence was never totally obscured at any point in the novel. Here again he is not just the story-teller who has presented the tale, but the artist-thinker who has suffered the story.

We have thrown all the light we could acquire upon the portent, and would gladly, now that it has done its office, erase its deep print out of our own brain; where long meditation has fixed it in very undesirable distinctness.

As one who has both told and suffered through the story, Hawthorne, not surprisingly, emerges with a moral somewhat different from the one with which he had begun: "Be true! Be true! Be true! Show freely to the world, if not your worst, yet some trait whereby the worst may be inferred!" He has not lost his hold on the principle of the sanctity of the heart, but in "A Flood of Sunshine" he gave that principle a kind of ultimate test. He submitted himself and us as fully as possible to the experience of freedom and new life which Hester held out. He created, cooperated to the full with her eloquent rhetoric. Ultimately, however he found both Hester and the principle limited and incomplete. Both fail in a fundamental relationship with reality. Hawthorne has given free play as well to the diffuse but inexorable power of nature. That too he tested to the full in the forest scene. Nature is an aspect of reality which will ultimately revenge itself on man if he fails to recognize its power, as it revenges itself on Dimmesdale and eventually on Puritanism. Still, even nature is but a vague and uncertain beacon.

There has been a refinement of Hawthorne's meaning, a modification of the principle which he set out to test in his allegory. Morality must be more than respect for the sanctity of the human heart, or rather one must respect it in all its dimensions by being ultimately and in all things true. In this very limited sense one can say that there is a moral lesson in *The Scarlet Letter*. This cuts in all directions, at Chillingworth, at Hester, at Dimmesdale, at Hawthorne himself and his own highly emotional commitment to the sanctity of the heart.

Perhaps, after our own critical journey through the novel and the forest of criticism which continues to grow up around it, we may be forced to return to the words of one of Hawthorne's earlier and better critics for our conclusion. George E. Woodberry finds Hawthorne almost as blind to the positive values of Puritanism as Hawthorne finds Puritanism blind to the values of the human heart. In emptying Puritanism of its Christian values Hawthorne has distorted "not so much the Puritan ideal—which were a little matter —but the spiritual life itself." And so Hawthorne concludes with an ultimate and despairing contradiction: It may even be true that hatred and love are at bottom the same. "In the spiritual world, the old physician and the minister—mutual victims as they have been —may, unawares, have found their earthly stock of hatred and antipathy transmuted into golden love."

In a kind of coda, we return to Hester. She has never been freed of the scar of the letter. When she returns from Europe to the settlement, she resumes it. She does gain a certain perspective, a historical perspective like Hawthorne's. Still it is radically incomplete. Hester dies in sorrow and is buried separately from her love "as if the dust of the two sleepers had no right to mingle."

Selected Bibliography

The bibliography which follows is highly selective and does not include items which have been excerpted in the body of this book since full bibliographical information has already been given. The most complete bibliography of Hawthorne is *Nathaniel Hawthorne: A Reference Bibliography, 1900–1971*, compiled by Beatrice Ricks, Joseph D. Adams, and Jack O. Hazlerig (Boston: G. K. Hall, 1972). Other convenient checklists of *Scarlet Letter* criticism are in Maurice Beebe and Jack Hardie, "Criticism of Nathaniel Hawthorne: A Selected Checklist," *Studies in the Novel*, 2 (1970), 519–87, and Buford Jones, *A Checklist of Hawthorne Criticism, 1951–1966* (Hartford, Conn.: Transcendental Books, 1967).

Abel, Darrel. "The Devil in Boston," *Philological Quarterly*, 32 (1953), 366–81.
———. "Hawthorne's Dimmesdale: Fugitive from Wrath," *Nineteenth-Century Fiction*, 11 (1956), 81–105.
———. "Hawthorne's Pearl: Symbol and Character," *ELH*, 18 (1951), 50–66.
———. "Hawthorne's *Scarlet Letter*," *North American Review*, 71 (1950), 135–48.
Andola, John A. "Pearl: Symbolic Link Between Two Worlds," *Ball State University Forum*, 13 (1972), 60–67.
Arvin, Newton. *Hawthorne*. Boston: 1929. Reprint, New York: Russell & Russell, 1961.
Austin, Allen. "Hester Prynne's Plan of Escape: The Moral Problem," *University of Kansas City Review*, 28 (1962), 317–18.
———. "Satire and Theme in *The Scarlet Letter*," *Philological Quarterly*, 41 (1962), 508–11.
Axelsson, Arne. *The Links in the Chain: Isolation and Interdependence in Nathaniel Hawthorne's Fictional Characters*. Uppsala: Universitets-biblioteket, 1974.
Baumgartner, Alex M. and Michael J. Hoffman. "Illusion and Role in *The Scarlet Letter*," *Papers on Language and Literature*, 7 (1971), 168–84.
Baym, Nina. "Passion and Authority in *The Scarlet Letter*," *New England Quarterly*, 43 (1970), 209–30. Reprinted in *The Shape of Hawthorne's Career*. Ithaca, N.Y.: Cornell University Press, 1976.
Bell, Michael Davitt. *Hawthorne and the Historical Romance of New England*. Princeton: Princeton University Press, 1971.
———. "The Young Minister and the Puritan Fathers: A Note on History in *The Scarlet Letter*," *Nathaniel Hawthorne Journal*, 1971, pp. 159–68.
Benoit, Raymond. *Single Nation's Double Name*. The Hague: Mouton, 1973.
———. "Theology and Literature: *The Scarlet Letter*," *Bucknell Review*, 20 (1972), 83–92.
Bewley, Marius. "Hawthorne's Novels," in *The Eccentric Design*. New York: Columbia University Press, 1959.
Black, Stephen A. "*The Scarlet Letter*: Death by Symbols," *Paunch*, 24 (1965), 51–74.
Bonham, Sister M. Hilda, I.H.M. "Hawthorne's Symbols *Sotto Voce*," *College English*, 20 (1959), 184–86.
Bowden, Edwin T. *The Dungeon of the Heart: Human Isolation and the American Novel*. New York: Macmillan, 1961.
Browning, Preston M. "Hester Prynne as a Secular Saint," *Midwest Quarterly*, 13 (1972), 351–62.
Canaday, Nicholas, Jr. "Ironic Humor as Defense in *The Scarlet Letter*," *Bulletin of the South Central Modern Language Association*, 21 (1961), 17–18.
———. " 'Some Sweet Moral Blossom': A Note on Hawthorne's Rose," *Papers on Language and Literature*, 3 (1967), 186–87.
Cecil, L. Moffitt. "*The Scarlet Letter*: A Puritan Love Story," *Reality and Myth: Essays in American Literature in Memory of Richard Croom Beatty*. Nashville, Tenn.: Vanderbilt University Press, 1964.
Chase, Richard. "Hawthorne and the Limits of Romance," *The American Novel and Its Tradition*. Garden City, N.Y.: Doubleday, 1957.

Coanda, Richard Joseph. "Hawthorne's Scarlet Alphabet," *Renascence,* 19 (1967), 161–66.

Cowley, Malcolm. "Five Acts of *The Scarlet Letter,*" *College English,* 19 (1957), 11–16. Reprinted in *Twelve Original Essays on Great American Novels,* Charles Shapiro, ed. Detroit: Wayne State University Press, 1958.

Cox, James M. "*The Scarlet Letter:* Through the Old Manse and the Custom House," *Virginia Quarterly Review,* 51 (1975), 432–47.

Cronin, Morton. "Hawthorne on Romantic Love and the Status of Women," *PMLA,* 69 (1954), 89–98.

Davidson, Edward H. "Dimmesdale's Fall," *New England Quarterly,* 26 (1963), 358–70.

———. "The Question of History in *The Scarlet Letter,*" *Emerson Society Quarterly* (Fourth Quarter, 1961), 2–3.

Dillingham, William B. "Arthur Dimmesdale's Confession," *Studies in the Literary Imagination,* 2, i (1969), 21–26.

Doubleday, Neal F. "Hawthorne's Hester and Feminism," *PMLA,* 54 (1939), 825–28.

Eakin, Paul J. "Hawthorne's Imagination and the Structure of 'The Custom-House,'" *American Literature,* 43 (1971), 346–58.

Eisinger, Chester E. "Pearl and the Puritan Heritage," *College English,* 12 (1951), 323–29.

Erlich, Gloria C. "Deadly Innocence: Hawthorne's Dark Women," *New England Quarterly,* 41 (1968), 163–79.

Folsom, James K. *Man's Accidents and God's Purposes: Multiplicity in Hawthorne's Fiction.* New Haven, Conn.: College and University Press, 1963, 1966.

Fossum, Robert H. *Hawthorne's Inviolable Circle.* Deland, Fla.: Everett/Edwards, 1972.

Garlitz, Barbara. "Pearl: 1850–1955," *PMLA,* 72 (1957), 689–99.

Gibson, William M. "The Art of Nathaniel Hawthorne: An Examination of *The Scarlet Letter,*" in *American Renaissance,* George Hendrick, ed. Frankfort: Diesterweg, 1961.

Grabo, Carl H. "The Omniscient Author—*The Scarlet Letter,*" *The Technique of the Novel.* New York: Charles Scribner's Sons, 1928.

Granger, Bruce Ingham. "Arthur Dimmesdale as Tragic Hero," *Nineteenth-Century Fiction,* 19 (1964), 197–203.

Grant, Douglas. *Purpose and Place: Essays on American Writers.* London: Macmillan, 1965.

Greenwood, Douglas. "The Heraldic Device in *The Scarlet Letter:* Hawthorne's Symbolical Use of the Past," *American Literature,* 46 (1974), 207–10.

Griffin, Gerald R. "Hawthorne and 'The New England Village': Internal Evidence and a New Genesis of *The Scarlet Letter,*" *Essex Institute Historical Collections,* 107 (1971), 268–79.

Hansen, Elaine T. "Ambiguity and the Narrator in *The Scarlet Letter,*" *Journal of Narrative Technique,* 5 (1975), 147–63.

Hardwick, Elizabeth. *Seduction and Betrayal: Women in Literature.* New York: Random House, 1974.

Hart, John E. "*The Scarlet Letter*—One Hundred Years After," *New England Quarterly,* 23 (1950), 381–95.

Henderson, Harry B. *Versions of the Past.* New York: Oxford University Press, 1974.

Hoeltje, Hubert H. "The Writing of *The Scarlet Letter,*" *New England Quarterly,* 27 (1954), 326–46.

Hoffman, Michael J. *The Subversive Vision.* Port Washington, N.Y.: Kennikat Press, 1973.

Houston, Neal B. "Hester Prynne as Eternal Feminine," *Discourse,* 9 (1966), 230–44.

Howells, William D. *Heroines of Fiction,* I. New York: Harper, 1901.

Huffman, Clifford C. "History in Hawthorne's 'Custom-House,'" *Clio,* 2 (1973), 161–69.

Janssen, James G. "Dimmesdale's 'Lurid Playfulness,'" *American Transcendental Quarterly,* 1 (1969), 30–34.

———. "Pride and Prophecy: The Final Irony of *The Scarlet Letter,*" *Nathaniel Hawthorne Journal,* 1975, pp. 241–47.

Katz, Seymour. "'Character,' 'Nature,' and Allegory in *The Scarlet Letter,*" *Nineteenth-Century Fiction,* 23 (1968), 3–17.

Kaul, A. N. "Character and Motive in *The Scarlet Letter,*" *Critical Quarterly,* 10 (1968), 373–84.

———. *The American Vision.* New Haven: Yale University Press, 1963.

Kummings, Donald D. "Hawthorne's 'The Custom House' and the Conditions of Fiction in America," *CEA Critic,* 33, iii (1971), 15–18.

Kushen, Betty. "Love's Martyrs: The Scarlet Letter as Secular Cross," *Literature and Psychology*, 22 (1972), 109–20.

Lane, Lauriat, Jr. "Allegory and Character in *The Scarlet Letter*," *Emerson Society Quarterly*, 25 (Fourth Quarter, 1961), 13–16.

Lawrence, D. H. *Studies in Classic American Literature*. Reprint, New York: Doubleday Anchor Books, 1955.

Lease, Benjamin. "Hawthorne and 'A Certain Venerable Personage': New Light on 'The Custom-House,'" *Jahrbuch für Amerikastudien*, 15 (1970), 201–7.

———. "Salem vs. Hawthorne: An Early Review of *The Scarlet Letter*," *New England Quarterly*, 44 (1971), 110–17.

———. "'The Whole Is a Prose Poem': An Early Review of *The Scarlet Letter*," *American Literature*, 44 (1972), 128–30.

Leavis, Q. D. "Hawthorne as Poet," *Sewanee Review*, 59 (1951), 426–40.

Levin, David. "Nathaniel Hawthorne, *The Scarlet Letter*," in *The American Novel from James Fenimore Cooper to William Faulkner*, Wallace Stegner, ed. New York: Basic Books, 1965.

Levin, Harry. *The Power of Blackness*. New York: Knopf, 1958.

Maclean, Hugh A. "Hawthorne's *Scarlet Letter*: 'The Dark Problem of This Life,'" *American Literature*, 27 (1955), 12–24.

MacShane, Frank. "The House of the Dead: Hawthorne's Custom House and *The Scarlet Letter*," *New England Quarterly*, 35 (1962), 93–101.

Manierre, William R. "The Role of Sympathy in *The Scarlet Letter*," *Texas Studies in Literature and Language*, 13 (1971), 497–507.

Martin, Terrence. "Dimmesdale's Ultimate Sermon," *Arizona Quarterly* 27 (1971), 230–40.

———. *Nathaniel Hawthorne*. New York: Twayne, 1965.

McAleer, John J. "Hester Prynne's Grave," *Descant*, 5 (1961), 29–33.

McCall, Dan. "The Design of Hawthorne's 'Custom-House,'" *Nineteenth-Century Fiction*, 21 (1967), 349–58.

McNamara, Anne Marie. "The Character of Flame: The Function of Pearl in *The Scarlet Letter*," *American Literature*, 27 (1956), 537–53.

McPherson, Hugo A. *Hawthorne as Myth-Maker*. Toronto: University of Toronto Press, 1969.

Mizener, Arthur. "Nathaniel Hawthorne—*The Scarlet Letter*," in *Twelve Great American Novels*. New York: New American Library, 1967.

Noble, David W. "The Analysis of Alienation by 20th Century Social Scientists and 19th Century Novelists: The Example of Hawthorne's *The Scarlet Letter*," *Myths and Realities: Conflicting Values in America*, Berkley Kalin and Clayton Robinson, eds. Memphis: Memphis State University, 1972.

———. *The Eternal Adam and the New World Garden*. New York: George Braziller, 1968.

Nolte, William H. "Hawthorne's Dimmesdale: A Small Man Gone Wrong," *New England Quarterly*, 38 (1965), 168–86.

O'Donnell, Charles R. "Hawthorne and Dimmesdale: The Search for the Realm of Quiet, *Nineteenth-Century Fiction*, 14 (1960), 317–32.

Rahv, Philip. "The Dark Lady of Salem," *Partisan Review*, 8 (1941), 362–81. Reprinted in *Image and Idea*. Norfolk, Conn.: New Directions, 1949.

Roper, Gordon. "The Originality of Hawthorne's *The Scarlet Letter*," *Dalhousie Review*, 30 (1950), 62–79.

Rovit, Earl. "Ambiguity in Hawthorne's *Scarlet Letter*," *Archiv für das Studium der neueren Sprachen und Literaturen*, 198 (1961), 76–88.

Sampson, Edward C. "Motivation in *The Scarlet Letter*," *American Literature*, 28 (1957), 511–13.

Scanlon, Lawrence E. "The Heart of *The Scarlet Letter*," *Texas Studies in Literature and Language*, 4 (1962), 198–213.

Sewall, Richard B. "*The Scarlet Letter*," *The Vision of Tragedy*. New Haven: Yale University Press, 1962.

Shear, W. "Characterization in *The Scarlet Letter*," *Midwest Quarterly*, 12 (1971), 437–54.

Slethaug, Gordon E. "*Felix Culpa* in Hawthorne's Custom House," *English Record*, 23, iii (1972), 32–41.

Stanton, Robert. "*The Scarlet Letter* as Dialectic of Temperament and Idea," *Studies in the Novel*, 2 (1970), 474–86.

Stein, William Bysshe. *Hawthorne's Faust*. Gainesville: University of Florida Press, 1953.

Stone, Edward. "The Antique Gentility of Hester Prynne," *Philological Quarterly*, 36 (1957), 90–96.

Steinke, Russell. "The Scarlet Letter of Puritanism," *University Review*, 31 (1965), 289–91.

Stephens, Rosemary. "*A* Is for Art in *The Scarlet Letter*," *American Transcendental Quarterly*, 1 (1969), 23–27.

Stubbs, John C. "Hawthorne's *The Scarlet Letter:* The Theory of the Romance and the Use of the New England Situation," *PMLA*, 83 (1968), 1439–47.

Swann, Charles. "Hawthorne: History versus Romance," *Journal of American Studies*, 7 (1973), 153–70.

Tanselle, G. Thomas. "A Note on the Structure of *The Scarlet Letter*," *Nineteenth-Century Fiction*, 17 (1962), 283–85.

Tharp, Jac. *Nathaniel Hawthorne: Identity and Knowledge.* Carbondale: Southern Illinois University Press, 1967.

Todd, Robert E. "The Magna Mater Archetype in *The Scarlet Letter*," *New England Quarterly*, 45 (1972), 421–29.

Vance, William. "Tragedy and 'The Tragic Power of Laughter': *The Scarlet Letter* and *The House of the Seven Gables*," *Nathaniel Hawthorne Journal* (1971), 232–54.

Van Doren, Mark. *Nathaniel Hawthorne.* New York: William Sloane, 1949, 1957.

Vogel, Dan. "Hawthorne's Concept of Tragedy in *The Scarlet Letter*," *Nathaniel Hawthorne Journal* (1972), 183–93.

———. "Roger Chillingworth: The Satanic Paradox in *The Scarlet Letter*," *Criticism*, 5 (1963), 272–80.

Von Abele, Rudolph. *The Death of the Artist: A Study of Hawthorne's Disintegration.* The Hague: Nijhoff, 1955.

Wagner, Linda W. "Embryonic Characterization in 'The Custom House,'" *English Record*, 16 (1966), 32–35.

Walcutt, Charles Child. "*The Scarlet Letter and Its Modern Critics*," *Nineteenth-Century Fiction*, 7 (1953), 251–64.

Walsh, Thomas F., Jr. "Dimmesdale's Election Sermon," *Emerson Society Quarterly*, 44 (Third Quarter, 1966), 64–66.

Warfel, Harry R. "Metaphysical Ideas in *The Scarlet Letter*," *College English*, 24 (1963), 421–25.

Warren, Austin. "*The Scarlet Letter:* A Literary Exercise in Moral Theology," *Southern Review*, 1 (1965), 22–45. Reprinted in *Connections*. Ann Arbor: University of Michigan Press, 1970.

Wellborn, Grace Pleasant. "The Golden Thread in *The Scarlet Letter*," *Southern Folklore Quarterly*, 29 (1965), 169–78.

———. "The Mystic Seven in *The Scarlet Letter*," *South Central Bulletin*, 23 (1963), 23–31.

———. "Plant Lore and *The Scarlet Letter*," *Southern Folklore Quarterly*, 27 (1963), 160–67.

———. "The Symbolic Three in *The Scarlet Letter*," *South Central Bulletin*, 23 (1963), 10–17.

Wentersdorf, Karl. P. "The Elements of Witchcraft in *The Scarlet Letter*," *Folklore*, 83 (1972), 132–53.

Whelan, Robert Emmet, Jr. "Hester Prynne's Little Pearl: Sacred and Profane Love," *American Literature*, 39 (1968), 488–505.

———. "Roger Chillingworth's Whole Business Is Reflection," *Research Studies*, 37 (1968), 298–312.

Whitford, Kathryn. "'On a Field, Sable, the Letter A, Gules,'" *Lock Haven Review*, 10 (1968), 33–8.

Willett, Maurita. "The Letter A, Gules, and the Black Bubble," in *Melville and Hawthorne in the Berkshires*, Howard P. Vincent, ed. Kent, Ohio: Kent State University Press, 1968.

Winters, Yvor. "Maule's Curse: Hawthorne and the Problem of Allegory," in *Maule's Curse*. Norfolk. Conn.: New Directions, 1938. Reprinted in *In Defense of Reason*. New York: Swallow, 1947.

Ziff, Larzer. "The Ethical Dimension of 'The Custom House,'" *Modern Language Notes*, 73 (1958), 338–44.